ing on Kendall's moving on Jessica's moving on Ken... moving on Rend...
ing on Nicki's moving on Chloë's moving on Amanda's moving on Demi's moving o
oving on Katherine's moving on Anne's moving on K... ...en's mo
oving on Dakota's moving on Katy's moving on S... nov
ing on Bethenny's moving on Marcia's moving on Chelsea's mo... mov
g on Kendall's moving on Jessica's moving on Kendra's moving on Elle's moving o
 Nicki's moving on Chloë's moving on Amanda's moving on Demi's moving on Sel
 on Katherine's moving on Anne's moving on Kristin's moving on Lauren's moving
ing on Dakota's moving on Katy's moving on Saoirse's moving on Snooki's moving
ing on Bethenny's moving on Marcia's moving on Chelsea's moving on Milla's mov
g on Kendall's moving on Jessica's moving on Kendra's moving on Elle's moving o
 Nicki's moving on Chloë's moving on Amanda's moving on Demi's moving on Sel
 on Katherine's moving on Anne's moving on Kristin's moving on Lauren's moving
ing on Dakota's moving on Katy's moving on Saoirse's moving on Snooki's moving
ing on Bethenny's moving on Marcia's moving on Chelsea's moving on Milla's mov
g on Kendall's moving on Jessica's moving on Kendra's moving on Elle's moving o
 Nicki's moving on Chloë's moving on Amanda's moving on Demi's moving on Sel
 on Katherine's moving on Anne's moving on Kristin's moving on Lauren's moving
ing on Dakota's moving on Katy's moving on Saoirse's moving on Snooki's moving
ing on Bethenny's moving on Marcia's moving on Chelsea's moving on Milla's mov
g on Kendall's moving on Jessica's moving on Kendra's moving on Elle's moving o
 Nicki's moving on Chloë's moving on Amanda's moving on Demi's moving on Sel
 on Katherine's moving on Anne's moving on Kristin's moving on Lauren's moving
ing on Dakota's moving on Katy's moving on Saoirse's moving on Snooki's moving
ing on Bethenny's moving on Marcia's moving on Chelsea's moving on Milla's mov
g on Kendall's moving on Jessica's moving on Kendra's moving on Elle's moving o
 Nicki's moving on Chloë's moving on Amanda's moving on Demi's moving on Sel
 on Katherine's moving on Anne's moving on Kristin's moving on Lauren's moving
ing on Dakota's moving on Katy's moving on Saoirse's moving on Snooki's moving
ing on Bethenny's moving on Marcia's moving on Chelsea's moving on Milla's mov
g on Kendall's moving on Jessica's moving on Kendra's moving on Elle's moving o
 Nicki's moving on Chloë's moving on Amanda's moving on Demi's moving on Sel
 on Katherine's moving on Anne's moving on Kristin's moving on Lauren's moving
ing on Dakota's moving on Katy's moving on Saoirse's moving on Snooki's moving
ing on Bethenny's moving on Marcia's moving on Chelsea's moving on Milla's mov
g on Kendall's moving on Jessica's moving on Kendra's moving on Elle's moving o
 Nicki's moving on Chloë's moving on Amanda's moving on Demi's moving on Sel
 on Katherine's moving on Anne's moving on Kristin's moving on Lauren's moving
ing on Dakota's moving on Katy's moving on Saoirse's moving on Snooki's moving
ing on Bethenny's moving on Marcia's moving on Chelsea's moving on Milla's mov

blue
rider
press

DEAD

★S

an entertainment

BRUCE WAGNER

BLUE RIDER PRESS
a member of Penguin Group (USA) Inc. New York

blue
rider
press

Published by the Penguin Group
Penguin Group (USA) Inc., 375 Hudson Street, New York, New York 10014, USA ·
Penguin Group (Canada), 90 Eglinton Avenue East, Suite 700, Toronto, Ontario M4P 2Y3,
Canada (a division of Pearson Penguin Canada Inc.) · Penguin Books Ltd, 80 Strand, London
WC2R 0RL, England · Penguin Ireland, 25 St Stephen's Green, Dublin 2, Ireland (a division of
Penguin Books Ltd) · Penguin Group (Australia), 250 Camberwell Road, Camberwell, Victoria
3124, Australia (a division of Pearson Australia Group Pty Ltd) · Penguin Books India Pvt Ltd,
11 Community Centre, Panchsheel Park, New Delhi–110 017, India · Penguin Group (NZ), 67
Apollo Drive, Rosedale, North Shore 0632, New Zealand (a division of Pearson New Zealand
Ltd) · Penguin Books (South Africa) (Pty) Ltd, 24 Sturdee Avenue, Rosebank,
Johannesburg 2196, South Africa

Penguin Books Ltd, Registered Offices: 80 Strand, London WC2R 0RL, England

Library of Congress Cataloging-in-Publication Data

Wagner, Bruce.
Dead stars : an entertainment / by Bruce Wagner.
p.   cm.
ISBN 978-0-399-15935-0 (alk. paper)
1. Cancer—Patients—Fiction.   2. Women photographers—Fiction.
3. Hollywood (Los Angeles, Calif.)—Fiction.   I. Title.
PS3573.A369D43   2012   2012016153
813'.54—dc23

Printed in the United States of America
1 3 5 7 9 10 8 6 4 2

BOOK DESIGN BY
CLAIRE NAYLON VACCARO

again, for Laura

Comments (6)

jolly roger

Some people forget there is a hell

August 11, 2012

Uhh get your jollies rodger?

You say that but you are on a porn site?

August 15, 2012

;===0

Omg shes so shy fuck her real gd dude

August 20, 2012

forever77

It is amazing how many of you slept through English class.

August 24, 2012

Der Spermin8tr

Once her hair is down, She getts pretty. No way those are C's, her tatt's don't look good. Great BJ skills. Lovd her hair down!!!!!

August 24, 2012

ketamean

if she has Cs, then I have f-cking Ds lol. So many of these small-breasted casting couch girls lie about their

again, for Gavin

and Yukimi, Taiyo & Zen de Becker

<u>Report Abuse</u>

to Clancy Imislund

841,294

people like this

Kylie Jenner, 13, Shows Off Her Legs In Fashion Shoot (PHOTOS)

Read More: Kylie Jenner Model, bikini, hot, legs, skimpy, sexy? Kim, Kendall, sex

and Carrie Fisher

adding comments has been disabled for this video

SparkNotes: **Inferno**: Important Quotations Explained

It is greatly significant that both Purgatorio and Paradiso end with the same word as **Inferno**: stele, or the **stars**. It is clear not only that **Dante** aspires to Heaven . . .

(GRAPHIC)

Help | About | Chronology | Gallery | Music | Forum | Your Bookmarks |
Share this site
Please Note: If you are seeing this page without a left frame, click here.

Notes

One of my favorite translations, by Dorothy Sayers, can be purchased from
Amazon.com via the following links: Hell, Purgatory, Paradise.

Contents

You should never

forget that

you're just a person.

Even though

you're not like

everyone else,

you are

just like

everyone else.

—Dakota Fanning

Click Here to watch

1st

Trimester

ICM

(Morning/Noontime)

Morning is the time of Man: *the Known*

salimmo sù, el primo e io secondo,

tanto ch'i' vidi de le cose belle

che porta 'l ciel, per un pertugio tondo.

E quindi uscimmo a riveder le **stelle.**

—I N F E R N O, XXXIV. 137–9

[Telma]

Hurt Boobies

Telma

just found out she was no longer the world's youngest breast cancer survivor (now 13, she had a radical mastectomy at 9, beating out Hannah Powell-Auslam who was diagnosed at age 10. They took the lymph nodes from under her arms too). Now here comes Mom saying there's a 4-year-old somewhere in Canada *as we speak* wearing the crazy uncoveted laurel of youngest juvie breast carcinoma vic. The news left Telma a little at sea, lil Telma with her little big C, wondering if her demoted standing might affect the awesome amazing cornucopia of pink-tie charity events—the gala balls & schmancy fundraisers, the private lunches at the Hotel Bel-Air/Soho House/fijiwater teleflora Resnick chateau on Sunset—she was asked to participate in all year round in LA, and points north, south and east. She was actually famous.

The irony was, her mother had a lumpy tit for months and was herself worried sick she'd been god-gifted with C. Gwen was one of those tiresome people forever skittish and terrified by doctors; it took almost a year for her to go in. She of course got an assist from her shrink who with more than a nudge from her client had prepped Gwen for a lumpectomy at the very least, any kind of maybe-ectomy, but all the oncologist did was some draining. She brought Telma

with her and at the last post-drama moment showed him the fleshy
pea under her kid's nipple. A week later, immediately after the unfathomable diagnosis, mother and daughter were sealed into the scar-
ifying rip-snorting over-the-falls barrel of ♥ break CancerWorld 2.0.
A half-dozen *shtarker* moms helped Gwen survive her baby's mastectomy (St. Ambrose Hosp/Westwood), for which she would be eternally damned/grateful.

(She can never forget: the hospital lobby had vitrines filled with a
traveling exhibit of Barbie dolls.)

(The gal who created Barbie and Ken got breast cancer & patented
a prosthetic called "Nearly Me.")

Telma was conceived in vitro when Gwen was 44. Her husband
froze his sperm before being zapped for prostate cancer; he succumbed, as they used to say, when his princess turned three, right on
her birthday. If Gwen was old when she conceived, now she was *fucking* old, an old broad old enough to remember the bookstore days.
The Sixties. She was what, 12ish? The Village, as they once called it,
had a profusion of bookstores (can ya imagine?) & head shops too,
with bongs and mushroom-lettered blacklight posters, the whole
deal steeped in that sexysubversive patchouli smell imported from
beyond—the foggy subversive motherlode of the Haight. In a sun-
shadowed courtyard the girlpacks could buy huaraches/leather san-
dals (but never did) *crafted* onsite by a fabulous furry freak, fresh
(seemingly) from the commune, or some commune or other, his
adobified kittycorner wafting with that leather smell, biker leather
smell (so the little girls they did guess) and when he got close to them
and leered, they could subversively smell scary sexy bearded man
smells, & triangulate from there. There was an on-campus bowling
alley, wax and pine-smelling, where Gwen and her gradeschool peeps
(they didn't call it middleschool then) sometimes hung on weekends,
instead of taking the 83 WILSHIRE or hitching to the beach. The
blast of AC hit you right when you walked in, odor of foodcourt and
future life, campus bookstore/indoor pool/bowlinglane sounds &
smells, a grand and grandly sunlit subversive world: Gwen remem-

bered thinking *This is the smell of college, the smell of being grown-up, the mysterious alluring subversive smell of the end of carefree days.* Her memories were saturated with the erotic energy unleashed by cliquish tween tribes venturing out on their own, testing wings with parental approval, the Village being a plaza that was considered safe for pubescent gazelles (back in the day when so many things were considered safe), their pairs upon perfect pair of rangy downy legs shod in magic markered Vans, perspiry hormone-blasted packs of flowerpower grrrls wearing chunky boyfriend I.D. bracelets (some of them) bought & engraved at P.O.P. on the pier, virgin wannabe wild childs out hunting and gathering for what they knew not.

Then her trips to Westwood became the stuff of nightmares. Gradually, with the brutal ardent fellowship of *kansurvivors* (Telma's portmanteau), dawn broke in Gwen's challenged kancermom life. The C community was extraordinarily strong and supportive and unflinching, knitting melanoma newbies into a single gargantuan gargantuanly heroic quilt. Aside from the 1,000 useful things Gwen was taught—to change dressings, what to look for in getting the jump on opportunistic infections, what to hope for & what not to hope for or what to hope and not to hope for too much, the useful trick of rolling down the window and screaming as you drove along the spine of Mulholland—the kansurvivors helped her develop a spiritual practice. For the first time in Gwen's life, she meditated. She yoga'd and breathworked & self-hypnotated. She alternately begged, bitched and railed at—& became inexplicably devoted to—her Higher Power. A mere month from ground zero (all the kancerfolk revved from zero to hero), she no longer needed to listen to CDs to trance out, she was a quick study and by then could guide her own meditation, levitating and vipassanating without aural aid to a private fantasy island, mystical cave or black sand beach, some safe bespoke exhilarating unicorny place, any airy-faerie (or not) conjuring that might serve as a light to shine its incorporeal voltage down on her daughter's wayward cells, defusing/disarming/disrupting with its otherworldly assassin energy, blasting all those fucked up cells to

Kingdom Come or wherever. At first, it was hard, so hard. Gwen was an unbeliever, not XXXL but L, maybe M, not a Hitchens but a large to medium agnostic, L/M, but you couldn't go through something like this without investing/believing/trusting in something other than unbelief, you just couldn't. She'd take Reiki, kancerkid Mom workshops, & wishing on falling stars in the Sedona sky over a vacuum any day. You'd have to be an asshole fool to go with vacuum over prayer. You'd have to be sick.

Then something turned. Suddenly she was an XXXL believer, she couldn't say how or why but Gwen became of an instant *grateful*, it was that simple, so simple————grateful Max had lived long enough to spend three years with their daughter, grateful for all her kansurvivor ladies (*and* kancer dads *and* kancerkids), grateful that after Telma's surgery the docs said her baby wouldn't have to go through chemo/radiation at *all*, seemingly *ever,* that was the first of a trickling stream of miracles that became a torrent: she could keep her beautiful nine-year-old hair. *O thank you thank you thank you, an XXXL thank you for nothing for something for everything.*

(Those baldhead, puff-cheeked, irradiated *Children of the Corn* gave her the willies & Gwen hated herself for that.)

(Ooh! *Bad*, bad kancer karma!)

So she sucked it up and became an *athlete.* Embraced the whole subversive *ha ha* crazysexy Kris Karr/Donna Karan let them eat Sheryl Krow kancer posse, embraced the *make C your bitch/I will fucking awesome tigermom* ACE *this for my baby!* shining, crappy creepiness of it all.

Made metastatic lemons into lemonade.

You never know how you'll behave in the face of the unspeakably shitty and Gwen took herself by surprise, flourishing somewhat in the most god-awful impossible suicide moments. Absolutely the *best* kind of kancermom—feisty and witty and wry, doggedly contagiously optimistic, a pulse and a beacon to all stricken stripes in all stages (or not) of recovery, because a lot of parents were just too passive to be properly posse'd, &/or constitutionally unwired for war-riorship, they could never be anything but flipped-out vics. Fearslaves. Gwen & Telma were soon ID'd by kansurvivor kommunity honchos as the dynamic duo, the LOOK WHO'S HOT! ones-to-watch tag-team on the fast-track to fundraiser glory, rising emo-superstars on the horizon of fatal shores.

. . .

First as patient then short-term into long(er)-term survivor, Telma was a bloody prodigy, a natural, a once-in-a-generation Justin Bieber of HOPE. Funny and fearless, she buoyed her in-patient flocks, be-coming unofficial "Hi!" priestess/ombudsgirl to the cause. She went to DC for stemcell hearings on the Hill & played with Sasha at the White House, *so much fun* tho she not so secretly wished Malia was there, because Malia was closer to her age and more likely to become a pen-pal, but Malia was somewhere with her grandmuh*ma*. *Why couldn't she have just brought Grandma back?* While Mom had tea with FLOTUS, Telma did younger-girl (younger than Malia) things with Sasha, hoping against hope they'd be asked to stay overnight but they only wound up spending an hour *in toto*. She bitched about it on the way back to the hotel and Gwen said *stop being so greedy.* Stop!

And now there was a *way* younger kansurvivor on the scene (Telma called the girls *hervivors*); she needed to take action. Do something BIG. The world needed to be tweeting about *her*, not the Kanadian Kancerkid *arriviste*, not Kylie Jenner (dyke-whore) or Mackenzie Foy (*so* gay, whore), the world needed to be blogging about *her,* not Abigail Breslin (has-been) or Hailee Steinfeld (hairy/Jewish Whore) or Chloë Moretz (OMG *such* a bi-whore!!!!! <3) or Elle (slut/SNOB) or Willow Smith (rich biatch/total racist [*LM-FAO!!!*]) or Willow Shields (so pathetic) or Bailee Madison (dwarfy jesusfreak) or the *next* Hailee Bailee or *next* Elle or *next* Willow (*Pink* just named her baby that, there was going to be a whole new wave of Willows) or the next *Next*. Next! And even though Telma had 4 years of non-recurrence and the interloper-ingenue's recovery had *just begun*——Telma wished her the best but survival odds were so *not* in her favor——*O Canada!*——Telma *especially* didn't want the world facebooking about whatshername's zero to hero so-called courage because 4-year-olds were too *young* to have (so-called) courage, you just *can't* be a kancerhero at 4! Besides, it was her experience that most kancerkids—she always spelled it with a *K,* to thumb her nose at it, make it fun, that was her trademark, she started a little movement, lots of people were using K now though she'd had the conversation with her mom that probably the Kardashians weren't wild about it, they thought they owned K-World, & that might be the one thing to keep the K/ancer thing from really katching on, at least not til one of the Kardashians got it in the ovaries or the tits—it was Telma's experience that most kancerkids were high-maintenance sympathy whores who went ballistic if you didn't tell them what brave soldiers they were 24/7. The only time they *weren't* wusses, snotting up their stuffed, lastminute giftshop animals, was a) when they were on a morphine drip; b) when they were being visited by the pro athlete/reality show star/Bieberish boy singer/*Twilight*/*Hunger Games* actor of their (make a) wishes. (The big *Twilighters* were never available so they always wound up with co-co-co-costars from the latest sequel.)

Telma was a warrior. It was time to enter the public eye again— she'd been away too long. Mom needed to touch base with that gal who did press for all the big ☆s, the gal who got them into *People* on Telma's 2nd anniversary of being kancerfree. Maybe now that it was Year IV *& counting* Telma could get a perfume, a *fragrance*, maybe call it *hero*™ or *warriorgrrl*™, Telma wanted someone savvy to pull out all the stops, wanted to do the Ellen Show victory dance with Flotus or Emma Stone or Greyson Chance, steal Greyson away from Jackie Evancho, she wanted more hits than *Charlie Bit My Finger*, wanted to rock together with Greyson or whoever, maybe Rihanna & Katy & Avril, to the SU2C (*Stand Up To C*) Manifesto to music . . .

This is where the end of cancer begins!

When together we become a force unmistakable
A movement undeniable
A light that cannot dim!
When we take our wild impossible dreams

And make them possible,
Make them true . . .
when together we rise as one.
When we stand up -
when we Stand Up To Cancer . . .

——it was *her* time, *hersurvivor* time, her mom loved watching Laura Linney have C on TV, kancer was in the *air,* kancer was hot, Telma wanted someone to orchestrate the swag, the kancerswag, copyrighted back-to-school backpacks, journals and calendars just like Taylor Swift, she wanted to go kancerdashian, entrepreneured greeting cards and keychains with hands in the shape of ♥s logos, t-shirts, headbands & lunchboxes, maybe her own *zero to hero* clothing line, bandaids & babypowder & pajamas & K(ancer)-Mart pajama jeans, maybe even design the bottles the medicine comes in———the wheels were turning . . .

. . . *everything old is new again*————

She got a big idea and maybe the genesis of the big idea had something to do with Lea Michele and (an unannounced) Barbra Streisand dueting on "Children Will Listen" at the NMJC! Ball (*No More Juvenile Carcinoma!*) at the Beverly Hilton—she was supposed to be there but that was the weekend she went with her mom to the White House——maybe it had something to do with Miley Cyrus, Drake, Jeff Bridges (Gwen *loved* Jeff Bridges), Chris Colfer (Telma *loved* Chris Colfer) and Rihanna taking the stage at that very same event . . . maybe it had something to do with (an unannounced) Steve Perry joining all the above ½way thru "Don't Stop Believin'"——or maybe it had something to do with the upstart Canuck's malicious personal best . . . because Telma wasn't interested in the silver: she wanted Olympic gold.

Whatever it had something to do with, she already had that tried & true familiar tingly feeling in her tummy, same as when Christina Applegate flew her & two other hersurvivors (dubbed "The Pink Bucket Brigade") to Louisville to lipsynch dance a raucous, hypomanic "Single Ladies" at KFC's lavish corporate HQ "Buckets For the Cure" Breast Cancer Awareness Brunch.

So her idea was to be on *Glee*.

Not as a guest, and not as a *Glee Project* loser doing a 4-part consolation arc. No way!

To be on *Glee—permanent cast member*.

They already had cripples and fags and fat sexless mountainous black monsters & whatever. They needed a spunky funny pretty girl being stalked by an unseen predator, the one that would come for us all, it'd be like Lea or Heather or Matthew suddenly got a fatal disease. It would be *hot* and awesome, & it would *rock*.

With newly minted brainstormy resolve, the fear receded—that wild, vicious little-girl-fearing-littler-girl poison fear—not rescinded but softly retreated, soaking her to the bone in *Ellen*ish Hope, & the ajar world opened wide like an awesome fragrant flower blooming in the night.

[Reeyonna]

*Everyone's a ★**

(*and deserves the right to twinkle)

Reeyonna's

mother insisted she go with her to the Central Library for an *event*.
She rolled her eyes and took more pills.

"You're going to go, Jerilynn, and you're going to like it. And *no
texting*. For one whole hour."

She used to call herself Jeri but it'd been Reeyonna for a while
now. Mom was the only person left who called her by the hideous
birthname. She could h8t on her twice—for calling her that, and for
naming her that.

Friends sometimes called her Ree, for ReeRee (the singer's nickname tho Rihanna spelled it *RiRi*; Rihanna's closest friends/family
called her Robyn). Every girl at middleschool had a mad crush on
the Rihannaissance Woman, with different cliques having different ogle alerts: Rihanna fashionwatch, (secret)body(spray)watch,
hair&wigwatch, chrisbrownwatch, S&Mwatch. Ree liked RiRi way
more than Nicki—Nicki was awesome, she was genius, an amazing
actress, a *comedienne*, OMG that song *shitted on em* was so hardcore*,*
LMFAO, but Nicki was kind of cartoony, she liked being cartoony,
all that Barbie stuff + she had that cartoony Kardashian ass—but

Rihanna was a *woman*, not that Nicki wasn't but maybe Rihanna was *more* of a woman. Sometimes it was just too hard to relate to Nicki, like she was moving too fast or whatever, but you could always relate to Rihanna, or aspire to be like her, or relate to aspiring to be like her. Plus she was more upfront sexier than Nicki, or maybe it's just that she was more upfront about sex period, you never really heard too much about Nicki's hookups, maybe Nicki had some hangups, but Rihanna was *out* there. ReeRee & her friends didn't like what Chris Brown did but they all *loved* Chris Brown & didn't care if they were fucking again as long as he didn't hit her, everyone thought it was swank when Rihanna changed the restraining order so it wouldn't interfere with Chris performing at award shows Rihanna was at because before she changed it he couldn't be like within 100 yards of her meaning he couldn't even go to the same award shows she went to even if he was nominated, swank that she could move on & swank that she told all the hashtag h8trs to *back the fuck off*. Besides, no one could dance like Chris flying thru the air on the VMA, Reeyonna'd been getting stoned and watching that performance every day for a year now——& that youtube of him dougie-ing OMG it made her cum, *Sex in the air I like the smell of it*, she was sure they'd get back together one day, a fairytale that began grimm but frog-princed in the end, Ree just wished she'd seen the hacked foto of his dick Chris sent her to make nice but Rikki couldn't find it on the Internet.

One day ReeRee wanted to be in a magazine with perfect abs, perfect tits, perfect tatts. Rihanna had about 20 of them so far, she & Chris Brown got matching ☆s, how awesome was that, hers was on the back of her neck, his behind his beautiful little ear. She kept it after he beat on her but added more stars. How awesome was that. (She loved the idea of getting a ☆ somewhere, maybe near her pussy, she loved the Marilyn quote Lindsay had *everyone's a star and deserves the right to twinkle*, Lindsay had a ☆ on her wrist too and a *live without regrets* and *clear as a crystal sharp as a knife I feel like I'm in the prime of my life* on her ribs but Rikki said rib tatts hurt like fuck no matter how loaded you got.) Ree had the idea to get one of those totally lifelike portrait tatts of her baby when it was created (the Kardashians used *created* instead of *born*), which was only like 7½ months away, no one but her 2 BFFs even knew she was pregnant, them and her bf Rikki. ReeRee wanted to get her baby's face on her arm or thigh or even maybe on her ribcage below the tit, they could do tatts of photos so amazingly real and eerie, she saw one on an old *LA Ink*, a gal got her nephew on her shoulderblade, he was thrown from the car & died when they were hit by a drunk——maybe a poem on the ribs that swept below her ♥, like in keltic or Hebrew or maybe in Buddhist, lots of movie stars had those, but how could you even pick a poem, there were so many? The trouble with getting a baby pic or a poem under your tit was one day your tit would sag & cover the pome ;(

Reeyonna googled what celebs had, Angelina had one about praying for the wild at ♥—Ree wanted something *trés femme* on her back, not the usual disgusting tramp stamp but like a psalm from the Bible, or whatever about a biblical woman—————huge-ass angelwings like Natalie Portman in *Black Swan*? or maybe was that Mila. Natalie probably doesn't have any in real life, she's the kind of girl who's too beautiful to get tatts. Angelina's beautiful too but tougher, Natalie you just want to protect. *I love you Natalie!* ReeRee thought it might be awesome to have something hardcore for the top of her butt (Rikki called them *ass antlers*) or the side of the V right above her puss or maybe wrapped around her thigh—something tight like a snake or barbed wire or lyrical like from a song by Drake or Eminem or even the bible that would be so tight—she imagined everybody clicking on her TMZ slideshows, looking so fly, topless or in a black&white Chanel bikini diving off Jay-Z/Beyoncé's (Queen B's nickname: JuJu) yacht (dubbed by Ree the *HMS Bed, Bath and Beyoncé*) in Martinique or Sardinia or Cannes (a circled ZOOM-IN pic of Ree's fresh raised-up skinswollen *"hooker"*/"𝖈𝖗𝖎𝖒𝖎𝖓𝖆𝖑" tatts, which would do in her mind until she found the right pome/lyric), with her new Justins friends Timberlake/Theroux/Bieber, Natalie

(Ree & Jujubee & Natalie could share the same nanny for their babies), and Gwyneth & Reb'l Fleur, which is the nickname meaning
wildflower given to Rihanna by her grandma, & the name of RiRi's
fragrance developed by or maybe just in partnership with Jay-Z.
Nicki & Beyoncé & Kreayshawn/Katy Perry/Gwen Stefani had fra-
grances too (& Marc Anthony, but you could only get it at
KOHL'S!!!!!!) . . . . she put Snoop, Kreayshawn & Usher on the
yacht, and Adele, and Rikki of course, Rikki the b.f., Rikki the
current&future father of her child, *their* child (soon to be Blue Ivy's
bff), tho maybe instead of its babyface tatted on *her* it'd be tatted on
Daddy instead, right on his sixpack, totally officially transforming
him into awesome BFFF (*Best Friend Father Forever* <3<3<3<3<3)
. . . . . . it'd be good to have him on the yacht to look after their baby
if the nanny was busy with the others', Ree didn't want to be worrying about changing diapers, not while she was gangbangin with
Eminem and Skylar Grey——& *Sasha Grey* too, like that video Rikki
showed her!!!!! Reeyonna sat there in the Central Library auditorium
& tripped on getting fucked by Drake/Dre & Fiddy, and that freak
Yelawolf too, DP'n til dawn. She thought it'd be weird getting fucked
by Lil Wayne, probably a taste you had to cultivate, she thought he
was so sweet but he was a *ugly*-looking nigga, like a devil, she wondered if he had bodystank, but if she tried which she sometimes did
when she was up in the trees getting fucked by Rikki she could make
herself come thinking of that youngmoney cashmoney cock . . . she
told herself (still in her little reverie) that if her b.f./father-and-
husband-to-be hooked up with Rihanna she'd be hella tight with
that ;D——in her fantasia she put a few others on the boat—Jennifer
Lawrence & Emily Watson & Robert Pattinson and Kristen, at the
OBGYN she read a *Vanity Fair* saying they earned 25 million each for
the last two *Twilights* which made them by far the poorest on the
HMS Bed, Bath and Beyoncé!!!!! (in Ree's dreams she and Rikki always had around 100 mill + another 35 coming in a year from where
she knew not, the music business/movies + merchandizing/concerts/
spatial appearances.) Now Nicki was on the yacht too, right? And Ye

& Kim Kardash . . . . . Rikki could Nickifuck *and* Kristenfuck too, Ree told herself it was only fair, she'd fuck Kristen too, Kristen Stewart was *hot,* she didn't usually go that way but now & again she'd fool around with her BFFs who were all shall we say *slightly broadminded,* she'd fuck Kimmy K & Skylar Grey & Nicki & Jenny L——— broadsminded broads on the mind *Heh heh heh*

M M M Money on my mind
M M M Money on My Mind
M M M Money on my Mind

Fuck bitches

Get money

Fuck bitches

GET MONEY

<3<3<3<3<3<3

. . .

Reeyonna's mom (Jacquie) was a photographer who became famous taking nude pre-pubescent pics of her daughter. It was a cyclical thing but back in the day there happened to be a whole crowd of arty photog moms who got their kicks from family nudies. Jacquie (that's what Ree called her, never Mom) always had legal problems when she showed at galleries which was kind of the point because it was good for sales. She had affairs with whatever 1st-Amendment lawyers represented her, just to give em a little more incentive heh heh. Jacquie *loved* when her work got banned, she came alive & glowed like she was preg (Ree wondered when *she* was going to start to glow, and worried if the glow started too soon it might be a giveaway). Once when they almost charged Jacquie with kidporn, the gallery got so much press it totally sold out of pics & Jacquie had to go print more. The whole mom putting you in nature *au snatchurel* at age 8 with your *Lord of the Flies* hair & no tits/nohair'd slit was a total creepathon. Which definitely got creepier as Ree grew older & more self-conscious of her body.

————now she was 16, way over the hill for the mom to cash in anymore. Plus Jacquie was really struggling, hadn't had a show in 5 years, didn't know what direction to take her Art. *Definitely* couldn't do the nudie thing again.

Reeyonna thought: *it's my time to shine.*

She was slowly coming into her own and the world was starting to take notice, to pay attention in funny little ways.

Dear Reeyonna,

We missed you so much, we've created an exclusive Proactiv® package—just for you . . .

.   .   .

The mom was always dragging her to *events*, like chambermusic performed in galleries, or artwalks&openings, art this's & art that's. The *events* of course being all about Jacquie promoting herself, or trying to anyway. Kind of sad. Her big brother Jerry (½brother from the mom's first marriage) joked about Jacquie lugging Ree along as pussybait. That was true; part of Jacquie's master plan. She called the mom *Pimp My Ride* to her face. Ree laughed when she saw the *Keeping Up With the Kardashians* where Kim gets a psoriasis outbreak before filming a commercial & their mom panicks and Kourtney tells their mom not to pretend to be worried about Kim's health when what she's *really* worried about is that the bad skin shit might ruin "the *moneymaker*, that *big fat ass.*" *I love Kourtney!*

But last month was cool because James Franco was the *event*— Central Library again—talking about a novel he wrote. Reeyonna didn't understand how or *why* (anyone) James Franco would want to

or could even *write* a novel, tho Kourtney, Kim & Khloé were writing one and asking their fans to name it. One of the perks of being
the World's Biggest Loser Artist and Has-Been was that sometimes
Jacquie could hang with whoever-famous after whatever *event*, which
was sometimes good and sometimes bad. So that was how they came
to hang with James Franco (definitely good). At *events*, there was always that torture moment (sweet revenge for Reeyonna) at the end
of each *event* when Jacquie slowly edged her way to the front of the
room toward whoever-famous while letting Reeyonna hang back,
she could tell Jacquie was shitting her thriftstore YSL slacks (Ree
thought that her mother seriously needed a swag coach) over whether
or not whoever-famous would recognize her—even if they once collected her back in the toast of the town nudie days. During those
post-*event* deathmarches Jacquie always tried to be cool, pretending
for her daughter she didn't *expect* to be recognized, didn't care if she
wasn't, when the truth was, if whoever-famouses were merely polite
upon self-introduction, Jacquie died 1,000 deaths & the ride home
would be skulky & sucky, her mother so preoccupied with her
bullshit that Ree could swallow pills without really too much bothering to conceal. But sometimes the moment of torture could be
avoided/mitigated by a little reconnoitering on Jacquie's part, say, if
she managed to contact the famous-whoever directly, *before* the
Event, by personal email or cell. If that happened and the famous-
whoever told her yes, do say hello, evincing a proper enthusiasm, one
that seemed *promising*, well then they'd approach the famous-whoever
at *event's* end, Jacquie hovering between fear & confidence/hopeful-
ness, & pathetically *not* let her daughter hang back, not just because
the possibility of rejection had (for the most part) been averted, but
the pussbait might just be the thing that tipped everything over in
her favor . . . . . . of course she'd kept her little secret—that contact
had been made—from Reeyonna—it was *so* pathetic!—fortunately,
in the case of James Franco, the mother's whorish maneuver had
been welcomed—by his smile and some of the little things he said
Ree could deduce that he knew Jacquie was coming, you could smell

her coming anyway, smell her panic and toady whoriness, *so* pathetic to be an old hooker no one wanted to fuck on *top* of even still having a *sliver* of the need to impress your daughter with the amazing legend of who you used to be. So sick & disgusting! So World's Biggest Loser!

Evidently James Franco apparently (supposedly) owned or once-owned a few of Jacquie's pics. It was embarrassing to be standing there with James Franco when he probably knew what her naked body looked like when she was 8 or 10 or 12, maybe he even re-freshed himself with ipad images on his way to the *event,* maybe the image was warmscreening in his pocket right while he was talking to them. Or while *Jacquie* was talking to *him,* because James wasn't really saying much. Maybe at home he had that famous pic of Reeyonna née Jerilynn standing in a swamp in Lafayette-St Martinville, the one that almost had her up on a porn charge, the one with her holding a toy gun next to her pee-hole while some anonymous 3-year-old tyke cupid-dick arc-pisses in the artily unfo-cussed b.g. Whenever Jacquie took particularly risqué pix she made sure to do them in silver gelatin or platinum/palladium or some such other obsolete pricey process/technique to dignify&justify&signify her shit. *So* fucking pretentious sick. While the World's Biggest Loser climbed up James Franco's asshole, Reeyonna stuffed embar-rassment by imagining herself sucking on his cock, then him lifting her by the armpits to do with her what he will. She pictured him going over his lines or writing a pome or the chapter of a novel while he fucked her up the ass, her other holes filled by Andrew Garfield & T Lautner, & Taylor Swift/Rooney Mara sucking on her tits too———————————————;D <3 lol

.   .   .

Tonight's *event's* whoever-famous was called Steve Martin, who she mos def did *not* want to fuck, suck *or* be sashagrey'd by. Jacquie said he was a famous comedian who played the banjo and used to work at Disneyland. *Whatever!* Oh: then she said he hosted *SNL* a lot, like maybe "I think he's hosted the most after Alec Baldwin," *so* Biggest Loser now ask me if I give a shit. But when her mom said *Steve Martin* sold a painting for 28 million dollars, one single painting by someone not Picasso who Reeyonna totally never heard of, that got her attention. For like 10 seconds. It made her think of the *Hollywood's Richest Teens* article she read in *People* about Miranda Cosgrove's multi-mill$$$$$ contract with Neutrogena/Justin Bieber's fragrance selling $3 mill in 3 weeks/Taylor L splurging on a 300K Mercedes-Benz ALS AMG Roadster.

Just before the *event* started, she excused herself to the bathroom to text & swallow 4 Percs and a 100 mills of adderall, washed down with a coke zero minican she always traveled with in her purse—the only way Ree was going to get through it. She went back to her seat and not-texted, letting her mind drift——————————— . . . .

. . . . the same pic of Whitney Port was in all the weeklies, lounging by a pool with her rockin body at a hotel in Hawaii. Ree wished she had Whitney's rockin hardbody, not Audrina's, even though Audrina's body was awesome, but Audrina had *issues,* and maybe a mom more horrible than even Jacquie (not quite). She had implants then had them taken *out,* a lot of stars did that, even Brittany from *Glee,* they put them *in* then have infections or whatever then take them *out,* only the smart ones like Natalie never think of it, they have too much class, or like Drew, Drew had to have a *reduction* because she was so stacked that she used to get backaches & whatever. But you never really believe Audrina, Audrina might *say* she took them out when they were really still *in.* Reeyonna drifted, wishing she had Whitney Port's face and body, even tho Whitney was kind of *over* . . . . Audrina was *definitely* over. No————— better to have a face like Blake Lively or Scarlett or Mila . . . . or a face/body like the Olivias: Olivia Palermo, Olivia Munn, Olivia Wilde, Olivia the pig . . . *LMFAO———I love Olivia the pig!* At home she'd trip out smoking the Blue Ivy weed that Rikki got her, googling | Q celebrity baby olivia? | to see who was having or already had *Olivia* babies, it was like *everyone*, like the *Scarface* guy Al Pacino, and Kirk Cameron & Chelsea Noble, the *Borat* guy & Isla— no wait! Is she called *Olive?*—& Justine Bateman (<3!!!), Lori Loughlin, James V Der Beek, Ben Stiller, (& Denzel & Kelsey Grammer) . . . . . . *oh shit*, she could *never* name her daughter Olivia which was *so sad* because she loved Olivia, tho maybe it didn't really even matter——————————————————the audience was laughing and she heard the faraway drone of Mr. Steve Martin as her head slopped & slurped around in the methoxycodone mishmash, flitting and drifting to the porn Rikki made her watch then pretending she was a judge on *The Voice* then just TV overall in general, warm dreamy pillworld backwash. Her BFFs were still totally into MacMainlining whole seasons, they had this rule where they only watched by the season, big clumps on the free tv sites, they were *obsessed* with that rad motocross chick Lisa Kelly on *Ice Road Truckers*, she was *awesome!* no one cared about *The New Girl* or *Glee* or *Idol* but they still liked *The Voice* and the Kardashians & sometimes watched *2½ Men* because they wanted to *so bad* fuck&suck Ashton . . . you watched different shows on different drugs, the drugs were your clicker. Rikki watched old *Dexters* & *Walking Deads* & weird Netflix DVD docs and made her watch when she didn't want to which was tight as long as they kushed, which they always did anyway before sex or after and even during, she was actually really trying not to smoke, even tho her BFFs said she had it wrong, she could smoke 4ever but stop the roxys & addies til after the baby. 2 fucking hard!!! When Rikki made her watch porn of course they smoked & usually started out with those crazy docs, making girls watch lame scary gross stuff on the internet or wherever was such a guy thing, she didn't even know how he found this shit, some were kind of interesting but some there was no way she could *even*, like the site with different drunk women being raped & it looked like *killed*, Rikki said it was fake but there was no way! or the one with movies spectators took on their iPhones after car crashes before the ambulance got there, poor little kids laying in the road their bodies all bent in the craziest sickeningest ways, people crying and screaming and barfing. He showed her one about a city in China that had this tradition that when a guy died & he was single, his parents would go out and find a woman who was dead to be his bride. They'd dig up her body and bury the two together so they could be a married couple in the afterlife! It was like a really gross, really sad version of *The Bachelor*. The doc said the dead guys needed to be at least 12 to be eligible, it was the law that you couldn't have a dead wife if you were like underage. Sometimes the parents of the dead girls could make money too, like if you had a daughter & she drowned or whatever, you could fish her out of the water and get money by selling the body like a dowry. *So* gross and *so* sad. If you lived in China and your wife died, now you had to worry about people digging her up and selling her like on Craigslist! *OMG!!!* ☹☹☹ She couldn't remember if there was the minimum age thing with girls, probably not, because girls were so discriminated against in Asia and the rest of everywhere, in school the teacher said sometimes in India or Africa or China if the woman has a girl the husband kills the baby right then and there, just like throws it against a wall. So sick and disgusting, so ratchet and *beyond!* If someone tried to kill *her* baby (if it was a girl, or even if it wasn't) she would so torture them forever! Whenever Reeyonna heard shit like that she was so happy and grateful to be living in America, no matter how fucked up things were like the economy. Another doc Rikki made her watch was about a British actress/model with a thing for serial killers—and well *of course* she lived in LA, where *else* would you go for your Dexter dreamdate? This girl like became *obsessed* with a truck driver who was in jail for killing prostitutes. They couldn't seem to catch him so he like wound up having to walk into the police station like the guy in *7even* who cut off Gwyneth's head, he walked straight in carrying a *breast* in a Ziploc bag!!!——*O M G*— like his last kill! *So gross* and *so sad.* It said that she visited him in jail and they sang Dwight Yoakam songs through the glass, which actually does go to show there's someone for everyone. (((;p lol))) Rikki cackled when the voice said the Brit in love with the Dexter used to model for "Herbal Grobust"———a company that made pills supposed to give you bigger tits!!!!!!!!!!!!!!!!!!!!!

Oh.   My.   God.

—————————the applause startled her—the *event* was over, at least the public part. Jacquie leaned into Reeyonna, never taking her eyes off Mr. Steven Martin, who was still onstage, already surrounded by brown-nosing Biggest Losers.

"Steve knows we're here," she said, surprising Reeyonna. She had that pathetic *lilt* in her voice.

Oh fuck that must mean he wants to hang. The thought of Mr 28 Million ever having seen her flat chest&braces was repulsive.

"Let's wait for the crowd to thin a little then see if maybe he wants to have a drink."

[Rikki]

Dirty Thumbnails

He'd

never been that into porn, not really, but lately he was, he liked to get up in the trees with ReeRee, future mother of his future child (*whoa!*) & watch xxxtreme Tube links on his fosterdad's iMac then fuck. Lately he made them watch clips on the *daughterdestruction* site & he'd get turned on by the way Ree overreacted, she'd freak about how *gross* it was, kind of overdoing it all the while eyes glaze-glued (*goo'd* to go) to the screen as the dads wreaked their anal havoc; suchwise Rikki knew she was completely into it. The contrary playacting made him go H.A.M., as they used to say.

There was always webtalk about celeb sextapes but that shit wasn't really on Rikki's radar. Why would he want to watch sicko fanboy slo-mo compilations of that sassy girl who starred in *Hugo* dancing on Jimmy Fallon or Kim Kardash getting off with Ray J (maybe for a minute) (maybe longer) (definitely would fuck Nicki M) when he could surf the lubesites & trip on dwarfchicks gettin facialed & creampie'd, or dudes with big bald heads vanishing into a bitch's pussy til you could only see their fat necks, or Sasha Grey getting

DP'd/ATM'd* (in HD), 14 lucky volunteers, bearded homeless-looking mutherfuckers with fixed stares and dilated eyes, hands idly jostling/tugging at dicks to keep their stiffies until it came their turn, buncha bums waiting on/line like they do at Midnight Mission mealtime, a cold, slow-moving queue snaking up to that batshit-crazy white girl, no condoms to be seen, the mini-marathon going down in one of those stuccoey porn safehouses, white & empty except for a mattress and maybe a couch, the biggest ugliest white pleather couch known to man in the known world. The Sasha Grey tape he liked most was the one with the guy laying on the floor on his back and her on top trademark-screaming *fuck yeah! fuck yeah!* the greased otherhole butt-up in its devilish pillow, ready for the ass-jacking, the xxxxxtreme home invasion, & when it came each bum's turn, the sorry-looking dude took his dick and sort of almost politely *placed* it in her bunghole, something almost rather *civil* about it, suddenly they were *in,* up & running, ruin-fucking the apple-sized void that was really just the deadmouth end of SG's large intestine, each bum bumfucking in perfect little segmenty moments of time, never over-staying/shooting their wad or their welcome, must have been someone off-camera giving them the wrap-it-up sign, afterall, this was a professional operation, and as the next-in-lines took their brothers' vacated place, the just-pulled-outs walked two steps to where her mouth was and Sasha Grey sucked them, by definition sucking the sheen of ass & pussy discharge that coated the bumdicks, by the 6th or 7th dipstick there couldn't have been all that much, rectally speaking, a friend of Rikki's told him that porn chicks did some enema detoxing before anal gangbangs, so there probably wasn't too much shit on the stick but naturally bits of blood & viscousy effluvia & whatever from the odd tear in the fabric so to speak, not to mention the dirty leakages/cum & pre-cum courtesy of the bum's rush, and while Sasha sucked (occasionally pausing to full-throat shout *fuck yeah! Fuck yeah!* between blowjobs, *fuck*-YEAH!-shouting with dead pottymouth that was a mouth yes plus being of

---

* Ass to Mouth

course the rank scarlet beginning of esophagus/little intestine) the next vagrant dick already politely proboscising, and so on & so on & so forth, on and on it went, a looped lubey-tube daisy-chain rondelay/square dance from Hell. When a buddy told Rikki that Sasha Grey had actually guest starred on *Entourage*, Rikki thought he was punking him. He never watched that old piece of shit show, couldn't find a Sasha clip on youtube, he'd have to Netflix, his fosters didn't have HBO anyway.

Rikki knew lots of kids at middleschool who did celeb sextapes, that's what everyone called em, "celeb sextapes," if you were a middleschooler & made one you could call yourself a celeb, just like how any porn actor's usually called a pornstar. He'd go on one of the XXXXXXwebcam tubes and there'd be videos they grabbed from stickam.com or some innocent social network site where home-alone girls or 3-girl sleepovers are in their bedrooms flirting and shit but occasionally they'd do more than that, and when they did, the webcam porntubes would capture & upload. Like a lion hiding in the grass. The girls didn't even look stoned to him, they were just sexed up, which made it even hornier. Rikki saw a few girls from school he sort of kind of knew, maybe they were two grades down. It was no big thing. ReeRee knew a chick who didn't even go to school anymore, webcamming from her room in panties and showing her stomach not even her tits, she never had to strip for men or use a dildo, they'd send money anyway, some would write and say she shouldn't be doing this cause you never can tell who was out there, all like *You know I have a daughter your age*, full-on I-want-to-protect-you shit as they squirt-jacked. She put a big teddy on the bed, all the chicks learned that from the live-chat/*barelylegal* sites, the cruddy stuffed animals shoved anywhere they could be seen, little pathetic clusters . . . . lots of middleschoolers FaceTimed themselves (*Face Times at Ridgemont High*) coming or dildo-ing or doing ATM or whatever or iPadded/MMS'd movies to each other. Rikki tried not to do that, the one or two times he did tho he made sure his face wasn't on camera, you could see the girl but not him, his friends

called him a pussy but whatever. Now that Ree was pregnant he
didn't especially want to disrespect her that way *whoa* he still hadn't
even been able to wrap his mind around having a baby (a *what?*), it
felt like a tiny fist punching his ♥ whenever he thought about it so he
tried not to think about it———at all——except when they were
together———————————(Tiny baby fist) . . . .
. . . . Rikki clicked a thumbnail with the caption
Exploited by school pediatrician. 26 minutes long, 92% thumbs-up,
1,549,351 views, 4.4 out of 5.0 rating. A Jap schoolgirl being examined by a doctor with a censored blurface. He fondled her, at first
subtly then crazy-brazen until Rikki was watching a full-on molest/
half-rape. Cams were hidden, three different angles, once in a while
changing POVs like security cameras at 7-Eleven. The call-his-shit-
Patricia/pediatrician looked like a retarded Jackie Chan. He fought
the girl over her bra, finally pulling it up til it sat strained twisted-
clumsy on top her tits, she kept crying crying crying as he tweaked
her nipples, kept resisting, but the Patricia kept on keepin on, fought
with her some more over pulling up her skirt but his fingers gave
him the upper hand *haha* crotchgroped but let her keep her panties
on, pain-swiping them aside to expose her stingy bubblegum-pink
Just Say No nippy lips. Jackie Chan Patricia kept jabbering the whole
time in Japanese & the schoolgirl squirmed and shifted and half-sat
up, squeal-crying as he turned to go fish something from a cabinet,
all you saw was the back of his lab coat, then the POV switched and
another cam showed him stick a butt probe in there but the poor
slopehead schoolgirl was no Sasha G. Plenty of cavities but all unco-
operative. Rikki numbly massaged his cock waiting for the reluctant
bitch to reciprocate Patricia's intense horniness, that's how they usually did it, the schoolgirl/cheerleader/babysitter or whoever resisted
for a while then got horny in spite of themselves, that's when the
clothes would come off and you'd see all the crappy tatts & piercings
or what have you. For Rikki it was always an especial hard-off bummer when a ho had those corkscrew, witchy fingernails, like anything but psycho trailercunt could think that was sexy to a man, think

it was sexy to be jacking themselves with those twisty fingernails held daintily *up & back*, he saw a nigger at the Children's Courthouse with that shit, she *worked* there too, they probably couldn't fire her because of some can't-discriminate-against-a-crazyass-Guinness-World-Record-Book-longnail'd-bitch-nigger law, nigger even'd figured out a way how to write with a pen, he had to stand there and watch this nigger fastidiously filling out a form, clickclack nails all tangled up like fuckin moose antlers, these longnailed *working* niggers were real pros with the nails shit——————the thing Rikki hated the most was when a pornstar put on a dumb devilface and talked shit like *that's right fuck my ass with that hard black cock*, Rikki always ✋'d MUTE when that shit happened (he never MUTEd on the goth & emo tubes. Found himself unexpectedly partial to suicide girls' pale white skin & bobbed black hair & the bright-colored tatts that shocked their milkywhiteness, plus they were usually tight, no longass nails + they never said stupid shit while they got raped, some of em even kept their glasses on which Rikki thought was way horny . . . .

But the girl kept crying crying crying, resisting and crying.

Rikki maximized and skipped ahead, dick in hand, still H.A.M. He moved the ✋ ahead on the 26-minute time bar but at 18.08 she was still resisting so he ➡'d some more til he was like a minute from the end but the bitch was still struggling, face looking all rapey & puffy as the ghostface killa/blurfaced pediatrician who probably called his shit Patricia hunched down & boned her on the examination table, his pants comically down around his ankles, why did that always look funny, type of thing that might bring you out of your trance-jack, at 25:28 the schoolgirl still enduring, writhing, suppressing panic while Dr. Phil/Patricia bad breath-whispered kamikaze shit in her ear, the muthafucka never even removed that grimy white coat.

Rikki ✋'d the time bar so he'd have more time to jack. Still strokin but partly creeped out. I mean it was horny but he wondered if it was really for real-real . . . . probably wouldn't be on one of the tubes if it was, cause they have ads running underneath for movies & shit, movies out now in the theaters, big ones like *The 3 Musketeers* & the new *American Pie* & shit, they couldn't do that if the shit was illegal. Cause it wasn't like one of those Russian sites with the girls being full-on underage, beat-up&raped, it had to be staged otherwise everyone who went online would be in trouble, whole muthafuckin *world*, tho he did puzzle over why Patricia's face was blurred out, tho if it was all pretend shit maybe that was just part of the pretend. Patricia likes to pretend. All the vids Rikki looked at usually had thousands of hits, sometimes hundreds of thousands or millions, no one could press charges against that many fuckin people for watching. There would always be some sketchy shit no *doubt*. Shady shit. Sometimes you'd click on a hinky thumbnail, a little bitch in braces with flat titties or whatever, & it'd say *this video has been deleted*. It might say something about the muthafuckas in it looked *too young,* no shit! No doubt. He'd clicked on just to see, just curious, cause it wasn't his thing, like watching dogs&pigs&horses fuck bitches (get money! fuck bitches! get money!) wasn't his thing but that doesn't mean he was never on the animal farm. And that shit could be *funny* if you were kickin it in the trees with your homies. Chicks trying to stuff pony cock into their pussies. But the Chester tubes . . . some of those lil-ass hookers looked like they were muthafuckin *ten years old*, what would happen is there were all these legit sites where kiddies did their chats, harmless rite of passage shit, talking to each other or whatever, you could always hear their parents bitchin at them from wherever & the kiddies would roll their eyes with *fuck you's* under their breath, tiny rebel shit, but sometimes kiddies got horny and nasty, everyone knew that biologically girls got sexed up way before the men, they were having their periods at six yrs old, & the xxxxxwebcum tubes would be out there prowlin, lions in the bush just waiting to pounce & *capture* the muthafuckin videos before the so-called legit sites found em & took em down . . . . Rikki went on a webcum site & found two slumberkiddies, webcummers titled the vid "2 hot home alone teens strip & shake their asses." The *home alone* category webcum vids always had the most hits . . . . the kiddies in this one had tatts too but the tatts were homemade, Sharpie'd shooting ☆s up and down their arms, one had Hebrew-type letters on her tummy like copying Lindsay or whomever——& sho' nuff they turned and shook their asses just like whores & strippers, busting little moves straight out of porn, all the little kids watched porn now. Tho even *that* tube had banners & shit announcing the latest flicks, ads and trailers that interrupted & Rikki had to wait for them to end before seeing the bitches giggle & shake their meatless asses at the iCam. One of the iKids—there was always one who was nastier than the other—one of em was on her way to being a pro, had two fingers up her ass, you could tell her little friend was kind of shocked/titillated, small-titsillated, whatever . . . . . . fucking poster of Bieber on the wall. Some shady shit. One of his homies said he went on this site called *tiny tiny tiny* and there were all these little bitches bending over to show their snatches, he said they were divided into categories like 'Age 6—12'—*damn.* No way he was gunna even get *near* that shit————————————————

   Rikki was back at 18:26 on the Jap schoolgirl timeline, he noticed his pants had fallen down around his ankles just like Dr. Patricia, he innerly laughed about that—you know, like, well that's how everybody winds up one way or the other, all the boys and the girls with their pants 'n panties down around their ankles, but he was too busy rubbing one off to let it brake the flow—bout to jizz then suddenly a tiny RON JEREMY popped up huddling next to an outrageously pink, boomerang-curved penis, looked like a 50-foot parenthesis . . . the skinternet had driven a stake through the ♥ of porn, the skeevy muthers were suffering (everyone but Sasha Grey), nothing more pitiful than an O.G. pornstar out of work, even Ron the Hedgehog Jeremy had been forced to diversify, putting silly putty penis elongator pills in his hornporn portfolio. Rikki was still jacking when the words of a satisfied customer crisscrossed the veiny hard-on: "This shit is like *steroids* for your dick! I'm almost 10" long!" Rikki x'd & ❮'d to get back to the violated schooljap but got one of those skanky live-videos instead, a titjobbed quiff in a cubicle with the ugliest curtains known to man in the known world strung up behind them like they do, hooker Bin Ladens making sure no one can identify their homely shit & locate what cave they're in, like anyone'd be *lookin*. He MUTEd to kill the tinny come-ons of the bitch who was trying to rope lonelyass pervs into paying for a private *chat*————————then right then *10 thumbnails* of big-jug skunky skanks popped up, fucking assault on his screen, dialog-box captions informing him they were all *in the vicinity*, scarily zipcode-close to Rikki's house, 2 white girls in Beverlywood, 1 in Castle Heights, 3 in Mar Vista, 7 (mixed bag) in Culver City, 4 in Santa Monica, 3 (cute) little niggers in Westchester, all asking if he was horny 2nite & wanted to fuck, he forgot to turn off the location thing but was near the end, too close to webcumming to ↗ to System Preferences, but then he got paranoid someone maybe just now hacked into his iCam & was already broadbanding his private home alone self-soothing jackfest to the world————————cock in hand, he refreshed the screen which now featured a banner celebrating the tech proficiency of the tube he had currently engaged, its corporate slogan crawled across the top of the screen: "WE INNOVATE—YOU MASTURBATE"—then it said CLOSE AD and he clicked the x but it was one of those new x's that were fake, when you ↗'d all it did was magic carpet you to a new site, you hadn't closed anything, you'd opened tubeworld & called in the horndog hounds from hell, they knew you were jacking, the whole world was, & all they wanted was to hyperlinkspam you right when you were cumming, *they had you by the balls in the palm of their hand*————*fuck these mutherfuckers*————Rikki was forced to esc, he closed the site & all the herds of x's that had silently sprouted like deathcaps while he was doing his Doc Patricia thing, closed all the open Windows, cleared all his ogling tubular Google history, logged out, shut down & walked away.

Without coming.

And felt like *whoa*, not too happy with himself. Spanking to girl-rape wasn't exactly a big self-esteem elongator. *You better than that nigger, you know you are.* The wetness in his underwear at the tip of his cock made him feel pervy, like when he got beat in a group home for nocturnaling on the sheets.

He jacked and came & rolled some purp. About a ½hour later, he jacked again. Then he watched incest porn and jacked.

[Michael]

Deep Throat

When

the letter arrived by pouch he was in Bermuda watching *Glee* with his son.

A copy came to three separate places: his agency, his publicist, and Sloan-Kettering, where he'd done his radiation and chemo. Written on flower-patterned stationery in the looping penmanship of a child, you could make out the inchoate cursive it would ripen into a few years down the line.

Mr. Michael Douglas,

My name is Telma Belle Peony Ballendyne. (Belle is my grandma's name & Peony is my mom's favorite flower and mine too! though Peony isn't really on my birth certificate, <u>but Belle is!!</u>) I am 13 years old and a <u>Kansurvivor</u>. (YES I KAN!) I became a <u>HERO</u> (not <u>victim</u>) of this terrible disease at the age of <u>9 years old</u> and have been <u>Kancer-free for 4 years now</u>, making me the <u>youngest Kansurvivor in America and maybe the world</u>! The doctors decided that it was medically necessary to perform a double mastectomy, for which I am also Guinness World Record Book-bound. My father succumbed to K (of his colon) when I was just 3-years-old. There is a LOT more of my story which I will not BORE you with (at this time! ☺) but that you can casually access on my webpage www.TelmaTheKancerSlayer. com, also there is a lot of interesting/fun/educational information on YoungestKansurvivor@TelmasKancerKidsArmy. My twitter is @ telmasurvivor and I currently have 48,000 FaceBook friends to date. I also currently blog for HuffPost, and many others, and was a contributer (the youngest) to a book for children called "I Don't Think We're in Kancer Anymore." If you google "Telma Ballendyne HERO Youngest Cancer" (my "K" hasn't caught on with everyone yet but just you wait, it will!), you'll find me on YouTube as keynote speaker at the CNBC Heroes Ball and numerous other events in Los Angeles, Sacramento, Boston and New York. My FaceBook page (13,469 friends!!!!! And counting!!!!!) has totally rad pics of me and my mom and FLOTUS (Michelle) at the White House, and me with Sasha. Malia is not in the pictures because she was with her grandma who wasn't feeling well that day ☹

. . . & by the way, if you're wondering why I spell this terrible disease with a "K" it is NOT to be kute but rather because I think we HEROES can take some of its power away. By not even respecting it enough to spell it rightly (korrectly?), we thumb our noses in its face ;D !! and also, it's not as scary with a "K," the Kancer Kidz use Ks for "kandy kane" and that is why I encourage all Kancer Kidz in Telma's Heroes to ALWAYS spell it this way.

Currently, I live alone together with my mom in the Cheviot Hills neighborhood of Los Angeles, which I am sure you have past through so many times (motoring on Motor Boulevard!) on your way to 20th-Century Fox Studios, the studio you chose to release some of your so many block-busters such as **Wall Street 2: Money Never Sleeps** (my favorite), **Romancing the Stone** (my mom's favorite) and so many others too numerable to mention! **Michael, I am SO GLAD AND HAPPY WE ARE KANSURVIVORS TOGETHER!!!!** (I am sorry I didn't write you when this first happened to you. Please forgive me, please☹☺)

There are TWO reasons I would like to now meet you and have lunch or dinner with you or if you don't have time I could come over for some tea. The more you get to know me you'll see how PUSHY I can be!!! But pushy people gets things done, don't they. I'm going to start a Telma's Pushy People HEROES Army!

Here are the TWO reasons of which I have spoken:

1) I believe it to be pearative that <u>ALL KANSURVIVOR-HEROES should meet each other</u> because we need to set the example of COURAGE in the face of Iniquity to those who have gone <u>before us</u> and those who will be <u>ahead</u>. We are FAMILY and there is as my Mom says STRENGTH IN NUMBERS!

2) My dream is to be a star on the amazing GLEE show (also made by your friends the 20-th Century Fox people. Is <u>Fox</u> different from <u>20th Century Fox</u>?!! Someone tell me please, I have always wanted to know!!!) Perhaps you might be able to aid me in this endeavor. GLEE I know is in decline but also know it can as my mom said recapture the national conversation. It is such a wonderful example to all kids, whatever be their diversity, & I know it would be such a cool place to spread the Word . . . of HOPE!!!!!! ☺ ♥♥♥

I thank you Michael Douglas for your time and have enclosed a paper with all of my contacts & information, and weblinks too. By the way confidentially speaking, my MOM has assured me that you are HER hero for so many reasons (I think she has a crush!!! ☺) but I would like to state that I am writing this MYSELF with NO OUTSIDE INSENTIVE and when I told her I was my Mom rolled her eyes and said, "Sweetheart, if Mr. Douglas contacts you I promise I will drop everything and take you to him for high tea, be it in Los Angeles or be it in New York or be it the Bermuda Islands."

ALL OF MY LOVE to you and your beautiful wife Catherine and your BEAUTIFUL children Dylan and Carys as well (I promise not to ever spell it Katherine Karys!!!) ☺☺☺

Love,

ME aka Telma aka Hervivor (my "coined" word for girl survivors!) aka the Kancer Slayer aka Just Plain GRRRRRRRRL

Gutsy little gal.

Helluva story there . . .

He had his own special needs kid. The letter really touched him.

Since going public with his illness, Michael had received thousands of beautiful emails & what have you, and made a personal vow to answer them all. The postcards and letters were easy enough (tho there was a mountain of them), but he had to put together a small webteam to triage everything else. Occasionally, a note like Telma's slipped under the transom and touched him— one person's karma touching another's, an interaction somehow meant to be. Nothing New Agey about it, either; after what he'd been through, the actor found himself letting go of a lot of formerly glib, judgey generalizations. Now his days were infused by an alchemy of subtle grace he'd never known. The good days, anyway.

Girl had some serious heart. A full mastectomy at nine—holy shit. *If we can find a way to bottle your courage,* he wrote back, *the two of us will never have to work again.* He said he'd probably be in LA sometime in the next few months and would absolutely take her up on her offer. *I'll supply the crumpets, and my friends Fortnum & Mason will take care of everything else.* "Hervivor"—that made him smile. She'd been through the ringer, that one, but still had hella spark, hella gumption.

He'd call Ryan to arrange a visit to the set, even a sitdown with the casting folks. Made him smile.

. . .

Funnily enough, there were just a couple things he could tolerate entertainment-wise during chemo/radiation. One was *Glee* and the other was the movie *All That Jazz*. (Who'd a thunk?) Amid all the nausea, weakness & general *tsuris*, he even managed to drop Ryan Murphy a line to tell him as much, something he probably never would have done if his kids weren't such fans of the show. He didn't know Ryan, but got a lovely note back the very next day saying how moved he was that Michael had taken the time. He said he'd love it if he dropped by, that the cast would be "absolutely thrilled."

Next month, he would be in LA making a film with Larry Fishburne. He asked Cat, Why don't we put out a feeler about you doing a guest thing? She said, Naw, they wouldn't want an old broad. He said, Don't be so modest, they'd kill to have you on the show. They're looking for guest stars in your age group: you're their next choice after Betty White. She laughed. But she was an actor, which meant she was worried about being rejected. *That's just the way we are, no matter how many awards they give us.* Professional hazard.

—You loved what it did for Gwyn. Totally revived her career.

—Is that what you're saying, baby? That my career needs reviving?

—Of course not. Wrong word. [light/fun] *Refreshing.* Your career needs *refreshing.* Refresh the page.

—[sexy, like a horse rearing up] Ho *ho!*

—I think it'd be *fun.* You could have fun with it. Gwyn went in and had *fun,* it was contagious, & suddenly she's singing on the Grammies and touring with Cee Lo. Ryan's writing her a *musical* for chrissake.

—[sassy/blood up] Is that what I'm supposed to be doing? Touring? You know, maybe you're right, maybe I *should* be touring. Or better yet, why don't we see if I can do *Dancing With the Stars.*

—Come on, Cat, you just won a fucking *Tony*.

—[all Welsh & fiery] Or maybe I should just latch on to Beyoncé. Isn't she Gwyn's bestie? Chill with Gwyn & Jay-Z and do *fuck-all*———

As an actor, he *got* it, that fear of being shot down thing, or even the living up to Gwyneth thing. Probably dumb to have brought up. *But does she really think I wouldn't protect her?* Afterall, he was Michael Douglas, and knew a few things. His wife was still hurting after all the crap people wrote on the Internet (Oh She Bipolar NOT!!! Just spoiled & beautiful can be the Problem sometime she wonts attention What a way to get it!!)(It may very well be that she is in the process of being replaced with a younger woman. Given his history, this would not surprise me in the least)(she is Roman Catholic he is Jew they are lost christ is the only one who brings peace) but he knew she'd have a blast. Maybe he'd approach Ryan—if he didn't spark to it, that would be that. Catherine would never know.

Ryan Murphy, *Glee*'s creator, was some kind of multifarious genius. A few years back he had a show on cable called *Nip/Tuck*, a superlatively sophisticated "plastic surgeons gone wild" soap that MD thought was inordinately, outrageously great. It was super-sexual, super-smart, super out-there, & for a while (to his mind) there was nothing on HBO or anywhere else that could touch it. The show didn't just break taboos, it diced, sliced, fucked, & burned them, then fucked them again. (His favorite arc was Famke Janssen as a transexual life coach who was sleeping with her stepson.) It took a moment, but Ryan made the seamless transition to network—*Glee*—where the zeitgeist (and the money) was. And just when *Glee* was becoming a cultural phenom, off he went to direct Julia in *Eat, Pray, Love*. Didn't seem to be anything the man couldn't do.

Glee was fun & frothy & rude, with that kick musicals always gave him. Watching it with his kids was a gas. But where did *All That Jazz* come from, & why now? Why would he find himself reveling in that chronicle of a death foretold, during *chemo* no less? Michael had always been riveted by Fosse, he related to the drugs and Ziegfeldian crash&burn grandeur, the eyes-wide-open chronicle of self-destruct, he was held in thrall by the outsized, nakedly romantic, hypersexually sustained self-takedown. *Art as intervention* . . . he felt deeply the trajectory of Fosse's career as well: from unknown dancer to unknown actor to *wham!* genius of American dance *blam!* Academy Award-winning film director who worked maguslike without a net but never (not really) fell to earth. In the cold heat of Fosse's shadow, Michael was humbly reminded of his own (supremely successful) professional life: from unknown actor to unknown-then-*wham!*-known TV actor to *blam!* Academy Award-winning producer to Academy Award-winning actor—albeit it *sans* defining genius, at least in his own eyes. If anything, the actor's genius resided in the shrewd custodianship of his instincts. He had no problem acknowledging that somewhere in there was real talent, but had privately fretted over his creative quotient for years. Since the cancer (all the awards & past acclaim aside), he'd begun believing (with some chagrin) that his entire *legacy* was in danger of slipsliding away into a sort of mega-televisionistic triumph, a *Cuckoo's Nest* producer's credit & a **HERE LIES GORDON GEKKO** written on his grave. *Hey, Michael, not fair to compare,* he'd say, becoming his own life coach. *And to Bob Fosse no less! What's more important? A man's work or how he lives and loves? You came back from the dead. You're shits and giggles rich. Your wife is beyond beautiful & you love her like you thought you could never love a woman before. Two beautiful kids whose rollicking wildhearted innocence feeds you and breaks your heart . . . . so eff being a fuckin genius, it's too late anyway, you're old old old, you're* done. *Time to rest on the laurels and smell the cancerfree roses*———

———NOPE.

Sorry . . . .

Still mesmerized:

still covetous:

of Fosse's *psycho panache.*

That petite, coiled *athleticism;* those god-perfect reflexes; that aesthetic of the twitchy, animal-pawed psychosexual dance. Michael never told anyone, but he'd always wanted to move like that—*who wouldn't?*—black derby, black bodysuit, black malice/mischief pulsing thru intricate, ladder-hanging routines, the impossible legerdemain that made it look easy. (Hell, Michael *Jackson* wanted to be Bob Fosse.) The actor ached to dance like him, had that closeted, heavy, sell-your-soul yearning, the way some people would kill to be able to *sing.* To be a rock star . . . . Michael was almost *religiously enamored* of that distinctive, distinctively American genius of how Fosse moved, glided, hunched, lurched, swaggered, carom'd, winked, locked, loaded & sprung, the soaring sex of his fight and flight, the ravenous twinkling gaiety (his passion for dance surprised Catherine when she learned of it, & was the thing that really won her over). More than anything, MD admired the balls-out vulnerability of the man, the fearless transparency, the diamondhard chestpained breathless rockface nobility of shared sheer risk. No one knew it, but his decades-old man-crush was the reason he took on the role of Zach, the director in *A Chorus Line*; the offer to embody his hero was irresistible. Nicole Fosse was a dancer in the film, and he spent as much time as he could talking to her about her dad.

All his life he'd prided himself on being a chameleon. Ambition and good fortune had allowed him to do spectacularly well with the middling artistic hand he'd been dealt, and for that he was grateful; *his* genius lay not in the art of his craft but in the seasonal confounding & upending of expectations, a nearly mischievous, overreaching, against-the-odds grab at the brass ring. Another thing he'd never shared with anyone, not even his wife (especially not her, he had his pride): the vain notion there was the possibility of a discernible, other-than-entrepreneurial genius nestled in some frozenly findable place within, an aspect of *MD* transcending his populist i*MD*b filmography. There came days now where he felt tough enough to storm the gates of heaven & snatch his prize from the gods; & (mostly) nights when all he sought was sleep. It was always said to seize the day, but why not seize the night? The cancer war had bestowed upon him strength and validation, & the spoils necessary to affect his new venture—an excavation of long-buried things. He would drag them into the moonshadows. It was time to dig for hidden codices & calendars, forgotten scriptures, scripts & sundials bearing signs & symbols written in a mother tongue he'd never bothered to learn. He would need to draw on that same courage he had summoned in the dark public noon of his disease, and see himself at last for what he was: either artist or quixotic fool—a brutal, delicate, holy enterprise.

Now it was time, & it felt like only a short walk from the community plunge to the ocean. He would leave the pool, with its useless, obsolescent lifeguards, to go swim with the ancient salt-water giants, living and dead . . .

.　.　.

All That Jazz.

The movie Michael had watched probably 30 times in as many years was still talismanic, still incantatory, still possessed the thaumaturgical effect of sponging up his anguished depression, preventing it from overpuddling—regulating and distracting. After the shock of diagnosis, he gravitated (again) toward the fatal themes of monomania & greasepaint grandiosity running through *Jazz* like a funhouse burglar. Fosse was writing about the *dexe*dream years when he simultaneously put on *Chicago* while editing *Lenny*—the choreographer's *Love in the Time of Cardiac.* He hadn't watched the movie in a while & *this* time was amazed to see it for what it was, as an unmitigated failure, a stupendously conceived, curdlingly self-indulgent, terribly written, crassly executed mess. A FAIL from the likes of Fosse was magnificently riveting; yet, because *Jazz* was so egregiously flawed, this mortal wound of a film left ample room for other voices, other rooms.

As they blasted the tumor from his tongue, he began to conceive himself as the chain-smoking black-shirted paws-up King of the Dance. *(Who'd a thunk?)* Made him smile. He immediately saw Catherine in the rôle limned by Jessica Lange—the white-gowned gossamer-veiled Angel of Death, the protagonist's last seduction. His wife would make an iconic, dusky, sensuous angel indeed. His medical travails had made their marriage stronger & the *Jazz* variations would memorialize that. Show the world they weren't afraid to meet The End clear-eyed & unafraid, that love was stronger than death. Cat seemed a natural to play another part as well, the dancer-mistress that Fosse cast his ex Ann Reinking in, but that was tough. He knew she'd prefer *that* rôle over beckoning Death—plus, in the Reinking part, she'd be able to dance, pull out all the stops. But it would be tough for *him*, & he had to think of himself. He needed to marshal his energies and protect his heart. He saw the Angel of Death as a caricature, which was OK—but for Cat to play a beautiful dancer/lover felt too close to the bone. Besides, he hadn't conceived *All That* as a project for husband & wife. No: the notion was born in a place far from commerce and calculation, shamanic, mysterious, & much was unclear. He did not know if it was meant to save his life, or save his death.

In those perilous, ghoulish dog days when malignant thoughts of recurrence stuttered on the tip of his insulted tongue, his jazzy desire coalesced; such was his cancer's sequelae. It gave him something to shoot for, a *major* pursuit. He knew if he trained very hard he might just be able to pull off—with merit—a personification of that swagged-out Fosse Swagger of derbied, softshoe'd nomadic royalty. Fosse wrote the book to *Chicago* as well, which gave Michael the encouraging nod to begin a 1st draft of *Jazz*, a potentially radical reimagining. He would show it to friends—Aaron (Sorkin) & Tom (Stoppard) & Steve (Kloves) for feedback, suggestions & general help. *What was there to lose? If the cancer don't kill me, I'll be 80-years-old in the blink of a wet macular degenerated eye—————————*

It came to him out of the blue (where the best ideas always seemed to live) (that mysterious, excavated out of the blue place), from irradiated sleep (Week 7 of radiation, & after the three chemo seshes):

Michael Douglas   Catherine Zeta-Jones

All That Jazz

Heather Morris

. . . . Heather Morris AKA Brittany Pierce, *Glee*'s drop-dead funny deadpan surrealspeak gal. (Cat & the kids were gaga for all things Brittany.) A fresh face with no feature experience to speak of, a working dancer turned improbable, show-stealing comedienne, she was an inspired choice (and one helluva dancer) to play the Reinking-mistress.

Maybe deliriousness in the wake of the cytotoxic campaign the doctors waged had beckoned him manically knit together the karmic thread that weirdly sewed it all together: 1) his wife won an Oscar for her performance as Velma in the movie based on *Chicago**; 2) when Beyoncé came across an old curiosity on YouTube—three dancers (including Fosse's wife Gwen Verdon) doing one of the master's signature, flirty, muscularly jaunty, thrown-away routines—she liked it so much she copped it for the famous "Single Ladies" video; 3) Beyoncé hired pre-*Glee* Heather Morris to go on tour & be one of the back-up dancers replicating the dance clip; and 4) the karmic circle was complete when the *Glee* people asked Heather to teach the cast the "Single Ladies" moves, a road that eventually led to Brittany S. Pierce. Lately, Michael found himself making connections like that, big and little, whimsical and not, as if something alien had given him a tune-up. How extraordinary was the world! Not too long ago, he

---

*The Internet informed that Bill Condon, who adapted the musical to film, happened once to have lived with Ryan Murphy—one of the detours of MD's bewitched, bewitching reverie.

was certain he would die before his father, unthinkable, but now he felt more alive than he'd ever been.

The critics would have a field day, they always did.

Let them eat cancer.

How could he care?

.   .   .

He dozed into cancer dreams.

Steve Jobs approached him on the street, asking for money. He had huge tits.

"It's for Aaron Sorkin," he said. "He needs the money for his mastectomy."

Jobs' smile was vulpine, his beard sickly, his breath rotten and prodromal.

"What's the matter, Michael? Aren't you going to help Aaron?"

DikiLeaks

"**I**already *got* her sis, & now I want *Elle*, I want to see her *cunt*, know what I'm saying? Dakota's cunt we *have*. But her *sister* . . . I see her in *Vogue* with her slutfriends Hailee & Chloë, I watch her goo-goo giggly on Leno in her Chanel & I pray to *God* those parents are hiding *sixteen* more lil orphan Fannings in Sleepy Hollow! Cause let me tell you something straight up: Harry Middleton *WILL NOT SLEEP* until he sees *every hair* on their chinny-chin-*chins*. And *you're* the one who's gunna make sure that I do! *You're the one* who's gunna show it to the *world*. As the song goes, *Baby, it's you!*"

He took a deep breath and focused.

"You are the Chosen One. Make no mistake, I have not had a hand in this. *God* has chosen you to *memorialize* all the cunning Lady Fanning cunts." He bounced in his chair & sang; he burst into song all day. *All the single ladies! All the single ladies . . . All the single ladies! All the single ladies. Now put your hands UP—*"

Sometimes he sang the whole deal, every verse, and you just had to sit there. *Well let him.* Jerzy was shocked. Hired just 10 minutes into the interview. Never happened. Like, ever.

His birthname was Jerry, Jerry *Jr.* to make things worse, from Jerome, his dead dad. Their mom gave them shitty names, Jerilynn sounded supertrash (which Jerzy thought was supersick, in that *Jeri-*

lynn was yet *another* nod to dead dad, only problem being, his ½ sister's dad's name was *Ronny*) and *Jerry* just sounded Jewy & forgettable, a name that should fucking be suppressed, like J.D. (*Jerry*) Salinger suppressed *his*. Even more fucked up and insidious of the mom was that *Jerilynn* & *Jerry* were sort of the *same. Victor/Victoria*———... growing up, his assmates at school idiot-brilliantly called him *Jerry's Deli*, the local place families went on the weekends so *fuck* that loser name. When he was a senior he read *The Painted Bird* by Jerzy Kosinski & dug the name. So he did a little reinventing, tweaked an *r* to a *z* & called it a night. He wouldn't respond to anything but Jerzy, not to his teachers or bitch mother or *anyone* & if friends fucked around and called him Jerry or Jerome he'd just slap their fucking faces till they got it right. Which they did soon enough.

Jerzy Kosinski was a rich & famous author who made up everything about his own life. Jerzy the Second wiki'd the shit out of the guy & there was like *nothing* about him that was real, it was such fucking genius! He had college kids writing his novels and *still* won all the awards. The guy was married to some sort of heiress, he played polo & acted in movies, & was handsome too. You'd think life was perfect but he killed himself—took a bunch of dope, got in the tub & put a bag over his head. Jerzy the Sequel took his hat off to anyone with that kind of schweddy balls, really admired them, he'd wanted to die so many times in life but was too gaping a pussy to do anything about it. He was kind of fascinated too by the *way* people offed themselves: gun, dope, gas, jumping, hanging, drowning . . . occasionally there'd be a fucked up one on the internet, like that chick stabbing herself over and over or the bullied fagteen who chugged Drano.

In contrast, the man interviewing him—owner of **http://www .TheHoneyshot!.com/**—veritable duke of his *domain*—THE HONEYSHOT!, proudly serving horndogs online since 2003—in *contrast*, you could call *him* whatever the fuck you wanted to and he probably wouldn't mind, probably wouldn't even *notice*. Plus nobody cared enough to even hang a bogus, brilliantly retarded nickname on

his perved, grody ass. His name was Harry, Harry Middleton, &
Jerzy nicknamed him Harry around the Middleton but kept that to
himself. Come to think of it, J2 didn't know which was worse, Jerry
or Harry. If you had em both, you might just have to commit Jerry-
Harry *hahahahaha*.

THE HONEYSHOT! paid cash money for their niche-market
specialty, celebskin flashes, of which the *genus* he trafficked in Harry
cannily estimated to be 95% accidental (the remaining 5 percent being exhibitionistic/PR-ploy dross), all submissions welcome but only
nipple slips & xxxtreme wardrobe malfunctions need apply. Harry
called his boys the Smarmy Sidewalk Army—but his happiest coin-
age & contribution to the skinternet was and would remain *papsmearazzi*, perforce THE HONEYSHOT!s distinct, some may call it
obsessive, emphasis on the mossy, shrouded nether regions. You
clicked on the homepage & the 1st thing heard was the Stones singing *"It's just a shot away!"*—THE HONEYSHOT!—with its *Cash
Money MondayShots!* (Mondays were big after a weekend of pre-
mieres/celeb debauches etc)—THE HONEYSHOT!—with its
Thighs on the Prize deep page *CUNTdown to Victory!*-IBL to *Cradle-
Snatch!*, Harry's controversial bonus rogue gallery of underage star-
let/up-&-*cumming* HONEYSHOT!s-to-be (each one represented by
the most tasteful & demure shots Harry could find—such was his
brilliance!)—THE HONEYSHOT!—with its Times Square tote-
board of the ticking hours/minutes/seconds left before his *"hairly legal hits & Missies!"* turned 18—THE HONEYSHOT!—with its
splash page banner searchandizing all cummers to a nostalgic subweb
showcasing commemorative 18th-b'day papsmearazzi *honeyshot!s* of
years gone by: the Em&Em's (Emma Watson & Emma Roberts) &
iHoneys (Miranda & Victoria Justice) Dakota & Katniss & Selena,
Bianca *Ryan* AND fuckin *Sunshine Corazon* & so & so & such &
such . . . . . . well, THE HONEYSHOT! was hot hot *hot*. Daily
traffic was definitely on the upskirt Upton upswing.*

---

* Even Harry was caught off-guard by the rampant success of THE HONEYSHOT!s webpage

THE HONEYSHOT! posted celebrity skin of *all* ilk, with that *very* special emphasis on the classic Bermuda Δ crotchshot, a cash crop that yielded panty shots & the occasional much-coveted, *crème de la crème* panty-less twat shocker. If you were 18 showing cameltoe by the pool in Maui (Xmas in Hawaii was a *very* busy time for papsmearazzi: tis the Four Seasons to be jolly!), scuba-diving in Sorrento, aimless in Amalfi or aqua-marooned in the Maldives, one of Harry's minions would be on you like ants on feta—"Wherever there's a wench with an uncovered stench-trench," said Harry, in his best Tom Joad, "I'll be there." If a papsmearazzo looked perplexed, he'd say, "What's the matter? Didn't you ever see Henry Fonda in *The Rapes of Grath*?" Then (of course) he'd bust into *I'll Be There* (Jackson 5).

It worked like this:

Cum 18-years of age, all the single lady ☆let crotches were fair game, and it was Harry's Hairy Crusade to webmorialize each fresh minty smell moment. Looking back on his collection of legendary *Honeyshot!* V-Days, he almost got teary-eyed. He remembered Emma Watson's like it was yesterday. They got her exactly 45 minutes after her 18th, in Mayfair, disembarking from a Maybach. Emma was the kind of girl who didn't need to be coached, tidy & proper & properly gamine, she'd been carefully sliding out of cars for years . . . but *this* time, in the *wee* morning hours of her *birthday* she'd been out celebrating & simply wasn't careful *enough*————revealing in the process a sliver of hairy (very) pot- and Pottered poody tat. Harry told his papsmearazzi that if you were hunting hairpie you damn well better know that your best bet was shooting it as it debarked a Range Rover, Benz or SUV. Do it right, & it's fish in a barrel. He promised to show Jerzy the *technique* tomorrow, give him a crotch course in the me-

---

Honeyshot! Olden Goldies (Ms. Hawn's two faces conjoined at the top of the page like those of comedy&tragedy, her *Laugh-In*-era face with her Medicare one), said page being wholly devoted to peeholes of a certain age as they stepped from their cars—Helen Mirren, Julie Christie, Diane Keaton, Susan Sarandon, Debra Winger. Zsa Zsa got hers as she was lifted from wheelchair to gurney, but that was more of a goof—Harry, who always wrote the webtext, called it a *funnyshot!*

chanics of getting the classic out-of-backseat snatchy snapshot! Harry made it a point to train all of his bushmen personally. He'd throw on panties & a Loehmann's skirt, park his Audi at the curb and position his boys while scuttling from the backseat. He made them shout "Elle! Chloë! Hailee!" for that certain *Je ne sais queef.* It was important to know the right stance and GPS (Global-labial Position) for the perfect ({})*shot!*—it was really just vectors and math. Another cool thing about the backseat exit experience was that lots of times just when you thought you screwed the pooch, you'd bagged the hooch.

"See," said Harry. "Sometimes it feels like hit & miss. You think the night's a bust. You get home, fix yourself a drink, & stare at your navel. But then you play it back & *see:* that big paycheck of blow-dried pussy, so fresh, monied and young! Coddled, cosseted & guarded for *fucking years* by *parents, handlers, agents, lawyers, personal managers, publicists* . . . but now it's *yours for the taking.* Know how we bagged Emma? She let her guard down. That simple. Would've happened sooner or later, ain' no stopping it. Sooner or later the hairpie *will* be placed in the bakery display case. Cause once they're legal, I don't *sleep* till we got it. Can't sleep or eat, can't even *shit.* See, cause know I'm *on* it. And they didn't even used to have to even *think* about this shit, streetside celebrity piss flap shots didn't even *exist* until THE HONEYSHOT! came along. I'm the pioneer. And as smart as they were, Emma's people weren't *on* it . . . . . who can blame em? I mean to know that someone was lying in wait to *skate* your sacrosanct client's stink rink—we used to call it the 'wizard's sleeve'—well Jesus!——*Hermione Granger* slid out of backseats a *million* times without incident, why *would* there have been any incidences, *all* my single ladies have! But comes a time they cum of age . . . . & they're distracted. Maybe they just had a fight with the boyfriend, just hung up, & now they're stepping out of the limo for the premiere . . . or maybe they were just watching a video of supermodels falling on the runway, maybe they're even a little *stoned*—or they weren't *talking* to the boyfriend, they were just *thinking* about him, maybe things aren't going so well or maybe they're going *too* well, maybe they're thinking about dick, cause a lot of my single ladies have been getting dick'd since they were 13, I can *guarantee you* that, nothing wrong with it, I don't pass judgment on my girls, kids grow up quicker these days especially in show biz but a girl like *Emma*, a good girl, upper class—upper class with a lower crust!—maybe she only just *started* getting dicked, maybe only even like just a few weeks before her 18th, so maybe right before she's about to step out of the car she's thinking about getting a little *more*. After the premiere, or whenever. Which is a lot to be thinking about. There are other potentially distracting states of mind. Like maybe one of my single ladies is a little remorseful she didn't take Petra Ecclestone up on wanting to throw her a boffo 18th, with Kanye & whomever, & deadmau5 DJing. Because they didn't really even know Petra that well. But maybe it would have been a goof to have had the party at the old Spelling mansion instead of just with friends & family. These are the quality of problems accorded my single ladies. Or maybe they're wondering about the burning lately when they pee, if it's chlamydia or maybe their throat's a little sore & they're paranoid about maybe having smoked a New Year's sparkler with HPV or who knows they could be beating themselves up for not having listened to management & waiting till they were 21 but just going for it and dressing like a sick whore for a *Maxim* shoot . . . . or maybe they're pondering what it's like to get fucked up the ass, which, no offense, might even cross the mind of a gal like Emma who hasn't maybe been getting dick that long, how can we know what's in the mind of Mrs. Weasley? I doubt if it's Emma's thing, but that don't mean she's never fancied taking it in the mugglerump, please keep in mind that all the single ladies usually *do* go thru a somewhat rebellious phase, after all those years of being *branded* and *pimped*, it wouldn't surprise me if they spent a month trying it, fucked in the starfish, could be a bucket list thing for girls these days . . . who knows, maybe right before they leave the Town Car they were cogitating about the rumor that Lea Michele *only* likes it up the ass and is saving her pussy for marriage— that's one of those urban myths, every few years there's some rumor

about a starlet who only takes it in the ass, now it's Lea, Selena Go-
mez, and Jennifer Lawrence, I remember when it was Sarah Michelle
Gellar & Jennifer Love Hewitt and before that it was Sarah Jessica &
Kyra Sedgwick I think . . . Jesus, I'm getting myself horny now, I'm
thinking about Hailee Steinfeld about to climb out of a Bentley shifting those Jewish *animal haunches* on the seat———

> *oh oh oh -*
>> & still:
>>>> he can remember
>>>> (like it was yesterday)
>>>> when his dear dear
>>>> Emma, when dear
>>>> Emma got out
>>>> of the back of
>>>> the Maybach
>>> *oooooo*
>> *slither-leathersliding*

Slip-Sliding-Away (Harry loved to sing that song) over the expen-
sively slaughteredskin seats, but that maneuver (just getting out of
the fucking car!) has never been an elegant thing for homo s'apes,
you may as well still be getting out of a horse & buggy, but who *gives*
a shit if it's elegant 'cause it was never hyperscrutinized . . . . . . until
NOW———no easy solution not unless handlers hang up sheets to
shield the celeb til they're out of the papsmear-free zone, same as it
ever was, at least until some engineer thinks to make a seat that pneu-
matically telescopes out the back onto the sidewalk then slowly tilts
like those geriatric TV Guide La-Z-Boys, it ain't like GM's gunna
get right on it, but until *somebody* did, Harry's Heroes would keep
stirrin' the honeypot & smoking the cracks, exercising their rights in
this great Uptonian upskirt democracy.

Harry had no patience for the truculent managers and hypocrite
PR flaks who tried to put him down when the truth was he respected
those kids more than their handlers. They were shown from an early

age how to be ladylike when leaving a car but now, in the ticking weeks before each one's 18th, all the single ladies had to have that embarrassing parental/management office conversation about the birds and the papsmearazzi bees, you know, one by one, all the Hailees and the Bailees and the Chloës, Mackenzies, Abigails & Olivias were told to be *mindful* to cover the goods with whatever was handy—Missoni scarf or Prada/Hermès/Chanel clutch held discreetly just *so* to make sure the unmentionables wouldn't be mentioned in the global conversation. What was so great about Emma's virgin frontgryffindoor honeyshot, *unmentionably* so, wasn't merely the hosiery (which Harry internet I.D.'d as a seamless silicone-beaded cat-girlish Wolford bodysuit. Emma was a Wolford/Smythson/Burberry Prorsum lass), the *unmentionably* perfect thing was, Harry got her by *fluke*, it was a new-hire schlep in the right place at the right time tho not yet fully trained, one of those sophomore in high school kids Harry liked to break in because the ☆s let their guards down when they saw them, "He was a newbie just like you, Jerzy Shores"—his nickname for him & Jerzy took it because it could have been so much worse—"the newbie didn't actually think he got the *honeyshot!* The newbie thought it was a FAIL but I knew better, I had this *feeling* . . ." So he took the kid's camera for a little late-night alone-time in the privacy of his bedroom & gorged on the the iMage, gorged, enlarged it & engorged————*and and and and an . . . . . .*
. . . . O O O *ooooooooooooo*—there—*there*—perfect English rose, wilding of heathery soap-scrubbed slit hair, peach of an unimpeachable patch sequestered behind Santa Maria Novella-powdered briefs, dampish twittering #tagged coming-out panties, evocative (to Harry, such were his passions) of mulch-dank Lake District moors, "or shall I say *s'mores,*" a perfectly manicured mons that never saw nor ever thought it would the light of online-day———————————————————but no no no! what was unmentionably mentionably awesome about Hermione's *honeyshot!* was that once in a blue moon, an unsuspecting, *very* fortunate papsmearazzo captures the *honeyshot!* holy Grail: that epiphany of

smushed candlewick, the sanitary napkin—a *rara avis* indeed! *Early bird caught the worm*—tail of the kite—by my *word*, Lord Middleton almost had a ♥ attack when he saw it, for never in his wildest dreams—his Hermione!

Misty-eyed, he related this exuberantly memorable anecdote to young Jerzy—he'd waited *so long* for that moment—Emma's moment—and how much it meant to him that he'd been there to see it first, before it entered eternal history, "and *that*, my new friend, they can never take away. We will always be connected in a way she will never know, & I shall love & cherish it, & carry it to my grave." He went on to speak of that difficult moment before posting, when he knew she'd no longer be his: in the bedroom, Harry's features illumined by dandelion (milky latex) pussywillow (furry catkins), alone with the image, before **Send** would rob him of the sacral intimacy of fumbling promnight ecstasy, before he shared her with the world—*if you love them let them go*—to **Send** was, afterall, his bold and righteous duty—but still—for a few shining hours she was his. He, Harry, his Highness of lowness, he, Harry, high priest of yeast, sat in bed woefully staring at the rectangular cloud of the Mac that lapdanced him in those tenebrous hours, he, Harry, could practically *taste* the bloodwort copperiness of Emma's new moon menses—for it *was* a new moon: a tender, slender crescent—and oh! that infernal cotton string! His God and his Devil had given him that. He was deserving, & forever grateful.

He was certain he'd live to be very old. The single ladies gave him *life*, each and every one of them, but he had always loved Emma the most, nothing untoward, nothing that was a problem, he took his sons to see all the Potter movies, and the 1st time he saw her he was struck by her beauty, he *saw* what she would look like as a single lady & full-blown adult woman ☆ yet he *never* objectified her, promised himself he never would, not until her 18th, in thought nor in action, instead he would wait for her on the sidewalks (Harry sang: *If it takes forever I will wait for you, for a thousand summers I will wait for you*), not

with the SmArmy but with the *fans*—her fairytale crocodile prince
at river's bottom, patiently biding his time . . . . before devouring & disseminating that toothsome, magian *honeyshot!*—a Julian
Assange of cunt, acting on behalf of the millions of boys, men, &
boys-to-men who adored her, grew *up* with her, and would forever
keep her in their hearts.

.   .   .

He was a late-starter, Jerzy was, he'd frittered away so many years in
the shadow of his mother.

Jacquie Crelle-Vomes was famous, one of the phonies of her gen
who achieved notoriety for taking snaps of pre-stacked progeny. Pre-
Jerry's Deli Jerzy hated that she'd taken nudies of his little sis, saw
straight thru all her bullshit. He knew that his mother's one-time
obsession was to have a show at MoMA—she thought her daughter's
underage body could catapault her over the museum's walls—that's
when he started calling her MoMA instead of Momma, which irritated her to no end. O how he loved to tweak her shit. Still, MoMA
went further than her firstborn thought she would. Had to hand it to
her, the woman was a real hustler. She really knew how to work the
wealthy adolescephiles, & acquired (marginal) fame in the process.
She was famous enough to have a Wikipedia page anyway (not even
Harry around the Mersey had one) even if it was stubby, with a
giant ⓘ *This biographical article needs additional citations for verification.* It
didn't even have her picture.

MoMA used to have him assist on some of the shoots, which felt
weird toward the end when his sister was getting tits. He would at
least have respected her if she'd taken skinnygirl pornshots but apparently MoMA never had the heart; her shit turned out like "subversive" David Hamilton. *How fucking pathetic. The bitch who thought she
was so incendiary couldn't even light the fuse. Total rampant pussification.*

It *was* far out, tho, to watch her work, a real education that maybe
he could learn from. From his teens, he scoped haughty MoMA's

cynical traveling circus with its floating galleries & carefully orchestrated, county-by-county 1st Amendment uproars; the ensuing
staged-for-maximum-PR-effect local library bans of her books; the
rote howls of the conservative media; the rote, smug rebuttals of the
liberal media; the pious ACLU voices advocating in her behalf,
shoved between sports and weather—and there was MoMA, ever
MoMA, with her recondite emotions, quietly nobly preening,
stealthily thrilled with herself, all her bullshit-fancy monographs
frontloaded with fancy bullshitting essays by bullshit-fancy fake geniuses, fake poets and incomprehensible tenured pervs—skunkhaired
Sontag lites + other sundry putative superstars, meaning anyone
MoMA deemed worthy to co-opt/seduce/fuck into sponsoring her
barfy, exploitative, flat-chested body of work—well, Jerzy thought
his new boss was *so* much cleaner in the pursuit and publication of his
quarry, *so* much more the accidental *artiste* than MoMA because he
didn't try to hide behind Art *or* his upskirts, didn't dress it up to be
anything but what it was: xxxxxtreme pervation. Pervomatical per-
vatoriness. His nocturnal prey *signifying* what MoMA was too chickenshit to nail to the wall. MoMA hung out in the shadows. MoMA
cockteased her collectors with a silver gelatin tween's sexless come-
on. MoMA pimped out her oblivious daughter's cobalt palladian
thighs.

There was a space in time when Jerzy aspired to be the new Weegee—or Son of Johnny Pigozzi, anyway—but it never worked out.
He was a vulturazzo in Manhattan for a while, staking out hospitals
& clinics & the offices of Park Ave docs with a camera, waiting for
skulking celebs. Facelifts, freakouts & O.D.s. He shot Michael Douglas in the subway, scrawny & disoriented from chemo, poor schmuck,
leaning on one of his kids. (Jerzy used to buy coke from his son
Cameron.) Stalked Michael J. Fox when the actor was in town, waiting for that elusive Parkinsonian pantspiss, which sadly never came.
Would've paid the rent for a year.

But it was cold in NY and Jerzy was burned out. The streets didn't make him feel brand new, no dreams to be made, nothing he could do—not the Jay-Z experience. The move to LA felt right, but nothing had clicked. Nothing until he met Harry.

On the way home from the apartment office of THE HONEYSHOT! he got the idea of his life. He'd become Harry's secret weapon, his sniper, his 5-☆ *honeyshot* General, Commander-in-chief of the Smarmy Army. He would enlist for 18 months, then hopefully, with his patron's blessing, gather up his edited work—nip slips, honied moneyshots & everything in-between—and show them at Gagosian.

He'd take another new name.

Some kinda cross between Weegee & Banksy: Squeegee, maybe.

MoMA won't even know what hit her.

.   .   .

"For me," said Harry, "after Emma, I got a bit depressed. It was like, *Where can you go from here?* But I'm moving on. You know what *honeyshot!* I'd like to get? I'll tell you. And it ain't Kate or Pippa, let somebody else get em, it'll be soon enough. Cause Emma was the *real* royalty. And it ain't Amanda Knox, either. You know who I'd like? Gabrielle Giffords. That's right—my ♥ belongs to Gabby. Jesus, did you see the picture of her in *People?* Post-headwound *svelte.* Wearing denim, with that little trake scar . . . thumb hooked in her jeans, like one of those hot bored MILFs you see at Anthropologie or Trader Joe's . . . I'd like to hook *my* thumb in her jeans! Cause I ain't all about the juvies. Like to get that perimenopausal kite string—a clear shot. Ain' never gunna happen. A guy can dream, can't he?"

"Sure, Harry. Got to."

"You can make 200,000 a year, minimum."

Jerzy pulled out a joint and lit up. He had the very strong notion it was OK & it was.

"Minimum. *Guaranteed.* But you gotta be *serious.* You gotta be diligent. You gotta eat, sleep & drink THE HONEYSHOT! It's all about longevity, Jerzy Shores, & persistence of vision. You want to do right by all the *beauties*. All the babes in toyland soon to be appearing in a chauffeured Escalade near you: I'm talking Hailee Steinfeld. I'm talking Elle. I'm talking *Madonna's kid*—Jesus H! Between the two of em, Hailee and Lourdes could support the depilatory industry without any help! I am guessing there are rumored *bales* of hair down there. And Elle ain't ethnic, as you know, Elle's *fair*, but sometimes the fair ones can surprise you in the southern regions . . . *Elle's fair in love and war*—

    mirror mirror on the wall

      who's the hairest . . . .

————————there is a *serious* bumper crop a-comin! New muffs & mufflers, *major* single lady bidness up ahead! Kylie Jenner *is seriously* on the tote—she's *five-ten,* did you know that? Of course, my Christmas wish would be to have something *beforehand*, a sextape, or a topless— I can dream, right? O Jesus, I want that one almost as much as I wanted Emma. Maybe just as much, who knows, the ♥'s a funny thing.

    "I'm gunna give you a special assignment, Jerzy Shores, think you're ready for a special assignment? I don't want to wait anymore. As long as I don't put em out there, don't got to wait for the single ladies to be legal. Understand? I'll pay *5,000* for any you bring in, no one's gunna have a clue what you're up to, how could they. It ain't even against the law unless you *upload.* That's what got Perez in trouble, he should have kept Miley to himself. This is between you and me—little keepsakes. Because the world is going to hell & I don't want to wait anymore, it's fuckin too hard on me. I want to see what I can *now.* I want to see the *world.* I don't want to wait for the Willows. I want Judy Moody's too . . . . that's right, go out and get me Chloë, get me Hailee, get me Elle! Get me little Sally Draper, get me fuckin Ariel Winter . . . don't be shy! I'll take Rebecca Black, she's got a forest growing down there. Kendall too. Kylie I'm more interested in but I wouldn't turn my nose up at Kendall. I'd do *something* with my nose, but I wouldn't turn it up! Get me Janet *Devlin* . . . the devlin made me do it! Get me *Drew Ryniewicz* . . . get me Sophia Grace and Rosie the Hype Girl! Rosie the Riveter! I wanna see *axe wounds*, I wanna see *movie SCARS* . . . get me to the *geek*. Marc Anthony's kid—Ariana's 18 soon. Michael Fox's twins. Get *palsy* with em—should be a walk in the parkinsons! I want to see the Depp kid. A little depp'l do me. And the Baldwin girl, Ireland. Go ahead, get your 30 rocks off & *pig out* on that thoughtless pig!

"But I'm thinking ahead, son, *way* ahead. About all the little ones who become part of the family, the national quilt, over the years, cause it takes a village. I'm thinking of all the little ones, the Suris and the Shilohs! (The Suri with the fringe on bottom.) The Obama girls—they are not ungettable nor are they sacrosanct. THE HONEYSHOT! is *out* there, THE HONEYSHOT! is its own rite of passage, THE HONEYSHOT! is a *visionquest*, out there like a tidal wave of baby beaver bounty: Here come the Gosselins! Here comes Honor Alba! Here comes Nahla Berry! Here comes Naleigh Heigl! Here comes Violet & Seraphina Affleck! Here comes Ava Witherspoon! (We just got her mother's cunt sliding out of the car to do a Kimmel.) Here comes Ella Bleu Preston-*Travolta!* Here comes Sadie & Sunny *Sandler!* Here comes Cleo *Schwimmer!* Here comes Satyana *Hannigan* & Billie Beatrice/Georgia Geraldine *Gayheart-Dane* & Savannah & Eden *Cross!* Here comes Indiana & Clementine *Hawke!* 'Ever' *Jovovich!* Harper Renn *Thiessen!* Here comes Vida *McConaughey,* and Charlotte *Gellar-Prinze Jr.*—here comes Britney's *sister's* fucking kid—a girl, right? And Haven cashwarren *Alba*—*thank Haven for little girls*—& Harlow & Apple . . . . yeah yeah yeah, the HONEYSHOT! *needs* an Apple a day——oops! Here comes Maddie Duchovny! Amaya Hargitay! Vivienne Jolie-Pitt! Stella Luna Pompeo! Jessica Springsteen! Vida McConaughey! Destry Spielberg! Evie *Bono* Hewson! Krishna *Lakshmi*! Archie *Poehler* & Alice *Fey!* Coco

"Coochie" Arquette-Cox! The little bitch from *Modern Family*, what's her name? *Aubrey. Aubrey Anderson-Emmons*. Coming down the pike and legal in just 12 short years! Rebecca Romijn's got *twins*—of *course* she does, she's 65 years-old—Charlie & Dolly! Sarah Jessica's got *twins*—of *course* she does, she's *82*—Tabitha & Loretta! Don't you see what we're sitting on? THE HONEYSHOT!s gotta keep the faith . . . . . . which brings me to Faith *Kidman-Urban*—— and let us not forget Sunday Rose *Urban-Kidman*, it's a *month* of Sundays, kid! Tobey Maguire's got *Ruby*, Salma Hayek's got *Valentina*, Tori Spelling's got *Stella*, Diddy's got *D'Lila* & *Jessie*—both girl-childs—J-Lo's got an *Emme*, Heidi & Seal got Leni & Lou—*Lou's a girlchild*. Bethenny Frankel's got a *Bryn* . . . . if I live long enough, I'll see Blue Ivy's black velvet . . . cause you see we get to know them from the time they're babes, we watch em laugh, we watch em cry, we see em dragged thru Barneys, see em squirm in rich and famous arms leaving Starbucks & Whole Foods & the fucking Malibu Lumber Yard, see em tousle-haired & toddler-jogging beside their toned-up yoga moms in the Colony, see em in Sandra Bullock's arms, Jesus, Bullock's arms must be more ripped than Cameron Diaz cause all I ever see is her hoisting that blackie like a kettlebell. We feel their joy & we feel their pain (*and I am telling you, Jerzy Shores, the day you hand over a shot of Paris, Michael Jackson's kid, that will be a day of celebration, a day of healing, of giving thanks to the Divine!*)——————we watch em grow up & grow tits, watch their teeth come in, buy our kids whatever style crap they're wearing . . . . then before you know it, they're staring out at us with their dead, hungry eyes from *Vogue* and *W*, in their Rodarte & Manolos, their Margielas & Louboutins, & they're leaving Starbucks or Whole Foods or the fucking Malibu Lumber Yard under their own power. Suddenly, our babies are going to premieres & museum costume ball fundraisers, I am telling you my new friend that it takes a village, & the village, *We the People of the United Village of Honeyshot!s* hold our breaths watching each little career begin, & we wish the best for our sisters, that's what they are, our little soul sisters—our daughters too & our future Moms—and we cushion the falls—the rehabs, DUIs, botched surgeries, 4-month marriages—just as we tally their triumphs . . . . until one day it's *time*, time for me to show their cunts to the world.

"And when that time comes, we are there to help. We are there to help them from our heads & our ♥s."

[Bud]

The Art of Fiction, Part One

Steve

Martin had a new book out; a bad bug forced Joyce Carol Oates to cancel her interview with him at the Central Library in LA. Oates had recently compared him to Edith Wharton, and Steve was looking forward to the Q&A.

JCO was one of those writers Bud was certain he would never read yet perversely enjoyed reading *about*. Everyone knew she had written a thousand books; a slow reader to begin with, Bud just couldn't see the point. Besides, he hadn't even read all of Dickens, and Dickens was in his Top Five. (It took a full 40 years for Bud to admit to himself that he would never—never, ever—read Proust. Capote supposedly never did either.) Still, he drew ironic comfort from the *Believe-it-or-Not!* aspect of Ms Oates's tsunami œuvre, & the trademark *shtick* pathology behind its creation. Which was somewhat of a shame (Bud thought charitably) because it wasn't so much the books that were being reviewed anymore, as it was the Brobdingnagian output. Every writer deserved a fair shake, yet he supposed the mother of so many *oaters* only had herself to blame. JCO often wrote under pseudonyms; you couldn't keep up with her *nom de spew'ems* either. Maybe that was sort of the whole point—staying ahead of your readers and critics. It was better than staying *behind* them, which is what Bud Wiggins had done.

. . .

He was turning 60 this year. A screenwriter since his mid-20s, Bud had a sole "written by" to his name, a co-credit (one of four others) on a forgotten horror film of the late 80s. When he turned 55, out of desperation, Bud took an early retirement, allowing him to collect a pension of $1,140 a month. The beauty was that WGA rules allowed him to continue to work, without being penalized. In fact, any income received *post*-pension would automatically be applied to a *second* retirement, collectible when he turned 65. The problem was, he was virtually unemployable. Until he found a job, he would have to keep living with his mother in the below-Wilshire apartment he grew up in as a boy. Dolly had lived there since the divorce, practically since Kennedy was shot (when the rent was $235 a month). Her husband Morris—Bud's father—killed himself back in '77.

A few years ago, with the help of a therapist, Bud Wiggins arrived at the mature, painful conclusion that he lacked talent as a screenwriter. He'd been given so many chances to soar yet each time fell to earth. And now, through an uncertain alchemy, he transformed defeat into liberation—the liberation that came with admitting he was finished, done, his sojourn in the Business was over. Of late, mortality was very much on his mind. Just how did he want to spend the years he had left? He decided at last to try his hand at what he felt he'd been put on earth to do—novel writing. Bud smiled to himself at the inept timing of his strategem: fiction was becoming a dead thing before his & the world's eyes, a faster death than anyone had imagined or been prepared for. But what could he do? *You can't fight the feeling.*

It used to be a cliché that actor-waiters, CPAs and dentists were all working on screenplays; then came the old joke ". . . but what I really want to do is to direct." Now it seemed that no one cared about writing scripts *or* directing. They only wanted to be novelists.

Novels were the new screenplays.

.   .   .

Truman Capote was such a fan that he famously declared Joyce Carol Oates to be "a joke monster who ought to be beheaded in a public auditorium."* Bud wasn't as opinionated. He *did* like the idea of writers whose work, either paraphrased or quoted, existed only in reviews; it had a Borgesian (Bolañoesque?) ring. Maybe he'd try his hand at a short metafiction with that theme.

The halogen bulb of JCO's industry attracted the moths of novelists *manqué*, old infants no longer so terrible who'd given up the ghost of authorial fame in mid-life, instead finding peace in the green-enough pastures of *TLS* and *The London Review of Books*. These gentlemen and gentle ladies inadvertently began their Sunday reviews of JCO's latest eructation with a winking bow to her promiscuity on the page, which depending on individual temperament or even the mood of the moment, could be a swipe or a grovel.

Bud thought her ageless, gazelle-necked, bug-eyed flap photos never really did synch with the characterization of her work. (He saw her as a Victorian figure on display in the *Quality Lit* wing of Tussaud's, alongside other prodigies of indefatigable overprolificity: Cartland, Simenon, Dumas, King.) He gathered from reviews read over time that Oates's *thing* was ultraviolent, hypersexual Gothic. With each long novel and long short story, the writer apparently upped the ante of outlandish narrative, her new releases storming the marketplace sometimes three at a time like soccer thugs intent on

---

* The kitty-clawed Capote's comments were prescient, prefiguring the fad of live-streaming *Allah Akbar!* decapitation, the extreme sport of extremist enthusiasts. The go-go years of online decaps straddled the millennium, peaking with the martyrdom of Daniel Pearl. Bud had planned to write a novella-length fantasia—in the genre critics call "Swiftian meditation"—about a headless man, but nothing ever came of it.

breaking the skulls of the books that came before them. The complex, superheated plotlines that Bud was able to skim from reviews placed her indeed in the prinicipality of the Grand Guignol soap. It was the vexing habit of the woman's fiercely loyal critics to provide bizarrely fussy *précis* of whatever book they'd been engaged to appraise—much like competing technical manual writers vying for the prize of Best Instructions in the matter of operation of delicate scientific equipment. When it came to *Shakti Oates*, Mother Goddess of fertility, they shared a freemason-like covenant, a moral-ethical philosophy binding them together in an erotomanic rigor of thoroughness and *objectivity*. The sheer meticulousness of their endeavors launched them—obliviously—into cultism. It was a hobby of Bud's to read all of her reviews, though sometimes just finishing them was daunting, as if her prolixity had gone viral, paralyzing the very coolies vested in carrying the palanquin.

As a novelist, Bud wanted—needed—to study and profit from her example. The woman was some kind of witch. Her defamers were legion yet, in the end, through devilry, the nastiest cavils were massaged into batty, ecclesiastical pronouncements placing her squarely among the Immortals. So, aside from said carpings—the periodic hoots, hisses, graffiti, buckshot and urine-splashing afforded any writer worth their salt (cf: obsolescent belle-lettres blogsites)—the Oatress was critically bulletproof. She was a member of good standing in that country club Bud only dreamt of one day belonging, with its tenured, critically sun-kissed topnotchers: Auster, Vollman & McEwan, Cormac McC & Lorrie Moore . . . though Bud *did* remember that JCO's memoir of her husband's death* got respectfully

---

* He thought it ludicrously ironic that the deceased was a frustrated writer whose unfinished novel JCO found and read after his death. (He began writing it before they met, a half century back.) Even though the deceased was an editor by profession, he supposedly never read any of her books. Any. Bud thought that was passive-aggressive o'plenty; there must have been a lot of rage there. Apparently, JCO was remorseful that she hadn't better encouraged his creative side. Reading between the lines—and there were a lot of lines!—Bud thought it sounded like the poor fellow had literally been crushed by his wife's productivity—outgunned, deballed & anonymized. (His surname being Smith, he left the world as blandly as he had entered it.)

slammed in the *Times Sunday Book Review* (front cover, no less!), second-fiddled to *The Year of Magical Thinking.* Well, you can't have everything. Anyhow, Joyce was no Joan. Joan had *another* book out about the death of her daughter—take *that*, JCO! When it came to LA freeways, fires, & losing loved ones, Didion had the lock.*

When JCO bailed, the Central Library suggested T. Coraghessan Boyle or Neil LaBute; Steve wasn't thrilled. He rallied on learning Salman was in town to do Bill Maher, but the logistics didn't work & Salman sadly declined. In six hours, the auditorium would be filled. The hosts were starting to sweat. Norman Lear, Carolyn See and James Franco were rejected out of hand.

Steve had just given the (tepid) thumbs-up to Arianna, when Dave Eggers returned his call.

They met in 2009, when Dave won the $100,000 TED "Wish" Prize. (Steve emceed the ceremony and later became a big supporter of 826 Valencia.) Dave said he'd loved to have done the Q&A but was home nursing a sick child. But he said he managed to get in touch with another winner of the TED award, Karen Armstrong. Karen was a former nun, a scholar of comparative religion who created the *Charter for Compassion*, a project that was dedicated to promoting awareness of the universality of the Golden Rule in world religions. Steve actually met Karen a few years before on Necker Island. Richard Branson invited a whole group to bat around ideas that might further the cause of reducing hate and extremism. It was a great time: Steve already knew Bono and, of course, Lou and Laurie—& Aby Rosen and his wife, the socialite psychiatrist Samantha Boardman. He'd never met Jimmy and Rosalynn Carter, or Queen Noor, who had an elegant, California girl beauty. Steve also knew Peter Gabriel, Peter Morton and Michael J. Fox (& wife Tracy) but had never met Sean Parker, who he really only knew through Justin's

---

* JCO became engaged to her 2nd husband just 11 months after Mr. Smith passed—while the body of her meditation on grief was still warm.

neat performance in *The Social Network*. Steve and Oliver Sachs marveled at how *they'd* never met, & happened to be big fans of each other's work, though admittedly, Dr. Sachs wasn't entirely *au courant* with his new friend's literary contributions. The actor-comedian-novelist's biggest love connection on that Necker Island trip was Desmond Tutu. The bishop was brilliantly congenial, with sunny, elastic features and a comedian's natural timing. There was something of the impish forest elf in him, and he smelled like an animal. He told Steve he'd retired and was "completely over the moon" about spending his days doing nothing but watching movies with his grandkids. He told him their favorite was *¡Three Amigos!* and Steve chose to believe him. Why would the bishop lie about something like that?

Karen Armstrong was in LA and *thrilled* to pinch hit. She was perfect: Steve loved the idea of being interviewed by a Fellow of the Royal Society of Literature, an organization founded by King George IV boasting Coleridge, Kipling, Hardy and Shaw in its lineage of Fellows. Rocking good company.

.   .   .

Bud Wiggins sat in the audience listening, yet found it hard to focus—one of the downsides of ADD. He began a casual catalogue of his miseries.

He had zero savings and hadn't sold a network pitch in years. His old school chum Michael Tolkin was an important ICM client, and Bud was convinced it was only Michael's quiet interventions that had kept him on the ICM books. Back in the day, it'd have been Bud doing the good deed; back in the day, for about six months, Bud was hot. That was a long time ago, when Ovitzsauruses roamed the Earth, Arabs were the only billionaires, & Teri Garr didn't have MS.

He was $200,000 in debt. His mother, the top earner at Neimans in Beverly Hills until she reluctantly retired at the age of 83, had managed to save over a million dollars. "That," she liked to say, regally, "is your legacy." Dolly was 92 now—op-ed sociologists were calling anyone over 85 "the old old." The doctors had learned their trade too well; the old old had become a ruinous drain on the nation's resources; the old old were very tough to kill. Dolly got nastier by the week. Like blood to a vampire, foulness gave her sustenance, and a certain *élan*.

Just this morning she'd railed against one of her Salvadoran caregivers. "I told her that she was now *required to wipe my ass*. Do you know why? Because I want her hands in my shit."

Bud was 59 (the young old), and desperately eager to trade the burnt-out dream of Hollywood screenwriter for a new one, the dream of being a novelist. Since he was a boy, he'd thought of himself as a prose writer. Even a published one—when he was in his 20s, driving a limousine at the Beverly Hills Hotel, Bud wrote an article for *New West* magazine about what it was like to chauffeur the stars. He got fired for that, but gained confidence as a writer. He began writing long monologues in the voice of various habitués of a bar he frequented: Fast Eddie, wheelchaired as the result of a parking lot shooting; Aesop, the bearded hippie & sometime movie actor who went table to table selling turquoise jewelry; Soledad, the waitress whose bartender husband was shot and killed; Seymour, the bystander who got winged in the gunfight that killed Soledad's husband, & squandered his settlement money on pinball machines. He was in the planning stages of writing a novel about those people, when fate intervened. He fell in love with an actress in a comedy group. They did improvisations in her living room and started to write up dialogue, scenes, & situations. They linked the sketches and a producer bought the results. A movie was made, and it didn't really matter that it would never be released—for a while, they were an employable team. ICM gave their script to other writer-clients as the template to be aspired to.

Bud never lost the sense that prose was his raison d'être. He felt like the proverbial woman who sacrificed a brilliant singing career to have babies; his babies were his scripts and they were all mongoloids. It was time to sing again. He knew he had a novel in him, but what kind? What genre? What kind of style, what type of characters? What would it be about? Sometimes when he got too crazy, Bud enjoyed going to events like the one at the Central Library because the grueling process of writing was usually presented in a relatable, somewhat entertaining light, and it relieved the pressure, at least for a little while. He already knew the life of a writer was arduous, and lonely too. You could be lonely working on some shitty TV script— if that was the way it was going to be, why not end up with a novel? With a novel, you at least had people's respect.

He tuned back in. Steve was telling Karen about the important lesson he was taught by Carl Reiner . . .

What was the connection between Steve and Carl? He rooted around in the IMDB section of his brain to come up with the answer and found it: Reiner directed Steve in *The Jerk* and *The Man With Two Brains*. (Bud was impressed by his ability to access movie trivia, even though it felt a little like being in a convalescent home doing daily mental aerobics.) Carl Reiner, Sid Caesar, Mel Brooks, Larry Gelbart—all these guys were in a small file shoved in an unmemorable section of Bud's amygdala. When he was a kid, Bud remembered how they all used to be on top of the world, the whole country knew who they were, and now that generation was finished, a living cemetery of dementia'd old olds, sequestered in falling-down Holmby Hills mansions, moldy and unkempt, horizontal hospice heads & groupies confined to their beds in stinky, understaffed, memorabilia-hoarded rooms, thousands of garish, encrusted picture frames with signed photos of the dead and dying, and the questionably alive: Carol O'Connor, Gilda and Gene, Bernie Brillstein, Brandon Tartikoff, Sandy Duncan, Karen Valentine, Mel and Anne, Sid and Imogene, Steve & Edie, Mickey & Judy, Kovacs and Freiberg, Roddy McDowell, Orson Welles, Chuck Connors & Orson Bean, Pat McCormack, Jack Paar, Pat Paulsen, *herrrrrrre's* Johnny—all current enlistees and recruits to the Double Void: that terrifying 2nd erasure following career death————————

> . . . . *Steve Martin was telling Karen Armstrong how he applied the simple advice Carl Reiner gave him about screenwriting to his novels: Give 'em the rules in the first few minutes—*

Maybe someone told Kafka, *Leave 'em laughing* . . . .

Bud drifted again.

He'd read in an article that morning in HuffPost about Steve selling a Hopper for 28 mill. But Steve said the Hopper he *really* cared about, "The Lighthouse," was still hanging in his living room. Bud idly wondered what a thing like that would cost to insure . . . . .

Last week, he wangled his way into an Art of Fiction Q&A with James Franco. (Sold-out, at the Chateau.) The actor had a new novel out, & was being interviewed by Liz Phair, a pre-millennium rockstar who supposedly made her name—Bud didn't have much of a file on her—by doing an album that mirrored *Exile on Main Street*, song for song. Which explained how a few years ago she wound up reviewing Keith Richards' memoir for the front page of *The New York Times Book Review*. At the time, Bud was surprised they engaged in that sort of "stunt reviewing."* He quickly emailed the editor, touching briefly on his career as a journeyman screenwriter (currently in mid-novel), suggesting it might be "great fun" to pair him with any Hollywood books coming down the pike—unauthorized biographies of stars, say, or the more respectable A. Scott Berg–type histories of agencies and studios, of Jews in the business, even Hollywood

---

* Of course, the *Times* routinely turned to Toni Bentley when it came to books on ballet, and in the realm of the overtly or mildly incestuous, had Kathryn Harrison on permanent tap; the estimable Julian Barnes recently carved himself a nice little niche when it came to mourning & death. He in fact reviewed Joyce Carol Oates's memoir of widowhood for *The New York Review of Books*. Barnes rather gently took JCO to task for omitting mention of her remarriage, which predated publication of her memoir, a criticism JCO initially rebuffed before eventually reconsidering. She set the record straight in reprintings of the mem. Still, the pairing of Liz Phair and Keith Richards did strike Bud as borderline.

fiction. Bud had the whimsical idea of enclosing a satirical *Shouts &*
Murmurs–style essay (to give the editor a sample of what he could do)
on the reality star Lauren Conrad's *New York Times Best Seller* trilogy
L.A. Candy. Ultimately, he decided not to, because he didn't want to
look like he was auditioning. He did his best to lay the groundwork.
You never knew. Maybe the next time they were casting around for
a "Hollywood insider" take on a new novel by Lauren or Snooki or
the Kardashian family, they'd give him a shout (not a murmur).

There was another writer Bud wanted to study: Fran Lebowitz.
Some days he was of a mind that he could learn even more from
Fran than from JCO. Fran was an examplar of a phenomena Bud
always found as puzzling as it was terrifying: to *wit,* the counterfeit
being taken for the real. Fran *signified* for the culturati, complicit in
promoting the myth that she was of the same bloodline as Thurber
and Wilde. Pundits and benefactors to whom those men were as
foreign as Bud was to Proust had inexplicably anointed her as such
and Fran made sure to sit very still as they lowered the papier-mâché
crown upon her epigrammatically-challenged head. Because *Bud*
was a writer who hadn't really written, not in the way he was *about*
to, not just *yet*, it was galling that Fran became famous—lionized—
for (not) doing the very same. Bud was alternately in awe and en-
raged, & obsessed with solving the riddle of how she had managed
to pull that off. Bud felt that as a preemptive measure, should he
never be able to finish his book, he could sit at her feet and take
notes. Why kid himself? He *too* wanted a hagiographic HBO documentary, he *too* wanted a Nobel Prize-winning friend singing his
praises! Bud went online and scrolled through Fran's aphorisms:
Calling a taxi in Texas is like calling a rabbi in Iraq . . . Humility is no
substitute for a good personality . . . Your life story would not make a good
book—don't even try . . . Bud thought: The tables are not round at
the Waverly!——but why was he so angry? Was it mere jealousy?
What business was it of his if the Empress's new clothes were
Weejuns & 501s? Why was it that her papal, erroneous mini-lectures

on the difference between *witty* and *funny*—unseemly advertise-ments for herself—set Bud's teeth on edge? Why, when what Fran had was what he wanted? Maybe he resented her because he wrote comedy for so many years. (Occasionally, Johnny Carson and Jay Leno used his stuff, though most of Bud's material never made it to air.) Fran despised the very thing she was: *a comic*. She was no Louis C.K., nor was she George Carlin or a cross between—she was weak borscht, a third-string *tummler* in a tux, a poor man's Steven Wright. An impressionist——no, an impersonator——no, *illusionist*——an Oscar Wiener Oscar Wilde. But just when he was in the thrall of h8ting on Fran, he fell into awe again . . . he had to admit his guru was possessed by social genius. She sure could pick friends. Hang-ing with Toni Morrison *fifteen years before* the Nobel. The perfect marriage: the bride wore black. Now Steve and Karen were talking about W. G. Sebald as the writer who influenced Steve's placement of paintings throughout *An Object of Beauty* . . . Bud checked out again, letting the African ladies carry him down a ruminative stream . . . *Toni Morrison, Alice Walker, Maya Angelou . . . Toni Angelou, Maya Walker, Alice Morrisangelalker—more* writers whose books he'd never crack . . . *crazed black swans dressed as royalty (but don't forget the royalties)—best look out when they hit the ground runnin' to collect their awards. Cause dese bitches'll run you* down. *Deez* scary bitches are award-*crayzuh*, ebony & ivory don't mean *nuthin* to dese bitches but *black- & white-tie*, as in *gala*, as in neverending *shitstorm* of tributes & lifetime achieve-ments hoohahs celebrating mediocre lyrical gifts, shameless sha-mans mainlinin Kennedy Center Honors like heroin, bitches never had to go too far to cop, cause more *mutherfuckin* awards be waitin on every street corner! But the *Nobel* . . . woo woo woo! Toni & her *Nobel*——uh, well, *whoa*. Nuff said. Nobel be duh Big One, bigger than der Bingle, fo sho. So big nobody *dared to dream*, nor pay heed, nobody had the *vision*, nobody saw it *comin*—nobody but Fran! The *Nobel!* Took *everybody* by surprise . . . . . everybody but——

Hey ho Hey ho
It's off to Sweden we go.

With S. J. (Ron) Perelman in tow
Hey ho!

She would offer him lessons not just in patience but endurance. A long-distance careerist, Fran knew how to pace herself to win. Bud dreamed of that moment when his *own* Nobelist would be climbing up his ass in a sold-out Q&A at the New York Public Library . . . the air crackling with pulse pounding chic, that nearly unbearable, blackout-inducing, *we-have-no-more-tickets-folks, I-can't-believe-I-am-here! they-are-legends-and-this-is-history!* mania. Fran astonished him. Only a serious hairdon't kept her from being the 4th Kardashian ——————————————————————————Steve and Karen were standing now and awkwardly embraced. As they held hands, Steve playfully mimed an exhortation for the audience to stand in ovation, which it did, the appreciative mob laughing and applauding. The talk had been rather serious, at times *strenuous*, a bit heavy going—the mood suddenly lightened, and pleasant relief abounded. Karen couldn't help herself from cracking up as Steve, clown prince, mugged for the crowd, clapping back at them. The applause grew rhythmic as Steve began the Zorba dance. Egged on by her interviewee, Karen Zorba'd too. Sweet pandemonium.

Steve would be signing books. Bud thought about waiting in line, but there were too many people.

MISSED CALL/VOICEMAIL was on the face of his phone.

He listened on the way to the lot.

It was the office of Chris Silbermann, leaving word.

The president of ICM.

[Reeyonna]

gossip girls*

*(white girl mobbin)

She

sat next to Rikki in the school auditorium where some early *Glee* episodes were filmed. Rikki, lightskinned pharaoh-looking Rikki, father of her relatively soon-to-be-born child, gender unknown. The speaker was a darkerskinned handsome-ish young man who was once a child soldier in Sierra Leone. He evidently slaughtered a lot of people (so he said) not just because the commanders of various so-called Lord's Armies brainwashed him to but because he and his murderous schoolboy friends were loaded on some kind of gunpowder he said they were forced (yeah right) to snort by their leaders, that was like snorting coke. *Oh, is that your excuse?* It was like *The Hunger Games*, but all black and without the games.

His name was Ishmael Beah.

The darkerskinned handsome boy stood at the lectern in coat and tie saying he/they killed men, women and children, even members of their own families. Rikki was more interested in what he had to say than she was, which was actually an understatement, it looked like Rikki was *obsessed, studying* the fellow. Man-boy crush time.

Rikki & his friends were enjoying hearing about the drugs & the killing, and how this fellow—his name was Ishmael—never even had to go to jail. He wrote a book about it instead that made him rich & famous and now he worked for the U.N. Ishmael went on to say that there were other (former) childsoldiers, all his rehabilitated homies, who now lived in Seattle or wherever, pursuing careers in rap.

. . .

Afterschool, Reeyonna and her girlfriends kicked it at the house, & smoked purp.

 — Did you know about Laurence Fishburne's daughter?

 — I can't remember who Laurence Fishburne is. In my head.

 — He's an actor. Lemme use your phone.

 — No—I have it. Oh! Yeah! He's on *CSI*?

 — But not anymore.

 — He was in *The Matrix*——

 — That is one *ug-guh-lee* nigga.

 — He is *not*. I think he's *hot*.

 — You think *Steve Tyler* is hot.

 — His money is.

 — Money makes the man.

 — *M-m-m-money on my mind, money on my mind* . . .

 — Youngmoney cashmoney.

 — Who's that actor with the eye—the freaky eye—

 — Forest Whitaker.

 — Shit, you gotta a *lot* of information in your head, girl.

 — I think his daughter used to go to John Burroughs. I think she was a senior when we were freshmen.

 — *So* much information.

 — Forest Whitaker is *really* good. He won an Academy Award for Best Actor.

 — Really?!?!

— What was Laurence Fishburne in? *The Purple Mile? Shawshank Whatever?*

— Hahahaha! It's *Green Mile!* Hahaha!

— She's got purp on the brain.

— *The Purp Mile . . .*

— That's funny.

— *The Color Purp*—hahahahahahaha!

— The color perp-walk.

— I *loved The Color Purple.*

— Yeah well now you're lovin the color.

— Isn't that a Prince song? *Purp Rain.* Ahahahahahahaha.

— Was Whoopi in that, or Oprah?

— Whoopi wasn't in *Purple Rain.*

— I love her on *The View.*

— This shit is *strong.* I am *so stoned . . .*

— Yeah it's good. *No sticks, no seeds, just Al Green . . .*

— *That purp, that bomb, that kush—*

— Psycho*denk . . .*

— I never saw *The Matrix.*

— Netflix it, girl. Stream on. Get on it.

— It's kind of like *Inception.*

— No, you can't instant it, it's only on DVD.

— O bullshit. Really?

— No, look—see?

— I totally watched that on my phone last week. Totally!!!

— Can someone tell me what the fuck a *Blu-ray* is?!?!

— I didn't like *Inception.* I hate that girl Natalie Portman.

— *Oh my God, you are so stoned.*

— That's not Natalie Portman! It was the girl who played the pregnant girl—

— from Canada?

— *Juno . . .*

— I loved that movie! What's her name?

– Ellen! Ellen Page.

– Look—she's from Halifax. Nova Scotia.

– Can I see?

– Oooh she's pretty.

– *I* want to be from Nova Scotia, I *love* Nova Scotia—

– Oh my God, she's like *twenty-five.*

– Really? I can't believe she's so old!

– It says 1987. February 21.

– That's my brother's birthday!

– She looks so young. She's one of those women who will look exactly the same until they're, like, seventy.

– *Natalie Portman!* ReeRee is fucked up. You saw *Juno,* didn't you, Ree?

– She gets pregnant while she's in high school?

– Um, gee, doesn't that sound familiar?

– But she's really *responsible* about it. I mean it's *so* not *Teen Mom.* She is so not psycho white trash!

– What about Laurence Fishburne's daughter?

– Why does he call himself *Laurence*? It should be *Larry,* right?

– It's like he wants to be all *English.* Like Dr. House.

– Dr. House is not English.

– He *totally* is. The guy who plays him? Oh my God, he is *so* English!

– Tallyho.

– Tally *ho's!!!*

– Would anybody care for a spot of tea?

– Sir Laurence Fishburne would love a spot of tea!

– *Sir Laurence of Arabia Fishburne.*

– Sir Lawrence of a Labia.

– That is disgusting!

– My little brother said that to me. I don't even think he knew what it meant!

– Why doesn't he just call himself Larry.

— Because Larry smells like *ass*. Movie stars do *not* name themselves Larry.

— Right?

— I can't think of any. *I can't think. I can't. Of any.* Oh my god I am so stoned.

— Larry Fishburne's daughter! What were you going to say!

— She's a pornstar.

— Yeah, that's old.

— Wazzup witt huh?

— Yeah! Tell us wazzup with huh!

— I was listening to huh on Shade. & she's like promoting huh porno, whatever. Huh real name's Montana but huh porn name be Chippy D.

— Whoa. It's like a Ben & Jerry's. Schweddy balls . . .

— Chocolate fudge brownie—

— Banana *split*—schweddy clit . . . . .

— Boston CREAM pie!

— *Muddddd sliiiiiiiiiide!*

— That's a good pornstar name! *Mudslide.*

— It's quite evocative, as the English say.

— She should just call herself Larry!

— Have you seen her movies?

— Rikki has. On his iphone. I told him I don't want to *see* that shit. I do *not* want to see Chippy D chomping on a dick!

— Didn't she go crazy?

— I think she went to a mental hospital but they said she was faking it. She tried to kill herself?

— I feel sorry for her.

— Feel sorry for her *dad!*

— Can you imagine how fucked up it must be for him? I mean, your daughter's supposed to be going off to college, but she decides to stay home & major in dick-riding!

— O! I mean, anywhere he shows his face, someone's gunna— people are like *snickering* . . .

– She said on this show—on Eminem's show—that her dad would one day see, like, her *Big Plan*, & they would totally mend their relationship.

– Whatever. I really feel sorry for her. He must have had to totally have done some shit in her upbringing for her to be doing that shit she does tho.

– Like molesting?

– No. I mean he *could* have. Don't all dads molest their daughters?

– That's gross.

– But he doesn't seem the *type*. & she probably would have been talking about that already, bitch so *crazy*. I'm just sayin he must have done *something*. I'm jus sayin.

– She's jus sayin.

– Maybe he *didn't*. Sometimes you can be a really good parent and your kid winds up shooting kids at school or whatever.

– Oh my god, Reeyonna, what if your kid does that? That would be so weird!

– I'm just gunna do my best to be a loving mom—

– We could give it a list of who to shoot.

– Ooh hoo! You better *hope* he doesn't *columbine*—

– All I know is, I don't want to put any pressure on the baby. And I don't want him to have expectations.

– Him? Is it a boy? Are you going to have a boy?

– I don't want him *or her* to have expectations!

– Expectations about *what*? Girl, you cray-zee.

– You Jay-Z.

– She doesn't want to know. She told the doctor and nurses not to tell her like what the gender would be.

– I could *never* do that. *I would totally need to know!*

– Well if it's a girl, don't name her Montana.

– Hahahahahahahahahahah—

– AHAHAHAHAHAHA—

– *hahahahahahahahahahaha*—

– So she was on the *Shade*.

– That's Eminem's channel?—

– And she's telling em porn is like a *stepping stone* in her career. You know, like it was for Paris and Kim.

– Did you see the Kim tape?

– No but now I *want* to.

– Did you know he's Brandy's little brother?

– Who is.

– Ray J Ray J Ray J Ray J.

– Gimme some of that, Swisher Queen.

– Lissen to her! She thinks she's Kreayshawn, but you just a basic bitch!

– Girl, I'm a *bad* bitch. I'm *fag swag.*

– *Fag swag* HAHAHAHAHAHAHAH

– The guy in the tape with Kim.

– He's an *asshole.* Didn't he leak that to the internet?

– He leaked a lot.

– Hahahahahahahahaha!

– He leaked it all over.

– And Chippy D . . . she talks about Sasha Grey too—

– OMG Sasha Grey is *such a slut!*

– Montana talks about her like she's Meryl Streep!

– Montana is just *dumb.* She looks like a donkey.

– That's mean.

– Sasha Grey is *nasty.* Rikki showed me a gangbang tape she did— I got *totally traumatized* just watching it! There was like this whole *roomful* of guys in line to fuck her in her butt! & *nobody* was wearing a condom.

– That is so disgusting.

– It's sick. It's like—*sick.*

– She is beyond slutdom.

– The d.p. queen.

– She needs an exorcist.

– And like, the DJs are saying—one of them's saying, like, "Montana, I was jacking off to one of your movies this morning"—

– Oh my God, he *said* that? On the *radio*?

– It's satellite.

– You can say anything on satellite.

– O my god.

– He like just totally says "I was jacking off to one of your movies but like I kept seeing your dad's *face* cause you really kinda *look* like him"—

– *Oh my God.*

– Hahahahahahahaha!

– *ahahahahahahahahahahahaaahahahah*—

– So what did she say?

– She said she was proud of her new "feature," that's what she called it, a *feature film*—

– That is *so, so sad* . . .

– Sick.

– They ask her about the *feature* and she says she does *everything* in it, you know, facials, anal, she even *squirts*—

– *What* is *squirting?!?!!!*

– You know how like some girls can *gush* when they cum.

– Rikki showed me this *compilation*—have you seen that?

– Where would I have seen *that?!?!*

– I don't know, maybe he showed you.

– You should just ask him!

– But I——do you mean *water* squirts when they cum?

– Water, *whatever.*

– Diet Squirt.

– Rikki said Louie told him that he had a girlfriend once who could squirt, like the shit that came out was *hot*, like *hot water*, & they had to always have like two *big towels* next to him when they fucked, & sometimes before they even finished the towels would be *soaked*—

– *Oh my God* . . .

– That is *beyond* disgusting.

– Like Yellowstone.

– Thar . . . she———

— *Blowwwwwwwwwwwwws!!!!!!!!!!!!!!*

— *ahahahahahahahahahahahaahahahahahahahah*

— Old Faithful . . .

— Right, the geyser—what do they—

— You know that actress Thora Birch?

— Is she in *True Blood*?

— No. That's Anna Paquin.

— I *love True Blood*.

— Anna Paquin?

— Oh my God, you are *so stoned*, just shut the fuck *up*. Thora Birch was in *American Beauty*.

— I didn't see that. I know of it but I haven't seen it.

— Get your Netflix game on, biatch. We watched it on Raymundo's iPad. Anyway, her parents are total pornstars.

— Her parents? Really?

— Yeah, I think her mom was in *Deep Throat*.

— I'm looking her up on *Wickedpedia*—

— They should adopt Chocolate Chippy D!

— Totally! She's probably their real kid . . .

— It should have been Thora *Fishburne*—

— Switched at birth!

— *ahahahahahahahahaah*—

— O my God, you won't believe this—

— She's too white to be his daughter.

— *What?*

— It says she went to *New Roads*.

— Are you kidding?!?!

— Who did.

— Thora.

— I think it's so trippy when you can have a black father and still look totally white if your mom's white. I saw a picture of Drake's mom—

— Thora Birch's parents *totally* need to adopt Chippy D!

– —look. See? He's a Jew.

– That's Drake's mom? She's so totally a blond!

– President Obama's mom is *totally white* like that.

– Are they still seriously porned out? Thora's mom & dad?

– I don't think they like *perform* anymore, they just manage her. Her dad does. Her career.

– If she has one.

– See if she's on twitter.

– Are you *sure* she is not in *True Blood*?

– O my God, you're *serious!* You are so stoned!

– No one can be managed by their *parents*. Well maybe when you're really young but then it gets fucked up. They like snap to the fact that their parents are totally trying to control them or steal their money. They wind up having to sue.

– I would *love* to sue my parents.

– ReeRee, when are you going to tell your mom you're pregnant?

– When I start to show. I have like this whole *plan*.

– Like how you're going to tell her?

– I'm supposed to get all this money when I'm 18? From when I was a model in all of her photographs? She's been like setting aside money for me, and putting it in a trust? She said I deserved to have some of the money.

– That is so cool of her.

– Your mom is so kewl.

– I mean, do you know, did she say how much? How much you're going to have?

– I think around like $200,000—

– *whoa whoa whoa*—

– but that was like 4 years ago. So there's probably interest . . .

– Reeyonna, that is *so much money*.

– I'm not supposed to get it til I turn 18, but I'm going to ask her to give it to me earlier.

– What are you going to do with it?

— Buy a house. Like a little cottage in Silverlake or the Holly-wood hills.

— Like a bungalow?

— O my God, I *love* that.

— I just think you need a house if you're going to start a family. Rikki and I need to *live* together, he needs to feel like the man of the house. You know, not a *boy* who doesn't have any responsibilities.

— Do you think she'll give it to you? Early? Your mom?

— It's *my money.* I'll fucking sue her if she doesn't!

— Hahahahahahahahaha!

— Sue the bitch.

— *Beeyotch.*

— She's a MILS—*Mom I'd Like to Sue.*

— *ahahahahahahahahahahahahah—*

— TMZ said Robert Pattinson and Kristen Stewart made like *$30 million* last year each—

— Yeah but Taylor Swift—no, Taylor Lautner made, like, *50 million.*

— Who said?

— *Dlisted.* And TMZ too.

— Johnny Depp made 125.

— Thousand?

— *Million*, you spaz.

— O. My. God.

— You are *spastic. In Touch* said that works out to like 40,000 an hour for a whole *year*, 24-hours around the clock!

— O my God.

— That is *so crazy.* Then Jennifer Lawrence is probably a billion-aire!

— No, the internet said she got totally fucked, she's only making like a million dollars for like the first three.

— Eminem probably made more than a billion.

— Would you fuck Eminem?

– Are you kidding? Of course!

– No, I mean if you could *marry* him, and you found out he *really likes* it when girls don't, just, like, *fuck* him right away—

– Do you mean could I *not* fuck him?

– Like do you think you could *not* fuck Em if you thought there was a chance he would marry you?

– What if you didn't fuck him and he *didn't* marry you?!?!

– If it was between fucking him or *not* fucking him but the marriage wasn't, like, guaranteed?

– I'd fuck Drake.

– I would *so* fuck Drake. He got *so* hurt by Rihanna.

– Slut.

– Drake's a Jew.

– Nuh *uh*.

– He is, he's a Jew.

– How could he be.

– But why is Eminem so pissed off all the time? Eminem is *so angry*. He has so much money!

– He's probably a pussycat. It's just that he's been hurt in love. You know, love is, like, heavy on his heart.

– I used to think he was gay.

– You thought Em was *gay?!?!*

– When "I Need A Doctor" came out, they said "doctor" was like code for "dick"—

– *Who* said?!?!

– It was on the internet . . .

– That is *so lame*. "Doctor" is Dr. Dre.

– I'm just sayin—

– The song is *totally gay*, tho. You know, Dre says "All I need is *him*" and Eminem's all like "Come back, Dre, you're the only one who believed in me, why should we care what other people think, let's just like, you know, fuck—"

– You are *so crazy*!!!

— I think it's *sweet*, they're really good *friends*, Em's just saying to Dre that he needs him. It's so like *vulnerable*. I mean, rap *never* talks about man love—

— & Royce sayin he loves Em like Em loves Dre & how he would kill for him *it is so gay!*

— Eminem gave Elton John a *cock ring* made of *diamonds*—

— O that is such BULLSHIT—

— No, he did, it was in the *Rolling Stone* . . .

— Eminem is like *so stuck up*. I mean like every song he's on that has other people, it's like so funny, he's always talking about how he's the *best*, like the others'll just be talking about weed or cars or bitches or *whatever*, and all Marshall Mathers talks about is how he's like the most amazing rapper who ever lived!

— Whoa! What is your *issue*.

— Cause you're talking—she's talking like she's been—what do they say—"a woman spurned"!

— A woman *spermed*—

— Squirted!

— A woman spurted!

— She *wishes!*

— If I had $100 million trust me I would *not* be angry.

— Maybe you would be! Maybe you'd be Charlotte Sheen!

— Who?

— *Charlotte Sheen.* Sister of Charlie!

— Oh! Charlotte! Hahahahahaha!

— *Charlene.* That would be *Charlene.*

— Charlene! Charlene! Charlene Sheen!

— Fuck *yeah!*—

— I'd fuck Hov and Ye before I did Eminem.

— Look at *choo*. Look @ dis biatch! "Hov" & "-ye"! Lissen to *choo*. Girl think she a nigga.

— Nicki Mee-naj. Nicki *Ménage à twaht.*

— What about Johnny Depp.

— What about him.

– Would you let him d.p.?

– I'll tell you my dream d.p. . . . I'm on top of Robert Pattinson & the guy on *In Treatment* is in my butt. Up to the nuts!!!!

– *Tea baggggggggg!*

– What is *In Treatment?!?!*

– Gabriel Byrne is *so sexy.*

– I'm kinda over Johnny Depp.

– *He's* over *you. And his* wife.

– I'm over that swashbuckling shit. I need uh *ass-buckling . . .*

– Have you seen his wife? She's *hot.* She's a singer.

– *Voolay-voo coushay ahveck m'wah, çe swa.*

– I wonder if she's been d.p.'d.

– Totally. She's been totally Johnny D'p.'d! That's why they're breaking up. She's over it.

– French people *invented* the d.p.

– "The" d.p.—————————ha!

– And Americans perfected it.

– This smoke is *amazing*—

– It's from Rikki's stash.

– *That purp, that bomb, that kush . . .*

– Gimme that blunt. Gimme gimme gimme.

– Ree, do you have any Adderall?

– No!

– O please O please O pretty pretty please?

– Do you think Laurence Fishburne ever saw any of Chippy D's *feature films*?

– O, gross!

– I mean don't you think he would've had to see something, like even by *mistake?*—

– Please ReeRee please? *Ollie Ollie Addie, oxen free . . .*

– Wouldn't a father be *curious* about his *daughter*—I mean, he's already *seen* her nude, he's *washed her* in a tub when she was little, he's already *seen* that nasty vadge . . .

– ewwwwwwwwwwwwwwwwww!

– ReeRee, *pleeeeeeeeeeease*?

– What?!

– Please can I *please* have some Adderall?

– Wouldn't a father be curious to see his baby take it in both holes & SQUIRT?

– You are so sick!

– Thar she blows!

– *Thar she blows——*

– *[all together now]* THARRRRRRR SHEEEEEEEEE BLOW-WWWWWWWWS!!!

[Jacquie]

The Family of Mann

Jacquie

lied when she told Steve Martin she was almost finished with a suite of new photographs she'd been working on the last few years—the culmination of everything she was as an artist. When Steve said he'd be *very* interested in seeing them, she knew he was lying too. They exchanged energized hellos while he was in the middle of signing books after the Library event. Jacquie waited half-an-hour longer for him to finish, standing a discreet distance apart, watching him autograph, with an old courtesan's half-smile. When he was done, a dozen giggling fans lingered, taking cellphone pics with the author for their Facebook pages. With the help of a library staffer, Steve finally disengaged, and Jacquie approached. He was warm and polite. They spent a few minutes catching up, then he said he had to rush to a business dinner. *Another lie,* she thought. He gave her a contact number.

What happened?

For a while, she'd had such a good run . . .

. . .

Jacquie grew up poor, in Ocala.

DOB: 1960.

Dad was a short order cook. Migratory. Worked up and down those beaches in the summers—

Pompano, Vero, Cocoa, Daytona, Satellite, Neptune, Boynton. She had no ambition. All roads led to Ocala.

Dropped out of (the evocatively named) *Junior College of Central Florida* & became a Wal-Mart worker. At least it gave her the ability to live away from them.

Perfect timing because right about then her father got disabled & became a stay-at-home dad. Seemed like everybody's dad had a fucked up spine.

The irony was, she met that married professor not at (the lyrically christened) *Junior College of Central Florida*, but at Wal-Mart. He was handsome, angry, boyishly hurt, sophisticated. 63, with a full head of hair gone professorially grey-white. Even looking back, Jacquie believes it to be true: that the outsized, sensuous quality of her remembrance of his outsized, sensual (boozy) cynicism wasn't some trick that youth played on her mind. The man actually smoked a pipe, wore a tweed jacket with elbow patches. Now, she smiles to herself & says, Can you believe it? It really worked on him though (the look); and he really worked on *her.* Everything worked & was working. His pipe-stem breath smelled like sex & mouthwash. The professor was her 1st big physical love affair, she didn't really have too many more after that, not on that scale, with that resonance. To this day, the Professor essentially was *it,* for a multifariousity of reasons. Jacquie got hooked emotionally too, oh did she did.

His wife found out but didn't leave him.

The not so nutty professor gave Jacquie a camera.

And a boy—Jerry (Jr.) AKA Jerzy. DOB: 1984.

And child support; his wife found out about that too.

What are you gunna do.

She fooled around in her backyard with the Rolleiflex 2¼. Took lots of pics of cats and spiders in their webs. The film wasn't cheap, she had to find a fancy camera store that stocked it. She lugged the thing to work. During lunchbreaks, she took arty parking lot (Wal-

Mart) pics: shopping carts, crap cars, asphalt detritus. Everything but people, she never liked people in the shot, not if she could help it. (She wasn't ready for people pics.) Her co-workers thought she was an agreeable dufus. Which she was. Got along with everybody and never made waves. The emptier the lots, the better. Jacquie *loved* her an empty parking lot, the slanty dividing lines, & empty curbside metered spaces too.

Oh and she went through a dumpster-pic phase.

Then she started getting her kicks on weekends (only when the professor wasn't able to see her). Took pics of all the beach places where her daddy short-ordered, up and down. Obsessive. She was like someone who assiduously studied guitar; one day, mysterious moment, they just can *play*, suddenly they're *guitar players*. Without knowing what she was doing, she'd given herself a carefully calibrated apprenticeship, & there came that moment of mystery when she effortlessly knew more or less what she was doing with the shutterspeed, the light, the artfulness of it. Self-consciousness lifted away. No agenda anymore. She went driving for hours, taking pics of anything, even people. Even the professor, but never the professor's wife.

Her father died. Became a stay-underground dad.

Then, exactly 2 weeks after renting a bungalow (a belated gesture, but still) for Jacquie and their son, her beloved had an aneurysm. She went to the hospital & sat in the car in the lot, not knowing what to do. Most definitely *not* up for encountering the wife. Beleaguered. Weeping & listening to wrong songs on the radio. Taking pictures of parking places to soothe herself.

When a tall woman of officious mien strode toward her, she thought, *She's going to tell me to stop. It's probably that you're not allowed to take pics on hospital grounds.*

Instead:

"I'm Jerome's wife."

(She'd never heard *Jerome*. He/she always used *Jerry*.)

The widow invited Jacquie to visit her comatose husband's room.

She never asked about Jacquie's son. Only saying, "You know, we have no children," which broke Jacquie's heart.

(She wished she had brought her camera up.)

(The widow even left her alone with the body, because that's what it was, just a body.)

When she got back to her car, the glass was broken, the camera gone. Even as she sobbed, she realized how textbook symbolic was the theft. She sat behind the wheel, collecting herself. Cheap glass diamonds littered the vinyl seat. She focused on the (less than half-empty) parking lot. That familiar, reflexive, self-medicating urge to get out and take pics, which was not to be. She kept thinking about the widow's kindness. To come get her, to leave her with her professor, alone. A simple act of grace that still glows deep inside her to this day, providing warmth.

She bought a new camera, but her heart wasn't in it. Hardly used it . . .

1990. Now 30 years-old— *oh!* Waitressing (again).

So unhappy, such unhappiness.

Single mom with a 6-year-old.

She decides to drive to NY and stay at the Chelsea Hotel. Has approx $3,458.52 in savings. (Left nothing by the Professor, for whom she held no resentments, he'd just leased her & Jerry Jr. the bungalow, Jacquie was certain he had plans to further provide, how could he have known he had a bleedy brain?)

She sets off, leaves Jerry Jr. with her mom.

On the way up (on the 95), she takes pics of kitschy outdoor volcanoes/miniature golf courses & all the tourist traps lining beach town main drags. More pics of where Dad worked, and the sunny desolate apartment houses they used to live in. Lonely moonshots, camp & lovely: the Burt Reynolds Dinner Theater—the exquisite nearby homes of Jupiter Island, hidden behind privets & parterres. Forgotten Kennedy Space Center parking lot outback, forgotten custodians who worked at the Astronaut Hall of Fame. St Augustine

Fountain of Youth giftshop pics. Swamps, plantations, & cemeteries, & pics of folks who spoke Gullah and could tell a good Gullah ghost story. (They were all good.) She goes to Jekyll Island & Cape Fear, she always wanted to because of their names—Cape Fear was a wash, nothing frightening about Cape Fear at all, there didn't need to be, the name was perfect enough, gothy frightening name, frightful beacon in the imagination.

The Ava Gardner Museum. Yes. The old woman who works there—an Ava lookalike. The lonely parking lot. Yes. Of a castle in what they call the low country. A crazy-baroque synagogue in Savannah. On the beaches, she succumbs, like a teenager, to taking pics of shells: harps, pagodas & turbans, sundials, nutmegs, periwinkles.

There: a newish prison in the middle of a city, and the bailed-out blacks who pour forth. There was actually some kind of museum of slavery next door, & the just-released prisoners would bump right into it.

She drives & drives under gusty civil war skies.

Where am I going, where have I been.

She doesn't bother with Atlantic City. Atlantic City will do very well without her. Besides, she's running out of film.

She settles into her room at the Chelsea. (The Professor told her he stayed there a whole month once, that's how Jacquie got the idea.) She hates it.

She's lost, exhausted. Wants/needs to be touched. She puts on her sexiest dress and goes to a bar, fancy one, sleeps with the first man who tries to pick her up—a DP. Movie cameraman. Two weeks later, she's living in his apartment. All the while, she's watching herself, watching the insane speed at which things are happening, the whole crazy city, a million miles an hour, & now Jacquie a part of it. She loves it.

Ronny hires her for his camera crew, commercials & indies. (The beginning of indie golden years/Parker Poseydom.) She loses the ambition to document her world, hangs up her lenses, still in that world though by default. (Her job. Her man.) (Which she eventually takes for a "sign.") Getting her bearings . . . missing her son. Wants/ needs to forget about the Professor, which is tough, especially when Ronny's fucking her—he's the only one she'd been with since her beloved—Ronny fucks her well but not with the freight/impact/ import of Jerome. Needs/wants to make a life for herself, a real life, a city life, still not feeling that's what she has or even getting close. *It looks like I do but I don't.* And it's late, late, *I'm getting old, how could I have stayed in Florida so long, oh how* how——————————all this time shuttling to Ocala every six weeks, that's about as long as she can stand being away from him, Jerry Jr., wanting of course her son to be with her in the big city, maybe it's out of respect for his father, allegiance maybe, loyalty, fear, before she puts a man in his life, before she gives him another dad, Jacquie just wants to make sure (as sure as she can) this thing with Ronny is real. She finally brings him to NYC for better for worse, to have & to hold. Ronny of course saying all along how cool he was with it, bringing the boy up, he'd been very sweet, & Jacquie believed him but still needed to know, to see, if it's real, needed Ronny to *demonstrate* it was real. But Ronny was fine, & so was Jerry Jr., they were good together, it was Jacquie's own skittishness, reluctance to change/go forward, the *definitive change*, really nothing to do with Ronny *at all.*

He starts working on bigger movies, studio ones. (Going to ball games with Jerry Jr.) Now she can get in the union. She needs that security for her son, that's real. Starts taking pics again, Ronny's encouraging. When they move into a big loft—shit, Tribeca, frickin *huge* space, today there would be no way!—they move in & Ronny builds her a darkroom. She gets busy. Dusts herself off and takes cityscapes. The usual. Pigeons & vagrants on Central Park benches. Gap-toothed smiling cabbies. Penn Station porters/couples. Children at the zoo, eyes filled with wonder. *Ugh when she thinks back.* But really *enjoying* herself. When she shows him her pics, Ronny settles into an armchair with a joint and says *I really like that.* That's what he always says. Which is annoyingly gratifying. Because she hates the idea of being the asst cameragirl girlfriend with the kid from another whatever who takes dumbass black&white pics on the weekends, she knows where *that* will end, and it does: Ronny renting a whitewashed gallery space & hanging her pix, inviting friends, colleagues, people from the neighborhood, the cheap plastic glasses with screw-in stems, cheap wine, cheap cheese, cheap crackers, cheap smell in the air, cheap art. Ronny was so sweet, he even put those little red dots beside half the pics so it looked like they were already sold, it's very loud inside that whitewashed makeshift gallery space, a DJ, people spilling into the sidewalk, after a while nobody looks at the walls & Jacquie runs into friends there who don't even know that's *why* they're there, because it's her show, of her pics . . . as it turned out, most of what she chose to hang were from that first trip, on the road from Ocala, the Myrtle Beach pics, the sad-faced astronaut janitors & gullahville folk, & the shells (she couldn't believe all the pics of shells!) & even a heartbreakingly empty parking lot or two, for old time's sake. She sells seven of them, though as far as she knows her old man snatched them up himself, as far as she knows he lied when he told her a guy came off the street & bought em—some were bought by a few of her friends, & as far as she knows maybe Ronny's *reimbursing them*, that's how she was thinking, a low self-esteem thing.

On Monday, she's back at Ronny's gig (McDonald's commercial) loading film, checking exposure, all that, effin' with the *f*-stop, there she is again, the girlfriend with the kid from another planet (though girlfriend was probably better than "wife") *whose real passion is photography*, yuck, & someone on the set, some prop person that's always on his crew that she never particularly liked says, *Oh, how was the show? I heard—I knew it was Saturday, but couldn't—I tried to go, but——did you sell any—oh that's so exciting! Ronny told me you did—————all of it so, so, so* . . . .

—————depressorama.

She befriends the director of a gallery that sells Mapplethorpes & various others, your Nan Goldins & Sally Manns, your Arbus & your Eggleston, premium photogs if not dead then living in the city, the South, the etc. But the gal likes Jacquie more as friend than artist. She says viz Jacquie's stuff that everything's there but the *point of view*.

The dreaded POV . . . .

So——

Jacquie decides on a project: she'll take a pic a day (fixed tripod), from the window of their loft that looks out over the city & a little park—*her point of view*—deciding to do that for an entire year. She thinks that maybe she'll—well no, she'll *definitely* have a book at the end of it. *Maybe call it "365 Days."* Having a book might—no, would *definitely*—make it easier to get a gallery show, she'd wind up with a slick portfolio *at the very least*.

Meanwhile, she sells a few pictures to a downtown zine for $25 each, a quarterly of short stories & poems, her image graces the cover, they spell her name wrong, Jacqui no e.

She's excited about her project. Her biggest challenge is to make sure Jerry Jr. doesn't run into the tripod, Ronny builds a bumper box around it, and every couple of days she gives Jerry Jr. the big stern lecture about being careful.

When she gets to Month Four of the POV project, Jacquie sees a book at the Strand by a photog who took pics from her *own* window every day, fixed tripod, called "The Four Seasons." She pokes around and finds three others, same deal, photographer's POV, fixed tripod, one from a 5th-floor walk-up in Hell's Kitchen, the other from a brownstone on the Upper West Side, & cannot *believe* she didn't know about the little sub-genre. Apparently Ronny didn't either, or if he did, didn't tell her. She felt like a fool.

(At least she didn't tell her gallery friend.)

(Her plan was to wait until she was closer to the year-end mark before she told her gallery friend.)

She's pregnant.

Ronny's mood turns dark when she starts to show.

She has a little girl in 1997, Jerilynn. Her mom dies that year, never having met her granddaughter. Her mom's name was Lynn.

Jacquie is 37.

Jerry Jr. is 13.

She stays with Ronny a full year before they officially end it. He's been fucking the gal who gets him the big commercials, that was going on way before Jerilynn was born. She even thinks about moving back to Ocala. She's *sentimentally ill.*

She moves to Brooklyn instead. It's affordable & there's a community of single moms who made the disgusted exodus from the island. The moms were bitter, & bitterly hilarious. Sexy too, and lifted her spirits.

She's at a gallery opening in the city. A handsome older man is staring at her. Short. Looks familiar. She looks away, that coquettish reflex to The Gaze. She's looking good if she must say so. That week she happened to have dyed her hair black, her hair is bangin' like Louise Brooks. He approaches, says she looks like his wife when she was young. Very charming, thick accent, elfin eyes. He asks if she's a photog, quickly interjecting "Oh, I hope not!" She says, "Well I am, but no one takes my work seriously. *Because I don't have a point of view.*" He spittle-laughs. He appreciates the humor & that makes her feel good. She forgot what that felt like; to feel good from the attentions of a man. He asks her to call him. She looks at the card after he leaves: Helmut Newton. Hah! She feels like an ass for not knowing, a *flattered* ass anyway. Her Brooklyn friends egg her on, they have a field day. That he's twice her age & married for a hundred years gets them in heat. They're ferocious & funny & she doesn't think she could live without them.

They begin a platonic relationship that lasts until his death. It seems to Jacquie that he never stops moving; he sends her obscene vintage postcards from France, Belgium, Monte Carlo, Morocco, Africa, the Canary Islands. For a man with a heart condition, rather astonishing. Whenever he's in NYC, he calls for drinks or an early dinner. Invariably, just after she gets home, one of his assistants phones to say "Helmut needs you for a photo shoot in the city." The jobs were always for three, four, sometimes five full days. She does anything asked of her: setting backdrops, changing cameras/lenses, even going for pastries. He loves that she's unpretentious, there was something about her he admired.

He's a bright spot in her life . . .

One day, she invites him for a serious coffee. A curious man, he immediately accepts. She's nervous. It's hard for her. She tells him that she's thinking about taking pics again. He winces, then sees the depth of her terror and desire.

She dares to tell him her problem:

I have no real point of view.

"Then you weren't kidding!" (A pause. His eyes rabidly twinkling.) "That was what you said the first time we met."

Her lip wriggles as she speaks of her travails. She bares all, even tells him about the professor. She says she has the feeling that this is *it* for her (she's 41 now)—either she makes her mark, or fades away.

I am old . . . .

"No," he says, "*I* am old!"

She begs him to be serious.

And here is what he said:

"I understand, dearest. *I understand.* You can't think I don't understand, can you? No. I know. I'm glad you had the guts to tell me what you did. It takes *guts,* I know. Not easy, not easy. It is *never* easy, it isn't *supposed* to. Now you've got this off your chest, but you're open—to advice, no? That is why you shared these things with me? Yes? Because there is something you can *do* about this——*existential* difficulty.

"This 'lack of a point of view'——"

"Do you know what you need, Jacquie dear? To be *banned.* You need to create such a *scandale* that *everyone* knows your name! To make something *truly disturbing,* to make your own *Sacre du Printemps,* your 'Rite of Spring.' To cause a commotion, understood? You need to make art for the FBI! Art that *forces* the police to *raid the gallery* that was brave enough to exhibit *the forbidden fruits* of Jacquie Crelle! My dearest *Jacqueline, listen* to what I am telling you. You need to be *threatened with prosecution and jail* . . . .

"You must know the work of Nan Goldin? Of course. I really am *very* fond of Nan, she has a *marvelous* gift. *Realism* is not my *thing*—there is enough of it in everyday life! I spend my days trying to *get away from it!* But Nan really is *very* good at what she does. Do you know the photo of the belly-dancing kids? Have you seen her picture of the little girl? The little girl in the picture is about 4, no? She *bends* to show her little *chat*—bare as only a 4-year-old vulva can be! All very *'playful,'* very *'innocent.'* Ha! Well, Nan is one of those people who know *just* what they are doing. *I* am like that as well, or I like to think so. Here is where Elton John enters the picture—so to speak. Now, you *must* know I *adore* Elton, he is absolutely *adorable*, June & I got *very close* to him, & my *God*, the *voice*, the *music*, he has the *whole package*. It's true he doesn't collect my work, but I forgive him! He doesn't want pictures of leather & tits & women holding whips on the wall. Well, maybe leather! *Understood.* I have no problems with it.

"Elton owns a few hundred of her pictures, I believe. Nan's. More or less. Some place in England wanted to show her work—not a *big* place, I think it may even have been *outside* of London. Being the patron of the arts that he is, Elton graciously loaned 150 images to wherever. To the venue. And of *course*, there was the usual complaint. Someone didn't like the little vulva! You see, the little vulva did its job, the little vulva works very well! The *gendarmes* say they received a complaint—& *in* came the storm troopers to *pry* the offending photograph off the wall! They took a few others with them too. A bare vulva leaves a bare wall! Now this photo of which I speak has quite a *spread*—Nan was very *thorough*. You can see the tiny pisser, even the darling shithole . . . well as you can imagine, an *uproar* ensued. You have the *fascists* on one side & the *libertines* on the other. It's always the same, no? The fascists shout: *Pornografi!* Isn't it what they always say?

I am telling you, it's true. *'The artist must be prosecuted to the full extent of the law!'* Oh, how they *rail,* Jacqueline. And the *libertines,* they say: *These are innocent portraits! To suppress them will have a*—they always are using this phrase—*chilling effect on terrestrial life as we know it!* Chilling effect! They love that phrase! It rolls trippingly off the libertine's tongue . . . oh, the two parties put on quite a show. And I don't need to tell you what happened, *Jacqueline,* do I. You can guess. There *was* no prosecution . . . the *sturm und drang* came & went, like a summer storm. But the price of those pictures! They went through the roof!

"I'm telling you, *cher,* England is always a wonderful place for ground zero. Because these *tempests* are closely watched by Americans—American media—like BBC costume dramas slowly making their way to the shores of American television . . . those English accents lend *credence*—they class it up, oh how the Brits can class up bare vulvas and shitholes! Ha! *Saatchi* is always a *wonderful* venue to have your ground zero. There was a *skirmish* in 2001—Nan, again! the woman is indefatigable!—the bobbies *insisted* the gallery remove the offending images *toute suite!* Saatchi refused; Goldin *triumphed.* And the prices? Up and up and up, up, up & away!

"Please listen, Jacquie dearest. Because I am being *utterly serious.* David Hamilton. *I bow my head to the Master.* But now I speak of *peri-pubescence,* which is a *littered field.* You'd have no chance there, no chance at all, & besides, there's no time, you would have to twiddle your twat waiting for Jerilynn to grow up. Where did you get this name, 'Jerilynn'? It's *horrid!* Hamilton—I've known him for years, he lives in St. Tropez—peri-pubescence has been good to him! What they call 'the sweet cusp of pubescence.' For me, it is *intensely* boring—I call it The Blah Lagoon. Hamilton once had a *stranglehold,* an absolute *monopoly* of the market. 11-year-old blondes with nipples a *bit* too large for their tiny chests—most of them viewed through linen curtains, nonetheless . . . what can one say? It's nice work if you can get it! Haha! Hamilton is absurd, but *attention must be paid.* His work is a *litigation perennial.* Every year, somewhere in the world there's a fuss, like clockwork, the man doesn't need to lift a finger (or a di-aphanous curtain!), doesn't even have to leave his *balcony*. David is the king of the 'landmark ruling'—you are *always* in need of the landmark ruling, darling! A landmark ruling in the UK declared his work indecent (which of course it is, but for *aesthetical* reasons!), it was so far-reaching that anyone who had his books *displayed* on their coffee-tables—that's a lot of coffee-tables!—if you had the Master's book in the privacy of your own home, you were at risk of arrest! The bobbies went on a *rampage*, clearing the bookstore shelves. David released one of those statements—oh, *that* you must do as well, the 'released statement'—what they call a *measured statement of protest* re-leased through one's *spokesperson*. We shall find you a spokesperson, my dear Jacqueline!

"Others soon got *wise*. Frankly, I don't know what *took* them so long. Jock Sturges . . . his pictures were *terrible*, terribly banal, in some ways far worse than David's. Because they *aspired*. To *Art!* He puts the kids on the *beach*—the beach! The mind staggers at the auda-cious paucity of imagination. Better they be posed reading a book through damned Victorian curtains than be *lollygaggling* on the beach . . . they're just nudies—you've seen nudist colony magazines? With the occasional hairy bush thrown in to give *absolution* to anyone who may have had a seizure of *guilt* when they found themselves lin-gering over the delicate line-drawn y of the hairless pubis at rest . . . or he throws in a Mom. You know, 'If *Mom's* in the shot, she must have approved!' That way, you get the good housekeeping seal. *Very* clever. Wouldn't you like the good housekeeping seal, cher? There's Larry Clark—a *real* pervert, not a fake one like myself! But let's not talk about Mr. Clark, frankly I'm not too interested in exploring the endless mystery of unwashed 13-year-old boys, particularly not when they're shooting up!

"Cher Jacqueline, you will some day have a book of your own. We must find a title for it. One must always pay attention to the *titles*, they're *very* important. *The Age of Innocence*—that's David, of course. El Maestro! *The Last Days of Summer* is Sturges. A wonderful title, I have to say. I'll help you with that . . . you see, the title must let the people know what you're up to, what it's all about. They went after Sturges—was it '91? In San Francisco, of all places! They went completely *berserk*, it was a *crusade*, they were carrying torches! And yet . . . and yet . . . can you guess what's coming, my dearest? 'The grand jury has refused to indict.' I am *telling* you, the grand jury *always* refuses to indict! It's a marvelous *game*, Jacquie, and you must start to play *toute suite!* Because it is a *very* lucrative one. Sturges made *millions* off the shenanigans. But the field is *too crowded*, cheri. Giants walked the earth before you; the ground is littered with scorched peri-pubescent & prepubescent cunts. You've got to go one better. Jerilynn—horrid name!—she's just turned 5, no? Little Jerilynn? Take courage! Take heart! The *pre*-prepubescent playing field is wide open! Why at the moment, I believe there is *no one on it at all!* Jerilynn's your ticket . . .

"*Jerilynn is your point of view! ça va?* Take courage, Jacqueline!

"And you *must* have a cold, hard look at Sally Mann. She is the Ideal—*the* class act. That's what you want to shoot for. Sally's the template, the Gold standard. She lives in Virginia. She was thrown by a horse & broke her back. A terrible thing. We spoke *every week* of her convalescence, for 2 years. I called from wherever I was in the world. Sally made her bones with those family shots—the Huck Finn nudies. *At Twelve: Portraits of Young Women.* Can't beat that for a title, can you? I'm telling you, titles are everything. That was something Sally knew very well . . . now, I don't believe they ever went after Sally in the *courts,* not as far as I *know,* but she was *banned in the media.* (Which is what we hope for *you.*) Banned by Artforum—*Artforum!* Can you imagine? A superstar! She worked in wetplate collodion. Used a very old camera, an *antique*, an 8 × 10 bellows. Which I think is very shrewd. You see, when you *embark* on this sort of thing, it is my *strong feeling* that it is a *very* good idea to approach the work via a *defunct process* or *difficult-to-use camera.* Don't go Goldin. And the most *important* part of Sally's example—listen closely, Jacqueline!—was that she shot her children, then *moved on.* She didn't make a fucking *career* of it. Take a lesson from that, Jacquie! She's doing *wonderful* work at this time, she's in her prime, hasn't a *thing* to do with naked kiddies . . . & *that's* where you want to land, Jacquie dear. Sally Mann showed there can be light at the end of the vulva!

"In summary:

"A gallery shows your pics. Someone *complains*—& if they don't, pick up the phone & complain *yourself,* just don't tell em it's you! The gallery gets raided—by *gendarmes* or even better, the FBI. (Scotland Yard's a coup.) Then: the tiresome wave of fascists & libertines. A celebrity speaks out in your favor, crying 'It's just a mom keeping an innocent diary of her babies!'—they're always good for a sound byte. Because it's important in this *phase* that you stay out of the fray. An articulate celebrity gets you lots of mileage, that's money in the bank. They're First Amendment *whores* . . . but it doesn't really matter, because that storied 'fierce debate' will follow, & if you're lucky—a media firestorm! *Jacquie, there's one thing that is guaranteed—people will know your name.* Your supporters will invoke Caravaggio and Degas; there'll be sidebar editorials in the *Times* on Nabokov & Charles Dodgson; 'chilling effects' and 'landmark rulings'; the sound & fury of grand juries, signifying nothing . . . *sales, sales, sales!*"

> *Cherry ripe, cherry ripe,*
> *Ripe I cry,*
> *Full and fair ones,*
> *Come and Buy!*

Stars Without Makeup

Ooo-woo ▪ ▪ ▪

. . . his stomach had that perfect, empty, racy feeling, & the ♥*flit,* skipping beats. *Ooooo.* The reason being, the reason why, because what he did was put the crystal in a sheet of toilet paper, a little mound, & then he swallowed it. Swallowed the little biscuit. What he was doing *now* was, he got a tweet from a trusted twat that Renée Zellweger was at Peet's—Montana & 14th—sitting in a chair at a farthest-away outdoor table, reading. Hunched over, deglammed, in a North Face vest. No makeup. *Incognito.* (Same Peet's frequented by the over-the-hills: Molly Ringwald, Marcia Cross, Kate Capshaw.) Though Renée's time was over (her *cognito* place in the sun), she hadn't *quite* entered the Where Are They Now? newstand magazine cycle; but was *definitely* in the Fast Track To Washed-Out Hagdom internet rinse n spin. Not so wonderful a place to be, because any missteps came across as global FAILS.

730AM . . . got the tweet, swallowed the speed, & waited. Then, *BLASTED* out of bed & into his 2002 grody-interior'd Range Rover, rocketing to Peet's (she wasn't there, might be in the head), then over to Whole Foods—Montana & 15th—to wait. Radio on: hip hop. Frank Ocean. Hip hop could actually make good white person morning music, if you played it lowish.

The women darted in & out of Whole Foods like exotic luminous fish in an aquarium castle: to and from the Yogaworks above the Starbucks across the street, to & from Peet's, Caffe Luxxe, & Sweet Lady Jane's . . . they didn't have to wish they were California girls. They were insanely preserved & insanely rich, and if no longer in the zip code of beautiful, they were residents of the posh, gated community of Old Town—most were in their 50s. Lotta divorcées. No need to cry for em either, cause on *Montana adjacent* that usually meant a $25 mill+ settlement.

Sometimes if things were slow & Jerzy wanted to hang at the beach, he'd hit this very spot. Last week he got Phoebe Cates pushing a shopping cart & turned it around to one of the *STARS— They're Just Like US!* dillios. In these parts, you got people like Madeleine Stowe, Jamie Lee Curtis . . . or Renée. An older crowd, so he usually avoided the area. Come to think of it, lots of strollerpushing pussy today tho maybe they're au pairs . . . he swung back to Peet's but still no sign of————*here she comes*. She looks so *un-Renée*, he almost missed her. Whips around & parks residential, so he can telephoto. *Got* her . . . . she looks dumpy, shitty, preoccupied. Not a complete disaster—what the business calls a "gasper." There were "hooters" and there were "gaspers." Kirstie Alley at 600 lbs was a gasper. Clint Eastwood's disgusto-looking vericose veins on the golf course in Carmel was a gasper. A *hooter* would make you *hoot* aloud, like, say, when Jerzy took a perfectly photogenic image of Katie Holmes and advanced it forward or backward frame by frame til she looked zombily scientologized and/or disheveled, weird-eyed, blinky-weepy, psycho or whatever. By the same means, he made Gwyneth look homely & bag lady-bitter, cellu-lumpy, agespotted. Jerzy was *good*; he sold a pic of Michelle Obama looking wild-eyed indigent that really made the supermarket shoppers hoot.

But the Renée he got was neither. More of what they call a *pageturner*—filler *between* the Hooters and the Gaspers, you stare at it, you take it in, you register the shittiness and dumpiness of it, you get that quick, pleasant little hit that reminds you, stars can be dumpy & shitty-looking, *just like you & me*. Stars can be dumpy, shitty-looking, plastic surgery-deformed, sad, binge-eating cunts, but they're just like you and me, only with more money.

Like a million times more.

Jerzy had his own Smarmy Army of twittering sickos—he called them shitters, twitfarts, twittiefucks, what have you—on the payroll, some of them bonafide bottomfeeders but most just 14 & 15 year-old kids who got a (small, *very* small) % whenever Jerzy sold a pic they had tipped him on. They were easy to cheat. They were middle-schoolers (one was his weed connect), fucking *sk8trs* who were in it for the sport—just another computer game. Stalking the wild celeb gave em that GPS spy-high . . .

More tweets now as he rolled down Sunset toward Beverly Hills. Paula Abdul was at Fred Joaillier on Rodeo *(go, Paula!)* . . . Trent Reznor @ CB2, Santa Monica Mall *(why would anyone give a shit)* . . . Piers Morgan *(hate that dipshit)* b-fasting at the Polo Lounge w/Carl Bernstein *(you needed to be 70+ to know who Bernstein was)* . . . slow morning. *Fuck it . . .*

He parked on Burton Way, across from the *L'Ermitage*. Nice green grass, in the island between lanes . . . Burton always made him feel peaceful. He snorts some coke, leaves the truck, & strolls to the "park" (10 yards away). Sits down cross-legged in the sun. *My place in the sun.* Feels nice. All buddha-buddha.

The stars will never be . . . . just like ME.

Harry Middleton "hired" him but that didn't really mean a thing. H around the M would buy pics from *anyone*, you could be a serial childkiller or a Muslim shoebomber, Harry didn't give a *honeyshot!* badger shit, as long as you delivered, Harry would pay the long green. The man had "hired" Jerzy because he liked the idea of *staff*, he liked playing the big pasha, the poobah, the grand vizier commanding his Smarmy of papsmearazzi, all that horseshit appealed to the freak's baroque sense of e-trepreneurialism. What being "hired" *really* meant was that Jerzy could hang at Harry's apt (an awesome thing) & use it as a pitstop, a place to smoke a joint between Olsen twins, do his meth in the john while H was in the middle of *spieling* pussymania. But man could not live by *honeyshot!* alone.

All in all, being a Hollywood paparazzo suited him. Jerzy liked the perpetual motion. Before Mom was MoMA, she lugged him along on photo expeditions (so she said; he was too young to remember) on the Floridian coast; maybe that had something to do with it. *O right, of course! That explains why I'm a paparazzo & a speed freak. It's all because MoMA hauled my diapered ass along on her lame, peripatetic excursions!* Then she ditched him for New York. Jerzy was left in Ocala with his grandma & her Banquet® TV trays and *muy* depresso ways. And just so Jerzy wouldn't *forget* her, MoMA left a shoebox of warpy, sun-drenched Polaroids, some with her & *the Professor*—his father—in that rathole-looking place she always called "the bungalow," a few with the three of them—Jerzy, MoMA & Dad—*(dad, her married lover)*—one had Jerzy in the curly-haired arms of *the professor*—the name he *still* called his father in his head (that's what MoMA called him) . . . MoMA & the Professor all squinty-eyed and happy, staring down the camera in the white-out FL sun. He wondered who took the pics. Maybe a neighbor . . . when he entered toddlerdom, the Professor dropped dead; more Polaroids now, with Jerzy, MoMA and the grandparents staring down the camera, MoMA squinting no longer smiling into the once-paradisal unbearable brightness of Sunkist Florida sun. Then Gramps collapsed & died, and MoMA left. There were no pics from that time.

He fought a lot in school, they called him a bastard, like the cliché goes, the kids and teachers always find that shit out, & everybody finds a way to torture you about it. Jerzy fought hard, but all he learned was, when you fought you lost. Never a correlation between fighting & winning/only fighting & defeat & humiliation. That's what he learned. At least they didn't call him bastard in Néw York, everybody was probably a bastard, even though he became a rechristened bastard because MoMA forgot to marry Ronny the DP— Ronny Vomes. "Vomes"—what an assholish moniker . . . MoMA used Crelle-Vomes as her "professional name," but never married either one of them. What a *load*. So now he was a bastard two times over, and his baby sister was a bitch.

After MoMA and the DP broke up, they moved to Brooklyn. Ronny was still in their lives, being Jerilynn's real father & Jerzy's fake one. Sometimes Jerzy worked on the camera crew like his mother once did, that's how he got an aptitude, even fantasized about getting into the union. Jerzy went to Baja on a shoot & Ronny fired him for not showing up on the 1st day of principal photography. Those were (the beginning of) the Heroin Years, now he was in the (middle of the?) Tweak Years (still mix 'n matched with H), Jerzy'd always been way into both but now he was super-grateful into the joyful, joyous ♥*SLAM* Days & GBH/Xanax Nights.

He got loaded in Costa Rica, Belize, BC, Krakow, Colorado, Crete. Detoxed in UK, Rome, Colorado, Crete, Krakow, BC, the Cape. Returned to New York at 28, took all those years just to find his true calling, that of celebrity craphouse *creep*. A creeperazzo makes his own sked. Creeperazzi are *independent contractors*. But the very best part of being a Creeperazzo creeper is you have the where-withal to do R_x *all day long*.

The Master Plan was to fuck with/edit down the *Best of the Best* of Jerzy's vanilla creeperazzi & (still to cum) *papsmearshots!* then assemble them into a gallery show. Oh, that would righteously piss MoMA off! She might never recover from the blow! He'd call the exhibition *Jerzy Shores*—Harry would love that he used his nickname, he'd give him credit for his cleverness in the catalogue. Jerzy would show his work in LA as *Jer-Z* or *Squeegee* or *Jeezy*, or maybe he'd use all three just to confuse people. He was going to shoot for the *top*—he wanted to be repped by the Gagosian. He wanted to be the 1st (& last) one on the block to legitimize/commodify/artworld-monetize the *moneyshots*. Jerzy'd done a bit of late-night tweakstudying about the Gagosian on the web, they had a client that took pics of Lindsay, Sasha Grey, & whomever—made short shitty videos of them too—real dumbass shit—Jerzy thought *no way* could the guy compete with him. Another Gagosian guy named Richard Prince did paintings of nurses & stenciled jokes that went for millions—& Jerzy was convinced that the *reason* it went for millions was because the guy was *Number Uno*, he must have been the *1st* to be totally serious about making a nurse-and-stenciled-joke painting—or if somebody else *had*, then this guy's paintings of nurses & stenciled jokes were the 1st *breakthrough* nurse-and-tell-an-actual-joke paintings, that's all you needed, it was all about *breakthrough*, maybe the other guys who did that kind of painting—paintings of nurses and whole jokes—maybe the other guys blew it because they *used the wrong jokes,* knock-knock jokes or whatever with *doctors* instead of *nurses* . . . but Jerzy thought: more power to him, more power to this guy Richard Prince *and* to Larry Gagosian—Larry Gagosian was King—all he (Jerzy) had to do was have that *breakthrough*, be the *1st*, or the *1st breakthrough* anyway, like Jean-Michel Basketcase was with graffiti, or Arbus & her freak-show folk———*no one* (so far) (to his knowledge) had thought to hang their altered/fucked with/edited papsmeary vulturazzo creep-shots in a *major gallery of art* (tho it must be said that Jerzy didn't really do a thorough internet search of it because he didn't want to come across someone who *had* already done or was just *about* to do the very same thing that was his Gagosian Dream) but it was a *fairly safe bet* that no one had. Certainly none of Jerzy's esteemed *colleagues* could in their pathetic minds even come *close* to imagining such a thing. The collective Smarmy Army brain was unfathomably clueless & ill-developed in the realm of this degree of sophistication. How could any of them even know about or understand the genius and the cultural force Larry Gagosian, who was King?

He'd spent a lot of time in galleries, afterall MoMA made her splashy little sensations when he was just turning 18, right around the time she was ab-/using his baby ½sis who he loved, Jerilynn, whom he always had protected from harm but had failed to against the MoMA machinations. These days mother and son were estranged, but big brother and little sister IM'd, little sis told big bro MoMA was getting desperate, which gave him a kind of wicked pleasure, and while big bro did not tell little sis his Master Plan, little sis *did* know that big bro was a creeperazzo but big bro *distinctly* told little sis *not* to tell MoMA that's what he did for a living, he didn't want that bitch anywhere *near* knowing how he was paying the rent (MoMA did know—just how, he forgot—that her son wasn't on the East Coast, & was living somewhere in LA), he wanted her to know as little about him as *pah-see-blay*. What he *prayed* for was for MoMA to wake up one LA chelsea morning to see that her son's *creepshots!* had been declared A R T—she could come to Gagosian's with everybody else & *kiss the ring, the ring of my hem'rrhoided shithole.*

.   .   .

Three tweaking tweeters said Michael Douglas was at Sur. *With who?* he twittered back from his twat. *Did not rec* was the teetering reply. Did not recognize. Meaning it was probably an agent, manager, lawyer, whoever, though J's twitshit troops *should* be able to recog even *them.*

Re selling Douglas pics to the e-/print tabloids, the demand had leveled off. They still paid okay, nothing like what they did in the six months after the Big C, but the $$$ was still okay, tho the prices had begun to drop the further the actor got in recovery. Still, they paid. The tabloids wanted a stockpile of the actor *lookin good* because the more shots they had of him *lookin good*, the bigger would be the fall (for their readers). They knew the fall would come—one way or another. They knew their readers (& non-readers too) were just *waiting* for a recurrence. How long had it been? A few years already? The actor was already overdue, it was *time*, he'd been cancerfree long enough, & their readership—*public drama demanded* a recurrence, only one that wouldn't be so easy to be licked, Patrick Swayze-style, & one where he wouldn't be able to keep his hair . . . public drama demanded a recurrence that maybe ended in a Roger Ebert-style mutilation. *Jesus* . . . if Douglas lost the whole lower jaw, whoever got that

1st photo of Catherine OBE holding a stained scarf over the missing bottom of his face—Jesus, that was probably worth $5 mill.

. . . . Jerzy got another tweet from one of his twats saying Mary Murphy was there, at a different table. Jerzy never saw *So You Think You Can Dance* but knew that her thyroid cancer had supposedly been successfully ZAPPED . . . . Jerzy still held to his personal axiom that whenever a celeb declared themselves cancer-free, the devil woke from his nap————

Sur, on Robertson . . .

Big Sur, *yessur.*

Creeperazzi crowding & papsmearing the sidewalk.

"Paparazzi"—dumb word from another era, *La Dolce Vita* word, era of Cinemascopic glamour and arclights strafing Hollywood premiere nights, era of MGM oldschool grandeur/oldschool restraint (era before the internet), era before they sawed off Zsa Zsa's feet, era before Liz became a rouged-up, roughed-up canteloupehead, era before a stoned nurse tamped his cock into Mickey Rooney's crack-lipped hundred-year-old mouth for webcam kicks. Reagan was still chopping wood for chrissake . . . but time & TMZ wait for no man . . . & they're *very* young, these jeepers-creepersazzi Jerzy uses— they're, like, lone wolves with ADD, tense & smelly & fuckin crazy, with their SUPREME t-shirts, $500 hightops & threadbare vintage American Apparel————now, one of em who's standing in front of Sur *sees* something—someone deliberately stepping out of a car *down the street,* seemingly to avoid the————*RachelBilson Rachel-Weisz RachelMcAdams? LisaEdelstein LisaRinna LisaD'Amato? Ryan-Gosling RyanReynolds RyanSheckler? AshleeSimpson (AshleeWentz) AshleyGreene AshleyTisdale Ashley*————*?*—& one of the lone wolf creepers *tears* across the street, sweaty relay runner *solitaire,* infernal Olympiad. . . .

Jerzy stands outside the restaurant . . . in the world of creepers but not of it. Oxycodone-dreaming of being interviewed in *Interview* by Richard Prince: RICHARD PRINCE Talks To Art World's Latest Bad Boy Genius, Papsmearanarchist SQUEEGEE/

JERZY SHORES. But until then, to make the rent, he needs something tweet & potatoes, needs to start building up his photo archive for reasons of Gagosianocity. And if along the way he so happens to score some of that happy accident poon for Harry Middleton's Private Stock Vineyard, well that would just be icing on Elle's or whomever's cupcakes, a big payday no doubt, Harry said he'd pay a premium, Jesus, might be high as fifteen-thou for a Hailee or a Chloë or a Kendall, but it's very hit and miss, that kind of work. Jerzy knew enough to know you could never chase that kind of *honeyshot!*—you had to let them *happen*.

He didn't talk about it with Harry, or really much with anyone, but he considered his specialization, that *true calling*, to be the *sick celeb* (that's why Mr. Douglas *à table* @ Sur got his attention). He loved the moment that came weeks—or, if he was fortunate enough, days, or even hours—before death, when, with sniper's telephoto viewfinder, he caught their eye. *The moment they looked back.* When Harry spoke of his *own* epiphany—that private moment shared with Emma Watson—tho the *content* was dissimilar, that was when Jerzy knew him to be a kindred spirit. Maybe the two Moments weren't so different; maybe they were really just the same. In the wee, wee hours, when he was very stoned, Jerzy would google *recent celebrity deaths* ["About 90,100,000 results (0.06 seconds)"], clicking from site to site, scanning the ebituaries of the month & those from years gone by. He read with nostalgia, for some he'd captured & been paid a bounty for; most were lost for all Eternity, residing in *honeyshot!* Heaven. He usually checked www.deathlist.net/; last night, Kirk Douglas was #5 on the Top 50 of those most likely to expire.

The list comprises celebrities thought most likely to pass away during 2012. Candidates must be famous in their own right such that their death is expected to be reported by the media, however candidates cannot be famous purely for the fact they are likely to expire shortly. DeathList 2011 was a big disappointment, chalking up its lowest score for over a decade, but, with the performance in the latter half of the year, surely there are signs that the dry season is behind us.

That strange & special *moment* . . .

The beauty of his Moment with Farrah still haunted him.

For weeks, the vulturazzi camped outside her pre-cadaverous home. She was returning to St John's in the morning, & (somehow) slipped out without being noticed. The night before checking into the hospital she would spend at her hairdresser's, an old & dear friend. But Jerzy got a tip. (It wound up costing him $10,000, but was worth it.) He stayed up all night in the SUV, smoking crack & waiting. At 9AM, beyond the modest hedge of the modest house, there was a commotion at the front door: Farrah & 3 others. He readied himself to leave his truck. The others were already climbing into the station wagon that was in the drive . . . suddenly, without warning, *Farrah walked into the street.* What was she doing? Jerzy was thrown off-guard. One of the group paused beside the car & called out to Farrah; from the tone of it, he wasn't very happy. It wasn't Ryan O'Neal . . . *but what was she doing?* She looked—well—*lovely*—or—well—there were *aspects* of loveliness, easily reminding of the youth & great beauty that once was. She wore jogging pants—the hair of course was perfectly done up by her friend—and was leaning down at the curb . . . to pick up a blue-wrapped *New York Times* from the gutter.

She looked all around her, as if seeing the world for the first time & knowing it would be the last, that she wouldn't be returning from her morning trip to St John's. Jerzy had tried a thousand times to re-member those seconds during & after he sprung from the car with his camera. From the seconds he'd been watching her pick up the paper to the *instant* he found himself in front of her, only 5 or 6 feet be-tween them. But he couldn't—it was like a black-out. It was as if he had been teleported before her just so that he could look in her eyes. She startled for a moment, her instincts not knowing if he was an as-sailant—friend or foe—but when she saw his camera, she unmistak-ably Farrah-smiled, there was relief, not foe but friend, he was part of her tribe. He began to shoot her, & she was gracious enough to *give* him the shot—like a kiss—he recalled that after 30 seconds or so she said, "Is that enough? Do you have enough?" Then she said, "I'm tired," but he kept shooting. And that was when it happened: every showbiz cell in her body bade her smile, graciously and valiantly, even during a rape such as this, & at the very end the swimsuitfamous smile collapsed into the tender rictus belonging to one already launched into oncoming oblivion. She fought it from happening, but sheer weakness of flesh, not of mind or of spirit or of heart, betrayed—that axiom of teeth & lips, timeless equation of Americana/girl-next-door majesty which had rallied (not just by decades-old celebrity reflex, but by impulse of simple humanity, & pretty girl/neighborhood sweetness) to hold in place (for him, for Jerzy) the curbside illusion of an icon still vibrant (which Jerzy in these seconds had *believed*, it had worked on him until now, until this very Moment) crashed into the grimace in a rotten death's head.

The man came from nowhere, pushing Jerzy to the ground, foaming & messy & hitting & lurching for the camera, but Jerzy hung on for life (the strap around his neck) plus who knew, maybe he could get a ¼ of a mill for the hairdresserhouse curb pics (well, not quite that, & he spent it all on drugs), Farrah was shouting at her friend to stop, can you believe it? Shouting at her friend to let Jerzy be, & by then the others were erupting from the car shouting "Shame on you!"/"You are an *asshole!*"—Jerzy was only worried about his camera being seized, the man had homicidal fury in his eyes, but must have been worried if he kept it up his friend Farrah might be so stressed out she would die right there in the street . . . . *he understood him when Harry said he would carry that Moment with him forever—the Emma communion Moment—the looking at her nakedness—how they could never take that Moment away from him.*

He was a master of the dead man walking shot: a recklessly unguarded Chris Reeves or Patrick Swayze, using walkers to drag themselves to the terraces of their hosp rooms. They would turn unbidden & look into the ether—Jerzy would be in a tree with his snip-

erscope—they couldn't see him. They had *sensed* something out there. You could see it in their features, gaunt hopeless animal look, wounded gazelles who knew they would soon be culled from the herd by jackals. His only regret was not getting Steve Jobs, in any way, shape or form, not even close. Not getting to stare into those Da Vinci eyes. Jobs had been *his* grail, *his* Hermione: a good pic of the dying animal would have been historic. Apple might even have bought it directly, just so it wouldn't be out there. Jesus, he hadn't thought of that until now, they'd probably pay tens of mill————
————he was coming on to another speed biscuit, & it was as if it had been laced with regret. He said to himself, *Jobs would have been the show-stopper, the centerpiece of my Gagosian. Jobs'd have been the draw. If I'da got Jobs, my name'd have been made. I'da done a mash-up/mixtape of the sorrowsfull Job poisoned app Gaze & my coven of barely legal papsnatch, called the show The Naked & the Dead . . . . . .*

. . . . . . standing on the sidewalk in front of Sur with the rest of the loserazzi, contemplating a retreat to his car to snort some lines, when he saw her. She was petite & wore her hair in one of those piled up ponytails. She was an odd one; if you blinked, you could think maybe she *wasn't* a little girl, maybe really a tiny freak like Kristin Chenoweth, ultra-petite, unwizened, middle-age chick. But a second blink brought you back to the objective truth—she was probably 11 or 12.

Something about her jammed the frequencies, & could throw a person off.

"Is anyone from *Glee* inside?"

"I don't know."

"I read that Heather Morris & Ashley Madekwe like this restaurant."

"Ashley *who*?"

"Madekwe."

He thought she said *"my dickweed."*

"Well, that could be."

"I'm probably going to be on the show next year."

"Oh yeah? On the *Project*?"

"No, the *real* show."

"What's your name?"

"Telma. What's *yours*?"

"Jerzy."

"Is that Russian or Polish?"

"Yeah."

"Yeah what?"

"Russian & Polish. It's both."

"Did you see *Never Say Never*?"

"The Bieber movie? Yeah."

"I was the girl—*one* of the girls—Justin brought onstage to sing 'One Less Lonely Girl.' But they had to cut it. They told my mom there was a scratch in the negative."

"Bummer when that happens."

"Telma!"

The voice came from across the street. Jerzy looked up. "Telma, come on!"

He attached a middle-aged face to it.

"What's your last name?" she asked.

"Kosinski."

"Are you on FaceBook?"

"Nope."

"How can you not be on Facebook? Do you tweet?"

"Yup."

"What are you?"

"Telma!!!!"—the woman from across the street.

"@jerzythelenzer12."

"@Telma.i.m_iWillSurvive."

She handed him a card with the info, then strode to the crosswalk, appeasing her mother.

"I'll tweet u!"

"Right on," he said, under his breath.

Tweet me. Tumblr me. I'll tumble for yuh. Twick or tweet. Tweet or twat. I'm tweaking, I'm twikileaking. I'm twiki-licky take a leak-ing . . .

Seconds later, his confederates went apeshit—Michael Douglas was leaving Sur.

He looked great. His hair was a perfect, tousled celebrity in *itself,* as recognizable as the Biebercut, a snowy, stylish pompadour that shouted, "Cancer-free!" *One day the man will die,* thought Jerzy, *but his hair will live on.*

Lunchtime.

Time to go home & smokeswallow some *biscuits.*

[Tom-Tom & Jerzy]

Sit.com

"Why

can't you get *newly buff.*"

Tom-Tom, Jerzy's roommate, was on the couch smoking crack & watching a new show about realtors competing to see who could off-load houses with *colorful histories* first: like the one with the pool William Shatner's wife drowned in, or the place Phil Hartman got shot or the condo Eric Douglas had in escrow when he OD'd, supposedly now haunted because someone forgot to give his ghost the memo about escrow being cancelled.

"Jerzy, I'm asking you a *very simple question.* Why, in *God's* name, do you *refuse* to be *newly buff*?"

"What the fuck are you talking about?"

Tom-Tom was 30. (Created in '82.)

She was/is still pretty.

She scratched (at) herself.

"You know what you need to be doing? You need to be doing *upper body work*, dude. I clipped some pictures, from *People.* They're in your room. Rick Rubin—Rick Rubin is *newly buff.* Remember how fat Rick Rubin was?"

"Who's Rick Rubin?"

"O come on, dude. Rick Rubin the *rap* producer. *You* know who he is———"

"Yeah def jam."

"Well there you go. Remember how *fat* he used to be? Well Rick Rubin used to be *fat*, but now he's *newly buff*. OK? You're following me, right? Drew Carey? Marc Jacobs? and OMG Perez Hilton—*all newly buff*. Fuckin *sculpted*. Well actually I guess Marc Jacobs has been buff for a while, he's *still* buff but I guess just not so newly. Shit, you know how fags love to look good? Well when a superrich fag—and Marc Jacobs is *superfuckinrich*—when a superrich fag sheds the poundage & gets all *newly buff* it's like—dude, it probably feels so good it's like they're doin *speedballs* 24/7. All sexed up & on-the-prowl beautiful & newly buff. Shit, *I'd* like me to be a superrich fag *anyday*."

He slow-bopped to the kitchen for a bite. He wasn't hungry *at all* but that *forward movement toward the kitchen* reflex, whatever kitchen in wherever he was living/crashing, that itinerant reflex kicked in & off he went. (Not thrilling to the newly buff rap either.) The boys on the sitcoms he used to watch always did that, home from school & gravitationally pulled to the kitchen for some laughtrack-accompanied dialogue. Reaching his destination, he picked at some new Wheat Thins already going stale having been shoved back into their box without being properly sealed. He had 3 baked potato chips & washed it down with a coke, he'd bought two dozen of those expensive commemorative cokes in brushed aluminum bottles, they were lined up in a rack in the fridge like beautiful missiles, & Tom-Tom wafted in and sat on a bar stool at the counter & they dialogued, just like sitcom/normal people would. She could gauge how high he was and even *what* he was high on by studying the minutiae of his behavior under the fluorescent lights; Tom-Tom's kitchen was like one of those vacuum rooms that astronauts hang in when they're fresh in from space & the Captain comes to debrief them or whatever while they change out of their spacesuits.

Ground control to Major Tom-Tom . . .

Tom-Tom used to be his dealer in NYC. They once were roman-
tically involved, and even tho they weren't anymore, they still fucked
on & off because they were so *jacked* all the time, but the fucking
wasn't epic, more like creative masturbation. Tom-Tom's deal was
that she got fired off Season 3 of *American Idol* for misrepresenting her
life situation, what they call pity-party plying. (At the time, Jerzy was
so completely amazed, she never told him/anyone she was auditioning) (He fucking *hated* that show but still forced himself to watch *for
professional reasons* so as to familiarize himself with the contestants
because the tabloids tended to pay premium for pics of these jerkoffs
especially in the last weeks before a winner was picked) Tom-Tom
always used to sing to her clients when they copped; her voice had a
cool tumblr *timbre* but Jerzy never knew that she actually had *ambition*. All the rappers used to deal dope & they became huge, right, so
why not Tom-Tom? She auditioned in Arkansas because she thought
outside of NYC she'd have a better chance. (As shit turned out *Simon*
was the one who really loved her.) So she a-capella'd Stefani *Don't
Speak* & you're-going-to-Hollywooded. When she got there, she had
a frienemy roommate, & the frienemesis' dad came out from Akron
to be supportive & wound up getting killed by a drunk on Delong-
pre & the frienemy daughter refused not to continue, & totally slayed
with nilsson/*can't live (if living is without you)*. To make matters worse,
there was a kid, black kid from DC, fat gospel perennial type had a
fuckin *bullet* lodged in his head from random 4th of July shot, the
docs said it was too dangerous to remove. A lot of sob stories that
year, more than usual. Tom-Tom started getting spooked because she
didn't have a *story*, well she *did*, but not a hum-dinger, the irony being that everyone in her fucked up family had somehow managed to
stay *alive*, and she just didn't want to go the route of, you know, "I'm
a dope dealer, I've been raped 3 times, I like to dyke, I've had 7 miscarriages, but I have *such hope*" & all that. So Tom-Tom got in touch
with an ex-girlfriend who lived in Long Beach, girl she used to
swing/scam businessmen with, they'd double-team them at bars, go
back to their rooms & blow em not fuck em, dose em with GBH and

take their money. Tom-Tom got back in touch with the swinger because she knew the swinger had a brother who was a 3-quarter quad. They hatch their little plan & get their stories straight. And Tom-Tom tells the producers that she has to go home, its urgent, her *fiancé's* having *health issues*, they want to know why she didn't tell them she had a fiancé with health issues & she works it, deliberately holds back the details, strategically thinking it's better if they have to *pry* it out of her, finally she has her pre-planned breakdown in front of them, "I didn't want anyone to think I was playing the sympathy card!" The idea was wack to begin with but it's starting to go off the rails. The producers tell her to stay put (like she knew they would), they will *absolutely* fly the fiancé out—smelling the sellable blood of tribal TV tragedy. Tom-Tom said OK & they sent a car to take her to the airport. With cameras, they were going to film the whole thing, the shit was spiraling out of control! Tom-Tom panicked. She called the producers and said that her fiancé's parents were *frantic*, they had just called to tell her their son went completely against doctors orders and was on his way to Hollywood *as we speak* with his sister in tow. Oh! The producers said just give us the airline info and we'll take care of it, we'll pick em up (w/camera crew), but Tom-Tom said no, they're not flying, they're driving in like this *especially outfitted for-quads van* & she didn't know where they were at this point in time! The cockamamie backstory being (hatched with the swinger), the ¾-quad fiancé was rushing home on Valentine's Day, a dozen roses on the seat beside him, when he swerved to avoid a squirrel & went straight into a telephone pole . . . of course the truth & the *problem* with this storyhatch being, the disabled bro of her ex-criminal she-lover turns out only to be a *semi*-quad, not from an *accident*, but from botched anaesthesia during a *lap band* procedure, *plus* he's got advancing MS. Which *could've* or *should've* worked in Tom-Tom's favor if she'd given the whole thing more careful thought i.e. been more on her hustling game, not amping up her usage when she started to panic. Someone on the *Idol* staff thought the half-quads thigh/calves looked too atrophied and spastick for someone who was supposedly a *recent* quad & when they found out about the MS they dug a little deeper & interrogated Tom-Tom's ex-, who didn't have the skills/chops to act her part very well either, the house of cards began to crumble then *BOOM* she's off the show. Looking back in solitude & therapeutic meditation she came to the conclusion she had classically self-sabotaged, that she was afraid of success, Dr. Phil did a whole show on it which she almost got on but was dropped from the last minute.

–That's what I want to do.

Back in the dining room now, watching TV, her attention fully on *Million Dollar Listing* while Jerzy's on the bong.

–What. Be a realtor?

–*Housedresser.* Home *stylist.* That's who the realtors call when they're trying to sell an empty house and they need to make it look *lived* in.

–You mean like housesitters?

–No! Those are *different. Anyone* can sit in a fucking house. That's a different deal. *Housedressers* are the ones who like get the *props.* They're like set decorators. Production designers. It's like a play! What the realtors do if they can't sell the house because maybe the furniture's shitty or it's got funky fungshwee—*some* of these realtors try and sell a house without even filling the *pool,* oh! big mistake!—the homestylist goes in and makes sure the pool is filled & even makes sure there's like expensive *shit* floating in it—floating chaise lounges from Restoration, or whatever. And they bring in *shitloads* of flowers, they even put framed pictures of fake families on the *fireplace,* in the *bedrooms,* all around the house, Jerzy *I am serious.* They do *whatever it takes* to make the house *desirable.* I'd come in and *work it,* like, they say you be in & out in a *day.* The people on this show? The people on this show? The people on this show just paid $35,000 to get their house dressed & BAMBAMBAM *the house sold the next day!* Jerzy, I want to start a company! I want a housedresser website! You feel me? Can you feel me?

–Yeah, I'll fuckin feel you. Whip em out for me.

Tom-Tom was shooting Demerol too. She was a nurse at the VA & not only stole it directly but took surplus from C patients when they died.

–So I *still* want you to tell me why you can't be *newly buff.* Or why you can't *wave off Oscar talk.* And if you can't wave off Oscar talk and you can't be newly buff, then tell me why you can't be *linked*—to a, you know, reality star bimbo. Dude, you got to lower the bar. Get your ass linked to *Kelly Osborne.* Fuckin scavenger *bitch* can only do *four* things: gain weight, lose weight, eat dope, & go to fuckin celebrity funerals. If you're famous, look out if Kelly wants you as a friend! Cause she'll crawl up your ass to die but you'll die first! Have you seen pics of her at the burials? Front and center, like front row fashion week in fuckin Paris 'cept the tears drop down from that chubby face—can you imagine what that face *smells* like?!—the tears drop down & puddle in that vulture vadge . . . but no shit, I would *love* to have my ass *linked.* Please, Lord, link me! And if the good Lord don't see my ass fit to link, than maybe Lord Jesus can at least let me be Emily Deschanel, just for like a hot minute, so I can talk about my rockin new body, & my sister's rockin success, & my rockin new life as a mom!

–You know what you oughta get your head out of the ass of those fuckin magazines.

–Zooey Deschanel needs to be fuckin *raped* by *fags.* See how adickable she is with her ass blown out from multiple unadorkable dicks. [*her attention went back to the show*] Did you know the guy who used to be the *host* got busted for stealing *paintings* & shit from dead people's houses?!?!?!

–What show.

–This *show.* 'Million Dollar Listing'! I *love* him!!! They said this house {eyes glued to the set} was rented by *Natalie Portman* while she was *pregnant,* but I'm not sure I believe that. Tho you know what? If you tell someone who's *interested,* you know, a potential *buyer,* you say, "Natalie Portman once lived here," well that actually *is* a form of housedressing, right? That's like *extreme housedressing,* right? I mean, even if it isn't true. If she didn't *live* there or lease it or whatever, she might have actually *stayed* there, how would anyone know but her? You have to like *ask Natalie*, if you were ever trying to prove it in court. Because you don't have to have your name on the lease to live someplace, not that she *ever* has her name on anything, the stars always list shit under their company or lawyer's name or whatever. And even if you lied about it, that's proably not even illegal. Because it could be *hearsay*, right? Yeah, I'd say that was completely acceptable . . . hey how was your day baby?

—Aw-ite.

—Get anybody good?

—No. Marisa Tomei. Sky Ferreira.

—Who's that.

—Just a bitch. A model. Oh, Chelsea Handler—

—She's so mean! I *love* what she said about Angelina! She & Jennifer are tight, & that is *so loyal*. And her fuckin body *rocks*.

—Who else, who else!

—The kid from *The Big Bang Theory*.

—I will never watch that shit.

—Got Michael Douglas, at lunch.

—O, he's cool! How's he doin?

—OK I guess.

—Sick again?

—I don't know. He looked OK.

—There's a gal with a *vlog* somewhere, someone sent it to me—I think she had cancer. She was saying if you had *bread*, you could fuck with it. With cancer. But I mean *seriously* fuck with it. I mean that's no great newsflash, right? Cause everybody knows that if you got money for a good lawyer, you aint goin to prison, right? But obviously if you have bread, you can fuck with the cancer or the whatever by *delaying* it. Delay the inevitable. Like, Steve Jobs got a new liver, remember that? Had a Whipple first, they take out the pancreas, cut off its head, then stuff it back inside. But with the liver the internet chick said he got around the list, cuz there is a *shitload* of people on the list in California, she said he couldn't buy the top spot cuz too many people would've found out so he went to Tennessee & bought *their* top of the list & had it done in Tennessee—all in, like, a week, he was in&out . . . Do you want to know what I think, Jerzy? I'm a nurse, right? And we sell private information to the media *all the time.* I mean, we don't *talk* about it but we do, cuz everybody's hurting. Everyone's pockets are fuckin light. & they *know* they can't regulate that shit. There's just no way. You just need to be careful, cuz man it is *hard times,* & you cannot regulate people and stop em from doing what they need to do to feed their families. Well I don't think people are different in Tennessee. Human nature don't change from state to state. People in Tennessee are—how do they say it?—'just like you and me'! So here's what I think. I think Apple went in there, to Tennessee, whatever city, I think Apple went in and *bought a whole hospital and everyone in it!* How else could you get away with that shit without anyone finding out? I think Apple was planning it for a *longass* time, I mean he was sick for, what, like 10 years, right? But he didn't *need* the liver til later. Right? And the money for all the hospital workers had to be big enough so no one was going to pick up the phone to TMZ. What they did—I've thought about all this—they probably paid everyone X and told em, you know, if it doesn't leak, everyone'll get Y. Like half now, half when the deed is done. As an incentive to keep their mouths shut. Makes sense, right? They bought a little private hospital with 200 people & Apple gave em, say, a million each, which they could do without even feeling it. $200 million aint *shit* to them—300, 400, *five hundred* aint shit—they're big as Russia & bigger than all the oil companies put together. And it's not really the doctors you need to worry about leaking the shit, it's the RNs and the LVNs and all the techs, but if you give the techs a quarter of a mill & you give the LVNs 500 thou & the nurses a million each, then you got to give the doctors probably 5 million each, again, not because they would be the source, but because they would be *pissed off* when they heard everyone was getting the bucks from Apple but them. Human fuckin nature. If Steve Jobs didn't have the long green, he'd have been up there dirty dancing with Patrick Swayze a long time ago.

That man really touched me. I bawled when he was on 20/20 with his wife & they were walking around their beautiful property . . . David Crosby had *two* fuckin liver transplants, right here in LA! And that was before they were throwing livers around like they was fuckin Vicodin. I think Charlie Watts had the same thing Michael Douglas has—in the throat. Probably when cancer got to Keith Richards, it said: "Uh-uh. Fuck *that!*" Even *cancer* don't want to fuck with Keith Richards! And Nurse Jackie? What's her name? Mrs. Soprano?

  —Edie Falco.

  —You've gotten her, right? Taken her picture?

  —Yeah, a few. You mostly get her at award shows.

  —She's so great. She don't have tits no more, but she don't whine or talk about it . . . Blake Lively got new tits, but she don't have breast cancer. But Michael Douglas is *rich*, dude, & *money never sleeps.* Money compounds daily & nightly! The dufflebags are always waitin at SunLife!

  He started for his room.

  —You know what I saw on the Internet about Jobs?

  —What.

  —What they did was—and it's totally legal, Apple found a way to make it legal—they broke down a patch of Jobs' skin into cells & started putting the cells in all their new shit. iPhones, iPads, iPods, i-whatever. So that like in 10 years, maybe less, there won't be any Apple products that literally don't have his body in em. Isn't that a trip? And they say that if you see anyone with a t-shirt that says, "Create JOBS," it aint about the economy. Nuh-uh. If you see that t-shirt, that means whoever's wearing it was a part of that special team. The Internet has some whack shit, but *that*, I *totally believe.*

  —Hey, goodnight.

  Tom-Tom shouted after him:

  —I put those pictures on your bed!

                  .   .   .

There were some pages torn from magazines, with red marker circles drawn around the abs of Perez Hilton, Rick Rubin, & Marc Jacobs, and there was one of Matthew McConaughey taking his body for a walk at the beach . . . on slow days, the beacherazzi set up Camp Mc-Conaughey, for that *US Weekly* dog/Frisbee/young son on-the-sand shot. Let them eat beefcake. Mostly though you just hung out, gossiped & smoked weed/crack with your fellow fellows. But you *could* get lucky, & get collateral shit—last month Jerzy got Brooklyn Beckham romping with dog/bodyguard; Hailee Steinfeld (pre-Harry) walking at the edge of waves in deep conversation with Ron Howard; a frail-looking Charlie Rose. He had fond memories of Charlie—Jerzy spent a week in scrubs, hanging in the back of the hospital after the ♥ surgery, hoping that when he was released, they'd wheel Charlie out the rear entrance. Which they did. The magazines paid a higher price than he thought they would because Charlie, always the gent, was kind enough to cooperate by looking like warmed-over shit.

He snorted some meth & sat in front of the laptop. The image was frozen where he left off, a website called http://behindthecasting couch.com. Each "casting" session began with a note to the viewer that the women they were about to watch were all there looking for a job but there *was* no job. The crawl said tuff titties, the poor bitches ended up fucking and sucking for nothing. The way it worked was this guy sits at his desk in an office in a business park. He has all these appts set up with women who answered an ad saying they could make fifteen hundred to 5,000 a day as *models* in the adult film business. Cameras are hidden all over the office, the guy even holds one the whole time, keeps it trained on them kind of dufusly because eventually he's naked, with this camera strapped to his wrist. So they come in, he interviews them, he says, Why do you want to be a model, they usually say it's for the money, but sometimes they say it's for the experience. They're (usually) nervous, he asks do you swallow, most say yes, do you do anal, most say yes or at least they've tried w/their bfs or if they haven't tried that they're willing (probably) to, then he asks them to strip. After they strip he tells them to bend over, which they do, hands bracing the wall, brownishpink unprofessional unpowdered ingrown-hair privates ready for their (extreme) closeup, manicured or shaved (most the time), pimply ass (some of the time), whatever. Some ugly, some fat, some petite w/big-toe-size nipples. The ones without the tatts make Jerzy the horniest because they're the ones who are easiest to imagine being hoodwinked. The guy has em spread everything with their hands, & he leans over with the camera to look, like a trader looking at horse- or slave teeth. Then he just says it, lays it on the line, *What I want you to do now is suck my cock.* In the one Jerzy just unpaused, the chick was taken aback. Not a tattoo on her, a real hottie. The guy had to like *talk her into it.* "Am I going to get money for this? Today?" The guy just says "NO but this is how they do it, & if you don't do a tape you're not going to get the opportunity to make fifteen hundred to 5,000 a day." Says there's lots of pretty faces out there but the producers want to see if you can take direction. I've been doing this for 5 years. It's pretty much what I do. I can guarantee you work, but you don't get paid for today. Then he hardballs em, says they can go home right now if they're not up for it. They agree, because they're already naked on the couch of an office in a building in a business park, it's like already being on the burro halfway to the bottom of the Grand Canyon, & he tells em to unbuckle his pants and fish it out. And they're suckin him like real pros while he dufus-holds the camera so we get that nice POV of the b.j., the old death-from-above shot, then he says "Well, I guess you know what's coming next." & he fucks em right there on the creepy nut-creamed couch. Or sometimes on the hard desk. He even has them hold the camera while he's fucking them! You know, hold it on their own action. *Then* he says he's going to fuck them in the ass, no one ever asks for lube & no one ever asks him to put a condom on (Jerzy loved the COMMENTS *this is fake people get real no girl in her right mind is gonna do what you just seen with all the sexual std's we have these days* & a guy wrote under that *last girl I took home from a bar didn't ask if I had any stds and I didn't ask her about stds. Welcome to reality*) There's a fixed camera on the table, he tells them to look in the lens. At this stage of the tape, most are rectalwincing in pain as they get pounded. If he pulls out, he comes on the small of their backs, but mostly on their faces, the "facial" was what men wanted to see, a guy pulling it out of slut ass & shooting on & into the mouth, on & in the nostrils, straight into the eyes.

Jerzy watched free, shorter versions of the auditions; you could view the unedited original if you paid to join, but he made a habit of never paying for sexsites. He got *close* to paypal/ing tho, with *backroomcasting*. No shit. He tweaked on it for days, & from everything he'd read on the internet & the *feeling* he got from having watched so many of them he fully believed 1000% the shit was for real. No way could these lame chicks be acting, you'd need to be Meryl Streep. Plus the guy's face was always fuzzed out, which Jerzy felt was too subtle a game to be running, whoever was behind the site would have to be, like, "These are fake but to make people think they aren't, let's take the time/expense to fuzz out Ed's face in every single frame." Like why would they even give a shit if you didn't believe they were real? They probably liked to keep em guessing, better for biz.

Jerzy clicked on another one. A superMILF redhead. Before you see her come in, the camera in the office shows the scammer already on his cellphone telling an associate he's about to interview a soccer mom, he tells his friend that he went on facebook & she's *definitely* a fuckin soccer mom who's into her children & her marriage, the guy's almost breathless, Jerzy never saw him excited like this before in any of the other videos. The office phone rings & it's the mom & the guy hangs up his cell & gives her directions how to find him, which walkways and whatever, because it's a business park. The mom comes in & she's a total fox. He asks if she told any of her friends where she was going & she laughs and says no, she told them she was going to the mall. He asks why she came and she said sometimes she got tired of soccer mom life & wanted to explore "the naughty side." The guy goes thru all the bullshit, the take your clothes off & bend over, the now-I-want-you-to-suck-my-cock, & BAM he's fucking soccermilf—a ceiling camera shows him pulling out and coming, he was only in there about 20 seconds, a premature ejack. In case you missed it, the producers drew a red PowerPoint circle around fearless leader's dick (*and* cum, now Elmer'd on her lower back) then wrote an OOPS!!! above the circle, with little arrows pointing to the cum. The guy kept fucking soccermilf anyway, but Jerzy thought there probably was some editing there. Had to be.

He didn't have any meth so he ate 3 orange sweet-tasting addies, did a little coke, & masturbated to the casting sessions (a school friend of Rikki's texted him that a guy who helped recruit chicks for the castingcouch just got busted for kiddie porn. Plus the friend texted that the internet said the guy with the fuzzed out face had major Herpes), sampling/toggling between **Related Videos** til 4AM. Then he snorted some of Tom-Tom's H, nodding out in front of the castingporn til the alarm woke him: Shade 45, slowly getting louder til it twitched his consciousness:

I just wanna talk, and conversate
Cause I usually just stalk you and masturbate
And I finally got the courage to ask you on a date
So just say yes, let the future fall into place . . . CUNT.

[Jacquie & Reeyonna]

MILF-to-be

"I didn't see you on the couch!"

"What *is* that? Is that a nametag?"

"O! Yeah—"

"O my God, it says *Sears*. Did you get a job at Sears?!?!"

"Yes, I did."

"O my god! Mom, are that bad?"

"It's—I'm doing it for work. For my work."

"Doing *what?*"

"I had this funny idea. For some images—photographs. Then it got less & less funny and more just *interesting*."

"What!"

"Well, Sears has a portrait studio. Whole families come in."

"O my god, it's getting *worse*—"

"You'll get a prom queen, or newlyweds, or new moms bringing in their babies . . ."

"So, like, you were like an *art* photographer, & now you're taking pictures of *families* at *Sears*?!"

"I am & I'm not. And don't be such a snob. I don't really know yet. But I think I *can* make art—there's art *in* there. I just need to find it."

"So you're like going to have an exhibition of the family portraits or whatever that you take at *Sears*? Sears won't even *let* you, they would totally *own* them."

"I don't know what I'm doing, Jerilynn. I'm just following my nose. Going by my lights."

Jerilynn/Reeyonna softened.

"I guess I *kind* of get it."

"All I know is that I'm *excited* about something. For the 1st time in I don't know how long."

"Then that's cool. I'm happy for you, Mom."

"Thank you, honey."

"I just hope none of my friends see you."

"They won't, unless they're in Valencia."

"Mom, can I talk to you about something?"

"What is it?"

"Uhm. I don't know how to—this is really weird."

"Sweetie, what is it?"

Reeyonna/Jerilynn stiffened.

"I'm gunna have a baby."

"No."

"I am. I'm almost three months pregnant."

"You are? O Jerilynn—"

"I didn't tell you—I haven't really told *anyone*—because I was afraid I'd get talked out of having it."

"Do you know who the father is?"

"Of *course* I know, *oh my god* I am *not* a *slut*."

"Jerilynn, is it Rikki?"

"No, it's the *football team*."

"Don't fuck with me, Jerilynn! GODDAMMIT, don't *fuck* with me on this, you're not in the *position* to *fuck* with me!"

"All *RIGHT*. O-KAY. I'm *SORRY*. I'm *SO SO SORRY*——"

"Don't cry. Please don't cry. I didn't mean to yell."

"I am *NOT CRYING! God!*"

"O Jesus. Shit. I'm sorry, honey."

"You're so *MEAN*. I don't want you to be *MEAN* to me!"

"I won't. I just need to think. I'm just—I just came home & you dropped this on me."

"I'm *REALLY REALLY SORRY!*————"

"No!—I'm really glad you did, I'm *happy* that you did. I'm really glad you told me. OK, Jerilynn? Did you hear that? Can you hear that? I am *very, very* glad. Tho I wished you'd told me *sooner*————"

"I'm sorry! I'm sorry!"

"*You don't have to have it. You can have an abortion after* TWELVE *weeks. A friend of mine's daughter had hers at* FIFTEEN—— . . . . . ."

"I AM NOT GOING TO KILL MY BABY!!!!! WHY DID I EVER TELL YOU WHY DID I EVEN EVER TELL YOU I SHOULDN'T HAVE TOLD YOU———————————!!!!!!!"

"All right. Calm down. Calm down now. Let's just take—let's take—let's take some time here. OK? Can we do that, Jerilynn? Let's breathe. Can you stop crying & go wash your face? I should have known you were pregnant. The acne . . . and you lost your hips . . . *stand straight.* Lift your shirt————"

"*No!*"

"What is the matter with me? The throwing up in the mornings . . . I thought you were *bulimic*—I feel like *such* an ass."

"I'm *sorry*—"

"It's not *your* fault, it's *mine*. & would you please stop saying you're *sorry*? Can you just STOP?"

"I'm SORRY! I'm SORRY, I *will.*"

"————just let me just think. Let me just sit & gather my thoughts. Can you do that? Can you go wash your face and let me gather my thoughts? Because—there needs—we need, we'll need to . . . oy. *Oy yoy* YOY. *Oy yoy yoy yoy* YOY. The school . . . we have to————"

"Can we go out for dinner?"

"Yeah. Maybe that's a good idea. Let's go out for dinner."

"Can we go to Du-par's for pancakes?"

"Yes. We can go to Du-par's."

"Thanks."

"Thank *you*. For talking about—for telling me, for talking to me. I really commend you for that. I really do, Jerilynn."

"Thanks . . ."

"Let's go to Taylor's—the steakhouse. Do you want to go to Taylor's?"

"Can't we go to Du-par's?"

"You can't get good steak at Du-par's."

"OK."

"Dinner'll be expensive, but so what. You're eating for two."

"Maybe *three*," she said savagely. "Maybe it's *twins!*"

"Jerilynn, don't *even*—nice to see you laugh anyway. I'll get there in a minute. Or maybe a day. Or a week. To laughing. O boy. O well. *Well well well well well*. Go wash your face & we'll go."

"K."

[Reeyonna EXITS. A beat, then, Jacquie calls after]

"Jeri? Have you seen my Klonopins, do you know what happened to my Klonopins?"

"No but I'll look!"

[sotto, to Self]

"I cannot find my Klonopins. & I really fucking need them."

[Reeyonna & Rikki]

Pregnant ⏸

"**My** mom's going to call. Did she call them yet?"

"I don't know. I don't think so."

"She said she was going to call."

"For what."

"I guess it's a *Meet the Parents* moment."

"Yeah. Okay . . ."

"So have they said anything to you?"

"About what?"

"About the *baby*. How are they dealing?"

"My mom won't come out of her room."

"Wow, really?"

"Yeah, she cries."

"Bummer."

"Yeah . . ."

"You sound fucked up. Are you like, totally fucked up?"

"No. Just some weed. Why."

"You just sound fucked up."

"I'm good. Are you?"

"Not *really*."

"Yeah . . ."

"Are you watching porn?"

"No."

"You don't have to lie."

"I'm not lying."

"I don't care if you watch porn."

"Then why do you ask? If you don't care why do you ask me if I'm watching it?"

"I don't know. Maybe I'm horny."

"Maybe you just like being in my business."

Pause.

"I just think . . . the sooner we move out the better. But I'm going to wait a week. Before. A week *before*."

"Wait for what."

"To ask."

[Telma]

We Don't Need Another Hero

Of all the stars with cancer that Telma reached out to in her campaign to join the cast of *Glee*, Michael Douglas was the biggest, and the first responder. Another one she heard back from right away was Grant Achatz, the famous chef; he had tongue cancer too. The doctors wanted to cut out the jaw and the tongue but Grant said no because he didn't want to lose his tastebuds. Grant got chemo *and* radiation instead. He said the lining of his esophagus shed like a snake & part of the getting-well ritual was peeling the lining out of his throat like smelly clingy cellophane while he choked & vomited. Now, *that's* a hero. She liked Grant, & she liked Christina Applegate, & she liked Will Reiser, & she liked the guy from *Dexter*, & any one of them could have gotten her on the *Glee* set. But Michael was the only one she had shared her aspirations with.

At night, she read his letter over and over (he handwrote it the same as Telma had, & her mom thought that was such a wonderful way of showing solidarity), wondering when he was going to call to ask her to tea. She already knew what she was going to wear. Her mom said, be patient.

It was Saturday, and she was doing her usual weekend tour at St Ambrose (pediatric oncology, or, as Telma liked to call it, *ped-OINK! OINK! OINK!*), going from bed to bed with Sir Vivor, her three-legged English terrier that she got at the shelter, & Bunny, the real-life floppy-eared cocker spaniel that was the official ward mascot, putting kids (& parents) at ease. Telma knew how to make the frightened children laugh, settle their moms' & dads' nerves, instill hope. Showing everyone how to pull the courage trigger. She loved her weekend warriorship.

The Bertram & Bonnie Brainard Family Center for Pediatrics was *hers*: she owned it. But Telma didn't define or limit herself by ped-*oink* alone—she had toured/ombudsgirl'd through them all: The Rick & Tina Caruso Family Research & Critical Care, AEG Extended Care (clinical outpatient), The Stewart and Lynda Resnick Pavilion (neuropsychiatric), the Verizon Towers (imaging center), & Twitter House (extended residence for families with kancerkidz undergoing treatment)—& most weekends could be found crisscrossing & cross-pollinating the sprawling campus, faithfully fulfilling her duties exercising authority, not only as the Wizard of Brainard, but the mayor of St Ambrose & all its environs. The cafeteria staff plied her with frozen yogurt; elderly volunteers thrust flowers into her tiny hands; there was even a special place where she could nap, covered by a quilt stitched together with the names of kancerheroes embroidered on every square. The RNs called themselves *Telma's Troopers*—most of them were on the *20/20* that featured Telma five years back. Elizabeth Vargas and a camera crew followed the (then) 4 foot titan thru the rooms & corridors of Brainard as she cajoled and consoled, struggling to keep up.

But that was . . .

. . . a while ago.

Too long, thought Telma.

Time for a comeback.

Anyway—what was good for Telma, was good for kancer.

.   .   .

A nurse told her that Biggie Brainard (pushing 13, real name, Colt Brainard III) (5'3"/165 lbs) happened to be "at hospital" today, and would she like to meet him? *(Well, duh.)* Biggie's dad, Bertram Brainard, was an inventor who disappeared from public view after fully endowing construction of the *oink-oink* building 10 years back.

Now *this* was going to be really something! Telma had never given much *thought* to the Brainards, & with this development, was, well, nearly ashamed at having neglected to ever have *inquired* after her benefactors. Until now, they had no flesh at all, flat and bloodless as the walls of the edifice on which their name was engraved. Telma immediately asked where she might *find* Mr. Biggie Brainard, & the nurse replied that he happened to be in the basement getting an MRI, or trying to anyway. She explained that he was mortally terrified of the hellaciously noisy apparatus that, to his mind (his *mind* being the very thing the machine was attempting to observe, record, interpret, & diagnose), swallowed a person prematurely, like an overeager coffin.

Biggie lived with his older brother Brando on a vast estate in Bel-Air. The brother, his de facto guardian, lately noticed that Biggie was having subtle cognitive difficulties, the most pronounced being in the realm of short-term memory. He hadn't struck his head on anything (as far as anyone knew) & the doctors had already ruled out diabetes. Now, they wanted to take a look at the brain.

All this was transmitted to the Mayor, who of course enjoyed a privileged standing when it came to hospital staff sharing certain confidentialities. Once she got the *brainard* tumor joke out of her system, she was on her merry way.

She was introduced to Camino (nanny/caregiver) & then Biggie (overweight but not yet morbidly obese, though heading for it) in a doctor's lounge. The nurses' ♥s broke in unison when they saw how sweet the two looked together—Telma's fearless, charismatic, firecracker Laurel to his poignantly fearful, socially awkward, shrinking-violet Hardy. Having been briefed on Biggie's MRI jitters, she lost no time suggesting they go for yogurt in the "café."

The nurses shook their heads in respect.

The Mayor was alarmingly proactive.
That's our girl.

                              .   .   .

—So did they say if you can have kids?

    —Probably. I had surgery but I didn't have any chemo.

    —Radiation?

    —Nuh-uh. Christina Applegate had what I had & she had a baby. I met her when we were in Washington. The doctors said one day I might have to have my ovaries taken out but I can still carry. Christina might have to have hers out too.

    —What kind of surgery. Did you have.

    —A mastectomy.

    —Oh. (*Pause*) I saw this little girl on the Ellen show. She's like four years—old & got it too. Breast cancer.

    —She was on Ellen?

    —I didn't see it but my brother sent me a link. He thought it would make a good telemovie.

    —She's from Canada. But she's not really a survivor.

    —I didn't even think four year old girls *had* breasts.

    —I mean, you have to be kancerfree for at least three years before you can be called a survivor.

    —But I mean if you're still alive after your surgery or your chemo & whatever, doesn't that make you a survivor?

    —*Technically.* In layman's terms. But if someone has something cut out & then it never spreads anywhere else—like me, so far—it takes *three years* before you're allowed to say you're kancerfree. The rule is, you have to be kancerfree for *three years* before you're allowed to call yourself a survivor, & *five* years before you're allowed to say you're cured.

    —Allowed?

    —Those are the cancer organization *rules,* & they're very strict. You can't just go and change them. It's like the Olympics. And that girl won't know for *three years*. I mean, I hope she *is*—a survivor. That would be so rad. She's already a hero. She's got swag.

—Swag? What is that?

—That she's cool. But right now she's just a kid with kancer.

—Yeah I guess.

—So where do you go to school?

—At home.

—At home?

—I have a tutor.

—That is *hella tight*.

—It's OK.

—I want your life! So what else?

—What else?

—Like, about your parents. Doesn't your mom come to the hospital when you have tests?

—She doesn't really live with us.

—Now I *know* I want your life! Where does she live?

—London. Near London, I think. And Paris. Her business takes her away a lot.

—What's her business?

—I don't know.

—What about your dad?

—He lives at home. We live with him. My brother and me.

—Your father paid for this *whole building*?

—Yeah.

—He must be a billionaire.

—I guess.

—What does he do?

—Invents ideas.

—*Coolio.* So what do *you* do?

—What do I do?

—For fun?

—Well I help my brother.

—How.

—With ideas.

—For what?

—Movies and television.

—You *invent* ideas?

—I guess.

—Rad! What kind.

—My brother has a production company? And I come up with ideas? For projects.

—That's so awesome! What kind of ideas?

—Did you see *Turndown Service*?

—The movie?

—With Zach Galifianakis and Tosh? And Kristen Wiig?

—I *almost* saw it. Is it on Netflix?

—Only Apple TV.

—What's it about again?

—These people own a fancy hotel? That's Tosh & his wife, Kristen Wiig. His wife in the movie. But they're going bankrupt? And they have this son who's a loser, who they never respected? That's Zach Galifianakis. And when he tells them he's going to save the hotel for them they just laugh. So he starts this service where people pay him to break up with their girlfriends. Instead of breaking up by texting. I mean, he has to find the girls then break up with them face-to-face. But I mean, the girls who are getting dumped are face-to-face with *him*, not with the guys who are dumping them.

—Like, how much does he charge?

—A lot, because most of the people who hire him are rich.

—But how could you make enough money to save a hotel, just by breaking up with people?

—They do in the movie. There's blackmail and stuff I left out.

—Coolio.

—It's not really so great. I mean parts of it are funny. It made $430 million in the world but only 160 in the States, & I think the studio

thought it'd do better. In North America. It was sort of a disappointment. They weren't really disappointed, they just thought it would
do better.

—Does it say it's written by you? In the credits?

—I didn't write it, it was just my idea. But it *does* say, From an Idea
by Biggie Brainard. My brother said I could have a From a Story by
but I liked From an Idea by.

—So where do you get your ideas?

—I don't know. It depends. Usually from the internet. I mean not
literally. The internet makes me think of ideas.

—Coolio.

—My brother's pitching *You Rule!* today, I think to NBC.

—What's *You Rule?*

—That's why Brando couldn't come, because he's pitching *You
Rule!*

—Is it from your idea?

—Uh huh. It's about a high school student who I guess is kind of a
loser who finds out that he's actually king of an island in the South
Pacific.

—That's awesome.

—We're doing a big movie with Michael Douglas & Larry Fishburne. It's in preproduction. Robert Pattinson might do a cameo.

—What's a cameo?

—When a big star is only, like, in one or two scenes. Sometimes
they don't even want a credit. They usually get a percentage.

—What's it called?

—A cameo.

—I mean the movie.

—*The Treasure of Sierra Leone.* It's in preproduction. The guy from
Twilight might be doing a cameo. Robert Pattinson.

They talked some more & had their yogurt. Telma scrutinized
him, attributing his occasional redundancies to nervousness. She had
the feeling he was maybe more nervous because of *her* than he was

about the MRI, at the moment anyway, sweetly so. But it was time, & she gently nudged Biggie over to the dreaded topic of *magnetic resonance imaging*. I've had a hundred of em, she said. She said she knew he was supposed to have one today, and do you want me to go with?

A little in love with her (or maybe a lot), he said he did.

And that was that.

. . .

There wasn't any phone service until she went back to the ward to get her purse & jacket.

The text was from her mom.

> MICHEAL DOUGLAS
> CALKED!!!!! u did it :D i
> HAVE DETAILS!!!!!

Then

> I MEANT CALLED!!!!!!!

Telma let out a whoop and ran down the corridor shouting "I'm *gleeful*, I'm so *gleeful*! I'm *gleeful gleeful gleeful!*"

The RNs nodded their heads, smiling at their favorite kook.

Snubbing the elevator, the littlest breast kancer hervivor who could flew down all five flights, bursting out of the lobby into the wild freedom/explosive normalcy of the deep blue day.

[Rikki]

Zen and the Art of Go Fuck Yourself

Dawn,

Rikki's foster, the woman he started calling Mom just 2 wee into his placement—Dawn, soon to become his legal mother, her husband Jim his legal dad, both having agreed to the sacred, irrevocable process of adoption—hadn't left her room in almost 5 days. Rikki practically wanted to die. He had heartache-headaches & even stopped watching porn. He never thought she would take the news of ReeRee's pregnancy so hard.

Jim, sitting in the darkened living room, TV on low. Shows about houses: redoing houses, buying houses, flipping houses, razing houses. Dance show and singing show competitions. All America was singing and dancing and competing. All America was famous and winning, and if they weren't, they were famously failing, all America was looking for someplace to compete and to win and be famous, or famously fail. There were only two groups left in America-World: the billionaires and the singing show contestants. Jim, laughing at Geico commercials in spite of himself. Jim, laughing at his favorite show, *Family Guy*. Jim even hauling out the old DVDs of his

2nd favorite show, *Sealab 2021*, but not laughing, busy now listening through walls—you could be anywhere in the house and hear it—listening morosely to his wife/fits and starts/cries and moans. Rikki knew where it was heading: soon, he'd be disadopted. (First maladapted then disadopted.) All he wanted was to make it easier on these people, these beautiful people Dawn & Jim, who only happened to fucking be the only ones who ever treated him like a motherfucking human being, the only ones who ever loved him, ever *risked* loving him.

The only ones he ever loved back.

"Dad."

"Come in, Rikki. Come sit."

"How's Dawn."

"Been better." (*Soft fatherly smile of understanding*)

"Dad. I'm sorry . . . about—things."

(*As if he hadn't heard*) "Rikki, I've been wanting to talk to you. You're going through a lot & I feel somewhat guilty that I haven't been able to devote much energy to what's going on in your life. Because I know there's a *lot* going on, big, big stuff. But I want you to know that's not for a lack of concern. Dawn's having a rough patch (as you well by now know) & I've got to see her thru."

"If you guys don't want to adopt me, that's cool. I don't want you to stress."

"You're saying this because of Reeyonna? The pregnancy?"

"I didn't mean to hurt Mom. It really hurts me to give her pain."

"O. I see. You think she's having trouble because of that."

(*Sweet suite of fatherly smiles*)

"What can I do to make her stop crying? Should I go talk to her? Will she talk to me? Dad—should I move away? I'll move away, with Reeyonna. Would it be better if I moved away?"

Jim sighs. Then: "Dawn's in some trouble, but it's nothing to do with the pregnancy." (*Rikki subtly reacts, unprepared for the remark*) "What happened was, she applied for a job up in San Francisco. Not a job, really—a 'position.' In the field that was—is—her calling. The position requires training, & you can take a course up there in the Bay Area. It's a Buddhist orientation, which is perfect for Dawn because she's been a meditator for years, as you are probably aware of. (*Of course he was. That was just Jim's conversational way.*) And she's just, well, your mother's *very* much up to speed on proper breathing— 'yogic' breathing—she's done the 'Art of Living' workshops over at the big church. She's an inveterate fan of the Dalai Lama, & Thich Nhat Hanh, & Pema Chödrön, all those people. The Levines— they're that couple, Buddhist couple, who are both—who both happen to be dying. They live in New Mexico I believe. And the fellow who had a stroke, in Hawaii . . . the Leary fellow, he was with Leary—Ram Dass. *Be Here Now.* Terrific book.

"So I would say that your mother is more than a *neophyte.*

"The course takes 9 months, it's very comprehensive. Now, you know Dawnie's been depressed since she stopped teaching. That's not a secret. You can't live in this house & not know that. She's had troubles on & off all her life with depression. Rikki, it's a disease. And I think that taking this course, this going-back-to-school, but this time as a *student,* really lifted her out of the gloom. The gloom & doom. She *probably* needs to change her medication, up it a little, I'm getting into that. But this place—up north—is a Buddhist operation, the people who run it are all Buddhists. Dawnie printed out the application from their website and went through it *very* thoroughly. They asked her—they asked *everyone* who applied—to write an essay—we *both* had the impression it wasn't, the essay wasn't, it wasn't an *audition* for the course. Not strictly speaking. They just asked that you write a personal essay conveying why you wanted to take the course & do the work, what you expected to get out of it, that sort of thing. They wanted to know a little what you imagined your plans were for the future, in the sense of utilizing whatever you learned with them. But not in any serious detail. I think it was more about hearing you explain your passion. *That's* what they wanted to hear. Maybe a little about your experience too, in life. With the 'great mystery.' Because you may not know this but Dawnie's had a lot of death in her life. Her mom at an early age, her brother—a drunk took him out—her dad, just a few years ago. She had a little sister who died at five months. Dawnie was 4. She'll never talk about it, but believe me, she remembers it *vividly*.

"Dawnie was *very* excited about it; the course is only a few months away. That's what our trip was about last month—looking for an apartment close to the Zen Center, a single. Dawnie called it her 'room with a view.' *A room of one's own*. It's a long time since she felt her independence, that sense of herself as a unique & separate individual on the planet, someone worthy and productive, a *woman* not just a wife, mom, teacher, or whatever the world chooses to describe her. She showed me the essay she wrote for those people, & Rikki, I tell you it was *really something*. Really something. One day, I'll ask her to show it to you. *Spectacular* piece of writing. I didn't think she was capable of that—no, that sounds wrong, that's not exactly what I meant. I knew she was capable, let's just say I didn't think she had the *tools*. Rikki? I was completely floored by it.

"Long story short, Dawnie didn't get in. I don't think they really even considered her. They wrote her a letter saying they were sorry but the course was only open to *professionals* at this time. We were floored. I asked her if she wanted me to call, you know, speak to someone at the Center, to push a little and find out what the hell was going on, but she was adamantly against it. So, it completely—her plans were completely thwarted and I think there was some embarrassment too because she was so confident, and told some friends as well. Where she was going, & how long she would be away. The whole idea of going up there to be engaged in that kind of work touched her soul . . . I looked at the ad, the one clipped from the magazine, Buddhist magazine, looked at it *very carefully*, & to be honest, I still think it can be read either way. In other words, there aren't any flashing lights that say CIVILIANS NEED NOT APPLY. I think someone in their outfit needs to take a closer look at *wording*, at how things are *worded*. Because I'm an engineer, I pay attention to that sort of thing. But evidently, we both misunderstood. Because I read the ad right along with her.

"That's what put her to bed. It has nothing to do with your situation with Reeyonna. In fact, Dawnie said something to me about it this morning. She hasn't talked much, but she was worried you'd think you weren't on her mind or that she wasn't going to offer any support or guidance. She wanted me to convey that. Because I know she *plans* to, soon as she pulls out of this little nosedive. This has happened a few times before. It's a lot of darkness, what the therapists call 'family of origin' stuff. Early trauma, all that PTSD rigmarole. It's real, but I don't think knowing the reasons behind it helps.

"I'm not going to let her go on like this forever. If she doesn't improve by next week, I'll take her to see someone."

Jim heard his wife crying & excused himself to go to her. He got as a far as the hallway then turned back to Rikki.

"I keep kicking myself. Wondering if it was a mistake to include the check—the tuition was $5,000 & I sent a check along with Dawnie's application. The check of course was returned. I keep second-guessing that maybe they thought that was arrogant or presumptuous. Sending along the check, like it was a fait accompli. But it was a completely innocent thing! We *both* were excited, I was excited *for* her. See, I thought it was essentially a done deal, we *both* did. But jeez, maybe someone thought it was a bribe! I need to stop kicking myself. Still, it's there. 'If I hadn't sent the check, then she'd be in.' What they call magical thinking. Isn't that dumb?"

.   .   .

The selfish relief Rikki felt was quickly overtaken by apprehension about his fostermother's condition.

He went to his room and called Reeyonna because he'd been giving her updates & wanted to tell her it wasn't the baby thing that was freaking his mom, but something else. *I mean, she probably is flipped about the baby, but right now my dad said she's flipped she lost this job that she thought she was gunna get. Or this job she was* paying *for to get. She thought she got hired but she didn't. My dad was telling me.*

Ree said she was almost ready to ask her mom for the trust money. He didn't say anything; that was her business. The whole reason *behind* her asking for the trust money made him overall nervous. Having a kid was huge enough, but now ReeRee was talking about moving out & getting a place of their own. They were going to buy a bungalow in Hollywood, depending on how much money she got from her mom. And if they didn't buy the *bungalow*, Ree said they'd rent a *duplex*, maybe over on Fairfax. He never had his own place like that, didn't know shit about it. When he pictured the new place, he saw himself sitting on the bare floors wondering who you even called to set up the wireless. And *plus*, he was going to be a father. It was all so huge & fucked up he couldn't even deal.

Rikki smoked & got his email. A friend sent a video of four guys in A&F/HOLLISTER hoodies banging this girl at school who never turned down a rape. They were all wearing Obama masks, it was kinda funny, kind of okay. He scanned the stickamgirls/facebookam/ *Talk To A Stranger* sites where the screen's split into webcam twos: like, a girl would be in her bedroom on the top screen, watching the stranger in his bedroom on the bottom, & there'd be a scroll of whatever they were keyboarding each other usually just shit like *show it to me, you're so fuckin hot, show me your tits*—bullshit like that. For some reason the girls always showed their faces but the strangers typically made sure the webcam cut em off at the neck so that all you usually could see was their hands strobe-stroking their big dicks. The one he started to watch was funny because the girl's little sister burst into the room in the middle of it & saw what was going on and shouted "Perv!" at her sis then left, slamming the door. A 9-year old calling a 12 year-old a perv cracked him up.

Rikki got out the bong & settled in for some hardcore tubin' but suddenly got hungry. Went to the kitchen and made a bigass sandwich—double turkey, double roast beef, beaucoup Jarlsberg, lettuce

& tomatoes & jalapeños & grey poupon. Big bag of honey mustard kettle chips. A water pitcher filled with crushed ice & coke zero. He tried picturing the kitchen as the one in the new bungalow/duplex, but it wasn't a nice fantasy, it made him bummed.

On his way out, he saw the letter on the breakfast table.

ZEN HOSPICE PROJECT

Dear Dawn,

Thank you for submitting your application for our End-of-Life Counselor Program. Regrettably we will not be able to include you in our fall training. We are very pleased to have received an enthusiastic response to our Call for Candidates including applications from hospice caregivers, psychotherapists, chaplains, and healthcare professionals.

In order to select participants we carefully review each application assessing each candidate's established experience, commitment to end-of-life care and the merits of their proposed plan for use of the training. We appreciate the obvious attention you gave to preparing your application.

Please understand that this decision is not meant to discourage your interest in caring for those with life-threatening illness. On the contrary we feel that the culture needs more people with your demonstrated dedication to improving end-of-life care. We hope you will continue your efforts in service and that you will remain in contact with *Zen Hospice Project* and *The Institute on Dying*.

Yours,
Frank Ostaseski
Founder & Guiding Teacher
Zen Hospice Project/Institute on Dying

Back in his room, Rikki fell into his own kind of funk. He was even more guiltstricken now for laying the pregnancy trip on his fosterfolks. The timing was so shitty—right in the middle of his mom's depressathon. He'd always wanted to make them proud; now *this* was how he chose to repay their loyalty and commitment, their unconditional kindnesses. He wouldn't *let* them adopt him, he'd spare them of that additional hassle-y heartache.

He felt like a monkey, not a man.

That's right: they had a monkey in their house, a *ganja*-smoking monkey that ate their food & yanked his dick & got his load off watching Jap schoolgirls getting raped.

It was time to put away childish things.

·   ·   ·

New father, new baby, new life.

(*Permanent new legal parents, Dawn & Jim.*)

New dreams, new ambition.

(Uhm, there weren't really any old ones.)

All these ☆lets and shit were always buying houses for their parents. They'd turn, like, 18, & say, "The birthday present I got myself was buying a house for my mom & dad. It was the best present ever," some such shit, & Rikki would smirk and call them dicks but now it was like *Who the fuck am* I, *they're out there* doin *shit & I'm just smokin weed and pullin my pud.* Mom 'ould damn well come out from her room if I knocked & said, *hey moms, it's Rikki, can I talk to you a sec? I, uh, I just, well uhm I just bought this house for you & Dad. It like has a pool? It's, like, a mansion in (Malibu) (Hancock Park) (the Holly Hills)—so many rooms (in my father's new house)—you know I don't mean to break confidences but Dad told me about those buddhahead mutherfuckers. Sorry for the language Mom. But like, uh, I made a donation? And they wrote another letter, I'll show it to you, it said they were* REALLY SORRY *for what they did, they want you to* COME UP *& do that job they originally didn't want you for. I bought a ticket for you, 1st-Class, for you and Dad. Got you a*

*room too at the 4 Seasons right near where the buddhaheads are doing their
bullshit.*

He suddenly had an Idea, the Idea of his young life.

Rikki's epiphany was to seek out his heroes & take counsel from
those bigger-than-life fathers whose movies had sustained him during the Lost Years when he wandered the DCFS* desert of dark,
crappy, DVD-stocked dens, trekking by court order from group- to
residential- to assigned-family homes, till (free at last) he reached the
promised land (Dawn&Jim): Laurence Fish., Denzel W., Forest
Whit., Morgan F., Wesley Snipe. He knew they were approach-
able—if he could find them!—& would see themselves in little boy
Rikki, crying for help. Wikipedia said Fishburne lied about his age
to get his first part in that war movie, said he was 17 but he was
14 . . . *could I do something whack like that? Something dope/fucked up for
real? Naw, prolly I'm just a punkbitch.* He needed to go hunting for
courage like the lion in *Wizard of Oz.* He'd yellowbrick it to the
Wizard—his BIGGEST role model hero Antwone Fisher—the man
whose mama was in jail when she gave birth to him, & whose papa
was a gangsta just like Rikki's (Antw.'s daddy got shot before Antw.
was even born) . . . . *Antwone Fisher*, soul brother/teacher/father,
raised in the System just like Rikki was except Antw.'s best foster
family happened to be his *very first one*, but the state (like they do)
took him away from the *good fam* & put him in with *hella bads* &
Antw.'s life went to shit till he joined the Navy . . . whereas *Rikki's*
best placement wasn't till the very *end*, the rest of them before, before Dawn & Jim, the rest being multitudinous shitholes—though,
no matter how shitty or crazy the placements, each made sure to
have its dark, DVD-stocked den, not only because it kept the kids
occupied, but for the show&tell required to impress the [very] occasional visiting social worker . . . a key difference being that Rikki

---

* Department of Children & Family Services.

didn't join the Navy, not yet anyway, & didn't see how he ever would———

Antwone made himself a player out of sheer guts, got a job as a studio guard, *infiltrated* the Hollywood System so he'd be heartbeat-close to what was going on. Sitting there daydreaming in front of the paused porn, he started to think maybe he would even apply for a job like that once they got settled in their new space.

He'd write a script about his life just like Antw. did, then get Antw.'s advice if the script was any good & see maybe if Antw. could help get someone to direct it into a movie the same way he got Denzel to direct his. Or maybe Antw. would read Rikki's screenplay and want to direct it himself.

It was all good.

He knew he had a shot with those niggers, especially Antwone because of the whole shared hard knocks/DCFS/gangsta dad/crack-head mom/adoption thing. Yeah yeah he would sure to have a shot because

he *will*see*hisself*in my

eyes

[Bud]

Bud Wiggins, Returning

Tolstoy

was wrong. That's what Bud thought, anyway.

As he mulled it over on the way back to Dolly's, he saw a laughing bum on a bus bench on La Brea, just south of Sunset. More like a laughing Buddha than bum (though maybe they were one & the same), for he was ecstatic; his jaw opened in ravenous hilarity, arms & fingers gesticulated wildly, eyes on fire as he stared ahead at the invisible movie playing on a screen that only *he* could see—blockbuster comedy of Eternity. The peculiar thing was that just before he turned right on Olympic toward Beverly Hills, Bud passed *another* ecstatic bum in a FUTURE CELEBRITY t-shirt, this one even *more* extreme than the last in his appreciation of whatever was being unreeled. For 35 years, Bud had been knee-jerk monetizing his daily experience through a screenwriter's filter, & *this* one quickly coalesced into a pitch about a "happy virus" descending upon the meek & the homeless then worked its way up from there. He quickly rejected it, remembering he was no longer in the business that bore him such meager fruit through the decades. Besides, he suddenly recalled that David Foster Wallace's big book touched on that; Bud never liked being accused of general plagiarism.*

He thought of Tolstoy because he'd seen plenty of *unhappy* bums of the paranoid type who rage in public places. It was easy for Bud to come up with reasons behind their display of insanity: a fire and brimstone fervor of religious psychosis; anger at the intrusion of Homeland Security, whose voice spoke through their teeth or the radios of passing cars; disgust at Women, whose gender was the source of all disease, all misery. But when it came to imagining what was behind the *happy* bums' façade, well, he was fairly certain, if asked, they would not say, "I am at one with the beautiful absurdity of the cosmos!" or even "I am Jesus & I shall save you!"—because, at least in the *latter*, what would be so hysterically funny about that? No, the difficulty was in discerning *what was on the screen* that caused such insane joviality. Clearly each was having a singular experience; each was seeing something *specific to himself* that tickled his madhouse funnybone.

Hence:

Unhappy bums are all alike; every happy bum is happy in his own way.

Take that, Tolstoy.

. . .

Nothing had changed, really, in those 35 years. Bud was still addicted to pills and living in the downstairs room of his mother's rent-controlled, split-level apartment—*The Charleville Manor*—in Beverly Hills. He couldn't find work, any kind of work, and relied on the kindness of almost-strangers; friends in the Industry who'd mostly slipped away. A few times a week, he awakened to his own high-

---

* Not having read the novel, Bud checked it on Wikipedia when he got home. Wallace wrote about a *movie*, not a virus, which was actually closer to Bud's initial observations of the bums' "watching" something on an invisible screen. The plot synopsis said that viewing the film rendered its audience not *happy*, but *lifeless*, but it was enough in the ballpark to discourage Bud (for the moment) from further "pitch" fantasies. He remembered a Python bit as well, something about a joke that was so funny that it killed whoever heard it.

pitched screams. The only thing that was different was suddenly being 59 years-old. Recently, the dentist told Bud he was grinding his
teeth, and asked if he wanted a night guard. Bud joked, "Why bother?
I've only got about 15 years left." Instead of cracking a smile (the
dentist's assistant remained stoic as well), the dentist just shrugged, as
if to say, *You've got a valid point there.*

The building Dolly lived in was now owned by a Vietnamese
woman with serious OCD. The reign of the Jewish landlord—the
building was once owned by the furrier Abe Lipsey—was long over.
The VC drove a little Mercedes & her face bore an agéd, frozen,
mani-pedi smile; she was as anxious for Dolly to die as Bud was.
Dolly had been in that apartment more than 4 decades. Her rent
could only be increased x-amount per year, the results being, to the
VC's immense consternation, that she paid less than ½ what the other
tenants did—the dogged, nest-building, penurious Dolly (Chinese
Year of the Ox) rolled over any financial obstacles in her way. In
time, she became Neimans' highest earner, having fleeced the company through an elaborate system of purchases, returns & swap-outs
that involved the bedazzling, bedizened expertise of the aforemen-
tioned Mr. Lipsey, furrier & landlord to the dying stars. (Broderick
Crawford's ex-wife, the starlet Joan Tabor, had died in one of Lipsey's
buildings, a suicide Bud remembered *The Beverly Hills Courier* writing up as an accidental OD of influenza R_x.) When she retired at 83,
she had a tad more than a million in savings; now, she was a relatively
spry nonagenarian whose only fear was falling. Bud hoped she'd soon
take a dive because the longer she lived, the more her savings were
depleted by the round-the-clock caregivers she'd hired specifically to
prevent her from taking a tumble.

Dolly was half-blind and half-deaf but enjoyed her TV golf. She
would sit in her chair in front of the set—a $1,300 lazyboy with a
motor allowing it to tilt on a 45° angle that made sitting down & getting up fun—and rip into the physical traits of the linksmen. Though
if a handsome one was playing, her voice turned creepy & horny.

He sat on the carpet holding her hand. In the last few years, Bud learned something strange & poignantly sad about his mother—she literally didn't know *how* to hold a hand, or how to let someone hold hers (like a girl who never learned how to kiss). She would dig with her thumb into his flesh until Bud nearly yelped in pain. Most of the time he endured it, simply by using the mantra *the money the money the money is coming* but often he was compelled to give brief tutorials on the art of handholding. For a few minutes she'd listen, with a proper sort of acquiescence, before suddenly digging into his flesh again with a cartoon villain's gleeful. Dolly's senses may have been dulled but her acuity ferociously lived on. The moment Bud entered her room, she scanned his body, his grooming, his clothes. *Are you going to grow a beard? Are those boots or are those high heels that you're wearing? They're ugly! Ugly! Ugly!* When she wasn't being critical, she leered, and told him how *thin* and *gorgeous* he was. He cringed.

How did it happen that after 60 years, this rancorous crone, this snapping turtle, this weird, decaying dominatrix, this *virago* still dominated his life?

Bud had been on a daily "maintenance dose" of opiates since the dawn of time. There were five or six doctors he could count on for refills—they'd been treating him for "migraines" for so many years that Bud believed he actually had the malady. He *did* have migraines but they were what are called "rebound headaches," *caused* by the pills. He bought R$_x$ off the Internet once and wished he hadn't because twice a day he got emails from the "fulfillment department": *Bud, your prescription is ready!*

Opiates were constipating, to say the least—a friend of his with AIDS was prescribed liquid opium because it was the only thing that effectively stopped the diarrhea—so Bud had always been rather fussy about his prematurely geriatric toilet. He took 1000 mg of magnesium a day and never traveled too far from his stash of stool softeners and MOM (milk of magnesia). Impaction was a ring of hell to be avoided at all cost. In his day, he'd been forced to go to the emergency room more than once; one visit ended in provoking an attractive young RN to announce, post-enema, "You've just given birth!" Bud got chills when he read about the obese woman who died writhing & obstructed on the floor of an ER waiting room. A zeppelin of shit had accreted in her gut for days but the Hugh Laurie at King-Harbor said it was probably gallstones and gave her Vicodin. Her husband begged them to treat her but it must have been a busy night, everyone knows how the triage thing goes. The guy was so frustrated he actually called 911. When they asked for the address, the poor schmuck told them they were in the waiting room of the King-Harbor ER. Bud heard the tape on a website; the dispatcher couldn't wrap her head around him calling from a *hospital*, you know, it was like, what a dorkus! Somebody call *America's Funniest 911s*! Of course, she said there was no *way* they could send paramedics to an ER . . . a security camera captured everything, she falls off her seat half-conscious, puking feces, and the janitor comes and just mops up around her like in a silent film! Meanwhile, the zeppelin's exploding through the sluice ("O, the humanity!"), a razored bowling ball of rockhard shit slipping the surly bonds of bowel to touch the face of God and waxed linoleum. The hour-long footage got *leaked*—another soupçon offering to the webgods, to the daily unquenchable fatal reality show planet. The woman had three kids, and mischievous hackerh8trs spammed their emails with mash-ups of Mom seizing on the floor, adding *Blair Witch* screams & Howard Stern farts.

.   .   .

It took a few days for Bud to connect with his agent. He had called right after listening to the message at the end of the Steve Martin event—it was already 9:30. Sometimes the assistants were still working late, but not *that* late; he left word. It felt good to say, "Bud Wiggins, returning."

Bud had made a study of his rise and fall in the Business, by virtue of the way the assistants addressed him. When he was at his hottest as a Hollywood screenwriter, he'd call and get, "O hi, Bud! He's *just* finishing a call but I know he *really* wants to talk to you. Can you hold? Oh—wait, he's just wrapping up!" (Which meant the agent was *physically gesturing* to the assistant *not to lose Bud*.) "Okay! I'm putting you through . . ." It wasn't unusual—back then—for the excited agent to hop on before the assistant even finished talking. But as the workless months dropped from the calendar like dead leaves falling, the assistants stopped using his name. It became "Hi" or "Oh hi," the personal touch gone. The agent would invariably be on a conference call (the quaint, pre-wired era when conference calls denoted power and status) and they'd put Bud on hold for *long* fucking minutes. Then, "It looks like it's going to be a while, can I have him return?" In the years that followed, they'd put Bud on hold and wouldn't come back to check with him at all . . . after a few minutes of holding the Void to his ear, they'd pierce the silence with an angry, clinical slap: *He'll have to call you back.* The days of unquiet desperation had begun. Somewhere near the fin de siècle, a new idiom was born—Bud found himself awash in a sea of "I don't have hims." Depending on one's status or the assistant's disposition, he or she might choose to customize and embellish, such as, "You know right now I *actually* don't have him . . . can he return?" (If you had *some* heat, they had a wink in their voice one could translate as seductive.) As time went on & Bud got colder (if a frozen corpse possibly could), the "actually" became a curt *I don't have him* until one day, all that was left was the lightspeed *He's not available*—no flirty apologies, only barely suppressed, deadened annoyance: end of the line.

Agents were usually in early, and when Bud hadn't heard back by 10 A.M., he decided to call in. Who knew, maybe the voicemail wasn't working or whatever.

"Bud Wiggins, returning."

The assistant was cheerful enough. The new hires gave you the least amount of shit. They didn't know who the losers were.

"Bud, I'm putting you through to Chris."

His gut flipped.

"Hey, Bud! How are you?"

"I'm good, Chris. How are they treating you?"

"Well. Very well. Life is good. I'm gonna have to jump, but here's why I'm calling. I got a call from Rod Fulbright, at CAA. David Simon's doing a new series about Hollywood and wants to meet with you."

"Who's David Simon?"

"*The Wire*. And *Treme*. He's a very talented guy, but not our client. So *call* him—call Rod—tell him that we spoke, and he'll give you the information."

"Why does David Simon want to talk to me?"

"It's probably about the Hollywood show. Maybe he wants you to work on it. I really have to jump."

"Chris, it doesn't make sense—I mean, it's *great*, but——"

"Oh—do you know Michael Tolkin?"

"Sure I know Michael."

"That's it then, I forgot, sorry about that. David got your name through Michael. Michael's executive producing."

"Oh. Okay."

"Call Rod."

. . .

He knew Tolkin from gradeschool.

Thirty years ago, when Bud self-published his book of short stories about wash-ups in the Business, for a brief moment he was the toast of the town. He remembered Tolkin coming up to him at a party and saying, "I really think you're onto something there." Over the months that followed, there was a lot of interest in Bud writing the screenplay: Oliver Stone, Barry Levinson, Bob Altman. Altman had supposedly considered adapting the book himself but decided to make *The Player* instead.

Bud called Rod, but only spoke to his assistant. Xochilt said the meeting with David Simon was set for next week, a Thursday, at one o'clock, at the Polo Lounge.

"Rod asked me to pass this along," she said. "When David talks about *The Wire*, he refers to it as a *novel*."

"You mean it's based on a novel?"

"I'm actually not sure. I can get back to you on that. But apparently when David discusses it, he prefers to call it a novel instead of a series. You should do the same. OK?"

"Perfect."

He thought he should probably call Tolkin. They'd been out of touch; he could get his number through the agency. He watched the pilot of *The Wire* on his computer then lay down to ponder the plot of his own work-in-progress. *Though maybe I should call my novel a cable series,* he thought, almost cracking himself up.

Thursday, 1PM, the Polo Lounge . . . back in the game.

He treated himself to 6 Norcos and 6 klonopins, in celebration. He was in his bedroom, but heard his mother singing a childhood song. Her voice carried over the baby monitors her caregivers had placed in the living room and kitchen.

Bud pictured himself in one of the storied booths of the fabled pink palace, & said a recently youtubed Gleason line outloud:

Howwwwwwwww sweet it is!

[Jacquie]

Seared

She

got lucky with the Sears job because it wasn't a slamdunk, not even close, especially not at her age. But there she was, amidst the dolorous big box retail funk—the perfect storm of 3 (count em) *just-fired* employees + a gay manager who was way into her from the presentation/gate . . . during the interview she charmed by reminiscing about those adolescent darkroom days plus *very carefully* alluding to perhaps being a bit overqualified, not of course summoning googleable glory days but rather pulling a few savvy foto technique remarks out of the hat, simple but effective enough (she hoped) to seal the deal. She was mindful to keep her comments modest and leave her ego out of it, which was hard, *is* hard, & kept reminding herself she was on a down-low mission from the muses. To offset any potential Brahmin vibe/takeaway, Jacquie humbly stressed that she was super-trainable (knowing that training was always management's bane), even tho probably just an hour's tutelage on the machines would do—i.e. the girl was camera-ready. And she flirted a little the way fag hags do: those superheated moments in the early stages of any wild, drama-strewn romance between a gay man and hetero woman. All's fair in art and war, & the art of war too.

She just wanted to get hired.

.   .   .

Moms brought their babies—lots of baby portraits. (Everything was called *portraits* and *portraiture*.) Family pets even. On Saturdays, families came in for their formal sittings. On Sundays, they came after church, & Jacquie got that feeling of real Americana. She thought, in 100 years, her work would be featured at flea markets & yard sales, anon family portraits, circa early 21st-century. Young couples sauntered in, cholos & cholitas, fewer though than Jacquie would have thought. They were almost always at the store shopping for something else. They'd pass the photo studio & the girl would get the idea and not let it go until her boyfriend caved.

The manager was one of those dream homos—shockingly ascerbic, hilariously brilliant, borderline heartbreaking homely. Shaved head, big butt, tender heart. ("I cry at the drop of a pillbox hat," he told her. "Make that an *Isabella Blow* hat.") They began to lunch together in the mall, telling stories from their lives, stock shards & bravura fragments typically kept on reserve for a crush, or a simpatico new acquaintance; the broken pieces soon conflating into the unwashed picture windows & stained glass one risks sharing with a veritable new friend. Such as: before coming to Sears, Albie worked for an online company that turned photo submissions of pets/family into large, hangable prints in the style of Warhol & Lichtenstein. Such as, he spoke reasonably fluent Japanese, courtesy of an older man who took Albie as a lover when he was just 14. (They were together 10 years.) He was 38 now, & a widower. His husband Francesco recently died of AIDS, & Francesco's grandmother was a famous black panther, which Albie thought ironic, in that Francesco was an albino. (Albie honed and exploited the albino–Black Panther routine through the years to great comic effect.) Albie was HIV-positive himself, coming up on 23 years . . .

Fragments & shards.

Jacquie came clean, telling him the whole certiwikifiable truth &

nothing but, ending with the confession that once upon a time she was a celestial body (but no more), one of those shooting stars fated to arc across diurnal skies, consigned to perpetual underexposure. Albie surprised her by saying that he already knew, because he was required to websearch all job applicants. "There was something *about* you," he added. "You remind me of Anne Sexton! But I'd have looked you up *anyway*. I look *everyone* up."

Of course he does. Because that's what people do—they look you up. Everyone looks everyone up, that's what *she* should start doing.

No—too late.

Suddenly, Jacquie felt old, uncertain, unsophisticated.

Undernourished, underwater, underexposed.

Washed up & washed down.

That most pitiable thing:

A performance artist without a concept.

. . . menopausal Sears employee.

A familiar fog rolled in & clung to her coast.

·   ·   ·

—I got your note. And I'm sorry that I haven't been more present.

—That's OK.

—No, it isn't. Because we have a lot to talk about. First of all, how are you?

—Fine.

—Are you really?

—Yeah—why . . .

—You're going through changes in your body. Any changes in your head?

—Like what?

—I don't know. It's not my head.

—Sometimes I feel really *sad*. Then sometimes like I am *so happy*. That I'm going to have this baby. & being a mother scares me? But I think it's something I'll be really good at?

—(*Smiles*) Is that a question?

—(*Smiles*) No. It's a statement? (*They laugh*) It's a *statement*.

—I got a call from—is it Eliza? Hirschorn?

—The social worker.

—Is she the one who works with all the parents? Of the girls who are expecting?

—Uh huh. She's really nice. I mean *really* nice.

—Good, good, that's great. How many girls over there are expecting?

—Just Marisol. She's six months . . . last year there was I think three. No! Four. Yeah there were four. Remember Toleda?

—From Salvador? Those big green eyes? What happened to her?

—She had a little girl, I think. No! A little boy. She went back. To Salvador.

—I talked to Rikki's dad.

—You *did*?

—We've had *several* conversations. I'm off tomorrow, and we're having lunch.

—Cool. Is his mom going?

—I don't know. I don't think so.

—How's Rikki.

—He's good.

—Can you bring him by this weekend? For lunch? Because now he is *definitely* in my life! I want to know him. We've hardly had a conversation. Is he smart? His father's smart.

—O my god, Rikki is *so smart*.

—Not that it's a prerequisite . . . it's all about the heart. Does he have a good heart? Is he a good man?

—He's got a *really* big heart. O my god, he is *so generous*.

—Terrific.

—So how's it going? I mean work.

—Fine. Work is fine. Your note said you wanted to talk.

—Okay. I—yeah. I wanted—

—Sorry to interrupt but are you going to tell your father?

—I guess. Maybe. You mean, now?

—Yes, I mean now. Have you thought about it?

—Kind of. It's not like he—I haven't talked to him in like, 3 months.

—You do what you need to do. I'm not advocating either way, but that's his grandchild. If I talk to him, I certainly won't discuss it without your permission.

—Oh my god, please don't!

—OK, I'm done.

—Mama, I wanted to ask you . . . it's just something—you know, we can talk about it another time.

—What is it? (Reeyonna looks down at carpet/stressed out) Jerilynn? What's going on?

—Well I've been thinking. I've been doing a lot of thinking, &—I've been thinking about how we're going to *live*, Rikki and I, when, when the baby's born. You know, where we're going to *live*———

—(*Doesn't know where this is going*) Okay?

—& I thought we could get an apartment, we could get an apartment that's like really close, or not too far away . . . .

—You're going to need *a lot of help*, Jerilynn, I don't think you *realize*———

—. . . . . . . because if I just keep living here & Rikki keeps staying at his house, I *totally know* what's going to happen from watching all those *Teen Mom* shows—————

—You're *you,* Jerilynn, you're *not* a TV show.

—They're *reality* shows. They show what—what happens—what *can* happen. In *reality.* And it's because they stay at *home* and are dependant on their *moms.* There's, like, no *consequences.*

—Well, I think it's good you're having these thoughts, but—

—I just think it will be *so much better* if we live in an apartment.

—And how do you expect to pay for that? Is Rikki working? Are his parents going to give you money?

−I don't *think* so.

−And I don't have it, Jerilynn, I just don't have it. I'm working at Sears! I think it's a sweet—it's a good idea, I mean it's *sound*, but there's—the baby is *already* going to be a big expense. The baby is a *hardship*. You really need to start to realize. There are *diapers*, there—

−I know! And I don't—I wasn't going to *ask* you for any money. I want to use my *own* money.

−(*A kind of crazy look*) Your own money?

−From my trust.

−What do you mean trust?

−For the money. For the pictures—

−What pictures—

−The ones you *took*. Of *me*. The *photographs*. Remember when you said you were going to put money away? Because you said you wanted me to *benefit*? You said you wanted me to *benefit* from your work—

−Oh. Yeah. OK. Okay—this—this is . . . .

−I'm not *asking* for your money. I'm not asking for anyone's money but my *own*. And I know I might not be able to have it until I'm 21 or 18, legally or whatever, but what I wanted to ask you was if you— if they—the bank or whomever—if they could give me my money *early* because of my—because of my *circumstances*. I can even help *you* with it, I mean, if you need money, so you don't have to work at Sears anymore, it would take off *such* a burden from everyone's shoul- ders . . . or I can even take *part* of, like, whatever it is, I could take just like 125,000 or even a hundred—

−(*Trancelike*) A hundred and twenty-five thousand . . .

−Mom, I don't *care* what it is, you can release to me *whatever*, it'll just make things so much *easier*—I mean, so people—you & Rikki's parents—so no one has to *worry* . . .

−Jerilynn, I want you to listen to me. I want you to hear this. I really want you to hear this. For a lot of years, I raised you and your brother alone. Your father gave me money for a while & then that stopped. And I was desperate. I was very, very depressed. I felt like the world passed me by. It's a terrible feeling to have. I started taking pictures again because it was the only thing that stopped me from spiraling down. I started taking pictures of *you* because you were my light, my little faerie, my little blond angel. I had *no idea* anyone would be interested in those photographs. Because they were really just for me. Are you listening? *Because I really want you to listen, Jerilynn, you really need to listen.* I was absolutely—I couldn't believe they got so much attention, even acclaim. And it allowed me to begin a new life, it let *us* begin a new life. But what you need to know is that I did not become rich. Not me, not the galleries, not anybody. It was more—it's like my career has been more— more a *cause célèbre* than anything else. Do you know what a *cause célèbre* is, Jerilynn? It's when something's *controversial* but not necessarily *profitable*. You know, so I traveled to England to show my work, to *tremendous* expense, & everywhere we went—it wasn't cheap bringing you on these trips, that's why I had your brother stay with Ronny in NY—there were always these little *tempests* when I showed my work, & it seemed that as long as the pictures were *controversial*, people were more apt to buy. They sold for twenty-five hundred up to $12,000. We didn't sell too many $12,000 ones, we sold a lot in the midrange & even more in the lower, the lower prices. And the galleries took 50%. *50% . . .*

–If what you're saying is there's less of the money left, I already told you that's OK, because—

–I didn't *have* to put you in a private school, but I *did*. Do you know how much New Crossroads cost? $23,000 *a year*. For a 12-year-old!—

–Mom, it doesn't matter, I'll just take whatever's there—

–Jerilynn, I don't even remember, but that's not—

–You don't remember how much is there? In the trust?

–I don't remember . . . *promising* that—because I knew what our *situation* was. But that I don't remember isn't the point—I'll take your word for it, & it *does* sound like something I would have definitely wanted to do if I could—

–There isn't any money?

–Jerilynn, I'll go over my bank statements with you, I'll have the *accountant* go over them with you. Right now, I'm carrying $90,000 in credit card debt.

–O my god. You totally lied. You totally scammed your own daughter . . . .

–Jerilynn—

–O my god, I *hate* you————

–That isn't fair. Apparently, you weren't listening when— (*Reeyonna starts to SCREAM*) Jerilynn—Jerilynn, *stop*. Stop!

–You *piece of shit! You stole money from me!*

–I didn't st—

–My own mother actually stole money from me! O my god! O my god— *———I want you to DIE, you BITCH! I want you to DIE! You piece of shit bitch! You will NEVER see your grandchild EVER I would NEVER let you see her even if I had a MILLION DOLLARS! I would never let you see her because you are so SICK, you are so FUCKING SICK that you would probably take NUDE PICTURES of it & try to SELL them on the INTERNET! because you're CRAZY you're CRAZY you're a fucking SICK CRAZY SLUT & I fucking HATE YOU! You are the biggest WHORE, you always make a FOOL out of yourself Steve Martin was LAUGHING at you & James Franco wanted to fuck ME not YOU even tho he could tell you were a fucking OLD WHORE! [sustained screams, then] YOU FUCKING FUCKING FUCKING PIECE OF SHIT [a sustained scream, then] you should just DIE why don't you go somewhere and DIE you are the WORST & the SICKEST you have NO TALENT and everyone thinks you're CRAZY they KNOW you are no one even wants to be SEEN with you all you have is how SICK you are, you are the WORST MOTHER, O my god I would rather be ADOPTED like RIKKI than have YOU as a MOTHER! You will NEVER meet my baby, you will go to your grave without seeing my baby & when my baby is older I will tell him*

that his grandma was a SICK PIECE OF SHIT and how HAPPY he should be that you never held him—you will NEVER EVER EVER hold him, do you understand? Are you listening? You better! You better! Because you ARE A SICK FUCKING WHORE AND I HOPE YOU DIE! I HOPE YOU DIE! I HOPE YOU DIE!!!!!!!!!!!!!!!!!!!!!!!!!!!!!

2nd

Trimester

CAA

(Afternoon/Dusk)

Afternoon is the time of Woman: *the Unknown*

Io ritornai da la santissima onda

Rifatto sì come piante novelle

Rinovellate di novella fronda,

puro e disposto a salire a le **stelle**.
— P U R G A T O R I O, XXXIII. 142–5

Dancing With The Stars

He

was in LA, in preproduction on a film. Catherine was shooting a Fosse-themed *Glee*. Ryan told him that a guest stint by Catherine had been in play long before Michael sent his fan letter.

Karma.

.   .   .

He met the little cancer gal & her mom for tea at the Peninsula.

Then he did something that surprised him.

Michael told the driver to take him to the little cemetery in West-wood where his half-brother was buried. (He didn't question his instincts anymore.) Anyway, now was as good a time as any to pay his respects to the dead; he wasn't able to make the Reaper's recent gala, and had respectfully RSVP'd his regrets. He'd be attending soon enough.

The actor's asst called the park to make sure he wouldn't be disrupting a funeral by his presence. The coast was clear. A caretaker met him at the car & walked him to Eric's flat stone. The mood of that shitty day—Eric's funeral—washed over him. He knelt a moment, running a finger over the grass on the grave.

The actor meandered through the modestly-scaled tombs. It felt like a minefield. He stepped over, around & in-between the engraved invitations in a superstitious foxtrot (or minuet, holding Death's hand like a child without knowing it), which was more or less what he'd done with cancer—with sure foot and unwavering eye, he picked his way through the cellsplitting grunge & muck that tried to abduct and to claim him, to snatch him back whence he came like an incensed parent denied custody. The fuckers on the Internet who laid virtual money that his time was nigh had already lost their shirts. He felt like Keith Richards. He'd outlive all the jackals, & have kicks along the way.

Everyone knew that Marilyn was buried here but as he walked and surveyed, the profusion of showbiz dead surprised him. His dad's time was well-represented: Malden & Matthau, Leigh, Lancaster, Lemmon. The manicured morgue was as eclectic as a guest list off the old *Tonight Show*—Capote, Coburn, Cassavetes—Gene Kelly, Don Knotts, Merv. Dominick Dunne's murdered daughter was here and he wondered why Nick buried himself in Connecticut instead of with his child. Michael couldn't bear the thought of being separated from his children, even in death. He shook his head at the Zappa & Joplin markers . . . *unfuckingreal.*

He soft-shoed between Natalie Wood and Billy Wilder, suddenly standing over Farrah. That was a tough death. It was one thing to go on Letterman and tell the world the cat got your tongue, & entirely another to announce the cat crawled up your ass and died and was taking you with it. In those first frightening months, MD thought of her a lot. He watched her documentary—all in all, a damn brave girl. Hella courage. And to have them film you like that, hella courage all around. He remembered something a friend said when the family was vacationing in Fiji. They were floating in a coral reef when a small, black&white-banded snake swam between his legs and disappeared. His buddy told him it was poisonous but not to worry, it had no interest in human beings. Michael asked where the hospital was, if you happened to get bit. "You could drive to the clinic in town," he answered, "but I wouldn't recommend it. It wouldn't be the best use of the hour you had left."

MD wondered how he'd behave in the face of losing numbers: that was the real *Hitch-22*. (Jesus, losing Christopher was a loss. What giantsized balls the man had.) He knew the producer in him—the warrior—would never want to concede, but the actor just might . . . He agonized over the question: When do you stop NetJetting to clinics in Switzerland, South Africa, Brazil for experimental treatment? When the only result is twitter rape, videos of your emaciated bodyhusk struggling in and out of vans, your haunted, anguished huffin and puffin visage HuffPosted to the world. Ryan O'Neal had stayed by her side, steadfast & true. MD laughed a little, thinking: he won't be by *my* side, least not if I can help it. There were so many things you'd lose control of once you crossed a certain threshold . . . Ryan had leukemia himself, for the last ten years, same type Ali had in *Love Story*. And now he's got prostate. It's Cancer's world, we just live in it. At least Ryan was still alive. Wasn't he?

He headed toward the car, pausing at another stone:

DOROTHY STRATTEN

FEBRUARY 28, 1960–AUGUST 14, 1980
IF PEOPLE BRING SO MUCH COURAGE TO THIS WORLD
THE WORLD HAS TO KILL THEM TO BREAK THEM, *SO*
OF COURSE IT KILLS THEM . . . IT KILLS THE VERY GOOD
AND THE VERY GENTLE AND THE VERY BRAVE IMPARTIALLY.
IF YOU ARE NONE OF THESE YOU CAN BE SURE THAT IT
WILL KILL YOU TOO BUT THERE WILL BE NO SPECIAL HURRY
WE LOVE YOU DR

Strange. He wondered if the mom had written it. Maybe. In a raging delirium of grief, no doubt.

Star 80 was probably Fosse's best film. His most *director*-like film, anyway.

She was only twenty. *Star 20* . . . .

Some were made like his dad, royal tortoises mobb deep in guardian angels, while others breathed ICU nursery O_2-tank air for a few
mayfly minutes before expiration.

One needn't be a philosopher to grasp the insignificance of tem-
poral goings-on; one needn't even be pretentious (tho sometimes
that helped). In the design of things, there was utterly no signifi-
cance in whether you lived an hour, a year or a hundred years—the
span of human life was cloud graffiti. Michael couldn't remember
the context, but one of his doctors in Montreal used a wonderful
word, *blessure*, which meant injury to tissue, a break in the skin.
(The actor rearranged it in his head as "surely blessed.") Last night
as he fell asleep, he meditated. If every soul who'd ever lived and
died on Earth—Yahoo! put it just over 100 billion—were to suddenly manifest & vaporize, the Unknown* would have no more
awareness of the thunderous lamentations accompanying their collective outgoing breath than an insect would have knowledge of a
microblog devoted to its industrious ways. The unfathomable ces-
sation would incur no celestial *blessure*, the Ineffable not suffer
the slightest bruising whatsoever. Something he read in his college days at UC Santa Barbara stayed with him all these years,
something one *did* have to be a philosopher to have said, or a
philosopher-poet, anyway. "Life is the rarest form of death." Wasn't
that wild? The old joke of life being a near-death experience. Was
that George Carlin? Or Mr. Nietzsche?

MD came out the other side of his catastrophe with the firm belief
that cancer was his teacher. Cancer had urged him to accept (or die
trying) earthly life for the dream it was—*fleeting*, as they say, tho such
a perception seemed impossible to achieve (if one could call it an
achievement) for anyone but saints, idiots & visionaries. Yet since the
diagnosis, he strove to live in that blissful, acquiescent state, that un-
reachable cliché of *presence in the moment*, yes, in *this* moment, not
moments past or moments to come. This moment was all he had. In

---

* He went on a "Rapture" site recently, out of curiosity. It said that the ascension to the Heavens
would come at dusk, or the late afternoon.

this moment, he was alive & cancer-free. In this moment, from a cemetery, he conjured his wife, beckoning. In this moment, he could see his children crying, laughing, sleeping. In this moment, he had more money than he could spend in a hundred lifetimes.

By the time a too-close bird ended his train of thought, the actor's tour was almost done. It wouldn't have been complete without Marilyn.

The plaque on the drawer of the cinerarium bore only her name, and the year of birth & death. Thirty-six years-old at the age of *blessure* . . . A long time ago, a businessman bought the space right above her. He told his wife to make sure they buried him facedown, in the missionary position—just for the kamikaze cosmo-comic eterno-skeleto-fuck jokey thrill of it—an inspired wish that his widow evidently wryly carried out. Then bogeyman Madoff swindled her and she had to auction off the spectral fuckpad penthouse, she got five million for it (if memory served) & buried him elsewhere—exhumation *in flagrante postmortem delicto*. It was common pop-cult knowledge that's where Hef was going, years ago he bought the crib beneath Monroe, so he could properly stick his candle in the wind. Karma was a funny thing: Norma Jean was molested as a child, & she'd be molested in the afterlife. It was ironic too that Dorothy Stratten always wanted to hang at the Playboy Mansion; now, Marilyn and Hef would be partying, with Dorothy just outside the gate, for all eternity.

The Wheel of Karma kept on turning.

MD understood those people who thought burial was for squares, for whom *cremation* was the magic word—to be sprinkled here & there, over the ground or into the wind & water of a place one loved. He understood the feelings of those who were stingy/proprietary about recycling theirs or loved ones' organs, even those who thought there might be bad voodoo in signing the donor's form on the back of a driver's license. He *understood* how a person could feel in their untransplanted heart that mutilation—that posthumously violent, non-consensual *blessure*—regardless of the alleviation of the suffering of the living, just wasn't the way to go.

He didn't care about any of that now. They could scoop his eyes & pluck his corneas, whittle his kidneys, grand theft his thorax, fry up his liver, & harvest his skin on a special edition of Piers Morgan. They could tear off cock&balls at the root and laminate them for teaching hospitals. They could feed him to the dogs & piss on him, because by then his soul would be in another dream.

He was over it.

[Gwen]

Ctrl + Z

Tea

with Michael Douglas was heaven.

Gwen was on Cloud 9, she'd had a crush on him forever. Telma wore her new Marc Jacobs dress and was so excited that getting a part on *Glee* was hardly discussed, even though she couldn't *believe* his wife was actually *guest-starring*. OMG! It was all so adorable, watching her daughter interact with the legendary star, & Gwen thought he couldn't have been more charming. Sylvester Stallone, Tilda Swinton & L.A. Reid were in different parts of the sunlit room having tea. It was beyond beyond.

When Telma got her diagnosis, a few people told Gwen that cancer was a gift. She wanted to strangle them, but now she understood.

·   ·   ·

A few days later, she got a call from an attorney who said he represented St. Ambrose. He wanted to talk; when Gwen pressed what for, he said it was a matter best discussed in person.

Century City was walkable from the house. The request for a rendezvous was strange and slightly mysterious. On the stroll over, she had fleeting, preposterous fantasies of why she'd been *summoned*. She had a feeling it was a good thing.

That feeling changed when Dr. Bessowichte entered the conference room. After a cold, rabbity greeting—no shake of her hand—his wan smile withdrew, skittering under a rock. "Dr. B" (St. Ambrose happened to be the patron saint of bees & beekeepers, and schoolchildren too) had been with them from the beginning, right there in the trenches. He was the *ex officio* tsar of Telma's Troopers, whose equanimity & genius for decision-making sustained them through all manner of bloody, crazy-making stratagems, artifices & bombardments of the cancer wars. In Gwen's eyes, he was the single person most responsible for having saved her daughter's life. He never retreated, not once. He was part of their family.

Something awful had happened . . . it came to her head that he was going to announce that he was sick, that he was going to die. But why wouldn't he call or just come to the house? Why wouldn't his wife Ruth have called? They could have asked her over to *their* house—they were all that close, it was that kind of bond.

Why would a *lawyer* call with that kind of news?

Nothing she came up with in a handful of seconds made any sense.

"What is it?" said Gwen. She was trembling now. "What's wrong?"

A sudden, monstrous shift within, as she thought the unthinkable.

"It's Telma . . . is it Telma? Did the cancer come back?"

But if it did, why are we here in Century City, why aren't we at the hospital, why aren't——————————

An attorney began to speak (there were 3 in the room), but Gwen stopped the world by imploring Dr. B with a beggar's brutalized eyes.

"No—no! Nothing like that," said the doc.

The eldest lawyer spoke up.

"Thank you for coming."

What? He's thanking me? Why he is——————

"I won't sugarcoat it, Mrs. Ballendyne"——*Mrs. Ballendyne? Huh?*——"this isn't going to be one of your best hours. And it's certainly not—not one of the hospital's finest. Dr. Bessowichte will be the first to tell you that."

Though it wasn't a cue for him to speak, the restless doctor squirmed & broke free of the muzzle.

"I wanted to come to the house, Gwen. I wanted to tell you at the house but they said no, that wasn't a good idea—the hospital forbade me. I didn't want to listen." He sighed, and repeated, "I didn't want to listen."

Gwen felt like she was watching a play.

"What is it, Donald, what's happened?"

He didn't seem to hear her.

"They tied my hands, Gwen—"

"What are you saying?"

"It has been a nightmare. Not just for me, but the other doctors on the team. On Telma's team . . ."

"GODDAMMIT, DONALD, you tell me what you're talking about & YOU TELL ME NOW."

Two of the lawyers spoke up.

She turned to them with ferocity.

"No! Don't talk! HE talks! Only HE talks."

"There was an error," said Dr. B. "A series of errors. 1 in 10,000,000. And I can walk you through it, when it's time. We have already constructed a *very specific timeline* of events."

He paused.

The air was brittle, frozen.

Everything got bigger and smaller (for Gwen), all at once.

"Gwen . . . Telma doesn't have cancer. She never did."

(*Almost inaudibly*)

(*As if jarred from a private thought*)

"What?"

"There was a mistake—a *series* of freak mistakes & *switch-ups*, on the clinical & the—on all levels."

"You're telling me that my baby never had cancer?"

"That's right," said the eldest lawyer, gingerly stepping in. "It is a *terrible, tragic event* based on both *human and machine error*. The hospital is heavily insured for this sort of—"

"*This sort of thing?*" railed the doctor at the men, as if suddenly, in the play, taking the rôle of the injured mother. "This sort of thing? *This sort of thing?* I don't think you *understand!*"

He pivoted toward Gwen in mid-monologue, as if to show her how eager he was to give voice to injustice, thus lending *her* a voice, until her own did come. As if seeking support for any effort he would make to redeem himself. As if asking forgiveness.

"'*This sort of thing' just doesn't happen*, it doesn't happen! In 45 *years*, I've never seen it—never! *Never.*"

Indeed, with this last word, this remark, the ruined doctor spoke as if it *hadn't*, that what they were discussing was a thing so far outside his and any other practitioner's realm of possibility and experience that it would, with calmer heads, inevitably be acknowledged even by the most aggrieved parties as the supernaturally statistical anomaly that it was; and that Dr. Bessowichte (& Team Telma) could not, in the end, have had any way of avoiding its preordained inevitability . . . for a few tortuous moments, the defenseless, prideful physician, himself mutilated, freefloated in a sphere beyond denial, speaking from his ethical, frightened ♥ no longer as a preacher but as a child who wishes to *think back together* something precious they had dropped and broken.

"O God. O my God!"

Someone pushed a box of Kleenex at her.

Dr. B stiffened, bracing for blows, & the dangerous pelting hail of oncoming tears.

"Gwen, I'm so sorry—"

"Then what *did* she have?" She wasn't fully comprehending. "If she didn't have it, what *did* she have?"

"Something that *looked* like cancer," said the doctor. He leaned bravely in, for the first time. "It's not simple—"

"Not *simple* . . . ."

"Gwen, I don't know how to express in words how sorry——————"

"You're *SORRY.* You're SORRY!—*O my God my God my God.* What am I supposed to do? How can I——*what am i o what am i supposed to do to do o what o what what am i——————*"

(*Her lamentations directed to the ether*)

"First, you get a lawyer," said the eldest partner. "There are a half-dozen the firm can recommend, all the best at what they do—medical malpractice. Until you're represented, we ask that you keep what we've shared today in confidence. Disclosure at this juncture would potentially do both you and the hospital great harm."

Dr. B, patron saint of bees & schoolchildren, of candlemakers, chandlers, & domestic animals, buried, as they say, his head in his hands.

"Great harm?" she said.

She stood, unwell.

The doctor rose along with her out of sheer clinical reflex, seeing/sensing even in his periphery that she was unsteady, she looked ill, she was a wounded human being, it did not matter that he had been her assailant, he was still a healer, by definition & by oath. In medical school they taught that *given an existing problem, it may be better to do nothing, than to risk causing more harm——————————*She went flush, she had no rage, no stratagems, no emotions. They tried getting her to sit back————————*primum nil nocere* . . . . *doctrine & principal of nonmaleficence reminding the physician he must consider the possible harm an intervention might do——————————* down, they tried giving her water, they tried to comfort. She struggled to keep the vomit from rising. They gave her a box of Kleenex that sat in her limp arms, her eyes like smidged window-panes————————*may thy rod & thy staff comfort you, rod of Asclepius, ancient symbol of medicine & healing, Hippocrates himself a worshipper of Asclepius—————————————ἐπὶ δηλήσει δὲ καὶ* ἀδικίη εἴρξειν/ἀσκέειν, περὶ τὰ νουσήματα, δύο, ὠφελέειν, ἢ μὴ βλάπτειν————————————————and all she could do was

send Telma for a sleepover at her grandma's. Of course not telling the grandma/her mother, telling her mother instead that a friend of hers had an emergency, her friend from Ojai, which friend asked her mother, what do you mean which friend, my friend from Ojai, my Ojai friend said Gwen, & I may be out of touch for a few days. It's an emergency, a family emergency, no she's fine, yes, it's marital trouble, yes, no I'll be fine. She took three 100-mg pills from an old bottle of Seroquel. She hadn't walloped herself w/Seroquel since the early days of Telma's surgery/recovery. She slept 16 hours & upon awakening, was curious to note she had no recollection of how she got home from that nightmare meeting.   .

It took her a while to replay the Century City horror film, which she did for about an hour, & then the phone rang.

If it was Dr. Bessowichte, she was going to hang up.

If it was a wrong #, she was going to blurt it all out.

If it was Mom, she was going to ask her to keep Telma another day. She wouldn't tell her what was going on, wouldn't even tell Phoebe, not yet. (Maybe Phoebe.) (But not yet.) She wouldn't tell anyone, how could she? She wasn't even sure she'd told herself.

"May I speak to Ms. Ballendyne?"

If it was Jenny Craig, she was going to blurt it all out. If it was Mary Kay, she was going to blurt it all out. If it was ProActiv, she was going to blurt it all out.

"This is she."

"Great! I'm Beth, Ryan Murphy's assistant, and the reason I'm calling is that Ryan wanted to know if you and your daughter would enjoy being *VIP guests* for a taping of the show! He's heard *so much* about Telma—from *Michael Douglas*—and is *very* excited to meet her."

Enjoy. Being VIPs. Yes we would.

"Thank you. Yes."

"Great! And I know that Ryan wanted to make sure both of you came for lunch with the cast and crew! Are there any days that are better for you than others?"

[Telma]

Brittelma

She

started "journaling" (the word that her therapists used) a few years before she got cancer. Telma wrote all thru pre- & post-surgical times, darkest times, and was determined to publish an edited version one day called *Diary of A Kancer Kid*. Everyone on the ped/oink ward kept journals, the on-ward psychologists encouraged them to write down their hopes & dreams, their fears & affirmations. Some of the pages of her notebooks were crinkly from dried tears—she hoped when it got published, a photo of one of those pages could be included. She knew it would be a bestseller, & was currently mad at herself for dropping the ball. It was too late to go on Oprah anymore.

When Telma got diagnosed, Phoebe, her outside shrink, asked her to pick a magic number. (Phoebe as opposed to Samuel, her ward shrink. She loved Samuel but loved Phoebe more.) When Telma picked 16—which was perfect because she watched *My Super Sweet 16* marathons on the weekends & was currently obsessing about her own Super Sweet 16 to come—Phoebe said to write an affirmation 16 times a day, and to go ahead & say each affirmation *outloud* 32 times a day, for good measure. Phoebe told her to pick a few, and write them down, but *not* say them outloud, to keep the affirmation a secret so it didn't lose its power, Super Sweet 16 Secret power affirmations were FOR TELMA ONLY, Telma and her diary, she wasn't even supposed to tell Phoebe. She wrote *KANCER-FREE* 16 times & *HERVIVOR!!!* 16 times (shouting them aloud as well) & wrote ~~VICTIM VICTIM VICTIM~~ (as in, NOT) 16 times (shouting *"NOT* a victim! *NOT* a victim!"), she wacky-scrawled affirmations & fancy penmanshipped declarations to the world 16 times a day, every morning, afternoon & evening, and sometimes even before going to bed at night. That's why she was in the middle of Journal #21, and the notebooks weren't thin either, they were thick, & lined.

Telma wrote about her dreams and her pets—like her fish Goldie & her parrot Mighty Man, & Sir Vivor, the cantankerous terrier, a tire-chaser who lost a leg as a result of his passion. Depending on what side of the bed he woke up on, Sir Vivor would accompany her on St. Ambrose "rounds." (When the fellow was obstreperous she had to leave him home because the hospital said there were liability issues if he bit a nurse or even one of the kids.) She wrote about her crushes too—currently, Biggie was looming *large,* though as yet had only bashfully been apportioned a few lines—and poems & little sto-ries/lyrics of songs (with affirmations in-between), and *original* songs too.

She wrote down her *Glee* fantasy, & didn't show it to her mom. She wasn't even going to share it with Phoebe (not yet), so it wouldn't lose its power:

When we arrive, the Oscar Awardwinning Mr. MICHAEL DOUG-LAS is waving, he's been waiting for me and my mom at the 20th-Century Fox Studio gate, which happens by an unusal twisting of fate to be only a few miles from where we make our home in Cheviot Hills. MICHAEL DOUG-LAS is sitting looking very handsome with that winning rogueish smile in one of those golfcarts with a canopey & wants me to come with him. Which of course I really do & yet I do not wish to be rude & leave my mom all alone there, but then my mom said to Mr. Douglas, "Why of COURSE she may go with you, let me simply park our car & meet you both 'on set.'" And off we go!!!

Weaving throughout the backlot streets (NOT "of San Francisco"!) The golfcart happens to have a bag of In-and-Out burgers fries & milkshakes that MICHAEL DOUGLAS has so kindly arranged to be on a nice tray and ready for consumptchion. "Dr. House," from the smash television show "House" waves to Michael & I as we zip past, shouting to Michael that he is a very big fan. I take this oportunity to wave back, & I can distinctly over-hear Dr. House whisper to someone next to him, "I do not know who she is, but I can simply tell you that I know she will one day be a huge star." It is only then that Michael informs me as we zip away that the gentleman Dr. House was whispering to was none other than Mr. Simon Cowell. Simon replies, "Yes, I don't know her name, but I saw her sing and dance to '(All the) Single Ladies' at a Kids With Kancer benefit—and you are right she was wonderful. I wonder how we may get in touch with her, and if she currently has an agent or manager?" To which Dr. House replies, "I believe they are headed for the GLEE stage, it should be later easy enough to find out."

All the people are waving as we continue on our way, everyone from janitors and guards to show biz superstars, it is just like being in a magical dream. But instead of driving to the set, Michael stops the golfcart in front of a big building. He steps off, extended an arm like a True Gentleman, or just like a knight would to a millady. We enter the glass building & a guard waves us through with a smile, saying, "I know who you are!" The elevator WHOOSHES us to the offices of Ryan Murphy, Creator. He is so very nice, & takes my hand like a knight would a millady's, and falls down on one knee and bows. We are corjually invited to a huge room where all of the doctors and nurses who ever took care of me are waiting.

Ryan said, "Telma, when Michael told me about you, I YouTubed your performance of '(All the) Single Ladies' in Kentucky and it was simply and utterly amazing. Perhaps you have heard that some viewers have been very upset that we did not hire a True handicapped person to play Artie because Artie is played by Kevin McHale an actor who just pretends to need a wheelchair. As opposed to the viewers liking very much that Coach Sue's niece was a real Down's Syndrome mongol. The viewers enjoyed that Glee had a cast member who did represent a pairaplegic boy (Artie), but now that the show is such a HUGE success (even tho it is now starting to die, & I know that you will help the show to continue to LIVE) & reaches—reaches out—to so many people, helping to raise awareness for so many causes not the least of which is tolerance toward the very fat and ugly, and all gays, well, this legitamate issue of our viewers has been keeping me awake at night. If I may say I had been hoping that THE GLEE PROJECT would have yeilded a True Handi-capped type but a lass, it did not. I ask myself, 'Why should we have to pre-tend?' And that was precisely when I got the call from Michael asking if I would meet you. And I said, you know, this is absolutely amazing, it was like God put you right there in front of me! God said, 'Ryan, you don't have to pretend anymore. (God the creator told RYAN THE CREATOR!!!!) I have brought you a girl who's a genuine hero. She's not pretending. She has been through Hell—the h-e-l-l of pediatric kancer—and come out the other side to be a CNN hero & example of courage not only to other kancer kids but to their parents & anyone struggling with disease and diversity.' [she did some cribbing from the introduction they gave her when she spoke at a Young Heroes Brunch in La Jolla] *So here is what I have done, & I have received the full permission & backing of all of the studio bosses. It is, as they say in the Business, a 'green light.' I have written a character, just for you. & I hope you don't mind but I've called her Telma!"*

Now comes the part where all of us walked—a whole mob!—to the GLEE soundstage, and it is incredibly dreamlike and like a dream. When we enter, it seems like the soundstage is a DARK MAZE but we keep walking, one of my hands is in that of MICHAEL DOUGLAS, the other hand is in that of RYAN THE CREATOR, I am in-between them and following them as if it is a dark, dark jungle, and when finally we emerge into the cave of the GLEE club set, all heads & eyes turn, and the creator Ryan is instantly applauded, which is what happened ANY time he danes come to set, because without RYAN THE CREATOR they would all be nothing.

And now, he stands in their midst quieting them.

"Guys and dolls," he says, "I would like you to meet someone VERY special, someone I have been TELLING you about for at least 2 weeks, ever since the Academy Awardwinning actor MICHAEL DOUGLAS informed

me of her by email, Twitter, Skype & the telephone. She is 4 foot ten & a real
hero. She happens to be, currently, the OFFICIALLY youngest known
SURVIVOR of breast kancer in the United States and the world. Please give
it up for the latest addition to the GLEE club: Telma Belle Ballendyne!

> {and then the applause, not just from Tina & Rachel & Finn
> & Kurt & Brittana, Artie & Becky the mongol, Blaine & Quinn
> & Will & Mercedes, Santana Puck Coach Shannon & Chord
> Overstreet and The GLEE PROJECT Damian Samuel Lind-
> say & Alex, and Oscarwinning GWYNETH PALTROW &
> Mr. John Stamos & too many to mention but all of the little people
> who cook the food for the craft service and do the makeup and cam-
> erawork and build the sets and the awardwinning CHOREOG-
> RAPHY of which much of the show's success is based on. & there
> is my mom standing back and smiling, she has been there all the
> time, and her face is wet with tears, for a minute I feel bad that I
> wasn't even thinking of her so swept away was I in the magic of
> this dream—my Mommy, who is my best friend, so kind & sweet
> & knowing enough to let her daughter have her as Nicki Minaj
> sang "moment4life." How far I—WE— have come! From kancer
> to GLEE, from hervivor & hero————hervivor Moms were
> heroes too . . . .

————then RYAN THE CREATOR is saying that he hates to tell
me this without proper notice (except as it turned out, he DID already tell my
mom), We are shooting your first episode as a full-time cast member of GLEE,
& do you happen to know the song 'Smile (While Your ♥ Is Breaking?)',
which of course I did so happen to, having sung it at the "Topeka Convention
Center" & on "Weekend Edition" & even with Kourtney Kardashian duet-
ting on Khloé's birthday (for which I was paid $25,000 for my services, of
which 100% of said fee went straight to the Telma's Warriors Scholarship
Fund), I just HAPPENED to know the song FRONTWARDS &
BACK!!! I even still to this day sing myself to sleep by it—& suddenly I hear
a voice, the voice of an ANGEL singing the very song & it takes me a few
moments to realize. . . . The person whose voice I hear is MY OWN!!!!!!!
It's ME who is singing, like a bird, without even knowing I had BEGUN.

And the beautiful set that they constructed starts to move and kind of crack open & I find myself still singing but standing upon a MOVING RUNWAY, and yet still never do I break my singing stride. . . . & I am dancing too!!! (I catch sight of myself in a mirror and magically, I am of a sudden in the MOST beautiful tuxedo, and I am wearing a derby and carrying a long black Kane . . . . . .)

Smile tho yr ♥ is aching
*Smile even though it's breaking**
xxxxxxxxxxxxxxxxx
xxxxxxxxx
xxxxxxxxxx
xxxxxxxxxxxxxxxxxxxxxxxxxxxxxxxx
xxxxxxxxxxxxxxxxxxxxxx
xxxxxxxxxxxxxxxxxxxxxxx—

——are those real tears? coming from amongst Awardwinning cast&camera&lighting crew? Are those real tears coming not just from my Mom, but from Academy Awardwinning MICHAEL DOUGLAS and Emmywinning CREATOR RYAN MURPHY and Academy Awardwinning GWYNETH PALTROW? All are frozen in positions and staring, at me, TELMA, (and how I am so very honored) there seems to be to my eye 100 people at least all told, Artie is standing now beside his wheelchair, having said he is embarrassed to be a pretender while the real thing, future Emmy and Oscarwinning TELMA BELLE BALLENDYNE's right there in front of him (how sweet!!!) he says outloud that it is now MY time it is now MY turn to take the throne, mettaforically to speak of, because of course I am not "handicapped" as the world considers the term to be, for example I am not wheelchair bound, but I am Kancervived, with all the Dignity, Hardships & uncertanties that go along . . . & even the Mongol seemed to grasp what was happening before hers and everyone's eyes, Becky the Down Mongol was born a hero, & standing there seems to grasp that she has already been

---

* Permission to reprint rest of lyrics denied by rights holder. —*author.*

recriuted into Telma's Troopers not RYAN THE CREATOR's. A tender button on the GLEE soldier's pea coat, the downy Mongol was a ♥felt punch-line who would never EVER be abused by Sue Sylvester, & sweetly funny too, whether the downed Mongol could voice it or not she could SENSE and FEEL that Telma, dancing & singing before her, was the real thing, a bonafied outsider like herself, the 2 of them left Artie the pretend-cripple in the dust . .

. . . .

All watched me in mid-song & dance in my Badgely Mischka tux, (I got the spelling right because I copied it from a magazine!!!) all still frozen in Show Business Time, but I kept singing & would not have been aware of the OTHER voice if a HUGE GASP & mass swivelling of eyes had not cued me.

I turn . . . & it is————— JUSTIN BIEBER, singing smile though your ♥ is xxxxxxx, xxxxxxxxxxxxxxxxxxxxxxxxxxxxxxxxxxxxxxxxxx xxx------------he is walking toward me, and my knees are SHAKING!!! but I can see clearly that JUSTIN is an Old Soul just like me, and I don't wait for him to approach ME but am BOLDLY approaching HIM until we are SO CLOSE that our NOSES almost TOUCH

That's xxxxxxxxxxxxxxxxxxxxxxxxx*

Smile, xxxxxxxxxxxxxxxxxxxxxx?

xxxxxxxxxxxxxxxxxxxxxxxxxxxx

xxxxxxxxxxx--------------------

And OMG when we finish you could hear a pin drop!!! JUSTIN kisses my cheek then touches my forehead with his forehead, & this dear Diary is when the audience can hold it no longer, there are many LOUD SIGHS fol-lowed by LITTERALL CRYING & APPLAUS, and JUSTIN BIEBER is bowing, he beckons me to follow his lead, he has taken my hand in his, someone through flowers to me, a WHOLE BOOQKAY but it hits JUSTIN by mistake!!!!! There is so much laughter from MICHAEL DOUGLAS and RYAN MURPHY, CREATOR, and HIS WIFE CATHERINE and GWYNETH and BRITTANY S. PIERCE and then more sighs as he (JUSTIN) gentlemanly presents the bouquet to his

---

* *Ibid.*

partner, ME, TELMA, hervivor, the creator Ryan turning now saying
Thank You JUSTIN BIEBER. . . . & Thank You MICHAEL DOUG-
LAS & Thank You CATHERINE & GWYNETH————————
but most of all we must thank GOD for the newest ADDITION to the
GLEE FAMILY, Miss TELMA BELLE BALLENDYNE & while the
applause continued, JUSTIN whispered, "TELMA, come let me give you a
ride home in my SWAG-filled Range Rover, and we

. . .

For whatever reason, they hadn't been left a drive-on. The gate
opened and Gwen was directed to park in a makeshift holding
area, so as not to further impede the already slow-moving line of
studio visitors. Gwen said *shit* under her breath, still (forever) reeling/
keening/plexus-punched from the obscene news, already on morbid
nauseating countdown in her head as to when she is going to tell her
daughter she'd been mutilated more or less on a whim, victim of extreme preventive care, they tore into that precious healthy body like
wolves, their teeth were needles of every gauge, needles & clamps &
forceps & retractors & scissors & saws & hooks & ligatures, fun and
games at Dachau Children's Hospital, St. Ambrose Frankenstein
Family Pediatric Care Center—Gwen basically on countdown of as-
yet unknown duration, she didn't want to deprive Telma of her *Glee*
moment. *We'll visit the set, then after, or maybe before she goes to bed, or*
maybe the next day, I'll tell her we have an appointment with Phoebe,
Phoebe, as of the last few hours, now privy to the situation, had to
be. Gwen wanted to tell her daughter in the *safety* of a *therapeutic envi-*
ronment, just in case (who knew) she had a nutso reaction, which she
really felt was doubtful though Gwen had one herself—*she'll have a*
lovely day on the Glee *set (if we ever get our frickin parking pass), maybe a*
few more lovely days, maybe a whole lovely (comparatively) week before———
SHIT the gal at Ryan Murphy's office or *someone* forgot to leave a
pass *shit shit* SHIT isn't that perfect?
     And when the guard tried to call production, for some perfect
reason no one answered (of course not!) & so finally the guard

reached someone on the set who told him to call the office back, a puissant/pissant command which he dutifully obeys in the way only a dumbass studio guard could. She watched it all unfold, her daughter in the seat beside her oblivious doing her instagrammy thing & Gwen expects no one at the prod. office will answer but *lo & behold* a person actually *does*, the dumbshit guard listens with all this *gravity* like on terrorist alert *Just print out the frickin pass you dumbshit* which in a moment he does, like *he's* the one who pulled strings, like he wants somebody to kiss his ring for it, & he tells her to drive over *there*, pointing way over yonder in the direction of Palm Springs, it's that far away, & just then Gwen remembers the Ryan Murphy gal *specifically telling her* she would be able to park close to the set, in fact *right in front of the production office* so they wouldn't have to hike over, subtext being, your daughter has or had cancer, neither of course anymore being the truth, *Oh man* Gwen thinks darkly, *we are certainly going to miss those cancer perks*. Even tho they long since gave up their handicapped parking permit, the one that was so hopeful during the months of surgery/recovery, the unnecessary months! they'd given it up because Telma, ever the warrior-ethicist, said she *wasn't* handicapped (anymore), it was an effrontery, & unfair to all the people who *did* need a handicapped permit, Gwen couldn't argue with her, and why should she? she was *cured!* Cured! CURED! Of *NOTH-ING* & when she deigns to mention this little detail to the ugly illiterate peanut-brained guard he acts like she's uppity, says *Well I don't know anything about that, & if it were true* (literally using that phrase, calling her a liar!), the woman he just spoke to would have said so. At least the Captain of Retardation offered to call back, but Gwen, not wishing to be further victimized, wisely said no, just let it be, she already had that general sinking feeling, sinking feeling upon sinking feeling, that this-is-as-good-as-it's-going-to-get feeling as he waved her through to the most distant parking structure known to man. Within that structure, awaiting within, was the single furthest-away-from-everything parking space, a 10K trudge in the shimmering heat, all those little golf carts speeding past with laughing passengers, bantering almost, sometimes they even whizzed by with only a driver, say, a personal assistant merrily whistling to himself in the midst of an insignificant errand, maybe even just on his way to lunch, or sometimes a cart passed with the name of a show on it, *X Factor*, *New Girl*, *Family Guy*, whatever, lowly intern at the wheel temporarily liberated from office humdrum to deliver a fat check/free swag to whomever bigshot . . . . then (still 8 minutes left in their walk to the set) Gwen sees a cart with *GLEE* on it speeding past, yet another galling solo driver no doubt heading in the direction *they* were going, to the soundstage, she shouts "Hey!" but he doesn't hear & she's suddenly a bit embarrassed—there goes the *Glee* production company driver without a care in the world, zooming past the Mom of the girl who survived cancer without actually *having* cancer—now *that's* a true survivor!—the girl that Michael Douglas (who *did* have cancer, though maybe not *anymore*) was so moved by, & had paved the way for their studio visit on this bright fraudulent high-end LA day with its traitorous bowling ball moon hanging in the sky-blue sky like a fuck-you to the night.

Michael Douglas would have been furious to see them walking like this in the hot sun.

At the soundstage, Ryan Murphy, Creator, was not there to greet them.

They stood stranded outside until a very, very sweet gal with lots of gear strapped on her smiled the *biggest* smile. "Are you Telma? You must be Telma!" & for a minute Gwen thought things would be better. (Wrong.) She began to say something but was startled by a loud BELL/ALARM. A big red light atop the stage door lit up & revolved like the ones on old ambulances & the sweet gal smiled but at the same time *seriously pantomimed* them NOT TO SAY A WORD, NOT EVEN TO MOVE. Telma heard (over the girl's walkie) someone shout "PLAYBACK!" and she & her mom stood there, Telma's ♥ racing, worried she was missing something, everything, then some big cranky guy ignored the light, opened the steel door & went in, which the sweet gal frowned on but permitted, in the sense that she didn't try to stop him. & for *just* a few seconds, everyone could hear Lea Michele's brassy voice, it sounded live but Telma was surprised when it squeaky-rewound & the bell alarm SOUNDED again, the red light went OFF, & the sweet tomgirl gal walked them in and advanced them to a temporary position where they could see without being in the camera or anyone's way.

The alarm sounded and . . . . . "PLAYBACK!"—& Telma saw Brittana & Lea & Artie, Colton, Mercedes & an older woman in black tights, patent-leather dance heels & derby, everyone was singing and dancing. This went on stutter-starting/stopping for about a half-hour. Then someone yelled "We have it!" and there was commotion but then that same person asked everyone to be *very still & quiet* for a moment, which they were, not a peep, it was all so exciting to her, Telma thought that's what Show Business is, there's only two ways it can ever be, it's either *very loud and crazy & all over the place*, or it's *very quiet & serious and organized & disciplined*. Then, after everyone had been *extremely* quiet for at least 60 seconds, the same person announced it was LUNCH.

Telma & Gwen were walked over to the director, not by the sweet gal, but someone else who was sweet but not *as* sweet, the director stayed in his chair & smiled & shook their hands. When they left, Telma thought he called her Aleisha. They were walked over to a cast member or two, but of the lesser variety. The famous ones had disappeared.

No one seemed to know exactly who Telma was. No one, not even the director, seemed in the least prepared viz her darling daughter, which puzzled/irritated Gwen . . . . . but the day was saved because the woman in the tights & derby came and graciously introduced herself, first to the mom *Hello! I'm Catherine* then to Telma, *So wonderful to meet you! My husband's talked so much about you, I heard you're a helluva dancer* (Telma thought, *OMG. It is Mrs. Michael Douglas, the Oscarwinning Catherine Zeta-Jones. OMG how could I have not known that, I am so embarrassed*) but then she got called away, as people in show business tend to, shrugging at Telma & Gwen as if she really truly didn't *want* to be called away but, as it was work, had no real say in the matter, which was the truth. At least leaving them with that lovely glow/feeling that they *mattered*. Gwen told Telma that was Michael Douglas's wife, Telma said *I know! I know!* She was just too all over the place keyed up to say anything in the moment, Telma knew she was his wife, knew she was doing a *Glee*, she was Welsh even though she sounded English, & that she was a bipolar Hero.

Catherine went away and it was back to

Mother and daughter

stranded

again

Telma said she wanted to walk around on her own for a while, do some exploring, Gwen said OK & Telma struck out.

She went in search of Artie/Kevin, and was shocked to actually see him only a minute into her peregrinations, out of his wheelchair (naturally). She went straight up & said she was here because she was a friend of Michael Douglas, she took the bull by the horns and informed him that she was currently the youngest breast cancer survivor in the world. Artie/Kevin seemed really interested, even tho Telma thought that might be partially because he thought she was a guest of Catherine's.

He said, "Wow, really?! He was here earlier, he's so great"—not actually really (fully) knowing a rejoinder to the little girl's breast-beating boast—asking instead how she knew Michael D. Telma told him the story, of how she wrote him a letter because he was a survivor too & how he wrote back. Artie/Kevin said, "Whoa, you guys are pen pals?" Telma nodded with a big smile and A/K said, "Pen pals with Michael Douglas! *Very* cool." Then *he* was called away. Artie Kevin ignored whoever was calling him as if to show Telma that he answered to no one, but they called him again and he shrugged like Catherine did and excused himself, telling her all the while that it was rude to just leave someone in the middle of a conversation, but again the shrug of *What can I do?*

Telma went & sat in his wheelchair but a property person came along. He was very nice about it but said he needed to take the chair away.

She went over to the snack table and picked up a gooey slice of honeydew melon. Too sweet. The bananas were gooey too, and the cantaloupe too hard. She grabbed a handful of almond M&Ms & baby pretzels. She was glad to see her mom talking to someone in the distance. A girl came to the table and started shoving soda cans into a big cooler filled with ice. Telma asked her if the creator Ryan was coming. Without looking at her & continuing to shove cans in the cooler, she said *O he doesn't tell us when he comes but he's usually here every day.* Then the tomgirl gal appeared & sweetly wagged a finger at Telma. *You guys are supposed to be having lunch with the Cheerios. You guys are gunna get me in trouble.*

She walked the young guest outside. Gwen was already sitting in a golf cart, waiting. The outdoor lunch tables were supposedly four or 5 whole soundstages away but you could smell the BBQ from here.

As she went toward the golfing cart, Telma saw Heather Morris. Heather/Brittany was one of her total role models because the dancer was cast permanently by accident. (Even though Telma wanted to be cast permanently *not* by accident.) Heather was the biggest testimony to the magic & miracles and *serendipity* of how ☆s are born, that was a word she loved that her mom told her meant a person's happy destiny. Heather was in Telma's opinion one of the friendliest & least jaded of the cast too because everything was so new to her, she had never set out to be a star. Telma had among others a Heather Morris Google Alert, in every YouTube clip or whatever interview with fans or press she always came across as crazy-kind because in her ♥ she must have known how blessed she was, that what had been given her could so easily be taken away, not necessarily by Ryan the Creator but by TV gods in general. (There would always be h8trs, trollers & flamebaiters, one of them was a Mean Girl who kept writing *heather's just a fame whore a total poser cant you people see?* & Telma wrote back *YOU are the whore can't YOU see? not heather* but felt kind of bad about it after, even though she knew she did the right thing because as a rule she didn't like to be a Mean Girl h8tr herself. What is a poser anyway, what does that even mean? How could Heather be fake! But she knew Heather was strong, & getting stronger each day as her fame grew, that Heather must know that such is the price one must pay for true ☆dom, be it be granted sudden or gradual.) As she became famouser, of late Telma could tell it *was* getting maybe a bit harder for Heather to be Heather. Like when she got googalerted to a *Glee* event in Beverly Hills at the Museum of Television. The whole cast was there & the fans could ask any question they wanted. When Heather left the event people were screaming for her to sign posters & whatever, they just wanted her attention, & Heather looked like maybe she wasn't feeling well, she just got into the limousine and crouched down, she ducked down hiding from everyone. At first you could hear the fans—if you could call them that because Telma read how so many of these so-called "fans" hunted down stars for autographs then promptly sold them on eBay—you could hear them say how cute it was that she was playing peekaboo from the limousine, everyone had so much good will toward Heather, more than the usual star, because she was always so nice, she always shined, and made whoever she was talking to shine too, but when the so-called "fans" realized she wasn't playing peekaboo, that she was just on the floor hiding & maybe having a tiny nervous breakdown, their voices grew louder, but the car pulled away. That's when Telma heard one of them shout, *There'll come a day when you'll WISH we wanted your autograph*———————how awful.

Heather was in a robe on her way to her trailer and Telma went right up. She was *so nice,* she looked Telma right in the eye like she was a real person, a big person not a little person, she was so *kind,* she said right away that her new friend Catherine already told her *all about* who she was, & Heather said she "loved warriorgirl" & was so impressed!

Telma asked if she could sit with her for lunch but Heather got a sad look and said she had to give an interview to a man who came all the way from Italy, and that she wasn't having lunch with everyone today ☹ Telma was hoping she would invite her into her trailer at least to hang out & maybe have a tiny lunch during her interview but Heather just kept on apologetically sad-smiling.

When she was finally excusing herself, Telma asked if she could give her a kiss & Heather said *Yeah!* but everything got superjumbled in Telma's grasping, desperately in the moment, overheated mind whether Heather was gay in real life, because *Brittany* was, maybe just like Ryan the Creator had written Lea's & Gwyneth's roles especially for them, maybe he did the same with Brittany basing her some or a lot on the *real* Heather, probably Heather was partly gay in real life, there'd been such a fuss over the original Brittana kiss, & with Kurt kissing Blaine, & Darren Kriss & everyone now always kissing, tho mostly it seemed girls kissing girls & boys kissing boys, so Telma, in heady, ♥felt, headrushed desperation thought maybe *that* could be the way to gain entrée, to leapfrog *Glee Project 2* & any *other* kind of project, person or thing Ryan & Dante were considering, the way to stand out from the pack, that maybe if she *did* then Heather would tell Creator Ryan, the creator Ryan was bold, a kiss between older & younger could be the new frontier because everyone was getting tired and bored (thought Telma, in that moment) with the boy-boy/girl-girl same-age kiss, this way maybe would be another way to help her to be permanently hired————————so——she put her tongue right in Brittany's mouth, deep, Brittany didn't see it coming, Telma had her eyes open as she pushed it further and further in, the expression on Heather's face was *total shock* which actually allowed

Telma to keep the thick pink muscle in there longer, even if it was only a *sliver* longer because as it turns out a sliver happens to be a *lot* in tonguetime, Telma only kissed once like that ever, one boy (not Biggie ☺), was kissed *by* him more than kissing him, that little swordfight first-time exploring tongues do, but not as deep as *this*, she twirled & swirled around in Brittany's mouth til Heather grabbed her & practically threw her off her to the ground saying *What are you doing are you* CRAZY?!?!?! Then she looked around declaiming to no one in particular *OMG* this little girl just kissed me with her *TONGUE* OMG HOW GROSS! THIS *is so* W E I R D, who *IS* she, where is her **GUARDIAN?**

the tomgirl gal rushed over, and a few stragglers too, half-smiling not knowing if it was a joke, Heather saying

shouldn't I tell someone, who should I tell? (half-smiling/half-spooked as Telma backs up in shock & embarrassment then falls on her ass but keeps backing up crab-like) WHO SHOULD I TELL??????!!!!!!!!!

. . .

On the long walk back to the car, all Gwen could do was ask her daughter why.

When Telma said she thought it would help get her on the show (tho her logic was torqued & perilous), Gwen's heart broke again. It broke all day long, every beat like a bone china teacup shattering against a wall.

A golf cart headed toward them, not from the soundstage but from the direction they'd originally come. Gwen saw the shaven head from a distance and knew it was Ryan Murphy. When Gwen told Telma who it was, her face dilated in tiny ecstasies.

He pulled up, smiling.

A tiny girl sat in front, with his asst & a mom in back.

"Sorry we missed you!" said Ryan.

Ryan shook hands with Telma from the cart. He turned to the tiny girl, who had some kind of harelip. The mom seemed to have something going on in that area as well.

"Gwen & Telma Ballendyne? Meet Melanie & Aleisha Hunter. You 2 'single ladies' have a lot in common." He spoke directly to Telma now. "Aleisha's a breast cancer survivor. Melanie, how old was she when she was diagnosed?"

"She was two."

"*Two-years-old,*" said Ryan, his sensuous lips in pouty incredulity. "I've heard of the terrible 2s . . . but *that* is ridiculous!"

(Ryan's relationship with Melanie & Aleisha was such that all seemed completely comfortable with him making 'light.')

"She's 6 now—aren't you, Aleisha? Our Aleisha happens to be *the youngest breast cancer survivor in the world.* We're on our way to introduce her to the cast. Do you two have time to come back for a little lunch?"

[Jerzy]

Spurts, Illustrated

Jerzy

got lucky & snatcherazzi'd Amanda Seyfried (27) sliding out of a friend's Tesla at the Brentwood Mart (that rare *passenger* seat *honeyshot!*)—no panties. He thought of photoshopping a kite string because at this time, Harry round the Ovaries was paying a premium for *Ragtime* pics. *HoneyRagtimers!* was a new link celebrating what Harry, authentic *Mad Men*-era–ish madman that he was, still, in conversation, quaintly called *the monthlies* AKA the red meanies, showcasing *rag hags* of the week (subheading: "They Got The World On A String!"), a riff on those pukeworthy stars-are-just-like-you-&-me features in the newsstand tabloids—pics of Tobey Maguire pumping his own gas, Demi Lovato scratching her own ass, Lena Headey leaving Ikea, Shailene Woodley leaving Café Gratitude, iCarly jaywalking, Jared Leto drilling for oil in his left nostril—Harry's banner victoriously proclaimed "They get periods!" Jerzy got eight grand for the Seyfried, a bit higher than usual because on closer inspection the pussyhair revealed itself to have a week's growth from a recent shave. Harry could be mollified but never satisfied. His latest dreamquarry was Her Anexo-Bulimic Hardbodied Highness Kate (unhairy around the) Middleton. Ever since he saw pix of her bikini bod on a yacht off Ibiza he coveted a royal *honeyshot!* "A fella can cream can't he?"

Jerzy knew how to keep HM happy. What he did was he snapped all the lolitas—the Chloës & the Elles & all the single hailees, the stylists always lagerfelded em up like jonbenets for premières & what-nots in freebie Miu-Miu/Marchesa/Prabal Gurung (Miss Hailee), Stella/Dior (Chloë M), YSL couture (Miss "Sally Draper"—Harry said he'd pay *25,000* for Kiernan Shipka's *honeyshot!*), Rodarte/Philip Lim/D&G/Ferretti/Chanel (Miss Elle), you could usually count on the *ensembles* being too revealing/sophisticated for their age, young money cash money *honeyshot!*s were easy pickins—though you could forget about a no-panties pic, the kids *always* wore panties, they were way too far as yet from that rebellious stage, probably for the best because an all-the-single-hailees pantiless *honeyshot!* would've given Harry an instant coronary.

In the meanwhile, Jerzy had his pumped-up kicks cause no one in their wildest dreams could've guessed he was angling for a young harpie's Hairpie around the Middle *honeyshot!* . . . . . . there was just no *legal market* for them. To make matters slightly more conducive to our patient, young money cash honey-seeking underagerazzo, all the clueless single hailees were of course as yet unschooled in the proper methodology, the Emily Postmenstrual *etiquette of* exiting a leather backseat whilst holding a clutch over Area 51, a maneuver that was the most-favored by publicists, the latter-day equivalent of the primly self-protective Bunny Dip of bygone days. Jerzy knew that H around the M could *never* post underage *honeyshot!*s for fear of prosecution— it was written into their secret handshake contract that any on-the-fly prepube portraits went *straight* to Harry's private reserve, do not pass *goo*.

> *A wine bought young & stored will cost less than to purchase*
> *the same wine once it is matured. It can also give great*
> *pleasure in anticipation (each time you check your cellar, you*
> *will see bottles growing in both taste & value) & when*
> *opened has a sense of occasion about it. Imagine the romance*

*when opening a bottle at a dinner party when you mention
how long you've been saving it & remember where & when
you bought it . . .*

The fearless bossman always bossed up & said *Get em!*

One of the things that kept him on his toes was Harry's intriguing unpredictability. Last week, Jerzy brought him a treat, no big thing, a little *aperitif,* just a snatchshot *soupçon* of Chloë Sevigny, not meant to be anything more than a cordial, a nice port, a nighttime sweet left under a hotel pillow—less prosaically, a retriever bringing his master a dead bird.

Harry *erupted*: "That's fucking coals to Newcastle! That's bringing *cunts* to an OB/GYN! She is a *hooker.* Have you seen her blowing Vincent Gallo? *That's* a pair to draw to. You oughta go on the internet a little more often, my friend, you'll get an education. What the fuck was it called? That movie he directed? You can watch the scene on the internet. That phony prick . . . . . *Brown Bunny!* Vincent Gallo directed a piece of shit called *Brown Bunny,* starring his girlfriend. That slimy piece of shit—can you imagine his personal hygiene?— she should have sued his skinny ass. But she didn't, cause she's a whore. Vincent Gallo: actor, model, director, phoney. I'm telling you, the guy was the James Franco of his time! Go on the internet, go, you'll see her gobble-gobble. & this ain't a sex tape, we're not talking about a Kardashian, we're talking about something *voluntary.* & *pretentious,* which in my book is the worst of sins.

"& don't *ever* bring me pictures of that cocksucker's cunt again!"

· · ·

His half-sister was crashing with him and Tom-Tom.

She told him *never* to call her Jerilynn, only Reeyonna or ReeRee, Hey fine with me, sis, remember who you're talkin to? Jerzy who used to be Jerry Jr. She said he could call her Ree, too, or Yonna or Reezy. *Yeah yeah, just don't call me Al, or maybe it's 'You can call me Al,' or whatever it is.* Ree was pregnant and moved out of MoMA's after MoMA told her about the grand theft art-o, lootin' the poor kid's legacy. Looks like l'il homie finally *got* what he'd been telling her for years: that MoMA's a douchebag. But he didn't gloat about it. Funny how nobody ever sees the *truth* till they get hit in the pocketbook, to borrow an antique phrase of Harry's.

Jerzy was sort of attracted to her, speed made him attracted to everything, & when Reeyonna wasn't there, he and Tom-Tom (who lyked to dyke) joked about an all in the family 3-way. ReeRee was hot but even hotter to Tom-Tom, being that she was already beginning to show. On weekends, ReeRee's black boyfriend stayed over and Jerzy & Tom-Tom listened to them fuck through the wall, then Jerzy & Tom-Tom would fuck like rutting dingoes while the teen lovebirds were all moanballing and mattressspringing. *Fun!* The black bf was hot too, though not to Jerzy. Not really. But with a little fairydusting of the ol' spackle m'gackle Jerzy could for sure find himself jacking to a thought bubble of the boy's brown washboard abs, imagining that sleeping giant, that eggplant, that Deep Purple napping below deck, with its rutabaga-, deflated punching bag–sized scrote, the whole deal fisting up from the loamy stank of Jockey Gardens.

One time the 3 of them—Tom-Tom, Jerzy & ReeRee—watched porn after the black bf went home. The internet was on the big plasma in the living room. They smoked dro & sat on beanbag chairs. Tom-Tom wanted to blow Ree *Witherspoon's* mind (she liked annoying Reeyonna by calling her that, but it was really only more like Reeyonna got *half*-annoyed because she liked the attention though she'd never admit it, liked to be half-teased by an attentive dyke even though she didn't run that way), she wanted to play some XXX shit because she knew ReeRee wasn't a pornhead. So first she went on one of the milkmaid sights & they watched pregnant chicks pump breast milk, tittie squirters, &tc. Reeyonna said it was disgusting. But Tom-Tom had a *plan*, a ground control to *major* plan, Jerzy couldn't *believe* what she cum up with, man a new low in frickin depravity. *Fun!*

This video they were suddenly looking at was super strange, shot outdoors, somewhere like up on Mulholland. There must have been *40* chicks milling around, just chatting away like they were getting mani-pedis, all nude except for high heels. Put em in jogging clothes & they'd look like a bunch of moms shootin shit at a dog run. The chicks on the *frontlines* were the only ones not being casual, these were like *savage bitches* they had this *savage energy* and they were all gathered around this Kreayshawnlooking white girl who was kneeling on the ground on a towel so she wouldn't scrape her knees, & this frontline of chicks was *circling* her like she was frickin *prey*, man they looked *badass.* And these chicks, they're all, like, mildly *jacking*, standing straight up & *mildly jacking*, it's like they're about to start a race, you know, gentlemen start your engines . . . then *one* of em, black chick, nasty-ass Tina Turner type, straight outta Compton, naked except for heels *breaks* from the line & struts forward toward White Girl like a singer taking—*owning*—the stage in the final finals of *The X Factor—The XXX Factor!* gets real close to White Girl like she's gunna do a solo, which she does, drum solo, she Han Solo hand solo hand so low starts to beat off, fanning that pussyclit with stiff longnailed lacquered nasty-ass fingers *man* she brutally *works* it, arm moving like a piston, then starts *yelling* too, fucking *Zulu*-style! & her chorus line buddies join in, they're jacking but still casual, you know, they don't want to steal their sister's thunder, they're not at bat yet, they're still on deck, &, like, they don't want to, you know, fuck up their turn when it comes, they don't want to fuck it up by coming before they're at bat, but this Zulu shit even got the attention of the desultory mani-pedi chicks six rows back, the Tina is *screaming* & *beating* herself & cussing out the pathetic cowering Kreayshawn———& then *WTF!!!* some *watery* shit frickin *GUSHES* from the Tina's hole, man it is a *horizontal geyser*, even Jerzy who's seen a lot of *porno* never seen anything like it & ReeRee says *O my God! What* is *that?* but Tom-Tom is not forthcoming with an explanation. Ree's eyes are glued to the screen anyway (whose wouldn't) (Jerzy watches Tom-Tom get off, watching Ree watching), man that Tina's like a broken fire hydrant, she's in White Girl's *face*, standing right over it, straddling the mousy chick's already soaked, dirty blond Kreayshawnscalp, the Tina's bending her knees, fuckin *awesome* quads, like she trains for the event by doing squats at the gym, she's got this tuffskin, murderous cool-looking face, & *lets another torrent rip*, fuckin *hydrant-hydrosquirts* on the retard cracker, Reeyonna still looking on in transfixed fascination, saying now, *"Is it pee? What* IS *that? Is it her pee?———"* Tom-Tom, ever the old pro/ black widow, white black widow, keeping on the downlow, saying nothing as the fountainspray diminishes though man it is *still* jetting out, Jerzy wondering/marveling where it's all coming from. The rearguard of mani-pedi freaks walks forward now like fresh infantry, like they used to in the Civil War, those old paintings, soldierly stepping up to replace their dead/bayonet musketwounded/spent comrades, all impressively nude & heel-shod. And they commence to beat off *together*, 5 bottle Rockettes at a time, blurry piston machine arms! then *OUT* pours the . . . *fluid*, granted not as much as the Tina who clearly was the heavyweight, the legend, the headliner, superstar spurtswoman of the day *cant touch that* & the watery shit (not called Patricia) is like jellyfish/insecticide *dusting* White Girl's idiot face, blond hair stuck & slick from waterbombs seeming called on command. Jerzy wanted to ask Tom-Tom if the squirty shit was the *result* of the bitches cumming, or could they get it to squirt *without* cumming, but he didn't. Later.

Tom-Tom, exspurt in such circus anomalies, bless her ♥, Tom-Tom then did proceed to *explain* the gynephenomenon to her sponsee, explain the ABCs/sex biological ed of it, coolly, calmly, clearheaded/clinically, ol' pro Tom-Tom, reeling in the fish by playing the dispassionate tutor, she might just as well have been explaining to a child why the sun comes up in the morning and the moon rises at night—he knew it was *exciting* for Tom² to be schooling Ree Witherspoon suchwise.

Jerzy snorted adderoxys off the base of his thumb whilst pondering a mystery right up there with the pyramids and Stonedhenge. Namely, *Where the fuck did somebody find FORTY chicks who could squirt?* I mean, just the logistics of getting em all in one place at one time . . . they couldn't have been paid much, probably some weren't paid nuthin at all . . . doing it for the love of the art I guess, you know, like, the love of the game. Jerzy himself never had the luck to fuck a squirter not even a *diet* squirt & wondered why, because he'd consorted with a fair amount of kinky ladies. So it did seem all the *moreso* to be no mean feat, tho he surmised that if your job was casting porn you were likely to have a file with 1000s of names, contact #'s and preferences—a *Who's Who* of who swallows, creampies, facials, fists, who DPs, grannies, shemales, ladyboys, gangbangs & BDSMs, who pisses, fatties, dwarfs&midgets, who racials, rape-o's, monster cocks, tortures, toilets, who old mans, & who so on & so on & so forth. Jerzy further surmised that if you were responsible for finding *talent* (not backroomcastingcouch sort of walk-in talent), you could probably do goo diligence & round up a squirtsquad.

But *still*—

Forty of em!

Sheesh . . . .

Reeyonna was uncomprehending and shocked, oblivious that Tom-Tom & her half-brother were getting off on watching her trip. Suffice to say that by now the cretinous, kneeling, whitetrash white-thrash'd blond was drenched. Jerzy was in the speedball sweetspot. He even jacked a little over his trousers making sure his sister wasn't looking. He went on an extended fantasy, like, the cops arrive on Mulholland but the others disperse & only White Girl is arrested. She's a runaway. The police call her parents who live in Utah. Super Mormons. Morm & dad fly in to bail her out, they're not really understanding what was her crime, & a cop starts to tell them what she was doing at the time of the arrest but decides that a picture's worth 1000 words. & Jerzy imagines himself gathered with the snickering

cops on the other side of a huge 2-way mirror watching Morm &
Dad look on as Tina & her Amazon sistuhs firehose their precious
baby———————————————Reeyonna now saying she *heard*
about something like this, but never actually *saw* it—Jerzy saw the
wheels beginning to turn, Tom-Tom's strategy already working, the
brilliance of it being that half the battle was getting ReeRee to start
talking about the pervy shit instead of just walking away in repul-
sion—ReeRee said a friend said Larry Fishburne's daughter did it in
a movie, squirted, & then Reeyonna's eyes mesmerically wandered
back to the screen and she said, "This is so completely gross!"

Jerzy, sinuses burning, took in the lovely pastoral scene, his ½sis
still glued to the set in spite of herself, even tho the rest of her body
was simultaneously trying to back itself out of the room&out the
door, Tom-Tom's eyes goo'd to ½sis, & glazed over too; he was afraid
he might do a little gushing himself.

.   .   .

Bristol Farms over on Beverly Boulevard & Doheny was always very
good to him.

He sat in his car & got em like sitting ducks: Lily Collins . . . Jon
Cryer . . . Alyson Hannigan . . . Tyler Perry (with bodyguards).

He drove back to his spot on Burton Way and parked.

Walked to Sprinkles for cupcakes.

Wandered into Gagosian . . . .

Oh!

. . . . large fotos on the walls snapped by a Jap named
Sugimoto—b&w pre-tsunami seascapes— + pics of empty movie
theaters. (All you saw were seats & screens, also pre-tsunami.) It was
spooky, especially the seascapes, because when Jerzy looked all he
could see in his head was the tsunami porn he watched on youtube
after that shit went down, it really did a number on him, he was
high in his room for 2 wks watching that 10-story blackwater tube
of water breaching the sea wall, trapped japs fluttering like moths in

sealed tombs of swept away cars. The big wave still gave him the creeps. One of the things that he still thought of at least one time a day was the people on the roofs of five-story buildings, which is exactly where *he* would have gone, he knew himself, he'd have totally thought "I'll be safe on the roof of this 5-story building" but when the camera came back the building was underwater & gone. That always hit him in the gut because he knew that kind of denial/ fantasy life/poor planning—an erroneous feeling the story will have a happy ending, of overall safety stemming from the childish view that reality can be regulated by thought/wish/need, that everything that happens is all a big dream he can choose to wake up from whenever he desires—Jerzy knew this feeling he carried around in daily life was nothing but a terrible bullshit weakness in character, a spineless character flaw born of pathological lassitude/inertia that would prevent him from ever becoming an adult, from becoming a man, from taking responsibility for his actions, he knew that he was missing whatever that thing is that fully grown men had, probably the same trait that would allow him w/o compunction to turn in friends & family if the fascists ever took over. He felt the familiar twinge at the end of this train of thought, & felt queasy.

Looking at the calmness of the eerie seascapes was sort of like looking at a chimp an hour before (or after) it tore off the zookeeper's face. Maybe that was the artist's point. *The chimp was chill.* It didn't take a giant leap of the imagination for Jerzy to see *his* pix on the walls (his "abstract" snatcherazzo *c*-scapes *hahahahaha*) and that instantly made him feel better. Reputation did not precede him, but revelation would. He had already begun to comb thru his image bank—thousands of verité celeb pix taken over the last 5 years. He was looking at the little batch of *honeyshot!*s too, taken to date.

A soft alarm went off in his head: time to leave the gallery.

(Bad karma to overstay his welcome.)

He was just on his way, when canned-sounding laughter raucoused the air, growing echo-louder as it attached itself to the flurry

of bodies walking thru the entrance. A white-haired man of sunny
disposition & ruddy, play-doh features emerged from the back &
strode briskly toward the entourage as it entered the main room.
Jerzy had a Special Moment: it was the man himself: *Larry G.*

Larry around the Gagosian. *Larry Gaga . . .*

Jerzy instinctively rapid-shrunk into wallflowered loseraazzo in-
visibility as Gaga greeted Michael Douglas and Catherine Zeta-
Jones, & a close-shaved middle-aged black in button down shirt &
Mr. Freedom jeans. King Larry shook hands with Zeta-Jones,
Douglas & the black but did *not* with the two who hover/dangled
on the nervous periphery. (They of the Serfdom/Personal Assistant
Class; they of the Disposable Intern fortunate enough in these times
of financial hardship & gluttonous starfuckery not just to be employed {even if paid nothing or next to nothing} but lucky to be
breathing the same *fucking air* as the celeb employers who rescued
them from the shame of their go-nowhere lives; they of the Indentured Class who sign contracts forbidding them to disclose via lawsuit or memoir whatever lame, embittered, perceived perceptions of
the famous hands that fed them they might claim to have conjured,
enumerating said benefactors' rudeness, frivolities, unsanitary hab-
its, sexual quirks, unsolicited come-ons, sadistic vulgarity, et alia
whilst in defamatory pursuit of financial gain or plain revenge by
leakage to TMZ, the DMZ, the NAACP, Triple A or any other
outlet including of course blogs & webloids, print tabloids & dying
pub houses still trafficking in the hardbacks & paperbooks of yes-
teryear. They of the parasitical Tolerated Class who eat the chores
& errands bacterium that colonize hourly around the mini-industry
of any celeb: dry cleaning fetchery, stopped-up toilets, party e-
vites, phone sheets, sending of flowers, packing of suitcases, ghost-
twittering &tc. For accomplishing those very things, their
congenital purposelessness is {amply} rewarded by being *lent* purpose & {more importantly} *identity* via the privilege of being allowed a priceless, special education wherein they may vicariously
experience what it's like to have an *actual life*, meaning one that is

fuller, richer & more exciting—*more lifelike*—in every way than theirs could or ever will be.*

Jerzy, skulking in a corner, watched the sexily muzzled, panicked-obsequious intern-lice crawl upon the skin of whatever host they were grooming, now & again lifting covetous heads to pause in their feast of bacteria, to observe with gimlet eyes the skilled quadrille of the gallerist & his visitors, the easy chummy social network of the rich, famous & powerful; that certain way they have of being googoo gaga for each other, each anticipating the others' emotional needs. Douglas said he was in town filming, adding that Catherine was shooting a *Glee*. (Gaga told them he & Shala were googoo for *Glee*.) From his post, Jerzy quickstudied Larry 'round the Gagosian as best he could, because one day he would be *selling* himself to the Man— to the impresario, ringleader & tastemaker, to the one-man *Gagosian's 11*.

Ogling Douglas' wife, who looked trampily deep into bipolar meds & high-end anti-aging *crêmes*, Jerzy thought: *Now that is a hot fuck*. He wondered if Douglas got his C by being wayback viral throatstroked by *papilloma* . . . . . seems like a person would have to go down on a boatload of broads to get the HPV in the gullet (well, do the math), if the actor scarfed half as much pussy as dimpled dad Kirk—King *Leer*, Kirk the lyin' King—then he just might have qualified.

Gagosian twice cast an *aware* eye Jerzy's way, which the speed-balling *ratsorizzo*razzo took as his cue to exit. On the way out, he came within 5 ft of the entourage, both ships passing gas in the night.

"We want to show Antwone how to spend money," said Douglas. "Cause I think he's too close with a buck. Don't you, Cat? Don't you

---

* Imagine the unendurable agony of the members of the above, the depressed, depressive Whores With No Name Class as they watch, like invalids, the hypnotic, rainy day, addictive, back-to-pack *X Factor* (UK & US) auditions on YouTube, going back so many years. Confronted by the spectacle of *other* (Non Chore-Whoring) No-Names bursting forth to become instant supernovas, their tears turn them into pillars of Loser Salt. Consider their anguish, watching—knowing—the fecundity of a universe that is constantly spitting out new stars . . . while they remain eternally condemned to the purgatory of the Stillborn.

They cannot even be *dead stars*, for they were never stars at all.

think Antwone's too close with a buck? He's not *flashy* enough. Fishburne & I are gunna take him under our wing & teach him how to be *flashy*. He's gunna learn how to play with the *big boys*. We're gunna show him how to spend, how to spend money & influence people.

"Cause it don't mean a thing if it ain't got that bling—right, Antwone?"

'Treasure' hunt ends

432PM PDT by Debi Rheng-Vatos

Douglas set for comedy

"The Treasure of Sierra Leone" locked its final principal lead in Antwone Fisher's helming debut. Megastar Michael Douglas joins Will Smith, Sandra Bullock, Laurence Fishburne and Hailee Steinfeld in what Fisher calls his "black comedy." Michael Tolkin penned, from an idea by Frederik "Biggie" Brainard III. Ishmael Beah consults. Ooh Baby Baby It's A Wild World Films' Brando Brainard produces. International sales are being handled by MGM/Paramount/Lion's Gate. The story, taking place in 1995, centers on a con man who needs to raise money for his daughter's heart surgery. He teaches an African American runaway how to impersonate a 'lost boy'/child soldier from the Ivory Coast—they hit the lecture circuit and make a bundle. Things begin to go terribly wrong when an Oprah-like character enters the picture and insists on flying the boy back to his Ivory Coast home in order to reunite with friends. (The producers would not comment on the rumor that Oprah Winfrey has privately expressed interest in a "cameo" role, as herself.) Tolkin wrote Robert Altman's *The Player*; his last novel was *The Return of the Player*. Fisher's recent credits are *Let's Go To Work!,* a doc about the black entrepreneur Leon T. Garr, and the bestseller, *A Boy Should Know How to Tie a Tie: and Other Lessons for Succeeding in Life* (Simon & Schuster). Brainard recently produced the megahit *Turndown Service,* has just formed a television division, Just Upon A Smile TV. Contact Debi Rheng-Vatos at debi.rheng-vatos@thehollywoodreporter.com

[Rikki&Tom-Tom]

*Call Me Ishmael**

*AKA *Konyshots!*

Rikki

couldn't fucking believe what he found online—Antwone Fisher was directing a movie starring, of all people, Larry Fishburne. (Too bad it didn't say anything about porndaughter co-☆ring.) It got weirder: there was a role for a black his age. **www.castingcallLA.com** said Antwone already saw 100s of boys but hadn't yet found "the one." "We'll know it when he walks through the door," said Fish (not Fishburne; "Fish" was Antwone's nickname) in an interview with **www.shootingstarz.com**.

WTF. Shit was *crazy.*

The timing was crazy cosmic too, but Rikki was stymied about how to proceed. He talked to ReeRee (somewhat reluctantly hipping her to his general plan; not too many people had ever known about his closely-concealed somewhat embarrassing ((to him)) ambitions to act, maybe just Dawn & Engineer Jim) and Ree tripped on it & loved him for it, because it was so unexpected, & a way of being proactive re them getting a house together, getting a life, getting on with their lives to come. Reeyonna then spoke to her bro who then spoke to his parttime g.f. Tom-Tom, who was *truly* hip to gaming the

Hollywood system. *The Treasure of Sierra Leone* had a Facebook page & casting link where you could upload your reel from tmblr or wherever. Tom-Tom even found verboten chunks of the script in the shady thickets of the webswamp (**www.scriptileaks.com**).

She ran down the synopsis for him: *Treasure* was about a failed character actor (Fishburne) whose estranged teenage daughter gets a virus that severely damages her heart. In order to raise the 300K required for meds & a transplant, Fishburne becomes a grifter. He hooks up with an old guy (Michael Douglas) recently fired from his job of 35 years—a daytime soap—whose livelihood now pretty much exclusively consists of seducing widows. Douglas never really has the heart to royally fleece the old ladies, settling instead for room, board & pocket $$$ in exchange for platonic companionship. Enter Fishburne, who wants to change all that *muy pronto*. The duo stage a bingo scam & are nearly out-hustled by a brilliant 15-year-old, an *agro* Afro-American runaway from some foster home hellhole. Impressed by his *mad skills*, they take the kid under their wing.

That night, Fishburne watches Oprah interview a former child soldier from Freetown. He's riveted by the charismatic young boy's articulate saga of being abducted by the Lord's Resistance Army and brainwashed to be a killer. Inspired, he calls his friend Douglas & proposes they set out on a scam tour of America—with the runaway impersonating a reformed child soldier, Fishburne playing his impoverished, dignified African father, & Douglas trodding the boards as the founder of the NGO responsible for the boy's rehab & redemption. At first Douglas is skeptical, but when Fishburne bares his soul & says that his daughter will die without the surgery, Douglas needs no further coaxing.

So they set out & the kid's a natural. Born for the part. As a warm-up, he practices on the widows, who practically hand over their pocketbooks. Fishburne & Douglas begin booking lectures in small auditoriums & concert halls, and pretty soon they've got a cash cow phenom on their hands. They're making local appearances, doing call-in radio shows, county fairs, all that. The fake warrior becomes

a burgeoning rockstar on the indomitable-human-spirit circuit, the
darling of liberal socialites' soirées, everybody hungering to hear the
lurid horrors of manchild in the unpromised land. The biggest problem becomes how to keep the whole floating crapgame below the
radar—Fishburne & Douglas want attention, just not the *wrong* kind.
Because the minute someone starts trying to verify details, the jig, as
they say, is up.

Tom-Tom read Rikki an online press release from a few weeks
back. It said that Ishmael Beah, the famous grownup child soldier
whom the script's impostor was based upon, signed on as a consultant
on the film. The name rang a bell. Weirdly enough, Rikki recalled
that some months ago, Beah visited John Crowe Ransom to give a
talk about his memoir, *A Long Way Gone.* The dude didn't seem too
much older than himself. During a special assembly, Beah shared his
story of the atrocities he was forced to commit as a young boy. He
remembered Beah talking about how the rebels hooked him & his
homies on some kind of speed mixed with gunpowder.

Killin & cokin'! *Fuckin bitchin . . .*

The web was awash with h8trs whining that Beah "went Hollywood"—not only was he cheapening his own story, but the stories of
all traumatized child soldiers & "lost boys." Blahdee-blahdee-blah.
The usual devils were busily obsessed with debunking the truthful-
ness of Ishmael's journey (http://oneminutebookreviews.wordpress.com/
ishmael-beahs-a-long-way-gone-is-a-long-way-from-the-truth-magazine-
says-in-report-raising-serious-doubts-about-memoir/)—but what Rikki
really liked was, Beah kept above the fray, rebutting, "sad to say, my
story is all true." In response to his lotusland-sellout critics (http://
whatisthewhat.org.african-stories/lost-in-america/ishmael-beah-chronicles-
his-role/), he said "sometimes painful truths must be 'wrapped' in
comedy in order to open people's eyes so they may learn & understand."

Tom-Tom thought Rikki's encounter with Beah, plus the fact
he'd already read (listened to, actually) the memoir, was some kind
of sign from God. (She was way off into omens & numerology.)

But Tom-Tom also knew they were seriously running out of time. Any day now she could get a Google Alert that Antwone Fisher found his *boy.* She gave them a firm 48-hr deadline, periodically setting out bumps to help Rikki get the job done. *Bumpin bumpin bumpin.*

Tom-Tom said the most important thing was for Rikki to listen to Beah's book on the iPod, like over and over, building a baseline of memory in his head of how the dude spoke, his rhythm & intonation, with particular emphasis on the content of stories & anecdotes, cause that was gonna be the source of his freestylin material. The rich, poetic details of Sierra Leone, its fauna&flora, Beah's friends, family & aborted childhood . . . *that's* where the gold was. She really wanted him to master the Beah *voice,* the glib, syrupy, transatlantic *inflection* that counterpoised so well with clipped, deadpan tales of random rape, torture & murder. Tom-Tom reminded Rikki that in the *movie,* Douglas and Fishburne put the (adopted!) boy through a similar crash course, accent & all.

Rikki didn't go home for 2 straight days. (He slept with Reeyonna at night but during the day Tom-Tom banned Ree from the *working area*, banned *everyone*, cause the shit they were up to was too serious to be distracted by people walking in & generally getting in their business.) The dro was dank, the blow was crank & the shit was crackin. They read aloud scenes from the script, a couple times she even jacked him off for real. Rikki wanted to keep it going but she said nope, back to work, maybe they'd fuck when they finished. Tom-Tom was a good improvver, she used to have a boyfriend in 2nd City, & Rikki turned out to have some flamboyant freestyle flair. V. good at voices & impressions. Tom-Tom got *way* into it . . . she pushed & pushed, and at the end of their mini-marathon told Rikki he was effing *awesome,* which he was thrilled to hear, he felt *good,* & came to believe she was telling the truth, too. Tom-Tom encouraged him to get cocky (*just don't let it show*), in this situation she said it was *totally okay* to get his cock on & be stuck-up/superconfident of his gifts. If he really wanted to get the part.

. . .

Rikki was krunked up in the trees, tripping on how no one knew how much Antwone Fisher meant to him.

It seemed like every soul-killing family placement/residential group home Rikki ever was at* had a copy of *Antwone Fisher*—the movie Hollywood made about Fish (not Fishburne)'s life—tucked into their shitty collections of donated cassettes & DVDs. Which was ironic, because Fish's spirit got nearly crushed by the foster mom they show in the film beatin on him & calling him a nigger 24/7 (a black bitch, too), & the foster sis (another black bitch) molesting him when she babysat. So Rikki grew up sort of watching a docudrama, *kind of*, not in detail but in *feeling*, the story of his own woebegone, borrowed life.

The internet said that the favorite all-time movie of dudes in the penitentiary was *The Shawshank Redemption*, which was about corrupt & homicidal jailers, but about escape & freedom too—well, that's how it was with foster kids and the *Antwone Fisher* flick. Seeing it for the first time, only 7-years-old, Rikki—stomach-punched, face-slapped, nigger-called, dick-in-fostermouth'd Rikki—was old enough to acquire the perverse, eager hope that his life might be survivable. He had fantasies of joining the Marines just like Antwone did; of having a strong man there for him like Denzel was for Fish, in the movie; & of meeting a girl who loved him, just like the girl in the flick did. Of course, they left out a lot of shit from the book. (Rikki kept a worn burnished copy of the autobio *Finding Fish* in his drawer—*Finding Fish* was Antwone's *A Long Way Gone*—in whatever drawer of whatever terrible transient home he found himself in any given year, kept it hidden beneath socks & underwear, like smuggled treasure.) They didn't show how Antwone wrote a screenplay of his life then got a job as a guard at a Hollywood studio so he could learn about the Business; or how he struggled to

---

* Before at long last being remanded to the loving care of Engineer Jim and his "Dawnie."

get someone to film his script. That would be a whole other movie.

(Rikki wondered if they ever showed *Shawshank* or *Ant. Fish.* up in Pelican Bay, & what maybe his father thought of them.)

. . . during his deformative years, young Rikki watched the sado-surroundsound saga of *Antwone Fisher* as he caromed from one foster placement to another—the melodrama of abuse on ironic TV room tap for the very kids busy being Rx drugged, beaten & sexed by their keepers, old pros at the *foster children reimbursement payment scale* game, squeezing every $ they could from their hopeless, helpless, ratfucked human cargo. As he grew older, Rikki grew puzzled too. He was happy for Antwone but couldn't understand why anyone would want to make a movie about such miseries, a movie that seemed to exist for the sole purpose of confirming he, Rikki, was a captive resident of fosterfucked Hell, & that what he watched on screen was a mirror/reminder (except with movie ☆s!) of his fosterfuckery life . . . movies were supposed to *entertain*, he supposed *someone* thought they might be entertained by watching this boy-to-manchild Antwone trapped in a nightmare different but the same as his own! The motion picture bore the Good Bad Housekeeping Seal of Approval, no doubt. But why? Rikki was sure there was a reason, otherwise Antwone surely would not have allowed this thing to be shot. See, *Antwone Fisher* was released more than 10 years ago—so maybe there had been an end result he hadn't heard, say, maybe the production brought Fish's abusers to justice. He searched online . . . or maybe the movie struck fear in the ♥s of the wicked, forcing them to be kinder, & seek forgiveness of those they murdered & destroyed, to amend their ways . . . but if that were true, what was the DVD doing in all those scarysick dens? (In one home, a retard night supervisor went suckin from dick to dick, *while* the lil homies watched *Ant. Fish* on the flatscreen.) Wouldn't the fostercrooks be afraid that viewing such a film would foment rebellion amongst their charges? What else *would* be the point of such an adaption to film, if not to inform & overturn? And if Denzel & Antwone & everyone else confabulated it *not* for political reasons but first & foremost to *entertain,* with each further viewing Rikki felt there to be something cruel in it: the notion that this movie *Antwone Fisher* might entertain—might ease the interminable misery of his borrowed days by whispering, *Watch & learn that you are not the only one bound by misery, misery is not a thing that can be confined to your stained, stinky couch & stained, stinky little life, no! Misery is all around you . . . misery, ordinary misery, as ordinary & crippling as nausea, ripples ever onward & outward*

As if the filmmakers were trying to tell him

Yes! Even though domestic hell is your world, the only one you know, the only one you will ever know, take ♥! Because all of Hell belongs to no one man or boy, it belongs to the world at large, not just the pukey smallness of your world within the bigger pukey world, but to the Universe & infinitude of undiscovered universes beyond, each mirroring the hell of the other

As if to say———

*this "entertainment" was concocted to show you there are infinitudes of mirrored, shitty Hells you will be forced to visit should you ever break free of this one, that which resides in the creepy stink-den where you wallow, friendless, unpopcorned, watching the Hell of your own reflection thrown back from the screen . . . your hero Antwone portrays you! He got out, yes! He escaped from the carcasstink rot of the borrowed living room couch, from the mouth of the caretaker, to the carcasstink rot of onscreen Hell you now see him cavort in on the Samsungscreen one hellboy watching another, until over it starts again, on some stained stinky shitty couch, in some other universe . . . .
. . . .*

Rikki gettin hella hyphy! He be swisher trippin———

He saw *Antwone Fisher* countless times tho only recently made the connection that not only was the film ☆'d in but *directed by* Denzel——Rikki wanted to be like *those* men, the *creators,* the *doers,* the actors & activists, if he tried *hard* enough he thought he maybe could, *knew* he could, he wanted to be like Denzel w/a Best Actor, Denz knew how to direct too, how the fuck could he do all that shit, he could do *anything* & could just go & do whatever he wanted, if it popped into his head he could just go mutherfuckin do it; he wanted to be like Jamie Foxx collabin' with the players, w/Ye&Ludakris&big boi, you know, Jamie could *sing*, Jamie was *funny*, he fuckin created *In Living Color*, & Jamie had his *own* Best Actor just like Denzel, Rikki wanted to be out there *being* somebody, like all *"Lil Wayne featuring Jamie Foxx, Rikki, Drake, Nicki and whomever,"* Rikki wanted to be like Don Cheadle, like Will Smith, like Wesley, like Affion, like *Tyler, the Creator*——————

——————*hey don't be greedy dude, don't get sacrilege.* You know the *true* one to aspire to, that's your real shot, more than anybody, & that's still Fish (he needed to aspire to be his own *version* of Fish, because he had to keep his individuality)—Antwone Fisher, stalwart unflashy boy of ambition (*just like me*), boy who broke free, boy become a man, a manchild who wrote & directed, wrote books too, dignified man & boychild who could do it all.

He never told Tom-Tom about any of that, never told anyone, because a person didn't have to share everything.

. . .

She put him in the shower, dressed him in levi's & a t-shirt that said YSL, they did more coke, swallowed some roxys & were good to go. Tom-Tom stood behind the camera, she'd moved the whole operation to the bathroom which had a tiny skylight & told Rikki to begin by giving his name, age, what school he went to, how he was in a few school plays/productions like *Rent* & *House of Blue Leaves*. (All bullshit) She thought it was a good idea to prompt him by asking questions O.C. She got to the meat of it right away because she knew he had to get their attention, about 10,000 other vids were probably being uploaded *right now* so his audition needed to stand out *from the gate.*

She made Rikki introduce himself, the key factoid being that in real life he actually *was* a foster child (just like Antwone F & the boy pretending to be the child soldier in the movie), but who *differs* from that character because of his very loving relationship with his foster-parents & their imminent plans to legally adopt him, a ceremony that was mere months away. Tom-Tom had concerns that whoever was watching the tape might think he was making this part up, so she took pains to have Rikki dwell on it, to inform directly to the camera that he would be doing some improvising but the shit he said about his upcoming adoption was not a part of it. That shit was true. Occasionally, when he froze up or got self-conscious, Tom-Tom turned off the camera to loosen him up, maybe give him more blow, *tiny* bit of H, once she even brained him which for some reason made him laugh inside while she was doing it, tripping on how she could really suck a dick straight up, deepthroating till his balls disappeared in her mouth, that's why they call him gutsy. When Tom-Tom turned the camera back on, she did some off-cam freestylin herself, like reading some of the dialog of a socialite in the movie who gets duped into believing the runaway's story of ex-childsoldierdom, the Miami Beach toryburch of her being titillated to the core whilst in the presence of this *very attractive* negro monster/killing machine who laid claim to being redeemed viz the help of loving dad Fishburne & intrepid U.N. worker-turned-NGO founder Douglas, parts of the script reminding Tom-Tom of that movie where Will Smith pretends to be Sidney Poitier's son. She'd have shown it to Rikki but they didn't have time.

He soon found his own cadence. He talked about being a student at John Crowe Ransom Middleschool, ordinary kid who did ordinary stuff, even mentioned his g.f. Reeyonna, Tom-Tom thought that was tight. In one part of the charming (she hoped) "novelty interview," she even had him lay out the strange *co-inky-dink* of Ishmael Beah coming to speak at his school assembly last year, it was too karmic not to mention, plus how *A Long Way Gone* had been on Rikki's iPod for like, a year already. Co-inky-dink? I think not. She was beguiled/captivated just filming/watching Rikki glide from middleschool plainspeak to cagey hustler to ruminatively remorseful, childsoldier-Beahspeak, patois-riffing freestylin monologues off the e-purloined script. She hoped the producers wouldn't take offense, because the screenplay wasn't supposed to be *out there*, tho Tom-Tom was 100% certain the prod co had already just shrugged its shoulders, everyone knew you couldn't keep anything off the internet, the world as we know it was now pure LeakiLeaks, all leaks all the time, & no one expected the genie to ever get back in the bottle. Tom-Tom was certain too that Rikki wouldn't be the only auditioner openly using it as source.

Then Tom-Tom said (prearranged), "I understand you & Ishmael were friends," so as to trigger/cue Rikki to rev up his patois freestylin & Rikki said

Yes . . . tiss is true. We trahvill'd to-get-hur in duh teek [thick] *forest, duh moon was hangin like a bloody banahna in duh black saffire pool of duh sky. Dat day I saw duh rebels snatch duh imam from deh mosk & tie heem to a pole & set heem on fie-uhr . . . we covered r ears from duh screemin. Duh rebels made me & Ishmael do many terrible tings, you know, like chop off duh arms & legs of duh moms & dads and duh cats & dogs* [Tom-Tom almost lost it right there]. *Dere were many daze when we hodd to go wid-out duh use of anti-perspirant. Sum times, before day sent me & Ishmael out to rape and to pillage duh village, duh nasty-ass rebels day feed us speedy dope & to make us angry, day force us to watch duh Justin Beeber cone-surt feelm—————*

Tom-Tom laughed, wondering if Rikki went too far. She decided it was perfect. *I mean hey! it's a frickin comedy, right?*

. Around noon of the 2nd day, she started to edit together an hour or so of footage. But when she replayed Rikki's hilarious monolog with the chopping of duh arms & legs of duh cats&dogs and duh Justin Beeber cone-surt feelm, she said fuck it, fuck the montage, and told Rikki *that's* what she was going to give em. Rikki started to protest, not even too much, but Tom-Tom told him it was now in the hands of the lord. With a wild eye she said

"TOO LATE! Already pusht SEND! It is now in the hands of the Lord, & the Lord's Resistance Army too. Nigger yo sweet black ass is *officially uploaded!* You gunna be a *moviestar.* Now come & get your reward, I'm gunna suck that beautiful black dick til your eyes roll up in your fuckin head. What are you smiling at, whats the matter, you don't want me to? What, you don't like the way I suck it? Cause nigger I know you *do.* Now how's *Reeyonna* gunna find out about that shit? Who's gunna tell her, you? Cuz I sure as hell don't plan to . . . don't you like the way I do you? Cause I know you aint *never* been done like the way I do. Well aw–ite, that's better now, nigger show me that you *mean* it, cause otherwise you gunna hurt my feelings. Ooh ooh *that's* better. Look at that muthafucker. Just *look.* And take a *long* look, cause you aint gunna see it for a while. That's right. Say 'Bye–Bye!' Say, 'Bye–Bye, Black Beauty!' Cause that muther is goin *in.*"

[Jerzy]

To Kill A Hummingbird

Jerzy's

intel, his twittinformers, twatsnitches, GPS-holes, whatever, had furnished him plate numbers & car descriptions, so he could still make the I.D. & give chase, even if they did a vehicle switcheroo, even if the windows were blacked out he could still follow them to Melrose Place or Giorgio Baldi or In-N-Out (the one by LAX had been good to him) or the plastic surgeon's or wherever. This late afternoon, he had cellpics of plates, dents, & scuffs on Rihanna's SUV, Reese's Audi wagon, V Beckham's Rolls, Colin Farrell's Fiat, Lindsay's Lex hybrid plus 100 more, all +/- the last 48 hrs at most, because anything later than that was untrustworthy intel.

A current one to watch was Michael Douglas, who *at this moment* was being chauffeured around in a Music Express Mercedes. Jerzy was one of a handful of people on planet Earth who knew Douglas was having dinner with Heather Morris at a private estate above the reservoir in Silverlake Hills. He told his twits&shouts to *sit* on that because if it was a romantic thing (more would be revealed), a furtive exit pic/shadowkiss could gross a fucking mill & if they didn't keep their mouths shut, they wouldn't get a penny, which was the only way to guarantee any kind of silence . . . the situation tho was *de facto*

way volatile, he couldn't keep a lid on it too long, it was a LeakyLeak
world like Tom-Tom said, the tomtom drums could be heard in every global village, the Douglas/Hemo *tête-à-teats* (he sent out a tweet:
does Hemo still have her implants?) would need to come to a head soon,
i.e., before his rival pack-o'-ratsies found out.

This, as Hyman Roth said, was the life he chose.

·   ·   ·

He cycled thru this kind of trouble a couple times a year when sleeping issues got out of hand.

He needed GBH to come down, GBH worked nicely, but heroin
or methadone was still preferable. Tom-Tom became his source, very
reliable, gave him just enough to mellow at the end of the day, then a
few hours later sleep, problem being eventually it wouldn't be
enough. He'd slide into smoking PCP (to further chill), which
worked for awhile, in that way everything works for awhile, until it
doesn't, until came the familiar visitations of paranoia&(mostly) au-
ditory hallucinations.

He knew a wave was coming, immense & unsurfable, when he
switched the sat radio in the truck from CNN manwhores Blitzer &
Cooper to *Shade 45*, the hardcore hip hop station belonging to racist
genius Eminem. It was important for him to listen because *Mr.
Mathers* was the enemy, the *Emeny*, *Mr. Mathers* (Jerzy always used his
white birthname) was the Trojan horse from which all coming racial
strife, bondage & pestilence would run havoc. Msquared was the
puppetmaster, biding his time with his white cohorts & consorts,
slaves too but of a higher class, Elton & David, Fallon/Fey, Ashton &
Demi (still together tho maintaining divorced personae per PuppetM's orders), Tom & Katie, Justins Bieber/Timberlake/Theroux,
the list was hella long . . . M²'s most ardent skill being his immense
instincts/knowledge of how to seduce the black, how to play on their
weaknesses, their whitelove of fame & money, their blackened obsession to be white, their white *obsession* with it, *Mr. Mathers* played it
like a Game of Thrones.

For Jerzy, the distant rolling thunder of conspiracy always had the same flavor: the Race Wars, newfangled, coming race wars, grandfather of that which Manson botched. Today, listening to *The Shade*, he could see the dark familiar funnel of it as yet far away, trunk of an F5, awesome furry black twister spiral-shimmer with untwinkling rhinestones along its wormy trunk which on closer look were up-spooling specks of debris, church pews, housesplinters, yard shard jetsam, John Deeres & orchard trees feeding the frivolous maw, Jerzy saw it change direction & begin its slow advance toward him, & it was a warning he recognized, the gargantuan drill-biting clang, the chomping pulverization of the ground in the syncopated broken circle of 4/4 time, ferocious machine shop tapdance roving over the checkerboard of his mindscape like a playstation *God of*——

Time to ready himself for his role of counterspy: the White thought he was spying for them on the Black but in actuality he was spying on the Whites for the Black, yessir, that is correct, gathering intel/conducting *cointelpro* on behalf of those few Black left who could be trusted, the few who hadn't been bootysnatched by M^2 & his minions Jay-Z (Hov), Kanye (Yahweh), Nicki (Miriam), Lil Wayne (Zion) . . . and now Tyler the Creator was owned by the Puppetmathers who came a-raping in the night, Odd Future no longer a collective but *collected,* oh the tragedy of it! for Tyler had the shiniest shine, for a moment, Suge had thought he was The One, but now it was done, the Odds weren't good & the goods were Odd, Wolf Gang still pretending to be heretical anarchists flying above their SUPREME t-shirts the SUPREME agitprop banner of Youth, all had succumbed, now blind sucklers of M^2's cock, tongue & tits. They be Gobblin———

> Even the Jackal will offer her teats and suckle her cubs
> (Lamentations 4:3).

Jerzy was one of the coveted outsiders (whites) accepted into the camp of the Black; in the manner Tom Hagen was accepted as the only non-Italian consigliere.

When he first saw him on *American Idol*, Jerzy looked into his eyes & his soul, down into the ratty mouth of him, & at once he knew—the knowledge electrifying him like a gust from another world, a stellar wind—knew *without question* that Jimmy Iovine was behind the erasures of Biggie & Tupac—it was I-Veen, with the help of minions Paula Abdul, Spike, Quincy, Arsenio & Eddie Murphy (Tupac said Eddie gave money to charity but the $$$ never ever found its way to the ghetto, Toop said ½ his fans were white & that Madonna was his homie, & Don McClean his mentor), who knocked down that 2nd domino of helter-skelter (Charlie M having pushed the 1st). I-Veen had 50 middleclass Whites standing by, each elected by a constituency of 100,000 Whites all across the land—across the breadbasket & ♥belt of this land my land your land this made for you & me land, by the end they stood for *5 million*, all told, but the skittish Black pointed Judaslike fingers at one of their own—Suge—my Suge, your Suge, their Suge, Suge Knight! Suge Knight, who was the only warrior meshugg enough to lead them out of the White darkness that had descended & enshrouded them, if only they had *listened*—but the water got too muddied, crafty I-Veen knew the triumphant surfacing of the White *at that time* would have read lunatic-racist-fringey instead of sober-consensus-of-the-White-Mass—so, like a judicious climber who because of inclement weather conditions, turns back a mere 500 feet from Everest's peak, the wisdom & even-keeled brilliance of General I-Veen bade his infantry retreat. The dominos were scattered, many tin soldiers fell, the Race War was not to be waged.

Not on that day . . . .

It will keep, said the General.

He would pass the torch to his sons, Ricky Ruben & Liar Cohan, and *son* of sons Martial Law Mathers. I-Veen the Father, Liar & Little Ricky the Sons, MM the Holy Ghost.

The blind complacency of the Black set the stage for the rise of Marshall Mathers, his marriage to the assassin Fiddy, & the shame and humiliation that followed of Jay-Z, Drs. Dre/ake, Lil Wayne, Snoop, T.I., Ludacris, Nicki, Rihanna, and so many others by his hands. (The beating she suffered was owing to the talented Mr Brown's explosive displeasure upon learning the news that had been concealed from him; that she had crossed over to the Puppetmathers' world. He did not love the way she lied. If one were to make a timeline, it would be clear to see that Rihanna's easing/lifting of the restraining order coincided to the very *day* she received word from Jay-Z-hova that her contrite beloved had been made a boss on Mathers' plantation. Alack, another sad day for Suge Templar Knight, who until that moment had been so impressed with Mr Brown, & now spent sleepless nights bemoaning the fate of *all* of his once brave brethren.)

Jerzy kept a diary in a close, careful hand; the wild history clarified things for him. He wrote about Mr Mathers living in his Oz-like home in Detroit, serviced by Black&White slaves. Like an emperor, his every need was made manifest: in the middle of each of his many labs there sat a fountain which spewed forth Splenda-flavored diet Coke. Mr Mathers has gone on record that he keeps vast files of wordplay rhymes on index cards for future anthems; Jerzy wrote in his journal other hidden details that he felt must come to light should something happen to him during one of his missions—mainly, that a whole room in itself was dedicated to those troves of songs to be written & played at a future date when the War is over & peace descends upon the land. These are the songs that contain the word nigger; the Puppetmathers would fold them into the compositional theme he used so effectively, time & again, of his dominance over the thickheaded thugs & tatted pickanninies of rapdom. *He dreamed he was King, woke up, he was still King* . . . . . of those he enslaved. *Watch the (game of) throne* . . . as White infiltrate & co-commander of Black Cointelpro, Jerzy had done an exceedingly careful study of Mr Mathers' manner of speech, his inflections when he talkshowed or spoke to radio press—the Puppetmathers has a playful side, but likes

to keep his interviewers on edge, enjoys making them feel honored
he has spared them from his whipsaw rage & violent whitened black-
henchmen—Jerzy noted that when M² was being serious, his broody
face formed words with peculiar, post-modern wigger phrasing, odd
& somewhat somehow blackified, & strange sounding . . . *it isn't
quite white trash not exactly but then what is it?* Jerzy realized what
caused Mr Mathers' baffling, unplaceable argot: simply the effect
upon his regular speech—a compression or distortion or displace-
ment of sound—by that of an *alternate* speechifying: as he spoke to
whatever obsequious interlocutor to promote himself, he was *at the
same time sending messages to his slaves.* One day there would be a machine not yet born (Suge's scientists were working on it) able to split
his voice in two, & isolate the *2nd speaker*: exposing, for the cynics,
the pep talk/marching orders he dispenses to plantation workers, in
all media & venue.

So artful was Mr Marshall Mathers, that to his father I-Veen's
pleasure, a 3rd domino need not even be touched by his hand—they
were already falling by metempsychosis.

The love of Jerzy's life was a black Jew (he called her Blue) whom he
lived with for a time in Brooklyn. He destroyed that love with the
necessary, poignant sacrifices of War, forever paying the remorseful
price. When the Great Wave came over him—such as it was beginning to lap at him now, & such as it had before he was hospitalized
for his small, secret ♥ attack—he called her Blue, yet came to believe
her true name to be Zadie Smith.

Zadie Bluesmith sometimes helped him, the memory of her
helped clear his head so he could set down thoughts & analyses which
in Time he knew would be historical. He wished she could be with
him but he'd lost track of where she was, didn't even know if she
were still alive, sometimes had a *feeling* she wasn't, then heard she got
married, but when he heard she got married he preferred to believe
she was dead, that his *feeling* she was no longer living had been cor-

rect, preferred that awful thing over believing or learning she had married. She sometimes helped him during his compositions, the close & careful journaling he did to make sense of his inspirited crusade. Because it was lonely, solitary work. She helped with his *Lamentations,* & encouraged him to carry with him at all times the acrostic alphabet of which the League of Informers & Betrayers was composed—those who it had been written would stand in the way of the Suge-led Black, the warriors who one day, after much bloodshed, would storm Heaven & achieve their place in Paradise *for there is no pain like their pain.* He kept the laminated cheatsheet in a drawer, it'd been there since he came home from his small, secret ♥ attack, but when he saw the dark distant funnel & heard the faraway rolling thunder he placed it on his person & wore it all the days. An eerie roll call & reminder of MCs who had fallen:

Plantation Lamentations

א (Aleph) **Eminem, Master/Overseer/Puppetmathers**
ב (Beth) *Big Pun, Bone th., Busta Rhymes, Beasties, birdman*
ג *(Gimel) Geto boyz, the Game*
ד (Daleth) *Dre, Drizzy, DMC, dmx*
ה (He) *Hov-Jay-Z*
ו (Waw) *Weezy, Waka Flocka Fl., Wiz Kh., Warren G*
ז (Zayin) *Ye, Yelawolf*
ח (Heth) *Ice Cube*
ט (Teth) *T.I., Tyler the Creator/T-Pain*
י (Yod) *B.o.B.*
כ (Kaph) *Common, Chris Brown*
ל (Lamed) *Lauryn Hill, Luda, LLCool J, lil kim, Jeezy*
מ (Mem) *Method M., Mase, Mos Def, Mob deep, Maybach Music, MIA*
נ (Nun) *NWA, Nicki-Barbie, Nate dogg*
ס (Samek) *Snoop*
ע (Ayin) *Naas, Andre 3K, Eazy E, OFWGKTA*
פ (Pe) *50 çent, Puff*
צ (Sadhe) *Scarface, Soulja boy, Salt N Pepa*
ק (Qof) *[The Martyrs 2pac/Biggie & Warrior Archangel Suge Knight]*
ר (Resh) *Raekwon, Rakim, (Rihanna), Royce da 5'9", Rick Ross*
ש (Shin) *Slick Rick*

And then Blue I.V. was born, a black blueblood whom the Puppet-master could not transfuse, resistant to his plantation platelets, & that was when he was certain his Zadie Blue had transmogrified, had come to him, & it would not matter if he would no longer be living when Blue I.V. came of age in the Days of Majestic Rage & over-threw those who bore and betrayed her, the Bé & the Hov—the chosen cloven—the *béhooven*.

· · ·

He toggled between CNN faggot panicwhores & *Shade 45*, reawak-ened to *la causa* as he listened sorrowfully to converted slaves singing on Marshall Mathers' plantation.

Royce da 5 9's voice rang out from the fields:

"Tell Shady I love him the same way that he did Dr Dre on the chronic, tell him how real he is or how high I am or how I would kill for him to know it."

Proud Black warriors who once stood tall now grew spreadcunts for the Puppetmathers, speaking in tongues and Code.

Suge Knight's head hung in sadness & steely resolve.

· · ·

If he could help them triumph, his place in history was secure.

(That's where his head would go.)

(The cheatsheet laminate)

(A year ago, while hospitalized for his small, secret ♥ attack, Jerzy spoke with Suge & Suge Knight honored & thanked him, and told him he would contact him in Time.)

The dark funnel frightened him.

Jerzy had some little tricks to lighten up.

For example, he'd dig out a DVD, Biggie Smalls guest-starring on an old *Martin Lawrence*. No shit, Sherlock. It was *whack*. Biggie played his 24-year-old self. He drops by Martin's to tell him confidentially that he's looking for a back-up singer & the next thing he knows (loose mouths in the hood), there's 1,000 people outside the apt looking to audition. Gina & Pam diva their way in, & effin hilarity ensues. Jerzy loved it because it was so unabashed a tribute to *I Love Lucy,* one of his faves. Cunt MoMA used to plunk him down in front of the tube w/cold Banquet TV dinners & forget about him for the day *yeah, life's a Banquet, a beggar's banquet huh.* That show saved his life. To this day he fantasized it was *him* born to Lucy & Desi, primetime.

. . .

Home now.

Bootie bumpin—meth & warm water shpritzed up the ass.

3 pages torn from magazines, sitting on the low table between him and the flatscreen, for his perusal.

A tivo'd NatGeo doc was on, but he couldn't focus.

He was focused on the torn magazine pages.

"Second Look" was from *People*:

Two pix of Emma Watson placed side by side. The pix look identical, she's walking out the door of Whole Foods. The caption says, *Find the Differences in these two pics of Emma Watson, the latest face of Lancôme in Paris.* Hmmmm . . . try as he may, he couldn't. I bet Harry around the Middleton could find the difference hahahaha. He'd say *Oh shit yeah, she's got 653 hairs on the arm on the right, & 547 on the arm on the left . . .*

O. Yeah. Now Jerzy sees that in the 1st pic, her Hermès watch has a single strap; in the *other,* it's got *two.* Effin fascinatin, huh. Jerzy moved on to the side-by-side shtick Rob Lowe beach pics in the *Enquirer*'s "Two for the Road" knock-off. *Good ol Rob. Now there's a guy who always lands on his feet.* Jerzy took a closer look . . . is that a beauty mark on Rob's abs or is that a mark on the magazine paper? He spent a few minutes on it but couldn't find the diff, the 2 pix looked exactly alike. Shit. Hate it when that happens. Well if at first you don't succeed, fail, fail again. Hahaha. And for our next braincruncher, ladies & gentlemen, it's . . . *Lea Michele!* (featured in this week's In Touch *Double Takes*.) First thing Jerzy looked for was the photoshop nose-job. Nope, no photoshnozz. *Hahahahaha.* They left it intact. Took up a lotta space in the mag, tho. All the nose that fits to print, haha, the bitch got plenty o' proboscis. But *WTF,* he couldn't find any differences there either . . . .

He crushed/smoked an Addie then watched some of the *Martin Lawrence* ☆ing Notorious. Biggie looked fatcheeked & shiny-new as a baby, he wore a smart, XXXXXL well-pressed jumpsuit, his bigass feet stuck in a pair of pristine orange construction boots. *Swank.* Back & forth Jerzy went, twixt the *Martin* & the NatGeo doc . . . but it was sticky going. *Man, this tivo's a fuckin antique, what's the matter with her. Fuckin Tom-Tom. Must be the 1st one ever made.*

The NatGeo doc: a hummingbird was on screen.

He used to love reading NatGeo the Magazine but it started getting too sado-porn for his tastes. Fucking Rupert Murdoch bought it, fucking Murdoch ruins everything. Destroys. The last time he flipped through one was a few months ago in the waiting room of a pain doc. Foto of a farmer in the snow perched over the carcasses of two reindeer whose antlers became entangled. The old Swede said he figured it took them three days to die. *Fuckin Murdoch.*

Hummingbirds scared him—too much like fibrillating ♥s. They reminded him of what he thought his own ♥ must have looked like before the small, secret coronary. (Nobody even knew he'd had one except an RN he kept semi in touch with, she was a dope fiend, sometimes they FaceTime geni-cammed, she stuck a hairbrush up.) This deepvoiced narrator guy was talking about how a praying mantis could kill a hummingbird. *Say what?* Jerzy PAUSED the docu to google praying mantis because he got temporarily *fakakta* & thought maybe a _/|_ mantis really *wasn't* an insect like he fucking *thought*—but no! shit! It *was*—unpausing the Tivo so the narrator could say that mantises waited *in ambush*, fucking *waited!* at the feeders! for the hummingbirds to come! How the fuck could that be? How could it? because that demonstrates *intelligence*, how do you even *recognize* a hummingbird feeder if you're a fucking insect, how do you *lay in wait,* you're a mutherfucking *insect,* & if an *insect* can kill a *bird* then

maybe it could learn to recognize *the door to my fucking room* . . . .
. . . .

With stupendous effort, he kept reality checking to make sure he wasn't having a freak-hallucination. When it became too much, he MUTED (letting it continue to PLAY, hoping the mutherfucking docu would do him the favor of *ending* by the time he came back), & hit the kitchen for something to eat but of course he wasn't hungry. Decided to look for gum, looked in the drawer where Tom-Tom kept lightbulbs & screwdrivers & tacks, couldn't find any, actually didn't feel like gum anyway. Then he wanted a cookie, there happened to be an actual cookie jar on the counter (but no cookies, he'd need to remedy that, he'd pick up his latest fave, Tim Tams, Tim Tams for Tom-Tom, she'd get a kick out of that, *chewy caramel chewy fudge chewy baca Tim Tams——shit. Maybe I should just run out right now to the 24-hour Ralphs*) so he went back to his room to smoke, his attention back on the 3 torn *Can You Spot the Differences?* pages, couldn't remember if he'd torn them out or if Tom-Tom left em for him, Tom-Tom was always tearing mindless shit out of mags & leaving it for him to peruse . . . . he sat back down, eyes averted from the screen.

He tried calling T²'s cell, bored, horny, imagined it ringing beside her dead body, or *ringing ringing ringing* while she was being raped by the police. Hung up & went back to Biggie & Martin, the mantis (Biggie) & the hummingbird (Martin), lit the crack pipe, scoped the 3 torn-out pages, thought about going for TimTams, handfucked for a hot sec to Emma, jacked to Rob, Biggie Martin hummingbird MUTE *pipe jack/rob lowe's dick in his mouth emma back to rob back to emma back to rob back to emma he cums kitchencookie jar no gum in the hardware drawer useless phonecall to TomTom TimTams* UNMUTE

rub

just one

more

off (Lea Michele's hairyhaileejewish
arms&pussy he thought about going to the tube that featured CATEGORY:
HAIRY/JEWISH

There they are: side by side: the Mantis and the Hummingbird.
Can You Spot the Differences?
morephonecallstoTomTom   morekitchentrips   more
crackpipejacking   GBH   mantisjack biggie biggie martin i love
lucy who ate the fucking cookies   tries to jack can't cum finally
sleeps.

[Tom-Tom]

Domain Change

"**Hey,**

guest what, sunshine? Alice doesn't *live* here anymore! Not for long, anyway . . . that is *correct*, we are *moving*. We are movin & groovin— to Mt. Olympus! You heard me, *biatch*, we are *chariots on fucking* FIRE. Tell you more about it later, hon, you will not *believe* how it came down, the *opportunity*, man, it is all *gunna happen*, it's all *happening*, & you better start wishing *large*, Large Boy, cause right now there aint a ☆ in the sky that's gonna say no to you. Lotsa airplanes in the night sky, sunshine. *When you SWISHER 'pon a star, makes no diff*——& on *top* everything, it's a *moneybag year*, Chinese *moneybag year*, did you know that, Holmes? Bet you didn't. Young money, cash moneybag.

"Man *shit* Jerz, you look like shit warmed over. You gotta cut back, dude, cause I can't be bailin you outta no psych ward, I ain't got the *time*. And my shit's just gonna get busier . . . just take a shower, OK? you fuckin *smell*, can you please just take a frickin shower? Pretty please? Jesus pull up your fucking pants, that bumster shit aint gunna play up on Olympus, playground of the gods . . . here, let me help, that's a good boy, & no I will *not* suck your dick while I'm down there, you couldnt get it up anyway . . . see? See that? I sucked & it aint gettin close. You probably can't even feel it. That's one mushroom cryin in the rain, aint growin like the rest of em. That's one dead fuckin shroom. Straighten up, Jerzy! Straighten up your room, boy, straighten up your shroom! Straighten the fuck *up*. That's some short woody you got there, Woody. You aint gonna be peckin too much with *that* woodpecker, Woody.

"All right, come on, let's go sunshine, I'm puttin your skeevy un-showered ass to bed *right now*, *shit* man, you know maybe you need a girlfriend, a steady fuck might tighten you up, cause you're married to that pipe, you're becoming a sadsack eunuch mutherfucker, & I aint shittin you Jerzy, the Tom-Tom train is *on its way*, friendy-friend, bout to pull out the *station*. Today, I secured the mothership! We bout to take *legal possession*, & as you *know* sweet cheeks *possession* is 9/10s of the law . . . *choo* choo choo choo *choo* choo choo choo—that's right, baby boy, one foot after the other, you doin *real well*, we're putting you to beddy-bye cause the Tom-Tom train is leaving the station & you *best* not be running down the track all tryin to hop on . . .

"All aboard! Last stop: Mt. Olympus! We all gonna be Mounties, we be Mounties listenin to that Sermon on the Mount! & if you *expect* to have a place *onboard*, my friendy-friend-friend, you have *got* to get yourself *togethuh*. Cause *we are ☆dust, we are golden. & we got to get ourselves back to the———*ouch! Now *come on* tweety-pie, stop draggin your mutherfuckin feet, man you *are* a sorry-ass crackhead mutherfucker. What the fuck happened to you? You know we oughta see if your sister wants to fuck you, pregnant girls are always way horny, you see em rubbin up against posts like a cat when nobody's lookin . . . maybe ReeRee could use a little on the side! Maybe ReeRee needs your peepee HAHAHAHAHAHA! O don't look all like that, you *know* you'd *love* it. Hell, *I'd* love it. I might just lend a helping hand. *Like a good neighbor, Tom-Tom is there* . . . Cause I know how to cervix a pregnant gal, Sue Sylvester-style. Tell you what, when sissy & me are a happy couple, all cozy, I'll invite you over once in a while, you can help me give her head. Good help is tough to find these days. She'll already have had the kid, & by then another'll be on the way, but this time it'll be a celeb's baby, none of this teen mom boyfriend shit. We want a kid with an *annuity*. Get us like an Ashton love child. Make him pay through the nose . . . but I am telling you, once sissy's mine? There is *no way* I would let you tap that *solo*, no *fuckin way*.

"You know what you've got to learn, Jerzy? What *you* need to learn is how to move the fuck *on*. Stop your *cryin*. Man that shit is unbecoming. *I* know what time it is. You're still crying in your bong about Jigger Blue. *The night is bitter, & Jerzy lost his nigger* . . . oops I mean jigger . . . *and all because of the Jew-schvartzuh who got away!* Sunshine, you have got to *move on*—just like *Jennifer & Renée & Demi & Ashlee & Scarlett & Sandra*. Those girls know how to *get laid*, then *move the fuck on*. They make a movie with a guy, they're armored up cause they've been hurt too often, but he's gorgeous, never mind he's been married 4 times & cheated on his last wife while she was having chemo—you know, they're thinking maybe *this* is the one, they lower their guard, get all *vulnerable & involved*—the publicists already have the brakes on, cause the publicists know what's coming, they see the breakup even before the hookup, the pubs are smart, except for the one who got her ass shot on Sunset, & they start saying shit like *they're just friends* yoddy yoddy *they value each other like good friends*, all that yoddy yoddy horseshit, but suddenly the ☆ is head over heels, usually the guy she's tripping on is a ☆ of way lesser magnitude, the pubs are freaking because they know the whore's track record, but it's too late, PDA pics are flooding the internet *proving* the authenticity of their love, & why not, who would begrudge, doesn't the dirty whore deserve to have a boyfriend who's maybe going to lead her to marriage & babies? Hasn't she been unlucky in love *enough*? Hasn't she dodged every STD known to science in her career as a ☆ who ☆fucks lesser ☆s? Hasn't she succeeded in hiding the 2 miscarriages & the 2 ectopics? Hasn't she put that pussy through bootcamp, & isn't she old enough to be dead in the ovaries? Oh & she *tries* to go forward with a degree of caution because she's been burned before but this time *fuck* it sure does feel like it's going to *last*, the Bad Boy sucks & fucks every hole, ooh he's good at it too, even fucks the holes in her ♥, every hole the bitch has, & you *know* there must be holes only celebs have, I am *telling* you, Holmes, ☆s *are* different than you and me! And then *o shit* someone leaks that the relationship is *slipping away*, the pubs of course knew it was coming, they rush in and say no no no! That's bullshit, they've never been happier—as a couple—& here are pictures from their holiday in Hawaii to prove it! Then: *BLAM BLAM BLAM* they've got sperm & egg on their faces *both parties are moving on!* O they still think the world of each other, they're going to continue their relationship *as friends*, but they've decided to *move on* because—get this, Jerzy! I read it on the US Weekly website—shit I can't remember what couple it was about but it said, it said, they decided to move on *because 'at the end of the day, they weren't on the same page'*—At the end of the day they weren't on the same page!!!! I swear Jerzy that's what it said!

"And as we all know so very fucking *well*, you have *got* to be on the same fucking page—& if you aint, you better *move the fuck on.*

"So: know what we're gunna do, Jerzy boy? Aside from moving on but as friends or whatever? We are gonna *man up.* We are gonna *Jennifer out* & *Demi up*, & move the fuck on to your bedroom. Mama's gunna give you something for your beauty sleep. Cause if you're gonna help U-Haul us—if you're gonna help us *move* to the Sermon on the Mount, you have *got* to get your beauty sleep.

"Are we on the same page? Well, goodie! We're already on the same page, & it aint even the end of the day!"

[Jacquie]

Unstarry Night

Jerry Jr,

the son she had with the Professor, hated her. She never understood why. There was always a tension there; she told herself it was a blood thing, something in the blood. They'd been estranged for years. She knew he was living with a girl in Brooklyn, that he was a paparazzo. She knew that he moved to the West Coast a few years ago. She knew he was a drug addict.

She knew, she knew, she knew . . .

. . . that Jerry was in touch with his stepfather, Jerilynn's dad, & when her kid ran away—*Is that what I should call it?*—she called Ronny to get Jerry Jr.'s cellphone #. Ronny still lived in New York, working (fitfully) as a DP. When she told Ronny their daughter was pregnant, all he said was, "Oh. Wow." He sounded depressed.

She had a feeling Jerilynn might turn to her brother for help. She hoped so, anyway, because she'd been beside herself. She was grateful when Jerry Jr. left a message (an unexpected kindness) that she was with him, & was fine. Relieved, Jacquie let it go. It wasn't the time to reach out to Jerilynn.

Now her daughter hated her too . . . her daughter hated her and she was working in the portrait salon of Sears Roebuck. She wasn't even taking pictures, not strictly speaking, because the camera, lighting and various angles the customers chose from a booklet were fixed and calibrated. It was like flying a plane by instruments.

The world was cruel just now, & poised against her. Sally Mann had a piece in *The New York Times Magazine.* On the left of the page, a black&white portrait she took of herself & her two beautiful daughters; on the right, a color re-creation of the same, taken 10 years later. One's in law school, the other's a painter living in Brooklyn. Her daughters looked like they loved her so———————— *How could I have saved any money? I used every penny to live, so both of us could live! To eat and have a roof over our heads, & the occasional luxury. She gets pregnant and now I'm the villain. Well I'm sorry.*

Where did

I

go

wrong How did I——
    Transient fame transient transient transient
                        Years ago she befriended a woman named Tierney, Tierney Gearon, fabulous name, used to be a model, famously had a messy brood of kids, four of them famously with three different dads. They met at the beginning of Tierney's *meteoric,* as they say, rise to somethingness. (With indigent starless heart, Jacquie remembered her Shakespeare: *When beggars die there are no comets seen.*) She was covetous—the timing of it was maddening. Only weeks after Helmut delivered his Rosicrucian-cum-Barnum&Bailey secret sauce lecture, Tierney's nudies of her *own* bitsy babes erupted like fireworks in the alchemical skies of art & commerce. She never discussed it with Helmut (*or* Tierney), but it sure felt like Tierney got the memo. Those weeks and months got moldy with resentment/betrayal. A Kristallnacht of legal threats, repressive fanatacism & counterpoised Free Speech *hoohah* lit up the careering darkness, just as the oracle foretold . . . *beaten to the punch!* There was Tierney—gorgeous, sexy, famously scattered Tierney (scattered like a fox)—actually *doing* what Jacquie was only in the (bare) planning stages of. *Ma pauvre cher* Jac-

queline! Still fussing like a fool over which abstruse photographic technique to employ for her inchoate *Studies of A Daughter* suite; still hassling in her head/paralyzed over what venues & backdrops might effectively supplant the humdrum woodsy settings and empty beaches so thoroughly mined by the genre.

Pouring salt in the wound, Tierney's blitz shook the ether above the Saatchi Gallery in London—London!—the very city Helmut rhapsodized as the *ne plus ultra* when it came to firing ranges for that first, art-full shot heard round the world. Great theater dust-up: big-tent kerfuffle in the UK. It was awkward running into her mentor when the Tierney show traveled to New York. He elfin smiled, & said, *"See?"* She tried for days to interpret what he meant, uncertain if it was "I told you, but now it's too late" or *"You go girl!"* Tierney's story (& she was stickin to it) sounded as if it was torn from the Helmut playbook: her naïf protests that she had no real experience as a photographer, & didn't hardly consider herself an artist. Then how the kiddie nudes would have wound up at Saatchi, Jacquie hadn't a clue. Not that it made any difference. They were *there*, & so was Tierney, she had *arrived* (Jacquie not yet departed), hence proving Newton's First Law of Motion: your career will sit in the shit unless something comes along to knock over the outhouse.

She ruminated between customers at Sears.

Saatchi was further than she ever got. Jacquie *wanted* to show there but they turned her down, even with the fair-to-middling controversy she had going for her at that moment in time, even with Helmut's (supposed) intervention. Turned down by Gagosian too . . . if only. *If only she had achieved persecution on a grander scale*— Tierney had been threatened with jailtime! *Jacquie* never was, not for lack of trying, which made her furious. Thinking back, from her position behind the photo menu counter of the Sears Portrait Studio, l'affaire Gearon had an awfully deleterious effect. Seeing the woman's kiddlings on the beach (the beach! She had the courage to repurpose the beach!) in their birthday suits & fright-masks (for that never-out-of-fashion Meatyard-Arbus touch) made her wince; she recalled Helmut schooling her in the vital importance of pictorially referencing one's *progenitors*—"or do I mean *progenitals!*" he said, imp that he was. But the bugle had sounded the Call to Post. Tierney was off and running, while Jacquie brushed a hobbled horse in a forgotten stable.

Everything went Tierney's way: galleries teeming, barristers double-teaming, Scotland Yard's knickers twisted, Big Ben ala-ruming, bobbies on bicycles 2 by 2 . . . Tory threats & Saatchified fêtes . . . Jacquie still shared espressos with Helmut yet couldn't help wonder if the bloom fell off the rose, the *schaden* off the *freude*, the rider from her saddle. She became paranoid: could it be that when Helmut was away, he was a guest at the Gearon estate? Be-cause if it all wasn't so fucked enough, Tierney happened to be fa-mously wealthy, father lived on an island somewhere, father & daughter famously got along famously . . . Helmut probably had been not-so-secretly in love with her from the beginning, Jac-quie was 5th-string (if that), Tierney magnetized men, Jacquie enraged&repelled them, Tierney tethered them to the maypole of her gemütlich sexuality, why not add Helmut to the orb & fasten him by his own whip. Tierney was six years younger than she; Tierney was the Nude Kid on the Block (Jacquie wasn't even the girl next door); her naked progeny awash in bright stupendous Egglestonian progenicolors, with Jacquie left in the *dirt*.

  Brava Tierney,

                      brava————in the years that followed their ini-tial acquaintanceship—after Tierney made her bones—she had more time to hang out, & they saw each other a nice handful of times a year. Jacquie of course never told Tierney what she was working on, it would have come across as rip-offy. *Keep your work close but your frenemy closer.* She was relieved upon learning that Tierney's new oeu-vres was not of the prepubescent ilk. But it was Helmut—always Helmut!—who finally offered some helpful remarks. *Just do it, dear heart, you won't be ready to show for a few years, by then the wheel will have turned, the market will be ready again.* In the meantime, it was rough to watch Tierney's sold-out shows, when Jacquie had nothing to show but her unconvincing sangfroid————

Brava, Tierney!

Brava!

Sitting behind her little counter at Sears, on a slow morning, reliving when the *unthinkable* happened (Newton's Second Law of Motion): Scotland Yard swooped in, *The News of the World* demanded the gallery be closed, headline-blasting *'A revolting exhibition of perversion under the guise of art'*——

Take it down take it down take it down!

Now museum, now you don't.

Word circulated that Ms. Gearon was facing a possible 10 years for daring to thumb her nose at the Child Protection Act. Publishers were ordered to remove hundreds of copies from bookstore shelves . . . but the Sturgis Effect kicked in, each banned book acquiring a weedy, hard-to-kill, proliferative 2nd life . . . the numbers were climbing, the sales were soaring, and . . . she's . . . *off—& running!*—— Tierney played it demure & perplexed, *very* very smart, stating again & again for the record that she was *just a mom* . . . mom *first,* artist *second* . . . who are these people that wish to pillory a mom? To destroy her for daring to see her children through a child's eyes? *J'accuse!*

& *again* the unthinkable (Newton's Third):

THE CROWN RELENTS!
NO CHARGES FILED!

Tierney was actually supportive when Jacquie had her Media Moment in the tail end of 2003. She was gracious, never making Jacquie feel like she'd *appropriated TG's work.* She was one of the first people Jacquie showed her pictures to, inviting her over to the house to see them. Jacquie felt compelled to remark just once that she'd begun shooting her daughter before ever hearing about or seeing Tierney's portraits. Tierney was unruffled & even generous of spirit. *She can afford to be,* thought Jacquie. *She can famously fucking afford to.*

. . .

There she is, having a bite in the Sears employee lunchroom. She imagines forgetting why she sought the job in the first place, not that she knows exactly, only that her instincts told her *there is something here* . . . but now a greyish depression enfolds her like a flu & she imagines what it would be like to soon forget what her instincts said, just to have the job, no grandiose motive behind it . . . or even worse, to realize she *has* no viable instincts anymore—though maybe that would be better than where she found herself *now, today,* at this *moment*, being that place of beaten down, too-much awareness. So maybe it *would* be for the best to simply forget the vague, bullshitty reasons she made up for herself to explain why she'd been compelled to work at Sears, all for the best to just start forgetting a little day by day about who she was or *thought* she was, who she *imagined* herself to be by definition of her so-called career, maybe to forget or cut off at the root her impossible daydreams of resentment & impossible eventual triumph, forget about all that & just become a hardworking, pleasant demeanored, dreamless dumbass full-time employee, that would be better, much, might just work out, anything would be better than being the loser she'd begun, with unruly stamina, to consider herself these bygone days.

In the unmedicated flu of depression—like one of those Point Dume ladies who make Schnabelly collages from broken shells & hunks of yarn, or paint eternities of gloopy red acrylic valentine ♥s, Brentwood ladies who go thru "wearable art" phases, in their clunky La Jolla boutique-bought precious stoned necklaces & their *bold, striking color summer dresses* to wear on cruises—no—another fantasia intruded . . . she'd become the *maker* of those things, pathetic little craftswoman struggling to pay the rent on her Eagle Rock/Reseda/Studio City sublet, with the dusty clangy Calder knock-offs & a 70-lb. chalcedony purple-mawed healing shard plunked clumsily atop the corner of the welcome mat, New Age paperweight overkill . . . in her fever of insignificance, her fluish narrative of oblivion & loss of self, she became the servant of a widow who travels the world taking pictures for submission to *National Geographic*'s reader photo contest (a woman who'd won three times in 10 years): mist-filled, dentist's calendar-worthy, Cambodian temple ruins; fly-swarmy, cretinous-smiling, Machu Picchu vendors dressed in *bold, striking colors*; spectral Varanasi ghats neutered by that very calendarized eye. (It was telling that in her grim idyll, Jacquie's employer was the picture-taker, not she.)

Lots of gremlins today!

Another dismal reverie that somehow alarmed her with its aura of veracity began with Jacquie, improbable survivor of multiple metastasizing cancers, meeting a rich alcoholic slob on a cruise, the broken-bloodvesseled type who wears a captain's hat. Now when she gets tipsy, she gets maudlin (the figment of her in the scenario, because in real life she never got tipsy, in real life she got *shitfaced*), wondering what her charming new friend will think when she spills that her two grown children refuse to speak to her anymore, & she's never met her grandkids. *Will he judge me?* All she could do was see her with him in the dining room, then having an intimate talk on deck, saw herself breathe deeply, close her eyes & hope he maybe had a similar history—*some* kind of estrangement, wickedness, at least a little unexpected child death, something, *anything* but a healthy thriving relationship with his kids, *Lord please no, not that.* She already saw him (in her fluish head) nodding off in his ludicrous cap as she told him about Jerilynn & Jerry Jr., coming to from his nod, shaking his head in empathy, or making a damn good show of it, when the *truth* of it is he's muttering under his breath *Jesus* THIS *cunt must be some piece of* WORK. *To have* 2 *kids, not one, but* 2 *blow her off! She's probably fucking nuts but the crazy ones give the best head*

what would it be like *what would it be like to blow a rich, alcoholic, borderline-homely slob in a captain's hat on a cruise, the sheer desolation of it, the aloneness, she could taste the crud of his dickskin, what would it be like* what would it be like *what would it be like to be on a cruise in a stateroom blowing gagging swallowing & maybe embarrassingly upchucking a little afterward, hoping he didn't notice/*

hear but knowing he did, and even though he began each morning vomiting
the first drink before he put on his cap, even though, still, watching your *little*
barf he was almost as disgusted by you as you were of yourself, *though he'd*
never be able to be quite that disgusted, no one would, no one could possibly
be, what would it be like to be told right after emerging from the bathroom with
the heartburn of your miscarried puke what would it be like to be told that he
really needs to sleep, he's not feeling well, not at all, the best thing for him to
do when he feels this way is go to sleep. Alone——————

· · ·

She sat in the lunchroom with Albie, the fag boss she had seriously
contemplated proposing to, she loved the fags, they were so hurt, so
like her, so simpatico, she couldn't live in the world without the caus-
tic kindness of the fags. In the short time she'd known Albie, they'd
become galfriends, they shared passports to the same country, she
trusted him to listen to her tales of woe & conquest, to be on her side,
just as he trusted the same, they were instant co-conspirators, pain
buddies & art hounds. She was sitting in the lunchroom grimming
out, and when Albie came in, the tender, comical sight of him instantly lightened her load. He sat down beside her, they were the
only ones, more or less, Albie arranged it like that, he didn't relish
the company of fellow workmen, knew she wouldn't, and scheduled
them for late lunches.

They'd gossip about celebs or he'd tell her he wanted to die because he found out his husband took 2 boys to bed, *their* bed, while
Albie was away (he called him *husband*, tho they hadn't yet married),
& after the catharsis & general bloodletting he'd take Jacquie drinking at the Sports Club Bar & Grille, too many hanging flatscreens but
decent 330–8PM calamari, decent sarcastic peoplewatching—

She was going to pour a little bit of her misery heart into his
hands, but he spoke first, & with urgency. He looked drawn.

"What's wrong?"

"I'm closing early today."

"Albie, what happened?"

"My cousin Ginger—I'm *really close* to her and her husband Daniel—closer to *her*—she just had a baby & it was a stillborn."

"O!"

Now she could see he had been crying.

"Jacquie, it is *so horrible*. And Daniel said there's something wrong—with Ginger—that she's really, really *calm*, you know, *too* calm, & normally? I wouldn't trust Daniel's version of events? But this time I do? Because . . . Jacquie, can you come? Would you go with me?"

"Of course I will."

"Because she asked me to do something—Ginger got on the phone & asked me to do something—and it's *kind of* crazy? Right? & if it was someone else I could *kind of* see the value of it? But because it's *her* I can't even *go there*. But I'm the one she asked, so I need to kind of sort of like *honor that*? And I don't think I—I don't think that I can actually *do* it. I think *you*—I just really need you to be there."

"Albie, let's just go. Let's go and see her."

"Really? Jacquie, *thank you*, because I just really don't think I can *do* this—"

"What is it that she wants?"

"I'll tell you on the way over, we can go in one car? Can we just take one car? My car?"

"Sure."

"I won't be able to, I *know* myself, I would *fall apart*. And I thought *you* could maybe help, *specifically*. Because I know myself, I'll faint or just *lose* it in front of them, which would be *so tragically fucked up!*"

"Albie, what? What is—"

"She asked me to take pictures—of her & the baby. Like a portrait, a formal family portrait. So she can remember. Jacquie, it's so sad! (*Crying now*) Would you take them for me, Jacquie? The pictures? Because I know myself, I will *completely lose it*. I wouldn't want to do that to Daniel & Ginger! I wouldn't want to do that. Do you think you can help? Jacquie, can you take the pictures—the portrait? Can you take the family portrait?"

[Jacquie]

This Strange & Mournful Day

The

new mother, Ginger, was in bed sitting up, & the man, father, new dad, what have you—Daniel—he was sitting at bedside actually smoking a cigarette which Jacquie thought was impressive. Albie was already kissing Ginger, & Daniel was side-eyed checking out Jacquie, as if waiting—daring—for someone—anyone—to tell him to put out the cigarette. When Albie got out of the line of vision, Jacquie took one look & saw the mom holding the baby in her arms and said to herself *But he said it was a stillborn,* which only seconds later was confirmed by closer sight, energy & mood all at once, the woman was holding the baby, the baby didn't look malformed at all, the baby looked beautiful, but there it was, terminally malformed of life.

What Ginger had asked was if Albie would take their portrait: her, Daniel, & the baby, or just her and the baby should Daniel not consent, which was his prerogative, tho she hoped he would. But Albie knew that his nerves couldn't withstand it, he immediately thought of Jacquie, she was *famous* (in his mind, and it was the truth too, because he'd never met anyone who actually had a page in Wikipedia), if he could get her to do this, which in his heart he fairly knew he could, if Jacquie would do this for him & his cousin, that would be a blessing, good and right. When he told Ginger about his idea, & who he was working with, this famous photog and all—and of course this was before he'd even asked Jacquie if she'd come—when he told Ginger, she smiled so quietly, so beautifully, O! heartbreaking! saying "This is why God brought her into your life."

On the way to his car, Jacquie said they should go to her house first, she had a Hasselblad & a Leica there, & film too, but Albie always traveled with his Rolleiflex in the trunk, he was a hobbyist, the impulse purchase of the Rollciflex being one he regretted because it was so much money. He kept it wrapped in a towel wedged next to the spare, all they needed was to buy film. He asked if she was familiar with it & when she said yes, "very," he said, *Of course you are, sorry, don't mind me, I'm an idiot,* & she said no no, there were lots of cameras she didn't know but a Rollei was her 1st, a gift from the father of her 1stborn (Jerry Jr.), the (squirrely, tho) not so nutty Professor.

The nurses were leaving the new mom and dad alone, so the door remained shut & they didn't need to hassle intrusions and interruptions. Natural light. Albie was going to leave but Ginger told him to stay, & he hung back. O—natural light—the staggering sad beauty of it, the gruesome wondrous marvel & miracle, the outlandishness, the *Babyland*ishness, this mother had no tears in her at this beatitudinous moment, just stared not even with longing at that tiny expired thing, no longing *at this moment* because she had her, the little girl was in her arms, so what was there to long for?—she was like a superhero whose special power was a serene unhurried unrushed unbroken smile that could bring the bedrapéd dead back to life. Jacquie stared a while, not morbidly but taking in the scene before she began, the artist's prerogative. She wanted to take a respectful moment, plus she was curious, she'd never seen a dead baby, well who had, & the mom had *yes* a beatific smile as if in a tender sacramental state of show&tell, & knowing that a fellow mother might be curious, well who wouldn't be, & generously wishing to help sate it, such communal impulse in such a case was unnaturally natural. Jacquie smiled as she looked at the thing, its eyes were kind of open, she became aware of tears rising from a deep deep well but forced them down, an actual labor, reverse of child labor, she remembered once the Professor telling her (while he was schooling her in all things) that the sound of Bach's partitas were the sound of human tears . . . afterall the moment wasn't about her, it was about the pietà of mother & child, *the mother and child reunion* & the mother wasn't crying, so how dare Jacquie?

She got very close to it, the closer she got, the more the mom seemed to open up, her smile grew larger & her eyes watery, her big breasts exposed. The closer she got to the dead baby the more intimate was the two women's fleeting bond. The tiny girl's vulva was enormous, almost the size of a grown-up's, Jerilynn's had looked the same, swollen from the mother's hormones. For a few seconds, it looked roaringly healthy, thick rubber bumpers bracketing a deep decubitus ulcer, it looked like the thing that may have killed her.

The agitated husband didn't know what to do next *little darling of mine* smoke another cigarette or throw himself from the window. The wife beckoned him in that calm understated tender way and he couldn't refuse her, he said he'd get in the picture if he could keep smoking his cigarette. She said "smoke your cigarette sweetheart" & he did, squinting, smoke hung in the natural light, sirens in the distance, sound of Albie muffling his fag tears somewhere behind her— did the door open & close? Did Albie leave? It didn't matter, nothing mattered but the little family, & Daniel the husband, who was handsome as hell, quashed the cigarette on the floor & climbed deeper into the bed, he wasn't about to look at their babygirl, only a motion away, but he'd surrendered to the camera, & his wife's wishes.

She went through one roll of film, & then it was done.

[Reeyonna]

I Am A Camera

ReeRee

was panicking. Kind of. She was trying (failing) to turn the rage toward her mother into something useful, an engine that could power her into a trajectory, *any* kind of momentum, momentum of a *life*.

She needed money—she & Rikki did—her brother gave her $400 but that was 10 days ago & he was so fucked up he was scaring her. Kind of.

She was a prisoner held captive like Rapunzel in *Tangled*. Rikki had his crappy Craig'slist motorcycle but was only with her 3 or 4 times a week, his fostermom was hospitalized for depression & he needed to be there for Jim his dad. Which was sweet, pure Rikki. It's what is going to make him a great dad. But still, tho————*what about me. What about fucking me what about me and your* BABY. *You have time to do your little auditions but what about me with my throw-up.* She seemed to be having her morning sickness *now,* all these months later. They took his bike for chores&fun when he was there but when he wasn't all she could do was ride the bus which she *hated* because all the sad, scary people looked like dull mean ghosts patiently biding their time to lay claim to her. One day she would get on the bus &

never get off & nobody would even notice, sucked into the whorl of their grimy nowhere worlds.

Rikki said she should just come stay with him at his house, he talked to Dawn & Jim (well, to Jim) & they were totally cool, of course they were, they were kind, it was so much better to have kind fosters than a thieving bloodmother or faraway idiot uncaring blood-father, they gently lobbied Rikki to lobby ReeRee to come home, their home, *her* home, her 2nd home, a clean safe stressless environment because an expectant mom should not be wandering rootless, an expectant mom should be going to birth classes & cultivating friendships with other expectant moms through the affiliation of new parents and parents-to-be, an expectant mom needs to be going to the doctor regularly, an expectant mom needs to be close to her doctor's hospital when the baby came, or before if something went wrong, an expectant mom & the husband or partner & the whole extended family needed to have a *relationship* with a doctor. Rikki said that Jim wanted him to tell her that he knew she was having problems with her mom but to put that aside and come stay with them. If the proximity to her mom was the thing that was stopping her. They would take her to the doctor visits, they would take her to buy things for the baby (a stroller, a crib, there were so many things), she was having a baby, their *adopted son's* (soon) baby, she was giving them the divine gift of a grandson or granddaughter, they weren't pushy, she knew they weren't, the mom was nice, a little distant, but the dad especially wasn't pushy, he was always kind and gentle, a good man, *Please Ree,* said Rikki, *please just won't you just come? Cause this shit is getting crazy* she knew a portion of his ardor, of exerting his/their influence, was a measure of how far he was outside his comfort zone, he'd been freaked out about the baby thing from the beginning & now the moving away had freaked him out further *plus* Reeyonna knew that for some reason he felt guilty, he still felt the baby & all were somewhere in there behind his foster mom's depression, & she knew he thought a baby would cheer her up when/if she ever got home, cheer his dad up too (which it would), which was sweet,

Rikki couldn't help himself, and ReeRee even felt a little bad for being so stubborn about just staying where she was but her new mother's instincts bade her be selfish, bade her be protective, bade her keep as far away from that thieving cunt as she possibly could, *but what about me, Rikki, what about me & our fucking baby. I mean who's having this baby, Dawn & Jim?*

Reeyonna said no.

She was adamant. That would be the worst kind of defeat.

That would put her inside a mile of her mother's home—the bitch would soon find a way to wander over and establish a fucking détente—*No way*—defeat defeat defeat. But she loved Rikki's parents & felt bad for the mom who was going through a really hard time. *I'm going through a hard time too goddammit.* She even called Jim to thank him & tell him why she couldn't & got off the phone sooner than she planned when he made the mistake of saying he had talked to Jacquie who he assured was quite concerned re her welfare. O! The thieving cunt was trying to jump on the *caring* bandwagon—*Hi y'all! It's just me! Grandma!*—which, by the way was impossible because all she ever thought about was herself. *Too fucking little too fucking late. Rikki's mom & dad care more about me than you* ever *did, you psycho, I am going to disendaughter myself from you, & become their daughter. And they will agree to my terms, they will have to if they want to see their grandchild, they will agree to my terms which are that NO ONE WILL HAVE CONTACT WITH YOU EVER.* BECAUSE YOU ARE A FUCKING PSYCHOTHIEF WHO STOLE YOUR DAUGHTER AND YOUR COULD-HAVE-BEEN GRANDCHILD'S LIVES.

She was going to make a lot of money as a forensic detective then sue the bitch. (All of her friends basically either wanted to become pornstars or CSI forenz detectives. They called her a basic bitch for liking *The Closer* but Kyra Sedgwick had such amazing hair.) By then she'd be tight with the district attorney, & it would be easier for her, she would try to get her mom a jail sentence, not house arrest but JAIL because at least in jail she could get raped by a dyke, & if she ever got sick, the medical care was so shitty she read on the internet that sometimes they just let the prisoners die writhing in pain in their cells. She wished Kim Kardashian's dad was still alive, she recently found out by watching an E! biography that he was a big lawyer & friend of that football player who murdered his wife, ReeRee googled while she was watching & it said the killer even stayed at Robert Kardashian's *house* when he was out on bail or whatever. (She would totally try to make it so that her mom could *not* get bail.) She wondered if Kim, Kourtney & Khloé were even born yet, she hoped not, because it would have been sick to have someone in your house like that who everyone thought killed his wife (which he *did*, & at first got off for but was later rearrested) but she guessed it was fine because after all their dad was the O.G., the original Kardashian, the *O.K.*, & she concluded he would be perfect to handle the case against that selfish bitch, her soon-to-no-longer-be mom. ReeRee would sue & win, maybe even be awarded the house, which would certainly be a twist. Mr. Kardashian would petition the court & have her mom ordered to vacate & take all her shit her fucking useless cameras for her useless career with her, & ReeRee would get a restraining order against her for *life* just to rub it in *you cannot come within 100 miles of me & my child maybe children by then* she & Rikki and her friends & even his fosters (by then his adopted true parents) would commence to paint & scrub & garden-redo, maybe even winning an *Extreme Home Makeover* removing every vestigial trace of the paroled, restraining-ordered Thief of Dreams . . . her grandmotherless baby (on Ree's side, not on Rikki's) might even wind up going to John Crowe Ransom, she'd fix it so if Bitch Thief ever even came *close* to the school-grounds to pathetically glimpse sight of her non-grandchild (all filial relations to Reeyonna by then, with the help of Ree's D.A. friend & others, having been totally legally severed . . . Rikki once told her about the whole process, she didn't want to be ruled an emancipated minor, "emancipated minor" was some bullshit for cranky young ☆lets trying to get away from their own thieving parents, no, she wanted the real thing, her *blood connection* to Bitch Thief to be *totally stricken from the record*)—& if she *did* show up an old, raped, makeup-less just-released-from-prison hag to glimpse her tweenage grandchild, well then she would risk rearrest & detainment & imprisonment. For it was now *Reeyonna's* turn to steal from her mother, steal her time, her years, her life, her breath, her world.

· · ·

Sometimes the baby kicked like a motherfucker then it would suddenly STOP, not just for a little but for it seemed *like a whole day* and she'd freak & call Rikki who would have to stop what he was doing which was probably smoking an executive branch & wacking off to Korean porn & come over. They'd kawasaki to the free family clinic in Venice. She always loved the beach, wanted to live at the beach, right on Speedway, even though they'd probably end up in Hollywood because the beach was so expensive. But she knew you could probably still find cool places if you used the service Ashton Kutcher talked about on Jimmy Kimmel.

She/they needed money. Initially Rikki's fosters gave them $2,500 but that was like 45 days ago & Rikki was worried to ask for more because his fostermom maybe had to go to some kind of rehab that cost like $39,000 & insurance didn't pay. He was hoping/waiting/expecting for Jim to present another check soon, or at least to ask if any monies were needed by the young couple. Reeyonna didn't like the idea of asking them again anyway, though she did consider getting married, just for a moment, thinking that would be a new & genuine/acceptable reason for them to hand over more cash.

She was unsettled & a little depressed, taking Vicodin now just to feel better. Tom-Tom said as a nurse that Vicodin wouldn't hurt the baby, a doc at the clinic said that too, cuz she asked him. Then he asked if she was an addict, & when she laughed & said no, the look on his face was like she'd said *yes,* he said it would be best *not to* ingest of course not just street drugs but *any* R_x drugs that had not been prescribed, he said there were safer drugs for pain that he *might* prescribe if she had the *demonstrable need*, but generally, Vicodin was relatively safe re the fetus, & if she was going to do that, if she was going to *ingest,* which he of course did not recommend, then Vicodin was better than something she might get *from the street.* She laughed no no no & he smiled, but not broadly.

They/she now were living on a hill called Mt Olympus in an *awesome* house Tom-Tom said belonged to the old woman Betty White who won that contest to host *SNL* a few years ago, which ReeRee & her friends actually saw, very stoned, never until then having heard of her. Tom-Tom said they (even tho Rikki didn't even stay over so much) couldn't stay for free anymore & it pissed her off that her brother didn't lift a finger to say a word. Tom-Tom said they needed to pay *$750 a month* for their room there, which was *half* as much as any apts she was already looking at for Rikki & her online, but she was tired, & with her unabated morning throw-up which left her sour and weakened for the rest of each day relieved just to be able to stay in one place. But she was proud that at the peak of her discomfort & feelings of being wronged she not *once* considered crawling back to her old neighborhood to throw in the towel & stay at Rikki's, a stone's throw from Hooker Queen.

The roof had a beautiful glimmering view of the city, she swishered it all from the top of the house, there was a safe way up there that Tom-Tom hadn't even thought about yet because she was still so busy getting overall settled, but it was so beautiful & peaceful at night for Ree to have her solitude, & to smoke and look out at the city which held her destiny. And yet, stonerviewed, everything seemed through a darkly glass wrong-way-up, meaning, the trillions of winky little stars could not compete with the carpetwavy staccato citybrightness thus throwing in their own celestial towels & changing partners with the frippery earth, that had long abandoned its natural state of loamy black pitch & countrynight mysteries, *this* earth was too showy & shiny to stay put, out of vanity, *this* earth obliged by flipping over to take the crown of (now) starspackled sky.

The house deadended on Vulcan Drive. ReeRee thought it was named after StarTrek but Tom-Tom said all the streets in Mt Olympus were named for the Gods & that she should google Vulcan. She did, it said Vulcan was a god having to do with fire but it was so boring.

. . .

So she called Sears in Valencia and asked for the portrait studio & when a man answered she asked if *Jacquie* was there, & when he said who may I ask is calling she hung up.

She took a cab straight to her old house. It cost so much money because the cab had to take her back but she didn't want to involve Rikki, didn't want her mother to have that on him. She knew what she was going to take, she needed something of value to sell on craigslist, & if she at the same time could deliver a blow to Hooker Bitch Thief, so much the better.

She knew where they were, some were hidden, some always kept (somewhat) in the open, because Hooker liked to see them, hold them, for comfort, she loved them more than she ever loved her children, especially her daughter, who she saw fit to fuck over by taking kidporn & robbing without qualm.

Reeyonna felt nothing, why should she, eye for an eye, they were reparations, & their spoils could not even come *close* to making whole ReeRee's loss. *Mutherfuck that old stinkyass whore.* She found a soccer duffel bag from her closet & hooliganized Jacquie's makeup into it, writing *ThiefWHORE* in lipstick on the mirror like in a horror movie. Then she went to the special place they were hidden, a total of about 6 cameras & long lenses & battery packs, & she took them all.

[Bud]

The Mother Load

Naturally,

Bud followed ICM's lead & contacted the office of Rod Fulbright, David Simon's rep. In a two-week period, meetings were set, bumped, reset, and bumped again. Because both cancellations had been last minute, Fulbright's asst phoned *and* emailed.

The meeting was set for 8AM at Soho House. The phone rang at nine on the night before; when caller ID announced "C A A," the burgeoning novelist jumped out of his skin, fearing the worst. In Bud's experience, a 3rd strike signaled the end of a meeting's life cycle. The good news was, the agency was confirming.

There was always the chance it could abort in the morning. Bud told himself that wasn't likely because of the earliness of the set hour— a bullshit rationale that still managed to provide feeble comfort.

. . .

His golf ball-size, precancerous prostate nearly had him under house arrest; it ruled over him like a despot, forcing him to piss every 20 minutes. He envied his mother because at least she was diapered & didn't have to get up 17 times in the middle of the night. No wonder he was chronically fatigued.

The urologist never suggested medication that might help (even Dolly was on Renessa), and for some reason Bud always forgot to ask. Seemingly, the only arrow in Dr. Deconcini's quiver was a technique called "the double void." The maneuver entailed remaining at the urinal when you were done, & *willing* yourself to pee all over again. The first and only time he tried it was in a public restroom. As Bud stood idle, ruminating over his novel, his mother's money and his bladder, he eventually noticed a guy washing his hands a little too long, trying to catch Bud's eye in the mirror, like he was maybe looking for action.

He almost blew off Soho House, out of sheer exhaustion. Dolly's caregiver had a family emergency, and it was too late to find a replacement. Bud slept—or rather, didn't—on the fold-out couch in the living room. The baby monitor was stuck at an insanely loud pitch; putting cushions and pillows over it didn't much help. (He couldn't bring himself, morally, to shut it off.) Under the nonstop drone of Fox talking heads, he could hear Dolly farting and belching and muttering to herself. "They want me *dead*"—"Dirtycunt lying *bitch*"—"Then why don't you *go and fuck yourself*?" As he drifted off, she began to call out, at first shy & plaintive then insistent, imperious: "Bud? Bud . . . Bud? *Bud*. BUD!" When he asked with a shout what she wanted, Dolly's answer was always the same. In a pitiable Baby Jane voice, she cried, "I don't want to fall! I'm afraid, I'm afraid! They're all falling! Nancy Reagan! Betty White! Zsa Zsa! Hips are breaking, right and left, left and right!" He bellowed reassurances but she kept at it until he was forced to climb from the couch and go to her room. He'd tell her that she wasn't going to fall, that neither he nor her caregivers would *allow* it. Her mood instantly brightened, her wrinkleless face transforming to a sweet little girl's. Then she'd pass on a nugget or two from the tabloids he brought her each week.

"Who's the one on *Dancing With the Stars*? Not this year—the whore. The whore that was married to Hefner."

"Ma, I don't know."

"They threw her off . . . whenever it was. Why can't I remember her fucking *name*? Anyway, they say she *stinks*. In the magazine you brought. Her publicist said she has *bad b.o.*"

"Her publicist?"

"Not her publicist, her *stylist*. You know what I mean."

"I don't watch that show."

"Well you *should*. Kendra Wilkinson! I *knew* I'd remember. The whore with the cute little body. Letting herself be pawed at by that *old*, old man. Can you imagine? Well *I* can! I would have done the *exact same thing*. But first I would have had to get in line. I hope she got money out of it, she better have gotten *millions*. She's smart, I *admire* her—there's nothing wrong with being a whore, Bud! . . . and that little girl, who's that little girl? They said she doesn't like to wash—why can't I think of her name. Shit. What is it——*Reese Witherspoon*."

"Reese Witherspoon was on *Dancing With the Stars*?"

"No! I was *reading*. In your magazine. Apparently she has an allergy to *soap*, if you know what I mean. That's me being nice. And Uma, Uma *Thurman*, remember her? It said she stinks *even more*. Than the others. But you know who they say is the stinkiest of them all? Guess."

"I don't know. Who."

"*Sarah Jessica Parker*. They said she's *foul* & I *believe* it."

Dolly assiduously used a person's entire name, as a testimony to her mental acuity. She often recited out loud a random catechism of phone numbers, names/dates of holidays, & obscure family tree birthdays/wedding anniversaries—she wanted Bud (and the world, however small it'd become) to see that she was still *with* it.

"Bud, do you know who has fungus? On her fingernails? *Jennifer Aniston*. They're splitting right and left. I used to wait on women like that, I saw *everything*, in the dressing room at Neiman's. They were filthy under the arms and *everywhere else*. Anyone who has fungus on the fingers has it on the toes. O yes. You better believe if you have *finger* fungus, your hygiene *leaves something to be desired*. Because fungus doesn't come from out of the blue. And if you've got it on the *fingers*, you've got it on the *cunt*. These girls spend a fortune on waxing their holes, but they can't afford to buy a bar of soap? And her friend from *Friends*—what's-her-name who was married to the *kook*—she's got hairy feet. *Courteney Cox*. It says she's got hair on her toes, just like a man."

Instead of counting sheep, Bud counted the money he'd acquire upon her death. In his fantasy, he was merciful—instead of breaking a hip in a fall and succumbing to pneumonia, Dolly died peacefully in her sleep.

She had doled out some of her fortune over the last few years, a thousand here, a thousand there, always on unpredictable occasions. He felt like a waiter getting a tip but knew better than to ask for more. Dolly withheld her dowry, still intent on marrying him off "to money."

Dolly tried *marrying money* herself & failed. She regretted wasting her best years on Bud's father, a preening, narcissistic spendthrift. After the divorce, she confessed to Bud that she'd run a bit wild. She spent time in bars, and once brought Lloyd Bridges back to the apt for what she called a "c-hunt." She had a thing for rich, black-out drunks. Hook-ups frequently took her to Vegas where the scenario included Dolly being given a few thousand in hundred-dollar chips to play with while her paramours shatpisspuked themselves in the honeymoon suite. At night, crawling into the alcoholic bed, she told them she lost everything at the tables; the chips were safe at the bottom of her purse. (If stray chips dribbled from their pockets while they were out cold and she scooped them up, well that was OK too.) *Go where the money is* was her most important slice of parental wisdom. *You should have married the Duchess of Alba.* 85 years-old! *That's Hefner's age! If Kendra could do it, so can* YOU. *Do you want to know how old the groom was?* EXACTLY YOUR AGE. *She has palaces! She's so rich she doesn't have to kneel for the pope! She's allowed to ride a horse into the cathedral in Seville! You should have met her, Bud, why couldn't you have found a way to meet her? Because her husband's* HANDSOME *but he's faggy, he can't* HOLD A CANDLE, *he isn't* BUILT *like you. You should have met her & given her a good* FUCK, *you should have fucked her to death! Early death! Cause that's what* he's *planning, you better believe it!*

He rocked himself to sleep, fantasizing what he was going to do with Dolly's money. He knew he wanted to spend a few days walking around with a big wad, just to see how it felt to have 20 or thirty-thousand in his pocket. His father used to walk around with a wad & Dolly *hated* it. Now Bud understood the man's motivation. He empathized . . . . . .

————————**BLASTED** awake by his mother at 2AM, her voice triple-amplified by the monitor, singing in her sleep

> THE TEACHER TOLD HIS MOTHER
> SHE'D TAKE HIM RIGHT IN HAND,
> TEACH HIM A THING OR TWO!
> LIKE HIS OLDER BROTHER
> HE BEGAN TO UNDERSTAND,
> LEARNING EVERYTHING
> HE THOUGHT SHE KNEW . . . .

At a quarter to 4, awakened again————————
"Bud? Bud? *Bud?* Bud. *Bud?* Bud! BUD! Bud, I *need* you!"
He roused himself, practically stumbling into her room.
"Mom, what's wrong!"
"I need to *shit*," she whispered. "That's what's wrong."
It took 10 minutes to maneuver her onto the seat of the walker that was kept beside the bed for this very contingency. He told her to raise her feet up so he could wheel her to the powder room. When they reached the doorway, Dolly said she needed to stand & move herself to the toilet, on her own power. It didn't make much sense to Bud—it would have been easier just to push the walker past the tub to the bowl, but she wouldn't be swayed. "This is the way we do it! This is the way *Marta said* to do it."

When she reached her destination, he understood; much better that she was already standing. Dolly militantly barked orders—time was of the essence.

"Get rid of the walker!"

While she held tight to a diagonal safety bar on the wall, Bud removed the obstruction. She sighed, winced, & took a few pained breaths. He thought something might be wrong.

"Why are you wincing?"

"Because . . . because . . . *because I haven't had a shit in three days*, does that answer your question? Because if it doesn't, *I'll tell you again.*"

She gave him a hard stare, as if to poison his eyes. His stomach contracted then he let it go. She slo-mo pirouetted until she stood in front of the toilet facing him, barely covered by her stained, debris-splattered robe.

Bud averted his eyes in modesty & disgust.

"Now I hold the other bar, and you—*don't move! Why are you moving around?*—listen!* What I want you to do is *pull the diaper down around my ankles.* Then I'll grab your shoulders & you'll *lower me down.* That's how Marta does it."

Bud tried to lower it but there was some sort of tape on one side, and he had to fuss with it. He got it unstuck and began to push the diaper down with both hands as Dolly snapped, "Come on, come on! Don't be shy!"

Suddenly, she screamed. From his crouch, he looked up at her face, a mask of agony—he froze.

"Ow! Ow! Ow!"

On the fourth *Ow*, brown & yellow stool erupted from her anus, accompanied by a marching band of flatus. She began to lean backward; Bud reached around to brace her fall.

She hit the bowl with a muted *clunk.*

"Are you OK?"

She had the biggest smile on her face, & sang out:

"*Plop* plop, *fizz* fizz, O what a *relief* it is! Marta *said* I was due. She said, 'You're *expecting*. You're going to have a *baby*.' I said, 'Make it a little girl, will you? I already have a little boy—'"

He was winded & nauseous.

"Cry, Marta, & let slip the dogs of war!"

Another fusillade as she emptied her bowels again, & Bud stood, woozy. He felt the sharp sting of a pulled lower back. With ecstatic voice, Dolly picked the song up where it left off.

"All the kids to the teacher carried—candy & ice cream cones!— but who do ya think the teacher married?—*Wood'n* head *Puddin head* Jones!"

[Bud]

The Art of Fiction, Part Two

"**As** you know, David wrote the novels *The Wire* and *Treme*."

"They're novels? I mean, they were novels?" said Bud, flummoxed.

Michael Douglas was four tables away, having breakfast alone. The smell of his mother's shit was still in his nostrils.

"They weren't *book* novels, but David calls them—we *all* call them *novels* because of their dense narratives. And because of the *feeling* you have after you've watched them. It's indistinguishable from the feelings you have after reading a *novel*."

Bud kicked himself for spacing on Xochilt's caveat. He wondered if David Simon was late, or if he was coming at all.

"They're pretty much regarded by critics as *literature*. Did you know David won a Pulitzer Prize for fiction, for *The Wire?* They basically created a new category—*The Novel as Filmed Drama*." Bud didn't think Pulitzers were actually *won*, but why quibble? "David even did an 'Art of Fiction' interview for the *Paris Review*. You know Richard Price, don't you? His work? He's an *amazing* writer. He won a National Book Award. Or maybe it was a Pulitzer. Richard called *The Wire* a 'Russian novel'*—we *love* Richard, he wrote some of our

---

* As quoted in *London Review of Books*, May 27, 2010.

best shows. *The London Review of Books* and *The New York Review of Books* have practically devoted *whole issues* to *The Wire*. I think if you sit down & watch all seven seasons, there is *no way* you would say at the end, 'That was great *television*' or even 'That was great *cable* television,' because *The Wire* is no more a TV show than it is a drama about police or about drug dealers or about Baltimore. David always says it's not about *any* of those things! People make *a serious mistake* when they try to *summarize* what *The Wire* is about. You know, put it in a pigeonhole. If a gang of professors at Harvard, Cambridge & Oxford are still trying to figure it out—did you know they teach *The Wire* in universities all over the world?—then I really don't think that a television critic, or even our viewers"—she speedily corrected herself—"our *readers*, are going to be able to nail."

"Wow, no, I guess not."

"The syllabus for the course Joyce Carol Oates teaches on *The Wire* at Princeton says that David's book has *darkly glinting Aeschylean moral textures*. Don't you think that's perfect?"

"Very, very accurate."

"She says these *amazing* things about the show, even David doesn't understand some of the things she says! I shouldn't say that. Joyce is *beyond brilliant*, and so is David. I know that David got annoyed with her though—they're *crazygood friends* by the way, & he thinks she's *wonderful*—but David got a little peeved because she teaches a course on *Battlestar Galactica*, & tells her students that she thinks it's a 'sy-fy *Aeneid*.' David thought that was just a *little* over the top."

"Yeah. Just a little!"

"David thought the essay about *Mad Men* was crazy too. It talked about Don Draper's secret past creating *a real dramatic crisis in the Aristotelian sense* and *conflict with an elegantly Sophoclean geometry*.* David said, Get over yourself!"

"How many have you seen?"

"*The Wire?* All of them," he lied. "Big fan from early on."

"Have you seen *Treme*?"

---

* *The New York Review of Books*, February 24, 2011.

"*Love* it."

"*Treme*'s a really good *book* but I'm *emotionally* closer to *The Wire* because they were only in their 2nd season when I started interning for David."

"Wow. What an amazing opportunity."

"I'll send you the pilot. Toni Morrison's become a *very serious* fan. She is amazing."

"Of *Treme?*"

"Of *Treme* AND *The Wire*. She came to *The Wire* late—her friend Fran Lebowitz turned her on—Fran's a *huge* fan of *The Wire*. She was going to write something for us but for some reason it didn't happen. Though I guess Fran not writing something isn't so surprising!"

She arched her neck Michael Douglas's way.

"He looks *so great*. Amazing *man,* amazing *life*." Back to Bud. "Do you know Mike Schur?"

"Uhm, I don't *think* so," Bud said, tentatively.

"He's a showrunner—*The Office* and *Parks&Recreation*."

"O sure! We've met."

"Mike said he wished he'd created *The Wire*. Mike said *The Wire* was Shakespearean."

"Wow."

Bud wanted to make points, & wondered if now was a good time to bring up Lorrie Moore's essay on *Friday Night Lights* from *The New York Review of Books*, wherein she called *The Wire* a "visual novel."*

---

* When it's time for a cable auteur's fawning, metacritical dicksuck (usually coinciding with the release of the complete DVDs of his show), brain surgeon Ms. Moore makes a savory mouthpiece; there are few things sweeter than egghead head. The novelist has shown herself to be down with the squad/groupie—ready to traitorously jump the ship of her own craft: in a wet pantiesgyric to *The Wire* in the pages of *NYRB* (if only David Milch was still around for her to service!), she calls David Simon's Baltimore a "quiet rebuke to its own great [in the dialect of the Brownnose Indians, Moore employs "great" as a means of softening the already soft snarkiness of her takedown] living novelists, Anne Tyler and John Barth [is Barth great? is he living?]" and goes on to pamdesbarres the anus by asserting that her beloved show is "arguably biblical, Dantesque . . . the series's creators know what novelists know [ooh, I'll bet] . . . whether time comes [like a *jackhammer*] in the form of pages or hours. On DVD, it can be watched all at once, over 60 hours: this particular manner of viewing makes the literary accolades and comparisons to a novel more justified and true . . . *The Wire* has much in common with the plays of George Bernard Shaw. [It] embraces the Wildean

"Did you know John Updike was watching *The Wire* when he died?"

"Wow. Incredible. Uhm . . . what about *Mad Men*?"

She went cold.

"What about it?"

"I was just wondering what David calls *Mad Men*. I mean, is it, does he think of it as a book?"

"You're not joking?"

"No—I'm just trying to get a flavor of . . ."

"*Mad Men* is absolutely *not* a book—a novel. *Mad Men* is more like a *novelization*—no. Wait. I shouldn't even say *that*, because *David* is the only one who is writing novels for television. *Mad Men* is more like a . . . *cartoon*, a *manga. Mad Manga!* But *please*, if you meet—when you meet David, please don't talk about *Mad Men*."

"My agent said David was developing—is developing—a new . . . a new *novel* about Hollywood."

"Yes! That's why he wanted to talk to you. He *loved* the little book of short stories you did about Hollywood."

"He read that?"

"*Very* much."

"I'm flattered."

"When did you write that?"

"Probably about 25 years ago."

"David thought they were more a *novella* than a book of short stories. *But not a novel.* He wanted to know if there were any more you've written."

---

sense of art's cleverness as well as its uselessness." In a companion cockstroke/rimjob of *Friday Night Lights* offered in the same pub, the brainy, brain-giving plaster caster begins by sharing with the reader her slutty surprise and delight in finding herself at a Manhattan book party "locked in enthusiastic conversation in a corner with two other writers [Barth & Tyler? Toni & Fran?], all three of us, we discovered, solitary, isolated viewers of the NBC series *Friday Night Lights*." After referencing Janet Malcolm, *Wozzeck* & Daniel Mendelsohn, the pundit pantycreams about *FNL* being filled with actors who are "disconcertingly attractive young people with pink, wavy mouths." A final quote from Moore: "In fact, two characters on *The Wire* are murdered [Barth? Toni? Tyler? Fran?] in David Simon's Baltimore just in time for the excellent actors who play them to join *Friday Night Lights*." From *Friday Night Lights* to *The Wire* then back again—this gangbanger knows how to righteously 69!

"O yeah!" he lied. "A bunch. But I've really been focusing the last few years on, well, I guess you'd call it a *book*."

"Taking place in Hollywood?"

It sounded like that was what she wanted to hear—that he was working on a collection of "Hollywood" stories—so Bud decided to go with the flow. They'd apparently reached the meat of the interview.

"Yes! I was *calling* it a novel, but I guess it's not, really—not the kind David writes! Which are so layered & . . . well, Sophoclean! And *wonderful*. Would you excuse me a second?"

On his way to execute the tricky *Double Void* gambit, Bud was intercepted by Michael Tolkin.

They were high school chums who hadn't seen each other in years. Tolkin wrote movie scripts for seven figures (& dabbled in cable), and was an acclaimed novelist to boot. He had the sort of career Bud wanted—the respect and acclaim of the Industry *and* the book critics as well. Bud had long felt a rivalry there, which of course his old friend would have known nothing about.

Michael was also the ostensible instigator behind the still vague David Simon affair.

Bud embraced him, but Michael was in a hurry; a handshake probably would have been better.

"I'm right in the middle of the David Simon meeting! Hey, thank you for that—I was going to get your number from CAA, so I could take you to dinner."

"I'm late, Bud, so I don't have time to talk, we can talk later. But here's what's happening: David's doing a show about Hollywood, I may or may not be involved. It's scripted improv. He wants it to feel like *The Wire*, whatever *that* means, I *hate* it when people start talking about what shit should *feel* like, you know? I remembered those great short stories you wrote, and I was telling him about them, how funny and moving they were, & he just *jumped* on it. David wants there to be a protagonist like—like the one you wrote about

in your book. A down & out screenwriter, maybe addicted to narcotics or porn. I don't know what David's thinking—*nobody* does!—
we didn't talk all that much. My deal isn't even in place. I'm only
telling *you* this because, & I *love* the guy, but David's a *writer*, what
more can I say, that's what writers *do*, we steal from the best. And I
do think he's genuinely interested in *listening*, you know, hearing
stories about the bottomfeeders in the business. I only brought your
name up as an example of someone who really *captured*, who *knew*
those kind—that kind of character down to his *soul*. But I'm not so
sure, I don't think he'd ever, I shouldn't say *ever*, I just don't think
he's looking for you to write something for him for his *show*, to be
in on the *ground floor*. And I'm telling you this because I don't think
you should—Bud, you do what you *want*, you're a big boy—I just
don't think you should be giving your *stories* away."

"That's fine, Michael. It's fine. It's all good."

"Well, *I'm* not so happy about it. Is he in there?"

"No. His development gal."

"*Do not tell her any stories about Hollywood.* You know, I said to him,
either talk to Bud as a peer & potential writer on the show or don't
talk to him at all. Jesus, David! 'The art of storytelling is reaching its
end because truth and wisdom are dying'—Walter Benjamin said it, I
didn't! He also said that every work of art is an uncommitted crime.
Maybe that was Adorno."

"Don't even worry about it, I can handle myself."

"Bud, I gotta go."

"Hey, remember when you lived in that apt on Fountain? Where
Carl Gottlieb & Sela Ward used to live?"

"The La Fontaine! That was 30 years ago."

"Where are you living now?"

"Wendy and I have a house in Laughlin Park, but we spend most
of our time in Carpenteria. And I never gave up my seedy little office
in Malibu. We need to downsize—our girls are in college. You? Got
any kids?"

"No."

"And you're living . . ."

Bud said "Hancock Park" instead of "with my mother."

Tolkin broke away. "I'll call the end of the week, I want to put you in touch with someone."

"Great! Hey, who ya meetin' in there?"

What's a little *gauche* between old friends?

"Michael Douglas. I wrote the movie he's about to shoot, & he's got 'actor questions.' Ugh. Good guy, though. See you, Bud."

. . .

Tolkin called like he said he would. He felt bad about being inadvertently involved in Bud's "set up," & gave him a hot tip.

He told Bud that the company producing the Michael Douglas movie was relatively new, but already had a few hits under its belt. It was run by a kid named Brando—nice kid—the son of a billionaire. Michael said that Ooh Baby Baby* was practically "giving away" blind script deals, "which in this climate is unusual, to say the least." He told Bud that he'd already spoken to Brando about him.

"They should be calling you soon. I know you take jobs to make your monthly nut," he added thoughtfully.

Tolkin was a *mensch*. He would certainly have been aware of what terrible straits Bud was in—for years now—yet was handling the situation, such as it was, with enormous sensitivity. Bud felt awful for having had a moment's resentment toward the man who'd floated back into his life in the form of a fairy godfather, spirit guide and overall ministering angel.

"Do I need to come in with a pitch?" said Bud.

That hollow feeling began taking over, just like it used to. The

---

* Ooh Baby Baby It's A Wild World Films was named after Brando's mother's favorite song. Tolkin was of the opinion that naming a production company thus was "heinously charming—or charmingly heinous. Either way, something about it works."

despair of knowing that you didn't have what it took, that a beggar could never be a nobleman.

"No! Less is definitely more. Brando listens to me, & I said you were Charlie Kaufman before *Charlie* was Charlie Kaufman. He's *excited*. Just take a general meeting. Brando will pitch to *you*."

[Michael]

The Oaks

He

came to see her because he loved her. He wanted to talk about the project, of course, & about the *flopsweat* that seized hold of him in the last few weeks. The fear that he might be calling dark energy. He didn't like the witchy feeling of superstition that of a sudden descended upon him in regards to directing & starring in a film about the death of a maverick. *A maverick like him . . .*

Though he hadn't fully discussed it with his wife, Michael was certain he wanted her to play the Angel of Death. Still, he couldn't put his finger on it. There was something tawdry & graspy about this posthumous-feeling, pet project of his. An element of morbid kitsch . . . was he jumping headlong into a lot of meretricious nonsense? He aimed to cross Fosse with Cocteau, but was he really up for that? (Was anyone?) Because whenever he had that "genius" conversation with himself, he sure as hell came out on the losing end. Would he—*could* he—make some kind of wild theatrical poem, some messy, perfectly imperfect masterpiece? All he had to do was close his eyes & he could hear the jangle of a critical & financial fiasco, a lampoonable death rattle.

Whatever he was going to make, he sure the fuck didn't feel like falling on his ass. (Never did.) This wasn't a midlife gambol, it was an act of love, or was meant to be, as much as it was a *cri de coeur*. But the virus of doubt had infected him, and experience had shown that was a tough bug to kill. He'd awaken in the night, at that time Dr. Calliope always called the hour of the wolf, from a dream that he was walking alongside the catafalque bearing his body; the pallbearers looked at him sideways with contempt & he felt shame that he didn't have the courage to climb in the box. That *quality* of nightmare hadn't occurred since radiation.

With each passing hour, he saw himself engineering what the Internet called an epic FAIL, a professional, personal, spiritual blunder. But there he was, taking the meetings, there he was, already *out* there, making plans. Producing—he'd even hired someone to do a budget. Yes, yes, it was way preliminary, but *still* . . . he was doing the *act as if* that *All That Jazz* was going to happen, that it *had* to. That it must. Maybe he shouldn't be moving so fast. Maybe he should just *sit* with it for 6 months, even a year. He didn't want to be like Warren either. Warren had been talking about the Howard Hughes movie since Precambrian time. *I don't have the luxury. I may not have three years.* He needed a reality check. Could be he was just chickenshit, a classic case of the jitters. The trouble was, he couldn't sort out old fears (the ones long before his cancer, childhood ones mixed up with his father) from the new. If anyone could get to the bottom of it, Dr. Calliope could. She was a deepsea diver that way, deepsea diver *extraordinaire*.

He was her analysand in the early 70s, during *Streets*. Calliope Krohn was the shrink to the stars; she knew how to navigate the celeb mindset. No one intimidated her. The celebs appreciated that, it was a special gift.

Her old patients kept in touch by phone, some just to chat and check in, others to seek informal counsel. Former clients—what they used to call *marquee names*—were an aging tribe of legends, & the old Krohn was their Yodagirl. They'd all been through the wars together—in one-on-ones & weekly groups that she ran out of her office in Beverly Hills—their private, deeply personal melodramas often played out for the insatiable public, a public that, with the advent of the Internet, became a rapist, a rampaging, murderous home-invader. A remarkably high percentage of the Tribe had endured, managing to hold onto their seats at the cultural table, still rich, famous and recognizable by the dullwitted man-on-the-street of China, Finland, Capetown, where have you, & for that they credited the doctor's governance.

So they called & they called & they worried, & sent care packages: deli from Factor's, pasta from Dante's, takeaway from Spago's (a nostalgic nod to a man called Swifty), platters from Bristol Farms (nostalgia again, because it sat on the land where Chasen's used to be), cupcakes from Sprinkles, yogurt from Yogurtland, flowers from The Empty Vase. Because most were in the Academy, they sent DVDs of whatever films were up for awards that year, sometimes their own. They sent personal assistants to check up on her when they weren't checking up on her themselves because after all she was almost 90 & steadfastly refused to employ caregivers, she *barely* let in the twice-a-month housekeeper, & her Tribespeople (justifiably) worried she would fall, that when she didn't answer the phone she was in trouble, she'd fallen & couldn't get up, or was dead. Only a month ago, two Oscar-winning actresses & a Tony/Grammy doubleheader descended upon her Trousdale home at the same time, unbeknownst to each other, because they kept getting a busy signal, keystone kopping into the house through the sliding glass backdoor that was forever unlocked, startling her in her usual plunked-down spot, half-dozing/watching TV, always one of said hundreds of DVDs, starred in, produced, directed or written by her minions (in-home festival that revolved year-round), the phone hadn't been properly put back in its cradle, that's all, everyone had a laugh, perfect anecdote to be neatly folded & put away until employed on the day of the eulogies.

Dr. Calliope was in excellent health for her age, sharp as a tack as they say, still cutting to the heart of a problem with unsettling speed. She was always there for him, had helped him through so many dark times . . . those early years when his ability to dream froze in his father's formidable shadow; through the Oedipal crisis of *Cuckoo's Nest* & Dad's towering rage; the addictions and divorce & of late not just the cancer of course but the prison ordeal with his son . . . there for him in that hallucinatory time when he *became* Michael Douglas, walking/leading/guiding him through that obverse world of acclaim and peril. Because for an actor, sudden fame was a crucible, perilous as a slow fade to obscurity. The only fates possible for a supernova were joining a constellation or falling out of the sky.

He remembered talking to her just after the diagnosis. He was so angry at the doctors who missed it, angry that *Catherine* had to be so angry, for months they said it was something else, how could they miss a tumor the size of a walnut, then he was angry at God & so fatigued during the treatment, his anger turned inward and he grew depressed. Dr. Calliope had lost a son herself to cancer, Jesus, that must have been 40 years ago, she never discussed it until their recent phone calls, so poignant, moving, germane. (CK always sent lovely notes on the birthdays of the children Catherine had given him.) She was the first to tell him to divorce Diandra, years before the event finally happened. She rarely made any sort of pronouncement, not her style, not what therapy was about, never gave *advice,* not in that sense, in the concrete sense, she wasn't a codependent shrink & wasn't *invasive*, not too invested in the mechanics of her clients' daily lives (not really) so when she said he should *divorce her,* he thought she was being dramatic (she was, but that shouldn't have diluted the message), and in-trouble as the marriage was, that *irritated* him because *no one*, not even Dr. Calliope Krohn, told Michael Douglas what to do, or how to *live his life.* He was caught in a conundrum, because that's why he was seeing her, wasn't it? Not necessarily to be told what to do but to show him how to live, how to *love,* how to love *himself,* & how to live through things that might destroy him.

Not listening to her about Diandra became one of the larger regrets of his life.

When he was at St. Ambrose for his check-up, he made the mistake
of leafing through one of those embalmed vanity magazines for the
local rich, *Santa Barbara Living* (he thought *Santa Barbara Dying* was
more apt), & there she was—his ex, barefoot, sitting on a horse under
one of the huge oak trees on the estate they once shared. He really
missed his beloved oaks, more than he did the property itself, once
the magical backdrop of so many important events in his life. But the
oaks! He used to talk to them at night, he sought their counsel during the day too, right in front of the gardeners, he didn't give a shit,
they were potent spiritual beings, & he carried them in his heart,
proud to be a tree hugger to the end.

There she was: an absurd photograph, like one of those sad *Town &
Country* portraits of latefiftysomething socialites decked out in rich
hippie couture. They made sure their picture was always taken at the
optimal distance required for the photographic facelift . . . plus there
was something creepy/sexual about the pic, the old come hither, her
pre-Raphaelite hair still rich-hippie-shower-wet, barefoot, bare
legged slice of thigh, a little riding crop in her hand, submissive horse
head down, her orchestrated control/domination of mise-en-scène.

The article was called "My Santa Barbara Dream."

LOL!

Diandra was selling the house.

She had lots of bad press during those first cancer months when
she sued for *Wall St.* sequel profits; whatever she had of a pathetic image needed heavy rehabbing. *Someone* was advising her, *someone* must
have told her to take the bull by the horns, like they tell the CEOs
to just be open with the public after their products kill a bunch of
people—so she gave interviews saying she wanted the world to know
that she wasn't a greedy person *by nature*. But the quote Michael liked
the best was the one about the lawsuit she filed while he was in treat-

ment: *"I asked myself every night if I should walk away."* O man, the fuckin agonies! Nobody knows the trouble this bitch has seen! Upon the advice of *whomever,* she continued to dig a tidy little grave for herself by *clarifying* to all who'd listen that the *reason* she was suing— suing *again,* in the midst of his *treatment*—she kept flogging that litigious dead horse (*not* the one so MILF-ily straddled in *Santa Barbara Walking Dead*) was because none other than Bernie Madoff had cleaned her clock. Blame it on Rio.

Blame it on the bossa nova . . .

Morbidly curious, he skimmed the text. She talked about her Japanese garden, the one "never photographed" because she considered it a "sacred space." She said she hired—hired!—a Japanese priest to come have sake ceremonies and move rocks. He laughed out loud and one of the passing nurses said, *Hope it's a good one.* O yeah, O yeah, it's really really good.

"Already back then," she shared with her interviewer, "my interest was to grow organic vegetables & fruits. On the weekends, we used to go in the garden in our pjs & pick strawberries, for healthy shakes"————o ha! o ho!

He recounted the story to Dr. CK but what once was funny, turned. He could taste the bile rising.

"I didn't come here to talk about my former wife."

"You're doing a pretty good job."

"Ha!"

"Talk about anything. *No restrictions.* Better yet, you won't even be billed. Though that may depend on how long you stay."

"I'll put you in touch with my business manager. I don't think your files are current."

"Talk about the *oak trees.* Or we can just sit & navel gaze."

"I'll show you mine if you'll show me yours."

"I don't think mine is particularly alluring. I'm not so sure it *ever* was."

Time to get into it.

"Bob Fosse was a patient of yours, wasn't he?"

"Oh yes—back when I was still in New York. And after I moved my practice, but not so much. He did thank me from the podium when he won the Oscar."

"Really?"

"For *Cabaret*."

"I didn't know that. That he thanked you. Nice."

"Oh yes. You know that he beat out Francis for *The Godfather*. Bob beat him, can you imagine? & Francis was my client as well . . . awkward. His daughter called not long ago. Sofia. She invited me to a Hollywood screening of her movie. I thought that was darling. She's a *brilliant* girl. A darling."

"I'm thinking about doing a remake of one of his films."

"Oh?"

"Fosse's."

"Yes, I gathered that. Which one?"

"All That Jazz."

"To produce? To act in?"

"Both. But this one, I think I'd direct."

There. Got it out.

"Good for you! That movie could *use* a director."

He laughed. He'd forgotten about her right-on critical eye.

"Do you know my favorite of his? *Star 80*. It's a terribly hopeless film—his best too I think, by a longshot. It took *extreme* courage, & a *lot* of therapy to get him there. To that place where he could strip away all those extras, those bells & whistles he used, to *dazzle*. What's his name, Eric Roberts, Julia's brother. My God, what a performance! Then he disappeared, didn't he? I saw him on one of those awful celebrity rehab shows. He was *marvelous*, & so was the Hemingway girl. My God, what Bob teased out of her! She's no Meryl Streep, you know. Quite an amazing work. Bob stripped *everything* away. Only emptiness & savagery were left."

It was a pleasure listening, as long as she was talking about someone else. For the Tribe, debriefing Dr. Calliope after a private screening of their latest was far more stressful than waiting for reviews in *Variety* or the *Times.*

"All right. So. You want to do *All That Jazz.* To play the part Roy Scheider took—I'm assuming! And you plan to direct."

"Yes."

"What, then, is the problem, Michael?"

"I don't know if it's a *problem.* It's more a *concern.*"

"You're mincing words, playing with language."

"Look, Calliope, I'm just—unsure about it. I'm wondering if I'm biting off more than I can chew here! You know I *ask* myself, Is this really how I want to spend my time?"

"Well, I don't know. Is it?"

"Do I want to spend my time making another movie?"

"You're making movies all the time. Aren't you?"

"I'm *acting* in movies. I'm not *producing* and *directing.*"

"You ask if that's how you would like to spend your time. What else would you be doing? With your time?"

"I mean, instead of with the kids, & Catherine. You know how consuming that is, Calliope. This isn't just 'another movie.' I don't even know if I can pull it off! And I worry about the content, not just for Catherine, but for Dylan and Carys. I mean, you know suddenly the old man's making a movie but it ain't *Pirates of the Caribbean.* 'Then, what is it, Dad?' 'Well . . . remember when Daddy had that little *health scare?* Well, uh, in *this* movie, kids, well—y'see—Daddy dies!'"

They laughed.

She took a deep breath, & straightened her spine, readying to speak. Michael girded himself for feedback, the fingers on one hand moving like an anemone's in a light current.

"A sensitive, talented man—a producer and director—a man who has it *all* is *dying.* Does that sound familiar, Michael? Of course, you're not dying, not *now,* at least not more or less than the rest of us. Let's just say your *aptitude* for both *antipodes*—life & death—is presently running at a higher *pitch*, it's *keener* than most. Your *appreciation* of *extinction* has lit a *fire* under you; it has *humbled*, but *not* tamed. I'm sure it crossed your mind that *Jazz* might be too *on the nose*, you people in Hollywood used to *love* that phrase, do they use it still? *Perhaps* on one of your sleepless nights, I assume you've had many, you may have surmised there was something *distasteful* about the choice, the *idea* of it, something too *flamboyant*. The *reachiness* of it may have confused & depressed you."

Reachiness. Jesus. Dead on.

"That, I think, is its brilliance. Is it a risk? An *artistic* risk? Of course it is. What isn't? You wouldn't seriously be thinking about it if it weren't. So: the proof is already in the pudding. If you had sat there and told me you wanted to remake *Star 80*, then I'd say you had a problem. A big one. Because *Star 80* is already perfect, in its own way. But *I* think you could do something *spectacular* with *Jazz*. Not just because it's a *goddawful* movie. It's *dreadful*. It's a horror! As it happens, I watched it not too long ago & it fell flatter than a pancake. Cheap and egotistical in every wrong way. But his *intentions* were honorable, his intentions were *brilliant*. Bob *was* brilliant. The *concept* of the film is *brilliant*. I know what he was doing, he *told* me so, Bob strove to make his *8½* but all he got for his money was an *ego bath*, you know, flapping his wings in the water, all that chain-smoking and 'It's *showtime!*' inanity. A tacky cabaret, a *cartoon treatise* on sexing & workaholism, *completely* uninstructive & utterly, radiantly *charmless*. He was frustrated with his therapy. I was too; he never worked very hard with me. Wouldn't put in the time, not till toward the end. *Jazz* was '79, *Star 80* was '83. He died in '86 I think, maybe '87. And because of this *frustration*, he wanted *Scheider* to die at the end, so *Bob could live!* Bob thought that would be enough, you see we hadn't done our real *shadow work* at that time, he truly thought if he could kill himself off in the film he wouldn't have to do the hard work of looking at his life & where he came from & why he was so hell-bent on destroying himself & those around him, those he loved—he refused for a long time to do the kind of work I did with *you,* the work we did *together.* By the time he was ready, you see it was almost too late. Now if *Jazz* had been a better *movie,* maybe Bob's plan would have worked! Oh, I shouldn't have said that. I think I've been too hard on him . . . excuse me, Michael"—she looked heavenward—"& forgive me, Bob. I'm not sure I'm looking in the right direction, but do forgive me! He *was* brave, I will say that, oh yes, I will say that without *tergiversation.*

"But you—*you*—I *know* your courage, Michael, I've *seen* it. It's *real.* My *God,* you're a long-distance runner. With everything you've been through, you have *earned* the right to bargain with the Angel of Death. Even if she's your wife, *especially* if she's your lovely wife. And don't underestimate our Catherine. Don't you dare, you know better than that. You know how tough that girl is. You've *both* earned the right. To bargain for a little more time, time to watch your kids grow, time to be together. Time to make a *movie,* which is a fair portion of what I believe your purpose is on this planet, what you're meant to be doing. What *I* think you're meant to be doing, from all the *years,* & everything that I know, everything that I feel & know about *you.* You've earned the right to bargain for a little more time to make sense of your *life.* Because all you need is a *little more time,* to *see*—that there *is* no sense in life but *the doing of what you love,* & the *loving* of those you love. That clarity will come, Michael, it's *right around the corner* for you. You see, your gift is that you *captivate* people. You have marvelous *energy,* people love to *look* at you, to *listen.* Lord *knows* what you'll do when you make that terrible film your own! Now *that's* a challenge. You'll *captivate* us all!

"This fear you have is *not* in depicting yourself as a dying man—& who, by the way, says the *All That Jazz* Michael Douglas must die?— no. That's not what you're afraid of. That is distinctly *not* your fear. You've flirted with death so much lately . . . the world was practically shouting at you two to 'get a room'! Michael, you are an *artist.* I believe that has always been your central drama. 'Am I an artist?' *That* is the question that arises during your hour of the wolf. No? Do you remember we used to talk about the hour of the wolf? That terrible time between 3AM and 4AM when we are *completely alone*. 'Am I an artist?' Well, I'm going to give you the answer. I'm going to answer that question, and all you need to do is *accept it as truth*. As gospel. Because I know something about it. I know a *lot* about it. And I have never lied to you, ever. Not even once. Not even a *white* lie. Well, maybe I overbilled you now and then, but nothing too serious . . . *ha!* So here's the answer, like it or not: *Yes*. You, Michael Douglas, *are an artist*. And I say that before God. You have my one hundred percent *guarantee*.

"Every artist I've ever known has the same fear, I call it the *If I jump into the abyss, will I die?* fear. And do you know what the answer to that is? If you *don't* jump, you'll die."

The phone rang, and she broke away. Which was good because he needed a moment. When the old woman hung up, she turned to him and smiled. He knew that was the image of her he would carry with him into both their eternities.

"Thank you. Thank you, Calliope."

"Make this wonderful project a journey—for *you*."

Her eyes got mischievous.

"Can you dance?"

"I've been known."

"But can you cut a rug? That's what we called it when I was a girl." She reached to touch his arm. "I seem to have *opinions* lately."

"You *always* had opinions, girl."

"Maybe so. But I have even *more* of them today. It apparently comes with the territory of being *very*, very old." She took another deep breath. "I have one final piece of advice."

He girded himself again, a protective reflex he'd acquired during a lifetime of counsel from his straight-shooting mentor—and friend.

"Fire away."

Her eyes flared.

"I would *love* to see you do a turn on *Dancing With the Stars*. It's my favorite show! I think it'd be *marvelous preparation* for your movie. The sooner you begin cutting a rug, Michael Douglas, the better!"

[Gwen]

Falsies & False Positives

Across

town, Gwen saw her own therapist, the one she met at Our House, the grief center she'd gone to for support when her husband died. She felt blessed that Phoebe was already in her life when her daughter *became ill* (Gwen now choking on those words), because she really helped, & really helped Telma too.

"Have you cried yet?"

Gwen hated that question.

"No. Not really. I'm too angry."

"It's good that you're angry, you should be. I'd be worried if you weren't."

Silence, then again:

"Gwen, have you been able to cry?"

"No!"

The repetition some sort of therapist's ploy.

More silence.

"I'm afraid to. I'm afraid to."

"And why is that?"

"Because if I cry"—tremulous voice—"the anger might go away, & without the anger—"

Silence.

"Without the anger . . ." The shrink cued her to fill in the blank. The patient remained quiet. "Without the anger, you're afraid you'll fall apart. That you won't have the strength you need to see justice done."

. . .

Gwen wasn't really sleeping; she took sleep when it came, like coins being dropped into a half-conscious beggar's palm. Under siege, she spasmed awake with little starts & yelps, reacting to whatever movie flickered behind fitful shutlid eyes. It was one of the hellish cruelties human beings were subject to—to be unable to use sleep to escape from a waking nightmare, to find oneself in a place where nothing worked, there was no comfort, no alternatives, no let-up, like a person burned and tortured in such a way they cannot sit or stand or lie down without excruciating pain. She told her lawyers she needed time to think. Gwen couldn't *act* until certain things were handled.

Until Telma had been told . . .

She haunted the Internet's vast trove of horrific misdiagnoses & wanton, wrongful surgeries. A woman in the UK lost a breast by hospital blunder, something they knew right away but didn't tell her for nine years. In a ghoulish twist, she became a counselor to those with breast cancer. Her ballroom dancing pastime was no more; the beloved strapless dresses retired to the closet, a murdered raft of pretty girls, carefully, quietly hanged. She went through menopause without hormone replacement therapy because if you've had breast cancer, HRT is *out*. Insurance paid £100,000.

There were a lot of similar cases, closer to home. An L.A. woman had a double mastectomy & reconstructive surgery as the result of a misread biopsy. She was awarded $110,000 for each shorn tit. *Was that because she couldn't afford the right lawyer?* Gwen's counsel said Gwen needn't worry because her daughter's case had "unique & compelling attributes," and they believed a settlement of around $15 million was feasible. They also believed that a proviso of any settlement would be the hospital's insistence that the records of the case be sealed forever, as St. Ambrose would have trouble surviving the primal rage that such a bogus mutilaton of a child would engender, not to mention a child as charismatic as Telma; not to mention that child having become a beacon of hope for other children thus afflicted, & for their parents too; not to mention that Telma would become a poster child—an electronic billboard!—of the hospital's malfeasance and cynical desecration of the Hippocratic Oath. The calculus of the $15 million figure of course included restitution for the physical & emotional travails of reconstructive surgery that Telma would eventually endure in the relatively near future. If the records *weren't* sealed, the original error would never fade in public consciousness, to the contrary, it would compound yearly, *monthly*, as the press nurtured & obsessed, the maimed darling growing up under their exploitative sponsorship into a lovely young woman that *another* surgical team (the reconstructivists) would pounce on in the name of closure and healing, but the *people* wouldn't see it that way, the *people* would see it as Frankenstein redux.

It could be worse . . . in erratic, restless fits, Gwen joined the accursed orgy of the Web, Single Mom Seeking Stories Worse Than Mine. She read about a woman in Brooklyn who lost her husband & two daughters in a fire. She returned to the apartment the next day to retrieve the only thing she was afraid had melted: a silver urn containing the ashes of another daughter, dead of leukemia at 15. For a day, Gwen's mantra became *she lost three daughters my baby's alive she lost three daughters my baby's alive* the distraction made her feel better by the smallest of increments but it didn't sit well that it was on the back of that poor woman, at her expense. The feeling never lasted anyway.

"I just feel crazy, Phoebe. Completely crazy. The not-sleeping doesn't help."

"Are you taking the Xanax?"

"During the day, Seroquel at night."

"I want you to be careful with that."

"It doesn't *work,* Phoebe. It doesn't matter how much I take."

"I hear you, Gwen—but we need to talk about this at the end of our time today, OK? Because we really need to. Agreed?"

"Agreed."

Then:

"I've sent blood & tissue samples to *three different labs.* Telma thinks it's for something routine."

"Do your lawyers know you're doing that?"

"No."

"Didn't you agree you wouldn't—"

"Her name's not anywhere on it."

"You don't want to do something foolish that jeopardizes your settlement."

"It's all going through the office of a good friend. He was my husband's oncologist."

"Just be careful. What are you looking for?"

"Cancer."

"I don't understand."

"We've got some early results saying the likelihood is slim. Slim to none!"

"Your thinking is that if she *did*—if you can find out that she *does,* then—"

"Yes! Then at least what they did won't be for *nothing.* If they fucked up thinking she had it, maybe they fucked up thinking she *doesn't.* You know, I play this game, this *things could be worse* game in my head, I'm *trolling* the Internet—that evil woman in Massachusetts who had an autistic son with non-Hodgkin's. She wouldn't give him his meds because she couldn't stand caring for him anymore, she wanted him to die. And the housewife who got staph, one of those weird catastrophic infections, while she was in a coma the doctors told the husband she was going to die unless they chopped off her arms and legs & the husband had to decide right there. He finally said *Yeah,* you know, *let's do it.* And when she woke up, she was *so* grateful, she said all she wanted was to watch their baby grow!

"Phoebe! That woman had *kids*, she'd been *sexual*. She'd given boys & babies & men her breasts . . . she'd been suckled & *felt up.* Every girl remembers the first time she was felt up. Do you? Do you remember the first time you were felt up? Telma won't. Telma won't remember because Telma won't ever *have* that experience—my baby's never going to be felt up! She'll never be able to put on a bikini in the summer, I don't care what kind of fucking surgery they do, Phoebe, she will *never* be able to know what it's like when you finally get tits & you walk across the sand & all the eyes are on you, the boys are looking, that time of your life when you catch yourself in the mirror and you *love* what you see . . . I used to get *hickies* on my tits, Phoebe! Do *not* talk to me about prosthetics & fucking skin flaps! It's like fucking Auschwitz, like they're *experimenting*————[crying now]————cutting *into* her again! It isn't *FAIR*. It isn't————— [screams, then]————they went in there, Phoebe, I'll never forget that day, they went in there &————took her little————took her little titties & all the lymph nodes . . . those *assholes! Mutherfuckers!* Making themselves *saints*, everyone kowtowing & worshipping, *O God Bless you, doctor, you saved her life, you're helping all the children*—to live! . . . to live! To LIVE with the scars of your fucking sick *torture*—God Bless and may God *fuck* you and *YOUR* children, may God turn your babies into *monsters*—butchering my baby, it's a fucking *freakshow* over there! O Phoebe! What a fool I am! I didn't get a second opinion, why didn't I, I should've gotten a second opinion————"

"Remember that word 'should,' you know we need to be careful when we use that word. When I hear *should*—"

"I'm sick of hearing that! Should should should should should! Everyone gets so fucking militant about *should & should have*, everyone wants to fucking *punish* you for using the word! Well *should have* is probably the single most important word or phrase or whatever in the *English Language!* I'm going to use it until I *die!*————I remem-

ber when they said she didn't need chemo or radiation I was *crying* I
was *thanking them!* What an *idiot* . . . *[crying now for two full minutes,
then]* & they were *right*, Phoebe, they were *right,* she *didn't* need
chemo, she *didn't* need radiation, she didn't need *anything!* All of those
dinners, those $500 a plate *benefits*, at the Hilton, at the Beverly Hills
Hotel, Telma even *performed,* everyone on the medical team honored,
one by one, year by year, the dinners & the standing ovations! The
smug smiles of those high-flying butchers! That Michael Jackson
Conrad doctor looks like fucking *Dr. House* next to those sick mutherfuckers! And it's *my* fault this happened————————*don't you try
and tell me it isn't, Phoebe! Don't you dare!* Because I should have just
pulled her out of there. I'm not a mother, I'm as bad as them! I have no
maternal instincts, if I had maternal instincts, I would never have let
this happen! Never! I'm as sick and fucked as that woman who withheld the medicine from her son! To kill him! Do you want to know
how fucked up I am? How selfish & fucked up? The last few days I've
actually been *worrying* what people will think of me when this comes
out, & you better *believe* it's going to come out, I'll make *sure* of that
because *I'm going to bring them down.* I've actually been *worrying* that
people will think I'm a terrible mother, I *know* how people are, they'll
go on the internet & blog about *how it could have been prevented*—if the
parent—the *MOM*—had only done her *homework* . . . *& they'll be right!*
I've even been worrying what *Telma* is going to think of me too, you
know, she's going to HATE me————don't you try & tell me she
won't, Phoebe, it's her *right*, don't take away her *right*————or *worse,*
what if she goes into this whole resentment thing, which will be her
right, but she never really *mentions* it because she's that kind of kid,
such a good, sweet kid, but it's there, her mommy let her down,
her mommy let them *remove her breasts*, her mommy let them steal her
youth, her *mommy* stole her youth, *the doctors & her mommy stole her
beauty* . . . you know what she's being set up for? She's being set up to
be *a drug addict.* A maimed drug addict . . . at 18, the surgeries begin . . . how many surgeries will it take to make her whole again?
How many, Phoebe! A *million* fucking surgeries will *never* make her

whole————————don't ask me how I know, Phoebe, don't you ask me that! And there she is, with the skin graphs not taking, or maybe infections—'complications'—whatever—& she's *angry*, angry at me *as she should be*, angry at the *world*, they give her pain pills for the surgeries, she's depressed anyway, she's being *set up*, these stories do *not* end well——"

Gwen had exhausted herself, & Phoebe called for her to be calm. She told Gwen she was glad she had cried, but now she wanted her to take some deep breaths. Which Gwen did.

"You know, I don't see Telma as an addict." It was the only thing Phoebe could grab hold of; the rest was just too big. "I've worked with many, many children, & I don't see that for Telma."

"You don't *know* what can happen, you don't *know,* how *could* you, *no one* knows . . . O! Did I tell you what the woman said when they handed her the urn with her kid's ashes? She said, 'God is good.' *God is good.* That's what she said, Phoebe."

"You're right, Gwen. I *don't* know what will happen to Telma. None of us have a crystal ball." *Whenever she talked about crystal balls, Gwen recoiled inside.* "I can only hope for the best for her, the very best. That's all we can *ever* do, Gwen."

"You're right. How about rainbows and roses and whiskers on kittens . . . Do you want to hear *another* sick thing I've been thinking? I lay there in bed imagining Telma's 18. And she goes and gets her implants. They say some women get *breast cancer* from their implants, & the *sick* part is, I'm lying in bed *imagining* that when they're in for a few years—you know, she turns 21 or 22 or 23—*that's* when she gets cancer! Because of the implants! *That's* how fucked up I am, Phoebe! It's like now part of me wants her to get cancer! It's so *sick.*"

"You're depressed, Gwen. And when we're depressed, we get morbid. We catastrophize—"

" 'Catastrophize!' "

"We're filled with negative self-talk . . ."

"Just spare me, Phoebe. Please just fucking spare me. Why don't you admit it? You're probably *thinking* it, so why don't you just admit that I'm the one who let it happen? It *should not have happened,* that's the bottomline, but I *let it!* I am responsible, *1,000%.* Because *I am the mother.*"

"You didn't let *anything* happen."

"O Phoebe, Phoebe, what do I do? How can I tell her? How can I————what do I *say?*"

"You tell her the truth."

"I can't!"

"You can. Because the truth is that you brought her to the very best doctors in the world. And they determined, with all of their knowledge & all of their expertise, that Telma had breast cancer. And they found out that they were *wrong.* They found out too late. And that you wish you could change what happened, but you can't, because you're just a human being. You're just a mom. That's what you tell her. And you tell her as soon as possible. You can bring her here or I can come to the house. But before that happens, before you do have that talk with her, I want to see you in better shape."

"Phoebe, you have to help me."

"That's what I'm here for. You can do this, Gwen. You *have to.* Not just for Telma, but for *you.* Because she's sensitive, she's seen you depressed but she's never seen you like this. You can't keep her at her grandma's forever. I don't care how much you think you conceal it, Gwen, she knows something is *terribly wrong,* and it isn't fair to her for you to prolong this. And you can't go on beating yourself up either. The self-punishing has got to stop. The *rage,* the *false guilt,* will consume you. *[moments of silence]* Telma's strong. You know how we're always talking about her as an old soul? Well, I really believe that. Telma's an old, old soul. And she's tough. She must have been Cleopatra in another life."

Gwen allowed herself a smile, & the shrink matched her.

"No," said Gwen. "Mother *Teresa.* Did you know that she calls herself Daughter Teresa!"

"Ha! See? She's *tough* and she's *resilient.* But now I need *you* to be tough. I know you are, Gwen. I *know* you're tough through *observa-*

tion. I've seen you be tough—fierce—*heroic*—not just in this room, but in your *life.* I'm seeing it *now, you* just can't see it. I've seen you be a lioness, protecting your cub—yes I have, Gwen, & Telma had to get her courage from *somewhere,* no? That girl is a *survivor,* & so is her mom————————————"

"DON'T USE THAT WORD! DON'T EVER USE THAT WORD PHOEBE! I DON'T EVER WANT TO HEAR THAT WORD AGAIN FOR AS LONG AS I LIVE!"

paroxysm of sobs/moaning

empty boxes of Kleenex at her feet

then

Phoebe does something she usually avoids with patients, she walks around & kneels at the chair & holds her, rocking gently, like a mother, a mother & daughter . . . .

[Telma]

Cave Dwellers

"**Guess** who's coming over for a visit on Friday?"

"Who?"

"Phoebe."

"O Phoebe! I miss her!"

"Well, she misses you too. She wants to see you."

"We're not going to her office?"

"Nope."

"I *like* her office."

"She's making a housecall."

"Ratchet!"

"Ratchet? What does that mean?"

"Just—that it's *ratchet!*"

. . .

"Mom, that boy Biggie called & asked me out to lunch."

"Asked you out where?"

"Not really 'out.' He asked if I wanted to come to lunch at his house in Bel-Air."

"Who else is going to be there?"

"His nanny & I guess a chef? And maybe his brother."

"You said he was so shy. I think it's nice that he called, that must have been very hard for him."

"*Welllllllllll* . . . I actually called *him*."

"O you *did*. How very *forward* of you."

"Not to ask him *out*, just to talk. Then *he* asked *me*."

"Have they found out what's wrong with him?"

"No—I mean, I don't think so. I guess I don't really know. Maybe he'll tell me when I see him."

"And where are his parents again?"

"He lives with his dad. Him & his brother. His mom hasn't been————I think maybe she was *gay* & maybe left his father for a woman."

"This is something you were *told*, or something you've come up with using your *amazing powers*?"

"Sort of told. Kind of reading between the lines. I don't think she ever—I don't think the mom ever really came back. She, like, *disappeared*. As far as I know."

"Not at all? To see her sons?"

"It's sort of ratchety. That she never came home. Because from my understanding, it did happen a while ago."

"Strange."

"Biggie said that evidently his mom is a *spelunker*. A *spelunker* is a person who likes going into *caves*. Evidently, his *mom* & the *woman* are *spelunkers* who go all around the world finding *caves*. To explore. I don't really have the whole story. I don't even have *one quarter* of the story."

"Kind of interesting, anyway. Don't you think?"

"I don't really want to gossip."

"It's information, not gossip."

"It feels sorta gossipy."

"You're protective of your new friend, & that's good. That's a lovely quality, Telma."

"Can I go there for lunch?"

"Of course you can."

· · ·

"Should I ask Phoebe to the fundraiser?"

"What fundraiser?"

"Mom! The *Courage* Ball."

"When *is* that?"

"Mom, do you have Alzheimer's?"

"That's not very nice."

"Mom, you're on the *committee*. I'm going to *perform*."

"O! That snuck up so fast. . . ."

"Mom, we've been *talking* about it. I've been *rehearsing*."

"I've missed the last few meetings——"

"Steve *Martin* is hosting! Mom, you *love* Steve Martin! & they're giving an award to *Michael*. Michael *Douglas*. And O my God, Rihanna!"

"It's going to be an amazing evening."

"Ratchet! You don't seem very excited."

"I have a headache, that's all."

"Mommy?"

"What, honey."

"I'm sorry I asked if you had Alzheimer's."

"It really didn't bother me, sweetheart."

"*Good*. Anyway, we get two extra tickets & I thought it would be nice to ask Biggie Brainard. I mean, not that he couldn't get a ticket *himself*. Because he like *owns* the whole *hospital*. I thought it would be nice for him to come with."

"It's very nice. Very thoughtful."

"Can I give the *other* ticket to Phoebe when she comes over? Don't you think that's a good idea, Mom? Don't you think Phoebe would want to come?"

[Rikki]

Scripted Reality

Rikki

got an email from the Canoli-Maddin Casting Group, wanting him to come for an interview. They said that because they were seeing so many people, if the provided date & time didn't work for him, they would *not* be able to reschedule. A Googlemap of the Westside was attached, with a ★ near the intersection of Olympic & Centinela. The message closed with PLEASE DO NOT REPLY TO THIS EMAIL/DO NOT CONTACT BY PHONE.

He printed it out & showed it to Tom-Tom. She held it in her hand without reading, sitting on the couch stoned watching a "Behind the Scenes Feature Video!" on the *Pregnant In Heels* website streaming thru the flatscreen, sipping her Pharrell Williams strawberry Qream™ liqueur. Then she read Rikki's email whereupon she closed her eyes as if having a prayerful telepathic moment before opening them again whence returning her attention to the Samsung. All she said was *"knew it,"* rhythmically repeating *knew it, knew it, knew it,* dead-eyed, understated, faintly syncopated, smoked her joint & watched her program without looking at him, not a glance, just *knew it knew it knew it knew it knew it* now a murmur, gurgling of a fountain, *knew it,* she said, *cause it already happened.* (The only part for her to play, being, to witness the miracle{s} & be of service.) She added—still unlooking at Rikki—that she *knew it* in the very same way the *Mount Olympus* opportunity was going to happen, knew she'd be moving into this big empty house & taking everyone with her, her ragtag "dependents," & only the strong would survive, *everyone* would be forced to step up their game or leave. Funny or die. That meant Jerzy & (Rikki &) ReeRee too, cause she wasn't gunna play favorites & had no time or patience for anybody's shit. She was building an *empire*, she was *branding*, she was krisgenerating & putting her life on the *line*. And because of the energy she put out, things were moving *fast*. *The love you make = the love you take.* Tom-Tom had a vision *I had a vision of love* she would have her own hit reality show, Rikki was going to be a moviestar & she'd manage him on the side. (Tom-Tom had a lot of visions, some were so beautiful dark twisted fantasy she didn't even want to *summon* them, it was not yet their time.) One of her *visions* said Rikki was gunna be huge, he was gunna *POP*, & her reality show was gunna *BLOW the fuck UP*. Cause dont let em bullshit you life's a sprint not a marathon. *Life's a sprint nextel, you never know what's gunna be on the frickin verizon ahahahahaha-hah.* Yeah. *Yeah, baby.* This life is *stevejobshort*, my friends, so eat the freakin velvet cupcake.

   Don' worry bout me, & who I fire, It's my empire, & yes I call the shots, I am the umpire————

The Tom-Tom train was leaving the station.

[Reeyonna]

Our Love Is Here To Stay

"When's
your audition?"

"Wednesday."

"Next week?"

"This week."

"You mean tomorrow."

"Yeah."

"What're you gunna do if you win? I mean if you get the part."

"Be in the movie I guess."

"What're you gunna do, if you get famous."

"Be famous. I don't know. Be famous."

"What about us?"

"What about *you*?"

"*Us.* You, me & the baby."

"What about it."

"Are you gunna buy us a house?"

"Yeah I'll buy us a house."

"Would we get married?"

"I guess."

"O now you guess. Now that you're famous you have to *guess*."

"I'm not guessing. I'm not guessing."

"You said when you got *adopted*, after you were *adopted* we could get married."

"OK. We will. I said we will."

"I don't want this baby born out of wedlock, Rikki."

"It won't. We can go to Vegas. Get married at the Hard Rock or some shit."

"I don't want to live in this house anymore."

"What's wrong with the house the house is tight."

"I don't want to *be dependent* on other people. Especially not that *bitch*."

"I'll move you out."

"What do you mean you'll move *me* out."

"Move us both. I think my dad's gunna give me some more bread."

"Will you stop fucking other people?"

"What?"

"Are you going to stop fucking other people after we get married?"

"You're trippin."

"Like you do now?"

"Like I do now?"

"That's right, Rikki."

"O like I do now. & who am I supposed to be fucking?"

"Who? Who are you fucking? Should we start with Tom-Tom? Cause I don't *even* know where to go after that."

"I'm not fucking Tom-Tom."

"Lowlife snaky *bitch* who thinks it's cool to fuck my old man? Fucking *grenade*."

"I'm not fucking Tom-Tom."

"Rikki, don't *even*. What'd you guys do, make a porn tape while you were making the audition tape? Is that what you did, you made a little *porn tape* too? & does my *brother* know? Does my brother know his dyke grenade *girlfriend* is fucking the father of his sister's child? Rikki, you know you fucking make me *sick*."

"He's not even your full brother."

"*Fuck* you, Rikki——"

"& she's not even his girlfriend————"

"I *know*, she's YOURS!"

"ReeRee, come on . . . ."

"My brother's probably *happy* cause he probably can't fuck anyway."

"Nobody's fucking anyone, OK? You're paranoid. You're spending too much time in your room."

"O! Right! Because she fucking *banned* me from the rest of the house! And *don't tell me* you're not fucking the skank."

"There's nothing happening like that."

"Then whose blood was that on your dick two days ago?"

"Blood on my dick? I didn't have blood on my dick——"

"O! So sorry! I didn't mean to *offend*. Because from that look on your face, it's like, O! I said something to really insult you!"

"You're tripping, Reeyonna."

"Maybe it *wasn't* her blood. Maybe it was her *shit*. Maybe it's just *grenade* shit————"

"Man you're talking crazy."

"You haven't even *seen* crazy."

"You *know* she's a *dyke*."

"O yeah! I forgot! She's a dyke! That's why *she's been fucking my brother for like 14 years!* But maybe he has a pussy, maybe he's just a big pussy! I gotta give you the benefit of the doubt, right? Have you ever seen my brother's pussy?"

[*He shakes his head, pissed/loaded*]

"Skanksnake is *bi*. She's a *bi-sexual bi-polar* CUNT."

"And if I get the part in the movie, you're gunna have to kiss her *ass*."

"No, that would be *you*."

"Cause I couldn't have done *any* of that audition shit. I wouldn't be going down there tomorrow. She really helped me."

"Helped you get a disease maybe."

"Reeyonna, you know what? Fuck it. Whatever."

"Whatever? Whatever? You have *no sensitivity* to my feelings! You are *so mean to me*—"

"Come one Ree, don't cry. Come on now—"

"You better wear a condom when we fuck."

"Whatever."

"Whatever? Whatever you fucking PIG I fucking HATE you!"

"Don't be throwing shit at me—"

"Aren't you even *attracted* to me anymore? *[she went to Macy's & bought a limited edition Karl Lagerfeld Impulse dress, she bought it in a bigger size so her stomach would fit, & took in the rest by sewing by hand, he didn't even say anything, how nice she looked, she did up her hair too]* You'd rather fuck a 35-year-old?"

"She's 31."

"O my God, you're *defending* her————"

"I'm *not* defending her, Reeyonna. I'm not *fuckin* her either."

"Why don't we do it, we don't even do it anymore."

"I told you it's hard with your stomach getting big like that. Cause when I start I feel like man I can't put that in you cause it's all like *ooh whoa shit I'm gunna hurt the baby!* I know it *won't* but it's still in my head."

"Well try to get over it."

"I know. I will. I'm sorry."

"You are?"

"Yeah."

"You still love me?"

"Yeah. *Hell* yeah. You're gunna be the mother of my child."

"Not that way, the other way. Do you still love me the other way? Like do you still want to fuck me?"

"Yeah."

"Then say it."

"I love you the other way."

"You still want to fuck me?"

"Yeah."

"But do you love it, do you still love it?"

"Yeah I do."

"What do you love. Tell me what you love."

"To fuck you. I love to fuck you."

"Then why don't you. Why don't you fuck me."

"Like when like now?"

"Come on come on come on & FUCK me. Don't you want to make me come & suck my milk? I'll make you come so hard."

"Go in the bedroom, Ima get some weed."

"Where."

"From Jerzy."

"Is he home?"

"From his stash. He said it was OK."

"Not the joints that are dusted."

"You know I'm not down with KJ."

"It could hurt the baby. If he has roxys, can you bring me?"

"Are u even supposed to be doin that shit? Roxys n shit?"

"The doctor said they're cool. & I went online & there's a whole list of painkillers that are OK if you're pregnant."

"I'll look for em."

"Then you'll come back & fuck me?"

"Yeah."

"Wait—tell me what you're gunna do when you come back."

"Gunna fuck you. Ima gunna be all over you."

"*Who* you gunna come back & fuck?"

"You."

"*Reeyonna.*"

"*Reeyonna.* Ima come back & fuck Reeyonna."

"Where are you gunna fuck her? Where on her body . . . ."

"Ima fuck her pussy. Ima fuck her mouth & her ass. Ima fuck that baby out of you, bitch."

"You know I'm gunna let you, Rikki."

"Then you know I'm gunna be there. I'm gunna be there doin it to it."

"Ooh I really miss it Rikki. Ooh Rikki Ima gunna make you feel
so goooooodddddd . . . ."

"Then let me go 'n get that weed, girl. He got some Viagra & cia-
lis & shit too, Ima wanna smoke a while & let all that shit hit me so I
can get over it, you know help me to get over stickin my dick in &
pokin that baby in the eyeball. Ima smoke a little weed & you can
suck my dick."

"Our baby's gunna be really happy you dropped in."

"Ree, come on now, don't say that shit!!!!!!!!!"

"Hahahahahahahahahahaha!!!!!!!!!!!!!"

"Now you're gunna make me all *neurotic*————"

"Go on & get that *weed*, Mr. Neurotica. And dont forget the *Viagra*. And dont forget the *Roxys*."

[Jacquie & Reeyonna]

Celebrity Miscarriages

The

theft shocked & hurt, *embarrassed* her, but what could she do? Her daughter was out there in the world, five months pregnant—no way would she call the police. Even though her small circle of friends said she should. "On *Intervention*," said Albie, "they *always* tell the parents to call the police. They say if you don't, you're just helping your kid to stay sick." There was still no way.

After the initial shock, Jacquie had a good cry over the loss of the cameras themselves. She pictured them in her mind, saw them, felt them, the reaching for & the picking up, the straps even, the cold compact steely heft of their bodies, the exquisiteness of the machines, saw herself screwing/swiveling the lenses, the battery packs, the armatures as a soldier assembles his rifle, with love & respect, pride of ownership & mastery, stuffing their guts with film, attuned to each's quirks & hiccups, each its own idiosyncrasies, how she watched over them, like a good mother paying closer attention when they got subtle bugs or technical fevers & if it lasted or grew worse, bringing them to the camera doc, leaving them overnight or even for a week in CCU (camera care unit) to be healed, always worried she might never see whichever baby again, not due to failure or impossibility of repair, but fire in the camera hospital, or . . . theft. They were part of her & she, part of them, for better & worse; each helped carry her through chapters of her life. Yes, they were her children as well, & the irony was not lost.

She knew that Jerilynn felt

why had it been impossible to call her Reeyonna? She practically begged me & I wouldn't, I thought it was silly, to say 'Reeyonna,' + I didn't like her changing the name I had given her, even though it was a terrible slight to her father because the root was Jerry/Jerome, I named her as if she belonged to the Professor, & now, to not call her by her 'tween' name seems so utterly hurtful, sadistic, insane

betrayed not just by her mother but by *them*, treasure chest of cameras, tireless, ostensible instruments of *Reeyonna's* putative wealth & liberation, cheated by the mechanical eyes that had probed & proposed to her whorls of underage skin, she *allowed* them to with the innocence and capitulation of a child she let them in, she gave herself to them and they failed to protect. *Reeyonna* once told her that she read in school how the Indians wouldn't let their pictures be taken because they thought the camera stole their soul, & it had all come true all of it————————

In her loneliest late afternoon Mt. Olympus moments, palm of hand resting on the melon covered by the very same stretchedskin so thoroughly ogled by her mother's 1,000-eyed beastie battlework battalions, Reeyonna felt her young girl's soul still trapped within those leathery, hardbodied, unforgivingly stylish, monumentally indifferent machines. Well. She would not let that stand, no, not now, could not let it stand to have been cheated & disrespected, could no longer let that stand now that she was carrying her own camera in her belly, hatching her own witness/assassin/co-conspirator, could those cameras have been so arrogant not to conceive that by doing the bidding of their mistress they had doomed themselves to chattel? disposable robot trash pawed & pawned to/ by strangers for a fraction of their worth? Reeyonna went on **www.DigitalPawnshop.com** *& laughed as she brought them to market, Brothers Collateral Loans, right down there off the hill in W Hollywood, she goofed and chortled as the abducted children click-clanked in the cotton laundry bag* *they'd been carelessly thrown into, with no regard for their beauty, thrown in with a vandal's high-spirited abandon, now and then she opened the neck of the bag to literally spit inside it, she'd have handed out all perfectly engineered specimens on Skid Row or set each on a rail to iFilm a traincrush and put it on youtube for Thiefbitch to see, yes she would certainly have done that if she didn't need the money, she'd have drowned them in the water like in that Eminem song & recorded them screaming and pounding on the trunk of the car and dying, and sent the sounds to her mother & when you dream I hope you can't sleep & scream about it you could never EVER put a price on them, not for Bitchthief, for Bitchthief their worth was inestimable, incalculable, though they had ultimately failed to give Bitchthief her fortune either, still, Bitchthief had fetishized them, all that worn leather with the little rents here and there, the nicks and dents and whatnot just like or close enough to the vintage guitars of famous old rockers, each one's metal casings infinitesimally eroded by her mother's fingers, the cells of her mother's fingers, how could you how could you put a price on the metal of the ruggedly beautiful armatures each polished by exfoliation, the very cells her mother shed in their handling, the armatures protecting the sacred calibrated innerworkings that allowed Jacquie to memorialize Time itself!—no—one could not put a price on how they'd been prized, adored, ecstatically enlisted in erotic career worship, in sacrifice, human sacrifice! of she, Reeyonna!—all Reeyonna could do was hope that her mother's soul had been captured too, stolen by ReeRee's theft, & that Jacquie would die a little each day, each hour, each moment, that she would feel it in her heart & stomach feel the rape each time they were handled by uncouth foreign hands.*

· · ·

Jacquie cried——————————— . . . .
. . . .

The wash of memories.

The Rolleiflex the Professor gave her—her first—that stolen too, out of smashwindowed car while she sat with his dying body. (Dad's fry cook venues & childhood loneliness.) Her joy & dismay that an older, educated, married man would be interested in her, find her alluring. The rented bungalow, to her, then, the height of luxury—at

first—a lovenest—and then—the baby screaming it never stopped
screaming, & the adult loneliness. Punctuation of scary illicit raptur-
ously screaming sex. Being pregnant with Jerry. The fear/joy of baby
coming, illicit baby, boy baby, scary baby enraptured, screaming.
Her useless mother. The kindness of the Professor's wife, ushering
her to the hospital room, *Jerome's* hospital room, Jerome who insisted
on being *Jerry*, everyone has a secret name, everyone wants to be
called by something else. Real widow leaving fake widow alone to
say her goodbyes. A religious act, a saintly act. The Mary Magdelen-
ity of it all, of the 2 women. But Jacquie never thanked her, never
thanked the Professor's widow, never said a word, never even thought
a word, too shellshocked by her life.

.   .   .

She was all right after taking the pictures of the stillborn in the manger. The manger at Little Company of Mary Hospital. She was OK
in fact for two whole days, on a kind of strange eleemosynary high.
Energized. Everything was more vivid, colors, sounds, dreams. Ac-
cession of long abandoned hope. Albie said don't come in but she
insisted she was fine, work was good for her. She was grateful to him.
The experience left her feeling back in the art game as well. *Ah.
Hmm. So this is what the mysterious Sears thing was all about.*

Then she crashed.

She couldn't get out of bed and didn't realize she couldn't or that
she *hadn't* until Albie called to ask if she was okay—not because she
didn't show at work but because she didn't speak after picking up—
not because she had nothing to say but because in that instant she did
not know who or where she was. When he was 16 he answered
phones on a teen suicide hotline & the training handily came back.
He assessed whether Jacquie was a threat to herself or others and determined she wasn't.

He brought food over after work, a gesture that sent her riot-
weeping. He sat on the bed and the floodgates opened, she talked
about the dead baby, the proof sheets were all over the bedcovers, she

pushed them toward him but he didn't feel now was the time to look. He gathered them in a neat pile and set them on the bureau—a gesture that was executed with such civility that of course it elicited a (not so) fresh jag. Albie was patient, God bless; he wanted her to empty herself out. The blood came back into her body. She sat up against the headboard on the 4 pillows that he with warm and perfect faggotry had fluffed up & rearranged, alternately drinking the chicken soup he brought (Jerry's Deli!), & reading aloud from the glossy Sears portrait studio booklet not meant to be taken home by customers but only flipped through, called *These are a few of our favorite things,* reading aloud in a comic delirium of relief brought on by his visit, the sociability of it, of one who shared her experience, who loved her and cared.

A baby was on the cover, but now all babies looked dead; this one had a superfluous hair band, a decorative touch that to her jaded eye made it look even deader. She read aloud from the Book of Sears.

NEW BABY/BIRTHDAY
Are you ready for your close-up? We are! Our photographers are experts at capturing that winning expression you'll remember forever. Add instant drama with a custom enhancement!

The scandalous irony of the read did the job of catharsis in a different way than expected, she thought it would end in hilarity but the moment was as they say too soon, her policeman said flow my tears, copious antediluvian tears of remorse, & depthless worry not just for all martyred funerary mothers throughout time but for her *own*, remorse & tears for *her* baby, the one she disappointed, the one demoralized and demolished, the one who stole from her, her precious baby ~~Jerilynn~~ *Reeyonna*, 16 & pregnant somewhere in Hollywood wandering like a fugitive doing god knows what, the daughter who walked the streets as Jacquie's own stillalive stillborn.

She called Jerzy again, she got the idea to call him and asked Albie if he'd sit with her while she did (well of course he would, he wasn't

going anywhere), she said she wanted—*needed* to get in touch with
~~Jerilynn~~ Reeyonna, *had to see her,* no matter what. (The gift of focus
a dead baby can bestow.) She told him how grateful she was for having that experience, the privilege of it, & grateful again that he came
to see her unasked, she thought she was losing her mind just a little,
& there he was with the chicken soup & now she was feeling so
much better. (They hugged. He said he would make tea. She said to
wait until she called her son.) Jerzy didn't answer. She hung up. Albie
said to leave a message. She called again. She tried to be stoic yet im-
part urgency, the urgency that was her right, the Mother's Prerogative. *Jerry, please call me back.* Then, *Jerzy, can you please call?* More
plaintive that time + craftily using the name he preferred, hoping the
tactic wouldn't backfire. *Why didn't I call him Jerzy, ever? I resented that
he wanted to change the name I had given him . . . O Albie, I am a lunatic,
I am a stubborn & terrible woman, I am a terrible mother whose children have
become monstrous with hatred & anguish.* She didn't care if the *Jerzy* tack
did backfire, she was tired of fucking around, she wanted to see her
baby. *Albie, should I arrest her, should I have her arrested? For stealing my
things? Albie, should I? Should I just call the police?*

He said yes, knowing that she wouldn't.

In this moment, she had an awakening: time to *assert.* Get that
Mom mojo workin. She phoned Rikki's fosterparents, they hadn't
recently connected, yet another thing that made her feel remiss,
she'd been standoffish because she knew her daughter loved them
not her, maybe not loved but respected, always Jacquie's pride rampaging like Mothra, she phoned and Jim answered & while they
were talking she wave/whispered to Albie it was OK to go make
tea she really wanted tea so he left the room. Jim sounded cheerful,
she always had the sense he was careful in their dealings, as if thinking of/knowing her to be a bit of a loose cannon, Jim said that
Reeyonna *o my god he actually calls her that why didn't I call her that*
was staying with Jerzy *he called him that lord what was wrong with her
she was the only one Mothra the Destroyer* and his girlfriend?roommate.

That apparently, according to Rikki who was the source of all their information, they all moved from where they used to live, which wasn't per Rikki so wonderful, to a much nicer place called Mt Olympus in the Hollywood Hills. Jacquie right there lost her cannon & said too-assertively *Enough! This is enough already,* as if it all were Jim's fault—grew suddenly imperious, that talk-to-servants voice she hated in herself all the more pathetic for never having *had* servants, still she rationalized it was all right to use that tone, tone in the major key of Mother's Prerogative, she was trying to turn the engine over, engine of her Mothra-sized mojo, *I think we should just go & get her.* (Noting even as the words came out that she said "we" not I as in *I am just going to go get her.*) Jim said he understood her frustration, they'd had a lot of that themselves (he & Dawn) (of course they had) but the engineer said he thought it would be a mistake, he told her they'd already put an invitation on the table, already invited ReeRee *he actually called her that! the diminutive of a name that she, Jacquie, never gave her what is the matter with me what is wrong* to come live at the house. For a second she got pissed, thinking Jim & her daughter must be in open communication, chatting it up on the phone as he waged his little campaign, a campaign she hadn't even been privy to, so she asked if he was/had been directly in touch with *Reeyonna,* & Jim said only once when her daughter called him at the house. He went on in that analytic way to suggest that the best strategy was to wait them out. *Let's give it a few more days, Jacquie. I really do think she'll get tired of struggling out there, she'll get tired of running around, & I think that as time goes on, she will find our offer more conducive. We're praying on it, anyway. That's what we're praying on.* She reluctantly agreed *but not for more than a week* (mojo only a quarter workin but hey). The kettle whistled, a cup of tea sounded divine, served by her dear friend/servant right in bed, she could taste the honey, this new Australian honey she was all hung up on.

The conversation wound down. She rote-asked after Dawn. Jim said his wife was just back from the hospital and something in Jacquie remembered, barely, but enough to cause her to stifle the impulse to ask why, why was Dawn there, she had that scintilla-recollection, an inpatient stay would be of the nervous/mental variety, briefly awkward, then Jacquie's rote awkward wishing of Dawn well, Jacquie's rote kneejerk invite for the two of them to come for lunch or tea or supper or drinks or *something*, Jacquie's end-of-call attempt at humor re the whole fucked up situation being possibly/absolutely brightened by a grandchild at the end of the rainbow, & right when she hung up again came the remorse, guilt over her narcissistic ways, it was always about her, and there was Jim, so stoic & kind, the weight of manifold worlds upon him.

.   .   .

She surfed the web without leaving bed for two more days.

The Internet said Kirstie Alley got fat after her *mc*, mc being Internet for miscarriage. The Internet said Tori Amos wrote an album after her mc. The Internet said Pamela Anderson mc'd with Tommy Lee & with Kid Rock. The Internet said the *Enquirer* said Brad & Jen mc'd. The Internet said Valerie Bertinelli mc'd. The Internet said Amy Brenneman mc'd when she was 39. The Internet said Christie Brinkley had 3. The Internet said Nell Carter had 4. The Internet said Amanda Holden had 2 *fetal deaths*, the most recent in the 7th month. The Internet said Joan Chen had 6. The Internet said Jane Seymour had 2 before having twins/preeclampsia. The Internet said Linda Hamilton mc'd. The Internet said Nancy Kerrigan had 6 in 8 yrs but refused to talk about it. The Internet said Nicole Kidman had one in 2001. The Internet said Lucy Lawless mc'd right after filming the last episode of *Xena*. The Internet said Demi Moore mc'd in '97. The Internet said Jane Pratt mc'd twins. The Internet said Brooke had at least 5 & that her cervix was scarred. The Internet said Sharon Stone had a string of mcs. The Internet said Emma Thompson needed IVF because of PCOS (polycystic ovar. Syndrome) and mc'd in 1997. The Internet said Vanna White mc'd in 1992. The internet said that

Oprah mc'd when she was 14. The Internet said Sporty Spice had 5/
PCOS.

That's what the internet said.

. . .

Ginger sent her a beautiful email, thanking her. She also wanted to
know when she could see the proof sheets. Jacquie told her she was
sick & would it be all right if they met next week.

Ginger said of course and attached an article from *The New York
Times* written by a *mohel*. A Jewish couple had scheduled their baby
to be circumcised but it died 3 days after being born. They always do
the *bris* on the 8th day of life. The parents called the *mohel* and told
him what happened but said they wanted him to do the circumcision
anyway. The essay was about what a wreck he was but the parents
were calm and from them he drew strength. *isn't that interesting how he
said they were so calm?* she wrote. *thats the way it was with Daniel & me
when you were taking our picture. maybe you felt that too*

Jacquie googled *bris*, then wondered if the *mohel* had skipped the
prayer that welcomed the baby into the world.

[Jacquie&Jerzy]

Sicker Than the Remix

"Thank

you for meeting me. I appreciate that."

They were having lunch at El Pollo Loco in the crappy strip mall at the corner of Sunset & Crescent Heights. A depressing convenience zone at the bottom of the Mt called Olympus.

Her son was dead pale. Jerzy never quite met her gaze, which had the effect of rendering a boyish grin insidious. From the waist up, the body was calm; the legs thundered beneath the table, as if working the pedals that animated him.

"Have you seen her?"

"Just about every day. We live in the same house."

"Can you tell me what's going on?"

She just couldn't bring herself to say *Jerzy*.

"What's going on?" he said, genuinely puzzled.

"With Jerilynn. Reeyonna."

"Nuthin. I mean she's good, she's really good. I think she's been looking for work."

"Looking for work *how*," said Jacquie, with a bite. "She's five months *pregnant*."

"You can be pregnant & work. Porn stars do it all the time."

Deep breath. He is my son. He is damaged. He smells like chemicals. He despises me, & he is playing, a cat with a mouse. God, give me the strength to be grateful he agreed to see me. Help me not to blow it, God, at least not this far into the lunch.

"Jerzy"—it came out unbidden. "Do you think we can put our heads together?"

"Don't call me that."

"Don't call you Jerzy?"

"It's Jerry."

"I thought it was Jerzy."

"Not to you."

"OK. I didn't mean to call you the wrong thing."

"Don't worry about it."

"I just think we need to be kind of a team here. Because I think Jerilynn" (she only reverted because of what he just said. She was completely prepared to say *Reeyonna*) "is a little out of control. If it weren't for the baby, it'd be different. We probably wouldn't be sitting here. Though I'm very glad that we are."

"Sure, Jacquie."

His gaze was askew. He seemed to be grinning at something over her shoulder, as if an assassin just walked in—the one he'd hired to come from behind & slit her throat. He had already excused himself from the table three times, twice to the bathroom, & once to get the phone he supposedly left in the car even though it was visible in his pocket as he excused himself. She had no clue who this man was or where he'd come from, something aberrant in the Professor's seed. She fantasized about being that timid, withdrawn Ocalan girl climbing into a time machine, brought forward to *this* time, this *now*, her time machine guide pointing to the tweaky stinkweed deadskinned bum & saying

That. That. That is what your baby will grow up to be.

"Rikki's parents said she could stay with them."

"Uh, I don't really think she wants to do that."

"But why? Why doesn't she?"

"You'd have to ask her."

"She won't speak to me. She hangs up when I call."

"What can I say."

Neither of them made even a pretense of eating their food. Jacquie tap-tapped the tabletop. His thighs momentarily slowed, as if to acknowledge whatever message was being imparted by her table-tapping *tom tom*. He threw that smug, knowing sado-smile at her tippy-tapping fingers, which made her stop.

"Do you know what all this is about, ~~Jerzy?~~ Jerry? Has Reeyonna talked to you about it? Has *Jerilynn* talked to you?"

She was starting to lose it with the double names & the double bullshit.

"A little."

"What did she say?"

"You spent a bunch of money that was supposed to be hers?"

"Which isn't true. Not that a little thing like that matters! There never *was* any money, Jerry, *and none promised*. Whatever money I made from my work—& *believe me*, it wasn't a *lot*—whatever money I made was for the *household*. It was for *rent* and *clothes* and *necessities*. For you *and* your sister. Because Ronny wasn't exactly, your stepfather was *frugal*, he never went above & beyond what the court told him to pay, which was an *absurd* amount. $550, something like that." She stared down at the table at her own fingers, which weren't tapping anymore, they were just laying there. "O what's the use? What's the use, there's just no point. Your sister has this *conviction* in her head—and she's *stubborn*—and there's just no way to make her see anything different."

Some fake eating and pushing around of food (Jerzy) and some rattatattapping/tomtom *macoute* (Jacquie).

Jacquie shrugged, & threw in the towel.

"At this point, your sister can think what she wants to think. I don't have any control over that. If she wants to make me into the wicked witch, there's nothing I can do. But I *am* concerned about her taking *care* of herself. Because if she's not taking care of herself, she's not taking care of the baby. Is she going to the doctor? Do you know if she's been to see a doctor?"

"I think Rikki takes her to the free clinic. In Venice."

"Well that's nice to hear, that's *very* good to hear, thank you. Because she's got to be doing *some* kind of neonatal care. Because that's important. I just want my daughter to have a happy healthy baby & be healthy in the process."

"Right."

The waitress came along & refilled Jerzy's tea.

"So how are things going?"

Jacquie was surprised he asked.

"As well as can be. With diminished income and a fugitive daughter. And a son I never see."

"You're seeing me now."

"Yes. I'm seeing you now."

"So. Nuthin goin on with the career?" (That creepshow grin again.) "Any gallery shows coming up?"

She knew he knew that she didn't. *Please help me God to be gracious.* "No, but there's something I've just started to work on that I'm excited about. There's definitely something there, I'm just not sure what it is yet."

"Cool."

She felt like an ass for oversharing.

"And how are things with you?"

"Same old same old. Workin hard, hardly workin."

"Do you talk to your dad?"

"We kinda had a blow-out when I was in New York."

She heard about that from her ex & had zero desire to hear junior's side of the story.

"Still doing paparazzi work?"

"Yup," he said. "Still a proud *papa*."

"I saw a *60 Minutes.* Is it true about some of these people making small fortunes off a single picture?"

These people. Like saying: *So what do they exorbitantly pay these days for scraping dogshit off the sidewalk?*

"Yup. The folks you work for take most of it, but you can do all right. Depends on getting that *honeyshot.*"

"What's a honeyshot?"

"A paparazzi term," he said, goofing on her a little. "For a shot you know you can get at least 5,000 for."

"Have you ever gotten one?"

"My specialty," he said, *trés insouciant.*

MoMA paid the bill & they walked to the lot. She asked which one was his ride. He pointed to the gnarly van (*Honeyshot Central USA*).

She took a sealed envelope from her wallet.

"I'd be very grateful if you'd give it to Jerilynn."

Obvious from the heft that it was bread.

"Should I say it's from you?"

"No. Well—you *can.* I guess. Yeah, well why don't you. It doesn't really matter. She took some things from me, some very valuable things, but I still want her to know . . ."

Jacquie broke it off, her eyes tearing.

"That's really nice. Of you."

He put his hand on her arm for a moment; she smiled at the small tenderness. She got into her car & he stood there until she rolled down her window. His voice grew low & different; intimate, strangely focused, out of alignment, compelling.

"You know Ashton Kutcher? From *2½ Men?*"

"Uh huh."

"Who's supposedly no longer with his *old* lady?"

He lost her there.

"Have you heard him talk about the apocalypse?"

"No. I haven't."

"He talks about it on the Internet. Tho it's hard to find now; someone did a lot of scrubbing. & you know what kind of resources *that* takes . . . I think the original interview's in some kind of outdoor mag. You should google it. He talks all about how he's stockpiling food & water, building up his body."

"O my god, are you serious?"

She was glad he was engaging her conversationally, no matter how off the wall. Listening instead of talking relaxed her.

"For real. And that he's totally prepared to move his family—he and *Moore-Willis* are still *totally* together—to higher ground whenever it goes down."

"Really?"

"Don't believe everything you hear. They'll be together forever, you can't break your vows, not when you've been married by the Puppetmather. So Ashton gave that interview—*one interview*—about the coming Wars, & that was *it*. Not a single word *after*. I mean, Ashton *Kutcher* was saying this shit, not Gary Busey or Michael Lohan! Not even Mel Gibson . . . my point *being* it should have been *huge*. The guy's *still* in the Twitter Top 10, probably hanging on by his teeth, Taylor Swift, the mudsharkardashians *they can really hold their mud!*—Obama, Rihanna (all Puppetmather loyalists I might add), fucking *Shakira* pardon my language is higher on twitter than Ashton, still that's 8 million people or whatever, right? But *nope*: nuthin. Silencio! Ask yourself why. Next thing you know, Ashton & Demi are all about sex trafficking, the new spokescouple for saving little girls from pimps. They're all *over* it. Suddenly they have this *passion*, which is funny cause he inseminated those girls, Rumer 1st then Tallulah & Scout, to protect them from the black hooligans who will dominate the 1st segment of the Wars. To protect with the elixir of his blood—the 3rd horse of the Apocalypse. Suddenly they're all about child trafficking, a topic with that *rare quality* of being able to *captivate* and *bore the shit out of a person* at the same time. You can't even be cynical because you're just not going to pay attention long enough. Which is how it was engineered. You hear *child sex trafficking* and part of you checks out, you say *Huh? O—yeah yeah, right, yadda yadda, uh huh, good activism on ya Ashton & Demi* . . . like out of *nowhere* this became their pet cause, and here's the question to posit: Do you really think that was *their* decision? To suddenly be the impassioned spokespersons for child sex trafficking? Well *I* don't. Because *none* of these people—from Katy Perry to Suri Cruise to Gotye on down— *none* of these people do *anything* without being told, they don't even shit in their Totos pardon my language unless the *Puppetmathers* gives em a heads up. The whole trafficking thing was *brilliant* (who do you think came up with it? EeYo-Veen & M², um, duh), its goal being to deflect attention from Ashton's prematurely delivered *eschatology* because everything he said was *true* but wasn't meant to be heard *just yet.* Ashton marches to his own drum which M² actually likes, but this time he got in just a *bit* of hot water because he shot his mouth off before getting the heads-up, jus kinda went ahead & did his own thing & said what he said, the *text* of which Puppet-M approved but not the *timing.* So the Puppetmather reigned him in. But it all blew over, don't believe everything you hear, Ashton remains a beloved mascot, loyal court jester & perennial of the Plantation. Tho be assured the time *will* come when EeYo-Veen *will* say, *Do it, Ash. You go girl, do it* NOW! TALK *about it, good on ya.* There was a happy ending after all because they were relieved: I'm talking *Zuckerberg, Dorsey, Bezos,* Jada *Pinkett,* the Olsen/Russiangoogle twins, I'm talking *Sean John, Jay-Z, Gwyneth, Anne Hathaway,* the Widow Jobs, everyone at youngmoneycashmoney . . . the attention span of the public ain even short anymore, it *don't exist.* People can't be bothered, the Puppetmather counts on that, plus he wisely planted the seed that Ashton was colossally *punk'*ing himself."

"What are you saying."

(What could she say.)

"OK, the Four Horsemen. The 1st is *white*—victory. The Whites will be victorious, OK? *Duh.* The 2nd is *black*—famine. The Blacks will starve, OK? *Duh.* The 3rd is *red*, that's just blood, OK? Red is Black Blood being spilled. But the one you need to pay attention to, is the *4th.* The 4th horse is *pale*, like your grandchild's going to be. *That's* why the baby's going to be in danger. They will hunt down the remixes."

"Jerry, I need to go."

He became contrite.

"O. Sorry. I'm not really serious. I'm just thinking about this stuff all the time. Kinda just me playing chess in my head, but out loud. Hey thank you for buying lunch."

"Thank you for visiting."

"Stay foolish. Stay hungry. I wish you way more than luck."

"Will you please take care of yourself, Jerry?"

"All day long." He smiled and finally looked her in the eye. She caught a glimpse of the 11 year-old boy. "All day long."

"Please. Please take care."

"I will," he said. "I will." Then, "I will."

"If you need any help in doing that, I want you to promise to call, OK?"

"Yeah yeah, sure sure. Sorry I went off. I'm just fuckin around. With words. You should listen to 'Syllables'—Dre says *the torch is gunna burn out before it gets passed, Jay said it's his last, & 50, & Em, then what?*'—the Puppetmathers & all his slaves are on that song, the Puppetmathers is the very 1st one to sing, like he always is, you will notice that on songs he's always No. 1 & in concert he comes out *last* to upstage the shameful spectacle of the indentured minstrels he has ordained to precede him, but make no mistake, in *Syllables* the vastness of his armies are talking about the end of the *world* not just of rap, they're saying everything *Ashton* was saying, but in code. Meaning, the Wars will bring great suffering, there will be many dead on both sides but the Whites will rise like a Phoenix, the wind beneath its wings comprised of Black Archangel Slaves. *Some* of the code's on *2½ Men*, you just have to *watch and listen*, do *not* underestimate John Cryer's involvement, that would be what they call a Fatal Error. The 2 Chucks—Sheen & Lorre—were *made* from Cryer's rib, just as the 2 Carters—DWAYNE MICHAEL **CARTER** & SHAWN COREY **CARTER**—were made from O.G. Sammy Davis Jr . . . Cryer is as close to Puppetmathers as Ye is to Hov, as close as the blonde-rooted patsy ?uestlove is to his slavemaster Fallon,

?uestlove who cowers and kowtows to Tina Fey. Britney's so-called *dance till the world ends* is in code, preapproved by LA Reid . . . its true meaning that General (All-Seeing) Eye-Veen is willing to face the end of *Time*, which is his *strength*, Time, that echo of an axe in the wood. Learn from his example. *All see it coming.* The Deschanels will sit on the right of the throne, Eye-oh-Veen & L.A. Reid on the left. They are signing everyone up for the fires."

"Okay. Jerry—"

(Contrite and comical.)

"Ima jus playin! I'll shut up. Ima jus' playin . . . . ."

"Jerry, I really need to go. Maybe you should give me the envelope back."

"No, it's cool! I'll get it to her."

"Are you sure? Because I really need to count on you, I'm counting on you. You promise you'll get it to her?"

"No worries."

"OK then. Please take care."

"I will. I am. I will.i.am."

"Just please make sure you get that to Jerilynn."

[Jerzy]

Ebony and Ivory

From: Paparazzo Guy (jerzycrellevomes-final-gaze@hotmail.com)
Sent: Sat 4/21/12 1:30 PM
To: Suge Knight (SugeTemplarKnight@deathrow.org)
Inbox (131)

Dear Reverend Suge Knight (president, founder, CEO Deathrow Records).
My name is **Jerzy Crelle-Vomes**. For several reasons, not to be revealed, I shall be brief.

Perhaps you may remember our last meeting, at Cedars-Sinai Hospital in the CCU. I had a heart attack which wasn't too sever, & was forced to make my residence there for a period of one week. You were kind enough to be among my few and special visitors.

As you know, Reverend Knight, I am a professional photographer of some experience and well standing. My work brings me into contact with famed celebs of all size and stripe, notwithstanding otherwise notable people who have attached themselves (or wished to) throughout the many years to you with great determinedness in order to gain some of your luster, and move within your Many Spheres. Many of them would not even be known to the world without you having given them a wide birth.

Some of these Seekers are "with you" but the majority have Fallen & now suck at the Teat of Marshall the Puppet Mathers. I have recently come into knowledge of infornation I believe will be of great invaluable to you. I cannot put it in an email (naturallyI could but choose not to) because of the "sensitivy" of it the information. But I believe it will interest you as it involves the struggle of the Black & even "identifies" all the Black Parasites who have joined the Plantation of **I'Veen, PuppetM, jay-Z, Elton John** and so many more. I shall divulge (if given the chance) who these people are that claim to be involved in the struggle of the Black but are only self-interested & actually will march with the plantation owners when that day we are waiting for comes! They do not know that Puppetmathers has assured that their Deaths await them.

Much of this information is only known by agencies such as the **LAPD, CAA, ICM, and WME.** If NOT known by them you can believe they will be coming after it (me) with great gusto, and shall thrown everytning at me and my family they can, in order to pry it. Reverend, I must say that I feel like **Pvt Bradley Manning** who gave his info to **Julian Assange** and now lays rotting and tortured in his Levenworth cell!

Reverend Knight, you are my Knight in armor, my **Julian Assange** who I would die for please "allow" me be your **Pvt Bradley Manning**! I believe that with my informanion and your fearlessness and vision "for" the Black, we can triumph. BLACK shall equal TRIUMPH, and WHITE SHALL UNDERGO FAMINE, I know we can turn the tables it is Gods will. It is the same god who created the Mantis and the Hummmingbird. I look forward to sharing a fine cigar with you, & await you respond. I hope this gets to you relativly quick and finds you in excellent health & spirites!

With respect,

Pvt Crelle-Vomes
998 Rangely
West Hollywood CA
Please do not contact by cellphone by email only please

PS, Laurence Fishburne can be trusted, his head hangs low in sorrow
and anguish because his young daughter has been conscripted by the
Puppetmather troops.

.   .   .

He got lucky.

Not only was he the first snatcherazzo to get Dakota Fanning's barely legal (panty'd) *honeyshot!* but he scored a blitzkrieg of
nipslips too. The multiasstitted Ms. Fanning was crowded into the
backseat with some BFFs & had the misfortune of being pressed
against the door, which made awkward torquings of her upper
body fertile ground for whoredrobe galfunctions. Jerzy strobefroze
the peekanips through the car window, standard op procedure for
doubleheaders—pictorially, the blouse cherries would be served before the slice of pie.

Harry could barely contain himself; he'd been waiting more than
a decade—since *I Am Sam*—since the rape in *Hounddog*—since the
ad campaign wherein she was poised to insert a humungus bottle of
Lola by Marc Jacobs between her 15-yr-old legs—waiting with jag-
ged jailbated breath to see her *deep undercover*. He wrote Jerzy a check
for 5K johnny on the spot. Lately Jerzy had been missing days &
Harry wasn't too thrilled about it, openly expressing his displeasure
& avuncular advice to stop or slow down whatever he was doing;
now, Jerzy'd bought himself some time & good will. Upon delivery
of Decoded Fanny, Sir Middleton literally got down on his knees to
him & did the I-am-not-worthy hand move.

Harry was a hard one to read; he could go puritan on you when
least expected. Like when Jerzy was on his way out the door & one of
HM's snatcherazzi showed up with pics of Ashley Tisdale & Audrina,
each purporting to show them during or right after a "facial" . . . the
latest foto fad among the spunkerazzi was milky cum on the face of a
liteweight celeb. Which made Harry round the Middleton *furious*.
First of all he said it's all bullshit, the pics aint real, second of all
they're disgusting& degrading. He said, *Honeyshot! ain't about degrada-*

tion, it's about *defloration. About girls coming of age no pun intended. We come by our honeyshot!s HONESTLY no pun intended.* He was old school, a mons Corleone who refused to traffic in dope & facials.

When Jerzy got home he sent the Fanning link to some of his buds. He almost sent it to MoMA but thought twice. Then he had a cool idea. When Jerzy had his Gagosian show, the pics would all have little cards next to them like paintings do in museums except all that would be on them was whatever link was appropriate.

For example, *Suite* Dakota would have

http://harrymiddletonhoneyshot.com/entertainment/celebs/dakota-fanning-and-her-stella-mccartney-micromini-make-for-nipple-slips-&-a-very-special-private-opening-just-between-legs-and-friends-0071825922

Very cool.

. . .

He got stoked by the card/link idea and it fired him up to at least take a stab at beginning the inhumanly mammoth job of sifting, snorting & organizing the thousands of captures in his imagebank. To make such an impossible task manageable, he psyched himself that it was all for the *portfolio*—Larry Gaga would need to see a hard-core sample of Jerzy's work to whet his appetite—& that during this process he would most certainly alight on the core group of digital Weegees that would eventually embody the Trojan Magnum® opus of the actual show. He didn't yet have a fallback plan given the un-thinkable possibility that his hip didn't hop no more—say, his karma didn't gagosianiacally come together—because aside from the insane genius panache coup of hanging his massive (blown up) celebmash-ups on the high priest/high white tower walls of Our Lady Of Gaga Cathedral there just weren't any alternate spaces bitchin enough to rival/approximate/be viable. There were always spaces way down on Melrose or East Holly, other bogus Brewery artwalk schmuck arenas downtown, but those were for sk8tr art, not the real shit.

He was *almost about* to start that scary-daunting portfolio culling, but first things first.

He was in his room, bootie bumpin, & into the KJ a bit. (What's a boy to do?) He was on the floor, usual position, legs lotus-crossed, sitting before a low table, Japanese-style. The GUESS WHO'S OLDER? page Tom-Tom tore from *OK!* was splayed before him. Susan Boyle or Madonna? Rachel Bilson or Mischa B? Kate Hudson or Katie Holmes? AnnaLynne McCord or Ashley O? Kim Kardash or Gisele Bundch? Kristen Stewart or T Swift? He had to put tape over the bottom of the page because the idiots didn't print the answers upsidedown they printed them rightside up how fuckin lame. Somebody's head better roll *somebody's headshot heh heh.* What was going on was, he'd smoke a little, do his boo-tay bidness, whatever, but when he turned his attention back to GUESS WHO'S OLDER he would at first forget the premise, instead thinking the side-by-side pix were one of those CAN YOU SPOT THE DIFFERENCE? deals & he thought, *whoa, there's millions of differences between* that *face* (Kristen S) *and* that *one* (Taylor S), *where/how do I begin? Whoa————— their faces are so trillion-different-ways-different* but then he started to wonder, maybe no one's face was. Different.

Shit.

More clipped pages: Salma Hayek, Kim K & Jennifer Hudson were all wearing the same $4000 Alex McQueen ensemble, they asked 100 people at Rockefeller Center who wore it best. The thing had gold epaulets, maybe General I-Veen will be wearing that shit on Day One of *Battlefield Earth.* Jerzy thought Salma wore it best but Salma only got 15%. Jennifer got 34% & Kim got 51%. Everybody loved Kim, even the women h8trs, because she was unapologetically *zaftig.* All women knew that a big fat ass was about the only thing guaranteed to be waiting at the end of the rainbow. He smoked, did a little bidness, & when he went back to WHO WORE IT BEST the same thing happened as before, he thought he was doing a *spot the difference* puzzle, even though he'd never seen a triptych, it was always a diptych, like, how the fuck were you supposed to spot the differ-

ence between *three different fucking people*, there would be an infinitude. *Spot the Infinitesimal Infinitude.* There *were* a couple of diptychs
though, and that snapped him back to the *who wore it best* deal,
Gretchen Rossi & Aubrey O'Day, Gretchen wore it better 81%,
Nancy O'Dell & Victoria Justice, VJ rocked it at 61%. Readers
weighed in on who sizzles&who fizzles. They better just keep the
who wore it best to diptychs not triptychs the shit is getting out of
hand. But then he got spooked

&then he got

PISSED *freaked* addled-anxious, bothered
whatever & skipped to another Tom-Tom-torn page called MY
MINI-MAN. Tina Fey is 5-4: her hubby's 5 feet. Nicole K's 5-10: K
Urban's 5-8, and Tom the ex is 5-7. L'Wren Scott is 6-3, Mick's five-
10. It was dumbass though the thing about Tina's hubby being such a
dwarf was kinda interesting. *Zorba the Geek.* Tina Fey. Wow. Please
god may I pretty please rape that? He skimmed the ifotos . . . .
always enjoyed seeing his own pics . . . . . . *this* batch taken outside of
Harry's employ of course . . . fuckin schlep pix of Sandra Bullock &
that black baby, *hated* those schlep pics, black prop baby wedged in
there, jaw set in steely essence of *motherhood*, she *aint* a fuckin mother
& that *aint* her fuckin kid why doesn't the world talk about *that*. Like
where she bought it and the fact we all have to *play along that's it's really hers.* Fucking taboo bullshit. We're all supposed to ooh & ahh
well *fuck* them & their stolen black babies, Bullock & Jolie & fuckin
Madonna do what the Puppetmathers *behooves* them to do . . . .
. . . . WHAT'S IN AUDRINA'S
bag? Like anyone gives a shit. She's deader than fucking
Zsazsa+stevejobs put together. What the fuck tho, lookin for clues.
What's In Audrina's Bag? Aside from maybe the implants she took
out. Lookin for clues cause he had a dream Audrina was going to
hook up with a mandingo just like Khloé & Kim K *you know, like if
she was gunna pass the (Black) buck*—————nuthin but whoremasters
under the employ of M^2. What *is* in Audrina's frickin bag—————
hmmmmmm let's see now, there's a *YSL makeup kit* . . . .

Vikto&Rolf Flowerbomb perfume . . . . . . Pup-Peroni sticks for the teacup yorkie . . . . . . Batiste dry shampoo for volume Heather Morris now what's in Hemo's bag? She'll wind up with a nigger, they are no match for blond hardbodied white dancers, the latter's supreme powers of seduction being among the foremost armament & weaponry the Puppetmathers uses to ensnare) why can't the Blacks see it's like Body Snatchers *they close their eyes & when they open them it's too late they're on the Plantation. But what* IS *in Heather's bag? hmmmmm—Goody ouchless hair ties, Colorscience corrector palette, MAC mineralize skinfinish, bronzer, MAC impeccable brow pencil in blonde, Mason Pearson rake comb/smoke & mirrors NYC lash, Flirt! all that Lash mascara, Burt's Bees tinted lip balm, Flirt! Luv-a-licious perfume spray Flirt! all that Flirt! shit*——————one more shpritz up the ass, Jerzy goes for one more booty bump, *bumpin bumpin bumpin* yes please sir may I have another

.   .   .

Jacks.

Jackin' the *lolo* . . . LOL—————

Watches a youtube interview with Montana Fishburne, the actor's pornster daughter. Montana AKA Chippy D is sayin, "Porn is Art. Beautiful people touching each other in sensual ways. [*Like she's talking about a couples massage workshop in fucking Marin*] It's *all* Art: film, music, porn . . ." **www.hellobeautiful.com** says Chippy the chipper's mom still loves her anyway. Chippy thinks she's in the vanguard, that her *films* will rocket her to the starry stratospheres & in scholarly fashion cites the sextapes of Paris, Kim & Sasha Grey. **www.popeater.com** says that when Mr. Fishburne went to the emmys, he kept a far piece from Kim Kardash, who happens to be Chippy's callypygian mentor/entreprenOOZE—Double K-cup Kimmy.

His cock is fucked *up*. Hasn't been taking the Valtrex, recent flarecluster of herpes, tiny blisterbroken bubblewrap lesions, itchy/sting-y. Can't stop the marathon rub-offs so it never has time to scab over. Neosporin with lidocaine staves off infection (for now) but doesn't promote healing. Jerzy promotes healing by finding a 58-minute

Montana strokefest on xhamster.com (Tags: Ass, Blowjob, Celebrity, Cumshot, Dancing, Facial, Pornstar, Sex tape Categories: Ebony)— ooo-*WOO* what a skank. Chippy D commences to get buttfucked by a rappin fool. Acne on the ass. *Yuk.* On the chest too, like Mike the Zituation. Ewww. They call it chacne. As opposed to bacne (on/ between shoulderblades). Chippy's probably got that too. Stretchy-marks . . . yucky yucky *yuck.* Did she have a kid? Probably a bunch of late term aborts. Good decision, Chippy . . . . but let's not I mean why speculate (Q   does montana fishburne have any children) but the top hits were MOM STILL LOVES HER DESPITE PORN CAREER and LARRY FISHBURNE SHOULD BE PROUD OF DAUGHTER'S XXX-RATED CAREER! And MONTANA FISHBURNE: I WON'T HAVE A PROBLEM WITH MY KIDS WATCHING . . . it didn't say anything about offspring or aborts. Probably she just used to be fat, yeah that's it, chicks who were big tubs when they were kids are always fucked up. Though Mom & Dad must've been so proud when she lost that weight. *So proud that first time she got dp'd/squirted on camera . . .*

Toggling between the chacne-fied geyserfest & the Chippy D Q&A . . . the Question was, "Don't you realize this is hurting your father?" Chippy says, "Yes, and I feel bad. But I'm not going to let hurting his feelings stop me from living my dream."

Jerzy cums even better with the bitter herpes sting, smokes a blunt then sum GBH. Ponders the looming strife, Black famine subjuga-tion & White triumphal hegemony. Slow poisoning of Black kultur. Watched the shameful Tivo of Jamie Foxx playing a streetwise car-toon parrot in *Rio,* will.i.am was in there too. Watched shameful old youtube of Nicki superbowlwhoring for Madonna/opening for Brit-ney on Grammys (femcee Nicki astonishing impossible algebraic ge-nius of *Superbass*) then Britney flown in at the end perfect humiliating upstage of the slaveworking ass minajerie, Britney with angel of death wings, dance until the world ends deathwings of White tri-umph while Nicki stepped obeisantly aside, bowed down before her as if direct sight of White Goddess most certainly would blind her—she, Britney, who breathed (Puppetmather-ordered) life into Barbie—*two* Barbies now—by offering the blondhair'd poisonteat succor of opening for her on tour, which of course Nicki could not resist and of course was her subjugation & death. Jerzy knew that before it was done, Britney looked at Nicki's teeth then inspected her feet and genitals & only then did buy her slave.

(Everything fell into place when he read online that Nicki's child-hood crush was Bruce Willis . . .)

Jerzy especially sickened by the castration I'Vene performed on all Blacks upon their arrival at the Plantation, it was the very 1st thing that had to happen, it was in Plantation bylaws, & mandingatory upon being bought—this being the bootcamp wherein they were taught how to censor their own lyrics whilst performing on network TV or in venues that would not support the free speech *all* Blacks had fought 100s of years to be born into, I'Veen said, *If you are to suckle whitecocks of myself and Ryan Seacrest and Jimmy Fallon/Kimmel/so many others, not of course excluding that of your Overseer the Puppetmathers, if you are to worm yourself into the fresh princed hearts of White children by collab-ing with Katy P and Bruno M, Taylor and Justin, Charice & Celine and Britney and Josh Grob. and J Lo/the Sisters Deschanel, if you wish to one day duet with dead Tony Bennett (Tony had already taped record company-dictated variants of possible posthumous duets with himself), & Coachella with Sinatra/Winehouse/Whitney/Levon Helm/Donna holos, if you want to be SNL's beloved, if you dream of your own fragrance, liqueur, prêt-a-porter, net-a-porter, headphones beatboxees toothepaste Halloween cos-tume Superbowl halftime limited self-designed edition Maybach that forever carries your name, if these things you desire & untold dreams unimagined/ unimaginable then we shall school you* --------- meaning, of course, teach them the newfangled Plantation technique of artfully dubbing/ replacing/sanitizing their *own song lyrics*, killing the flow for money, a seizure of caesuras deforming the beauty & power of rhyme/ meaning by a shitstring of plosive fricative click-trills, just to get on primetime, the White made them *forget* that language was all they had, language had given them hope & riches, language had given

them *everything*, they'd cracked open White Kulchur with the rage of their language, the perfect violence of it, language was their *land*, it was the only thing they owned, & the Whites were better off for it, but in the end they must dominate. Now, as each arrived at the Plantation they were spayed & abridged right there on the porch while other Whites watch sipping mint jew lips. To becalm them, Cee Lo wore a playful Humpty Dumpty costume, & told them there was no real difference between *shhh* & *shit*, and that it had always been *I'm like forget him and forget you too* and that the transition from EXPLICIT to CLEAN was painless. Everything the Blacks had purchased with their birthright, all of their land, the millions of acres of hardcore poetry of their vowels & consonants, their *spit* as the Puppetmathers called it, the Language Land upon which they stood for good reason so tall and so proud, their ankles awash in the blood of hundreds of thousands of slaves whose words would never be heard, whose *lost syllables* came to nought, now there they stood, not on *their* land but on *his* land, the land of I'Veen, the porch of the Puppetmathers, in a fell swoop I'Veen's men stole their language land then stood at the ready with clamps, forceps and triple crush elastrators, and took everything that was left. Oh the elided lyrics—the *uninterrupted flow* demonstrated by the Puppetmathers was so perfect! All the *muthafuckas, bitches, fucks, nigger, shits* and *hard dicks* vanished—the new slaves were quick studies! Now avail on itunes: Kim Kardashian feat. Kanye/Jay-Z/Scarlett Johansson, Justin Bieber feat. Ludacris/Chris Rock/Susan Boyle/Zooey Deschanel—Lil Wayne featuring Rumer Willis/Drake/Blake Lively/Enrique Iglesias, T-Pain feat. Anderson Cooper/Charice/Ke$ha/The Game/Jennifer Aniston, shameful old *SNL* youtube of Weezy taking his seat in the back of EM's bus on the Ryan Seacrest/Plantation-approved "No Love" *yeah put a ~~dick~~ in their mouth, so I guess it's ~~fuck~~ what they say, I'm high as a ~~bitch~~, up up & away* .
. . . .
. . . . the peacock Puppetmathers spit *look at these rappers how I treat em* but Jerzy knew the Puppetmathers had censored *himself—*

such was his brilliance & the enormity of his vision!—Jerzy didn't
need to contact the martyr Suge Knight to know that the original
filecard in PuppetMathers' vast word-warehouse must have read *look
at these niggers*—a lyric he would reinstate with high pomp and ceremony when the Wars had ended victorious, & all Blacks who had not
Whitened were vanquished——————more collabs were comin:
Tyler the Creator feat. Taylor Swift/T.I./Whoop Goldberg/Busta
Rhymes . . . Mobb Deep feat. Jeff Bridges/Rick Ross/Karl Lagerfeld
& Kanye West . . . 50 Cent feat. Katy Perry & Russell Brand/Chris
Brown/Jerry Seinfeld . . . Wiz Khalifa feat. Pharrell/Paul McCart-
ney/Nicki Minaj/Selena Gomez/Drake/T.I./Matt Damon . . . Nas/
feat. The Mumford Brothers/Snoop/Jeff Bezos/Betty White . . .
MIA feat. AKON/Gwyneth/Jay-Z/Skylar Grey/Sasha Grey/Reese
Witherspoon/Homer Simpson/50 Cent/Drew Barrymore . . .
Gwyneth Paltrow feat. Dre/Eminem/Chippy D/Lupe Fiasco/Bruno
Mars/Nancy Grace/Cher Lloyd it

filled

him

with

DISGUST

　　　he wanted to set

fire *to the*

Plantation

he wondered when Suge Knight was gunna

　　　　　　　　　　　　　　　　　　　　　　　　call

[Rikki]

Dead Starfishes

"**I** *know* we're gunna find our boy—gon find him *today!*"

Larry Fishburne was in high spirits. He & Douglas had just come from lunch at Ago; they thought they'd drop into the Ooh Baby production offices unannounced & give Antwone a hard time. Fish (not Fishburne) was deep in the throes of casting, which made the ☆s even more impishly rambunctious.

Of course, all of the interns, gofers, staffers (especially Brando Brainard) were thrilled to see them. Their good-time energy boded well. They broke into Fish's casting session, intimidating whatever hopeful happened to be in the hotseat.

Which in this instance was Rikki.

"We're just busting our friend Antwone's balls," said Fishburne to Rikki. "We know *you* can take it—we just want to see if *he* can."

Antwone smiled, surrendering to the high-voltage hijinx. Douglas crept up behind Fishburne and stage-whispered to Rikki, as if inviting him into their special confidences. "We're just *taking the piss.* Ever heard that phrase, Rikki?"

He couldn't believe—didn't, actually—any of this was happening.

"It's veddy British," said Fishburne, "for *ball-busting.*"

"My wife uses it all the time," said Douglas.

"Is she a ball-buster?" said Fishburne.

"She's *Welsh*, what can I say?"

The director got the boys to settle down, which they did, mindful of the auditioner's nerves. There were two others in the room, casting people, both with big grins. One manned the camera while the other sat next to Fish, taking notes after each aspirant left the room.

"And by the way," said Fishburne to Rikki. "I'm *Fishburne*, he's *Fish*. Just so nobody's confused." Then he winked at him.

The scene they were in the middle of took place just after the boy almost takes the two grifters for 5K at a rigged bingo game. They outwit him but are intrigued. *Who* IS *this young flimflammer?* They take him to a steakhouse, where he has a long, moving monologue about his life as a foster child. The casting gal had been reading the lines of other characters, but Fishburne & Douglas insisted on jumping in.

Rikki read it through, & the director told him to do it again, but "a little lighter on your feet."

Michael Douglas (!) said, "That one was for free, because my uncouth friend and I rattled your cage. For which we apologize."

"Yes," said Fishburne, in earnest. "We were *taking the piss* out of our friend here, not you."

Rikki began the monologue, & had a good feeling in his stomach. When he reached the end, Douglas read his line:

> FALCONER (DOUGLAS)
> Well now, that's a helluva moving story, kid. But
> how do we know it's true?

> SLOOP (FISHBURNE)
> He's right. How do we know?

> JEROME (RIKKI)
> You don't.
> (Beat)
> And why is that a problem?

The men laughed too loudly at Rikki's deadpan delivery, told him he was *killer,* then left as noisily as they'd arrived.

He read with the casting woman for another 20 minutes, with Fish giving him very specific notes, as if to make up for the disruption. It was only after Rikki left the office and was getting on his motorcycle that he realized he hadn't said anything about their similar backgrounds or how much he loved the book Fish wrote and the movie they made about his life too—as he'd planned.

[Bud]

The Player

"Thanks

for coming in, Bud."

It'd been a long time since some showbizzer thanked him for coming in. Even though it was bullshit, it still felt good.

The offices of Ooh Baby Baby were in that luxe business pocket of Beverly Hills, a triangle made up of Burton Way, Santa Monica Boulevard & Doheny. The building was of the hipped up, minimal school, all concrete & open plan.

"It's a little crazy around here. We usually cast somewhere else but it's too boring to even talk about."

On the way in, Bud noted a clump of gangly, nervous-looking black teens with script pages in their hands.

"Are they here for Michael's movie?"

"'Michael's movie'! I like that."

"I meant—the movie he wrote for you."

"We've got two Fishes and two Michaels around here—*very* confusing. Tolkin'll love that, *Michael's movie!* In a sense, I suppose it is. Have you read the script? To *Treasure*? I'll give it to you. It's probably one of the most amazing screenplays I've ever read. Michael is writing on a *beyond* Aaron Sorkin level."

"He's pretty great."

"Did you ever see *The Rapture*? I'm a *huge* fan of *The Player*—that opening shot? But *The Rapture* . . . I think it's *better*. He's an *amazing director*. *The Rapture*'s one of my all-time favorites & I only saw it for the 1st time when Michael came onboard. Fucking *genius*."

Brando Brainard looked absolutely like a cheerleader—no: one of those tireless Jehovah's Witnesses who go door to door—no: the boy that played the Music Man when Bud was in junior high. Whatever he was, he was American through and through. His skin glowed with capital promise, hard, hopeful, shiny as a Granny apple. He was 28 but looked 18. Brando's fanboy élan, his peppy innocence, his unabashed *verve* were absolutely contagious—moreso when Bud refreshed the page to remind himself not just of the sweet kid's billions but of Tolkin's unswerving faith in the youngster's proclivity to make a deal. Bud felt suddenly lifted on a cushion of air, as if to get a better view of the inexorable rightness of the world. It wasn't so far a leap for him to see himself of the same class as Faulkner and Fitzgerald—a novelist preparing to moonlight as a screenwriter, for a little fast and easy cash.

"Here's the deal, Bud. And I'm going to pretend you know nothing about Ooh Baby, OK? I'm going to pretend you don't have a computer. That you don't even know what a search is. Old school. That's what I almost called the company, by the way. Old School. But my little brother liked Ooh Baby. So do I. It's funny, people come in here looking for jobs—not screenwriters, people who just want to work in production. By the time they're sitting in that chair, they've read so much shit on the Internet—and I don't care if it's favorable or unfavorable, I call it shit because it's a shitstorm of information with no human context. But they're somehow proud of themselves! Like they want me to know how much time they spent *Googling*. Really? So by the time they get in that chair, it's like *they've already had the whole experience*. I'm like, really? It's kind of like they've already *worked here*—because that's how these people talk, like they know *everything*, which is *true*, but they only know everything the

Internet told them—don't get me wrong, Bud, I *get* the Internet, I'm a Millennial, I'm an Internet *baby*—but it's like by the time they finish talking, I feel like*, Wow, I either need to fire this person or give them a raise!* OK. Sorry for the preamble.

"We've only been around two years and we've done very well for ourselves. *Turndown Service* made six hundred and fifty million worldwide, *before* DVDs, before *anything*. We're going into television, we're going into game design, we're going into web content. We might even produce a Broadway show. So now we're sophomores. And people *hate* us. They hate our *money,* they hate that we're *outsiders, right behind the smile,* you can *hear* them saying *Please God let him fail!* Now we're sophomores and those same haters who wanted us to crash and burn are praying we're just a one-hit wonder. Funny, huh. Really? They want to see you in that sophomore slump—*permanently.* Really? Sorry, guys. Afraid we're going to disappoint you. We have *twelve movies* in development and we're about to start shooting *The Treasure of Sierra Leone.* You know what we're calling our TV divisions, Bud? 'Hard To Get By' and 'Just Upon A Smile.'"

"Hard to get by—"

"Hard To Get By Television is for limited cable, like *Game of Thrones*; Just Upon A Smile is for network—sitcoms and reality shows."

"I love that."

"Because you *get* it. And if people don't *get* it, *fuck em!* Here's the deal, Bud. Wanna know who came up with the idea for *Turndown Service*? And the title? Which is genius? My little brother Biggie. He's 12 years-old. I shit you not. Wanna know who came up with the idea for *The Treasure of Sierra Leone*? And the title? Which is genius? Ditto. *My little brother Biggie.* Roger that. Do you know anything about savants? Mind you I didn't say *idiot savant* because my little brother is far from an idiot, he's fuckin *genius.* He's king. King Baby. There are all kinds of savants. *Musical* ones, *mathematical* ones—you know that woman Claire Danes played in the movie she got an Emmy for? Temple Grandin? I just saw it because we want to put Claire into something. Amazing performance. People don't know what Claire's capable of, *Homeland* just scratches the surface. So when they saw her in that movie, they were, like, *Really?* People say Temple Grandin's some kind of autistic, or Asperger, but I just think she's a savant. Her *thing* is that she can get into the heads of *animals*, she knows what they're *thinking*, what they're *feeling.* My brother Biggie happens to be a savant of *stories*, not *any* stories, but *Hollywood* stories, stories that lend themselves to the big or small screen. We just sold one to CBS called *You Rule*, about a slacker who finds out he's king of an island in the South Pacific. We actually have 14 projects in the TV hopper—I shit you not!—80% of which come *directly* from 'MSW.' *My Secret Weapon!*

"You know, I don't usually do the Biggie rap. Cause if I do, people are like *Really?* I guess I'm telling you because I have a feeling you could identify. With the underdog. Right? And that's a total compliment. Biggie's always been kind of an underdog, in a developmental sense. He has a tough time in social environments. He *can* have a tough time. Which doesn't mean he never comes out of his shell. I can get him to, but it takes a little *work*. I don't do it for me, I do it for him, because I'd like him to have relationships with *people*. He's all up in his head, which is an amazing place to be. But he's fine.

"So here's the deal. Biggie's given us a lot of comedy ideas but he has an idea for a drama. This one I don't get 100% but I'm not the genius either. What I'd like you to do—if you have the time, cause I know Michael said you're working on a novel, which I have total respect for by the way, I don't know how you guys do it—what I'd like you to do is maybe meet with him so you can get more of a flavor."

"Wow. Fantastic."

Bud had been down this road before. They always want you to do the monkey jig. So you do—but never get the job.

"I read those short stories you wrote in the 80s."

"Wow. Did Michael give them to you?"

Bud was thinking that pretty soon he would have to make a statue of Michael and put it in the living room, for easy access to prayer.

"eBay. But that's because Michael told me about it. What I liked about the stories was they were funny—but *dramatic*. Right?"

"That's sort of what I was trying to do."

"Well you succeeded, in *spades*. Like until James Perse I could never find a decent t-shirt or hoodie. I was like, *Really?* The universe *senses* shit, the *need* for certain shit, and *poof*, one day there's a guy named James Perse who steps up to fill the whatever need. Anyway, here's the deal: my little brother has an idea for a *drama*, it's a little *morbid*, I don't *understand* it, but that wouldn't be the 1st time I didn't understand something Biggie came up with, nor will it be the last. I don't ever want to bet against my brother. So what I'd like, is for you two to meet. It can be one time or you could meet *ten* times, doesn't matter, hell, if you get along, we'll just move you in! Then *after* you meet with my brother and you've got it all in your head, I'd like you to write up a little story for a screenplay based on the idea. Right? See I don't mean to keep repeating myself but just because I don't *get* this particular idea doesn't mean *shit*. In fact, it almost makes me think more highly of it. All I know is I have a duty to honor my little brother, honor his genius. I need to follow through on *anything* he presents. Right?"

"Sure. You said write up a story, do you mean an outline?"

Outlines were always freebies, another way the writer got grinded. You worked your ass off giving away your best ideas, because they knew you weren't in the position to say no.

"I can do that."

"I don't need an outline. That's not what I meant. Look, Michael spoke *very* highly of you, & Michael's a genius. I don't need you to *audition*. Who's your agent again?"

Bud blurted out "CAA."

"O right—Rod Fulbright. I'll have business affairs call. Contact Biggie directly and set up a time to get together. Shelby'll give you his email. He's a very special kid. I think the two of you might hit it off."

.   .   .

He picked up a frantic caregiver message on his way home. Dolly had fallen and was at the Cedars ER. He turned the car around.

Bud noted how calm and steady he was. *So this is it.* He played out the scenario in his head. He would park in one of the spots reserved for ambulances, the scofflaw act of an anguished family member. He would walk into the waiting room with a loping, dignified gait. The first person he'd see would be the distraught caregiver kneading her hands and gnashing her teeth. "Ine sorry, Meester Bud! Ine sorry!"—because as much as old people fear falling, caregivers fear being blamed for allowing it to happen. In the low, calm tone of a minister, Bud would tell her it was OK, it couldn't be helped, it would have happened sooner or later, there was nothing to be done. *It isn't your fault.* He would approach the *maitre d'ER* and ask to speak with a nurse. When the RN came, he would say that he was the son of the old woman the paramedics brought in, the woman who fell. An in-scrutable flicker would cross the nurse's face. She would tell Bud to wait a moment, and vanish—then reappear, saying, "Dr. Weymouth wants to talk to you." The security guard would allow Bud passage to the ER and the same nurse would lead him into a small lounge just off from the general commotion. The doctor would say, "I'm afraid that your mother didn't make it. She took a *very* nasty fall. When she fractured the hip—it was broken on both sides by the way—I think what happened was just a very *small amount* of fat wiggled loose from the bone marrow, formed an embolus and entered the bloodstream, traveling to the lung. Which was ultimately what killed her."* Bud would thank the doctor, who himself was relieved to be dealing with a sane and sensible relative rather than a hysteric. "How old was she, 90?" "92," Bud would say. "That's a pretty great run. I've seen folks

---

* Bud's detailed fantasy drew on the results of research he once did for a still unfinished script.

her age try to mend from something like this. It isn't pretty. I hate to use cliché but she's in a better place now, that's for sure." Bud's rejoinder would be "Let's hope so," and the doctor would smile, appreciating the hint of dark humor. Maybe the doctor had even read his book of short stories way back when. He would ask Bud if he'd like to spend some time with her alone and Bud would say yes. The doctor would disappear for a moment before returning to tell him it would be just a few minutes, the nurses were "cleaning her up, getting rid of all those tubes" and Bud should have a seat in the waiting room. Not wanting to encounter the caregivers—not having the energy to tell them of Dolly's demise and endure further histrionics—he would quietly step outside. There'd be a smoker there and Bud would ask for a cigarette. He hadn't smoked in 30 years. The smoke would feel good in his lungs. He would thank him, then stroll into the perfect Santa Ana-ruffled night air, toward Jerry's Deli. May as well have a sandwich before seeing the body. The paramedics were putting a gurney back into their truck. Bud would overhear one of them say "Jesus, could that old bitch *scream.*" "You'd scream too if two inches of bone was sticking out of your skin." "It sounded like an animal being slaughtered . . . *incorrectly.*" "You'd think the Dilaudid would have chilled her out." "O *shit,*" one would say. "I never pushed it! Fuck! She started gurgling blood & I had to deal with it— so I never fucking pushed the Dilaudid!" Bud had already ducked into shadow. "Whoa!" "You have *got* to keep that between you and me." "Don't worry about it. I did that same shit 3 weeks ago. I literally hadn't slept in 48 hours." *"Fuck.* How long did it take to get her from the house to here?" His partner punched a few numbers into his phone. "53 minutes! Cause she wouldn't stabilize? Then we had to bounce her down those stairs . . . 53 minutes, with nothing for pain!" The paramedics would devolve into laughter and grannyfuck jokes and Bud would snuff the cig. On his way back inside he would think about calling his mother's attorney. He would want to get the ball rolling on the inheritance but didn't want to come off as mercenary. He would decide that the way to handle it was to call in the morning to inform of Dolly's passing under the pretext of inviting him to the small service to be held at her interment. Bud actually hadn't even thought about a service, and would probably only end up having one if the attorney said he could make it. Back in the ER, an orderly would lead him to her draped enclosure, then make a hasty, respectful exit. There she would lie with a bluish tinge, a large patch covering where the bone broke thru. Her muff would be partially displayed—that old woman concentration camp corpse-muff, a dead bush still compelling him to look.

Goodbye Mother . . . .

The LVN escorted him to the triage area. Bud heard raucous laughter that he identified as the caregiver's. When he reached the open enclosure, Dolly was sitting upright on the exam bed. Marta was feeding her grapes.

"My son! My son!"

"Heyyyyy—what's going on? What *happened*?"

"Where *were* you," said Dolly. "Where *were* you—"

She pretend-bawled like a little girl.

"I was at a meeting. I came right after I got the message."

"He was in a *meeting*," she said, turning to Marta with exaggerated hauteur. "Did you hear? My precious son was in a *meeting*. Tell me, precious son, was it an *unemployment* meeting?"

Dolly arched her head, cuing Marta for their festive shtick wherein the caregiver held the cluster of grapes above Dolly's mouth to nibble at Cleopatra-style. Marta howled with laughter; Dolly was enjoying her audience. (Marta even slept in Dolly's bed at night. The two women were enthralled with one another—soul sisters to the end.) He cut through the revelry to ask what had happened. Marta grew serious. She said she was in the kitchen when she heard a *thump* on the baby monitor. When she got to the bedroom, *"my big baby"* was already on the floor. Dolly had been watching TV in her special chair, and dropped a cookie; when she leaned to pick it up, she tumbled onto the carpet. Marta pointed to the subtle bruise on Dolly's forehead. It looked like a bindi. Marta told Bud that when she couldn't reach him, she thought it prudent to call 911 because "your mommy she say she was dizzy." She wagged her finger at the old woman. "No more! Tha's a *bad big baby*. Next time you call *me*, Big Baby! *Marta* gunna come pick up your cookie!"

The two erupted in laughter again. A doctor who looked like he could have been Bud's grandson came in.

"I heard everyone having such a good time that I just had to crash the party!"

"Doctor," said Dolly. "This is my handsome only son." He shook Bud's hand. "And he's *currently unemployed.* So if there are any single lady doctors you know who would marry a sexy, brilliant *writer,* I'd like you to introduce them. *Because he needs to marry money.*"

Bud cringed. He was used to it; he tried to let it go.

"I will *absolutely* keep an eye out," said the doctor. He turned solemnly to Bud, as if he was really going to look into it.

"It doesn't even have to be a *female.* As long as there's *money* there."

"When can she go home?" said Bud.

"We're just waiting for a catscan. My guess is it will be absolutely clear and Mom'll be good to go."

The doctor turned back to Dolly and at the same time, pointed to Marta. He pretended to scold.

"But I want you to promise to listen to this lovely young lady. (Marta was 63.) The next time you drop a cookie, you give her a shout, OK?"

Dolly nodded her head, coy, sheepish. "Doctor," she said. "Did anyone ever tell you you're a *very sexy man?*"

"Coming from you, I'm flattered. Because I know in your day, you had the pick of the litter. You can *still* pick & choose—you're a gorgeous lady." He looked at Bud. "Isn't she?"

Dolly smiled, almost tearfully, drinking it all in.

"She's amazing," said the doctor. "Has she always been like this?"

"Yeah," said Bud.

The doctor assumed a professional demeanor, reiterating that he thought Dolly would soon be on her way.

"Now 'soon' could mean a couple of hours in 'hospital time,' but I don't think so. I'll try to hurry things along."

He turned to go, then shook his head.

"Ninety-two-years old . . . you're my hero. Take good care." He shook Bud's hand again. "That's a wildcat. You watch, she's going to outlive us all."

. . .

Bud left word with Rod Fulbright. He wanted to tell him how the meeting went.

He wrote and rewrote in his head what he was going to say when the agent called back, and *how* he was going to say it (studied nonchalance): "Hi Rod. I guess it kinda looks like they want to make a deal." Then he thought maybe he should have waited to call. It wouldn't be the first time he'd heard someone invoke *business affairs* in a meeting, only to never hear from them—from anyone—again. Actually, though, he kind of *had* to call when he did, because Rod Fulbright did not yet know that Bud was his client.

His cellphone rang.

"Bud? I have Rod Fulbright, returning."

He prayed the connection would hold. Reception at Dolly's was always dicey.

"Hi, Bud."

"Hey Rod."

"Well, I just got a call from business affairs at Ooh Baby."

"You're kidding."

"They were really drinking your Kool-Aid over there!"

"Wow. Great. I guess it's kind of like a blind deal? I mean, in the sense I really don't have any idea what they want me to adapt."

"As long as their money's green."

Rod said CAA would act as his "pocket" agency for now, and that Chris—ICM—was fine with that.

"They've offered WGA scale, which is a little more than $39,000. I told them that just wasn't acceptable. We'll probably counter with a hundred." After all the years of famine, it was hard for Bud to accept a seat at the table, let alone that food was being served. "They really want you for this. I'd like to get you at least 50."

An hour later, he got an email.

Hi Bud

Brando wanted me to give you Biggie's info. He can be reached at biggie@oohbaby.com He's pretty much always on line! Brando had a great time this afternoon, and I'm sorry I wasn't able to attend. But I'm sure we'll meet soon, and welcome to the crazy Ooh Baby family!

Best,
Keira

Keira Thompson
Director of Development
Ooh Baby Baby Productions
14 Alden Drive
Beverly Hills, CA 90210
(Tel) 3105816889
www.oohbabybaby.com

[Michael]

Lovers

"It's an *awful* thing to go through."

Michael and Catherine were having dinner at Mr. Chow.

"Has he opened up?"

"Yeah he has. A little bit. Because I've talked about Cameron. So there's a bond: our *wayward children*."

"Did she really say she thought porn was 'art'?"

"Yes she did."

They nodded their heads in muted sorrowful stupefaction.

"Did I tell you I saw Calliope?"

"No!"

"Jesus. There's been too much goin on."

"How *is* she?"

"She's *fantastic*. We had a *very* interesting conversation—if you want to call me just sitting there listening a conversation."

"I love that woman. And you *never* just sit & listen."

"She sends her love. She said, '*There's* a brave one.'"

Catherine raised a devilish eyebrow.

"And *what* pray tell was this one-sided conversation *about*? If I may be so bold."

"You may, because you're the bold & the beautiful. I went to see her because it's been too long. I don't know how long she's planning to stick around. Plus I *miss* the old broad. I knew she wanted to see me—probably for the same reasons! I talked about *Jazz,* my *hesitations* of late, and solicited her *opinion.* She was very elegant in what she had to say. Which in a nutshell was, *Damn the torpedoes!* Kind of a 'Mikie, you're gonna go anyway, so you may as well go in a blaze of glory.' She gave *All That Jazz* the green light."

"Michael, *please* don't tell me you've seduced one of the most brilliant psychiatric minds of our time into managing your career."

"Ha! Not a bad idea though."

"*Oooo* I want to *kill* her!"

"I told her you weren't all that high on the idea."

"I didn't say that. What I *said* was, I wasn't sure I wanted to play the *Angel of Death.* At *my* age, it's the kind of rôle that tends to typecast."

"You know you're right. Those Angel of Death offers are gonna start pouring in." She swatted him. "Did you know Fosse was her patient?"

"Uh uh."

"For years."

"Well," she said, resolute. "You do what you do. As it should be. But nowhere is it written that I must come round to being keen on my husband playing *himself*—"

"I am not playing *myself.*"

"—*or a reasonable facsimile thereof,* in a film where he *dies* at the end."

"Who *says?* Who says I have to *die*? He doesn't have to *die.* Calliope said the character could *live.*"

"This woman should be a studio head! Or God."

"Try both."

"Actors frequently confuse them. Michael . . . I just want you to respect my decision. If I choose not to play that part, you must promise not to bully me. Promise?"

"Point taken."

"When I say 'Promise?' you're supposed to say 'I promise,' not 'Point taken.'"

"Point taken and promised."

"That's a gross point, I hope. Give me ten of those, and you just might have found a way into my heart."

"I'll need to run that past Calliope." (*Another swat*) "I still think Heather Morris would be phenomenal in the Reinking role. As the mistress. Girl has a *rockin* body—"

"O shush your noise!"

(*A double swat*)

"Hey, come on now, don't hit a cancer survivor. TMZ's gonna say you beat up your *gaunt, defenseless husband* in front of *shocked diners. Onlookers.* While in a bipolar frenzy."

"Hmm. I bet lots of women in this restaurant would like to do the very same with *their* fellas. You know, what's that line from *Harry and Sally*? 'I'll have what *she's* having'!"

She was funny and fiery and could really make him laugh.

"Young Heather as your mistress, & no doubt you'll cast some unknown hottie for your bespoke Angel of Death. You'll be in heaven, won't you?"

"You know who I think would choreograph?"

"Who."

"Benjamin, Natalie's husband."

"He's *wonderful.*"

"But you & me are going to have to hit the dance floor soon. You're going to have to show me some moves."

"I *was* going to make a *Dancing With the Stars* joke but it's all becoming a bit too close to home now, isn't it?"

"That's Calliope's favorite show!"

"Well of *course* it is. I suppose the world *is* coming to an end—the therapist I once revered as world-class has now completely regressed into little more than a Tinseltown svengali! How quickly they fall! She dropped like ninepins!"

"I talked to Annie—"

"Annie Reinking?"

"We've spoken a few times. She sent me some beautiful notes when I was in treatment, & one or two since."

"Are they still in Phoenix?"

"Yeah. Her son's a special needs kid—"

"Marfan. I know. She was wonderful about Dylan. Wonderful to talk to."

"—she's *very* much involved, on a national level. Raising Marfan awareness."

"I should call."

"Hey, when's the gala?" he asked.

Catherine knew she was about to get her funnybone tickled. Her husband raised an eyebrow—the couple raised lots of eyebrows when they were together—transforming himself into Master Thespian, an old character from *Saturday Night Live*.

"Woman, I demand a reply! I am please to be informed of the *time* and the *date* of the latest gala—there've been so many, I've lost count—the latest gala celebration of . . . ME!"

"If it's the *Courage Ball* you speak of, Lord Master Thespian," she said, using his favorite berserk maid-in-waiting voice. "I believe it to be the 23rd of this month."

"O how I love to be fêted!"

"You've been fêted so often, you've become *fetid*."

He resumed his normal self.

"Y'know, we oughta have a face off—Master Thespian vs Catherine Zeta-Jones, Commander of the British Empire."

"Let's not. Did you know Beyoncé is taking Rihanna's place?"

"At the ball? What happened?"

"She got terribly sick and had to cancel her tour. The doctors don't even want her *talking* for 3 weeks."

"Is Steve still hosting?"

"Far as I know. And that little girl is going to perform."

"My Telma? My sweetheart Telma?"

"The little girl from Canada. She's going to bring down the house."

[Telma]

To Reach the Unreachable Star

Telma had been practicing, you could hear her through her closed bedroom door, and all through the house. Gwen would stop whatever she was doing and listen, and it was nightmarish, almost more than she could bear.

> Smile tho yr ♥ is aching
> ☺ even tho it's breaking . . .

Where was Phoebe? She called to say she was stuck in traffic, but that was half an hour ago. She didn't know how much more she could endure———————————————————————

. . .

Mother and daughter in the kitchen. Telma starving, ladling peanut butter & jelly onto rye bread, her favorite. Bag of giant marshmallows out, her favorite. A big bowl of Hawaiian Sweet Maui onion chips, her favorite. Big open thermos of crushed ice/pink lemonade, her favorite.

She was going to sing *Smile* for her mom but since Phoebe was coming (supposedly) she decides to wait.

Picks up Gwen's energy.

"Mom, are you having *problems?*"

Gwen says no but her denials are becoming frayed. Old soul Telma continues to be respectful, thinking it's to do with Daddy, they're right around the anni of his death, so she leaves it alone. *The child is the mother of the woman.*

And all that.

Telephone rings.

Gwen grabs it, certain Phoebe's calling with another update from LA traffic hell. Hoping she'll say she was in a wreck: engine blew up, hit a pedestrian, got shot by a road rager—anything but "Be there soon."

But it isn't Phoebe, it's Jesselle, the gal who's coordinating talent for the Courage Ball . . .

Right then something occurs to her that is so obvious, so blatant, it unhinges. How could she have even *entertained* having The Conversation with her daughter *before*, before the Courage Ball? The *recklessness* of it, the lack of a sensible, coordinated plan, the flight from *rational* was suddenly disturbing, *mostly* because Phoebe hadn't come to the same *glaring* conclusion independently; it was a *terrible* idea, cruel and unworkable, and Phoebe should have shot it down the moment Gwen voiced it. The woman she was desperately relying on was in way over her personal & professional head. Gwen shivered with the cosmic aloneness of her realization; no cavalry to her calvary would come.

Telma made a joyous leap toward the phone, pressing SPEAKER.

"Hi Jesselle!!!!!!!"

"Is that my Telma-girl?"

"Queen Telma speaking." (*A not-so-great English accent*)

"Hello Your Highness! Hello Gwen."

"Hi Jesselle."

"You know I always have to say hello to Her Highness first, *that's* the protocol. Now, you can't *see* it, Telma, but I curtsied too, same as I would to Queen Elizabeth."

"You *better*," said Telma comically. "I can't see it but my *knaves* are there, & they report back to me."

"You're scaring me! Gwen, she's scaring me! I want my Telma-girl back!"

"Jesselle," said Telma. "When are we going to have dress rehearsal at the hotel?"

"Well that's one of the reasons I'm calling, guys. Sweetheart, you're not going to be too happy with me, but we need you to sing another song."

"Why?" (*Crestfallen not hopeless—yet*)

"You're doing 'Smile,' aren't you?"

"You *know* I am."

"Jesselle, what's going on?"

"Our problem is that 'Smile' is the only song the little girl Aleisha knows."

"She's not even supposed to be singing!" said Telma.

"I know, I know, darling, but she sang 'Smile' for Marcy and now Marcy insists that she sing it at the gala."

"But that isn't *fair!*"

"I know it isn't, baby. I know."

"Darling," said Gwen. "Can't you sing 'Over the Rainbow'?"

"'Over the Rainbow' isn't *ready*, Mama! And I sing 'Smile' *so much better*, you *know* I do! Tobey Maguire & Mrs. Biden sent me *flowers*. People brought bouquets to the *stage*. They *never* did that for 'Over the Rainbow'—"

"Honey," said Jesselle. "*You* are a *rockstar*. 'Over the Rainbow' is *so much more* of a big person song. There's still a few days, you can *nail* it."

"Of course she can."

"I *can't*."

"You *can*," said Gwen.

In the last handful of years, cheering Telma to walk on with hope in her heart had become an involuntary reflex. But now, the sickening absurdity of it hit Gwen hard. Here she was, dreaming the impossible dream, tilting at (nonfatal) cancerous windmills for her baby, grotesquely dreaming of permanent remission—a remission at least from *something!* Willing to march into hell for a heavenly cause . . .

To right the unrightable wrong—

"Jesselle, we'll work this out. Telma will steal the show like she always does. We'll regroup. She just wasn't expecting it."

Hearing her own voice ground Gwen down.

A Judas mom, leading her only one to slaughter . . .

"Your mother's right, Telma, *listen* to her. You *always* steal the show. Gwen, can you take me off speaker?"

Gwen held the phone to her ear and listened, saying nothing. Then, "Oh," "Uh huh," "OK," "That's definite?"

The doorbell rang.

"Uh huh . . . OK right, yes, I'll convey that. But I have to go now, we have company."

She hung up and opened the door. Phoebe stood there like the priest in *The Exorcist.* Instead of the usual effusive greeting, Telma ignored her, still *in process.*

"Mama, what did Jesselle say?"

"Nothing."

"Is *what* definite? Is *what* definite?"

Phoebe didn't interfere; she could see she'd walked into a little tempest that need be take its course.

"Not *now*, Telma—"

"What did she *say*, what did she *say!*"

"She said that—that Aleisha—the little girl—she said that the little girl was going to be the last performer, that Marcy wanted her to go on last. That you had to sing *before.*"

Telma blinked at her mother like a robot on the fritz.

That was when she gave Phoebe a proper if stormy greeting, running tearfully into her arms.

3rd

Trimester

WME

(Evening into Night)

Evening is the time of the merging of
Man and Woman: ***the Unknowable***

A l'alta fantasia qui moncò possa,

ma già volgeva il mio disio e ⏹l velle

sì come rota ch'igualmente è mossa.

l'amor che move il sole e l'altre **stelle**.

—P A R A D I S O, XXXIII. 142–5

[Tom-Tom]

What's Your Favorite ☆ Got In The Bank?*

*www.celebritynetworth.com

Tom-Tom

had a *feeling* about it in her gut, a feeling she'd grown to trust, an extrasensory *feeling* about Rikki & *The Treasure of Sierra Leone* from the beginning. How could she not?

There was no way to ignore the *facts*—that Rikki shared that battered fosterchild thing with Antwone Fisher, and had even read his *memoir* (over & over!); that the inspiration for the character Rikki was auditioning to portray was none other than Ishmael Beah, who had visited his middleschool; & that Rikki had thoroughly read/ iPod'd Mr. *Beah's* book as well. It all amounted to a heavy dose of what Tom-Tom called the propinquity of providence. She was especially convinced of the importance of her seductive ministrations during the making of the video that one day would have hundreds of millions of hits because people would watch the audition tape as an historical document/debut, like they did Bieber's first youtube or Susan Boyle's *I dreamed a dream*. She was certain their juices & commingled *ch'i* had set the stage for Rikki's brilliance, even *moreso* that their coupling was, with direct obliqueness, the actual cause of three outlandish pieces of recent good fortune: 1) Rikki's "accidental" read-through with Michael Douglas *and* Laurence Fishburne; 2) the bizarre, unexpected call from an old friend asking her to take up free residence in an empty, Greek-columned minimanse high atop Mt Olympus; 3) the unheralded arrival of a reality show convention in downtown LA, whose convenient appearance, as if custom-made, presented itself not merely as a gathering of like minds, workshops, hook-ups and industry connects, but as a one-stop casting shop for the washouts & almost-were's who would form the cornerstone and fountainhead of Tom-Tom's Big Idea.

.   .   .

What happened with the whole Mt Olympus thing is that Tom-Tom's friend Cherokee was a hair & makeup gal who Tom-Tom used to run with and Cherokee called out of the blue just like everything lately seemed out of the cosmicorgasmic blue, saying *Double T you gotta help me, I'm fucked.* For the last 5 yrs Cherokee pretty much exclusively worked for Betty White, Betty wouldn't let anyone touch her face & hair cept her. Sometimes when her boss was in New York or wherever but not working, Cherokee housesat Ms White's rundown still very groovy house on Mt Olympus, which was far groovier than Cherokee's shack in Studio City.

From what Tom-Tom heard, Mt Olympus used to be chichi but was kinda frayed now, counting dope dealers, pimps & MMA/cage-fight promoters among its denizens. Its entrance was right at the mouth of Laurel Canyon, you turned up the hill on Mt Olympus Drive, took Mt Olympus to Electra, Electra looped into Hercules, then hung a right on Jupiter, a left on Hermès, & you're there. Betty was on hiatus from that show she did with Valerie Bertinelli, she was in NYC getting ready to come home and suddenly got cast in an Adam Sandler movie shooting in Paris, Spain & Poland. (Boo-yuh!) It kinda sucked not being Betty White. Anyway, for ten fucking *weeks* Betty'd be flying back and forth to the States, but only to New York, LA was just too far. She bought her pad 40 years ago when the

Mount was the spanking new playground of Southland gods, more Trousdale at the time than Trousdale lite (which it quickly became), gone much further to seed in the interim. Betty told Cherokee she probably should have sold it before the bubble, now that would almost be impossible, the truth is she didn't mean a word of it because she adored that house, it reminded her of a certain lovely time in her life, it was a living museum of nostalgia and gave her a kick plus it wasn't like she needed the money from a sale. She was frickin rich. According to Cherokee, she didn't want to do a big makeover on it either, a decision Ms White was positive added 20 years to her life. Plus she liked that whenever her makeup & hair doll housesat, Cherokee made helpful, practical, incremental improvements such as putting in a new water heater or recaulking/resealing bathroom tiles or even just (as Cherokee reported back) walking around with a can of WD40 unsqueaking the squeaks. The thing of it was, Cherokee was now going to have to go with Betty to Europe, the doll was wonderful at making her look wonderful but *aside* from that, Betty out and out enjoyed her, she raised her spirits and (mysteriously) made her laugh. Kinda like the daughter or granddaughter or great granddaughter she never had. *The doll was a hoot.* Betty had it written into her contract that Cherokee was her doll, they had to pay for her travel, per diem, hotel, all that good stuff. It kinda sucked not being Cherokee.

Cherokee did h&m on Season 3 of *Idol* and was the only one who even called Tom-Tom when she got kicked off. (Fantasia and Jennifer were such cunts about Tom-Tom's failed subterfuge, which might even have been looked at in a humorous, forgiving light if they so chose. Clearly TT was coming from a desperate place, and one should *always* demonstrate compassion for desperate people, but *no*, they were in full-scheming skeevydiva mode. Tom-Tom never really told anyone except Cherokee but she was *happy* when Jennifer's family got killed and she was *happy* when TMZ said that Fantasia was getting random death threats & hoped she *suffered* when there was a rumor she made a sextape with a married man, that's what happens when you think you're above empathy and treat your peers with ill-respect.) So Cherokee called Tom-Tom after they threw her off A.I. and *pursued* her because she liked bad girls. They became lovers and running partners, they were all about smack and candyflipping. After 2 years of untold drama (long preceding the arrival of the angel Betty White in her life), Cherokee checked herself into Serenity House, upscale Laurel Canyon rehab, where she commenced to take inventory of her life and compose a long list of those whom she owed amends, Tom-Tom being foremost among them. The h&m doll grew rife with fantasies of red roses and white picket fences, audaciously reaching out & asking Tom-Tom to join her in trudging the road of happy recovery, which amazingly, Tom-Tom audaciously did. Sadly, T² was asked to leave (before Cherokee even had the chance to make formal amends, and before Tom-Tom began her own 4th Step) for failing a urine test *and* sleeping with two of the former-patients-turned-counselors, a 27 year-old male & a 62 year-old female, separately but within a 2-hour period. More amazingly and audaciously, Cherokee had remained sober in the 84-odd months since, all of her drug cravings/energy handily refocused on a wild animalistic sexual obsession with TT, which always clouded Cherokee's already unimpeccable vision, forcing her into a cyclical destructive dance of fight and flight, merging and separation, and who, by bestowing money and favors, manipulated Tom-Tom, at least *thought* she did, into agreeing/pretending/promising they might really have a future together. And now the gal was going away to be with her Angel, she'd been doing pretty well lately in protecting herself from the madness of her obsession but when the housesitter she arranged for (a friend of Amy Smart) bailed, & there was Cherokee leaving in 36 hours, & knowing Betty would be *very* unhappy if the house were left empty— it was an emotional thing, as long as she knew someone was staying there Betty was chill—knowing that however gracefully her angel reacted, anything short of a house sit would be a disaster.

So inadvertently she tapped into her god-sized obsession and everything old was new again. All was quickly arranged.

Tom-Tom GPS'd the greek salad of streets. The doll intro'd her to the house & its mild old-house eccentricities. Gave her the keys and told her which opened what. Showed her the ancient alarm system thingie, still in perfect working order. Showed her the museumpiece home intercom system, still in perfect working order. A little pool cover retraction demo. Then Tom-Tom devoured her in bed god she'd do anything Tom-Tom asked, she'd suck a napping dog's dick like in the Czech *Animal Gangbang* vid they watched before/during their fuck. She'd put a snake up her cunt like that other video, head in the cunt tail in the ass *how the fuck did they even get the snake to do that* she'd get reamed by a pig or a horse & do it *unloaded*. Tom-Tom always told her what riches lay ahead when they fucked, she'd whisper shit in her ear while she licked her clit and worked her dark ★ with a dildo, Tom-Tom's deliberate funny retail sextalk which actually *would* have been *hahaha* if she wasn't always on the verge of coming, like how she would buy her a $3,000 Katie Holmes–designed pantsuit or these $500 Opening Ceremony shoes by Chloë Sevigny or an Olsen twins $34,000 backpack or how some day she would lavish her with custom jewelry like the $25,000 diamond-encrusted pendant of Stewie from *Family Guy* that Justin Bieber had made. The Double T drove her to LAX & passionkissed her in Cherokee's SUV (she gave TT the keys), Tom-Tom put all kinds of subtle notes, flavors and colors in that kiss, going-away bonus tracks, freebies Tom-Tom threw in as acknowledgement and compensation for the seriousness of the scarily timed Mt Olympus aerie temp gifting, in that she knew *in her gut* just how large and important a part it was to play in her immediate plans & fortunes, notes, colors & flavors that implied *I think I might really love you, Cherokee, this time I'm not so blind I can't see, to* know *we can have a life together, so hurry home my love, hurry home from yr white angel to yr angel of meth . . .*

On the way back from the airport Tom-Tom thought about that whole period of her life: Season 3. Season of the witch, no doubt. She got suicidal when Fantasia leaked her *Idol* artifice to Perez H (she was *sure* it was *fatass*-ia) and in like 3 seconds it viral'd the web and national/international tabloids too . . . then backfired on the h8trs & she started getting calls like from Jimmy Kimmel, and Amy Poehler played her on *SNL* (Maya Rudolph did Fantasia & Ben Affleck played Simon). She got hundreds of emails from *Idol* h8trs—death threats too—she was having her quintessentially American-ironic Tonya Harding folk hero *Anti-Idol* t-shirt moment. Letterman even wanted her to read the Top 10 and she went to an office in Hollywood to be put on tape so they could see if she could do it. There weren't any Top 10 jokes written for her yet so she read a *Ten Questions You're Afraid to Ask Condoleezza Rice*. She read well so that they flew her to NYC & put her up in a hotel not far from the apt she used to deal out of. Tom-Tom was so nervous in the car that took her to the studio that she puked. Had to do a little unplanned smack. The studio was freezing, Letterman never talked to her backstage and introduced her by saying "We're happy to have Tom-Tom on the show with us tonight. She flew out from California in Ryan Seacrest's private jet . . . and if you believe that, I've got a bridge with multiple schlerosis to sell you." The crowd roared & something sour shifted in her. She could smell the stink waft up from her panic mouth.

**Top Ten Reasons Tom-Tom Should Have beaten Fantasia
To Become the "American Idol"
10. In porn, "Tom-Tom"'s a top; "Fantasia"'s a bottom . . .**

In a month, all the attention faded away. She became a self-h8tr whose dreams died stillborn.

Until now.

.   .   .

Her Big Showrunner Idea:

She was part of a loose network of *loosers* angling for their own reality show . . . well *Tom-Tom* was angling anyway. A sorority/fraternity house all composed (in her conception) of one-time *Idol* contestants—though lately she'd considered broadening her sights to be more inclusive of *The Voice*, *The Sing-Off*, *The Singing Bee*, *X-Factor*, *Going Platinum*, &tc—who were sent home late or even way early in the game. Naturally no one could necessarily compete with Tom-Tom's famous winnowing as a consequence of out-&-out larceny. No, the others would be more than content to make encore appearances, standard bearers of the usual sometimes-ludicrous sometimes-laughable always-lamentable hard-/softluck stories. Tom-Tom hadn't yet begun her official reach-out, she took the reality show convention as a sign, that's where she was intent on doing a major scout of minor talent. She believed in the ☆s and their signs, that one needed only to cultivate the innate ability to interpret their meanings; she recognized the convergence of the convention *and* the Betty White godsend in which she would house and film her loser brethren a la *Real Life/Big Brother* to be a karmic omen in itself.

She had a wishlist of losers and *loosers* & was checking it twice: A) That punkbitch from *Idol*'s very 1st year who "signed" "When I Fall in Love" to his shit for brains deafass parents; B) Chris Golightly (season 9), who was raised by like 10,000 foster families, & ultimately bounced because he was already under contract to some fagboyband; C) Asia'h Epperson (season 7th), she of the annoyingly spelled name whose father's head got Islam'd in a car wreck right before her audition so she changed the song to "How Do I Live Without You" & later got arrested for assaulting some ho at a *holly*wood club (which actually happened to be the night Asia'h & T'om-To'm f'irst m'et); D) Jamielynn (season the 6th), whose dad caught his wife with a lips-to-nuts dick in her mouth, so he agro-capped her then capped himself into below-the-chest paralysis, self-consigning to perma-bedsores, shit-stink rooms & morning hard-ons he probably never would even know he had, for the rest of his disgusto-burden life. And she really wanted to get Chris Medina, the shameless cunt who wheeled his useless, brainfucked wife onstage to blow Steve Tyler, and made Jenny from the Half-Black cry.

Tom-Tom knew it wouldn't be easy getting all the leave-it-to-

diva loosers to agree on what direction they should go viz her Master
Plan. Just two weeks ago, a stoned/stoked TT called one of her fellow *Idol* ejectees to float the idea of a houseful of underdogs, a chronicle of the lives of a merry band of inside-outsiders (she was calling it
Bad News Bears in her head, from one of her favorite movies), an odd
squad overcoming kicks in the face on the road to Tinseltown triumph. Pitch it to VH1, Starz or TRU, one of those *looser* channels,
they'd fuckin jump at it. Chrystle-Leigh (season 3) right away Debby
Downer'd her by opining like some freakin expert on constitutional
freakin law how Tom-Tom could never use *Bad News Bears* as the
title without getting permission from the studio that made the movie,
which of course . . . they never *would* grant, she said, no *way*. Like
that was the point of the phone call, to ask this cunt what she thought
of Tom-Tom's *provisional freakin title* for her genius freakin show.
Tom-Tom said, You know what? No one's even seen the movie [you
CUNT], no one even [fucking] remembers it [CUNT]. Wherein
Chrystle-Leigh, Visiting Professor of Cuntology said, *Well YOU did
plus they don't care if anyone remembers or not, they won't let you use it unless you give em money upfront & even then they're going to ask for ownership*. Own *this*, you fucking diseased hooker. Then of course the
cuntologist said ditto to Tom-Tom's fallback title, *Daydream Believers*,
TT felt like an ass for even bringing it up but she was loaded, she
liked the way it sounded, she was excited & just wanted to put it out
there. I don't give a shit what we call it, she rejoindered, which of
course wasn't true, before puckering up: *I think it'd be cool if you wanted
to be part of the show*. Tom-Tom knew she was going to have to kiss
some *looser* ass if she wanted to get things rolling.

Tom-Tom hated to have to align herself or even deal with her fellow loosers, she was more than just one of *them*, a loser mouseketeer,
she was the CREATOR, the one with the VISION that would
shower unknown riches down upon them if they were smart enough
to latch on and *go for it*. She was going to do them the insane favor of
frickin *hand carrying* their lame, out-of-work, no name selves from
obscurity into the crystal light. She knew what she wanted the show

to be, she wanted it to be poignant, but wild and woolly too, with that demented freewheeling super-spontaneous smells-like-Gary Busey spirit, the problem was she knew more about the *Looser* Syndrome than she cared to, knew she was going to have an uphill battle not because of the show's *concept*, which was trippy and dynamic, she was 1000% certain she could pitch it and sell it for real, no—*not* that, but rather because she knew all of the *loosers* had a deluded sense of importance, delusional self-worth came with the *looser* territory, the irony being they were incapable of seeing the *truth* (which in the end probably saved them), that they were drowning, and only by the *benevolence of the stars* (manifesting through Tom-Tom's dreams and actions) were they being thrown life preservers, in the shape and form of a *venue* in which they could once again but this time maybe finally succeed at being losers. Tom-Tom knew she needed to be patient and merely consider them as spoiled invalid children, she knew they wouldn't be able to shut up, they would be combative, they couldn't help themselves, they were barely in the position to maintain breath in this world let alone bargain with Tom-Tom over the size and color of their fucking floatation vests, which was *fine*, but she'd rather be dealing with all that when they were already in the *house*, and *filming*—Tom-Tom wanted a reality show, fuck *out-of-touch reality*, at least if you were going to be out of touch be out of touch while the show's *fucking filming*, though not *too* out of touch, because there wasn't *poignance* in that and *poignance* was part of her Vision—*not* surrealism, she wanted no part of *The Surreal Life*'s Asshole World, fuckin Omarosa living in that senile piece of shit Glen Campbell's old Holly estate, fuckin rickety Jerri Manthey, fuckin Ron Jeremy, fuckin Flavor Flav & mini-me, Tom-Tom wanted the folks at home to laugh *at* em then *for em* then *with* em, cry w/em too, tears were the secret sauce, Tom-Tom the creator/producer wanted to hit viewers in the gut & slap their hearts, wanted them to see *themselves* in the *looser* wrecking crew, you know, like all of us are only a fartbeat away from humiliation and defeat, & must then find the strength to pull ourselves up . . . *Bad News Bears/Daydream Believers/*whatever must present the same suspenseful indomitability of spirit as magnificently evinced by Marky Mark & Christopher Bale in *The Fighter,* ergo apprehension & delight, and finally, *invested emotion,* she wanted the preverbial audience at home to be completely in sync with the houseful of *loosers* as they underwent painful public transformation, their pitiable collective charms finally breaking thru losershells to catharsis & *chrysalis luminosity,* with that special excitement glow ascribable only to newborn ☆s and wingdusted butterflies taking virginal flight.

Tom-Tom knew she'd win, in the end, & bend the *loosers* to her will.

· · ·

She did her homework, heartened by what she learned.

Ooh Baby Baby It's A Wild World Films was run by Brando Brainard. BB was a party boy cum producer, bankrolled by his father. She thought it commendable he'd resisted 24/7 agency gangbang invites, all clamoring to rep. He used his dad's lawyers instead. When asked about that, Brainard said on http://www.a-billion-dollars-is-cool/interview/brando-brainard.html that he took his lead from Spielberg, who apocryphally operated without an agent for years.

Apparently (with the emphasis on *parent*), there was a lot of money there. Brando kept similar company cause it's lonely at the top. He hung with the son and daughter of Larry Ellison, the $50 billion oracular man. David & Megan Ellison each had their own company, Skydance Prods and Annapurna Pictures respectively. The boy was 28 and raised $350 million the year before; the chick was 25, rode horses & Harleys and worked out of a $14 million home bought with a loan from Daddy's Octopus Holdings ("octopus" sounded about right). It sucked not to be the Ellison kids. The key difference between them and Brando was that while Brando Brainard's father, or his money anyway, was the gorilla in the room nobody seemed to be able to find the gorilla. Bertram Brainard was a recluse, an inventor with over a thousand patents to his name from medical devices to *ideas.* Tom-Tom thought it was very cool that a person could patent an *idea*. She crawled the websighs, servered the Clouds, & surf Safari'd, resulting in the provocatively useless knowledge that Brainard Senior was the wiz who came up with the 3-number security code on the back of credit cards. Which wouldn't have been notable in itself, had it not been for the part about the information highway robbery allowing him to collect royalties on his innovative capitalistic tool *for 15 years* after the established copyright. Tom-Tom dragged, doubleclicked, triple beam surfed & snorted in an attempt to find out *what* royalties, and from *who*. As it turned out, the money gratefully poured forth from slaphappy banks & merchants who saved trillions in fraud. (She couldn't find a $ amount re Warlock Brainard's remuneration.) Another one of his frightening ideas was the concept of/ technology behind those scary-cheap 7Eleven-type plastic bags made in Myanmar by dying 6-year-olds, bags so thin they *just* met the technical definition of "bag"—it's hard to open them even if you're at the right end, that's because of their molecular structure, each time you tussle you're almost certain the cashier handed you a defective single sheet. Finally you *peel* it back, & unless you triple-bag it, the freak plastic's built-in genetic design code virtually commands it to tear open just as you're getting in the car. The bags somehow left one feeling disempowered, even spiritually bereft, yet were now in 83% of national convenient marts, shaving hundreds of millies off the stronger still-crap bags being used before. **www.wikicorpsleak .com** said Brainard's attorneys were warlock geniuses themselves, as inspired & militant in finding arcane ways to trademark ideas as were the legendary tax-dodge lobbyist shysters hired by G.E. . . . Brainard's men were pioneers of idea patenting, a relatively new area originally perceived by many as likely having the ½life of an ostrich blink. So far, no lawmakers had overturned it.

Larry Ellison always hovered in the Forbes Top 10 list of world billionaires (out of 500), while Bertram Brainard fluctuated in the hi-lo teens. Tom-Tom thought it was funny that both men's sons wanted not just to produce but to *act,* she admired them for that too, thought it kinda ballsy. More clicking & webdrowsy dowsing revealed that Ellison Jr had planned to make a flyboy flick with Taylor Lautner, he was going to give that wolfboy-faggot seven-point-five milli, but when Lautner found out his boss planned to costar, he walked—which pissed Tom-Tom off because the punk hadn't earned the right to such rude behavior (not that anyone ever has the right, but a guru using rudeness as a *teaching* tool is always welcome, and wolfboy aint no guru), he was acting like he was Kevin frickin Spacey when the frickin *reality* is you're just a neanderthal muscle-cunt who got *lucky*, no difference between you and the guy who picks up a mistakenly thrownaway winning lotto ticket while bending down to bag his dog's diarrhea. And *Brando* was going to pay Mila Kunis *five million* to be his love interest in a rags-to-rich-bitches lark called *The Ferrari Kid*, "from an idea by Biggie Brainard"—Dame Kunis walked too, the ol *conflict in schedule*. What bothered Tom-Tom the most was it'd been made clear to the hacktress from the *beginning* that her boss wanted to co-drive the vehicle (http://www.starpoopscoops.com) . . . what part of playing a sidekickwhore to Natalie Portman makes you think you're Helen Mirren?

TT did her ritualistic thing where she got down with the Tarots & called money, in the Year of the Moneybags she called $$$$$ and the ☆s and the spirits to fiduciarily bless her good works-to-come with untold bounty. She pounded H & nodded out in front of the http://www.celebritynetworth.com-displayed screen, just chilled a while like that, everything perfect, skagged feeling perfect now, even thinking *the cameras can show me slamming, cause that's me, Bad News needs to show the warts the good times & the bad times* maybe get a new butt buy one like Coco & Tahiri&Amber Rose . . . . still tho it was bothering her, not a lot but a little, that, try as she may, she hadn't yet arrived at that *unified theme,* like, what would she tell the networks was the big idea behind her Big Idea when they asked that kind of shit which they always do, she knew she could make a house full of (former) wannabe-wannabes *work* but before anybody commits to freakin *monetizing* they want to pick it apart, not like dumbcunt Crystal Lightweight, but in really *smart* ways, they knew how to pick

shit apart, they messed with your head until they wore you down &
even *you* started thinking your idea was so *loser.* Tom-Tom worried
that she needed a *fallback* when whatever entity she was pitching to
threw that fucked-up *But what's it really about?* curve in there, you
know *There needs to be a unifying goal, it's good that they want to be famous but for what, if it's just fame WE DON'T THINK THAT'S
ENOUGH* you know the Jews never made it easy on you, that was
their frickin job, that's why they were put on the planet, you always
needed to be a few steps ahead, to make you step up your game, if
they threw something at you you better catch it & throw it back
PDQ or they'll see you as *weak.* The Jews lived to watch you burn.

So on the couch Tom-Tom not nodding just gauzy smoking
blunt/Jack D crunkin the war between her and the Jews, back &
forth, it not being *enough,* her shit like not being patricia or *enough,* &
it being OK you know it's just *loosers* striving for *whatever,* fame or
normalcy or both together, just striving *not to be loosers,* same way a
fool on Celebrity Rehab strives for sobriety—no one would say trying to get/stay *sober* wasn't enough—you know it's all about the personalities & enmeshments anyhow, *that's* the fuckin Big Idea, Hymie,
the funny funky *drama* that hooks you, the frickin dramedy, like
don't get all hung up on the grand fucking *unified theme,* she went
back & forth like that thinking it/she was enough, & the *other,* that
anxiety-causing crazymaking still unformed hypothetical rejoinder
to the kikey producers' pigheaded insistence on a *unified field,* a Unifying Fucking Purpose, some endgame goal she was tripping on that
she/everyone would need to reach—*no no no, it was all good, it would
all work, it was all perfect,* EVERYTHING would work, the future was
the past the past was prologue the child was father to the man of the
future *perfect* which was all contained in the NOW, the show had *already frickin happened,* that's what she'd already read in the ☆s, she was
already the head of a *burgeoning empire,* all perfect, another little bump
to get the energy to call forth a few more $$$$ . . . . back to
the internet, googling sundry reality players, it said Snooki only had
$3 million which was a lot less than Tom-Tom thought, maybe they

didn't update the site yet in terms of endorsement bootie, though actually maybe the conservative estimates were probably more accurate, they *did* say she was making $33,000 an episode, Audrina had $12 million, *holyshit* you're fucking *Audrina* and you have *twelve million fucking dollars* how did *that* happen, Kelly Clarke had $24 million *ohhhhhhhh* she didn't even want to look up Carrie Underwood but she couldn't resist checking Adam Lambert, *oh oh oh* he had *$5 million*, okay that's enough with the false *Idols*—fucking *Omarosa* had ONE POINT FIVE . . . *milli*————may as well get lost in KardashianWorld, Kim only made forty an episode, that's what it said, she only had $35 million, Tom-Tom thought it'd be a lot higher tho the $$$$ pour in so fast for the Kardashes that it's probably hard for a site to keep up *keeping up with the Kardashian's money* anyway, that had to be wrong because Tom-Tom read that Kim was buying back her sextape for $30 million, their mom was an amazing businesswoman she would *never* allow Kim to spend all of her fortune that way plus the wedding *alone* cost $15 million, the divorce prolly netted 3 times that in PR, it said Kourtney & Khloé made twenty thousand an episode & each had four milli, that can't be right someone really needs to update this shit Tom-Tom thought she could reach 4 milli pretty fast, 4 milli seemed a reasonable short-term goal, Kris Jenner had $20 million which again needed to be seriously updated but that was only right, she's the mom, it was *her* pussy they clawed their way out of, *she* was the one who changed their diapies *and took their shit* hahahaahah! the son Rob was a real *looser,* maybe a good catch for *Bad News Bears*, even Rob Kardashian *Senior* had $3 million & he was fuckin *dead!!!!!* For some people the $$$$$ just keep raining down *no matter what*, even that sick fuck Scott Disick, who should have been taken into a basement & raped & tortured for stuffing money in that waiter's mouth, *never* treat food servers with anything less than *total respect*, that's how you take the measure of a man, the way he treats his *mother* & the way he treats *servers*, even that peacocking parasitical scarlet pimpernel FAIL Scott Disick had $2,000,000 USD net-worth——————& Olympian daddy *Bruce* had *one hundred million* in the bank, she wondered where they got *that* number, she hoped it *was* a hundred milli because that was fair too, he worked hard for it, plus he never lost his humility, he was a kind man, when she first started watching the show Tom-Tom h8ted on him because he looked like a tranny but now she knew he was going to be one of her heroes & guiding lights from her *own* Mount Olympus . . . .

. . . .

. . . . she typed in (Q̶ Brando Brainard net worth), the computer was sluggish, probably needed to RESTART but then the screen hiccups & she clicks on http://www.celebritynetworth.com/cate gory/richestbusinessmen/richest-billionaires/brando-brainard-net-worth/ and there it is: *THREE POINT EIGHT BILLION DOLLARS USD*!!!!!!!!!!!! (*INHERITANCE)*——*& with a little more fucking around she finds the press release*:

> Brando Brainard, CEO & Creative Head of Ooh Baby Baby Films, announced that Keira "Tommie" Thompson will be the new President & Head of Development of the company's two new television divisions, Hard To Get By Television and Just Upon A Smile TV. Brainard said Hard To Get By will focus on limited premium cable fare, while Just Upon A Smile will generate network and cable product, which includes reality and scripted reality programming. Thompson left SONY Pictures Television, where she was President & Head of Development for eight years. Before that she worked for Bernie Brillstein at Brillstein-Grey Entertainment.

Tommie Thompson . . . Tom Tom . . . Tom Tom Tommie . . . Thompson . . . ThomThom Tommie . . . Tom-Tom Tommie . . . Thompson Thompson---------

. . . everything was making sense. Coming full circle. Thus it was written . . . in the ☆s and the starz channel.

She'd make her move as soon as Rikki was cast.

She Google imaged Keira: *fuckin hottie* . . . .

Just Upon A Smile TV—future home of *Bad News Bears!*

It all felt so right that she felt like goofin, & typed it out. Made her own little hyperlink *fuck it'd already happened anyway right?* just to try it on for size & see what she could see:

http://www.celebritynetworth/richest-celebrities/tom-tom-hit-pop-singer-and-reality-star-BadNewsBears-net-worth/

YES.
She fell out.

[Reeyonna&Rikki]

I Had A Vision of Love

ReeRee

booked a table 10 days in advance but they still had to wait a ½ hour to be seated, which was OK because she loved to peoplewatch. She'd asked for one of the garden patio banquettes with silk pillows that yelp.com recommended, but the woman on the phone said those were all reserved. The woman also seemed to be pressing her to make her reservation online but Reeyonna liked connecting with a human voice.

They parked a few blocks away because it was hard for her to look elegant getting off a motorcycle plus she didn't like the judgment in people's eyes that she was a bad mom-to-be for riding one in the first place. (She did have a cool pink helmet though, which Rikki locked to the bike.) Reeyonna thought she would have been less self-conscious if it was a Harley because a pregnant gal on a Harley made kind of a bold, fun statement that people were more likely to accept as not being reckless. But the kawasaki was small & old, and the gas tank was dented.

ReeRee had the whole evening planned. After dinner they were going to stroll to Millions of Milkshakes. She didn't care that racist h8trs on urbanspoon said the servers were rude & poorly groomed; she watched Kim Kardashian & her mom open the Millions of Milkshakes in Dubai online, which was pretty amazing, and wanted to try a Kim Kardashian shake.

The hostess led them to a beautifully set table with fresh-cut flowers & candles, unlit as yet because it was still light out, and because she was peeing so much (her 7th month) it was actually really convenient to be next to the bathroom. She told Rikki that the "restauranteur"-owner was actually one of the real housewives of Beverly Hills, then wondered aloud if Lisa Vander-pump would be there tonight. Reeyonna skipped lunch to be extra hungry—5PM was the only time Sur had a free slot, and she guessed that was why the crowd looked older. Paparazzi weren't even there yet.

She felt rich. The pawnshop gave her $2,100 for probably $30,000 worth of cameras and equipment, maybe more (*ask me if I care*), in crisp one-hundreds. They hadn't done anything fancy or fun since she stopped living at home & Reeyonna decided to treat them to Sur. The JustSpotted app on her android was always telling her people like Lisa Collins and Heather Morris and Kevin Dillon and Sharon Stone & Chaz Bono were having lunch or dinner here & she had a file of vids too of Hayden & Paz and Emmy Ros. & Miley and Selena all leaving Sur at different times (**www.x17video.com/celebrity video/**). She really hoped she would see someone famous tonight as kind of a reward for all the hard times she/they'd been having. (Right after they ordered, her phone said Britney was leaving a movie theater with her kids at the Malibu Lumberyard, Julia Stiles was filming in Barstow and *justspotted* leaving a Starbucks there, & Shia LaBeouf was entering a steakhouse across the street from the Standard in New York City's glamorous meatpacking district.) Still, Reeyonna wasn't raising her hopes too high because when she made the reservation she was told they could seat them at 5 as long as they could be *out* by 630, it almost sounded like they would have to sign a contract when they got there. ReeRee knew that celebrities generally didn't eat until at least nine or 10, at least not younger ones.

She decided none of it really mattered because for the 1st time since leaving home, Reeyonna felt like a human being. They did some MDMA & went shopping before their early dinner. ReeRee bought herself a stunning dress from Ovum, the Kardashian's new maternity line, and really *did* feel JustSpotted redcarpet glamorous. (She got Rikki an *amazing* beautiful shirt from Kitson, & jeans from 7For All Mankind.) She always wanted to own a pair of Louboutins and last week found a barely pre-walked pair online for $165. She wore bangles and nugget earrings from Belle Noel, Kim's jewelry collection, with lots of beauty products knocking around in her purse, selecting what *People* said Kim and HeMo and Rachel Bilson had in *theirs*—FusionBeauty Lip Plump Color Shine in Flirt, Dior Style Liner liquid liner in Black, Motives pressed eyeshadow in Toast, Joico Flexible Shaping Spray & Joico hairspray. Getting rid of those cameras made her feel better too, like she had cut off another dead piece of her mother that was weighing her down.

Her grandma used to say, "Don't just do something—sit there!" It felt so magical to just *sit,* to sit with your man in the ☆y ambience of an amazing Hollywood restaurant and be waited on by pretty, young, happy-faced servers, talented, gorgeous people with probably the same exotic/normal hopes and dreams you had, actors, singer-songwriters & painters, plus Reeyonna thought a lot of them were more like her too in that they didn't necessarily think of themselves as "artists" but of the type, say, who might want to become crime scene investigators or forensic pathologists should they have the time and money to go to med school or whatever school or lab you needed to go train. The servers made you feel good about yourself, they wanted you to love the food and the ambience (how could you not?), they wanted you just to be *you,* & to love yourself because if you *did*, it would be so *obvious*, you would *shine*, and shine your light on *others*, thus making it easier for them to love *themselves* even if it looked like they already did because a person could always love themselves *more* and the more they loved *themselves* the greater their love could be for *you* and the whole *world*. From their table Reeyonna saw part of a huge stone statue in the garden dining area (the person she spoke to on the phone said the garden tables were booked 6 months ahead at minimum), which their server (an actor, gay, who said he'd just done a *New Girl*) told them was an Indian god called Shiva. Shiva was young and freshfaced handsome, just like one of the servers, he looked so amazing and peaceful, a little like Ryan Seacrest but more manly,

Shiva's smile reminded her of Adam Levine's right at that moment when his eyes are closed in blissful meditation and he's about to press the button before the others. As Reeyonna sat there taking everything in she decided not even to let the baby weight she put on—30 lbs.—upset her. On the ride over they passed a Nike billboard that said you are entirely up to you, make your body, make your life, make yourself. She'd learn a lot from Nike ads/affirmations & decided now was the perfect time to truly "make" this body—and this life—her own. Because suddenly it was *so clear* how a small ripple that began with a romantic dinner at Sur between two people who loved each other & loved their *servers* and all the patrons too on a faultless dusk soon-to-be (not soon enough!) night in West Hollywood (as Shiva & perhaps some older celebrities in the garden looked on) could expand and travel one knew not where, becoming a wave of light & love that helped to make the world a better place.

OMG the food was *crazy* good. She couldn't wait to bring her BFFs here, she missed them so much! Since she ran away everyone was planning to get together but something always happened and it got fucked up. ReeRee had the shrimp dumpling appetizer that http://www.twisting-the-nosh-away/sur-menu-faves/ said was a fave of the Olsens & Rikki had the calamari Jimmy Fallon scarfed whenever he was on the "Left Coast." For their salads, Rikki chose the Fantasia (HeMo said it was to die for) and Ree settled on the deceptively simple amazingly fresh house salad. A taste bud treat! For her entree, she ordered the vegetarian Arborio rice that Alicia Silverstone, Amber Tamblyn & Anna Paquin found so alluring (Mrs. Paquin Moyer also adored the lemon picada chicken) & Rikki got the Ahi tuna that Lamar & Khloé twittered about. For dessert? A blackberry cobbler that Sur's Facebook page said Dr. Drew always ordered "without fail" (also a fave of the late Jeff Conaway and the late Mike Starr), & a trio of sorbets which happened to be loved by the trio of Ivanka Trump, Ashlee Simpson & Lake Bell.

After three glasses of wine, ReeRee made up her mind to not just *do* something, *sit* there—meaning, past the verbally contracted 6:30PM ultimatum. It wasn't until 6:45 that the hostess approached with a sweetly pained expression to say she needed their table, which by then was totally fine. ReeRee had proved her point, that she was someone to be reckoned with.

They sauntered out. Still no paparazzi & the night was still bright.

. . .

They took Coldwater then turned left, west on Mulholland, tracing the mountain's spine until they reached a lookout with benches facing the Valley. Rikki lit a joint & they smoked for a while, standing/straddling the little bike like a wooden horse and staring into the glittertwink.

"Rikki, I want to move out of that house."

Silence.

Wind.

All of the lights, above & below.

She was buzzed from the weed and the 7.5 vikes.

The MDMA was fading . . .

"We can find like a little apt above a garage in Hollywood or even the Valley. On Craigslist month to month."

Silence & whistly wind between silences.

"I just keep having this *feeling*, I've had it since I got pregnant. That once we get a home of our *own,* good shit'll start to happen for us."

They got off the bike and stood on the lip of the lookout where the grass met the dirt of the hill. Teenage wastedland. A good 10 minutes standing & staring into the bejeweled voidspace of the world. Benched themselves. Took in cityscape & night sky. Finished the blunt. Bathed in ½-wind/½-breeze, ½-warm/½-cool. ReeRee goosebumpshivered. *Holyshit I am so loaded Rikki this shit is so intense I am so, soooooooooooo fucking stoned.*

Jus sittin on the dark of the bench . . . wastin' time. Wasted—

This bench is so weird . . .

. . . does it seem weird to you?

wind and silence wind and silence silence wind *swhoosh swhoosh swhoosh* what *IS* that. Oh. Cars. Three cars. That's so weird they're behind us but it totally sounded like they were in front of us. In the sky. A fourth one slows—a couple looking for their own empty lookout. They clock Ree & Rikki & then the car vanishes.

Half a *swhoosh* . . . .

"Rikki, you have *got* to promise me *one thing*, you *have to*. Our baby is going to be *beautiful* but if something's wrong with it which there will *not* be but if there *is* you have to *totally promise* you will love it like you would a baby who was *perfect*." *Crying now.* "Because what I'm saying is there is *no such thing* as a baby who isn't *totally fucking perfect*. Will you promise?"

"Shit yeah. Course I will."

She liked the firmness of his response. In that unexpected, cool voice she began to sing *I am beautiful no matter what they say* trailing it off to nothingness/voidspace again.

Then:

Quiet inward ruminations on both ends.

Then:

"You know, maybe I'll get that movie."

"OMG, wouldn't that be *insane?*" Her own voice startles her and she realizes how stoned she is again. But so *happy!* "How much do you think you'd get paid?"

"I don't know. Shit. They gotta give me sumthin," he said humbly, ever aware not to jinx.

"Probably like a hundred thousand? I am *so proud of you for doing that, Rikki*. I mean you fucking suited up & showed up, which is way more than *I've* been doing."

"You're doing a *lot*. You're fuckin having a *kid*. That's *amazing*. That's *serious*, I couldn't do that shit."

"Did I tell you that? How proud I was of you? OMG I don't

even think I *did*, I've been a total *fucking bitch*. Ima *crazy* hormones. But listen to me Rikki are you listening I really want you to listen and hear this, it is *so fucking amazing* you even *did* that & that your *audition* was with Michael Douglas & Laurence Fishburne! OMG! How bitchen and magical is that? Did I ever tell you I really only started getting into *CSI really late*? Like when *Laurence Fishburne* came on the show? He is *so totally* the reason I wanted to become a crime scene investigator. He was *totally* in my vision."

"Vision?"

She grabbed Rikki's hand & held it to her belly for the babykick.

"Whoa," said Rikki. "Boy's gunna be a soccer superstar."

"Unless it's a *girl*."

"Then *girl'll* be a soccer superstar."

Quiet. Just wind, light. Warm. Lovely. His arm around her.

"I had this *total vision* of our life. A few weeks ago. I mean, of the life we could have, *will* have. I didn't tell you about it because I thought you'd laugh."

"I wouldn't laugh, Ree."

He kissed her cheek & caressed her hair. Daubed an already flat tear on her cheekbone with one of his knuckles she liked that.

"We were in all the magazines————!"

"Is that right?" he said, happy to go along. Happy she was out of bitch mode, happy to be having kind of a chummy little bullshit romantic moment even if he wasn't attracted to her, even if he thought he never would be again, even if just the thought of fucking her made him want to puke. But happy and glad tho, just now, to be talkin about when they'd be ballin . . .

"I was pushing one of these really expensive strollers, with our toddler. & you were holding Baby #2 in your arms. & there were already all these articles about how fast I shed my baby weight."

"So we're gunna have two?"

"Maybe *more*," she smiled.

"Was I ripped? I mean, am I gunna be ripped? You can at least give me a six-pack."

"You already *have* one. But yeah, in my vision you're *totally* ripped, like Cameron Diaz!"

"Hey that ain't right."

"OK Jennifer Garner then. No seriously. In my *vision,* there was a toddler and a newborn. I can't explain it but it was like way *more* than a daydream. I saw in my head this magazine, right? And I wasn't even stoned. Well maybe a little. & in the magazine there was this shot of Tom, Katie & *Suri* next to a shot of Ben & Jennifer and Violet & Seraphina. And next to *them* was *you* & *me,* our *family.*"

"What did we name our kids?"

"It didn't say. In the vision. But *you* were the famous one, it was really clear about that."

"Famous for what?"

"Like, movies & television."

"Aw-*ite.* Tha's tight. I can live with that, without the Cameron Diaz part, I don't wanna be lookin like no Cammy D!"

"In the vision, Laurence Fishburne took you under his wing but you became more famous. And he was a gentleman about it, he didn't become envious or bare a grudge. In my vision, you're like as famous as Will Smith, who by the way we are going to be *very* close with, their kids are much older but like, Jada's gunna be our kids' godmom."

"Jada's one of their kids?"

"*No,* Jada *Pinkett,* Will's *wife*————"

"O yeah! The swingers & shit? The swinger shit's dope."

"————and I've already finished forensics school. I *could* have worked for the city like the city of Los Angeles, for the LAPD, the city really *wanted* me to but I decided to just, like, be a consultant on *CSI.* That way I can spend more time home with the kids. And even though he's not on the show anymore, because Laurence is our *friend,* he helped get me the *job.* On *CSI.* Right?"

"That's right, he's family. I mean the mutherfucker *made* me. Always did me a solid, just like Denzel to Antwone. Hey, are we gunna have a sextape?"

"*No.* Well———we *might* have. No, *I* know! Someone hacked nude pics that I took on my cell & sent you in middleschool, I was totally underage but they're these amazing———"

"I know the one's you're talking about."

"No you *don't*, not *these* ones, because I'm totally making it *up!* Anyway, I'm *amazing* looking & they're *totally tastefully done*, like Scarlett's, I totally look bitchen & our publicist—our publicist is going to say 'Reeyonna's not ashamed of those pictures' & I'll give interviews like Heather Morris and Kreayshawn did about theirs, saying very cool & calm that I knew they would eventually come to light. But in my vision, I probably have to change my *name*, there can't be *two* famous Reeyonnas!"

"*Say ma name same ma name*————how about using Jerilynn?"

(*playful*) "Fuck you!"

"Hey, in your vision, do you like have us goin into rehab and shit?"

"NO. Well . . . . *maybe*. It's not in my *vision* but maybe there's some kinda *drama* everybody's going to want to write about on the internet, you know, something that makes people feel closer to us, lets em see we're human beings too, you know, like 'stars are just like them'————& *o!* And we have like *6 million followers* on Twitter!"

"Right on."

"Maybe *you* go to rehab . . . . ."

"Hey now c'mon be fair."

"And our publicist like says 'Rikki realized he had a problem with the painkillers he was taking after recent surgery on his knee————
——'"

"Hey that's in *your* vision, not *mine*. *I* ain't goin to no rehab."

"—————all like 'Rikki *knew* he had to do something about it.' You'll like go to Promises right near our Malibu beach house but it's like a one-time thing. You get day passes anyway because you'll have one of those sober companions. If *I* went to rehab, it'd have to be like for something that wasn't drugs, like for bipolar or maybe outing myself for bulimia. And when I got out I'd go on all the talk-shows, like Ellen & Anderson Cooper & maybe even become a spokesperson for raising awareness in teens."

"Where did you say we were living again?"

"Well, we have a beach house in Malibu, like next to all our celebrity friends. But we'd have a house up *here* too, on Mulholland. And on weekends we'd go to the beach & barbecue with friends, like Scarlett & Naya & Minka & all the Kardashians, whoever's in town. And Katniss Everdeen! We'd be tight with Matthew McConaughey and his wife, our kids are gunna play with their kids. (Their kids are *Levi* & *Vida*, I *so* love those names.) Matthew would teach our son to surf. And Laird Hamilton, he lives in Malibu with Gabrielle. We'll probably have a house in Hawaii & also a big apt in NY, maybe in the same building as Carrie Bradshaw."

"I want to be friends with some *rappers*, girl. Are we tight with the youngmoney crew? I want to be all partying with Drizzy and shit."

Reeyonna froze, putting her palm flat on her pant pocket. Rikki said,

"Cause we need to be down with Weezy & Ye." He saw the blood run out of her face. "What's the matter girl?"

"My wallet————————————————"

"Your purse—in the pouch?"

"No, I don't *think*," she said, trancelike. "I've been carrying it with me. It has all the money . . . ."

"Hold on. Hold on. We'll find it. You had it at the restaurant cause that's how we paid, right? With the money."

Reeyonna didn't answer.

She got up and ran to the pouch—nothing. Shocky, she walked to where they 1st stood, where the hill begins to slope down. "Where's your phone?" she said.

They crouched down as he shined the phone here & there.

"We need to go back————————*OMG*. O M G!"

"Don't lose your wig, Ree. We'll find it. We're *gunna find it*. Cmon, let's go back. To the restaurant."

As they climbed on the bike he asked her why she was carrying all cashmoney anyway. She said because she thought Tom-Tom might go thru her shit & steal it.

"Rikki, if I lost that money I'm going to fucking kill myself."

"No you're not."

"I am. I'm serious."

This time it's lively at Sur.

6 or 7 paparrazzi out front . . . .

Rikki waits for the hostess while ReeRee goes to look in the bathroom. There is zero chance the wallet would be in there but in her dreamlike moment of desperation, she wouldn't be surprised to find herself checking her socks to see if the money found its way to the bottom of her foot or on the way home maybe searching the high branches of tall dark faraway trees.

The hostess is kind, but there's only a sad solitary set of keys in the makeshift lost & found drawer. *Have you asked the valet?* Rikki says, we didn't valet park. Oh, uhm, OK. *Well give me your name & your number & we'll call if it turns up. Sometimes things just turn up.*

Reeyonna tells him she's going back to where they 1st parked for dinner. She walks then runs. Two ♥s pounding, hers & the little one's . . . she actually starts getting hopeful because she's already visualizing the wallet in the gutter, she can *see* it fortuitously hidden in shadow from potential thieves. She has these strong *visions* . . . sees herself grabbing it with joyful expulsion of breath & preg-sprinting back to Sur screaming *I found it! Rikki, I found it!* Can *hear* herself saying that—both laughing at the averted horror then going to celebrate at Millions of Milkshakes which for some reason they'd fatefully forgotten to before . . .

Rikki decided he might as well take a piss. The hostess kind of eyed him as he came in again and walked past, that trespassy look subtly informing that a courtesy was being bestowed because his right to pee had expired.

He stood at the urinal. Someone flushed then opened the stall door, no stench. The man went to the sink to wash. Rikki stole a glance—Laurence Fishburne.

And the actor was gone.

[Jacquie]

Toiling, Spinning

The

family loved the hospital portraits. The experience of going to their Northridge home with proofsheets—watching Ginger bend like a scholar to look through the loupe—was something Jacquie would never forget. The husband was at work, & Jacquie was glad. For a man, the death of his infant was a cold, finite event; for two moms, a chance to commune with a firefly soul that seemed just then to be as present as it was incorporeal. Yet for all Jacquie's supernal rationalizations—the baby's quicksilver, inextinguishable life force must be grieved over yet not mourned, a specious riddle reinforced by the mom's truly spiritual equanimity, born, reasoned Jacquie, by the knowledge of the Great Mother that we are wont to finally seek that plot of infinite lilies of the field—for all Jacquie's tiny, supernatural theories, each calculated to minimize and repress, to expunge & make *palatable* the horror of what happened, on the way to her car she felt the unbearable, queasy sorrow of living-mother/dead-child aloneness like a gust of hot propeller wind at her back & feared with each step she might turn to stone.

· · ·

She was still searching for a way to reclaim her own firefly soul; that of the artist she'd begun to fear was no more. Her life had capsized, trapping her beneath.

Then she read something that yanked her back with some hilarity to HelmutWorld & the boomboom years of his mentorship, her artful schooling in the theory & practice of all things photoshock. According to DailyMailOnline, there'd been a great to-do down under. A peer of Jacquie's who'd shown at the Guggenheim and the Venice Biennale was in hot water. A major show in Sydney had been cancelled due to complaints over pics of a nude 13-year-old girl; a clear case (for Jacquie) of *déjà nu*. Child protection advocates were incensed; the exhibit was shut down; images seized by police under the Crimes Act. Naturally, the Newtonian Laws of Negative Press prevailed and held true—a censorship hurlyburly ensued on a national level and the revolted Prime Minister leapt dutifully into the fray. But the artist needn't fear, as celebrity help was on its way (Newton's 2nd Law) in nothing less than the form of Cate Blanchett captaining her team in pursuit of Australia's prestigious A Cup. Newton's *Third* wrapped things up nicely in the end with a press release: *The New South Wales Dept of Public Prosecutions announced that no charges would be filed.*

Jacquie had a wild, mad laugh about it, the kind of huge, careless, orgiastic, toxin-busting guffaws that borderline personalities are known to indulge in the privacy of their homes. She sorely missed the man, his dry wit and wry level-headedness, his kinks & light-hearted gravitas, the charm and wisdom of his cynically uncynical counsel too. Now that she was having another *non-career* crisis, where the fuck was Helmut when you really needed him? She had the great good fortune of supping with him the night before he died. Jacquie had been oeuvre-hustling in LA, she was a bit rusty and out of her league but Helmut graciously insisted she join them for dinner at Il Sole: he & his wife June, Uma Thurman & Andre Balazs, Benedikt/Angelika Taschen, plus Jacquie & her date Pieter Wogg, a specialist at

Christie's who was a fan of way more than Jacquie's pictures. (She used to say, "You only love me for my body of work.") Helmut told everyone at the table how excited he was because "tomorrow, Cadillac is *giving* me an Escalade!" The next day, pulling out of the Chateau garage presumably to take the car for a trial spin, he dropped dead behind the wheel and crashed into a retaining wall.

She tried to hear his voice in her head, telling her what to do next, propping her up like he used to with trilingual pep talks, propounding that she still had it, if only she could step out of her own way, promising her that inspiration would come as long as she cultivated that certain je ne sais quoi *shtick*-to-it-iveness. But it was an old CD. Jacquie had never really been able to escape Phase One of Newton's Master Plan. She'd never even made it from hairless to bush leagues . . . something happened, she'd lost her faith & self-confidence, & began to spend her days trying to figure out how not to die instead of how she might live. Whatever artistry left in her was stunted, remedial, irrelevant. She failed miserably at the 2.0 thing, failed to transform herself from Mann manqué cartographer of flat tit mysteries/pretween genito-urinary landscapes into a swan that knew exactly what it was—a mature artist, take her or leave her.

Lately, she'd come *close* to feeling the breath & hand of her wily mentor, in that she alit on a few things she thought he'd have heartily approved. Jacquie saw something on the CNN site about a 76-year-old Tokyo man, a former travel agent with a wife & children now making his living as an actor in the booming genre they called "elder porn." She seriously considered flying to Japan to take his portrait—& tracking down other *salami men*—but it took lots of money to travel around like that. Unless she had a really strong feeling about it, which she didn't, there wasn't much point. She couldn't afford to be lukewarm quixotic.

Another thing that got her attention was an article in *People* that came out in the weeks after Gabrielle Giffords got shot called I SURVIVED A BULLET TO THE HEAD. Among the gallery of unfortunates was a 21-year-old cheerleader turned dental assistant whose injury necessitated the removal of a bizarrely visible chunk of skull and brain; her head looked like a clock missing that slice of 9-to-midnight pie—nothing but airspace. She was fully functional, arriving at her own homecoming queen ceremony in wheelchair & helmet. Another fine specimen was a young man who miraculously recovered from a bullet fired into his cerebellum when he was 5 years-old—the shooter was his dad, who killed his brother, strangled his mom then shot himself to death. *Far be it from me to suggest psychotherapy.* Jacquie thought maybe she could hit the road with the goal of taking 25 portraits of Americans who survived those kind of head wounds. She clipped something the cheerleader had said, "This is my new normal," which Jacquie thought would make a helluva title for a book: *The New Normal.*

Um, well, I have a new normal too: career death & poverty, and severely damaged children who hate & rob me.

Ain't that a kick in the head?

. . .

She couldn't believe it: *Pieter* was friend requesting. They'd been out of touch for a few years. He was living in London now, coming to L.A. next week. *Hey let's just pick up where we left off,* he wrote, in a light & funny way, so he wouldn't feel so rejected if Jacquie was in a relationship or whatever.

He took her to a wonderful Moroccan restaurant called Tagine that he'd been "obsessing about." (A typically gay Pieter phrase.) He told her that James Franco recommended it to him—the actor recently collaborated with Gus Van Sant & Michael Stipe on a mixed media installation at the gallery Pieter worked for in the UK—as a place where the odds were good for running into cast members of *Glee,* the show he said he was unfortunately "*still* fucking obsessed with & *it's so over.*" *O boy,* he'd gotten *so much gayer* than she remembered. "James said the glee club gather at *three distinct* watering holes:

Tagine, Sur or The Little Door. So before I blow this town, I'm going to take you to each one."

They jogged/ambled down a rather short & narrow Memory
Lane—they'd only had a six-month thing. Oddly, the cork in the affair had been the dinner party at Il Sole; they spent the night together, & that was that. They'd only seen each other a handful of
times since Helmut died, in '04.

Pieter did most of the talking. He left Christie's a while ago & for
the last three years worked at Gagosian. He said he had "important,
ongoing relationships" with major collectors, but the *real* perks were
impulsive road trips with Damien Hirst, pubcrawl/clubbing with
Tracey Emin, and late night suppers with "the Richards," Serra &
Prince.

"I have never been so fulfilled *professionally*." He raised a ridiculous
eyebrow & *ahem'd*. "On the *personal*, um*hem*, *romantic* front . . . well,
it's been a bit of a bloody trainwreck. Tho the phrase *living hell* also
comes to mind. Yes, I think living hell is a bit closer to the mark. Not
closer to, really, but perhaps the mark *itself*." She loved it when he
lapsed into his Steve Coogan doing Hugh Grant/Hugh Laurie routine. "Wait a moment, wait a moment—somehow *living hell* doesn't
quite capture the full . . . *catta-strofe*. So let's just call it a *natural disaster*.
Let's then—no! an *unnatural* disaster. That's *much* better. A calamity,
a major *calamity*, a major *colostomy* . . . a fucking *eschatological colostomy*
of fucking *Biblical* proportions *i.e.* I believe that I can *safely say* that *on
a personal level* the last few years have been what historians of this sort
of thing will call the *tsunamification* of hope, of *any* hopes or dreams
that Pieter Wogg might have had that he would find love, and the
marriage & requisite children that often follow. Yes. This is that volume—I am *living* that volume—Volume 4, of the massive biography—this is that volume entitled *Dreams Deferred*. I continue to prowl
the night, of course. Hope springs nocturnal. As do many other . . .
things."

He was more adorable than handsome, which went a long way,
with a capacious bag of immensely personable tricks. Pieter always

made her laugh; Jacquie & Albie agreed the cliché was true—"funny" got laid first. It felt good being out in the world with an old lover. To feel like a woman again.

She'd almost forgotten.

He reminded her more than once when they got back to his suite at the Chateau. Memory Lane grew, hope sprang, all that.

She brought with her a 5 by 7 of the portrait she took of Ginger, Daniel & their baby. When she showed him Pieter got very quiet, & Jacquie wondered if a stillbirth or child death figured somewhere in his calamity of natural and unnatural disasters. She stepped out on the balcony, to let him be.

Good lord. How beautiful the city was! If she were a god, she'd have reached out and grabbed it to wear around her neck. Her cellphone rang & her heart leapt—it was 1:30AM & no one but Jerilynn would be calling (she'd been keeping the phone in her pocket not her purse for that very reason). She looked in at Pieter, to see if it was him being funny, but he was still completely engrossed.

"Hello?"

"May I speak with Jacquie Vomes?"

"This is she."

A hesitation, then:

"Did I wake you?"

"No. Who is this?"

"I'm so sorry to be calling this late. Ginger MacMannis gave me your number. Well actually she gave it to my son-in-law. She said you were enormously helpful."

"What's this about?"

"The doctors said they don't expect my grandchild to make it till the morning." Her voice broke. "We're all preparing for a loss."

"Where are you calling from?"

"Scottsdale. We're at the Mayo Clinic."

[Telma&Biggie]

The Children's Hour

Servers

set up lunch on a gilded, baroque table beside the large stream that flowed thru the grotto/cave (a continuous loop) at the far edge (*which* edge Telma knew not) of the property, an unthinkable 112-acres in the heart of the heart of Bel-Air. Biggie's dad bought the original 30-acre property from Louis Trotter, the waste & excavation king, adding on whenever adjacent parcels became available. The land and three houses sitting on it—all other homes had been razed upon purchase—were owned by Closely Held Holdings, a corporation whose sole shareholders were Biggie, his brother Brando, their father Bertram, and Bonnie the absentee mom.

The enormous structures were approximately a mile apart. Each was inhabited by a single resident (Brando in the Gehry, Biggie in the Neff, Bertram in the Paul Williams), conjoined by seamless Calatrava-commissioned glass corridors, though no one had actually ever used the walkways to go from house to house, at least not to anyone's memory. Brainard Sr. hadn't left his classic Hollywood Regency since Bonnie vanished (five years ago come spring), & in fact was rarely seen at all; occasionally, Brando would report to Biggie he espied their father at some ghastly hour of night during a storm, slowly, meditatively making his way a ¼-mile or so into the wind &

rain-battered, unbreakable glass cocoon, his Meerschaum Calabash in hand, an insomniac spurned by his succubus, a cuckolded Sherlock lacking the balm of opiates to alleviate the distress of cracking a case for which he would never be hired: The Wife Who Would Not Return.

"Was this here . . . *before?*" said an uncomprehending, nearly bug-eyed Telma, in reference to the cave and underground mini-river. They took an elevator to get there, and Telma noted it hadn't been a particularly *short* ride down.

"We finished last year. I think it's illegal—the city thought we were putting in retaining walls. My dad said it's some kind of architectural wonder."

Her salmon & watercress salad just sat there.

"But what's it *for?*"

"Uhm, my mom's a spelunker. She goes all over the world exploring caves, ones with rivers flowing through. She always sends post-cards. She sent me one from the Deer Cave in Borneo. And one from the Caucasus Mountains—it's the deepest in the world. She sent one from the *longest* cave. That's in Kentucky."

"Is that where she is *now?* Somewhere in a *cave?*"

"She sent one from Vietnam with a picture of where she and Marj were spelunking. The Vietnam cave is the *biggest* one in the *world*. But the card took really long to get here so maybe they already left. It's called Hang Son Doong, & it's in the Annamite Mountains. National Geographic said the ceilings are 800-feet high. It said you can fit six 40-story skyscrapers inside *one cave*."

"Who's Marj?"

"My mom's buddy."

"Doesn't your mom have email?"

"No. Not really. I don't think so. She never gave me one. I think she probably just writes postcards and letters."

"That's so weird."

He ignored her comment. Telma regretted having made it.

"Sometimes the only way from one cave to another is by an underground *river.* They have all kinds of breathing systems, you know, aqualungs, you can go for 5 hours without surfacing. But if you use the river to swim to a new cave, and you have to go underwater for 10 or 15 minutes to get there, and on the way back, after you're walking around and exploring the new cave, if on the way back something goes wrong with your equipment or you run out of oxygen, the cave becomes your tomb."

"How horrible!"

"Because there isn't any way back but through the river. That's why my mom and Marj use the buddy system. If one of them has an equipment failure, they can still get back because they could take turns with the oxygen on the way back. That's why they explore together. You just can't spelunk alone."

Telma thought *OMG so rad so crazy!* & for a moment was mindlessly giddy. She stood up, made a few scrunchy elastic gargoyle faces, then sprinted alongside the river, demonically pirouetting as she went.

She stopped, about half a 747 away from her host.

"Hull there!" she shouted.

There was a faint echo.

"Biggie! How *deep* is it? How *deep* is the *river!*"

"Maybe 4½, 5 feet?" He spoke normally but the subterranean acoustics made him easy to hear. "You can program how fast you want to make the current—or make it so there's no current at all."

"Can we *swim* in it?" she asked, slowly venturing back while doing a jig.

"*I* don't, but *you* can. I like to rowboat."

"Let's *rowboat!*" She was positively Dionysian. "But where does it *go*? Where does the river *go*?"

"It just loops around."

"This is so much radder than Disneyland!"

"The whole thing goes for like maybe four miles?"

"*O my God.*"

She could barely contain herself. After a few more cartwheels, she resumed her place at the table. Biggie was halfway through a 4-tiered club sandwich, the most beautiful club sandwich Telma had ever seen. She wanted to marry him.

"Will you come with me to the Courage Ball?"

"Sure. What is it?"

"It's St. Ambrose's annual fundraiser for pediatric oncology. I'm actually going to perform."

This, announced with less than usual verve, owing to the development with the Canadian girl.

"Will you tell Camino so she can put it in the calendar? I'm really bad at remembering that kind of stuff."

"*Beyoncé*'s performing too!"

The elevator opened and a server stepped out, along with Camino, who stood by while he cleared the table before setting down goblets of hot fudge sundaes.

"Camino, Telma wants me to come with her to . . ." He turned to his guest. "To what is it again?"

"The Courage Ball, on the 19th."

Telma wasn't sure if his forgetting was normal or maybe a part of what was wrong with him. Camino swiftly handed her a card with all her contact information and Telma said she would forward the invitation. Then Camino told Biggie that his other guest had arrived—"a Mr. Bud Wiggins."

"What does he want?"

"Your brother said it's about one of your projects. He said you made the appointment yourself."

"O! *I* know what it's about. My *Antigone*."

The server stepped back into the lift after setting down a fresh pitcher of pink lemonade. Camino followed him, and briefly held the door to keep it from closing.

"Shall I say that you're on the way up?"

"As soon as we finish our dessert."

Camino smiled, the door closed, & they ascended.

"What's *Antigone*?" asked Telma.

"It's a Greek play."

"What's it about?"

Biggie just shrugged. Telma thought he might be getting tired, but she'd be going soon & had to ask one more question.

"She didn't come home even when she was in Kentucky?"

Biggie didn't respond. It was as if he hadn't heard her. The silence was awkward but she decided to ride it out.

"Kentucky has the longest cave in the world. It's called the Mammoth Cave and it's over 350 miles long. I always Google Earth whatever cave my mom and Marj are exploring."

Telma wasn't sure if the oddness of his response was due to Asperger's (her mom put that in her head) or something as-yet undiagnosed & more serious.

"My mom sends me postcards, she doesn't do email. They're spelunkers," he said, wrinkling his forehead. "My mom and Marj. That's why we put the cave in. Because it's undiscovered, and she loves finding new caves. If you're going to be a spelunker, you have to live by the buddy system."

·   ·   ·

Biggie looked away as Bud shook his hand. They sat in the living room, Bud making awkward desultory talk while Biggie majorly fidgeted. Then Biggie stood, motioning for Bud to come along; the rest of the meeting was held in the boy's bedroom.

"Your brother tells me you're the idea man."

Bud felt like he was auditioning for a reality show.

Biggie was already engaged in front of the monitor; without taking his eyes from it, he told Bud to come closer. The writer wheeled up a chair and looked over Biggie's shoulder.

"Is that Google Earth?"

Bud never used it before. Biggie said he was in Vietnam, at a great cave. He used his "man on the street" cursor to fly over hillocks & mountains. The sea level indicator rose and fell.

"You can't go *inside* the caves, but you can see all around them. You can even see the parking lot where people leave their cars."

"Pretty amazing." (And it was.)

"You're not on Wikipedia," said Biggie.

Oy. "Thank God," said Bud—which would have been a not brilliant but OK response if Biggie had asked why he wasn't on Facebook or Twitter, those being things one could elect to be a part of or not. Whereas a Wiki page was created without one's participation or approval, based solely on the small or large mark one had made in general society. Bud prayed the boy would just let it go; he didn't feel like being busted.

"So," said Biggie. "My brother said that you—can you refresh me as to why you're here again?"

Whatever was wrong with the kid happened, at the moment, to work in Bud's favor.

"Your brother said you had an idea . . . Brando said you had *lots* of ideas—but I guess the one he said he wanted you to talk to me about was a drama. And not a comedy. He said it wasn't mainstream. Your brother's hiring me to write the script of it. He wanted us to meet, so you could pitch me the idea."

"O! Right! My *Antigone!*" He actually turned to look at Bud. "Have you read the play?"

"In college," Bud lied. He hadn't read it *or* gone to college.

"Can I just email you the article my idea is based on?"

"Whatever works."

He wrote down his email; Biggie sent the attachment right then.

"Your name's Bud," he said, swiveling in his chair again to face him.

"Correct."

"My brother likes *high concept* but I'm moving away from that. I'll still feed him ideas. Though it's starting not to feel right anymore."

Bud understood exactly what the kid meant. Maybe Brando was right. Maybe they *would* become soulmates. Maybe Bud would move in after all.

Biggie turned back to the screen. "What's your address? I mean, to where you live?"

He realized that his host wanted to travel to Bud's home via Google Earth. He gave him Dolly's address in the flats; if he was faster on his feet, he would have given him Tolkin's. As Biggie entered "111 S Cañon," Bud said, "It's a little apartment in Beverly Hills that I only use to write"—he knew the building was going to look shitty & radiate loserdom. The saving grace was, he had a feeling the kid's pathology precluded him from judgment.

Just when Bud was fantasizing that the satellite images would be fucked up or hopelessly scrambled, a perfect photo of the front of the apartment house coalesced into crystal clarity. You could even see the car that belonged to the Vietnamese owner parked in the driveway. Biggie did his man-on-the-street thing, and began to walk around the building. Bud had never seen anything like it. Suddenly, they were on the south side, looking into Bud's room, the room he had lived in intermittently for over 40 years. For a moment, the screenwriter panicked, thinking that Biggie could make an adjustment that might show Bud inside masturbating, an activity he engaged in four to five times a week to burn off nervous energy and facilitate creativity. Biggie continued his saunter around to the back of the building, where Dolly's old Lincoln Mark IV had been parked with two flat tires for the last five years. She no longer had a license (she wouldn't physically be able to drive it even if she did), but refused for nostalgic reasons to have it towed for the tax write-off. Bud asked Biggie to "walk" to the rear of the car and focus on the license plate—there it was, DOLLYXXX . Biggie flew to the front of the building to show him another feature, one that allowed you to go back in time and see what the place looked like from the first day that Google had photographed it ten years ago . . . they watched how the façade of the building had changed year to year with the Vietnamese woman's remodeling. Bud could recall each of those annual façades, viewing them beside the parallel timeline of his failure as a son, a man, an artist. *Jesus.*

Bud's gut tightened as the boy flew up to hover over the building—

all the shitty AC units, litter and sandwich wrappers left by slobby workmen—then *up* they went, hundreds of miles above the earth, back to the caves of Vietnam.

"Can you find your way out?"

Bud was so engrossed in his tech-triggered reveries that for a moment, he thought the boy was saying something about the cave or the script or the process.

"Yes! Right. Sure." Biggie was already cursor-deep in his spelunking dance. "I guess I'll call you after I read it."

"Or come by. Just email that you want to come by."

Bud shook his hand again; this time there was even less of the boy behind it than before. Then he left the room.

Biggie called out:

"You're not listed on Wikipedia. Why don't you have an entry?"

[Bud]

Add To Cart

Mr.

Wiggins drove home from Yogurtland, tweaking the satellite radio. He had the *60s on 6* channel on, without sound. It said THE TURTLES, *Happy Together* (1965). Almost fifty years ago—the music of his youth. The aged screenwriter remembered being 13. At 13, *fifty years ago* meant Charlie Chaplin and the vague beginnings of forever-vague World War 1, the general mist of what may as well have been pre-history. Now, fifty years ago meant Manson and "The 59th Street Bridge Song (Feelin' Groovy)." So it fucking goes.

He sorted through the mail as he walked from the lobby down the hallway to Apt #4—the usual *Bed, Bath & Beyond* coupons, junk flyers and come-ons printed on shit paper, take-out menus for a local Chinese, a local pizza, a not so local Thai.

He fished a stately little card from the pile:

Dear Dolly,

For a variety of reasons, more and more people are choosing cremation over traditional funeral arrangements. As they plan their final wishes and needs, almost 50% of Californians have selected cremation as their preference! The numbers are increasing every year!

Bud already did the legwork. A downtown mortuary called Arm-strong would pick the body up, haul it to Orange County for burn-ing then tote the ashes back for a loved one to pick up, all for just a bit over 600 bucks. Urns started at $200, hardly worth it since Dolly had always expressed an interest in being buried at sea. If you weren't a big *urner*, they'd throw in a plastic box, gratis. His research extended to hospices as well. Veritas had a lot of good online feedback. The minute Dolly's doctor called to say the old gal didn't have more than six months, RNs would descend upon the apartment to make sure she was pain-free and comfortable as possible. Bud liked hospices' general approach—doping patients to make them comfortable, which invariably hastened death. No one likes a long, drawn-out demise.

Her bank statement (Wells Fargo) was hidden between the cou-pons and throwaways. Bud waited until he was in the foyer to open the envelope. His mother's balance was $1,384,411.08, even more than he recalled. Boy, that interest really mounts up. He wondered what it would be like to have interest work for you and not against you. What a concept.

Bud wanted to go to bed early. He climbed the stairs to say good-night. He couldn't wait to tell her that she could suspend his allow-ance because he just got a job, a real job, a *writing* job, but now wasn't the time. She'd probably say something withering anyway. Still, nothing could change the fact that a hot production company com-missioned him to write a feature. His world had been stood on end; he could even tell people he was with CAA and not be lying.

Marta was at her "station" in the dining room, studying a bible. She was a robust, cheerful Salvadoran mother of five and grand-mother of 12 who praised god and suffered no fools. She was an ar-dent churchgoer and as far as Bud was concerned, a living saint. Marta actually slept in bed with her employer during the week—Bud guessed that was a cultural mother-veneration thing, but it still blew his mind—worrying that if *Big Baby* needed her in the middle of the night, the monitor might not be loud enough to wake her. Marta took off weekends to spend time with her family, which was tough because Dolly hated the other caregivers. If she gave the fill-ins too hard a time, Bud would have to call Marta, who'd drop what she was doing and rush over to admonish, soothe and sweet-talk. By the time she left, Big Baby was so docile that she practically *goo-goo*'d.

He poked his head in. Dolly was asleep in a chair in front of the TV. Her mouth was open and Bud softened; the face looked like a death mask. Poor Dolly—solitary, snobbish, sadistic, rancorous Dolly. Bud still marveled at how she hadn't cultivated a single friend in half-a-century. *A true misanthrope.* Her parents never showed affection of any kind so it was no wonder she was clueless. As one therapist after another had inculcated Bud, *she'd done the best that she could.* She'd worked like a dog in retail for more than half a century, squeezing out every dollar she could, accruing bonus upon bonus, bending, twisting and torturing the percentages in her favor, scrimping and saving and going without just as her own mother had during the Depression. One of her most striking memories as a little girl was getting scarlet fever; the health department taped the doors and windows, quarantining her family inside. She never forgot the shame of being forced to accept charity—baskets of food left on the doorstep by neighbors in the early morning. *And oh how they hated the Jews in Urbana-Champaign. How they hated us!*

He was touched that the Universe saw fit to provide Dolly with her first real mother—Marta Morales—at the tail end of her life. She called her Big Baby, and Dolly called her Mama, for real. They had a secret language and laughed at a thousand private things. Better late than never. Bud would be lucky to find his own Marta toward the end.

He was about to back out of the room when she stirred, as if sensing his presence.

"Bud?"

"Hi Mom."

"Hi! What time is it?"

"Only seven. I'm going to sleep early."

"That sounds like a wonderful idea." Her head remained fixed but her eyes lasciviously raked him over. "You're handsome, and you *know* it. That *beautiful jaw*—those *lips*. You really kind of turn me on."

He was determined not to tell her about the gig until they cut him a check.

"Last night I woke up with tears in my eyes. I teared up over your father. Can you imagine? I didn't think I had it in me. I think it was because I was watching *America's Most Talented*, & the ventriloquist was singing with the frog. They were singing that song, 'Crying Over You.' Do you know it?"

Dolly was focused on the television. Michael Douglas was being interviewed about *The Treasure of Sierra Leone*.

"Bud . . ." He recognized it as her *dark conspiracy* voice. "Do you think he's not telling the *truth?*"

"Who?"

"Michael *Douglas.*"

That familiar inflection of groundless contempt.

"About what?"

"I just think he's . . . *got it*. I think it *came back*."

"Why would he lie?"

"Who *knows*. And that *nut* he's married to—he can sure *pick em*. I think she *wants* him to have it—the *cancer. Because then she'll get all the money*. She's no dummy. He's an old man, Bud! She's still *young*. You can't fault her for that. Do you know what old men smell like? In bed? The *farts* and the *breath*? Well *I* can *tell* you. Because that was my *thing* after I divorced your father. The old men were my *thing*. I was looking for *money*."

"Mom, I think I'm gonna go to bed."

"*Terrible* taste in women. His father fooled around *puhlenty*. What was her name—*Diandra*. He went from *bitch* to *nut*. She was smart, the first one, *$45 million* she got. And she was *right* to sue again. She should sue a *third* time. Serve him with papers *right when he's taking his last breath*."

"Night, Mom."

"We need to find you a Diandra—or a Jamie McCourt. A *divorcée.*

The divorcées are good because most are *dying* for a good *fuck*. I don't care *who* they are as long as they're *monied*. Go for an *old one*. A *dowager*. Do you know what a dowager is? I'll pull out my Neiman's customer book and we'll go *shopping for dowagers*. How about the fag's mother? *Cooper*. His mother's, *you* know, a *Vanderbilt*. Gloria. How does it go, what they say about people on top? They fuck their way to the bottom! That's where *you* are, let her *fuck her way to the bottom*, *that's* when you *grab* her. She had a son, you know that, don't you? He jumped out a *window* just to get away from her. Why don't you go out there, Bud? Fly out there and give her a run for her money. Cause she's got to be as old as *I* am. In the meantime, *go find Jamie McCourt*."

He said goodnight to Marta and went straight to his bathroom for a bowel movement. He'd been constipated ever since Brando Brainard said he got the job. His body was in shock.

Bud sat there with the iPad. He unfroze the Franzen, which was the last thing he'd been looking at—Franzen on YouTube had become a weirdly addictive pastime. In this particular screed, the bloated, bestselling litterateur smirkily held forth on "overrated writers," casually shitting on Forster and Graham Greene. Bud noted JF's three-day grizzle gave him a smug, Craig's List coker's mien, reminding the over-the-hill aging scripter of those contestants who were certain they'd win The Dating Game—or maybe more like a death-row interviewee, one of those high-IQ serial killers talking on an A&E doc about the 11 undergrad guys and dolls he decapitated then raped back in the Santa Cruz glory days. He said Graham Greene's so-called important books like *The End of the Affair* were basically shit but maybe that was a function of being Brit vs. American, and how there was a lot of American writing that Brits didn't get either—writers like, oh, George Saunders, and, uhm, his pal Dave Wallace . . . again, he shit on his good friend! Not only deftly tucking him into a minor peer's camp but insinuating that DFW didn't have the universality—even in death, especially in death—of Jonathan Franzen! "They consider George and Dave to be, I don't know, puerile, or bratty, or too broad, or annoying . . ."

The gall of the man nearly gave Bud a hard-on, but instead, he squeezed out a few pellets followed by a record-breaking, sustained trumpet of gas—a personal best.

Bud ran a bath and printed out the attachment Biggie emailed, a two-page newspaper article entitled "Between Scylla and Charybdis." *Scylla & Charybdis* . . . the names were familiar. He'd google them later.

Instead of getting in the tub, he sat at his desk and flipped through a book called *The 90-Day Novel*. After his meeting with Biggie, Bud drove down to the beach and treated himself to an early dinner at a Thai place off the Promenade. Then he strolled to Barnes & Noble, where a placard by the escalator announced an "author's event." He took his seat in a crowd of studious-looking wannabes. It seemed strange to him that instead of writing a self-help book for burgeoning novelists, then going on to write fiction, Alan Watt did things in reverse; he wrote an acclaimed novel (in 3 months, of course), then took the self-help guru route. The author entered to applause, his ease in front of a crowd attesting to a former career in stand-up. He thanked his publicist, who sat in the front row, then began thanking the bookstore staff by name as if there to accept an award. *The 90-Day Novel* was published by The 90-Day Novel™ Press, the sign of an entrepreneur at work. The book was in 12 weekly sections, further broken down into Day 1 through Day 90, each with its own epigram by Mailer, Maugham, Flaubert, Fitzgerald, Hesse, Jung, Pearl Bailey, & the like. It even included a "story structure analysis" of the author's own novel, *Diamond Dogs*, winner of France's 2004 Prix Printemps for Best Foreign Novel. Bud hadn't heard of *Diamond Dogs*, nor had he heard of the Prix Printemps, nor any of the authors that provided blurbs, including the writer of the cover quote, "Frank B. Wilderson III, winner, 2008 American Book Award."

Bud put the book down and picked up *The Paris Review.*

He opened it to an interview with Jonathan Franzen, who was being asked about the influence of Don DeLillo on his work.

FRANZEN

I don't think my pages read like his, because I had a preference for rounder letters—*c*'s and *p*'s. I think of him as being more into *l*'s and *a*'s and *I*'s.

INTERVIEWER

C's and *p*'s?

FRANZEN

I kept seeing a plate of food with beet greens and liver and rutabaga—intense purple green, intense orange, rich rusty brown—and feeling a wish to write sentences that were juicy and sensuous.

INTERVIEWER

Do you mean the sound too?

FRANZEN

No, the way they looked, the roundness of *b*'s and *g*'s, the juiciness.

It depressed Bud that he hadn't thought of letters that way, having shapes and colors like food. He would never be able to talk about vowels and consonants with such sensual, specialized knowledge; he'd never be asked anything in *The Paris Review*, not even for his thoughts about *The Wire* or *Mad Men*. Bud felt all about *l*'s and *o*'s and *s*'s and *e*'s and *r*'s—like a *loser*.

Bud understood there were certain things he would simply have to accept. He might never finish, let alone publish a novel, and if he did, the odds of collecting an award—even a *Prix Printemps*—were stacked against him. He would never be asked to discuss his life and his craft at the Aspen Ideas Festival. He would never give a TED talk or be profiled in *The New York Times Magazine*. He would never be extolled, asskissed and fussed over in the pages of *Interview* by special people like Marina Abramović & Antony Hegarty; he would never hang with Patti Smith and Johnny Depp, nor would they gift him with photos of Genet's scrotum or original letters from Rimbaud's gunrunning years or uncracked ampoules once owned by Hunter Thompson. Lil Wayne would never refer to him as "my artist," and Ellen would never give him a frivolous, on-air gift. He would never be asked to deliver a commencement speech, like Franzen's boon friend David Foster Wallace. He'd probably never hang himself either.*

He watched some old *Britain's Got Talents* on YouTube. Everyone amazed. Everyone astonished. Everyone was unforgettable. Everyone was making their mark, everyone was being launched from the filth and petty madness of anonymity into eternal stardom, everyone had rounded letters and rutabagas. Everyone was a pauper and ventriloquist-assisted frog prince, plucked from the sewers of minimum-wage schlepdom and installed in castle keep of the Immortal Kingdom of (at least) 10,000,000+ Hits, a finger would hit the playback machine, their mouths would open and just a few soulfully sung notes later they'd each be born aloft on a magic carpet of judges' tears and thunderous standing ovations, relocated from the Götterdämmerung of murderously American small towns and deadend English villages, whose very names elicited a doom of mental retardation, perma-poverty & quicksand obscurity, from those sickening black holes to the supernovae pastures of galactic e-Lysiums & beyond. Bud was old enough to remember that astonishing bit of television history when Jennifer Holliday sang "And I Am Telling You I'm Not Going"—now every week there were chubby adenoidal 11 year-olds vomiting it up on *Good Morning America*, and vomiting it pretty well. God

* . . . . never be eulogized for having a big brain that finally crashed down around him like a chandelier, its footnotes scattering like gewgaw frippery.

wasn't dead, epiphany was. The Internet had bestowed the thumbnail-transcendent Epiphany Channel; giddy passion plays of two-minute portable pop-cult fairytales ruled, with their hyperlinks of fall and rise/rise and FAIL/rise & rise mythos, *appiphanies* the new opiate of the people.

Bud wondered if Franco, Franzen or Fran L could sing, *really* sing. Franzen probably had a voice like an angel. Franzen and DeLillo could probably do a kickass *Sesame St.* "Alphabet Soup."

He slipped into bed under fresh, Marta-laundered sheets. He noticed a crease. *Jesus, she ironed them. A fucking saint.*

Rihanna was on an old rerun of *Ellen.* Before Bud shut it off, Ellen said, "I hope you know how amazing you look."

He closed his eyes and pictured the cover of his book. He didn't know yet what he was going to call it, so he focused on the part that would go just below the title: *A Novel by Bud Wiggins.* He pictured a cover quote by Jonathan Franzen and blurbs on the back from David Simon and Michael Tolkin. A half-hour later his thoughts were still racing (too much Coke Zero), so Bud decided to listen to the guided meditation CD a couples therapist gave him back in the day, when he was coupled.

He turned on the light to retrieve it. That's when he saw a piece of mail Marta must have left for him some weeks back. It was from the Library Foundation, inviting him, for a small donation, to become a "Library Associate." The clever solicitation came in the form of book cover:

Small
Miracles:
*They happen
every day*

by

Mr. Bud Wiggins

They happen every day . . .

Indeed they do. The gods of his understanding were at work *and* at play. Only moments ago, he lay dreaming his book, and now the book was dreaming him.

He would take his miracles where he found them—small, medium or large.

[Tom-Tom&Reeyonna&Rikki]

The Social Network

So far, Tom-Tom hadn't had much luck drafting *loosers* for the cause. In the end, she had no choice but to cast a wider internet but was hampered in that she had to *intrigue* without giving her idea *away.* She spoke to idle *Idol* primadunces; crampy *Top Model* supermidols; erased *Amazing Racers*; uncaught *Deadliest Catch*es; bored *Hoarders* and belligerent *Bridezillas*; undercooked *Hell's Kitchen*ettes and stinky *Think You Can Dancers*. She even had the brainstorm of conscripting one of the "tribute" actors gonged out of *The Hunger Games*—didn't happen.

To date, she had but a single conscript for her troubles—Phil Dean, an affable 63-yr-old interventionist from *Intervention*'s 2nd season. Phil had suffered a heart attack after shooting just three episodes & took a "sabbatical" to have a quadruple bypass. A&E elected not to rehire. Back in the day, Tom-Tom's very own Dr Phil specialized in expediting the recovery of washed-out child stars (Johnny Whitaker of *Family Affair*, Todd Bridges of *Diff'rent Strokes*) and mentoring their new careers as drug counselors.

The first thing the *loosers* did after Tom-Tom called to pitch them was google her ass. (A lot of times they did it right during the call.) Not everyone had a sense of humor about her colorful past. So Tom-Tom started using an alias, introducing herself as the backer and producer of an as-yet-untitled reality show. A requisite for any decent candidate was a large, dysfunctional dose of narcissism so Tom-Tom made sure to climb up everyone's ass first thing, the whole rigmarole about how *amazing* they were, what a *following* they still had, how *aggrieved* everyone had been when he/she didn't make the cut, bla. Usually, the earlier in the season the *loosers* were sent packing, the easier they were to handle. (Tom-Tom *did* realize she might be forced to resort to the bottomless pool of contestants who never even made it to televised rounds.) When she managed to get hold of a late-rounder—someone who made it to the last month or so in the life of whatever show—the delusional *looser* invariably acted like they *couldn't* be frickin *bothered*, & Tom-Tom better cough up what she wanted & *fast*, because they were like in the middle of a frickin *world tour* & already late to catch the private jet that was taking them to the Giants of Reality Programming Crystal Frickin Award Ball in frickin Monte Carlo—you know, the oldschool Lear with Snooki, Bethenny, Ryan Seacrest & half the Kardash Klan onboard. Some of the *loosers* actually wanted to know—*demanded*—how Tom-Tom got their emails! Because you *netpuked* it to the *e-niverse*, you shitty *anus*. But she had to chill, reminding herself that however pathetic, they had something she potentially wanted. She had to remind herself that *she* was using *them*.

TT didn't want her idea plashed all over the web either, so she wouldn't do email, other than the initial contact—she insisted on talking on the phone or in person. Which again was trippy because the social distortion vibe of the loose coozers was still always like *I don't* DO *phone like* EVER *so you have* SIXTY SECONDS *& it better be worth my time*. She made sure to drop the BETTY WHITE bomb right away because that got their attention, *Betty White has graciously given us the use of her Mt. Olympus home yes Betty is a producer but a silent partner in the venture*. Everything after that required a little more tact. *What the show's really about* (she read from the text on her computer) *is the individual and collective journeys of an eclectic group of reality show veterans who find themselves under one roof on the Hollywood rollercoaster bonding*

over shared triumphs and broken dreams but never straying too far from em-
bracing the house motto: 'Tomorrow is another day.' The louche douches
would then get that *thing* in their voice, that seen it all done it all *thing*
like they were the ex-exec producer of the original *Survivor* or the
retired co-co-co-creator of *The Bachelor/The Voice* or Simon fucking
Fuller or the CEO in charge of grooming Christina Aguilera's *twat*—
already *brands*, ubiquitous cultural *touchstones*, perfect hundred-year
showbiz storms/entrepreneurial *f5 tornadoes*—you know, like they
wanted you to think they had all this hot shit in the hopper, just
around the corner, their shit was going to hit *large*, they didn't need
your shit, because while they were waiting for their own *major shit* to
hit, like while they were waiting, the Hard Rock was paying them
the same or maybe just a little bit less than what they paid *The Situation* to show up at some Joe Francis/Demi Lovato/Brenda Song
hooker-wannabe bday gangbang in Vegas so like hurry up with your
dumbass pitch *because I'm gonna be all late for the premiere launch of my
first fragrance for K-Mart . . . well is that it?* they'd say, all tightass dis-
gruntled. *Just people living in a house? People who were once on reality
shows? I don't understand what they're supposed to be doing like why would
anyone want to watch.* (Just what TT expected to hear but from the
Jewsers not the loosers.) *I mean is it supposed to be like* Real World *or*
Big Brother? *Can you please say again what everyone's supposed to be doing? Because it's really not making sense to me.* Sometimes Tom-Tom
would give them a tentative title, maybe say it was *Daydream Believers*
in hopes that would give it a simple soft cool dreamy spin but she really wanted to tell them the networks wanted to call it *House of Losers.*

. . .

The reality/unscripted Expo couldn't have come along at a better
time. The *loosers* would be out in desperate droves & wouldn't be able
to hide the stenk of their wretchedness from her like they (thought
they) could over the phone. It'd be easy to chase down the weak &
wounded. But *some* of the reality dropouts/throwouts were actually
very cool people, & the Double T was starting to look forward to the

hookups. She knew she'd be energized by her peers, there were a bunch of *Idol*s performing on the stages and when she (re)introduced herself & told them what she was up to, who knew? They might have some good ideas, even jump on the bandwagon. Another thing was she had that taste of notoriety & tho her shit went down 10 years ago she'd probably get recognized, people still came up to her on the street at least once a week . . . *another* thing was she might actually be cool again, it might be her time, the world had changed, shit was more cynical, all kinds of shit, everything had gotten crazier/more *tolerant*, people embraced various squalid shit they wouldn't have 10 years ago, they fuckin cheered it *on,* sordid psychopathic bad girl shit, squalor/sleaze, a *whole different world* now, one that worshipped abject moments of infamy . . . if she got thrown off *Idol* TODAY for her old chicanery, the reward wouldn't be t-shirts & Letterman, it'd be her own fuckin *show.* The *Tom-Tom: Notorious!* show. Cause you want notorious? Ima give it you. *Tori Spelling* ain't noTORIous. Tori Spelling's about as noTORIous as one of Petra Ecclestone's cuntfarts.

Tom-Tom dug being in the adult swim of it all again.

Once the White House was up & running with *looser live-ins* it would be important to get someone up to Mt Olympus, a show runner with a track record, to check it out. See what they were doing up there on the Mount in Loser Lab, see it up close, the place would serve as she'd meant it to from the start, a kind of "living pitch," if Tom-Tom could find someone at the Expo and get em up, someone who knew the reality business, even get em up without telling them *exactly* what the exact *nature* of the shit was, & they rang the doorbell and she took them on a little tour, nothing planned out, nothing elaborate, by then she'd try to have a full house, it'd be cool if most of the bedrooms were full, like a real *home,* that homey feeling, just like *Million Dollar Listing* with the house dressers, the home stylists, that's all she was really doing, she *knew* she'd be good at that all she needed was the chance the opportunity now here it *was,* here she was making it all more *presentable* more *livable* more *sellable,* everyone rehearsing and doing their thing, maybe even by then have a *camera crew* up & running, if she could just find someone who knew their shit, get em up there and give em the *tour* then walk them out to the pool—Tom-Tom could *see* it, she could *hear* it—and they'd say to her, *Okay, this is for sure kind of trip for real but what's really happening?* (During the tour she would provide whatever kind of dope, if they wanted it, or whatever sex was deemed appropriate to get them to commit) Tom-Tom would say, OK, here's the deal, *everyone you just met is someone who got* THROWN OFF A REALITY SHOW! She could *see* it, see their *smile* slowly become a *HA!*—then the nod of the head, the *many* nods, of *knowingness,* nods that said *OK. I get it.* And SO WILL THE NETWORK. *You, m'lady, are sitting on a fucking* MAJOR FRANCHISE. *So let the games and the brand-building begin!*

. . .

They rode to the Convention Center in the same car—Tom-Tom, Dr Phil, ReeRee & Rikki—not just because Rikki's scooter died—it wasn't really a scooter but was so lightweight Tom-Tom called it that—but because until Reeyonna could pay her share of the rent Tom-Tom was using her as a gofer & personal asst.

Dr Phil was an avuncular, calming presence, & really understood Tom-Tom's *vision.* Due to a mix-up/wrong address delivery of his social security checks, he'd been evicted from his Hollywood garden apt & was sleeping in his car. After their interview, Tom-Tom moved him right in. She already felt the vibe of the house benefiting from his presence. She needed someone trustworthy to be her eyes & ears when the prospective cast of *schmoosers* finally fell into place. Dr Phil was one of those people born with a happy disposition—Tom-Tom didn't want unhappy people around her anymore. Unhappy people & the Year of the Moneybags do *not* frickin mix. Besides, she was thinking he might do something to help Jerzy, not an intervention exactly but something. When you were around Dr Phil his energy made you not want to use. She'd already talked to him about it, even suggesting maybe they could shoot Todd Bridges doing an "assessment" on Jerzy as part of the show, for a little drama, you know, like what would he or Johnny Whitaker recommend, would it be a hospital or a treatment center or maybe Jerzy could even do a home detox which would be *really* great for the show. Only trouble was, things would probably have to get much worse for Jerzy to agree to something like that. Because Jerzy was a loser for real but not a reality show *schmooser* so he *definitely* wouldn't agree to being *filmed* for something like that, he'd probably have to OD for them to get his crazy drugshit on camera. The way he was going, that would probably happen too. Soon.

.   .   .   .

They came on the last day, Sunday, because that's when they were having all the workshops Tom-Tom wanted to go to.

There was a Q&A called *How to Create, Produce and Pitch Your Reality TV Show*; she also didn't want to miss *How to Become A Host/Reality Star—Parlay Your 15 minutes of Reality Fame into a Career* either. But Tom-Tom told Dr Phil the one she was looking forward to the most was *Where Are They Now? Catching up with Reality TV Stars and Their Lives Today.* That sounded the most promising—lots of rotten fruit on the ground for the takin, she hoped.

.   .   .

Rikki & ReeRee walked thru the empty Hall of Autographs. It was huge. There were dozens of roped off lanes, each ending at tables with the headshots & names of whoever was scheduled to be signing. R&R didn't recognize any of them.

They sat down and Sharpie-circled events in the Expo Guide, deciding which ones they wanted to attend. Rikki said he probably should check out *How to Make it in Hollywood.* Reeyonna started getting excited about meeting Audrina, who seemed to be the biggest star there. Rikki circled Manouschka Guerrier from *The Private Chefs of Beverly Hills.* (Lately he'd been thinking that if movies didn't work out he could become a personal chef to the stars.) Ree circled Eric Roberts from *Celebrity Rehab With Dr. Drew* because one of her BFFs said he was Julia Roberts's brother, which she still didn't believe. Julia Roberts didn't mean that much to her but she was *so* good in the *Eat, Pray, Love* movie she went to with her mom. She circled Gretchen Bonaduce too, not just because she was Danny Bonaduce's ex-wife (Ree & her friends liked getting up in the trees and watching *The Partridge Family*) but because the Guide said she was on *Gimme My Reality Show!* which Reeyonna never heard of but thought was a really funny title. Both wanted to meet Mischa Barton, who actually maybe was a bigger or maybe the same size ☆ as Audrina. It didn't say what reality show Mischa was on but ReeRee watched *The O.C.* on SoapNet. Rikki circled Tila Tequila from *Dance-off Pants-off.* "Don't even go there," said Ree.

· · ·

Tom-Tom & Dr Phil were upstairs trying to find Room 506. A crazy-looking couple started pointing at them. "O my God, I can't believe it!" The gal had magenta hair, a pierced nose & some kind of Wild West brassiere. The guy looked girlish and both wore skull bandannas. Tom-Tom girded herself for the pleasant rush of being *Idol* outed.

"It's Phil! From the second season of *Intervention!*"

"We *loved* you!"

"Your interventions were the only ones that didn't end in relapse!"

"Why did you *disappear?*"

They introduced themselves as Kent & Vyxsin from *The Amazing Race, Season 12.* They said they were going to be at Hooters on Sunday in Burbank offering live TV commentary when the show came on. They gave them little hot pink vouchers that said WATCH THE RACE WITH THE RACERS!!! ★★★ADMISSION IS FREE★★★

· · ·

R&R walked down one of the long, roped lanes. At this moment, they were literally the only visitors to the tent that held the vast Hall of Autographs.

When they reached the table, a jowly man with a big smile & big white teeth shook hands without getting up & gave them a glossy cardboard 5 × 7 of himself. They looked at the card—he was someone on ABC's Eyewitness News. He'd written, in festive silver marker, "ABC 7 CHEERS! George Pennacchio."

As they left the Hall of Autographs, Rikki grabbed a few postcards from another empty table.

> If we could make Snooki a star, just imagine what we could do with you . . . DON'T MISS YOUR CHANCE. Follow us on twitter—be the ☆ that you are

On the way to Audrina, they passed some people standing on a red carpet getting their picture taken by pretend paparazzi. Big posters on the wall behind them said OnTheRedCarpet.com.

A trio of skeevy *slores* walked by. (Kim K's word for slutty whores.) They had stickers slapped on their grimy bosoms, "Follow us @PlayboyTV."

. . .

They found 506, an enormous, empty room filled with hundreds of set up chairs. A staffer told them the event moved to 501. 501 was ten times smaller. It was SRO.

Omarosa was on a panel with reality stars from *True Beauty* and *Chef Academy*. She was frickin fierce. She said she beat out half a million people to get on *Celebrity Apprentice* & that her goal from the beginning was to get the most camera time, she was going to do whatever it took, & as it turned out becoming the 1st African-American reality show villainess was the deal that worked. Omarosa said she'd been on thirty-frickin-seven reality shows & Tom-Tom didn't even know if she was kidding. (She was even on a show about floral arrangements, on the Logo Channel, whatever the frick that was.) Omarosa was a mutherfuckin *trip*. She said that apart from whatever she was up to in RealityWorld, she was a full-time professor at her alma mater Howard U & taught an MBA program. *Say what?* She was also pursuing a freakin frickin doctorate in the frickin freakin ministry (Tom-Tom knew she wouldn't be kidding about any of that), confessing that her true purpose on Earth was to spread the word of Jesus. She started going on about how fortunate she was to have partnered "with my friend, Mr. Trump," & how she was always on the look-out for reality shows to develop. *Hey I should probably try & talk to her after, maybe ol Sasha Fierce would be interested in* Bad News Bears, *and Trump too.* Tom-Tom'd had way stranger bedfellows in her time. *She looks like she'd be a* nasty *fuck too be my villainess black* BI-ATCH. *Pound that nappy ponderosa for* days————————

The other reality mavens on the panel (she hadn't heard of any of their shows) possessed a cheerleading, bulletproof, nearly robotic self-confidence that Tom-Tom hoped would rub off. Most of the time she held it together pretty well but like a lot of artists, she had her bleak moments—something the thrilled-with-themselves panelists apparently knew nothing about. Tho maybe they were just hiding that shit cause it didn't play in public; maybe they'd share their darkness with her after the event, one on one. All she knew was that if she were to succeed, there'd be zero room for fear/self-doubt. She probably did a little more speed than she should have; her heart was hammered. Her focus went south and she flashed on joining Omarosa's seminary, licking the salty, Ubangi lip-sized clit of merciless Mother Africa while Ivanka & Donald did their father/tall drinka daughter Rump Tower thing. All those thighscrapers . . .

When Omarosa was done, they went down the line, & every single panelist said how lucky they were to have triumphed in doing whatever the fuck they were doing, how they "were flown all over the world" to cook, to DJ, to fuck, to suck, to bla. Tom-Tom was getting pissy.

A panelist said, "I'm an attentionwhore." *No shit.* Another said, "The lower you feel the higher you heal." *Huh?* Another said, "Life is short, eat the red velvet cupcake." *Gimme some.* Another said, "There will always be h8trs. They *love* to drink the H8torade."

. . .

Audrina's body was so tight it was scary. Reeyonna got self-conscious; her stomach was getting giant, her back was killing her, & she couldn't imagine looking or feeling glamorous ever again. She wasn't even sure she ever did.

The interviewer said, "What's *your* favorite reality show?"

Audrina said, *"Cake Boss."*

"O! *Cake Boss* was cancelled!"

"It *was?*"

"Yes! Audrina I'm so sorry!"

When the Q&A ended, Rikki thought Reeyonna wanted to meet her so he started drifting with the mob toward the stage. But when he looked back, ReeRee just shook her head and trudged to the EXIT.

. . .

www.mischabartonhandbags.com

. . .

There was a lot of casting going on but it was hard to tell for what. People were even signing up to be videotaped by casting agents. There were booths with different websites for actors—ones that told them what was being cast, ones that sent them audition sites, ones for uploading videos.

. . .

Tom-Tom had butterflies at the *American Idol* panel.

Blake Lewis was there, & Mikalah Gordon from Season 4. The rest were Season 9s except for Kimberley Locke. Kimberley was in *Tom-Tom's* season, Season 3. They were talking about how they bonded with fans. One *Idol* said she even became friends with her webmaster.

Tom-Tom wrote down random shit she heard in her trapper

keeper: *suddenly the show BLEW UP . . . <u>take it to the next level</u> . . . follow my dream, follow my passion . . . <u>Don't be underwhelming!</u> . . . I'm a girlie-girl . . . Karina Smirnoff/DWTS: dance studio, beauty line— 'girlactik'*

At the end, about twenty people went to the stage to have their picture taken with the *Idols.* Tom-Tom was going to say hello to Kimberley but decided to catch her after she performed, later in the day.

.　.　.

Reeyonna really wanted to see Kris & Bruce Jenner but they didn't show. Eric Roberts didn't show either, and neither did Mischa. Rikki said Tom-Tom said Bruce Jenner had a hundred-million dollars. ReeRee wanted to see what people looked like who had a hundred-million dollars, if they looked different.

They passed an *Extreme Makeover: Home Edition* booth. ReeRee said they should get those people to do Betty White's house. That really cracked Rikki up, which made ReeRee happy.

.　.　.

Tom-Tom was finally recognized by a handsome fortysomething actor who struck up a conversation. He said he almost made the cut of the *Gigolos* pilot, Showtime's reality series about male escorts servicing female clients in Las Vegas. He tried again for the second season, but it was a no-go. She was *very* anxious to hear his story.

.　.　.

Reeyonna dug into her beef enchiladas while Rikki was in the head. She felt like a fat pig. *Ew gross.* A youngish, wholesome-looking man with barbershop quartet muttonchops came over. He said he was a casting agent, looking for pregnant girls.

"You're not from MTV, are you?" she said with a smile.

"No but sometimes I wish I *was.*" He said it in an appealing, jokey way. Friendly, sweet, not pervy or pushy. "Say what you will, it's pretty darn hard to argue with their success. *And* longevity."

He gave her his card and left.

She felt like a *fatter* pig. *Gross.*

She saw Rikki throw something into the trash on his way over. She asked him what it was, and he wouldn't say. He had that look he gets when he huffs.

"Did you whip it?" He just smiled. He was blazed. "Where'd you get the can? Did you *bring* it?"

He just smiled.

.   .   .

That night Tom-Tom met him for a drink on Melrose at a restaurant owned supposedly by Lauren Conrad. He said he was "a working actor" & Mark Wahlberg's 2nd cousin and sometime camera double. He said his real passion was making furniture. Mark had a lot of his pieces. So did Robbie Robertson, Alanis Morissette, Moby, Eddie Vedder, Dave Grohl, & Rufus Wainwright's manager. She told him about her vision. He said he'd love to see the house so they went up.

Bolt had the biggest dick she'd ever seen.

[Jerzy&Rikki]

A Short History of Rap

"Larry

Fishburne didn't do you any favors you know."

He'd been spending time with Jerzy since he lost the part. He was bored & Jerzy let him ride along during work. (Plus J had more time to hang because he was spending less of it with Tom-Tom since the *Gigolos* reject moved in; tho Tom-Tom already gave Bolt his own room, he was staying with her in the master 96% of the time.) Rikki said to Reeyonna, *Your brother's crazy for real but he's cool. We're down.*

They sped from one location to another as Jerzy got tweeted various ☆ whereabouts. Rikki asked who was tweeting him & Jerzy said "my tweethearts." Rikki stayed in the car smoking Romulan Queen whenever Jerzy got out to do his pap thing.

"I think Larry Fishburne's a fuckin MANTIS. He saw you in that room sitting very still at the *feeder* & clocked you as a little black hummingbird."

Rikki was blazed; J's rap wasn't helping the zituation.

"Hummingbird. Dude what do you mean."

"What do *you* mean, 'what do you mean?'? What do *I* mean? What do YOU mean."

Jerzy never took his eyes off the road. His smile was cheap & voracious, like a 3rd cousin of the Joker.

They rocketed toward an odd threesome supposedly lunching at Ago: Heather Morris, Michael Douglas, & Natalie Portman's husband the dancer.

. . .

He thought Tom-Tom was kidding.

She said she read online that the role had been cast. He said *To who?* She said, *Nobody I know. Like, an unknown.* Rikki said, *But I was an unknown.* She said, *You still are, pumpkin.* Rikki kept echo chambering *What?* all puzzled-looking & kooky. *What? What? What?* Then he stopped saying *What?* & started saying *Fuck.* He moped/paced from room to room then out he'd go, walking the circumference of the pool like a schmuckfaced, loserkook, crowing, canting, barking, bitching, sighing, shrieking, ululating/murmuring *fuk*-FUK fuk*FUK*fuk like an actor trying on attitudes, searching for the inflection that best suited his role, now highvoiced, now low as Tyler duh Creator. He offered the guttural wordstring to the Void, dipped his stubbed toe in nothingness.

The boy who cried *fuk.*

. . .

Jerzy felt bad for him. Anyone could see the kid had hi apple pie in the sky hopes. Probably thought it was a lock. Gunna be the new black whom-evuh, nubian screen god, BET supersizeme superstar. Bangin Rihanna for real, not *Reeyonna*, I mean Jerzy loved his little sissy but that *Reeyonna* shit was fuckin retarded whitegirl shit. & not *even*, 'cause sissy wasn't even white trash, which would at least have given her ½ an excuse. *My little sissy calls herself Reeyonna* was not some shit he'd be hurrying to share with Suge.

Poor kid . . . probably thought he'd soon qualify to get served up some of that perfumed, perfectly-preserved Halle Berry cherry parfait on a platter. Jerzy partially blamed Tom-Tom for not prepping him, not schooling the callow young buck in Hollywood's scary sickly ways, hence encouraging—*enabling*—his painful naiveté to run riot on Sunset Strip. Tom-Tom was also upset but not for long cause she had lots of eggs in her basket. Like, this poor kid only has *two*, & one of em just broke on the sidewalk. The *remaining* egg (organic, fertilized) being dammed up and near drowning in ReeRee's beaver, closer each hour to crowning itself king (or maybe queen), tiny, efficient predator camouflaged under bawling cloak of helpless infancy, its instinct being to suck the life out of its mother and father, then mature to hate them, *hate* them for reasons justified, unjustified & imagined, to vilify and *overthrow* them, all the while concocting contradictory campaigns & stratagems to get their *love* and *attention*, all children grow into fools who want *unconditional love* from the demon-parents they've come to *unconditionally hate*, and so it goes, a dumb ceaseless schizoid dance of arrested adult-child development, always ending with the shrink-guided offspring smugly, compassionately *forgiving* errant momsters & dadbeats in the latters' final deathbed days, decades-long drama of guilt & fingerpointing at last wrapped in a perfect, perfectly convenient psychotherapeutic giftbag the kids reward themselves with at croaktime, allowing them—the once wounded now healed adult child—to *move on* . . . .

Jerzy asked, *Do you want to smoke?*

Rikki knew he meant crystal not kush.

"Naw, the shit is wack. Pretty soon I'm be talkin like you."

"Well at least you'd be gramatically correct."

.   .   .

He liked the old man Phil.

Jerzy usually detox'd a couple times a year, something he did in the privacy of his home with a major assist from benzos. Whenever J got clean, he literally slept for 2 weeks. For the hell of it, he told Dr Phil to organize his (off-camera) intervention—when the time was right. Just now, it wasn't.

"It rarely is, my friend," said Phil.

"True."

"I'll let you in on something. I know how smart you are. Yes, I do. But that wonderful gift, all that wonderful *brainpower* hasn't served you so well. It's even been a hindrance. In certain areas. You're too smart not to know where this is going to end."

"Where's that, Dr Phil?" he deadpanned.

"Right where the big book says it does—'jail, institutions or death.'"

"Promise me you'll never work a suicide hotline, Dr Phil."

.   .   .

He couldn't ask his fosterparents for any more money. They'd give it to him, but he couldn't ask.

School became impossible. He told his fosters he was going to stay with Reeyonna, & they said, "That's where you *should* be." Killing him softly with their unending kindness. He lived at the Mt Olympus house now.

Tom-Tom was bugging them for rent. Rikki didn't understand why she would, when she was staying for free. When he asked to barter with his body she just laughed, then looked at him funny like she was gunna steal his face. The memory of that hopeful time when they made the audition tape, when both of them were certain he was going to become a ☆ had completely faded. Without the motorcycle, they were trapped up there. Ree didn't want to go anywhere anyway. After she lost her wallet she got depressed & stayed in her room. She didn't even want to replace her stolen ID. If Rikki needed anything down the hill he had to rely on Jerzy or wait & get a ride with Dr Phil or whomever. The one person he refused to ask was Bolt.

Reeyonna&Rikki watched *The Town* on DirecTV. The dude got away with all the $$$ just like in *Shawshank* but in *The Town* he got the bitch too. ReeRee liked it but mostly watched peekaboo-style, hand over eyes, because she said it was "too real." It *did* make Rikki think about robbery & shit. *One big score, then I'm out.* That's what the heist movie crews always said, like in that bitchen movie *Heat*. Rikki talked about it, talked some shit, putting out feelers. Ree said *You better not. You better be there for your baby.* Rikki said *Our* baby. ReeRee said *Your* baby like *right, your baby,* to further make a point. Rikki said he wasn't serious about the heist shit, just fucking around.

He might float it by Tom-Tom, tho. She probably knew somebody with a crew. Maybe she'd even done it before, not a bank or anything, just a small business or somebody's house, not a home invasion, just a robbery when no one was there. He knew she used to rob dealers. He knew from Jerzy that she used googlearth to scope out celebrity mansions. Jerzy said she started doing that during *Million Dollar Listing* speedball marathons, then they started doing it together, virtual bling-ringing, they'd check out a celeb house or rental using an address one of his personal twats shittered to him & they could like totally case the back entrances & shit, places where the ☆ might sneak out in an attempt to dodge the frontyardarazzi, Jerzy would then be waiting in the back or wherever they'd scoped, Tom-Tom was so good at it she could like land them right in Courteney Cox's swimming pool & they'd just hang there a while scoping the house from every conceivable angle just like they were hangin for the weekend on a little raft, the googlearth let you look toward this or that neighbor then you could fly over to the house Colin Farrell was renting & just hang & then fly back to Courteney's or out to the beach to James Cameron's or The Edge's. Jerzy had T^2 do the same shit with restaurants too but now everyone was doing it, all the celebrigoogleartherazzi. Jerzy said Tom-Tom could zillow what a house cost, she could zillow when it was sold & to what bullshit shell company belonging to J Aniston, Lindsay, Olivia Wilde or whomever.

Then Rikki got prudent & thought, *If I'm gunna do a stickup it's gunna need to wait til after the baby & my adoption hearing. Cause I don't want to fuck either of those up.*

Ree was due right around the time his adoption court date was set.

.   .   .

Jerzy played the NatGeo doc for Rikki on his laptop. They were parked on Mulholland outside the gates of The Summit, waiting with 11 other britney*spearshooters* for her to leave the house. Everyone'd been there at least 6 hours; the papp-posse was starting to thin out. Britney wasn't Jerzy's thing but it'd been a slow day, all he got was Paz de la Huerta, Toni Collette & Mamie Gummer, anyway, he thought he'd show the scene to the kid.

He told Rikki that hummingbirds could only store enough energy to get them through the night so they were always just a few hours away from total starvation. *Just like dope fiends yuckyuck.* Jerzy asked how long he thought a hummingbird could live. Rikki said I don't know a week maybe a month? A year? Jerzy said they could go *10-years-PLUS* (the internet said) but that 1st yr was *oooh* it was TOUGH. *Hey tell me about it. Jesus H a 10 yr-old hummingbird has got to be having his share of senior moments. Probably get alzheimer's, water on the birdbrain, need to start leaving post-its on nests & feeders ahahahahaha.* Hey Dr Phil told me a good one. Guy with alzheimer's goes to a singles bar. He sees this chick & he's gunna hit on her. So he goes up & says "Do I come here often?" *teeheehee you don't get it do you. Well I ain't gunna splain. I ain't gunna explainate. Ain gunna explainify. Ain gunna explainobrag the explainentials. Ain gunna explain the giraffe—————* holy *SHIT* 10 fucking <u>YEARS</u> of flutterin n fibrillatin n fuckin *hustling* to meet your insane daily food nut, plus whatever's required to fuel your *insaner* metabolism like some adrenal torment devised by the GODS *10 FUCKING YEARS!* the very thought of it had Jerzy continuously tweak-freaking, half-worried that the pondering of it alone might bring on another hopefully nonfatal tachycardiac episode of his own.

Jerzy said (the internet said) that sometimes praying mantises were called devil's horses. They were cannibals & *meateaters* holy *shit* YES fucking insect *carnivores!* It was like some shit out of *Starship Troopers,* which happened to be one of his alltime faves, some *Starship Trooper* shit *come to life!* But more than that, it was *biblical*, it was *germane*, it was more of the *4 Horseman shit that Suge told him at Cedars, the same shit he tried to run down to MoMA: White was Victory/Mantis, Black was famine/Hummingbird, Red was hummingblood . . .* Mind you, the devil's horsemen were *not* scavengers, nope, *huh*-uh, they weren't like *jackals* either (hell-*O! Can* I *tell* you why they aren't like jackals, Rikki? They aren't like jackals *cause they're fucking* INSECTS! *Hel*-lo) because they don't eat *dead things*, that just aint kosher . . . though under *certain laboratory conditions*, when, say, a rat cadaver was *manipulated* by some bored entomologist to simulate movement, the mantis could be tricked into pigging out. *The Reanimators!* Yech. Mantises could hide in plain sight by *undulating* like leaves in the wind. Double yech. *Whoa creepy.* Jerzy told him he read on the internet that mantises could kill fucking field mice & tree frogs & *soft-shelled turtles*—triple ugh! They seemed to be OCD sticklers too: when random offal detachSPLAT'd to the ground during an hellacious arthropodal chow, the morsel *stayed* on the ground like when a society lady drops a fork, you know suddenly it's untouchable.

Hey Rikki do you feel me? Rikki? can you feel me?

Jerzy said the internet said Arabs thought mantises always prayed toward Mecca. The internet said Americans used to think or maybe still do that a mantis could blind a sleeping man & murder a baby in its crib. (*SID = Sudden Insect Death*) The internet said the French believed a praying mantis can point the direction home for a child who was lost. Well some of the French maybe . . . .

Rikki said "Hey dude, enough, I don't want this shit in my head."

Jerzy said "*I* didn't put shit in your head, bro, you put it in *mine*. You & *Fishburne*, right? I'm just *reminding* you of shit you *already know*. And you're going to *need to know it*, bro. So you better be listening."

Rikki said (with a smile at least) "Dude you are *seriously* fucked up. You oughta lay that PCP pipe down for a little. *Whatever* it is you're doin. Cause that shit is fuckin you *up*."

"If I lay it down you be pickin it up for sure."

. . .

Nighttime. Rikki did a bootie bump right there in the truck while Jerzy was off stalking the wild *honeyshot!*—Madonna & her daughter, at La Dolce Vita. J'd been after Lourdes' hirsute honeydew for a few months now, stalking the elusive Little Madge vadge, a rare vintage indeed for Harry's privates reserve. H 'round the M was in Jerzy's front pocket now, seeing that Jerzy was the 1st & only snatcherazzo Harry deigned reach out to, the only one he thought would *understand*, & not judge. Jerzy had been pleased to introdouche himself.

Before Jerzy jumped out, he handed his young cohort a syringe of YES *sans* the spike. The boy really took to the meth/roxie combo *where have I been all your life*. He was smoking crystal now too, he'd do it in Tom-Tom's room, he didn't want ReeRee to see-see, Tom-Tom would laugh her spooky laugh not her goodtime girl laugh, T^2 seemed to mind Rikki the least when he did dope in front of her. Some kind of control trip.

Rikki bootie-bumped at the house but never in a car. A car! *Dude! Get over yourself* . . . hiked his pants down under dark Bev Hills residential moon trees a hundred yards north of Sta Monica blvd. & *shazam* the deed was done. When Jerzy returned, Rikki was in some kind of reverie, & startled. His pants were still down, right above the knees, he had an oblivious deathclutch on the base of his rockhard dick, holding it there like a bouquet at Queer Prom. Jerzy cackled. *Get a room, bro.* Pretty good size camel on him tho, lotsa *explainin* to do down there . . . *très* deboner oops I mean debonair. What Rikki did next took Jerzy by surprise: he stroked it a few times & came, gluegunning the glove compartment. Rikki never did that in front of a man before but knew it was just business, the business of meth, when he got home there was some crap in his pants too, decent amount, what shocked Jerzy was that the kid had managed to spackle at all because sometimes he jacked 10 hrs straight w/o liftoff.

Kids today.

. . .

He invited Rikki to see his work.

Jerzy stayed in the poolhouse which actually was the coolest place to live but no one wanted to because a generator as big as an outhouse sat buttnext to it. The thing was connected to two frigidaire freezers Betty White bought in the 1800s and kept out in the garage. The old generator had a full personality; it'd been around long enough to have earned run of the house (at least of the poolhouse & areas adjacent), meaning it belched revved rebooted and refarted whenever it damn pleased.

Rikki was anxious to see his new BFF's art. Jerzy kept his various stashes in the poolhouse/garage & Rikki was anxious to see those too. Jerzy was now the official hostess w/the mostess.

The middleschool dropout, out-of-work actor & dad-to-be stepped back to take it all in while Jerzy rooted around for a pipe. Rikki was confused. He thought the photos would be shots of celebrities but couldn't tell *what* they were. Jerzy kept mum, he was otherwise engaged. Rikki's head was elsewhere too, he was thinking of his BFF's stash but knew he really needed to try & focus *solely* on the so-called artwork because the more sincere & attentive he was to the pictures on the wall, the sooner & larger the bowl of crystal awaited him as a reward to ignite his bones . . . so he made sure to stay respectfully *on* it, even tho each millisecond was a war waged against ripping his eyes away from the weird, perfectly hung images & swiveling around to google if Jerzy was still treasurehunting the pipe or if he'd found it & already moved on to tapping no-longer-a-Secret Stash #1. Rikki decided to pose a question, which would at least afford him a quick glance, all like very fake casual, doop-de-doop-de-doo, like why would he have *any* interest in whatever the fuck Jerzy was up to, you know, like, how Rikki *really* wanted to spend the next 4 days was writing up a little *critique* about Jerzy's fucked-up *art project*, the very *last* thing on his mind being to smoke a few bowls & get to the porn.

"Are you going to call it anything? I mean, it's like gunna be a show at a museum & shit?"

Not bad—the *actor* in him did a pretty good job too of not seeming too anxious you know like if Jerzy offered him a bowl, cool, but if not, that'd be cool too, which like it *wouldn't* because Rikki would probably fucking club Jerzy to death with whatever was at hand. But Jerzy had the pipe & bowl in hand; shit was looking up.

"'Bad News Bears.' No, I'm kidding. *Daydream Believers*. I'm kidding I'm kidding. Do you know what a 'captcha' is?" Rikki shook his head. "It's when you go online and there's like a word & maybe numbers in a box written in wavy letters? And before they give you access you have to type in what you think the numbers & letters are? They call that a *captcha*. It's how they can tell you're human & not a computer." Rikki didn't know what the fuck he was talking about. "It's how they separate the hummingbirds from the mantis. So right now that's what I'm calling it, 'Captcha.' And I'm calling myself *Squeegee*. 'Captcha by Squeegee.'"

"Cool."

"So do you want to smoke some of this?"

.   .   .

"Can you listen?"

"Yes."

"We'll get down some more after you listen."

"I'll listen. I'm listening."

"You have to *want* to listen."

"But I do, dude. I do."

"This is about the number 3. Are you ready for this?"

Rikki nods.

Then:

"*3* . . . is the *only* number with a *beginning, middle & end.*"

Rikki let it sink in. Jerzy watches it sink into Rikki.

"I'm going to give you a triad. Know what a triad is?"

Rikki shook his head.

"It's a *group* or *set* of *3 connected people* or *things.*"

Rikki was already so far out there *whoa why would I need why do I even need to why would I want to get more out there yes I need to get more more more out there I do—*

"OK. All I'm going to do is give you *one triad.* 1 set of 3."

"OK."

"Then we'll get down with the KJ."

"Okay."

"I got a hundred roxies."

"For real?"

"For real-real. For really-real real."

"You're the bomb."

"We cn get stardusted."

"Uh I don't know I don't think so."

"I'm going to give you a *triad.* But you need to be *ready.*"

"I am. I am. I'm ready."

"I'm just going to say it."

"I'm listening."

"Here it is: *Iovine, Mathers, Jay-Z.*"

"What?"

"Say it."

"You trippin dude you trippin."

"Say it."

"Man this is—shit—you—"

"Say it. *Iovine, Mathers, Jay-Z.*"

"Iovine, Mathers, Jay-Z. But dude you trippin—————"

"Jay-Z is *Hov.* Say it."

"Dude I just want to smoke."

"Jay-Z is *Hov.* Say it."

"Jay-Z is *Hov.*"

"Hov = *Jehovah*. Jay-*hov-uh*."

"Jay-hov-uh."

"Jehovah = YAHWEH."

"YAHWEH?"

"That's a triad. That's all you need to know."

"All right. All right. I'm down, dude. I'm down. I'm down."

"Take the pipe."

fuck dude thank you. (Smokes/coughs. Crazy/smokes. Crazy) o dude thank you o shit dude it/s good. thank you. all that shit is for real heavy all your art too man dude shit thank you. i fuckin LOVE *this shit hey hey hey dude, go for a ride let's just drive or whatever you want to do what do you need man what do you need I fuckin* LOVE *this shit if you want me to do like I'm not like that but if you want me to do whatever to you to make you feel good, to keep the bowls cummin that/s cool i don/t do that shit for real but i/d do for you for real to whatever because all this shit is for real serious thank you i* O! SHIT! *dude, let's go for a ride! let/s go back to britney/s cmon dude! but we don/t have to, we don/t have to but if we don/t can you like take me down the hill? can you maybe like take me down the hill in the morning or tonight or whenever? cause i forgot to get maxipads for ree she said to get maxipads she's leaking pee dude let/s smoke can we just another bowl*

Cancer Awareness

It was early in the game, but he had that old *feeling*, the feeling that things were coming together.

He was at Ago with Heather Morris, the screenwriter Steve Kloves and the dancer Benjamin Millepied. Ben's wife sent her regrets; home with a sick baby.

Though he still planned to write the script himself (he was working on it in his trailer between *Treasure* scenes), talking it out with Steve was invaluable—the man, as they say, not only knew his shit but remembered where he put it. They first got to know each other on the set of *Wonder Boys* and had loosely kept in touch. Through the years, Michael's family made it a tradition to have supper with Steve and Jo whenever *Harry Potter* had its UK premières.

He knew Benjamin's work long before *Black Swan*. Michael and Catherine were fans back when he was a soloist at the City Ballet. When they finally met, Ben shared that he'd performed in a Jerry Robbins piece. Michael was a friend of Jerry's and realized he must have seen the kid dance sometime in '95. It was fun to introduce him to Heather. She was sweetly nervous, and the dancer put her at ease. He told her that he and Natalie loved *Glee* (and especially her). Ben did his YouTube homework too; he was genuinely impressed by He-Mo's hip hop dance videos.

Benjamin got a call from his wife and left a bit early. Through a faraway window, Michael and his guests saw the explosion of flashes coinciding with Ben's exit. They even heard shouts, no doubt of the "Where's Natalie! Where's your wife!" variety. Heather was the next to go, and went alone as well. Michael wanted to keep his project under wraps & didn't want them to be photographed together.

· · ·

Whenever she left a restaurant, there were always professional autograph seekers begging her to sign all sorts of Brittany/HeMo glossies, posters, and promotional items. When she started getting famous, other ☆s cautioned her not to sign, telling her those "fans" just turned around and sold everything online. Heather didn't care. She felt so blessed that she always signed anyway as she walked to her car.

[strobe storm cell clusters, then:]

Heather!

Brittany!

Are you friends with Michael!

Why were you having dinner! Heather!

WHY

are you going to work together!

is Catherine returning to Glee?

is Michael going to be on Glee!

Brittany! Over

HERE!

Here!   *Smile! Does Catherine know*

does Catherine know

does Catherine know you had dinner

with Michael?———————————

She got in the car. The valet unsuccessfully tried to block the chubby sweetfaced woman now at her window. "Heather we *love* you but we read in *Us* what you keep in your bag, & I need to *warn* you that a lot of the ingredients *are not safe.* Your MAC Skinfinish has TALC&*retinyl palmitate* which is linked to *cancer*!   And *ethyl*

    "Heather!   Heather!!!!!

hexyl methoxycinnamate interferes with cellular signaling, &

"H E A T H E R————————————"   can cause

mutations & HH Heather HEA T H

    DEATH! Flirt Dreamy Eyes Eyeshadow has chlorphenesin chlorphenesin is a preservative that is restricted in Japan it is NOT recommended for pregnant or nursing wo

H - - - -

. . .

Initially, Michael was concerned when his agent told him the talented director Bryan Singer was developing a film drama about Fosse for HBO. "Bye Bye Life" didn't have a screenwriter yet, & would be based on the eponymous bio. They spent two hours on the phone—Bryan was in Europe—which began with trepidation and ended with the director's peppy *insistence* that Michael proceed. Bryan said it might be a tougher call if he wasn't making his film for cable; two Fosse biopics might be more than the feature marketplace could bear. By the end of their talk, both men were convinced that the approach of the two films was different enough for each to flourish in its own way. Bryan said that in light of Michael's fairly recent, very public cancer drama, the whole concept of him dancing through a remake was beyond brilliant. It was inspired.

"*That's* a movie I want to see," he said.

·   ·   ·

Post-*Glee*, Catherine and the kids flew to their home in Quebec. He was 3 wks into *Treasure*, a 4-month shoot in all, and thus far workdays had been heavy. The producers assured him that wouldn't last, or at least that his schedule would get light before it got heavy again.

Michael had a few long weekends coming up and was anxious to join his family.

·   ·   ·

He was booked on Jimmy Kimmel at the end of the week. Before going to bed, he watched a a clip on YouTube of his Kimmel appearance last year. He looked for a while then scrolled down, idly reading the comments. He'd trained himself not to do that, but tonight it just happened.

> whiteonwhite 4 days ago @j4902lovechild I always knew he should be on stage—STAGE FOUR!!!!! SOOO HAPPY as an actof he has always SUCKED
>
> catacomb12 4 days ago @vermilion 1 month ago you are SO SICK he is a brave soul&wonderfull MAN may god have mercy on your DISSEASED SOUL
>
> Destroyallcheese 2 weeks ago @2120juvenilia HE IS STILL SMOKING MARLBORRO REDS!!!!! that is not a fighter.
>
> Jerseywhore 3 weeks ago @ottawacentipede (I hate to say this), but RARELY have I seen people winning against cancer. Many people I know(includin my grandfather) died from cancer. he was diagnosed in 2005, he went into treatment, he then felt alot better (the cancer was

gone), but in 2009 the cancer "was back". He struggled ALOT, went
into treatment again, but he

Invisible forces led him to continue his scroll.

Someone said that Catherine wasn't bipolar, she was just a spoiled
cunt, & they hoped she got cancer right in her starting-to-droop tits
and in her waxed butthole too because that's what happens when you
sell your soul for $$$$ to a philandering kike with an HPV.

Someone said the divorce with Diandra was a ruse, they were still
married, & Kirk discovered that the greedy juices of Diandra's vagina
gave him eternal life. They said Michael didn't fall too far from the
jewjew tree because he bought Catherine at auction & everyone
groupsexed, Catherine got paid $2,000,000 each time Diandra held
her down for Kirk to rape her talentless, cellulite-strafed ass and another two mill whenever they did it in front of Michael and the
kids . . .

He walked to the balcony to shake it off.

He thought about calling Calliope but it was already after midnight. She might still be up watching one of her movies, or be dead
to the world. He didn't want to risk waking her.

He tried diluting the poison by staying up and meditating. He
went through the breaths Catherine taught him. (It really helped
during chemo.) With each inhalation God came in and with each
exhalation, the poison flushed out, from his head, his gut, his
heart.

When sleep came, he fell instantly into bad dreams.

*Backstage, waiting to go on. A producer approaches to tell him Jimmy Kimmel
went to the hospital for emergency cancer surgery. The last minute replacement
is Roger Ebert.*

*Michael hears himself being introduced. He takes the stage under glaring
lights. The audience rises to its feet but does not applaud or whoop—like
automatons standing formal sentinel. The actor knows he can soften them*

up with his famous icebreaker. He swivels on the couch, looking into the theater.

"There's gotta be an easier way to get a standing ovation."

His timing is perfect, but still no response.

Awkward.

He turns back to Ebert.

The film critic wears a black turtleneck whose collar ends at Ebert's pointy Thalidomide witch's half-chin. Above that, the we-never-close fishmouth, with an invisible hook pulling the lower lip into a goofy, sing-hallelujah-come-on-get-happy grin.

— Michael, thanks for dropping by! When did you first learn that the cancer came back?

The actor is nonplussed.

— It didn't, Roger. I'm still cancer-free.

An explosion of laughter from the dead vertical audience.

— Aren't we all!

Another volley of disembodied guffaws.

— Michael, let's talk a little about the American doctors who 'missed' it. I was fortunate enough to have doctors who missed mine too. Now, I know it wasn't until you had it looked at in Sierra Leone that—

— Beverly Hills.

— What?

— They diagnosed at the Beverly Hills Hotel.

— Were you angry?

— Very.

— Are you going to sue?

A pause, then:

— My wife Diandra will, on my behalf.

His timing is perfect. Ebert and the audience laugh in approval of his guest's droll wit. Michael is surprised, thrilled at the reaction, & swivels again to acknowledge them but is perplexed to be looking out at an empty theater— a vast barn, with no seats or people.

— Just one more thing, because I know you can't stay. [The host directed

*his words toward the infinity of windblown emptiness] Michael's going in for
his weekly check-up—let's pray with him that the cancer's back.*

The actor started getting angry.

He closed his eyes and tried the breathing meditation.

Ebert said:

– Michael? There's just one more thing I'd like you to share.

Mercifully, he awakened.

[Gwen&Telma]

California URLs

Gwen got a reprieve.

Phoebe agreed the truth could wait until after the Courage Ball, when the little Canadian girl who'd become Telma's nemesis had gone home. Phoebe said that Aleisha triggered Telma's attachment disorder, or something like that.

Hours after they aborted their plan, Gwen got a shot of clearheadedness in the tub. She'd already phoned Phoebe twice.

"Sorry Pheeb, I know I'm a broken record."

"You call as much as you need to, Gwen. I'm here for you."

"What I *wanted* to say was, there's another reason I'm glad we didn't tell her."

"What's that?"

"I'm just sitting here soaking, and—I remembered how *specific* they were, the attorneys, about not revealing anything to anyone—"

"Telma's hardly 'anyone,' Gwen."

Gwen loved that Phoebe never rolled over. She wasn't contentious, she just liked to advocate all different sides of an argument. She told Gwen that was how she got "clear."

"But I should really talk to my lawyer, shouldn't I Pheeb? I mean, before we tell her? At least sort of bring him in on what's going on, on what my *plans* are. Don't you think?"

"I kind of brought this up when you said you were getting more medical opinions. Is informing Telma what happened any of his business?"

"It could be—I think it probably is."

"Tell me your concern."

"There's going to be a settlement, Phoebe. That's a foregone conclusion. As soon as I can figure out what the hell to do, which may be never. But which kind of *has* to be soon, or so my lawyer—my *lawyers*, there's like *seven* of them—said. Or relatively. I just don't want, when they start to negotiate or whatever, I just don't want anyone saying, 'We told you not to discuss this with anyone and now we hear your daughter's been blogging & twittering'—which is *exactly* what she *would* do, Pheeb!—and then it gets picked up by the Huffington Post, with *The New York Times* not far behind . . . *I* don't know. I think maybe their plan, the hospital's plan, their *attorneys'*, is to *seal* it, you know seal the records once we agree to a settlement—I'm going to have to set up a trust—I'm sure that's probably what they would *want*, to seal the *record* so the hospital doesn't look bad. I just don't want to fuck that up, for Telma, I've already fucked so many *other* things up———*Jesus,* Phoebe, you know I'm just thinking, I think I might have even *signed* something, something *binding* to that effect."

"Ah. OK, right. Now I see."

"You do?"

"Yeah, & it's very smart. Talk to him. Talk to your lawyer."

"I will, in the morning. But how am I going to *ever* tell her?"

"What do you mean?"

"I can't *order* Telma not to talk about it. I can't say, OK honey, the doctors made this mistake but you can *never discuss it* with *anyone, ever*—"

"You won't have to say that. Gwen, St. Ambrose can't put a gag order on Telma. They'll never be able to suppress the truth of what happened anyway, not with the internet, and that's something they're going to need to come to terms with. That's what your lawyers are for—that's something to be negotiated. That if and when it *does* come out, there won't be any penalties. At the same time, I think your daughter is eminently capable of coming to certain understandings. I think she'll have no trouble seeing who needs to know what, & how much. Telma's still very much a kid, but in other ways she's very much a young lady."

"OK."

"I'm glad we had this discussion, because I think I probably did you a bit of a disservice. I might have leapt before I looked."

"*You* didn't do anything, Phoebe . . ."

"Not true, I got *emotional*. I wasn't coming from a very grounded place, which is what you—what *both* of you really need right now."

"Phoebe, I know how hard it—you love her *so much*—"

"I can't let that cloud my judgment, Gwen."

"I think you're being a little hard on yourself."

"*As I should.* Look, it happens. I know that. It just hasn't happened to *me*. Therapists are people too, that's why therapists have therapists. We're fallible. And because I have a very special relationship with your daughter—"

"She calls you Mama Bear #2, did you know that?"

"—we've been through the fire, all of us together. Which means I need to be *extra* careful, *extra* aware, I really do. To not let my feelings intrude. But that's no excuse, that doesn't excuse me being sloppy. I need to take a look at my codependency. Do some work. And I just need to call that out."

"Thank you. I love you, Phoebe."

"Would you like me to be on the phone when you talk to your attorney?"

. . .

im 12. and im a 32A. now all the guys like me but they are always like wow ur flat. im like ohk? so is there a push up bra for a 32A and where can i get them for not too expensive??? please girls.
1 year ago

Telma was multitasking: watching TV, shopping online, and writing a letter all at the same time.

She was looking at sites that sold pushup bras. She talked to her mom about getting one a few months ago but they never did. She was visiting a Y! Answers forum.

> Okay listen you 12 years old and apparently flat chested. If the guys like you then you shouldn't worry. If you got a push up bra to moderatly please the guys you are also building up a rep as a guchi mama to the girls. Wait they will grow trust me.
> 4 months ago

> if the boys like you already thats great you must be so beautiful, but if theyre disapointed that you are flat chested thats just too bad for them because the only reason people like big boobs is so they can take your bra off and do all sorts of things with and to them BUT if you use a push up bra the boys will be even more disapointed when you take off your bra cause they will be expecting you to have a nice pair of boobies but if you wear a normal bra atleast you know your boobs are real and you can even tell guys that if you want cause its the thruth and theyll like you more for your real boobs ;) plus trust me its only a matter of time before those A's turn into C's unless small boobs run in the family
> 8 months ago

She thought she might have erased *The Nine Lives of Chloe King.* She watched a little of *The Vampire Diaries* then tried finding *New Girl,* which was actually supposed to be on *right now* but it wasn't, so she watched one of those teen mom shows instead. (They were having a marathon, which she thought they only did on holidays.) Telma *never* watched them, they were so *boring and annoying,* the girls were all brats who held their babies like props when they weren't crying or hitting someone in the head (their BFs, BFFs, moms or grandmas) & the boys were big dumb liars, like, *seriously* retarded. Telma felt sorry for the babies because they were going to grow up to be just like their scary parents, with no idea about how to live or how to help people or how to anything except cry and hit people and take drugs and steal money from your girlfriend's granny so you could buy a pickup you were going to total anyway.

The teen mom show commercials were *really* weird. Like one for birth control that looked like it was a *hearing aid* you stuck inside. *OMG disgusting, I will NEVER!* At the end, a woman listed all the side effects and different ways the birth control thingie could be dangerous. They said don't use it if you had "certain cancers" and Telma thought that probably meant ovarian not breast. The birth control ad was *totally normal* compared to the ones that came on for "Wild Partyline" & "Livelink" which were *TOTALLY DISGUSTING.* OMG!!!!! She paused the TV and went right to the Livelinks Facebook page. It was a full-on dating site but maybe one where you only talked to people on the phone? "Immediate & exciting! Meet someone *tonight.*" So gross! But Wild Partyline was *sooooooooooo* completely gross and disgusting. Telma googled the URL & clicked on it: CONNECT WITH 100'S OF *HORNY EBONY BABES* & *SEXY LATINAS* NOW! *O. My. God.* "SWEET PHONE SEX WITH A HORNY OLDER SLUT" . . . . no! no! *nooooooo!!!!!!!!!!!!* . . . .

————Telma could understand why the show would have a birth control commercial because lots of teenaged and younger girls watched the teen moms . . . but why were the *other* ads there?????????

OMG

——————the TV people who paid for the teen mom shows must know that DIRTY OLD MEN ARE WATCHING??????!!!!!

Ewwwwwwwww!

Im gonna B A R F ! ! ! ! ! ! ! !

She turned it off and reread her letter.

It was in cursive, like the one she'd written to Michael. She wanted to stand out, not just be one more of a million emails. In some places she copied from the Michael letter verbatim. She made the decision to continue to refer to herself as the world's "youngest Kansurvivor," as technically, Aleisha hadn't been alive long enough after her surgery to earn that "sobriquet."

Kris Jenner
Life & Style Magazine
Ask Kris:
THE KARDASHIANS' MOM SOLVES YOUR PROBLEMS
askkris@lifeandstylemag.com

Dear Kris,

My name is Telma Belle Peony Ballendyne. (Belle is my grandma's name & Peony is my mom's favorite flower and mine too!) I am 13 years old and a <u>Kansurvivor</u>. I became a <u>HERO</u> (not <u>victim</u>) of this terrible disease at the age of <u>9 years old</u> and have been <u>Kancer-free for 4 years now</u>, making me the <u>youngest Kansurvivor in America and maybe the world</u>! The doctors decided that it was necessary to perform a double mastectomy, for which I am also Guiness World Record Book-bound. There is a LOT more of my story which I will not BORE you with (at this time!;D).

(As you can see, I LOVE LOVE LOVE "K"'s!!!!! Almost as much as the Kardashians!!!!!!!!!!!!!!!!!!!!!!!)

I had a mastectomy & was lucky not to need a course of chemo or radiation. The doctors say there is "NO REASON" why I could not one day concieve of a child—which I very much would, & a DAUGHTER & hopefully MORE daughters, so that one day I may start a Dynasty of my own like you and Bruce!!!!

I am not a fan of very thin, annorexic girls & actresses. I think it is for some people a VERY REAL SICKNESS, & they need all the help they can get. YOUR DAUGHTER Kim & ALL of your DAUGHTER'S are so beautiful & unself-concsious about their beautiful womanly bodies. I know they are like that because of what how carefully you taught to them, & the SHINING EXAMPLE that you set, which is SO laudable!! I read the Glamour.com interview where Kim said she had a C-cup when she was even

YOUNGER *than me & used to sit in the bathtub with hot towels over her boobies, pray-ing they did not grow. (I sit & pray that mine WILL!!! though alas it is impossibel until the days of medical miracles which may not be for 100 yrs. But maybe APPLE will come up with the iPADDED BRA!! ;D) What was so very lovely & beautiful, Kris, was when Kimberly said that you SAT WITH HER & told her how much she would love her VERY big boobies one day, you said Armenians are curvy, you said, "This is who you are." & Kim said that was what gave her the confidence to be who she was!!!!*

I am writing to you to ask your guidance in finding a plastic surgeon so that when I am of the proper age, I too may have a FULL WOMANLY CHEST, & comely & au-natural-looking like your daughters. I know that your daughters's many chests are REAL. But the reason I am asking is that I know that you only associate with the VERY BEST in whatever field they may toil, & THAT is why I feel confident in asking you this. I like my other features very much & do not anticipate having any face work done until I am very old (my 40s). So all that I am asking is for a recommendation or referral (perhaps it would be best if you could make an introductory call?) for the VERY BEST NEW BREAST DOCTOR or even <u>doctors</u>, so I can meet him or the whole Team, & we can all get to know each other. That way, when my time comes, he won't be operating on a stranger. I have many doctor friends & get along with them very well. They are real friends, not pre-tend friends. They are "Telma's Warriors."

I am not worrying about my flat chest (which is also somewhat scarred by the skin grafting but is not as bad as that sounds)—I am not worrying very much NOW because there are no men in my life but one day if a boy finds my person-ality to be attractive to him, & I like him back in the same way, I would enjoying being in the position to be a NORMAL girl. (My dream is to look like ALL YOUR DAUGHTERS above the WAIST!!!!) I would like to be able to wear a swimsuit on the beach in the summer too without attracting too many stairs. Do you think you could help me?

Thank you, KRIS! I could not ask my mother because she has been a little sad of late, & its not that I do not trust her or have faith in her decisions & taste (which I do to the 1000%!!!!), but I know the KARDASHIAN KLAN is "in the know" & that you would recommend to me a doctor with whom you would trust to work on your very own children, if they were in the position I am, which THANK GOD they are NOT! And THAT is why I decided to "<u>ASK KRIS</u>"!!!!

Thank you, & I love to keep up with the Kardashians & I love your show & ALL your shows there are so many I have LOST COUNT!!!!!!!!

Sincerely,

Telma Belle Ballendyne

P.S. I have more than enough money saved, I believe my mother has put away for me monies from various sources to the tune of $100,000, I wanted to tell you this so you could tell the doctors that I am not a fly-by-night (which used to be my Dad's favorite phrase or sobriquett) or charity case & can pay them their full fee. Glod Bless.

· · ·

The day had exhausted her.

She kept circling back to the taboo, the unspeakable.

In the week that followed the meeting in Century City, it was explained how the mistake had been made, the vague mechanics and diabolically shifting sands of it. (The parts that Gwen was able to understand only made it worse.) The most pressing thing she wanted answered was how long they'd been aware of their mistake. They said that their findings had been confirmed only a week before disclosure; though Gwen had no reason to believe *anything* they said, this she chose to accept. Now it was up to the hospital to learn from the incident so it wouldn't happen again—new safeguards and protocols, mandatory seminars for doctors and nurses, required classes for radiologists. The time would come when insurance paid whatever it was going to pay, & everyone moved on, everyone but Gwen. There would be no mob of outraged parents in the streets demanding justice, because Telma wasn't *their* child; not the child of the brilliant, winning, idiosyncratic oncologists; not the child of the superb, bosomy nurses, each at the top of their game, drenched in compassion. The RNs gave Telma *and* Gwen their hearts, and she knew how mortified they would be upon learning of the secret horrors perpetrated on their mascot, their soldier, their—well, *yes*—baby girl.

Telma hadn't been born to *any* of them and they owed her nothing. They went home at night to their families, the children they'd so carefully raised and kept safe from harm. For a long while, Telma didn't come home at all. She roamed the *peed onk* hallways with her dog, spreading good cheer, climbing every mountain, dreaming impossible dreams. She made her nest in that deathstar place, a mutilated pig-tailed Phantom of the Operating rooms, a roving Dora the explorer of strange- and sinister-smelling corridors, of cubbyholes housing exotic, pitiably young inhabitants, each one dying or healing from rarities, each with readymade story & fate, they captivated her because now Telma was one of them, only she was stronger, she was braver, the *New Girl*, brave new girl in a brave new world.

All these years Gwen had grown to believe she was a reasonably tough mom, a worthy adversary for the cause. Only now had she begun to realize how terribly matched she was, not against the disease but the rampaging medical superheroes, each one more confident than the next of the proposed course of action. What a charade! What a fool she was to be exhorting them from her ringside seat! *Why did I embrace the diagnosis so quickly, so deep? How dare I! Would I have just rolled over if they said the same things to me? If I got double-teamed by* vultures *who said they needed to cut off my tits & needed to do it* FAST *or I might die? Would I have been so awed? so cowed & resigned? She didn't want to think about this anymore because it was too much, she would have to learn some technique, train herself to permanently deepsix what was too shaming, damning, overwhelming, too suicide-baiting. It made her want to die and that was the one thing she could* not *do, not as long as Telma was alive. There was no use indulging in the repetitive argument, that was a form of madness, searching for balm where there was none, Gwen knew that Phoebe or anyone really would just keep telling her it wasn't her fault, none of it had been, she was being irrational, that she did what any mother would have (tho she'd always know in her heart that it wasn't true), if you Googled pediatric onc Telma's whole team would be on the very first page, they were world-class, they were unimpeachable, they were legendary. There was no use because after a while you become a bore and people rightfully began to shun you, all you had left was your therapist who now was really nothing more than a paid friend, since therapy had gone by the wayside, there could be no therapy for you anymore, you were cooked, you were done, you had graduated, into Hell. She knew people would grow tired of her, and the ones that hadn't run or disappeared completely would practically stage an intervention asking her beg-ging her to please think about Zoloft or whatever pill it was that would help during this tough time. (Translation: help them by making her less of an in-sane needy bother.) "This tough time"! After the intervention they'd go home, those repelled soon-to-no-longer-be friends she'd been abusing, home to the kids they guarded even more closely now than before, having had the enlight-ening experience of coming across the highway accident of Gwen's cautionary tale, moving slowly by in their vehicles, taking in the guttering flares & man-gled metal, their children wide-eyed in the backseat, eyes glued to windows, thank God this did not happen to me—————well, thought Gwen, at least it isn't like losing a child to a pool drowning, you turn your back & it's over, those marriages never survive because the parent who wasn't home blames the one who was—o thank god Max wasn't alive! for this! Thank god Max never saw them do this to his baby! At least that was something to be grateful for. And didn't Eric Clapton's—didn't he fall—from a win-dow———————NO! NO NO NO, Gwen HATED when she started doing that, trafficking in others' grief to benumb herself, hated that more than ANYTHING, it made her feel cruel, astringent, mon-strous———————who knew what those same friends & families said in the privacy of their homes . . . there was probably a whole group of them (in reverie, Gwen doubted if they'd even be aware of their same-held opinions because it just wasn't the sort of thing to openly gossip about or ex-change notes, a kind of primordial superstition would prevent them from giving voice to what happened at the accursed House of Ballendyne, especially when you had kids of your own, it would be pretty near taboo) who murmured/pil-lowtalked with their spouses in those intimate moments before sleep, I really don't think I would EVER have let that happen to my child, I don't care WHO the doctors were, I'd have gone to the ends of the Earth . . . Then the husband might say in that male way, "That woman was asleep at the FUCKING WHEEL. There is just NO WAY—" or maybe if he was the husband of one of her dwindling circle of BFFs, maybe for a minute the BFF*

would rally to Gwen's defense and say "Hey c'mon now hon that isn't fair"
but the retort would be limply politic because in actuality she would agree with
him but couldn't let on, so she mounted a little technical defense of Gwen, her
BFF-to-soon-no-longer-be, because as a mom & still-technical-BFF it was
just the karmically correct thing to do. Yet the wife's minuscule effort would do
nothing to obscure the fact that both instinctively knew in their secret husband-
wife/mom-dad language (their twins, Telma's age, asleep two walls away)
that "Hey c'mon now hon that isn't fair" translated to "Of course she was
asleep at the fucking wheel, she's no different than one of those moms who
drown their kids in the tub, she's NUTS, I just can't say that about my
friend because I'm superstitious about bringing energy to it, about something
then happening to our own kids," all of that unspoken, or spoken, but in code,
it would be so obvious, the wife's affirmation of a truth told that she shared but
dare not express, also not a rebuke to hubby but a way to say let's hush now
and go to sleep, let's not call the wrath of anyone's god, & the husband would
cease his banter, he'd shot his macho family-protecting Papa Bear wad, her
signal that it's time to spoon, he'd hold her from behind in solidarity & grati-
tude that it didn't happen to them, to their family, holding her in quiet holy
gratitude and respect for her loyalty & commendable discretion, that's just how
a great wife and stand-up friend's supposed to act, & they'd fall asleep like
that spooning, husb and wife and unmauled children, whereas Gwen would
toss and turn, husbandless, with her deformed Tel————

. . .

She xanaxscrolled through the CHANNEL MENU GUIDE: news, news,
infomercial, *Cheers* in Spanish, sports sports sports, *House*, Kardashian, Kardashian, *Hell's Kitchen*. Some anchorperson was offering
tips on how to explain political assassination to your kids. Julian
Assange was hosting *SNL*—no. Can it be? *Maybe that's Bill Maher.*
But why would Bill Maher be hosting SNL?

She scrolled down, down, down . . .

Michael Douglas and Laurence Fishburne were on Jimmy Kimmel. Everyone was in high antic spirits. Everyone was laughing, everyone was rich, everyone was cancer-free. Jimmy Kimmel kept

saying let's talk about your movie, why don't you want to talk about your movie, & Michael said I don't want to talk about it, ain't even a *movie* yet, we're still shooting. Jimmy Kimmel said something & Gwen missed it & Michael's response was *Don't be an asshole,* they bleeped out *asshole,* & Laurence Fishburne was laughing so hard (he hadn't said anything the whole time, he just laughed) that Gwen thought he looked stoned off his gourd. The audience was having a blast, they already loved Michael because of his cancer victory, his comic humility about it, his elegant courageousness, the model of how everyone dreamed they'd handle their *own* diagnosis, they loved that he didn't drop by the show to sell something. Gwen caught herself thinking, *Wouldn't it be funny if Michael didn't have cancer too? That would be so nice for Telma, to have a friend that went through the same thing* then stopped herself. Trafficking again . . .

Jimmy Kimmel got serious & said he understood that Michael had brought along a very special friend who was backstage. Michael said that's right, she's in the wings. He said he was hosting a fundraiser at the end of the week, the Courage Ball, they raise money every year for kids with cancer, & his friend was going to be the guest of honor. *She's got a helluva voice too but she's not gunna sing tonight, not for the kind of money you people offer.* She came all the way from Canada to be here. Jimmy Kimmel said he met her before the show, she's a very special girl, then he asked Michael if there was something *else* that made her special. Michael said yes, she's the youngest breast cancer survivor in the world *the audience gasped and applauded then cut short their applause, to save it for her* she was diagnosed at 2½ and had a modified radical mastectomy at three *the breath of the audience got choppy with that awful detail, a kind of groan and the taking back of the groan all at once, in decency & respect for the little girl because the audience didn't want her imminent arrival to have any air of spectacle, this child deserved being met at her level, with decency & respect, they didn't want to subject her ears to carnival sounds, because she was Everychild.* Then Michael, with playful irritation said, *Jesus, can we bring her out already, Jimmy?* The audience laughed & out she came (holdng Mom's hand) in her *dear* pink glasses, with her bear called Bear, in her party dress and hair done up atop her head, the audience *awwwww'd* like they do when animal experts bring out perfect tiny lorises, tiger cubs (& baby bears called Bear), they melted & stood on their feet as she clambered onto the couch and into Michael's arms.

[Reeyonna]

Subterranean Homesick Blues

Not

feeling well. Physically depressed, emo-depressed. Shit spiritual. Doesn't leave her room. Rikki brings melty Yogurtland. Rikki craigslistbought a new used motorcycle, where did he get the bread. ReeRee only eats Rocky Road. Rikki picks up Rocky Road from 7Eleven when he doesn't feel like riding over to Y-land on La Brea, she likes Ben & Jerry's but it's *ice cream,* I'm like 200 lbs overweight, *can you please just go to why can't you please just go to Yogurtland?* When he delivers the ice cream he tries to cheer her up but she hates that he's so wasted. *You're gunna die on that bike and your baby will never know you.* She can thank big brother for that. What an asshole. Loser. *Looser.*

. . .

YouTube tripping. Kat Stacks talking about how she fucked all the brokass niggers in youngmoney. Kreayshawn talking about Kat Stacks being a ratchet ho. A slideshow tour of Beyoncé's million-dollar Mercedes van. (It has a shower and toilet.) ReeRee still couldn't believe Brody Jenner was the ½brother of all the Kardashians, *everyone* in that family was famous. Reeyonna *hated* that she'd been born this way, Lady Gaga should have written a song not about people who were born different but about people who were born to remain *nothing* until they died. She used to think she could never get famous because she had no discernible talent, tho look at Kim, Khloé & Kourtney. But even *they* had talent, *major* talent, it was just harder to say what it was, & that was part of the mystique.

She cried herself to sleep after watching 3½ hours of Kendall & Kylie Jenner and Janet Devlin. There were hundreds of videos Kylie and Kendall uploaded, karaoking to Nicki Minaj, they made funny videos in their bikinis with their friends from different exotic places, jumping around & laughing, so beautiful were their bodies, sometimes they did the videos from their room which was bigger than her mother's house, they were always in front of the cameras, they were growing up on camera, it was a natural thing for them, like a second language, you could tell they were in Paradise, she wanted so much to be a Kardashian. Janet Devlin lived on a beautiful farm in N Ireland like Rapunzel in *Tangled*/her castle, she had long beautiful straw-red hair too & one day she flew to Liverpool for *The X Factor* auditions and became immortal. It was *exactly* like Bella Swan, Reeyonna had that same nightmarish feverpitched painful *yearning* in every fiber of her being for the elixir of fame, she wanted to be a Kardashian or Janet Devlin, she wanted to suddenly be inside their bodies, it was the same yearning she had for Vampire Life & the elixir of immortality when she saw her 1st *Twilight* at 12 years-old—OMG she'd watched *every single one* of the Kendall Kylie Janet Devlin YouTubes, Janet sang all of her songs in a small room of her isolated country home, millions & millions of people watched, you could see cars in the window whizzing by & the reflection of herds of goats in the glass. OMG when she sang that Regina Spektor song *Us* . . . .

I'll never be famous I'll never be thanking stadium fans for not giving up on me never be saying FUCK Y'ALL to my h8trs, I'll never even HAVE h8trs, I just want to die!

.   .   .

She got an email from a company that stored the blood from your baby's umbilical cord.

It's nature's own insurance

The umbilical cord delivers nutrients and oxygen to your unborn child and contains specialized cells with great potential to generate healthy new cells and aid in the treatment of numerous diseases. As a result, more and more parents are opting to collect and store their child's cord blood.

What were they even talking about?

. . .

Rikki's fosterdad called. Jim never presses, only *suggests*. He's cool & methodical, a retired engineer. Rikki said he used to work on rockets. Jim says, *You know there's a bed waiting for you here, Reeyonna. Your privacy would absolutely be respected, I make you that promise. No unexpected visitors & that means you know who. Dawn & I will make sure of that.* Ree just couldn't say yes, she knew it was only her stubbornness, she knew that staying with Jim & Dawn was the best idea, probably the best place to be at this *time*, the best place for her new little family. To get the help & support she needed. Cause Rikki sure as shit wasn't going to provide it, he couldn't even get her fuckin yogurt. Reeyonna said haltingly, *Did she say anything about the cameras?* She kind of thought he knew or she probably wouldn't have mentioned it. Jim said, *She wasn't too thrilled. If you wanted to hurt her, mission accomplished. But I think your mother understood why you did it from your point of view. That doesn't excuse or minimize it, Reeyonna, but she said she understood. Anyway, none of my business. I just called to say what I said—& I'm glad you picked up!* Reeyonna thought it was cool Jim didn't bring up the cameras until she did. She said, *Yeah, and it's funny I did pick up because I haven't really been using my phone like at all.* Jim said, *I just want you to know that my wife & I are offering you sanctuary. For our grandchild . . .* ReeRee said, *I'll think about it, Jim, thank you, let me think about it,* knowing she wouldn't. *We all* said Jim *just want that baby to be healthy, that's priority number 1.* Reeyonna said, *Absolutely, & thank you Jim, you've always been so great. I'll really think about it, OK?* (Knowing she wouldn't, that the weed of her pride prevented her.) *We don't want him or her growing up to be a gypsy because his mom was wandering around* (engineer humor). *Jim, I have to get off now.* He said, *All right, Reeyonna, thank you for hearing me out. We're here for you, for you & Rikki & the baby.* She said, *I know that, Jim, & I really appreciate it. You've always— you & Dawn—you've always been so good to me, so fair. You're like the parents I wish I could have had. How is Dawn, is she doing OK?* (Some awkwardness there for Ree.) Jim said, *Dawn's fine, doing well, thank you for asking.* (ReeRee knew about Dawn's troubles thru Rikki.) *And how are you?* inquired ReeRee, suddenly Our Miss Manners of selfless telephone etiquette. *You doin OK?* Jim said, Me? *Can't complain. I woke up this morning & said, Welp I'm still on the right side of the dirt, guess I'll make a pot of coffee.* ReeRee laughed. What a sweet man. She had a pig for a mother and an asshole father who sent her postcards on her bdays, it was so interesting to see there were good parents in the world. *Rikki said there was a court date set for the adoption.* Jim said, *Yup. We're finally going to make the boy legal.*

A few more lobs & volleys, then:

— Reeyonna, will you do me a favor?

— Totally.

— I've got a money order for $500 with your name on it.

— No no! Jim, that's OK———

— It's from Dawn & she wanted me to give it to Rikki to give to you. So that's what I'm going to do.

— No really Jim you've given too much al————

— Now here's the favor. You said you'd do me a favor.

— OK, yes. I will. What is it.

— The *favor* is, you have to accept Dawn's money order & say thank you.

— That's the favor? she said with a half-smile.

— Yup.

— OK. That's *so sweet.*

— That's terrific. Dawn will be very glad. Now you take care.

— I love you. And please say hi to Dawn. And thank her for the money order.

— You bet I will.

— I'm going to write her a little note. I'll give it to Rikki.

— She'd love to hear from you. It's not *necessary*, but I know that she would.

— I love you, Jim.

— You take care now Reeyonna. (*Hangs up*)

. . .

Tom-Tom started hounding them (again) about the rent. She wanted like *two-thousand-dollars*. Fucking outrageous.

They had a week to pay. To make things worse, Tom-Tom told Reeyonna she had to switch rooms with Bolt so he could have the bigger, nicer room (tho of course Tom-Tom didn't put it that way). Which pissed ReeRee off because it was just a bullshit powerplay, the dude-ho always slept w/Tom-Tom anyway. When Ree protested now no one *else* was paying rent, Tom-Tom said that her *brother* was, & that being her ☆s, *Daydream Believers* were exempt. Reeyonna said *Hey put me in the cast, you can just say I was a* Teen Mom *reject,* Tom-Tom thought about it for about a second before saying no. ReeRee couldn't understand why not, she thought it was a totally rad idea, maybe the best she'd ever had.

Tom-Tom said she was getting *lots* of responses from potential bad news bears & soon the temple on the Mount would be filled with righteous *loosers*. To date, she had just-a-*gigolo* Bolt (who Dr Phil joked had a screw loose); *Intervention* Dr Phil; a baker's apprentice from *Cake Boss* (coming next week from Portland); a kid from Season One of *Bait Car* who just got out of jail on grand theft auto, said he got time off for bad behavior *hawhawhaw* and would be Greyhounding from FL as soon as he could clear it with his probation officer; & a retired ticketing officer from *Parking Wars*. T² was still thinking about letting the Alaskan dyke with a semi-moustache who crashed her rig in *Ice Road Truckers* join their crew, she had to admit from their phone conversations that the chick was a hoot. She said the truckers called fuel "motion lotion." Tom-Tom said, Hey, we call it crank. But gimme some.

Tom-Tom was having a big romance with this creepy gel'd hair guy she met at that lame convention. His claim to fame was getting cut from the final round of auditions of a reality show about mostly menopausal women who hired hardish-bodied, orange-tanned man-whores for sex. *Barf.* (Reeyonna watched one of the episodes with Rikki, there was a married couple who got off having the husband watch his wife get fucked, only the husband didn't seem too happy about it, R&R couldn't even *believe* seemingly somewhat normalish people were agreeing to put their twisted shit on camera. Showtime probably had to pay them, Rikki thought maybe like $20,000.) Of course being the *looser* that he is, loose Bolt wasn't actually *in* any of the episodes, being featured instead on *Gigolos Behind the Scenes On-line* (onscreen time: 1 minute 48 seconds) throwing a hissy fit when they said pack your sixpack & your ding dong, amigo, cause you're *leaving Las Vegas.* How fucking lame was that?

Apparently Bolt was Tom-Tom's new exec prod. Supposedly he had all these *connects,* people who owed him favors and such. Rikki said Tom-Tom told him Bolt arranged for a crew to come next week & shoot footage of house hijinks. Tom-Tom wanted them to film for 3 days—the more footage she got, the better the pilot would be— she was putting together what they called a presentation reel but said she'd be happier if she could complete a 22-minute pilot. *Do you think the camera crew's gunna do it for FREE, Reeyonna? You know what nobody seems to be fucking cognizant of? Nobody is cognizant of the fact that* NO ONE BUT ME *is even supposed to fucking be* STAY-ING *here, which is what I promised Cherokee. I don't* BREAK PROM-ISES, *I keep my* WORD, *I* WILL *make it up to her, that's between* ME AND CHEROKEE, *that's* PERSONAL BUSINESS. *But I need you to be* COGNIZANT *that if you're* NOT PAYING RENT *then* TECHNICALLY *you are just a* SQUATTER *here & you can just go* SQUAT & *leak yr* PEE *someplace* ELSE. *Fuckin cloggin up the frickin*

TOILET *with yr freakin* NAPKINS. DON'T TELL ME YOU'RE NOT, YOU ARE! YOU ARE! I DON'T CARE WHAT YOU SAY, I KNOW THAT YOU ARE! YOU'RE FUCKIN CLOGGING THE TOILET & YOU'RE GOING TO PAY FOR THAT PLUMBER VISIT TOO, *$349! . . . you should just* MOVE BACK TO RIKKI'S, *he told me his parents have been asking you to do that, well that's* EXACTLY *what you're gunna have to frickin do if you don't come up with no fuckin* SKRILL. *And don't start* CRYIN *and shit,* OK? *Cause I don't have any* SYMPATHY. *As Bolt likes to say, All god's children don't get free lunch no more, due to* BUDGET CUTS. *Hahahahaha.*

When Ree snidely asked how much rent *Bolt* was paying, Tom-Tom exploded. *He isn't paying* ANY, *bitch, because if it weren't for* HIM *there would be* NO FUCKING PILOT OR CAMERA CREW *& if you give me anymore* SHIT *I'll throw you & that frickin* TUMOR *you're growing in your* ASS *on the frickin* STREET. *Understand?* (ReeRee had to nod and keep her head down, had to sit & take it because she didn't have a plan.) *Motherfuckin nigger wannabe wants to tell me my* BUSINESS. *16 & pregnant & she's all up in my* BUSINESS, *ain't* THAT *a bitch. You better keep a* LEASH *on her Rikki! You better keep a leash on that fat bitch cause I* SWEAR *I am gunna go* OFF. (back to Ree:) *& you* DO NOT *want to see that, no you* DON'T. *Because you couldn't* HANDLE *it. Little Miss Wiggermuffett wants to sit there on her fat leaky* TUFFETT *on* MY *bed in* MY *house & tell* ME *my* BUSINESS. *'Yeah ahm the best to ever* DO IT *bitch, & you the best at never doin* SHIT.' *Eatin my* FOOD, *doin my* DOPE—*don't tell me you* AINT *motherfucker I* KNOW *you been doin my dope, don't you think I* KNOW *that? Ain nobody else like to eat* ROXIES *like you do too, not even you're brother. That's* YOU. *You like eatin Roxies almost as much as you like eatin fucking* ENTEMANN'S FUDGE CAKE *y'fat* BITCH, *fuckin* POSER, *'Reeyonna,' you* WISH *you* LOOKED *like Rihanna, too bad you gotta hairline like* DRAKE. *Fuckin Eddie* MUNSTER. *Anybody ever tell you you got a hairline like Drake? So* FUCK *y'all, I don't wanna* HEAR *about it. I don't wanna hear* SHIT *from you, Mama Cass. Just get*

*me my MONEY & shut the fuck UP. Do you hear me? Hey! I'm talking to
you—"*

— (Rikki) *Lighten up on her, Tom-Tom.*

— *I'm talkin to* HER *not* YOU. *I'm talkin to* HER, *not you, do you*
HEAR ME? *(still to Rikki) Don't just move your* HEAD, *bitch—*

— *Don't be callin me no bitch.*

— *I'll call you what I call you, this is* MY *house. When I'm in* YOUR
house, you can call me what YOU *want to call me. Do you understand? Do
you hear me?*

— *Yeah I hear you. But don't be callin me a bitch.*

— *Get out of my face, boat ch'all. Go spread your elephant legs for my buoy
here. Otherwise he tends to go* ASTRAY. *He's the father of your child, ain
he? Better throw him some pussy or he'll go astray. Men are like that. How
do you eat that bitch. Bitch so fat her pussy lips like goin down there & finding
a steak pinned to her snatch. Hee* HEE! *Somebody liked to put a T-bone
down there! Now get out of my face boat ch'all.*

. . .

"Hello?"

"Hello? Hi! May I speak to Chuck Aaron?"

"Who may I ask is calling?"

"My name is Reeyonna? I met him at the convention?"

"What convention was that."

"The one for—the reality—the reality show convention."

"Oh! Right. & may I ask the purpose of the call?"

"He said he was casting something? He was, uhm, he was looking
for women who were pregnant?"

(*The officious voice suddenly effusive*)

"O *hi! This* is Chuck."

"O—hi."

"I remember *you*. You were worried I was from MTV."

"Well, not really."

"I'm so happy you called."

"Are they still—are you still casting?"

"We're always casting."

"I mean for the pregnant—"

"Yes ma'm. What month are you?"

"I'm going into my 8th."

"Well guess what, that actually sounds pretty perfect for what we need. Is that your real name? Rihanna?"

"I spell it different. I'm R-e-e-y-o-n-n-a."

"You're white, right?"

"White."

"Right, because I *remember*. But for a second there I'm going, *But she's white* . . . so I guess you're president of Reeyonna's fan club, huh."

"She's pretty awesome."

"She *is*—& I'll bet you are too. I *remember* you as being awesome." (*She telephonically blushed*) "What about today, later on today? Do you think you can make it out here?"

"Uhm—today?" (*Taken aback*) "*Today* . . . you know, I really don't think so. I've been having car trouble."

(*She would have to figure out a way to get there. She could take a cab, or maybe Dr Phil could take her, she trusted Phil. She didn't want Rikki to know she was trying out for something because she was embarrassed, it was something she would never do under so-called normal circumstances but there wasn't such a thing anymore, she'd left the world of normal circumstances the moment she got pregnant, & now with the break from her mother her banishment was permanent. There was a time not too long ago when she would have laughed at a pathetic pregnant girl calling some casting geek she met at a lameass convention but now everything was different, like for Dorothy in* The Wizard of Oz, *the house had fallen to Earth only she was stuck beneath, she needed money, they needed money, needed it bad & one never knew. Maybe it was for a commercial, Toyota or Apple or whatever, no, probably it was for a baby product, maybe even for the people with the umbilical cord blood company. Also, she didn't want Rikki to know because of the casting fiasco he'd just gone thru, she didn't want him to feel like the same thing was about to happen to her, the same heartbreak, or for him to think she was trying to up-stage him.)*

"Uhm, tomorrow?"

"To—*morrow* . . . let me look & see what we're *doing* to-*morrow* . . . aren't the iPhones somethin? I was synching mine the other day & it wiped my calendar & addressbook clean! Sorry it's taking me a moment—"

"That's *terrible.*"

She'd been so stiff; she wanted to at least sound somewhat per-sonable before they hung up.

". . . and 2 o'clock it *is!*"

"OK great!"

"Do you know where we are, Reeyonna?"

"It says Canoga Park on the card?"

"Correct. It's a pretty sprawling campus . . . I've been here 3 yrs & I *still* get lost!"

She was nauseous, not because of him but because of everything.

"Reeyonna, what's your email? I'll shoot you the directions."

"That's OK. We have GPS."

She said *we* because she didn't want him to think she was by her-self. He sounded totally cool but she wanted to be careful, and smart about it.

"Are you sure?"

"I'm okay. Is there anything special I should wear?"

"At this stage, I'd say anything you can fit into!"

The call wrapped & she pressed END.

She immediately got a text message from a number she didn't rec-ognize, and thought it was a good omen: MOVIE EXTRAS WANTED! Make up to $300/day. All looks, No Experience Re-quired! To register call 877-589-4432. to unsub reply STOP.

Then:

She tried to stop it but the sick came up, sternum-stinging & vile, bursting from nostrilsmouth into the futile catchbasin of her cupped beggar's hand, *roaring stinging stinking* thru the rolling hilled town of

her fattened body & into the toilet, bile train express, she flushed
flushed flushed and the sick swirled down in its spiraling hurry toward

                                        subterranean
                                                            stops
            at

                                                stations

                                                        un

                                                    known.

[Jacquie]

The Heart Is Unholy Hunter

When

Jacquie got home from Scottsdale, she went over to Jim & Dawn's for coffee.

Jim said he spoke with Reeyonna and got the sense she might be growing tired of what he called "the itinerant life." He suspected she'd soon take him up on his proposal, "hopefully sooner than later."

.   .   .

The Arizona woman was Ginger's 1st cousin. The timing of the deaths—Ginger's stillborn & her cousin's infant—was morbidly preordained. Jacquie was a little more certain of herself than before, but only a little. This was a far different tableau.

The baby was almost four months old. Mom wanted him to sleep in their bed but the dad thought that wasn't safe; he worried about them rolling over and suffocating it. Besides, they never did that with their toddlers. Both parents fell into a deep sleep. A few hours later, the mom had a nightmare and woke up. She went straight to the crib (foot of the bed) and snatched up her baby, knowing it would be dead.

A neighbor watched the kids while they brought their son to the hospital. In a quiet moment in the cafeteria, the father told Jacquie he kept speeding up, instinctively, as if something could still be done, then slowing down when his wife cautioned his speed. Each time he slowed, he would suddenly remember what sort of errand they were on, that his son was dying. His thoughts would drift to funerals and grieving before abruptly returning to the present, whereupon he would speed up again. *A father is not supposed to be the driver of his son's hearse.* That was a thought he couldn't at that moment give words to. On the 10-minute ride, the only words he *did* say were directed toward the road ahead. "Is this happening?" His wife didn't answer.

He was six hours dead by the time Jacquie got there. The doctors suspected SIDS but in these sorts of cases, an autopsy was standard. Child abuse needed to be ruled out; the place of death would be investigated like a crime scene. The presence of toxins, fungus and nitrogen dioxide would be thoroughly delineated. Large stuffed animals would be regarded as suspicious asthmatic triggers. A/C ducts and heating vents would be examined as carriers of mold and second-hand smoke. All manner of things would come into play before anyone might even begin to approach a reasonable conclusion.

The very phrase *Sudden Infant Death* gave Jacquie the heebie-jeebies. She remembered her own fears, especially when Jerry Jr. was born, back when SIDS seemed to be more talked about. (Perhaps it still was but if you didn't have babies you wouldn't hear about it.) It still seemed the stuff of folklore, like those Japanese ghost stories she read in college where red foxes came from the hills to carry off sleeping children. It was a freakish puzzling thing, like spontaneous combustion.

When the pastor explained to the hospital administrator their wishes—to have a portrait taken as a memento—he was given a compassionate response. Their request to take their son back to the house for the photo was denied, but the administrator said they could have use of a doctors lounge or the hospital chapel. They chose the chapel. After the session, they insisted Jacquie stay for supper. Their children were young and well-behaved, & the parents didn't censor themselves. The mother complimented Jacquie on the portraits she took of Ginger and Daniel's beloved; her cousin sent the images to her online. She said it was "God's will and God's way" that she saw those pictures because not in a million years would she even have thought of doing what they did today.

Toward the end of the meal, the three-year old said from his high-chair, "Is baby dead?"

. . .

She took a 10PM flight home. In the darkness, she held the Hassel-blad in her lap as she would a baby. It was new, a replacement for the one her daughter stole. She hoped it did right by her.

Jacquie scrolled through the nightlight of her iPad to the wikipage on SIDS that she loaded in the airport. *Statistical pre-natal risks: Teenage mother. Mother doesn't finish high school. Mother is unmarried. Exposure to nicotine. Absence of pre-natal care———————————————————————————————————————*

———————————————————————a strong JOLT. (*She'd fallen asleep*) The tires hit the runway, just like how it sounds in the movies. Then the thrilling, thundering melodrama of domesticated engines roaring anew to slow the plane down, one last shout-out to show the world they were still wild.

. . .

Jacquie kept her job at Sears. It grounded her. Albie liked having her around, & she liked being around Albie.

At home, she sequestered herself. She studied 19th-century post-mortem photography with its daguerreotypes of moms&dads posing with the deceased: newborns, infants, toddlers. The poses of the living were as stiff as those of the dead. The departed wore heartbreaking outfits, miniature breeches, bespoke three-piece munchkin suits and white doily-hemmed cotton smocks resembling pillowcases altered for the occasion, each dead star clothed in awkwardly sublime get-ups—raiments sewn with infinite loving care for those extirpated creatures now impossible to fathom, for softened husks were all that now remained after untold empyreal explosions, supertransmundane stellar remnants of quarky matter that cradled all things, novas and supernovas, beginnings and endings, darkness and light, tiny celestial bodies illumined & decayed. With a final, storm-tossed exhalation (the undomesticated roar of tiny celestial engines) the dead rose to drift and dissolve into the ineffable, the Cloud of Unknowing, which the medievalists declared (the internet did tell her so) could never be witnessed, for how can one see the face of God unless through expired yet still half-open eyes? But there they were, served up on photographic plates: eternally unphotogenic, captured like big (little) game, their lonely hunters— all the sad, benumbed, peculiar, frontier-looking relative-folk— memorialized with their kill.

. . .

She visited Woodlawn Cemetery because to do it all online—"research"— ultimately seemed cheap and disrespectful. The Internet seduced one into believing God was in the details, and nothing was more detailed than the Alexandrian archives of the web.

Mournful Shostakovich in the car to summon the mood. She loved the way cemeteries were always open, like churches used to be. Should she park close to the perimeter? Or go deeper in?——————she drove until she was in the heart of it. Left the car and strolled to an area of flat markers. The 1st stone said: MY DARLING BABY born August 3, 1962. That's all that was written, a single date would apply to those stillborn, or those who never breathed for an entire day. Then: she was swimming in a sea of darling babies (all flat markers), many with birth- and death dates just a few days or few weeks apart. She saw an engraving that told her this part of the cemetery was called "Babyland." It sounded like part of a cruel boardgame.

. . .

She pondered her camera's monstrance-eye, immersing herself in funerary ferrotypes & historical portraiture of the effigies of those who died before reaching the so-called age of reason. All such *angelitos* enter Paradise, unencumbered—in Mexico, the child's godparents crowned the head with orange-blossoms while firecrackers announced the coronation of a new angel in Heaven. It interested her how popular belief held that if parents shed tears for their loss, the little one's soul would never reach heaven. Both sets of parents Jacquie had encountered, both *mothers*, had that instinctive, preternatural calm, and perhaps this explained it. A calm transcending shock, alone.

That night, she read about a mother's struggle to get a birth certificate for her stillborn. The woman became a lobbyist for stillborns' right-of-dignity. (Such was her sad, sacred, postmortem activity—supplanting that of nursing her baby, cooing over it, *watching* as it slept with a mother's beautiful, fierce-loved, penetrating gaze.) She called them "angelic records," noting that such bureaucratic consecrations were the closest we might come to a divine census of souls. All she'd ever wanted was to be a mother, and now that she *was*—for chrissake, all you need to qualify was to have given birth!—they'd refused her, they'd defaced her motherhood, as womanness, her intangible mysteries. They seemed to be of hell-bent mind that the star she carried in her womb for 8½ months and nourished with her very blood had *never existed*. Apparently, she could apply for a fetal *death certificate* but nothing more . . . the records of death took precedence over those of life! The woman was contemptuous of the consolation prize being offered: a non-legally binding "Memorial Certificate of Birth Resulting In Stillbirth." She didn't care about the controversies and debates—Pro-Choice feared that with the State's sanctification Pro-Life would take the fetus-as-child football and run to the endzone—this gal didn't care a *whit*. Because once she had been young, daydreaming of the children she'd have after marrying. How could she have fathomed God's will, how could she ever have compre-

hended His plan, that her baby would rise into the Cloud of Unknowing at the beginning of its life, not the end?

.   .   .

Our photographers are experts at capturing that winning expression you'll remember forever . . . . check out our NEW BABY styles!

.   .   .

She got an email from Ginger.

> *"Your eyes saw my unformed substance; in your book were written, every one of them, the days that were formed for me, when as yet there was none of them"*

.   .   .

Pieter called.

Jacquie said, "Good Lord, what time is it there?"

"530AM. I'm on my way to the gym."

"Jesus. California's a bad influence on you."

"Can you speak?"

"Yep. And I've got moveable parts."

"Beth Rader wants to see the pictures."

"Huh?"

"Beth Rader—I thought you knew her. Well she said she knew *you,* but I guess she meant your work."

"She wants to see *what.*"

"That amazing 5 by 7 you showed me, at the Chateau."

"Pieter, I don't understand what you're trying to tell me."

He repeated himself *very slowly,* which was annoying.

"Beth Rader wants you to stop by the gallery and show her the photo you took of that family in the hospital."

"I'm not getting this, Pieter."

"She's at Gagosian in Beverly Hills. I took a picture of it with my iPhone & emailed it to her."

"You took a picture of what I showed you?"

"You can hate me, Jacquie, but *this is your major work.* I don't even think you know it yet. I think *part* of you does, *part* of you knows. Maybe the part that showed *me,* the part that let me in. And I'm just really honored to have been *able* to play that part. To have been in the right place at the right time. That's where *you* are too, Jacquie, that's where you *are.* The right place at the right time. I think it's finally all come together for you. But you *can't* do it alone—there's just no *reason* to."

When she spoke, her measured tone made it sound as if she were someone else. "That picture is *incredibly confidential,* Pieter. I cannot *believe* you did that. Those people gave me their trust! What if it shows up on the fucking Internet?"

"It's not going to happen. Look, all I'm asking is for you to give *me* what those people gave *you:* trust. Give me your *trust,* Jacquie. I'm not *gaming* you, I *love* you, you've been mucking about far too long, & now you're onto something *very special.* Jacquie, I want you to have a *career.* You *deserve* one. I want to see you come barreling back. Something in me just *knows.*"

Pause.

"That this is your time."

An Indecent Proposal

"Bitch

move out of her room? Are you in her room yet?"

"Yeah. She left some shit of hers there it's cool."

"Like left what."

"Just some clothes, whatever."

"Where'd she leave it."

"Mostly in the closet."

"So now I'm free storage too."

"Tommie (Bolt called her that, she let him call her that), an *opportunity* has come your way."

"Is that right."

"To make some bread."

"Is it legal?"

"Absolutely. You know the crew that's coming next week? Seth, the D.P.? That's Seth's crew. Anyway I been knowing Seth since we were in high school, he's my bro. & they do—he shoots porn—his crew, they do porn shoots to pick up xxxtra change."

"They want to shoot a porno up here? Ha! Is that what you're saying? *Hahahahahaha——*"

"5K. That's what they're offering. They fuckin *love* the house—I sent em a few pics of the interiors & shit. Seth said it's like a 9 to 5 deal, then wham they're *out*. They only want to use the living room & pool area, you can rope everything else off. Seth said they even put runners down on the carpets to protect them."

"From like the spunk and shit. The pussy run-off. Teehee."

"They have the shit down to a science."

"When do they want to do this?"

"Sunday."

"So this is like *before* they're gunna do *Believers*."

"It's kind of a cool way for you to meet him—Seth—see how he works. If you already have a relationship things will go smoother & faster for the *Daydream* shoot, right?"

"*Hahahahahahahahah!* Betty White—porn queen! I could probably sell this shit to TMZ."

"Should I tell em you want to do it? Or you can think about it—"

"Can they do 5 thou in cash?"

"They probably do cash a lot."

"You've done porn, right?"

"Little bit. I've *directed* porn."

"No shit."

"That's my passion. I've probably directed more porn than I've *participated* in."

"OK yeah. Far *out*. OK. I guess you're gunna be coming around for your finder's fee————"

"I'm not like that."

"I know you aren't, baby. I know you aren't. (*Strokes his head, seeing his feelings got a little bruised by her comment*) Baby? I love you. Baby? See if they'll come up when you talk to em, K? See if they'll come up to seventy-five hundred."

Miracle at the Hilton

3 modest one-bedroom suites on the 3rd floor of the Beverly Hilton reserved (donated by the hotel) for talent/rest/makeup/rehearsal *lite* lounges. One for Beyoncé, one for Steve Martin, one for the performing children—Telma & Aleisha. (When Biggie told his brother that Telma invited him, Brando promptly bought a $100,000 table.) A Courage Ball talent liaison told Gwen & Aleisha's mom that Michael Douglas and his wife were going to try to come up to the room to say hi but that never happened.

En suite: Telma and Gwen and Phoebe, Aleisha and her mom Melanie. Telma basically acts like Aleisha isn't there. Aleisha stares at Telma wide-eyed, as if in the presence of a ☆. 5-year-old Aleisha is hopelessly devoted to Telma. Aleisha doesn't *feel* ignored; how can you be ignored by the sun? How do you feel snubbed by rainbows, tigers and thunder? How can you be dissed & dumped on by beauty and magic? Gwen knows how delicate things are at this moment, how near the edge her daughter loiters. Every once in a while, she tries to get Telma to engage Aleisha in the smallest ways—Phoebe does the same—to no avail. The terrible thing for Gwen is, she'd be handling her daughter quite *differently* if not for the uncancerous sword of Damocles that was sharpening itself just over the girl's head.

If not for that, she'd warrant a bitchslap. Aleisha's obsequiousness toward her role model, who after all had/has the very same cancer she had/has, had pioneered & *vanquished* it, that awed virginal slavishness happens to be the only mitigating factor allowing Telma to be kind, if kindness may be defined as the covert omission of *flagrant* cruelties, and the why & wherefore Telma justified even bothering to share the same *airspace* with the dwarfy interloper. Aleisha's utter worshipfulness is so pure, if not exactly endearing (to Telma), then *appealing*; precisely what staved off full evisceration by her fellow Kansurvivor non-Kanadian Hero. For the moment anyway.

Colorful little Kate Spade "I'm courageous!" bags in the 3 suites filled with donated stuff: Geo-Girls anti-aging makeup (Walmart) (ages 8–12), push-up bras (Target), James Perse/Free City tee's, *Pirates of the Caribbean/Harry Potter/Alice In Wonderland* DVDs, Avril Lavigne&Katy Perry best-ofs, VTech KidiZoom digital cams (!!!), Justin Bieber's One Less Lonely Girl Collection nail polish. Aleisha watches transfixed as Telma assiduously applies "I'm a Belieber" on the tapered big-girl fingers of her left hand, "Give Me the First Dance" on the right. When Telma waves her nails to dry, Aleisha is tranced out by the sustained fanning/twitchy/hi-oscillating movements. (Entranced by everything about her.) Gwen says you know it might be nice, Telm, if you could do one of Aleisha's nails, just to get her started. Her daughter abstains, not by saying no but by pointedly ignoring the request. *Why should I?* She says it all in a sharp look to her mother, a look that says, *Don't make me say this outloud! Don't make me say she's technically not even a survivor! Don't make me say you're not supposed to even call yourself a survivor unless it doesn't come back after* THREE YEARS (*Telma keeps changing the kancerules*)——the one thing Gwen, Phoebe & Melanie don't understand (tho Melanie's being so understanding in *so many* ways) is that Aleisha does not, *cannot* feel h8ted on, she's baby sister-enthralled & can't register Telma's rage, Telma's wish that she'd never been born, Telma's night prayers to God *please make her cancer come back*, with speedy, fatal fury. Aleisha's mom never says a word, just sits grinning like there's a language

problem, which there sort of is, to put it mildly. Melanie's smile con-
veys that all's rosy with her world, *My baby girl's alive, what's not to be
joyous about.* Maybe that's Canadian or Christian, but whatever it is,
Gwen's grateful for Zen Mom of the North. Gwen's embarrassed
enough by her daughter's mean girl prima donna stylings and relieved
she doesn't have to deal with a parent's legitimate beef on top of it.
*Let her think she's a bitch. If only she knew—if only everyone knew, we'd
start an Arab spring right here, we'd topple those doctors & shut down that
fucking hospital forever! And tonight's shindig would be for* TELMA, *forever
the world's youngest mutilated-through-misdiagnosis survivor, they couldn't
take that away from her . . . .*

At her mom's prodding, Aleisha haltingly begins to rehearse
Smile. Telma makes sure to trample over the 1st few maudlin lyrics by
announcing, "I'm going exploring!" then stomping out the door.
Phoebe and Gwen exchange looks, then Phoebe goes after her.
Gwen stays in the room, shrugging her shoulders, flashing Melanie a
contrite *Sorry, what can I do it's hormones* smile. When the truth is,
that *Gwen's* (really) the only one forcing a smile while her heart is
breaking.

·   ·   ·

Rikki and Jerzy got to the hotel early.

Being it's a fundraiser for kids with cancer, he counted on a lot of
underage ☆lets showing up—Jerzy was there exclusively for private
reserve *honeyshot!*s. All day long he nonsensically sang *Some people call
me the spaced cowboy/Some people call me the gangbang of Love————*
Rikki asked Jerzy why he didn't use a videocamera because like
Tom-Tom said he could just shoot & isolate whatever frames had the
beavercleaver. Jerzy said, *cause I'm oldschool, my friend. Matter of pride.
Better to set the beaver trap by hand harharhar then 2 in the bush harharhar
. . . . you're the cutest thing I ever did see I really love
your peaches want to shake your tree . . . .*

While Jerzy does his spiderazzi thing at the hotel entrance w/all
the other papps—as ordinary-unknown richfolk *filler*/VIPs/celebs are

just beginning to arrive—Rikki sits in the Hilton lobby with a stolen Kindlefire, pretending he's, uhm, like a hotel guest *yeah right.* They smoked crack in the parking garage, toked some Don King & gummy bear too, he's blazed. Rikki contemplates the rumor he heard that current management was renting out the Whitney suite to billionaire Macao gambling-type Japs and sand niggers for a million a night, the tub she took a shit in and drowned was still there, everything laid out like a museum, crack pipe and personal effexors they got back from the LAPD evidence room, wallet pics of her little girl, all her stained lingerie, you could get loaded and fuck a loved one right in the tub. That's some morbid shit. He goes on **www.lobsterporn.com**, already super spackled–m'gackled & superhard from the meth&roxies, bolus of beef jerky in his cheek like chewing tobacco . . . *CATEGO-RIES A-Z: innocent teen/saggy tits/asian schoolgirl/doctor molest/daughter destruction/upskirt tampon/squirt/small tits/extreme taboo/by force/granny mature/dildoes insertions/small tits/farmyard/outside/voyeur/daughter sleeping/massage/schoolgirl med exam/monster cocks/tittyfuck/hentai/mother daughter incest (simulated).* He clicked on *Jewish* then *Turkish* but his heart wasn't in it. Suddenly the volume went CRAZY LOUD, he must have unmuted by accident, it's making all these *cum sounds,* a lady hears as she walks by & frowns Rikki still fumbling trying to MUTE which he finally does. (He'd have to remember to tell T², she would crack the fuck *up.*) Now there's a little pop-up onscreen from bi_the_way432. Probably some automated drone shit tracking his location, he didn't know how to turn that shit off on this device, *fuck the Navy seals, dude, they should've used the porn guys to go after Osama woulda nailed him right away shoulda sicced em on Kaddafi too.* The female drone wrote: *OMG are you in beverly hills?* 5 seconds later: *im a mile away.* 10 secs later: *innertube.com is the best site for free porn fyi!* 30 secs: *you realize im talking to you right?* 1 whole fucking minute later: *it's not polite to ignore a lady.* Last (automated) gasp—*Age: 18. Sexual pref: bi. Zodiac: scorpio. ethnicity: American Indian. Pubic hair: bald*——Rikki said *mother-*FUCK that surveillance shit. Oops. Now a banner's crawling across the top

MEET SOMEONE TO FUCK NOW!

Turns it off.

Rikki just sits there, spackle/staring into the borrowed lobby of a place he doesn't (even temporarily) belong. People coming & going, with glam lives, lives that aren't fucked. He's still freaking about the baby, about being a dad, but really now just mostly freaking about the $$$ more, even Jerzy can't get Tom-Tom to chill on the rent shit, he won't front his sis any money either, you'd think J could at least get Tom-Tom to chill until Ree has the kid, then they'll be out in a flash, straight from the hospital to his fosterfolks, she'll be too wasted giving birth to put up a fight. She's like due in like *five weeks,* dude, the minute she goes to the hosp that'll be the fucking last Tom-Tom *sees* or *hears* of her . . . . spackle m'gackled————————

————————maybe robbery? Thinking about that again, mostly because he watched *The Town* for the 6th time, *loved* that fuckin movie, never got a chance—made the time though—to speak with Tom-Tom about the whole crew-heist deal . . . his thoughts now becoming fantasies as Rikki tries to squelch all the bad vudu in his head, he starts to trip but in a good way about Jim and Dawn, about finally being their real son before God & the law, thinks his dad would maybe convert the garage into a guesthouse for them and the baby, maybe one of those *Extreme Makeover Home Edition* dillios like ReeRee joked about Betty White's, you know where a couple of trucks show up with a 50-man crew—now *that's* a fuckin righteous *crew*—& they build a *whole house,* with towel-warmers like Ree told him once that she wanted, & ambient heated bathroom tiles like he heard Tom-Tom say *she* was gonna have, Tom-Tom said Bill Gates had a heated *driveway* so the snow would melt. Rikki trips on hanging out in his new home—*their* new home—right there on Jim and Dawn's property. Jim & Dawn could babysit & shit if him and Ree wanted to go clubbin & candyflipin.

But ReeRee won't, EVER . . .

You're way too stubborn, dude.

. . .

Jerzy knows he's strung out way beyond the point he usually puts down, hearing voices of race war/rap though sometimes the voices lead him to breakthrus too, like how L.A. Reid's hard lacquered bodyshell sleeps in the sensuous recesses of Randy Jackson's arthropod flesh, so the voices cannot be discounted nor dismissed out of hand. Miasma & background Muzak of the Uncivil War between hummingbirds & mantises. Trying to formulate a grand theory to explain the *rôle* that hummingbirds & mantises will play, a overarching theory of General Relativity that explains and *describes* the exact connect between what historians one day will surely come to call The Puppetmathers/Iovine Wars—& the *pact* or *formal agreement* secured by the *demiurge* between *mantis* and *hummingbird*.

The insidious thing is Jerzy realizes he's in the nightbloom of amphetamine psychosis but powerless to stop its militancy; trapped inside an acrostic gnostic boardgame. He laughs, glad to at least be able to *watch* himself laugh *cackle! Cackle! m'gackle!* when the epiphany flashes there are messages written on each Chloë/Elle/Hailee pantyshield, it's up to him to *capture the images*, no other way but a *captcha* to string the codewords together . . . & flashes too that Harry around the Middleburg is a CAA operative close to breaking the code stitched or drawn by persons unknown & made visible only by virtue of the *honeyshot!*s, that Harry's website is a brilliant distraction, a throwing off of scent. *And yet what does this have to do with mantises & hummingbirds, what does this have to do with Suge, what does this have to do with I-Veen & the Puppetmathers it must have something there must be something*

Animal Planet had showed him so many things, other beings locked in civil war. Like that show Hillbilly Handfishin the men hold their breaths underwater reach into hollow logs wait for thirtypound catfish to bite down they surface with it just stuck on their hand like that then club it into the boat, the gators are cannibals a 600 lb one on Swamp People accidentally hanged itself on one of the gator hunter's lines damnedest thing if such a thing can be called an accident the hook wasn't even in it, there was a baby gator still in its mouth, that was cosmic retribution.

Tonight an award is being given to *Young Hollywood Stands Up for Cancer!* & Jerzy's targets stand out whilst he clocks the arriving guests: Minka, Whitney, Pia Toscano&McPhee **HAILEE FUCKTASTIC STEINFELD** Nicole Richie, Tom&Rita Hanks, Vince & Kyla Vaughn (their infant daughter Locklyn: a *honeyshot! of the future*), **KYLIE FREAKIN JENNER** Cher Lloyd, Matt&Luciana Damon, Ethan&Ryan Hawke, ABBY FRIGGIN BRESLIN Khloé Kardash, Kathryn Bigelow, Kate Hudson/Matt Bellamy, Diane Kruger **ELLE EFFING FANNING** Meghan McCain, Rob/Sheryl Berkoff-Lowe, **JORDANA BITCHIN BEATTY** Nina Dobrev, Sandra Bullo————

Goes back to the car for a blunt & a booty-bump. Meditates on why he likes to shove crack up his ass of late. As Harry likes to say, *the Devlin (Janet) made me do it.* Jerzy sends an email of all images just taken to his NY agency, in the morning the tabloids will negotiate a price on what they like. Doesn't matter if there's *honeyshot!*s among em cause they'd never use em, never even *think* of it. Tonight he'll print the hi-rez *honeyshot!*s himself, he'll nurse & conjure & cull, Harry didn't like to have any ol batch just thrown at him, reason being he was slowly losing his sight, irony of eye disease for the beholder of beauty, there could be no correction thru surgery/lenses & the fatfuck bless his heart was vain, who'da thunk it. So Jerzy distilled & uncorked only the finest of ripened honeyvintages————

He smokes the pipe, half-looking around for the dumbass security guard. *Cheesy ugly fuckin garage.* Offends his aesthetics. Where the fuck is Rikki. Still tripping on the Wars. Eminem, the *demiurge*, the Demi Moorge, the Demineminurge, the whole vexing mantis-hummingbird *problemo.* But an answer was coming, he could feel it, like a tsunami still 1000s of miles from land, before it top ramens whole cities.

Someone from Deathrow really needs to call me back. He looks at himself in the rearview, and says:

"They do, right?

. . .

Once inside the hotel, packs-o-publicists waited with simpering smiles (years of cowering & nearly being slapped/struck by stressed-out celeb junkies on junkets), tho as *ja rule*, ☆s were usually fairly well-behaved at cancer gigs, even moreso pediatric ones—said publicists waiting w/nervous hi-beam smiles to sweettalk and *o so very carefully* shepherd VIPs to the *inside* red carpet getting them to stand there with the backdrops sporting COURAGE BALL plus a stamped smattering of slogans, *Take Courage/Pledge to Wear Yellow Livestrong Day/Take the Pink Ribbon Challenge/Give Today, Cure Tomorrow* + all the usual suspect logos of all the compassionate usual suspect corps, TOYOTA HUFFPOST TWITTER BEN&JERRY'S PANDORA INSTAGRAM GROUPON FLKR&tc. On said backdropped *inside* red carpet they of course would be shot by a *2nd* group of parasiterazzi, these being of the less loose-cannoned more *inner circlish* variety, in bed with the pubbers, each prosecuted to take useable glamshots *not* those sometimes peskily problematic step from limo tableaux, certainly no reason of course for *Jerzy* to be taking pics on the *inside* red carpet because one could not procure a *honeyshot!* on the *inside* of the hotel, at least not unless a fear-stricken flak was given the unenviable task of persuading this or that ½–¼ ☆let to have a seat in the Fisker Karma that sat over there on a revolving lazy susan just beyond the ballroom doors on its *own* red carpet'd muff. (To be auctioned off later in the eve.) There was no way any of the old pros—translation: ☆lets over 30—would jump in the Fisker anyway because it would look like they were endorsing, most had never even heard of a Fisker, they'd have to be told that fucking *Leonardo* had one before it would get their attention, because *hey I don't do shit like that for free*. Jerzy already considered being on hand for such a contingency but wound up musing if Emma or Hailee or whomever *did* climb in, a Fisker "get" would be one tough panties get.

Perspirating stinkbreathed ulcer-prone scaredy-cat pub flaks delicately moved the celebs, demi-celebs & ¼celebs thru the open doors of the ballroom for cocktails and mingling . . . those same old-timey thirtyish ☆lets that avoided the Fisk Karm knew better to *mingle* for free & besides, OCD handlers were in place to rush them to their designated tables for some well-earned álonetime. Meanwhile, bids were being placed for the silent auction (a banjo signed by Steve Martin & all the banjo greats; you could win a round of golf with Jack Black or Alec Baldwin ((both couldn't make it tonight)); you could blind-bid on a box that said **The Kardashian Experience**, &tc.) then everyone was hustled to eat 1st so there would be no clinking & table-clearing once the show began.

.   .   .

Sitting at the other $100,000 table (the one Brando didn't buy) were Michael and Catherine; Steve Martin (who'd flown in from NY where just hours after being voted president of PEN American Center); Joyce Carol Oates & husband No. 2 (who, in solidarity w/ husband No. 1 has refused to read any of JCO's work "because if I open that door I'll have to walk thru it"); Tom & Rita Hanks; Sandra Bullock (*sans* black baby arm candy) with what the mags call Unidentified Friend; Nobel Prizewinner & former PEN American Center President Toni Morrison; Sol and Tiffany Koster. Tiff was President of the organization that puts on the Courage Ball, the very same who had the effrontery to perform a partial mastectomy on Telma's appearance in tonight's show.

For a long while, there'd been a bubble of speculation about whether the Nobel Committee would come to their senses & just *give it to her*—to Joyce—but the bubble always burst. Each time it happened, sycophantic friends made the tiresome, toadying remark that JCO was the Nobel's Susan Lucci, the same they said about Julian Barnes before he finally won the Booker. Common sense had forced Mrs. Oates to the unpleasant truth: Queen Toni's investiture had knocked her out of the box for at least 30 years, because Oslo doesn't *do* nationality-wins that close together, which means she'd be 85 when finally becoming eligible for consideration. The Committee was famously unpredictable but the line in front of her did seem rather long: there was Rushdie & Roth, not to mention the usual darkhorse bevy of unpronounceables writing in dead languages in civil war-torn stamp-sized countries too new or too old for anyone to have even heard of (anyone except for JCO).

. . .

They were giving Michael Douglas the Take Heart Award tonight for his fundraising efforts, whose most recent focus was on children. "Mine are coming of age," he told *Entertainment Tonight*. "So it feels like a natural progression. Some of these kids are going to be the same doctors, researchers and scientists who'll find that missing piece we're still looking for in so many of these diseases we're struggling to understand."

. . .

At the *Ooh Baby* table: Biggie & Telma, Gwen & Phoebe, Aleisha & her parents, Biggie's brother Brando, Wendy Mogel & budding author Bud Wiggins.

Wendy was married to Michael Tolkin. Bud was her date tonight because her husband had to fly to New Zealand for the weekend, where a $125 million film was being shot from his script. There'd been a few skirmishes between director & ☆, serious enough that they almost came to blows. Tolkin & the lead actor had a good relationship so the studio asked him to intervene. Wendy wryly said that he agreed to do "emotional triage." Tolkin & one of his agents flew over, plus 2 studio semi-chieftains, plus 3 of the film's producers, plus the actor's & director's agents. They were all staying at the same lodge, which Tolkin had christened "Olympic Village."

Wendy had written a number of bestsellers on healthy parenting. (Bud told her, "Where were you when my mother needed you!") He knew Wendy all the way back to when she and Michael started dating. She was always kind to Bud, even when she knew he was down and out, something he never forgot. She looked Bud in the eye when he spoke, and generally treated him like a human being worthy of attention and respect.

. . .

Michael Douglas saw the documentary about Fran Lebowitz that Toni was in. He thought it was hilarious. He particularly loved the part where Fran talked about what it was like to accompany Toni & her retinue to Oslo for the Nobel ceremony. Ms. Morrison knew that Michael and Catherine hosted the Nobel Peace Prize Concert in 2003, for the Iranian woman.

"Shirin Ebadi," said Michael. "Brave lady. We had a great time with her. She's Muslim. *Yusuf Islam* sang *Peace Train*."

"Isn't that Cat Stevens?" said Toni.

"Right. I don't think the audience knew though."

"Of course they did!" said Catherine.

"A lot of em didn't. But I never argue with my wife."

"The hell you don't," said the firebrand.

"Because I know it'll end in blood. And it won't be hers."

She swatted him, as was her wont.

"We had a *wonderful* party in Oslo," said the laureate. "Lou & Laurie—Lou Reed and Laurie Anderson—and Bono."

"Bono is such a giver," said Catherine.

"He sang 'One,' " said Toni.

"That's what *I* sang!" said Catherine.

"Not *that* 'One.' The *U2* 'One,' " he said.

"I *know*. I was just being silly."

"Fran should have emceed," said the actor to Toni. "I take it back—that might have been dangerous! She should have sung a little ditty with Lou."

"Did you know that she's a *wonderful* lyricist? Fran is one of the great unsungs—literally!"

"That's funny."

"That woman *astonishes me with her gifts*. In my mind, she's right up there with Sondheim & Noël Coward. But inevitably, unmistak-ably . . . *Fran*." Her delivery was throaty and expansive, as was her laugh.

"Catherine sang 'One'—from *A Chorus Line*—when we were over there hosting the Peace Concert. Remember how much fun you had, Cat?"

"Marvin Hamlisch wrote me new lyrics, so it made sense when I sung it to Shirin. But he didn't really have to change too much. 'She walks into a room & you know she's uncommonly rare, very unique'—well that *is* Shirin. Marvin didn't have to touch that."

". . . peripatetic, poetic & chic," said Joyce, finishing the lyric.

"You *know* it!" said Catherine.

"I do," she said. "I actually reviewed *A Chorus Line* for *The Times Literary Supplement*."

. . .

Telma got up from the table and ran off, dragging Biggie along.

Brando said to Bud, "Did you get an email from my little brother?"

"He sent it to me right after we met."

"So what do you think? Did you read it?"

"I did. It's an amazing story. It's dark."

"Tell me about it. Welcome to my nightmare!"

Bud said, "It made me think of *Antigone*."

Of course it *hadn't*; it was Biggie who referenced the play. Bud read the detailed synopsis in SparkNotes online.

"What's *Antigone*?" asked Brando.

"A Greek play," said Bud, with casual assurance. "About a king who refuses to bury the body of his son. Antigone's the sister, who tries to get her brother a decent burial."

"Jesus," said Brando.

"Everyone in it dies, don't they?" said Wendy, almost rhetorically. She was easygoing, comfortably chiming in without having to know a whole backstory. "Antigone's *brother* dies, then *Antigone* dies . . . doesn't she hang herself? I think even the *king* dies. And the king's *son,* & the king's *wife*——————"

Bud thought it was classy that Wendy always downplayed the scope of her knowledge. She probably spoke Greek.

"Do you think there's a *movie* there?" said Brando. The question was directed at Wendy as much as it was toward Bud. "Or maybe I should ask, do you think there's a *script*."

Before Bud could answer, Telma roared up to the table holding a tall, ostrich-looking man's hand. Biggie was right behind her, panting. He plunked down beside his brother while Telma stood between Phoebe & Gwen.

"Mom! Look who I found! It's Dr. Bessowichte!"

The awkward Bessowichte shifted on his shifty feet.

He was nothing to her but *Dr. Mengele* now.

Gwen froze him out.

"Mom? What's the matter?"

"Nothing sweetheart."

"But you're being rude!"

"The doctor and I aren't speaking. We had a difference of opinion."

"About *what*?"

Gwen hesitated a moment, then:

"Obama."

·   ·   ·

Telma on the run again, a sugarless people high.

OMG she saw Khloé Kardashian. OMG!!! They hugged and hugged, hadn't seen each other since the KKs took over Lucy's El Adobe for Kourtney's birthday. Ryan Seacrest paid Khloé and Telma $25,000 to sing "Smile," & all the money went to the ped-*OINK* Research wing of St. Ambrose's.

Telma told Khloé she was singing "Over the Rainbow" tonight and was going on right after *Beyoncé*. Khloé said she already *knew* that, because it was in the *program* (it was too late to print the change re the Aleisha finale). *OMG you're CLOSING the SHOW!* said Khloé, which made Telma feel funny/sick in her stomach. *You're my*

little STAR! I cannot BELIEVE that BEYONCÉ is your opening act!!!
Telma said, *Yeah I know, I'm at the very end, well not the VERY end but
ALMOST (unable to bring herself to tell Khloé that in fact she, Telma, was
the opening act for ALEISHA, she felt funny in her stomach again, sick &
less-than & ashamed).* Then Telma had an idea how she could *totally*
steal the show from Aleisha if Khloé sang "Rainbow" with her like
they did for Kourtney's bday. *Khloé! Khloé! Do you want to sing it with
me do you WANT TO do you want to do a DUET with me?!?!* Khloé
laughed, Telma was so *happy,* she knew she'd found a *perfect solution,* a
way out of the nightmare, Telma hung on Khloé saying how much
everyone would *love* it but Khloé held firm, she said she hated her
voice & that she'd "officially retired as a singer. Too painful!" *But
what if someone pays us $25,000?!* Khloé laughed again. *I'm totally seri-
ous, Biggie will! My friend Biggie & his brother will, they'll probably give us
a MILLION dollars if we sang————My little HUSTLER!* said Khloé
with great affection. No, she couldn't, she really just wanted to sit &
enjoy & not have the spotlight on her, it was *such* a relief not to even
have the cameras there tonight (the absence of which had initially
depressed Telma but then she was glad because all they would do was
capture Aleisha's performance and make a ☆ out of her), Lamar was
in NYC & all she wanted to do tonight was be *entertained* by Telma
& "your opening act, Beyoncé."

Then Telma remembered with a *shock* the *letter* she wrote to
Khloé's mom, she was going to send it to askkris @ Life&Style mag,
but *why,* what a *lame plan,* what was *wrong* with her, why didn't she
just think of getting it to Khloé to give to Kris there were a *hundred*
different ways she could have done that, but this was so *easy* because
Telma had actually *known* for *two weeks now* that Khloé was probably
coming to the Courage Ball—or why didn't she even think of just
leaving it in the Kardashian *mailbox* (which on 2nd thought probably
wasn't the easiest thing to do, with the security they probably had at
the house) with a note that said something like "*Pass it on!* signed
Telma El Adobe." Luckily, Telma hadn't yet mailed it anywhere so
she ran back to the table & told Khloé she had a letter she wanted her

to pass onto her mom, it was very *personal,* & Khloé said of *course* she would, Telma said she couldn't give it to her *tonight* because it was back at the house & Khloé said not a problem, tomorrow she'd send a *courier,* not a *messenger*—the Kardashians know how to do <u>EVERY-THING</u>!!!!) to Telma's house in Cheviot Hills. Khloé said, "But honey why send a letter when you can just talk to Mom directly?" Telma said *OMG* do you think she would have the *time?* & Khloé laughed and said "She's *my mom.* I *think* I know her schedule better than you do! Mom'll *make* the time, or I will kick her fat ass. She will *always* have time for *you!*"

It was all too much to compute, Khloé was saying her mom always had time for her but Telma barely remembered even saying that much of a hello to Kris at Kourtney's party, not that she supposed it really mattered, & besides, Telma was really starting to spin *out* on her crazed sugarfree people-high (she was actually a "vegan Nazi"—she stopped eating sugar when she learned she had kancer, the nutritionist told her to stay away from all karcinogenic or "kancer-friendly" items *especially* sugar, Telma was always telling everyone ((*especially* the parents of kancerkidz)) ((except not Aleisha's mom)) that sugar was THE ABSOLUTE WORST for the human body & *along with dairy which human beings were not meant to consume* could *literally* FEED THE KANCER AND *KILL* you). She thanked Khloé & said she had to hurry and go find Michael Douglas before the show began & Khloé laughed, saying *My little hustler* again then turned to the *unidentified friend* sitting next to her to say, *This girl's gunna* GO *places.* As Telma left she extracted/confirmed Khloé's promise that once she got the letter, she would *hand-courier* it to Mama Bear. Khloé said she *absolutely* would but to *please call* if she wanted her to just pick her up & drive her to Kris' house (OMG!!!!!!!!) adding with a wink how it was all very *mysterious,* this mysterious *letter,* & what a mysterious *girl* she was & how *adorable*—turning again to her unidentifed friend to say: *Agent Telma—International Woman of Mystery!*

The excitable little gal flitted from the table, like a bee moving on to another flower.

. . .

Dessert and coffee were being served.

Bud had a few ideas for movies in his back pocket that he wanted to float past Brando. *Hey why not, I'm a made man, already in the Ooh Baby stable.* Real smooth and casual . . . just plant a seed. You never know.

"What do you think about doing a kind of *prequel* to *The Social Network*, except it's about the early days of *Microsoft*. When the cracks in the business—*and* the personal relationship between Gates & Paul Allen—are just starting to show. Gates was trying to get *rid* of Allen, even if he had to lie and cheat. And Allen has *cancer!* Bill Gates *is* Mark Zuckerberg."

"Then who's Eduardo Saverin?"

"Paul Allen."

"And who's the Winklevoss twins?"

"I don't know if we need *twins*," said Bud. "But if what you're asking is did Gates fuck anyone else over there are *lots* of people out there. But we *could* have a pair of twins . . ." Bud didn't want to talk about actual story anymore; he wanted to get to the mechanics of a potential deal. "I don't think we need the rights to the Paul Allen book—it's all public record. We *would* need to get permission from De Luca and Scott Rudin. I know them both, for years," Bud lied, knowing such a detail was irrelevant. "We should obviously pitch Columbia, cause they already own it."

Brando thought a moment, then said, "You think that's something *Sorkin* would want to write?"

"Uhm, maybe." Even though it seemed obvious to Bud that he was pitching *himself* to script it, he thought he should have been clearer. "This whole area's actually *totally* in my *wheelhouse.* [A word the agents used 30 years ago, though Bud wasn't sure if it was still *en vogue*] "I really think I could ace this. And I've got a great title: *Hotmail.* I don't think we'd even need to get permission from Microsoft, because it's 'fair use.' Isn't that a cool title? *Hotmail?*"

.   .   .

Telma finally finds Michael and Catherine.

Big hugs.

Michael turns to Rita Wilson and says: "That's my tea partner. My tea partner in crime."

He formally introduced Telma to Tom and Rita. "Aha!" said Tom, waving the program. "So *you're* the one who's closing the show! I gotta warn you, though, Telma, Beyoncé can be a tough act to follow."

"Talk to Beyoncé, Tom," said Michael. "Have a few words."

"I'll tell her to bring it down a few notches," said Tom. "I'll tell her to sit on it."

"I'll bet you will," said Michael. Catherine instantly swatted him.

"I'm sorry, Cat," said Tom re Michael's penchant for double entendre. "Apparently, it doesn't take much to get this guy started."

"Don't listen to these two clowns," said Catherine to Telma. "You're going to blow Beyoncé out of the water."

"Of course she is," said Rita.

"Don't you worry about *Telma*," said Michael. "She can hold her own. She's a showstopper, this one. Aren't you."

.   .   .

Suzanne Somers storms over to Gwen—a woman on a mission. They've known each other for years but never really outside of the benefit machine. Tho watching Suzanne playfully grab hold of Gwen's arm for all to see, you'd think they were sisters.

"Come with me NOW."

Suzanne's putting on a little show, the way celebrities do, holding Gwen's hand as she weaves them through tables with an *oomfy* stride, everything sped up, just a *smidgen* larger than life, acceptable theater, low-watt, kicky spectacle. Gwen feels the eyes of the diners on them and it feels good; like having a small serving of how celebs must feel *most* of the time. In this case, everyone knows Suzanne, of course, but no one knows Gwen . . . she must be *somebody*, but who? Gwen loves the ambiguity.

As they head for god knows which table, Suzanne says, "He's *amazing.*"

"Who?" says Gwen, a bit breathless, pleasantly distracted by each fresh set of spectator eyes.

"He worked with Tina on her chanting album."

"Tina?"

"*Turner.* It's called *Beyond.* Tina's a Buddhist, no one really knows that, she doesn't *talk* about it. She made a CD of her own personal chants, it is *so* beautiful. Barry almost produced it." (Gwen knew she was close to Barry Manilow.) "Will you promise me you'll download it?"

"I will."

"He's also an *incredible* jewelry designer. He's basically become Donna Karan's jeweler and spiritual advisor!"

They reached a table that was empty except for one man. (The show was about to begin and the bathrooms were being used en masse.)

"*This,*" says Suzanne, "is Montenegro. Montenegro? Meet Gwen."

Then she leaves.

He's sixtysomething, ruddy and sweetsmelling, impeccably turned out. He too is larger than life: big white wolf teeth, big wide beard, big wide spicy eyes. One dangly gold earring.

"Please! Sit."

She does. And right away he takes her hand.

"You're *suffering.* Because you want to—*need* to—tell *someone you love more than life* a painful truth. And he—*she?*—*she* has already suffered so much. *Too* much! And for what? But there is no *choice,* you cannot live in *lies,* you can only live in *truth.* You need to live in *truth* or you'll cause more damage, more harm. Not just to the one you *love,* but to *you.* The *truth* will be the gift you can give her. Do you understand?"

. . .

How, *how* did he know those things?

And *why* did Suzanne Somers lead her to him?

She felt like a ruin, dizzy, all clogged up.

She's had enough of herself, she's just had—enough.

There goes Steve Martin to the stage, there goes laughter and ap-plause, there go the doctors, doctors and more doctors, there go the *tributes* to the doctors, and now there goes a short film projected on the giant wall panels featuring herds of bald children w/eyes big as Montenegro's. There goes *Young Hollywood*—& more awards . . . she tells Phoebe she can't take much more. But she does not tell her she wants to die.

She's been thinking about dying, about dying and taking Telma with her.

Suddenly Catherine Zeta-Jones is onstage in top hat and tails, singing at Michael.

"ONE *singular sensation, at the bot-tom of the tongue—*"

Gwen tuned in long enough to recall reading something about how furious Catherine was at all the American doctors for missing it, how close their bumbling bullshit came to killing him, triggering *another* internal jag (one more in a series) of Gwen's . . . mother*fuck* American doctors, *boy o boy* could she relate, a person had a better chance of surviving heart surgery in the fucking Sudan, she was de-termined one day to bond with Catherine over mutual nightmares. *But at least theirs had a happy ending . . . .*

Gwen looked up at the monitors. The camera was on Michael watching Catherine from his table, eating it up. He loved his wife's passion and mischiefmaking.

"—THREE *wrongful di-ag-NO-ses, every test that he takes!*"

Lots of laughter, a bit awkward in that doctors never quite warm to indictments of their own . . . so many things could happen . . . those tumors were so hard to————Gwen reverting, retreating into her fog, Michael accepting his award, Michael with tears in his eyes, Michael stressing the importance of head&neck checkups . . . so so foggy. She looks around—Aleisha and Telma already gone, and Phoebe too. Phoebe probably saw the condition she was in & made an executive decision to be one of the adults accompanying the kids to the green room backstage where they would be wired for sound and generally prepped for their tearjerky rockstar finale. Gwen *wants* to be with them backstage, waiting in the wings for their cue, *wants* to be with Aleisha&Melanie, *wants* to be supportive, propping up her own sweet tragic maimed and mutilated daughter but doesn't for the moment have the strength to move from her chair.

>*Beyoncé!*
>*sings a medley when she gets to*
>>*"Single Ladies" the audience EXPLODES and then*
>>*she begins Run the World (Girls), kickass tribute to the up-*
>>*coming Telma & Aleisha . . .*

————WTF Gwen's arm is grabbed *HARD* by Jesselle, who says there's a *problem.* Gwen follows her to the far side of the ballroom then down, almost sprints to keep up, she's saying Telma won't go on, she's refusing, she won't sing unless Aleisha comes on *before,* Telma said everyone in the audience Michael Douglas and Khloé Kardashian read the program and thinks SHE'S closing the show. Gwen is mortified . . . "So you know what?" says Jesselle, with contempt. *"That's* what we're going to do. *Aleisha* will come out and sing 'Smile' then *Telma* will sing 'Somewhere Over the Rainbow.' OK?" It's a testy rhetorical question, Gwen doesn't say anything because if Jesselle's already made up her mind Gwen doesn't even know why she went and grabbed her or what she's supposed to even *do,* unless Jesselle just came up with that *now,* of Aleisha coming out first and Telma going *after,* but Gwen is surprised to find herself thinking *there is just no way, this has gone too far, Telma's going to go on* BEFORE *Aleisha or not at all because darlin you're just too young to be a diva*————————————————O SHIT there they are! Aleisha's mom's Zen grin turned to mush, Telma crying/stomping her foot in deep rhythmic tantrum, Aleisha watching her, watching

Telma's alien movements so closely, still devoted, still in awe, still helpless—

"What is the *matter* with you!" shouts Gwen. She takes Telma by the shoulders & shakes her. Telma: unplacable, opaque, insistent. So wounded in so many ways. Gwen *angry*, then remembering the mutilation—angry, then remembering—angry, then remembering. But the words come out *Don't do this to her Telma it isn't fair*————but nothing NOTHING moves her, & it's T I M E

SHIT! A hush falls like silent snow, everyone knows what's coming, it's in the program, it's Telma closing the show, that's what the program says, the Courage people (mostly Tiff Koster) had the idea for Aleisha to sing but it was too late to change it in the program, they hadn't even printed up inserts, the *plan* was for Telma to go out there and do "Somewhere Over the Rainbow" and at the very end (as abortively rehearsed) Telma would intro "my new BFF from Ontario Canada" (Tiff Koster's awkward wording) but now that wasn't going to happen, the *trouble* was that Steve was still going to intro Telma as planned (as written in the program) but because Telma refused to go and sing "Somewhere Over the Rainbow" and at the end of it intro little Aleisha, now little *Aleisha* was going to be the one who went out onstage as Steve intro'd *Telma*, which would require some quick explaining (by Steve or *someone*), you know, like, *as you can see this isn't Telma, before we bring Telma out please meet our very special guest who flew all the way from Ontario Canada to be with us tonight, she's actually the youngest breast cancer survivor in the world and she's going to sing "Smile"* but how was THAT even going to work unless Jesselle practically walked out onstage *with* Aleisha and used the mic for her remarks before handing it off to the beleaguered child . . .

. . . NOW Steve Martin says, We have someone very special with us tonight, I'm sure she's familiar to many of you in her official role of the Mayor of St. Ambrose's (already in the script, & written by

Tiff K) . . . ladies and gentlemen, without further ado . . . .
. . . . . *TELMA BALLENDYNE!!!!!!!!!!!!!!!!!!!*——————
"Telma, you are NOT *going on after her! You are* NOT*!"*
——————Aleisha & her mom walk on-
stage prematurely, Melanie confused, Jesselle too distracted to stop
them, everything's going to hell, plus the collective gasp at how tiny
Aleisha is also gives way to murmurry puzzlement, as 15% of the audience knows *this is not Telma.* Jesselle walks out after them to make
the proper intro, the audience laughs at the sweet nonpro logistical
snafu but lovely, the laughter *with* them in their ordinariness, their
simple sacred commonplaceness, the heroic example set by their most
uncommon commonplace courage which is what the ball is about
TAKE COURAGE Steve Martin's eyes already look like they might
be tearing up, so moved how can you not be moved—*Ladies & Gentleman* says Jesselle, having been handed the mic, *we have a very special
guest from Ontario Canada, Miss Aleisha Hunter* the heart is unlonely
hun——*Aleisha was diagnosed with breast cancer when she was 2½ (AUDI-
ENCE GASP) now she's five, she's the world's youngest breast cancer survivor (Gwen forever of course by Telma's side, now paranoid/reading Jesselle's
words as deliberate salts in the wound of your bitch daughter) (THE AUDI-
ENCE ROARS, HALF OF THEM ON THEIR FEET IN OVA-
TION, THE REST SAVING IT ALSO NOT WANTING TO
SPOOK THE LITTLE ONE WHO IS* VERY *LITTLE).* In
the clutch, Melanie has reacquired her Zen game face, the audience
now fairly gasping with the sentimentality&grandeur/impossible
bravery of the moment————————Mama Melanie leans down to
her baby & whispers *Are you OK?* meaning, *to be alone by yourself onstage?* Aleisha nods & Mom walks off————more than half the
audience dies a little because they didn't want Mom to go, someone
should have told Mom to just stay, the child looks so stranded, so
vulnerable, so perfect, so——————————the orchestra begins, a
small not overbearing arrangement, Aleisha makes a tentative start,
a few fits starts & hiccups then audience tenses, tears rolling already,

audience *WILLING* her to be OK, for *everything* to be all right *she will be, won't she? She's a trooper, right? The powers that be would not have thrown her to the lions, would they? I mean she must have done benefits before, performed at benefits before, no? Right?* The whole room *straining* with her, rooting for her, dying in their lonely flooded unhunted hearts for her, then

Smile tho yr ♥ is aching

the tiny *tiny* voice but NO! something's wrong with her mic! A technician elegantly creeps onstage, fixes it in a jiffy, now garble of terrorstricken loving anticipatory sounds that Gwen's never even heard from audience or crowd or anything ever——whalish sounds of primal anxiety&love&fear&primal love

Smile even tho it's breaking

————& that. is. it.
The child can take no more.
The nightmare moment the audience thought would never come

is here.

     Aleisha stares into the wings stage right, from the ballroom audience a ¼viewable spasmy clump of people is discernible there. Melanie. Gwen. Phoebe. Jesselle. Stage manager. Others. And Telma: unblinking, unstomping, uncrying, raging no more. Recipient of Aleisha's beaten begging onstage eyes.

     It happens so quickly, it's only seconds, she was about to rescue her daughter, Jesselle was going to go out there too, hell even Gwen was but Telma tamped the mom's arm & took the stage. The audience has not exhaled. They know this is no longer scripted. No one knows what's going to happen, not even Gwen, but more than a few think they do: *the big girl's going to help the little girl walk offstage*
NO.

Telma kneels to enfold her. Aleisha
trembles.

Loud silence, then Telma begins

:) tho your heart is aching

Smile even tho it's breaking

. . . . . . but won't go any further without her, her new BFF from Ontario CN. The silence grows louder. Telma gets *behind* her, still on her knees, arms enfolding/encircling her like a necklace, protecting, soothing, loving—& begins again—*warbling whispering entreating lullaby-beseeching* in Aleisha's ear—*MOTHERING*—Gwen out of her fog now and into a dream, all of it dreamy————————after a few false starts Telma gets her to talk—then talk-sing—then sing, her voice a thread of love entangled with Aleisha's *protecting loving* loving *LOVE*

[they sing lyrics describing weather,

suggesting that as long as

*there are skies above, one may persevere]**

Masterfully, the accompaniment recedes (quickly, plaintively, ♥breakingly) the conductor must've made that decision) until there is only

a

single

violin.

{Telma&Aleisha (together)}

[they sing lyrics suggesting

to remain steadfast

thru difficulties, the gloom

may lift and the

sun come out again]†

---

* Permission to reprint lyrics denied by rights holder. —*Author.*

† *Ibid.*

& then it's over.

Telma holds Aleisha
Aleisha holds back
burying her face in Telma/s blasted lam-
basted chest.
The mothers take the stage

& then:

pandemonium.

[Bud]

Fall Guy

Dolly

fell again. This time she sprained an arm and got what the doctor called a scalp hematoma; she bled beneath the skin. She got lucky, though, yet again—nothing broken. *Nothing broken, nothing gained*, said Bud aloud, in front of the caregiver with the worst English.

Bud sat on the edge of the bed. Mom looked all played out.

"Do you know what this is?"

"This?"

"This *phase*."

She sounded almost lighthearted. Jaunty.

"No. What is it?"

"This is *the deterioration-death* phase. It's old age. *That's* what it is: *the deterioration-death* phase. If there was a coffin, you'd just crawl right in."

"I can have one here tomorrow."

"Go fuck yourself."

They watched TV together, then Bud flipped through channels while Dolly slept. Reality show after reality show; the world was overdosing on reality. Once faddish, the New (filmed) Reality was the norm. Bud's little theory was that the "blooper" was to blame. When he was a boy, he remembered John Wayne dropping by *The*

Tonight Show with a blooper reel from his latest film—take after take of the Duke unable to make it through one scene or other without laughing. When he finally regained his composure, the virus had already passed to whoever was acting opposite him and the cycle began again. That sort of thing used to be a *goof*, a bonusburger you'd bring Johnny for kicks. It was fun, the folks at home liked the idea of being "in" on something plus it was sexy watching the squeaky gears of fame machinery at work. But when they started using blooper reels as "stingers" at the end of big feature comedies (a montage of mistakes, gaffes, and unprovoked hysteria over final credits), it was like climbing into a Philip K. Dick short story: the beginning of a fatal reality leak. If reality was the *PDF*, the blooper reel was the *end of PDF inviolability*, a gateway drug that hacked into reality to produce a highly addictive hybrid—reality programming—more potent than tired old reality itself. Cinematography died and gave birth to *the photography of everything.* Footage of the DP waking up in the morning, taking a shit and arguing with his wife before leaving for work (as DP on a feature film) was now as or more compelling than whatever fictional narrative he'd be hired to shoot. Formal storytelling no longer existed outside reality but had nestled *inside*; writers gave TED talks on creating narratives that could be altered by the shake of an iPad. The wiki page on bloopers said the English called it "corpsing"—trying to make the live actor playing the corpse onstage laugh. Well, someone had hacked into fiction and contaminated it with reality; now fiction was the fata morgana, the ghostly relic on the laptop screen; the untampered PDF was a fanatical construction, at last thankfully extinct.

He stopped on a TNT doc about John Ford. There was a montage of men, galloping on horses. Suddenly the narrator was talking about horses that were specially trained to fall without injuring themselves. They called them—what else?—*falling horses.* He pictured Dolly on one, strapped to the saddle on the cover of an Hermès catalogue.

·   ·   ·

Bud knew Michael would be jetlagged and was surprised when he agreed to meet. He said he needed to force himself to stay up because they were throwing a long-planned dinner party tonight for a writer who just published an acclaimed translation of *Madame Bovary*. Michael suggested the Coffee Bean, on Larchmont.

As it turned out, all the fuss in New Zealand was nothing more than—surprise—the actor wanting more to do. So Michael wrote three new scenes and elongated five more, without leaving the actor's trailer. All the bullshit between star & director went *poof*.

"Wendy said the movie's called *Misericord* . . ."

"That's just a working title. Did Ooh Baby close your deal?"

"Yeah. I've already commenced."

"I *told* you. What did I tell you?"

"Yes, you did. And I really thank you."

"It's from Biggie's story? What they want you to adapt?"

"*Kind* of. It's a *real* story that Biggie found on the Internet. He made a few . . . *changes*."

"Have you seen the two of them together?"

"Yeah, at the cancer thing."

"Right! There's something about them—the two of them, to-gether—that's *terribly* moving. Biggie's sick, you know."

"Something with his head?"

"They thought it was NPC, Niemann-Pick, but it isn't. They don't know *what* it is. If it was NPC, he'd be having seizures, & prob-ably be fairly incapacitated by now. But he hasn't had any seizures. *Physically* he seems to be fine. It's a mystery."

"Wow."

"The doctors told him it's going to look, smell & feel very much like Alzheimer's. I mean, in the end. Whenever *that* is, also some-thing no one seems to know."

"Gee, you know I'd rather write a script about *that*."

"Yours is not to reason why."

"Michael . . . I know you just got back. I know you did a lot of writing over there, and that you're jetlagged. But I just wanted to tell you the story. Can I tell you this story they want me to adapt? It's a very weird story. I mean it's *compelling*, but . . . I guess I just need to talk it out. Maybe you'll have a take on it."

"Sure."

"Are you sure it's OK? I don't want to burden you. We can do it another time—"

"No! Now's perfect."

"I'm really going to condense this, OK?"

"Condense away."

"This is really kind of you, Michael. I really appreciate—"

"Bud! You're killin me!"

"OK. The whole thing's based on this newspaper article. Fifteen, maybe 20 years ago. Takes place in South Carolina, the Blue Ridge Mountains. These two 16 year-olds are hiking. Boyfriend-girlfriend. Pretty rough rapids there—remember *Deliverance*? They shot *Deliverance* around there too. And the rapids? Long story short: the girl slips and falls, they *both* fall trying to cross the river, he gets spit out, whatever, but she goes down. And what *happens* is, she—her *body*—gets stuck in this . . . *whirlpool*, feet first."

"And the water *keeps* her like that, right? I've heard of stuff like this. It keeps her vertical."

"Yeah, it's like a washing machine. She's 8 feet under, whatever, and they can *see the body* but they just can't get to it. And her father comes and camps by the river. They make a few attempts to get her out—the men from town, and these are experienced men—but they can't do it, some of them almost die trying. So they have to call it off. The father goes nuts."

"Because he can't bury his little girl."

"Right."

"It's *Antigone*."

"Exactly! And the river's protected, so they can't dam it up. But the dad goes to the senator who happens to be Strom Thurmond. Thurmond lost his daughter not too long before in a car accident, so he's got a sympathetic ear. And Thurmond says, *Do whatever it takes.*

So they dam it up but the dam doesn't work either. And *more* of these guys come close to drowning. So finally, they just say, *The river will give her up.* No—they say, 'the river always gives up its dead.'"

"Jesus."

"Biggie made some notes about what he wants—"

"What are they?"

"—for the adaptation. First of all, he wants the whole thing to take place in one of these huge caves. So it's actually a river that runs *under ground*."

"Interesting."

"But this is the weirdest: instead of father & daughter, he wants it to be mother & son."

"I can guess which side of the river Mom's on."

This is where he needed Michael's input so Bud kept quiet. Michael began to subtly rock in his chair, eyes slowly opening & shutting, lost in thought. After a few minutes of that, he got up from the table, ordered another latte and a chocolate croissant, and sat back down with the same intensely focused demeanor—as if having placed himself in a twilight state where creative solutions might be accessed. He was definitely engaged in some sort of *process*, and Bud only hoped it was one that might benefit him.

They didn't give him 2 million a script for nothing.

Bud saw that the latte was ready, and fetched it. He set it down in front of his old friend, waited a few respectful moments then said, "So what do you think? I mean how the fuck do you make a movie out of *that*? Because from everything I know, everything I've *heard* and *seen*, Brando Brainard & Ooh Baby Baby aren't really in the business of making dark little *indies*."

"*No they are not.* You've got that right. You know, I talked to Brando—I think it may have been the day after you went over to the house and met Biggie. Brando said he came home from work and asked Biggie how your meeting went. *Biggie didn't remember you being there.* Brando said that his brother doesn't even really remember anymore the story of the girl in the river, either—he just remembers the broad strokes. Brando thinks Biggie's fixated on the story in that autistic way. I *do* think that most of the time, *details* elude him. I mean, unless Biggie brings up the page on his screen, he only remembers the broad strokes: mother, son, river."

"What does it all mean, Michael?"

Bud felt like he was on the pier, talking to a psychic.

"What it *means* is, you've got to make it work. Make it work for *you*. Because if it doesn't work for *you,* it sure as hell ain't gunna work for *Brando.* Now, that doesn't mean you don't take Brando's *input,* because you should. As much as possible. Because that's what will allow you to form an idea of what he wants. He won't tell you *directly*—producers never do. It's something he won't be able to *articulate.* Plus, I think he may be a little leery of encroaching on his brother, not that Biggie would even be *aware,* but I have a feeling Brando's a little superstitious. Biggie's the golden calf, the so-called idiot savant (unfortunately beginning to skew more toward *idiot*) and Brando's probably a bit reluctant to fuck with that. On some deep, brotherly level. But as long as the story is approached with *respect,* especially *at the beginning of the process*—which is clearly what you're already doing—as long as Brando can *see* that the material was approached with *respect,* you'll be fine. Make *mother, son, river* your mantra, then you're free. Sky's the limit."

He was flummoxed. There was some awkwardness there as well, because Bud felt like he was walking that fine, perilous line between asking for guidance and outright begging for help.

"Free . . . free to do *what,* exactly?"

Maybe it's for the best that he's jetlagged. He probably wouldn't have met with me if he wasn't. Maybe he'll come up with some kind of fix, out of sheer exhaustion.

Michael smiled to himself before taking a ragged bite from his croissant. Bud was starving. He hadn't eaten much in the last few days; he was saving food as a reward for when he found a solution to

his approach to the script. He resisted the impulse to reach over &
tear off a hunk of Michael's bread.

"A comedy," said Michael.

"A comedy?"

"Comedies are in Brando's wheelhouse. [*OMG. They're still using
the word! A nice omen*] They're pretty much the only thing Brando
responds to."

"You're saying I should write a comedy?"

"Yup."

"But how do I walk away from this? And how do I get him to
agree to let me substitute something *else*?"

"No, no, no. You write a *comedy* from the *river* story."

"The drowned girl—I mean, the drowned *mom*?"

"You got it. Are you following me?"

Bud was trying; he had to.

"A comedy?"

"Why not?" said Michael. He looked like one of those wild, ex-
ultant *tzaddiks* from rabbinical lore. *"Why not?"*

He fixed Bud with a secret fraternity smile, happy that he saw, or
pretended to, the light.

"Jesus, Michael, it's brilliant. But *how*? How do I make a comedy
out of something like that?"

Michael said, "Who was it that said 'comedy is tragedy, plus
time'?"

Bud looked it up on his iPhone while Michael excused himself to
the restroom. Well, it was either Woody Allen or Carol Burnett,
which probably meant neither. Other quotes were "If it bends, it's
comedy. If it breaks, it isn't" and "Life is a tragedy in close-up, a
comedy in long-shot." Bud racked his brain. He knew Michael was
right, but realized their conversation would need to have a sequel, at
another time; he didn't want to overstay his query. Michael returned
to the table.

"OK, fucking *brilliant*. I'm not sure exactly how I'm going to apply it—I need to *reframe*—but this whole *world* just opened up. Do you think we can have just one more talk about this? I mean, once I figure it out? Just to run past you?"

"Sure. Anytime."

"Because now I'm thinking the river can be in an *amusement park*. Like a Pirates of the Caribbean ride . . ."

"Ha! That's good!"

Bud felt a flush of excitement, that feeling of worthiness, that he & Michael were peers in the same trade.

"And if you fall off the ride, you enter this other world—"

"It's great, Bud. It's like Miyazaki. *Spirited Away* . . ."

He made a mental note to watch the masterful animated film; he'd never gotten around to seeing it.

"Michael, *thank* you! I mean, thank you for *everything*."

"We're writers, Bud. That's what writers do, we talk to each other. We steal from each other. You'd do the same for me."

Bud's eyes drifted to the half-eaten croissant on his friend's plate.

"Can I tear off a piece of that? All I want is a tiny bite."

"I'm all done."

"Are you sure?"

"Go for it."

"You're sure you don't mind?"

[Gwen]

How to Fix A Fatal Error

After

the Courage Ball, Telma couldn't stop throwing up. Gwen took her to the doctor and he started an IV because she was dehydrated. They put her in one of the examination rooms, & Gwen sat with her as she slept.

At home, she was listless. She stayed in bed, skyping with Biggie. She wouldn't talk to or even text or email anyone else. A messenger came to pick up a letter but Telma told her mom she didn't have any letter. When Khloé Kardashian was told there wasn't, she thought there must be some miscommunication. She got Gwen's number from Tiff Koster & called to ask what was happening. Gwen told Khloé her daughter had been sick, and would need to take a rain-check. Khloé asked if she could say a quick hello but when Gwen told Telma who was on the line her daughter said to *please tell her I'm asleep.* A bouquet of flowers was delivered later that day, from all the Kardashians. Written on the envelope was *to Telma, from Kris.* Telma never opened it.

. . .

On the day everything was to be settled, Gwen and Phoebe talked on the phone. The meeting was just after lunch. This time there would be no doctors, only lawyers from opposing sides.

"What did your attorney say?"

"That I shouldn't be there. That I should just stay home & let him handle it. That he'd call from the meeting if he needed to talk to me."

"And so?"

"Ain't gonna happen. I'll be there, with bells on."

"And you're going to talk to her after?"

"As soon as it's done."

"Sure you don't want me to be there?"

Gwen nodded. "I'll be OK. This is something I need to do for her, *and* for me. I need to have the courage she's had all this time. And Telma needs to see *me* being strong."

"Well . . . call me. After. OK, hon?"

Without warning, they cried together, a brief downpour through the wire—*to the limit, to the wall*—a summer storm. They still managed to get a few laughs off before hanging up.

On her way to Century City, Gwen went upstairs to give her daughter a kiss. Telma sat up in bed asleep, the computer on her lap, one stilled hand on the keyboard.

Gwen looked at the screen and saw what she assumed to be Biggie's bedroom. She startled when he lumbered in from off-camera & sat down at his desk. (Gwen ducked out of frame.) She watched from afar; he was engrossed online while Telma slept. It was so obvious that the two were calmed by each other's presence. There was something so sad and so sweet about it. Gwen stroked Telma's cheek with the back of her hand, then kissed her brow; Biggie's gaze subtly shifted in time to see it. At this moment—*just this moment*—Telma was an innocent, but the age of innocence was coming to a close. A new age and new time would soon begin. Gwen prayed for the strength to face it.

She prayed for them both.

[Mt Olympus mixtape]

Animal House

Rikki

had his cock in Montana Fishburne's ass & was *grateful* to Jerzy for giving him the Viagra because he was so loaded he'd never have been able to get it up *plus* he thought he'd be too shy or somehow *disturbed* to be fucking in front of people, he'd never done that before & wasn't sure his dick would even work in that type of situation *plus* he was never in a *gangbang* either. The tailend of that *If* poem he memorized for school got stuck in his head ". . . and which is more, you'll be a man, my son!"

> *To every season, turn turn turn the fuck* OVER.

The weed had something *in* it; or maybe the *meth*, he *heard* & SAW things, nothing too heavy. It wasn't all bad but it wasn't all good, which more or less described the experience of plugging Montana Fishburne's shit chute. *Plus* knowing Ree was up*stairs* was another bit of a hard-off . . . not cause he worried she might come down, which she *wouldn't*, it was just the just *knowing* of it—that she was up there—that was weird. But *everything* was effin weird today.

. . .

Jerzy went over his booty from the Hilton *honeyshot!*s.

. . . a veritable motherlode, a motherdaughterload, motherdaughtershootyourload. All the stinkle ladies nearest & dearest to Harry's abnormal ♥ signified & represented, or should he say *presented,* as in young pussycat baboonettes: Hailee, Chloë, Elle. He'd tell Harry to pony up 15K for the lot, & Harry'd give it to him too, because Jerzy had dared in drug-besotted boldness to fuck with the *Hailee* honey-pot, dared to photoshop a tampon string, perfect & undetectable in its digi-fakery, reflecting the unutterably ineffable influence of the darkside of the moon. *That* would be the tipping point, & allow J to demonstrate his Trojan Magnumnimity by offering it at a *rate,* just 150 yards . . .

Dirty Harry would no doubt Sinatra-serenade his thanks:

. . . got the world on a string, sittin on a rainbow———

In the midst of his photocumshot labors, the crotchety crotcherazzo found himself on the horniness of a dillemmawatson.

After sliding out of a hybrid SUV, a little girl approached him at the Hilton while Jerzy was in the thick of it, the fur was starting to fly, somewhere between Elle & Chloë. The kid strode right up and said *Hi!* like she was family then reminded him how they'd met a few months ago outside of Sur, she was that *gleek* with the funny old/young look hanging around waiting for ☆ gleesters to come in & out while Mom was across the street shopping. The naggy kid chastised him *again* about not being on Facebook then said all would be for-given if he took her pic, which he did, causing a bit of rubbernecking amongst tourists congregated on the other side of the glass inside the lobby of the hotel. The fuss—that she seemed to be "someone" (which of course she was, but only in *KancerWorld,* & not yet in the *rest* of the world, where she of course *would* be, soon enough (was just what the little gal wanted, & he'd been happy to oblige).

What she didn't know was that he'd already memorialized her, his m.o. being to machinegunfire *anyone* stepping from the back of a car, shoot now, look later. As he sorted everything from that night for his boss, he came across some pix of the gleek arriving at the gala with her mom . . . the tried&tru *stepping out* shots, and the little gleek did not disappoint. She was an unknown, & usually Jerzy threw some civvie stinkweed into Harry's snatch batch to sweeten the punch. Giftbag swagger jagger. Upskirt warmer-uppers. Twatcherazzi twizzle sticks. But *this* time, he destroyed all of the illicit images of the gleek, even those she asked him to take on the sidewalk. It just felt like the right thing to do.

He pulled on the glass dick & coughed out the smoke, & when he was finally able he said outloud "You're a good man Charlie Brown."

.   .   .

Harry's problemo was one thing, THE PROBLEM *was another.*

Jerzy turned over THE PROBLEM *in his head,* THE PROBLEM *being: How to see the face of God? At least he'd identified it, which had taken a lot of luck & hardwork. The answer was out there like the xxx-files once said. Jerzy wanted to see the face of G-d*—NOT *the false American Idols before him* not Hov, not I-Veen, not Puppetmathers *(making them smaller & smaller in his* ♥*)*, *but the face of The Eternal.*

But one thing haunted him:

What if he was allowed to see the face of G-d & did so, righteous & transcendent, w/o realizing it was the WRONG G-d?

The hummingbird & the mantis held the answer.

After careful meth odical scrutiny & further accumulation of much crack plaque Jerzy unpacked the disturbing parable of bird & insect. (He called it parable because in so doing it placed mantis & hummingbird outside of Time. It was easier to consider them if they resided in a place outside Time, in parable form.) G-d said to an as-yet-formless thing: Give me your Soul, your Spirit, your Energy, & I will make you into that magnificat *of Mystery: blurry venerated magnificence called Hummingbird. All who see you will know I touched you, that you did know me & saw my face, & that I did favor you. In you I shall be forever immanent. And the 1st formless thing said, "I accept & do praise you, forever & ever." & G-d said to another as-yet-formless thing: Give me your Soul, your Spirit, your Energy, & I will make you into that* magnificat *of Mystery: patient, aloof, anomalous gladiator, that vatic king called Mantis. All who see you will know I touched you, that you did know me & saw my face, & that I did favor you. In you I shall be immanent. And the 2nd formless thing said, "I accept, & do praise you, forever and ever." And upon assuming those forms he had bestowed like raiments they wondered when they would be allowed to see His face. But until then, they happily did go about their new lives, fulfilling their natures & natural destinies.*

The mantis was patient, & assumed the position of prayer, whether on wings in flight or at rest upon hillside ground or poised in acquiescence upon leaves dead, or still green. And the mantis heard a Voice say, Come, stand by the sugarwater of this bird feeder, & take care to hide, for that is where you shall see my face. So the mantis took up near-invisible sentry by the sugarwater of bird feeders, wherever he might find them. The hummingbird was patient too, though the G-d saw fit to place upon its tiny quivering shoulder the mantle of impatience, & while impatience appeared to be its nature such was His art in camouflaging the hummingbird's supreme forbearance. The hummingbird heard a Voice too & the Voice said, Follow me to the place where you shall soon see my face, but the Voice was always careful to be a flower away. Still, the faithful thing beat its wings ceaselessly toward It, for that too was its nature, an unending faithfulness to the G-d that gave it form. And the mantis prayed by the bird feeder in monk's simple cloak to see the face that His Maker had promised would manifest, & G-d said to him, You must kill the thing that comes to nourish and feed from this sugar, this water, & the mantis listened blindly, an assassin of His love, & did murder the hummingbird. But in the cruel & unforgiving instant of its kill, the mantis understood he would never see the face of G-d, and that he had killed his sister, the sister who had been promised the same as he; the G-d that had given them both life had taken care to make certain his sister, in her last moments, was fully aware that her brother was going to impale her, that she would die poleaxed by her brother's spiked leg as it hairtriggered from just beneath the very arm that it prayed with, her brother had been ordered by the G-d that made them to kill his sister for sport, & at the same time she realized she too would have done the same, that was her only solace (one which the G-d did not anticipate), that if ordered so she would have massacred her brother in obedience to her G-d, their Maker.

& now the mantis was alone, and alone with his revelation. In the horror of his predicament, he cannibalized himself—in merciful mercilessness their G-d had made it his nature to devour other mantises & so devouring itself was both a penitence & a cleansing of Soul and Spirit, thus ending the cycle of betrayal (until He chose for it to begin again, which He always did, out of boredom & for sport). Before the mantis died he cursed such a G-d, & for such heresy his G-d reconstituted him long enough to promise the mantis he would make him into the hummingbird, the mantis' sister, mother & wife, he would make him a flower-hoverer next time, and promised too that before the hour of his im-palement & death, his heartbreak at the further revelations of the perfect sense-lessness & sadism of this our life would be so much more exquisite than the suffering the mantis had last experienced, the G-d saw fit to tell his creation the misery he'd endured before cannibalizing itself would be increased a mil-lionfold—out of G-d's boredom, & for His sport.

Jerzy read that a motto of the Navy Seals is, "3 is 2, 2 is 1, & 1 is none." What does it mean? That one should never enter a battle alone, without an ally, & one should assume that before victory or even before battle allies will be lost.

You can't do 1 of anything . . . "1 is the loneliest number." Who sang it? 3 Dog Night. The 3 again: (A whisper: 1ovine, 2-Hov, 3-Em) "3 is 2, 2 is 1 & 1 is none." Listen to Ecclesiastes: "2 are better than 1, because they have a good reward for their toil. For if they fall, 1 will lift up the other. But woe to 1 who is alone & falls & does not have another to help. If 2 lie together, they keep warm; but how can 1 keep warm alone? & tho 1 might prevail against another, 2 will withstand 1. A 3-fold cord is not quickly broken."

(A whispernet: 1-Suge, 2-Pac, 3-Jerzy)

Listen to the rhythm of the trimesters:

1, 2 & 3.

The Known, the Unknown, the Unknowable.

He, she, them—the merging.

ICM, CAA, WME.

Listen to the secret language of <u>the 4th Trimester</u>.

Listen.

Listen, & you will hear the demiurge, the golem . . . .

. . .

Earlier, Bolt told Tom-Tom that someone from production had asked how old Rikki was. He was guessing they might want him to join in the fun. Tom-Tom said *I'm his fucking manager & he aint doin nuthin for FREE. Somebody wants to give him a bj, they're gunna have to PAY, & guess what, they pay* ME.

She told Rikki to find the ID she got made in MacArthur Park for when he was auditioning on that piece of shit movie, just in case Antwone Fisher wanted to hire him but had trouble with him being a minor. Tom-Tom knew they never liked using minors if they could help it cause you always had to provide a teacher, give em nappy breaks, yadda yadda, all this xtra costly dumbshit. When she learned the star of the porno was the one who wanted to confirm that Rikki was legal, Tom-Tom wasn't surprised. Early on, she saw the two hanging out between takes, & it was clear from their body language that they were in the courtship phase so often preceding consensual unprotected double-pen.

T^2 had them over a barrel. Bolt asked for $7,500 like she told him to but they wouldn't budge from the 5. Bolt probably betrayed her, bothsides-playing punkbitch that he was, probably just told them he knew she needed the bread & would do it for 5. Now it was *payback* time. When Tom-Tom said she was Rikki's *manager* & puttin him in the *show* would cost a thousand *for client services*, they *seriously* balked. They gave her the evil don't-fuck-with-us-lady eye but she knew that if they wanted to keep Chippy D in chapstix they would have to deliver. Montana looked none too pleased with these assholeproducers from the get-go, *Rikki* told her that, he said Chippy was cool, if you'll notice she never talks to the fuckers she just *texts* em, so when Tom-Tom saw Missy Montana Fishsmellrugburn workin her android with that anvil face she knew some shit was goin down about the producers tellin her they didn't want to buy Rikki for a g, Tom-

Tom would have loved to read *that* text, her money was on *monstana from the gate, wish I could eavesdrop, love to be a fly on the wall of that pussy join the crowd or should I say swarm tee hee*. Montana was anvilface retexting, like maybe she was saying *You wouldn't pull this shit with Kim Kardashian and Sasha Grey*, after all she was still Larry Fishburne's daughter, she had diva dna, no matter how humble her upbringing or how far the fall, it would have been *impossible* not to grow up without a sense of xxxxtreme entitlement.

Bolt came & talked to the double T about the whole Rikki deal. *Perfect.* She knew he'd pussy out. Bolt was one of these man hookers who didn't have the stomach for *conflict* but she knew he probably already got a $1,000 finder's fee for the house, or maybe they *did* come up to seventy-five hundred & he fuckin *pocketed* it . . . *Just a gigolo* was fucking wearing out his welcome. Tom-Tom would have evicted him if she wasn't having trouble getting *loosers* to sign on, just when she thought she'd signed some up they never showed, & besides, Bolt had a few plusses, aside from being generally telegenic, his cock was fat as a can of Coke Zero. *Cock* Zero *hahahaha* new nickname tee hee. Right when Bolt began his predictable-ass limpdick supplication not to make waves, she looked at him with irritation & said "Outta my face, bee-atch." From the corner of her eye, Tom-Tom caught cameraman Seth sniggering like he was glad somebody took a wrench to jigabolt. She'd dug him on first sight, & Seth being simpatico bode well for the *Daydream Believers* shoot.

Montana came through just like she thought. When they grudgegave her the envelope of cash, Tom-Tom made herself scarce for a while to give em a little time to untwist their panties. *Tee hee . . .*

She strolled over to the poolhouse, singing

> *Cheer up, Sleepy Jean*
> *O*
> > *what can it*
> > > *mean*

Dr Phil popped up, out of nowhere. He wanted to talk about doing an intervention on Jerzy for the show.

"What people won't *expect* is me turning to *Rikki* at the end, after Jerzy agrees to go in for treatment (*hopefully!*), & saying, 'It's all taken care of, my young friend—you're going in too.'"

. . .

"I was almost in one of your dad's movies."

"Really? Which one?"

"The Treasure of Sierra Leone."

"Really?"

"Do you & your dad talk about his movies?"

"We used to. Well, we still sort of, but it's more in my head because right now we're not really talking too much. I like to keep up with him, things he's doing, on the internet—tho sometimes he's hard to keep up with!"

Rikki was way high & feeling uncomfortable in his skin. It prolly was the four beans Tom-Tom gave him, he kept seeing this gold fringe shimmering in the air next to her a Kanye West kind of gold, it was all around her body like the gold painted around some of those plaster Madonnas/Jesuses, the golden fringe came & went but when it came it sounded like unfriendly windchimes & was super-real. He was more loaded for real than he wanted but pushed himself to be careful to maintain a respectful, profesh demeanor, especially when conversating with Chippy D, he wanted to be the consummate self-effacing gentleman. Cause if he did OK this might lead to other jobs, it seemed like a pretty good way to earn $$$ until ReeRee & him were on their feet like kiss my a$$ & my anus cause it/s finally famous.

The strange shall we say circumstances added to his discomfort & budding mild paranoia. He & Montana were having a normal conversate like any 2 people who just met would or might, the peculiar a$$peck of course being they could/would be interrupted any moment by a person/persons unknown ordering them to enter a zituation wherein he would inevitably be placing/ramming his dick into her mouth, pussy or a$$-ho while other gentlemen he did not know (and had not had the pleasure yet of conversating with or introdouche-ing himself) would be doing the same.

"So you were going to be in my dad/s movie?"

"Yeah."

"Who were you going to play?"

"The orphan boy who pretends to be a child soldier."

"That's a *big* part!"

"Yeah."

"Like what happened."

"I read my scene with your dad."

"You *did*? Well you must/ve got pretty far. Now I'm *impressed*."

"I read w/ Michael Douglas too."

"You read with dad *and* Gordon Gekko? You the man! Were you nervous you musta been nervous. I know *I'da* been."

"I guess. Do you ever get nervous? doing movies?"

"O I think *every* actress does—every *artist*. I think something/s wrong if you don't. Because it doesn't matter what your medium is: *acting* or *painting* or *writing*, doing *porn* or being a *sculptor* . . . it's all pretty much the same. & the *artists* are the ones—we're the ones who put ourselves *out* there, we put *everything* on the line. & I don't think that *ever* gets easier."

A boy-looking girl with a clipboard came over.

"We're good to go, Montana. Need body makeup?"

"I'm fine."

"You're squirtin on this one," said boygirl, a crooked little un-smile.

"OH! Oh *shit*—okay . . ."

"We have tons of towels."

"You got towels?" said chirpy Chippy, in her best worst Barba-dian Barbie accent, a Rihannabe. "Now all we need is a radio, sand, & sunscreen."

.   .   .

Tom-Tom & Phil dropped by the poolhouse. (The blow-ups once on the wall had been bubble-wrapped & stacked/stored in the garage.) Jerzy was watching TV; Nicki Minaj just got *Punk'd*, which confused & surprised him because he didn't think the show was even on anymore. Maybe at this point it was self-generating.

"Did you know," he said, "that human beings were meant to gestate for 12 months? . . . *the 4th trimester.* But women's hips can't handle it. *Duh! Design flaw!*"

She asked Jerzy how he was doing, & he said, "It's a numbers game." Tom-Tom said that Dr Phil had the cool idea of staging an intervention & she wished he would please consider for her sake because they were shooting inside a week and thus far all she had confirmed were Dr Phil & the schmigolo, and a raft of thin promises from 2nd&3rd-string players off *Supermarket Sweep, Shedding for the Wedding, Little People Big World, Can You Duet?* and *Find My Family*, plus maybe a fired, acne-pitted queen from *Hair Battle Spectacular*.

"You don't even have to go. To rehab. We'll get shots of you on a plane or a minivan, whatever, then say, you know, 'after 4 days, he relapsed & is now living back on Mt Olympus.'"

"Sure."

"*Sure?* Like in yes? Well no shit *that's* no fun. I thought you'd at least have offered up a little resistance. Jeez, Phil, he really *does* need a frickin intervention!"

.   .   .

The $500 money order from Rikki's fostermom came & Ree gave it to Rikki to go cash but somehow it wound up with Tom-Tom who told Reeyonna "your accounts have been credited for amounts past due." (She never even remotely knew about the 2K her mom laid on her, tho Jerzy planned one day to repay her out of Gagosian funds.) ReeRee had to eat it because she was still wary of being thrown off Mt. O, which would have put a serious crimp in things, & been deleterious too, at this point, in her baby bumpitude. When Tom-Tom made the amounts past due remark, ReeRee responded w/a simple, vacant "Thank you" that if not dripping in sarcasm was damp enough. Tom-Tom said, *Hey I kicked $50 back to Rikki so don't say I got no* ♥. *Why don't you use it to buy something for the baby*—T²'s line delivery of the last, if not dripping, most assuredly wet. Ree said "How did you even cash it?" "Friends in low places. Teehee."

Reeyonna was depresso-sleeping in Bolt's shitty old room, which smelled like Bolt, Betty White mothballs & sick catshit. Or maybe Bolt smelled like Milk Duds, catshit & sick Betty White. Tom-Tom decided to make a political move because after Jerzy agreed to his intervention, Double T suddenly had what she thought was her own stupendously brilliant brainstorm (even tho it was Reeyonna's) of doing a *Teen Mom*-type deal w/Rikki & Ree. T² couldn't believe she hadn't thought of it before, it was so right there in front of her nose, a fat, catshit-smelling cash cow waddling around right there in front of her nostrilarium. & when Reeyonna heard it she didn't even have the energy to say *I told you that shit a fuckin month ago.*

"Here's two-fifty"—she peeled off the bills—"if you agree to be in the shoot this week." (Like, how would they *not*.) "& there's another $250 waiting for you plus I'll waive the rent you owe. *Which*, if you add it all up, is something like a 35-hundred-dollar package. Hey as your brother said, 'It's a numbers game!' So think about it. But tell me soon or I'm gunna have to move you out & move other folks in."

·   ·   ·

On top of her now. It's all good. Grinding her. The booty bump on the break seems to have rallied all other hallucinogens/narco-intoxicants/beans&benzos into a huge crowd that fills a town square, ready for its leader to appear. *Is she still golden-glowing?* Yeah but it was all good . . . just a week ago . . . *where's the camera?* At the moment, the lens is trained on her face—pulling a train—for her *fuck yeah!* closeup before drifting down to the foul coal-fueled engines of the ship, dark bloodswollen mechanism that gives the vessel life & speed, multiple shovels shoveling, never letting the fires go out, never allowing the wound time to close.

There's another camera down there too, exclusively for the genital area, it does not drift up, reserved solely for cuntfucking CUs plus showing the asshole full or empty *some see the ass ½ empty, some see it ½ full* Mr Cleanwax'd & surrounded by pimply hillocks/errant in-growns, *hey Chippy D get on THIS ingrown————now there's a guy (fat, white) with his dick in her mouth so she can't say "fuck yeah!" cause it's poor manners to talk with food in yr mouth, now the director tells her to lay on her side, Bolt's right beside Joey von spermberg wearing a very serious look, like he's either learning or mentoring . . . she makes the adjustment & is now on her side, everyone has to make a little adjustment & settle in, all these hardons suddenly like a bunch of baby commas thrown off the sentence teat now having to wigglefight their way back, fight for the teat/holes, even the cameraman adjusting to the new light & angles, whatever, & part of Rikki's adjustment is he balances himself a little, holding her left leg up by the ankle like you would an animal's during a veterinary procedure, the director loves it because they hate when porn☆s aren't mindful of keeping that geni-space un-obstructed, Rikki's a natural, he's really drilling her & even forgetting how stoned he is when this dude comes from the other side with his long pink dick w/its lubed helmet & without a fairtheewell the dude's in her butthole whoa no* SHIT, *a* DUDE, *she's got to have a two-room apt in there because it looks like his* BALLS *have almost moved in, this is the moment Rikki feared! feeling somebody else's hardon right through the tendon-y bitchtissue . . . but the viag/cialis combo* + *all the other shit in his system including fatburger fries&shake is majorly workin* WHOA *if he thinks about it (the dick next door) which he tries not to then thinks about it for just a second, if he thinks about it his blackpink, spotted, veiny hardcock is really only separated from the other old, white, gross pud by sin & sinew whoa whoa* WHOA *it's cool, thas cool, just don't think about the other dude, dude, now* EVERYBODY'S *got the gold fringe on em & Rikki starts hearing* SIRENS *too, like heading to-ward the house & then like they're retreating . . . & oops now yet a 4th dude (hardbodied, tattooed, Aryan-white, Eddard Starklooking motherfucker) is up there now on the other side of Montana's 3rd-dick-stuffed mouth, the men bookending her crazy whorehead, but she knows/animal-senses there's a new dude behind her & wants to welcome him to the neighborhood* it's a beautiful day for a neighbor would you be mine could you be *so she reaches back an arm & starts to shaftjack him* Fuck Yeah! *& so: 1) dick in her mouth 2) eyes shut reachback/neighborly jacking of unseen shaft; 3) double-pen c/o Rikki & Otherdude (later Seth tells Rikki that's called a full house) . . . . then she turns her head to blow the new neighbor she was just jacking now reachback jacks the FIRST dude she was blowing, total of 3 cameras now, Seth's + 2 hand-held Circuit City specials, one xxxclusive to giving head & ramminglickingrimming hindquarters, c.u.s that look like cartoon microscopic slide image blow-ups—or fat wormslugs/anemones—or naked mole rats diving burrowing into gopherholes—the stereo dicks at Chippy's head reminding Rikki of the 1st time a gradeschool slut jacked him & a friend (but nothing like this!), they were at the movies, it was dark, she sat between them, it was so wildly heartbeating FRESH that the boys hardly even considered the other nor would they have particularly cared they were glue-spattering so qwik . . . . Rikki's nostalgic train of thought interrupted when WHOA, sudden sensation of falling, his body startle-twitches like when you wake yourself from falling in a dream, you jerk awake, whoa whoa whoa now WAIT—blackness for a moment, he can't get his mooring tho aware he's still managing to pound her pussy he hears himself making alien generator-like sounds of consciousness, emerging from the utter blackness, the generator or whatever starts UP gasoline-crackle carburetor throat-clearing sounds (to him) like 1,000 windowsheets of cellophane crackle-rustling all at once in each stereophonic ear & when he resurfaces just like a child in a pool forced under by bullying brother, Rikki hears FUCK yeah! FUCK yeah! but it's a man's voice he looks up & Montana's head is arched back, she's got her hands on the 2 aforemunchin'd dicks just like she's in a rowboat now she's sucking a 5th dude (bearded, homeless-looking) standing right in front of her—dick in mouth, dick in ass, dick in pussy, hands on dicks, what the boygirl clipboard later said they call a royal flush, & she stops her arched-back-neck sucking raising up her head for Rikki to see the face of Laurence Fishburne the one who disowned her for the shame & madness of her public transgressions WHOA WHOA WHOA WHOA WHOA Rikki closes his eyes hoping the image will dissolve—opening them again—no luck!—she's still Larry, still Laurence, what have you, even the body feels thicker bigger & heavier as* *he fucks it, it* FEELS *like the weightier different-smelling stenk cavity body of a man, Rikki's left hand still holding her big brown boney ankle* W H O A ! *lets the ankle go let my people go!* telling himself it's just the KJ or maybe the ketamine (Jerzy said there was a "taste" of it somewhere in there with the meth) or was it the PCP-soaked pot—the Thai Dragon White Russian Bubbleberry Blue Ivy Grand Daddy Purple Elvis Gummy Bear Don Cornelius kush . . . *when he was talking to Montana, he never told her his friend Jerzy said her daddy was the one responsible for him not getting the part, lately Rikki listened harder to Jerzy than he had the right to because Jerzy was the only one who listened to* HIM *& besides J was his connect now for everything&everything, the roxies, coke, beans, meth, the dilaudid lollipops a nurse connect of J's provided, even the viagcialis, the whole dillio, Rikki never even asked J what he meant or how did he know Laurence Fishburne was responsible, you'd think that he would have asked but he hadn't. Rikki never mentioned it to Montana because she spoke of her pops in such far-gone morose loving words that Rikki didn't want to emphasize possible bad traits maybe being passed down from her father's side not only just that it was important to maintain professionality & total respectfulism (why jeopardize future employment or create problems) but because there wasn't anything Chippy D could fuckin do about it anyway* F U C K Y E A H! *Laurence looking down at him now, still, the patriarchal movie* ☆*'s hands still on the 2 shaftcocks same way his daughter (who completely disappeared) had em & it didn't matter, Rikki told himself it was just the dope because Laurence Fishburne was* TOO REAL, *Rikki was consensual raping Laurence Fishburne, as Rikki rabbited Laurence he felt the movie* ☆*'s dick like a stale croissant against his ripped flatstomach yechhh & Laurence seemed to like it, he said* "Rikki! *[Rikki saw/heard it in his head] Your buddy was right,* I AM *the one who told em not to hire you, baby you were* TOO GOOD *there's only room for one nigger on that show, one king, one king nigger, how could I let a young nigger like yourself steal my* SCENES *but I'm glad we hooked up like this cause now I give you mad props for that mad prick you doin me witt* FUCK *yeah* FUCK *yeah* F U C K Y E AH *everything spinning now, something awful rising up from geni-regions sirens coming & going, gold fringe waving in dead-strangefruit-smelling winds, the fuckface under-*

neath him now fritzing from Chippy to Laurence, Chippy to Laurence, father to daughter, father of the bride, til Rikki PULL OUT! PULL OUT! *recognized that awful thing that was rising feeling both dishonor & relief, when he came to consciousness Montana was cumming boygirl/someone/others yelling* PULL OUT *then actually grabbing him, big hands yanking him out/off Laurence Montana, her cumming & squirting, that's why they pulled Rikki off so they could get that spurtsillustrated moneyshot, Montana furiously rubbing her clit just like Rikki had seen on pornhub.com or was it lobstertube or was it 3rat.com, rubbing it out out damp spot in order to sustain the concurrent copious horizontal eruption—Rikki returning the favor & drenching her with vomit*————————————————————

————————————————————————————

————————————————————————————

————————————————————————————

————————————————————————————

————————————————————————————

————————————————————————————

————————————————————————————

————————————————————————————

——————————————————————— *(ruining the shot.)*

[Dramatic Personae: The Cedars of Lebanon]

Deliverance

ReeRee

bled on the eve of the *Daydream Believers* shoot. Tom-Tom poked her head in the room, groggily clocked the paramedics, & went back to sleep. Rikki borrowed Dr Phil's old VW & followed the ambulance down. The winds were furious. The city below was bright & its landmarks brilliantly identifiable, like a city in a dream. He felt like he was slaloming down an xmas tree. 3AM.

They admitted her right away. Who should he call? Rikki didn't ask Reeyonna because he knew she wouldn't want him to call *any-one*. He didn't want to wake his parents either, no need, so he waited til 730. They were there by 9.

The 3 of them—Dawn, Jim & Ree's mom—had cellphone-strategized the best way for Jacquie to make her entrance but in the end she just strode in a minute or so after the fosters. When Reeyonna at 1st saw her, her features broke lose from their tenuous corral and spasmscattered, roving mountainscapes parched & dead. Mother Jacquie imperturbably rounded them up. At bedside, thankfully, merci-fully, unpredictably, the child in Jerilynn, in *Reeyonna* (still so much child in her!), couldn't bear it any longer & held out its arms. They cried together. Everything—embrace, misery, love—was primordial, in full knowledge the ooze & ahhhs of babydom approached at cosmic velocity. Rikki and his parents left them to their unexpurgated *I'm sorrys* duet, the melody flooded the bone-dry hills and made creeks again, it fed the grasses & herded the lambs, the mother touched her daughter's wet face—its features finally come home, and safely fenced—Mother's hands palmed over innocent flesh like a witch warming its hands at a fire it never thought it could ignite, remorseful crone who'd lost faith in her powers, but now had conjured *this*. The bewitched daughter *letting* herself be touched. The cosmic velocity of it.

.　.　.

At last, the claque, perfectly imperfectly reunited: Rikki and Reeyonna, Jim and Dawn, Jacquie and Jerilynn. An overwhelming sense of relief—group exhalation (Rikki&ReeRee exempt). Fear, yes, for the baby—as they wheeled her off, a nurse said something that made them fearful—but relief at the dismantling of a monumental impasse. Hopefulness, despite Jacquie occasionally (quietly) projecting forward to the days after the baby's birth, roughly sketching the destructive return of ~~Jerilynn's~~ rage. *Don't go there. Stay in the moment. In this moment, you have your daughter back. Isn't that enough?*

.　.　.

In labor now.

Jacquie's naked freefloating fear for the baby returns, like when you wonder if you left home with candles still burning, were they too close to curtains, did you leave the bathwater on or inadvertently cover the vents on delicate machinery, was the handle not removed from the discarded refrigerator, did you leave your child or someone else's in the car.

Rikki's just relieved to have the focus off.

He was going to drive Dr Phil's car back home but guesses he should probably stay. He only has roxies & weed. He wonders now that everyone's here if he should go back for sum yayo.

. . .

Jacquie & Dawn in the delivery room.

The gentlemen were invited, but abstained.

The gentlemen wait . . .

One hour, 2 hours—Rikki says he needs to get something from home, leaves—3 hours—shift change—Jim asks what's happening—stonewalled. *Why doesn't Dawn come out? I can understand why Jacquie wouldn't but come on, Dawn, what the hell's the matter? don't you think I'm going a little crazy out here?* Cellphones do not work in hospital zones. But he even steps outside the building to see if Dawn texted him: nothing. The engineer is nothing if not logical. An unwelcome voice bubbles up: *She probably hasn't had any decent prenatal care, to speak of.* He does not like the voice but does not silence it. He hopes that she did. Decent prenatal care. Or more decent than he thought. Engineer Jim takes deep breaths—Dawn calls them yoga breaths, she learned when she was in treatment for depression—just now it's the only way he can cope, the only way to forestall hyperventilation.

To dispel the *unnecessary* from his head.

A fresh nurse comes.

She says:

She's in critical care.

But did she have the baby?

She says:

She's in critical care.

. . .

The nurse says Jim can't go back, she says there's already 2 (Jacquie, Dawn) in there with her. So he waits in a family lounge outside the CCU. He wonders, *Where the hell is that kid? Where the hell is Rikki?* He starts to call Rikki's cell, but doesn't have it in him. Something in him is tired & broken.

Jacquie sits in a vinyl chair at Jerilynn's bedside.

Jerilynn looks bleached, beached, fattened, flattened; her mother looks the same. *She got so heavy, I never got this heavy. When I had her, I think I gained even less, I weighed more when I had Jerry. But that was just 10 lbs, not even.* Jerilynn has tubes in each arm (one backed up w/ blood), a see-thru celery green one in her nose (O_2), bright yellow one under the bed (cath). The urine shot through with sunshine, *but some blood in it now is that blood in it.* The machine monitoring her heart beats time in brash strident tones that almost seem threatening. Angry harbingers . . . the thousands of forgettable scenes from television & movies where an aberrant rhythm breaks from the pack like a dark horse, shrill, screechy, sped-up, doctors nurses & crashcarts come flying, then: the flatlining. Forgettable scenes too with teens going from delivery room to CCU, though much less of those. Right?

Jerilynn in quiet delirium, Jacquie tamped down, crazed, benumbed, Dawn stroking the girl's sweaty crown of hair, Dawn's eyes involuntarily sweeping what she can see of the bedsheet for blackmaroon blood, (Rikki's) black amour blackamoor blood—praying not to see a stain appear then spread like those helicopter shots of land-devouring blackwater tsunami—and the folly of Dawn's rage & offendedness return with galling sting, her rejection by the Buddhists, the vanity of it, the daily shame she experiences upon recreating her impotence at the hospice program's *snub,* her lonely preening pitiful *entitlement* burns her throat as it regurgitates . . . *she cannot let go.* That was the lesson to learn, how to let go, but she cannot, she learned nothing, she got a 2-week stay in the hospital for her trouble, of course they were right, she wasn't fit to keep vigil with the living let alone the dying, *she had learned nothing.* Only *now* does it come to her, only *now* can she see what a great gift it was, how it came in disguise at the only time she could have accepted it, the only time she could hold the gift in her arms even though she was not ready to open it—but now she *was.*

The online literature had been eminently clear, her resentments

were all bullshit, the course had been established for professionals in
the field, even *unestablished* professionals. She'd pretended, she'd *con-*
vinced herself (and even her poor Jim, & everyone else) they had dis-
sembled, *the Buddhists had lied,* when all she had to do was suck it up
and volunteer at a VA, pick a VA, *any* VA, or a thousand other places,
even those affiliated with the hospice she had applied to, she could
have done that, could have gone up to the Bay Area and done hospice
work with any of those places the Buddhists would recommend, but
no, she had elected to use her time differently, she had elected to
commit herself to a psych ward for other whiny entitled self-indulgent
assholes, oh she'd put her poor wonderful Jim through pure hell! And
God *knows* the effect her clownish crybaby collapse had on Rikki, at
a time when he needed her the most. He'd acted as if somehow it was
his fault that her application was denied.

Jerilynn is talking now.

Jacquie comes awake.

Jerilynn stares at Dawn, callling her *Mother*?

In her midlife midwife mid-death bones, Dawn knows the girl is
dying. *She must now open the terrible beautiful gift. She must now unwrap*
the paper. How perfectly imperfect that it is here, that she is here, that they are
here. Jacquie watches their interplay, but does not compete, allowing
Dawn to shadow ~~Jerilyn's~~ shade *day is done, gone the sun. Day is Dawn,*
gone the swan. From the lake from the pills from this guy Jerilynn says, *I*
don't understand where I am. Dawn says, *You don't have to. You don't have*
to understand or know The othermother marveling at the tenderness of
the exchange the perfect imperfect poetry of give & take the *fading*
light dims the sight & dead stars gem the skygleaming bright Mother, says
Jerilynn (to Dawn, why won't she look at me, I'm here baby), *I took*
your cameras all your cameras Jacquie gulps down breaths she is drowning, Jacquie says *I don't care about the cameras!* ~~Jerilynn,~~ *it doesn't matter!*
I don't care about the cameras! Reeyonna! it's the 1st time she interjects,
but daughter does not turn toward mother's panicked voice, nor look
at or even toward the mother, nor even voice-attends. She only has

encrypted eyes for Dawn, she calls Dawn *mommy, mama* at least she's
calling out for that, for mommy/mama *hari Krishna Krishna hari hari
mama mama* –

                                        *mama I took your
cameras, I don't know where I am, where am I supposed to be?* Dawn
says, *Right where you are sweetheart you're right where you're supposed
to be you're perfect* the give & take, the taking the giving (of)
thanks & praise. *for our days. neath the sun, neath deadstars, neath the sky*
now ~~Jerilynn~~ is drowning, Jacquie says, *Should we call someone?
Dawn, should we call?*————~~Jerilynn~~ shouting at Dawn Mom
*You! don't! know! none of you! none! of! you! know! where! where I am
going!* DOCTOR! DOCTOR! mama-mommy rushes out Dawn
says it's *all right baby it's all right to let go* never would Dawn have
dreamt she'd have such surety at end-of-life, end of others', never
never ever, she just knew, she now knows, now she knows &
prays dispassionately compassionate end-of-life will H A P P E N,
soon, at least before they come barging————*son has set———
shadows come———time has fled, sheets are red, in the beds* now the
scrubs rush in on cue, of course they do, the thousands of forgettable scenes, they crashcart-gallop after the dark star dark horse,
though more it's the dragon of flatlineshrieking machine they
chase, the machine sent them code babyblue, not the heed of
shocky grandma's alarum . . . . Dawn knows they're too
late to catch that blackened horse, to reign & subdue it, giving
her measure of comfort that her surrogate child will not (cannot)
be brought back to suffer more indignities of the flesh, hadn't she
sacrificed enough? hadn't she already bled out? hadn't she summoned the atrocious grace to leave a perfectly imperfect yawping
pink thing behind? one that would look like her (& Rikki) &
make her same mistakes, and make some she hadn't (not that
Jeri wouldn't have, she just wouldn't have the time), who'd grow
up in darkness, yes, but in the brightness of gods&glories too,

gods&glories her mother would have died too young to feel or to know, never would Dawn have imagined she would be blessed with the knowledge the gift of knowing when was too late, never dreamed she'd have such surety, in hurricane's eye Dawn is calm *how how why is it so I never dreamed I could be this calm* she needs to be, calm & centered, because ~~Reeyonna~~ is still connected to Dawn by the eyes, the girl's still staring, stormwindow eyes silently lushly dischordantly singing *while the eyes fade from sight, & dead-stars, gleaming rays, softly send* the tiresome code blue crashcart heroism can do nothing to stop the last verse *to thine hands*

we, our souls

Lord come in.

[mixtape]

Who Wore It Best?

Rikki

gets back to the hospital late because they smoked & got caught up in Jerzy's numerological bullshit. J comes with, they go to obstetrics, a nurse says *Are you the father? Yes, I'm the father (which actually sounded cool to say). Wait one moment.* [Then] *OK, they're in the family lounge outside CCU, L-14.*

When they get there his fosterfolks are kinda drapey on the couch, oddly spent, redrimmed eyes, Dawn sort of jowly, the only thing on Rikki's clouded hammery mind is to apologize for being late, for missing the birth, it never even occurs to him the birth maybe didn't happen yet, he knows he should see the baby, in a few mins he expects (thousands of forgettable scenes) to see the tiny rugrat on her tit, Ree sitting up in bed with that rosy-cheeked narcoticky postmarathon race look (the thousands of forgettable scenes in everybody's head)—*Hey is it a boy?* Dawn says no it's a girl *well can I see her? Let's go see him! No,* says Dawn, *her mom's in there with her now,* & just when Jerzy's going to utter some turdacious words of wisdom, Dawn tells them Reeyonna is dead.

& right then, a nurse brings the baby into the lounge, special circumstances, to show new life where there has been premature death.

The nurse smiles as if she hasn't a clue what has happened. She wants to hand the bawling deal off.

"Who's the father?"

.   .   .

She went to the car because they told her they were going to clean her daughter up. They didn't put it quite that way however they were as gentle and tactful as could be hoped for *if* one had to be told that the body of one's daughter was going to be made presentable by the sponging of excrement & bloodsweat & the removal of the needles & tubes that violated during her abrupt descent.

Sitting in her car in a hospital parking lot again, that was what defined Jacquie's lives and her deaths. Sitting in her car she listens to the sound of her breath, observes the rising fall of her breast. She remembers Jeri nursing, the recollection so vivid she suddenly feels the sting of infected nipple, impacted tit. She had both with Jerilynn.

From the parking lot, Jacquie talks to one of the girls at Opening Ceremony. Last minute bday gift, all that. She selects a few promising things by phone, they send some jpegs. She has Jerzy drive over to pick them up: a Rag&Bone, a Lim, a Wang. An Aubry top & Maxi Desert skirt, all earthtones, a raw-edged gray scarf, a Jacklyn dress. Other options: print tie-front dress/open back, cropped boyfriend pullover, silk blend deep V tank w/asymmetric hem/cut-out back. Silk & cotton.

All modest but not staid.

Feminine.

.   .   .

She approaches the shift leader (who of course knows all about the tragic situation) and requests time alone with her daughter. The shift leader of course says yes & please let me know if there are other ways they might accommodate. Jacquie has no intention of telling them her plans.

She gathers the family in the lounge. She tells them about the parish of portraits she's taken, the baby here, the infant in Arizona. She explains what she wants—what she's *going* to do. The ragtaggy dramatic personae solemnly accede without hassly questions, for which she is grateful. Everyone's in shock anyway plus she's the tribal chieftress, whatever she says is Word.

She tells Dawn that she needs her help.

She tells the men they will come back for them.

.   .   .

Both fight back tears as they dress their daughter.

Unfathomable delicacy.

Boundless love.

How heavy the body.

How heavy the body to make them break sweat.

Jacquie occasionally stops to examine the skin, as an appraiser admiring/cataloguing the stitches, patterns & imperfections of a vintage quilt—vaccine scar, birthmark, explosion of freckles, earlobe battered by years of repiercings/infections, a single chronically ingrown pubis hair Jeri always fussed with . . . the tattoo that surprises her. Rikki said the singer Rihanna had the same, a tiny ☆ on the inside of her left ear. The scanning & commenting to her helpmeet busies her mind. Dawn is grateful she can be of service.

A sound comes from Jacquie, a moany *o* from the O of her mouth as they came to the bulky, cellophaned cotton the RNs used to seal now bloodless Caesarean lips; they would need to cut the dress to get around that. Dawn says she'll go find scissors but Jacquie impatiently tears the fabric of the Wang. They laugh at the grisly absurdity.

Champagne wishes & cadaver dreams.

A last pass over seams and buttons before pushbutton raising the bed so that she's half-sitting, half-laying.

Jacquie brushes Jerilynn's hair.

"Pretty," she says, on unwitting verge of babytalk.

Dawn takes a step back & watches.

"Pretty, pretty girl," says Jacquie. "Pretty, pretty girl."

. . .

A nurse brings in the baby, hands it to Jacquie and leaves. She believes the two women are giving the dead girl a chance to say goodbye to the daughter she never touched, heard, smelled.

Jacquie gives the baby to Dawn, then prepares her daughter's arms. Dawn lowers it down while Jacquie sets up her camera. Dawn supports the baby but realizes she can let go. The baby stays cradled in its mother's arms.

. . .

Rikki, Jerzy & Jim come in. (Photo session over, camera and tripod hidden.) Jim is restrained, the boys gimlet-eyed. Too mindblowing even for heartache. So off-the-charts it's one of the few predicaments where a so-called normal response might cause them to actually look just as whacked out as they already did. The men wonder what they're supposed to feel, what they're supposed to feel.

Rikki's the 1st to come close, looking confused. He shakes his head and keeps muttering, *So fucked up it's so fucked up.*

Jerzy joins him bedside, like a boy band, about to sing into the same mic. He stares at his sister & says *Whoa.* Flashes on the dead naked body beneath the cool-looking dress before lurching back into the present. "Beautiful dress," he says. "Good choice. Great choice."

Not sure what he's supposed to say or feel but a compliment to Jacquie seems like the right thing. He flashes how if no one else was there he would probably lift up the dress and have a look.

Almost 15 minutes of people—*dramatis personae*—coming close then backing away, coming close then backing away. Rikki wonders is this a viewing. Is this official? That's why she's in the dress? Is this like a last time? Am I acting OK how do you act at a viewing? When is the funeral is there going to be a funeral?

Dawn says, "We're going to go see the baby. Are you OK?"

Jacquie says that she is.

The men linger a moment, as if leaving on Dawn's command would compromise their grieving manhoods. When Rikki finally goes, Jerzy follows after. Jim approaches the body a final time; Rikki and Jerzy turn to see that but decide in their whackitude & laziness to let him have his unmalecompanioned moment. Jim looks at her face, closes his eyes.

"It isn't fair. So young, so young—too young."

Laconic, clichéd, normal-engineer-type griefy editorials.

Dawn catches her husband's eye to let him know it's time to leave her now. They close the door behind them.

Jacquie stares out the window, the very same harmless idle way a visitor stares out the window when the patient is sleeping. You come with gift or flowers but they're sleeping and you let thcm because they need to sleep, and also you have things to do, it's a busy day, you can get more things done if you leave soon and instead just call and tell them later that you stopped by but they were sleeping & you didn't want to disturb. Tell them that you sat there very peacefully, which would be true, except you might imply you sat there longer than you did. Stretch the truth just a little, what was the harm. The patient is dozing and you turn to look out the window at the world, at life, the dull sun-slanty roar of it. You stare out the window & contemplate the brevity and strangeness, the richness and beauty, the fresh insults and horrors of it.

And then your friend wakes up.

.   .   .

Jerzy & Rikki walk to the van. Jerzy hates the hospital lot & parked off Robertson, just around the corner from the Ivy. His professional stomping grounds. They walk in silence, still in a bubble of intense weirdness.

A kid in Vans sprints by, clutching a camera. Then two more, then another . . . not kids, but fellow pros. 2 figures come toward them, surrounded by fly swarmerazzi. For once, Jerzy's happy not to have his camera.

"Leighton! Leighton!"

Jerzy pauses to watch with bemusement—like he's being given a tour of his life by the Ghost of *Honeyshot!*s Past.

"Who is it?" asks Rikki.

"Leighton Meester. From *Gossip Girl*."

"ReeRee loves that show."

Leighton gets closer, then fakes out the fotogs & goes lateral, tearing across the street.

"Wow," says Jerzy, staring at the receding ☆ & the pursuing hordes. "Did you see that?"

"What?"

"Her dress—same as Reeyonna's. The Alexander Wang!"

"So?"

"So . . . ReeRee totally rocked it. Leighton looked shitty. I give Ree an 87% & Leighton a *thirteen*—a 20% at *most*."

O shit, thinks Rikki, the dude's into his numbers again.

"87% of what?"

"Of the *vote*, nigger, what do you *think* I'm talking about?" Jerzy hugely smiles. "ReeRee *rocked it*."

BETTER BODY AFTER BABY

MOTHERHOOD CERTAINLY AGREES WITH HOLLYWOOD'S SEXY STARS! HERE'S HOW THESE HOT MAMAS LOST THEIR BABY WEIGHT—AND THEN SOME!

[Bud]

Til Your Hip Don't Hop Anymore

Bud

read somewhere on the Internet that last year there were 23,000 murders in Mexico. It made him think about his novel; maybe he should take a stab at dystopian sci-fi. He could write about how in the future, 80% of the world's population will be murdered annually. How in the future, there'd be no new pop songs, as all melodies/lyrics would be exhausted. In the future, Dolly will be dead too but the interest generated by multiple accounts would live on.

A fear both justifiable and irrational—the fear of falling—seized his mother, preventing her from leaving bed. The occasional diaper Marta taped her into was no longer only for bouts of diarrhea or leaky one-offs, as it had been the last six months or so; it was now her permanent toilet. When the caregivers informed him of this new development, Bud's first thought was, *How can she fall and die if she never leaves the bed?* He actually had a lot of guilt over what had become his own obsession—Dolly falling and dying—and spoke about it to a female therapist he was referred to by Michael's wife. Dr. Pelka said that with adult children, a death wish for one's elderly parents was fairly normal. (Bud wondered what other cultures would have made of her pronouncement.) She told him it was a common response to "caregiver burnout," which apparently sons and daughters can have even if they weren't strictly caregivers.

With Mom pretty much bedridden, Bud had to chuck the fantasies of her falling, instead imagining death from bedsore infection or pulmonary embolism due to inactivity.

.   .   .

Bud was feeling vulnerable and a little sorry for himself when the envelope from CAA arrived by messenger, to cheer him—the Ooh Baby contract. He scanned the pages. Ooh Baby and even CAA took it for granted Bud was an artist: beside each place that required his signature was written *Bud Wiggins ("artist")*, which gave him a pang of pride as well as one of doubt that he'd ever be worthy of the appellation. What would it take to fulfill that promise?

Lydia Davis, the author Michael and Wendy Tolkin threw a dinner party for, was at Barnes & Noble signing a new trade paperback edition of her acclaimed translation of *Madame Bovary*. She was in the middle of a 27-city tour and Bud thought he'd stop by; it was either that or the Central Library where David Ulin had undertaken interviewing the undertaker Joan Didion. Whereas authors like James Salter and Barry Hannah had been certified by academia as "writer's writers" (i.e. doomed to *nyrb classic* status), Davis was considered to be that *rara avis,* a writer's writer's writer. Apart from translating Flaubert, Blanchot and Proust, she had tried her hand at the art of the novel *and* short story, efforts, critics duly noted, for which the world was a better, more perfect place.

A lot of her followers were comfortable in asserting that her *Madame Bovary* translation was best approached as a novel *by Lydia Davis*, not Flaubert. In her own fiction, her stories were "famously short." In one essay Bud read, a reviewer excerpted in its entirety what he called "one of her more famous stories, 'Collaboration With Fly'":

I put that word on the page, but he added the apostrophe.

The MacArthur Foundation gave her the genius grant.

Her famously short stories . . . one of her more famous stories . . . famous to whom? Bud ruminated that all things must be famous in their own way to someone or other, a notion which had the comforting effect of making his dream of achieving fame as a novelist closer to becoming a reality than he thought. Based on Davis's example, Bud took heart that it might be feasible to release a book of exceedingly short stories of his own culled from the work-in-progress that was currently giving him such a headache. He'd call it *Some Extremely Short Stories—A Pop-Up Book, by Bud Wiggins,* and sell it out of a pop-up bookshop on Melrose funded by his inheritance. Maybe Barnes & Noble would carry it too, one of those little "humor" items on sale next to the cash register. *A Book of Short Torys, by Bud Wiggins* (with illustrations by the author). He'd take a little trip to the UK for research on Dolly's dime.*

During the Q&A, a witty Davis groupie stood up and said, "Do you think it's *possible* Flaubert's book is actually a French translation of a novel by *Lydia Davis* called *Madame Bovary?*"

Hilarity ensued.

·   ·   ·

He took long walks in the evenings now. He began at dusk, looping down Gregory to Rexford, then over to Charleville, back up to Reeves.

The turnaround point was Horace Mann, his old elementary school.

As he passed the various houses where he spent much of his childhood, he thought of all the sons and daughters who had lived in them, the progeny of the famous, crushed beneath their legacies. A good friend from those days was Eric Douglas. A sad case—the obits said handsome Eric was 300 lbs when the police found him, dead of

---

* Or write one of those short books about salt or the word bullshit. "A Brief History of *Brief Histories*" by Bud Wiggins was another possibility.

an overdose in his hotel room. He was Kirk's firstborn . . . Kirk had a new book out, a memoir. He'd written a bunch of other memoirs, novels as well. Bud thought he should probably have a look. You never know, maybe there's something to be learned. Michael Douglas told Brando Brainard that the stroke finally gave his father peace. Bud thought, *I wouldn't mind a stroke, though it'd probably be better to publish first.* Brando said Kirk had a second bar mitzvah when he was 83, something having to do with the biblical lifespan of 70. Thus far, the strokeless Bud had only been bar mitzvah'd once. He felt like a sluggard.

Someone forgot to lock one of the playground gates. Bud sat in the well-worn leather strop of a swing and propelled himself, letting his thoughts wander. Things were looking up. True, he'd been staying with his mother in the same room where he lived as a boy, but his days there were numbered. He was *Bud Wiggins ("artist"),* a working writer again. His novel would either come together or not, and Bud had surrendered to both outcomes. He was having a little trouble with the *Antigone* script though wasn't too worried; Michael said they could get together again soon to shoot the shit. Also, the pressure was off because Biggie, bless his soul, was preparing to have surgery to remove the tumor that'd been affecting his memory. Brando was completely caught up in that. No one would be breathing down Bud's neck. It gave him more time to work on the script *and* his novel.

He couldn't remember the last time he'd been on a swing. 50 years? He was never a daredevil like the other kids. In fact, swings scared him. No doubt those fears could be traced back to the days when his father installed a set in the backyard of their first house. Morris, a sadistic drunk, gave his son powerful push-offs and refused to stop, even when Bud screamed and cried and the swings shook, partially breaking free of their foundation————————————————————————of an instant, he was on the asphalt. *What?* Confused. What happened . . . how silly!—the swing had broken. Well of course it did, it was old, and made for 100 lb kids. Bud fell hard on his ass and it hurt like hell. *What a fool.* Dad was probably laughing his ass off, or at least the rotting coccyx it was once attached to.

. . .

Bud was invited to a Sunday brunch at Michael and Wendy's.

The house in Hancock Park was beautifully done. He was a bit rusty on the social side so when Michael's wife playfully chided him for being a wallflower, Bud forced himself to mix. He wound up talking to the writer Scott Berg and his partner Kevin. Bud hadn't read any of Berg's work but knew he'd gotten the Pulitzer for a bio having something to do with Scott Fitzgerald. He also knew that his brother Jeff was the bookish head of ICM.

Michael came over and asked Berg if he enjoyed teaching at Princeton. The conversation led to the great Dante scholar Robert Hollander, a professor emeritus there. Though in pain from his fall and higher on oxycodone than usual, Bud wanted to join in. He had more than a passing knowledge of the Italian poet. In the last few years, he'd pushed himself through a pastiche of different *Infernos*—Pinsky, Mandelbaum, Longfellow—and read most of the SparkNotes to *Purgatorio* and *Paradiso*.

The conversation was heady and he held his own.

"I've read the Hollander translation," Bud lied. Though it probably *was* true he at least owned the volume. Whenever a new translation of *La Commedia* appeared, he OCD-*one-clicked.* "It's always been a dream of mine to give a Dante lecture."

Bud made it clear he was being wry, but not entirely. Why not? Why *couldn't* he one day lecture on Dante? And why shouldn't they take such an aspiration seriously? Michael was an esteemed novelist, Berg, an honored author of nonfiction. While not as celebrated, Bud was a working writer—a journeyman peer.

Berg twitched. It was only the discreet, gently admonitory touch of his partner that softened his scowl.

"*You* want to lecture on *Dante*?" said Berg. Already Bud felt like he'd been stung. *"Really?* Somehow, I don't *think* so. *Durante*, maybe! You can lecture on Jimmy *Durante*. Maybe."

. . .

The soreness from the fall didn't go away.

Bud didn't have a doctor, so he went to Dolly's internist, Dr. Fine. He'd have to ask her for money because his Writers Guild insurance wouldn't kick in till next quarter.

He was back in the examination room putting on his shirt when the doc came in holding x-rays.

"Congratulations! You've got a break."

"Really?"

"It's classic."

"What do we do?"

"You're going to need surgery."

"Jesus, you're kidding."

"See the break?" He held up the film. Bud was too perturbed to focus. "We don't see it too much in people your age. It's literally called an 'Old Man' fracture. You're a little young—I'd expect to see it in your *mom*. The *good* news is, it's eminently repairable. I'm sending you over to Moe Ravitz. He's in the Cedars Towers. Great bone guy."

"Moe Ravitz?"

"Best geriatric orthopedist on the Westside."

[Gwen]

High Resolution

Gwen's

lawyer had already been given an inkling of "the number," but wanted the other side to go ahead and present its case. There was of course no question of the hospital's wrongdoing. A heretofore unbreakable chain of checks and balances had been torn asunder by human error, each link's failure more improbable than the next. The day of reckoning had come.

The timing couldn't have been worse for the plaintiff. St. Ambrose was compellingly forthright, telling Gwen and counsel that a philanthropist and longtime donor was about to make the largest gift to a private teaching hospital on record—a billion dollars. Bertram Brainard, whose name already graced one of their buildings, was deeply grateful that its doctors had discovered a rare, sesame seed–sized brain tumor in his son that had failed to be detected by the world-famous Houston clinic Biggie was initially brought to after exhibiting signs of memory loss. (There was no reason the hospital attorneys would have known that Biggie and her daughter had become fast friends, and no reason to enlighten them either.) Gwen got the sense they'd told her more than was needed—they could have just mentioned the billion-dollar gift and stopped there—

because they wanted to state, almost for the record, that catastrophic mistakes can and *do* happen, and are not in the domain of any single institution; nor was it a conspiracy of negligence that brought them to this room, on this day, but rather the banality of events—lab reports read in haste and fatigue, faulty calibrations and equipment, malignant interpretations of benign processes—that accreted to provide an evil end.

The hospital was convinced that any public revelation of Telma's case would do more than cause the sort of damage to an institution and its caregivers that takes at least a generation to heal; it would result in the catastrophic loss of the Brainard endowment. Attorneys for the plaintiff informed that because of the gift's magnitude, the hospital board had approved putting a $35 million settlement on the table. The money could come monthly, quarterly or annually, in a formula to be determined by defendants' design. (Compounding interest assured that the amount paid out over the girl's lifetime would more than double the offer.) There were two caveats. St. Ambrose wanted the entire case sealed forever. Secondly, Gwen must agree to sign a document stipulating the settlement would be diminished by two-thirds should its details ever go public by virtue of memoir, interview, blog, et alia, traceable to the injured parties.

The men finished, leaving Gwen and her lawyer alone in the conference room.

"It's blackmail, isn't it?"

"A form thereof."

"They don't even want me telling her! It's so *smarmy*. They're dictating the choices I have in sharing with Telma what happened—what they did that changed her life."

"What you say is true. Though I'm not sure I'd have quite put it that way."

"And what if I say no? What if I say go *fuck* yourselves, we're having a press conference. News at 11."

"You'd still get a settlement. You'd still be rich—Telma would be rich. I can't visualize a scenario where you'll walk away with less than $25 million. There are always unknowns. Insurance companies can be tough. They'll put forth the argument that she's got an excellent quality of life."

"Peter, she's a *fighter*. She wouldn't want me to take the money and run."

"That may very well be. But I don't think you can effectively solicit her opinion at this time."

"And *they* get a billion dollars. To fuck up more kids."

"You could look at it that way. Or you could look at it as maybe saving a thousand kids—5,000 kids—for every one they get wrong." He sucked on his electric cigarette. "If we go that route, you need to be prepared to go to trial. It's unlikely that would happen, Gwen, but you'd have to be prepared."

"How much did the boy who Michael Jackson molested get? The dentist's kid."

"Twenty million. In 1993 dollars."

"So: *20* years ago, a boy—how old was he?"

"13."

"Ha! A boy *Telma's* age gets $20 million for an *alleged* molestation. And *my* baby has a radical *mastectomy* for *no medical reason*. If you take inflation into account, it's probably the *same amount*."

"That's a pretty fair representation."

Long pause. The lawyer speaks up again.

"Why don't you go home, Gwen. Let me see how serious they are. I'll ask for a 5% penalty if word gets out. Let's see what they counter with."

"I don't want this going on and on, Peter. I've lost 20 pounds, and I'm losing hunks of hair."

"Let me talk to them."

.   .   .

Phoebe what did I do what did I do what did I do I made a terrible mistake! I made another mistake! He just called and said "its up to you but if it were me I/d take it," they always say its up to you but if it was them theyd take *it, they just say it so you dont think theyre coercing, the man gets millions, Peter gets millions his percentage but now I/m blaming him! O Phoebe I/m so selfish I told him I just couldn't take it anymore I just said do it you know how I/ve been since we found out but what difference does it make how I/ve been what difference does it make I cant take it anymore? of course I can of course I can take anything they throw if I was any kind of mother can you imagine my baby suffering, how she suffered, the surgeries the pain the crying herself to sleep compared with my little problems my big problem! Ha, my little bullshit depressions or whatever Phoebe its so sick my saying to him even to you that I cant take it anymore just do it I cant take it anymore & thinking knowing what shes been through! Phoebe all I have in life is my daughter my relationship with/to my daughter, when she got diagnosed I said I swore before that horrible god because He was the only one I knew I cursed Him and said nothing will ever come between my daughter and me nothing & now they've bought me off thats what theyve done they bought & sold my relationship with my daughter my sacred relationship o my god my god my god they didn't buy it off I did I bought & sold my daughters trust I cant put that on them I can't blame them or anyone for anything anymore O Phoebe what do I do what do I do what do I say how can I look at her how do I even ever explain all the money, the mastectomoney Phoebe Phoebe what if something happens to me, what if I die of cancer wouldnt that just be so perfect? We need to make sure that youre the guardian should something happen to me you not my mother, & when Im dead and gone they say O & by the way sweetheart you have like 50 million dollars, we just dont know where it came from O Phoebe I want to die its too late I think its too late I tried to call & Peter said it was too late he said I made the right decision of course he would say that because he just got $10 million fucking or whatever dollars, he said to calm down, he used that phrase buyers remorse Phoebe why would he use such a detestable phrase? Im the golden calf so of course he said Id done a noble thing ugh he used that word, noble, he said that I provided for her I assured my daughters future her education her security o these guys are so slick you know all I did Phoebe all I did was assure HIS daughters future, thats what I assured, HIS daughters education, he said I assured her grandchildrens future too Telmas grandchildren thank god she didnt get chemo or there wouldnt BE any grandchildren Phoebe*

Phoebe yes yes please come over I think this is one of those things people kill themselves over no yes no I promise no I don't feel like harming myself not yet Im just saying, I took all the mirrors down I just cant look at myself Telmas with her grandma Phoebe how do I explain to Telma why Mommy took down the mirrors because she couldnt look at herself anymore because instead of telling you the truth Mama took the money Mama ran with the money & now your whole life is going to be built on a lie a terrible dark cheap soap opera secret, I know what happens when families keep secrets Phoebe I know you know I know it isn't good no good can come of it O Telma Telma I am so sorry I was so selfish and so weak okay OK yes Phoebe yes come but dont you think I should just tell her whatever the consequences? Theres a legal penalty, they engineered it that way fucking brilliant like they already knew me, like they had insider information like they already knew Id go for the money! Shes a whore she/ll go for the money, just watch and see . . . Phoebe I don't care anymore we dont need that money, not all of it, its an obscene amount, I dont really care I/ll show them I dont care maybe thats the way I can fix it okay now I feel a little better but still come over no I wont make any calls I promise, & if I dont want to do it all I probably need to do is call the attorney, I dont care what Peter said, I/ll get another lawyer, you cant tell me, you cant tell me they can say no because no money has exchanged hands and even if it had I could just give it back, thats what tells me somethings wrong, thats what tells me I fucked up that Im thinking about how to no I wont make that call not until you get here Im so greedy Im just a greedy bullshitter Im a whore isnt that what I am? Im a whore who wants the money maybe I/ll just tell her maybe I/ll just talk to Telma & ask what she thinks we should do maybe she/ll say just let them just let them pay Mama or maybe she won't, maybe she wouldnt maybe she/d just say Mama you sold my breasts why did you sell my breasts you sold them to the highest bidder! oh Phoebe hurry hurry no I wont I wont do anything I promise, I/ll just sit here no I wont just come just hurry please just come

[Telma]

Wanderlust

She

brushes her mother's hair. Not a real brushing, really just a way of caressing. Gwen's been in bed for a number of days.

"Mama, are you still sick?"

"I'm sad. I'm just sad."

"Why are you sad?"

"Sometimes it just happens. Sometimes people get sad, & then they have to take care of themselves. That's what Mama's doing— taking care."

"You're not sad about something that happened?"

"No, sweetheart. Not at all. Darling, would you like to do some traveling?"

"Like where?"

"I was watching *Eat, Pray, Love,* and thought it might be wonderful to go to Italy."

"Sure."

"Or maybe Bora Bora or the south of France. Or China. We could go to China. Is there anyplace you'd like to go?"

"I want to go to St. Petersburg in Russia!"

"Oh?"

"We've been reading about the *tsars* and Catherine the *Great*. I want to go to Russia and be *Telma* the Great!"

"I think that can be arranged."

"But I can't go now, we have to go later."

"And why is that."

"OMG I didn't *tell* you. Biggie has to have surgery."

"What's wrong?"

"He has a brain tumor! I didn't tell you because I just found out."

She remembered what the attorneys said, but played dumb. *I will play dumb, for the rest of my life. Play dumb, for the rest of her life. Play dumb, for the rest of our lives.*

"O! Is that what's been causing his memory problems?"

"Uh huh. But it's really small and it isn't cancerous."

"Well, *that's* good news."

"And everyone *missed* it but St. Ambrose! Biggie went to a hospital in Houston and they *totally missed it*."

"That's awful."

"St. Ambrose said that if Brando didn't bring him in to see them, Biggie could have *died*."

"I guess things like that happen."

"They *shouldn't*. Mama, I was thinking—and I wouldn't talk to Biggie about it, but—I don't understand what a hospital is *for* if it isn't to *help* people, and find out what's *wrong* with them? It's not like his brother brought him to the *dentist* or to *Whole Foods*, and *they* couldn't find anything. He brought him to a *hospital* that has *specialists* who are supposedly *trained*. Even if the doctors *couldn't* find it, they have *machines* that are supposed to be able to. How can the doctors not have *seen it* when a *machine* sees it *for them!*"

"That's awful. But as long as the tumor isn't—"

"The doctors at *St. Ambrose* found it. Yay, team! Yay Team Telma!"

"I hope it all turns out . . ."

"I would be *so angry*. I don't even think the mom knows yet, Biggie said he thinks his dad or his brother's going to try to tell her, but

I don't see *why*. I think it's a waste of time. And Biggie's only going to get hurt because she's *never* coming home and I just think it's wrong to use his problems, *whatever* they are, to bring her back. She's a horrible mom and she doesn't sound like a good person either. If *I* were his dad or Brando, *I* wouldn't tell her. But I would be *so mad*. I would *totally sue* that hospital in Houston!"

[Michael]

What I Tell You In Darkness,
Speak In the Light

—Matthew 10:27

He

had five days off and was on his way to New York to spend the long weekend with Catherine and the kids. Brando was going to New York so Michael hitched a ride on the Ooh Baby jet. On the way to Van Nuys, Brando called to say he had to bail, something having to do with his kid brother, but the plane was at Michael's disposal. "Enjoy the weekend." Classy kid.

It was great to have it to himself.

He was feeling reflective.

He looked at his email.

Oliver Stone had forwarded a prospectus for something wild. An American architect refurbished a few dozen "peasant houses" (some were 5,000 square feet) in a village about an hour from Beijing. Each fully modernized home, with views of the Great Wall, were for rent. Oliver's email had just one word in SUBJECT: *Timeshare?* He knew Ollie was kidding, but it sounded like *the next cool thing*. He wouldn't be surprised if he heard that Bryan Lourd or George Clooney snapped one up.

www.headandneck.org wanted him to tape a segment about early detection, for their new app.

His reply:

Done.

The iPad chimed a new email from his daughter Carys:

hurry!

·   ·   ·

If he had the energy, the actor planned to visit his son. Since the bust, Cameron had been caught using in prison, and a tough judge had doubled his sentence, giving him another 4½ years; the kid was obviously so sick, but all they knew how to do was punish. Until this, Michael had been breathing easier because of a transfer to a minimum security camp, one without fences. The jail in Manhattan was rough on the kid—the Douglas men weren't too fond of confined spaces, especially when mandatory. But now everything was bad again. His hopes that Cam might be out in time to have a part in *Jazz* were dashed.

·   ·   ·

An art consultant he sometimes worked with sent him images of the work of an 18th-century Italian artist called Piranesi, best-known for a series of prints with the overall title *Carceri d'invenzione*—"Imaginary Prisons." The drawings were simply that: darkly baroque, labyrinthine, finely detailed renderings of jails that didn't exist, at least not outside Piranesi's mind.

Michael was captivated by the metaphor. These days it had become especially clear to him how zealously a man worked to customize the "cell" in which he served out his life sentence. His downfall is that he imagines he's safe behind bars; he becomes accustomed to counting himself the king of finite space. When the actor was a student at UC Santa Barbara, he wrote a paper on Plato's *Allegory of the Cave*. The philosopher put forth a world where men grew up shackled and facing the wall of a cave, unable even to turn their heads. Behind them was a great fire; figures walked across a foot-bridge, and the chained men took the shadowy forms to be reality. *For the very substance of the ambitious is merely the shadow of a dream . . .*

What *was* real? (He felt like an undergrad again.) Being a movie star? Cancer? The motorized chair that became a bed for him to lie down on inside a machine with metal wings that flew 40,000 feet above the Earth? His wife and children? Sages said the only thing one could be certain of was the Self—who was Plato to say that form preceded shadow, and not reverse? In the end, every-thing was taken away. A drunk driver, a blow to the head from an unlucky fall, a rogue clot ended all discussion. The imaginary prisons of Piranesi underscored the folly of belonging to the Church of Realism, that cult of forms and shadows which seduces us into believing we have some control over our lives. *Hey I ought to give a lecture on this shit . . . afraid I'd disappoint. They only want to hear about cuckoo's nests and throat cancer, not imaginary prisons or flick-erings in a cave . . .*

The clichéd *moment* was the only thing that was real. And if you could be lucky enough to be in the moment it was best to be happy, or at least at peace. It was best to love: he loved his wife and his chil-dren, and the blue planet that held all their beating hearts in its earthen hands.

And that was that.

.   .   .

On Tuesday, he'd be at Sloan-Kettering for his check-up.

Anyone in remission (or "cancer-free") had been through the drill a hundred times, playing the nightmarish variations in their heads as if to inoculate themselves: *OK here's what's going on: I saw something on the scan that I didn't like. Or, We're all kind of surprised at the speed of the recurrence—you were in three months ago, no? Or, I'm not going to dress this up for you; the cancer's returned. Having said that, I'm not going to doom and gloom you, either. Cause we're gonna sic the Navy Seals on this thing.*

The iPad chimed with another email.

Did you get me anything?

He'd forgotten. Which only meant his daughter was going to make him pay for his lapse, at FAO Schwarz. Big-time.

Thinking of her, his whole being smiled. The two brave little ones—Aleisha and Telma—followed Carys into his head. What would he do if something like that happened to one of his own? Such occasional musings were a hazard of parenthood. It was important to remember to be in the *moment*; not even forms that threw shadows were real . . . *and nothing to get hung about.* Maybe cancer was just another bar of an imaginary cell. The uncontrolled division of abnormal cells . . .

He was prepared to believe it. What would be the harm? The New Age parable said each of us had two wolves fighting inside. One was dark and evil, the other was light and filled with love. The winner of the battle is whichever wolf you feed.

.   .   .

Lately, he didn't like being called *survivor.* He was mildly superstitious that the very word fed the wrong wolf.

It was challenging enough just to live on the planet. As far as he was concerned, being vertical and breathing conferred full survivor status. Why should the word be reserved for victims of rape, incest, the Holocaust? Every human being struggled to get through the random blessings and scourges of the day, to live through the night to see the sun. *Hero* was the other word that put a hair up his ass. Everyone was a hero. We were all survivors—until one day, we weren't. It was probably the hubris of it that bothered him.

He'd take Telma and her mom to tea again. *We're cancer-free, right Telma? So let's forget the whole survivor deal—I never liked the "Nice try, cancer/I kicked cancer's butt" thing anyway. Let's forget being survivors and just be people who happen to be living their lives, people lucky enough to be surrounded by family and friends who they love. Maybe we don't even need to be cancer-free, how about just "free"? I guess what I'm saying is that I had a whole life before this thing and now I'm having one after. You're having one too, sweetheart, you're having it now, and believe me, there's going to be a lot more to come. And just because we don't use the words anymore, just because we don't say survivors and cancer-free, that doesn't mean we don't get our check-ups. "Trust in God, but lock your front door." Ever hear that saying, Gwen? So we go and get our check-ups, and when we get a clean bill of health we kick up our heels. Kick em up anyway! Cause we can just be people now, citizens of the world, not survivors or some kind of heroes. Kid, I think that's a jersey we can retire."*

He would take her on all the talk shows—start a new anti-hero movement . . . hell, they'd shout it from the rooftops!

I used to be cancer-free—now I'm just free.

Malibu Slumberyard

Rikki

named the baby girl Nikki, after one of ReeRee's favorites, Nicki Minaj. That it rhymed with his name was a bonus. Tom-Tom said she thought that's why maybe he picked it tho.

Nikki lived at Jim & Dawn's. Jacquie visited everyday. Rikki lived at the house again too. He had a job that paid good money (so he said). He told his soon to be lawful parents he was working for a "no profit" involved with the rehab of former child soldiers. Among his new friends were will.i.am & Emmanuel Jal, a rapper from Sudan who was featured on MTV. Rikki had a newfound confidence about him that Dawn attributed to fatherhood & the death of Reeyonna. Jim worried he was dealing drugs because he never heard of anyone making "good money" working for an NGO, especially someone w/ no experience.

Reeyonna's girlfriends loved to visit. The mood was heavy those 1st few weeks but then their laughter filled the house. They even taught Rikki how to change a diaper. He fucked 2 of them.

.   .   .

Jacquie hadn't yet developed the pictures she took at Cedars. She thought about burning the film but Albie said don't you dare. He was

the only one other than Dawn who knew. It was monumentally un-
real.

Nikki was gorgeous. Sometimes she called her "Lynnie" by mistake. (What she called Jerilynn as a newborn.) She thanked God for
Dawn & Jim.

Albie helped disperse the ashes. At 1st she said no but he insisted &
she was so glad. Jacquie knew how head-over-heels Jerilynn was for
Malibu. Jeri used to say one day she was going to make enough
money to buy a house there, "for weekends." Jacquie told Albie about
the day she drove Jeri & 2 girlfriends to the Malibu Lumber Yard.
The girls squealed & carried on because they saw one of the kids
from *The Vampire Diaries* at James Perse.

She wound up scattering the ashes in different places. Jacquie
was always intrigued by a private neighborhood in the Malibu hills
called the Serra Retreat. It used to be Old Hollywood—people like
Roddy McDowall, Loretta Young, Ray Walston & Karl Malden
used to live there. Now, it was James Cameron, Eva Longoria, Steven Tyler. At the top of the mountain was a beautiful old Catholic
monastery, with grounds overlooking the Pacific. It was open to
the public.

When it came time, Albie walked a respectful distance behind.
She reached into the container &, grabbing a fistful of her daughter,
nervously looked around like a 1st-time shoplifter. When Jacquie finally let the ashes go, she burst into unbidden tears. Albie ran over &
held her in his arms.

They drove to the Malibu Lumber Yard & walked around. She
left a lot of Jerilynn there: in front of James Perse, in front of Kitson,
in front of the yogurt place & the movieplex & the Coffee Bean. Her
mood lightened. They saw Vincent D'Onofrio.

The last most important spot was the ocean. Her bare feet felt
good in the sand. When it was done, they had drinks at Gladstone's.
Albie got excited because he thought he saw Colton Dixon from
Idol in one of the booths. He took the long way to the bathroom
to get a closer look. When he passed the table he looked over at

Jacquie with a trademark pukey face & shook his head. He made her laugh.

It was dark when they got home. She brought Albie next door and introduced him to Jim, Dawn & Nikki. Rikki wasn't there. They all had dinner together. After, Jacquie asked Albie if he'd spend the night. She made up the couch and they watched 3 saved *Glee*s.

She went to bed but Albie stayed up & watched 2 more.

. . .

With the help of a hospice newsletter she subscribed to, Dawn prepared a few things for Jacquie to journal about:

What I will miss about you is . . .
What I will remember most about you is . . .
What you meant to me was . . .
The hardest thing about letting go is . . .
I am angry at you for . . .
I feel guilty that . . .
I regret that . . .

She would wait for the right time.

She got an email from the Metta Institute.

Subject: WE'RE ALMOST FULL! . . . They were having their annual 6-day Cultivating Presence Retreat in San Rafael. The email said "Retreat Almost FULL, Commuter Places Now Open." The cost for the commuter package was "only $900." She thought, *Don't be silly, you can't do that now, how could you leave Nikki.* A few other retreats were coming up that looked tantalizing, and she'd already shared some of them with Jim. "The Great Matter of Birth & Death" was taking place in Turin, in Italy.

She phoned anyway. Dawn felt different now, a part of. A bonafide member of the community that once denied her.

"I'm interested in the Cultivating Presence retreat."

"Do you have hospice experience?"

"Yes," she said, wondering if the woman could read the sorrow in her voice. "Yes, I do."

"*Wonderful.* Can you hold a moment?"

Wonderful was an odd word in this instance, but why not? After-all, she'd just read an article in a Buddhist magazine about a student who told his guru he'd been diagnosed with cancer. The guru said, "Congratulations!"

"Thank you for waiting. Our computers are a little sluggish today. They seem to have minds of their own."

"Hate it when that happens," said Dawn affably.

"Don't you?" said the woman. "Ah—here we are. The Cultivating Presence Workshop . . ." She was slowly reading from the screen, stalling while the software fired up. "I know our literature says 're-treat' but most people just call it a workshop. Ah—okay. It looks like we are completely full."

"Even the commuters?"

"I don't know why we had so much interest this year. It's *wonder-ful*, but I can't put my finger on it. Can I put you on a wait list?"

"Yes. How many—"

"Now just wait a moment . . . it says that there's 40 people on it already—can that be? Well, it *must*, because the iMac tells me so! That doesn't look so terrific . . . don't think it will happen. I like to tell people the truth, what's the point in leading folks on? Now we've got *another* workshop—excuse me, *retreat!*—coming up in around 6 months. That's a *very special one*, people like it as much if not *more* than the Cultivating Presence training—oops. Wait—now, hold on—isn't that crazy? I spoke too soon. Aren't we having a time of it today?"

.   .   .

Jacquie had sent him to pick up the ashes. She told him that if he wanted to, he could take a portion before dropping them off at the house. Rikki expected an urn, but they were in a brown plastic container instead, about the size of a rural mailbox. A sticker on it said WE HEREBY CERTIFY THAT THE CREMATED REMAINS ARE THOSE OF JERI-LYNN CRELLE-VOMES. The box was *heavy.*

He sat in the car for about a ½hour, smoking a blunt and sniffing the last gram of yay. He broke the seal on the box. The ashes were in a plastic bag with the same affixed certification. He'd planned to take some but now he wasn't so sure. 1st things 1st tho: he drove to Tom-Tom's to get more blow. She was staying in a Travelodge in Mar Vista. She had an emaciated stray cat over there & was nursing it back to health. Rikki hadn't seen that side of her.

He brought in Ree's ashes. They set them on the table and tripped a while. They smoked some weed & crack, then balled. Her pussy was infected so she only wanted her ass fucked, which was cool. Rikki thought about the ashes. Kind of like Ree was watching.

He got his 8ball and on the way out, Tom-Tom said, "Did you forget something?" They both laughed at the lameness & the stonedness. Rikki went to the side of the bed & bent over to get the box. It was tipped on its side. He thought they must have knocked it over while they were fucking. Then he saw the plastic bag protruding, with clawed holes on top. Rikki said *Hey!* Tom-Tom came over & looked. She went to the head where the kitty cowered behind the toilet with its paltry, fastidiously created litter. The room stank from its humid, sickly droppings.

"Goddammit!" shouted Tom-Tom. *"Not* OK! *Not fuckin OK!"* As she rousted it, she told Rikki to open the front door. She tried chasing it out but it hunkered under the bed and hissed when she reached for it. She gave up & inspected the box in Rikki's hands. He'd shoved the bag all the way back in.

"Just get some scissors and cut around the holes—clean up the edges. Say it broke while you were taking your share."

· · ·

Beth Rader, the woman from Gagosian to whom Pieter emailed the image of the dead newborn, was persistent. She told Jacquie to let her know if she ever changed her mind.

Jacquie knew there was no way. She was done with that part of her life. She didn't know where she was going, but she knew where she'd been.

As scary as it was, she'd take the not-knowing every time.

.   .   .

Jacquie and Nikki went to court for the adoption hearing. To see the motley family collected together, and to know their poignant history, as the judge did, was not without impact. He was friendly, almost folksy, which made sense to Jim. In this courtroom, gentility & care should and did reign.

"I was made aware of your situation," he said to Rikki, "from a lovely note your soon-to-be-legal father sent to the court. You've had a heck of a lot thrown at you—everyone in the family has— that's quite an ordeal to go thru. You've probably had to grow up a little faster than you'd have liked. But Mom & Dad say you're stepping up to the plate. Handling yourself like a man."

"Yes, sir—I mean Your Honor sir. I'm trying."

"Fake it till you make it. Ever heard that one, son? 'Fake it till you make it'?"

"No sir your Honor sir."

"Well now you have. That's one beautiful baby. Bring her closer, ma'm, can you bring her a little closer? Oh, now she's a little doll now, isn't she. What's her name?"

"Nikki," he said.

"*Excellent* name—I have a goddaughter named Nicki, so good choice! I like your taste in women. In women's names, anyway. Ours is Nicole but everybody calls her Nicki. How do you like the experience of being a father? I know you haven't been one for long, but how do you find it so far?"

"Uhm . . . it's—pretty good."

His tentativeness caused laughter from those waiting for their own cases to be heard. The judge laughed a bit himself.

"All right," he said. "If the parties are willing, I approve, & wish you good luck. And I want you to take a good look at your Mom and Dad, son, remember this day. I hope you know how fortunate you are. Because these two people saved your life. They gave birth to you as surely as the mother who gave birth to your Nikki."

"Yes your Honor sir."

"Good luck to yall. And don't forget! Fake it till you make it."

As they left, a bailiff came forward & whispered to the judge, whose visage went from startled to dour. Rikki was arrested just outside the court.

[Jerzy]

Number Our Days

Mt Olympus was a memory. Betty White's groomer got so horny for T^2 that she flew back from Prague for an unannounced 48-hour booty call. A chaotic eviction followed; the squatters were no more.

The whole deal went down the day after Reeyonna met her moneymaker. Jerzy was helping Rikki throw his ½sister's clothes and whatever into some Hefty bags when the chick Cherokee got there & went apeshit. Tom-Tom smacked her in the face and Bolt & Dr Phil got between em whilst sundry tweaking daydream believers didst scatter. General fucking bedlam ensued. Rikki said he was gonna cut and run because Ree didn't have anything of value in her room anyway, it wasn't like she had a wallet or ID & credit cards to steal (he left the bloody sheets on her bed as a fuck you to whomever). Jerzy got real calm and went to the poolhouse for his stash & his $$$. Jerzy came from a long line of . . . coke, so he did some, took his prints from the garage, carried them to the van. On the way out, he ran into a shirtless Bolt who was in a panic because the broad was threatening to call the police. Jerzy clocked how Bolt's stubbly back was overdue for a wax. Phil tried his lame-o diplomat thing on the front porch but Cherokee shoved him and he fell on the ground. Tom-

Tom literally shouted to Cherokee she would fuck her and let her eat her pussy RIGHT NOW if she just promised to let everyone go without doing the 911 thing. The shit was too fuckin funny.

Jerzy sat in the van & smoked, a few houses up. You had to laugh: the premature arrival of Miss Hair & makeup-sex had the effect of poking a stick in an anthill of *loosers*. He let rip some longass farts but his raucous mood changed when he flashed on his dead sis in her postmortem duds. Even tho she rocked the frock. *The wacka flocka.* What the fuck . . .

.   .   .

At this moment, his Gagosianical *honeyshot!s* grace the walls (stacked against them anyway) of his crampy room at the Sunset Motel, an inn which can be found on the south side of its namesake blvd, between Normandie & Mariposa . . . a 7Eleven on the left, a Hollywood Dialysis on the right, (just shittycorner from) a Zankou Chicken; beside that an Auto Chek, beside that a Stor-Quest Self-Storage, beside that an Iglesia Evangelica Penteco, beside that a Lucky Liquorama, & assorted sordid strip mall anchors, anchorites&anchorettes.

But what is Jerzy doing there?

He no longer works, nor answers his android, nor leaves his funky domain except to purchase crack cocaine during the occasional paranoid ramble/walkabout under cover of darkness—but at civil hours i.e. not after midnight so as not to arouse suspicion amongst those who protect & serve.

Harry Middleton is concerned.

Jerzy came to the Sunset Motel for a reason.

As the 12-Steppers say:

He came.
He came to.
He came to believe.
That he couldn't stop cumming.

Sleasy does it . . .

Jerzy goes on extended head riffs. His latest fave is the torture of tyler the creator. In his latest, he & suge capture tyler the creator, who begins crying like a bitch. suge asks created tyler why he's always writing songs about killing & torturing & does he want to really know what that shits about instead of playing pretend like a mischievous little bitch. creator tyler just starts begging rite away please don't hurt me please please dont hurt me and suge's disgusted & turns to jerzy his trusted lieutenant & says deal with the nigger. and suge leaves & jerzy tapes created tyler's mouth & arms & legs to a chair & they bring in created tyler's mom & right away slice her tits off and stuff them in her pussy and jerzy cauterizes the wound so moms wont bleed to death and moms screamin & Jerzy pokes a syringe in created tyler that has Viagra + botox so he's paralyzed but gets a giant hardon. and they maneuver created tyler so hes fucking mutilated screamin moms in her not-so-famous-anus and onedirection & bruno mars are brought in to fuck created tyler too and they start pulling out created tylers teeth while bruno's brutalizing. ooh the screams be bone chillin thug/harmony. jerzy plays out variations on this dream riff, each one ending with creator tyler's rape, genitorture & death but right before tyler is uncreated jerzy makes sure the nigger understands that his betrayal has come at the hands of the puppetmathers & his cronies especially lil wayne just like when in the godfather tony rosato says before killing frankie pentangeli *michael corleone says hello.*

·   ·   ·

Jerzy has cracked the code & decoded the crack.

His discovery is epic.

So simple—it was staring him in the face.

(He has now seen the face of G-d.)

The hour is nigh . . .

He's been trying to leave his room (paid in full for 2 wks upon check-in) for 5 days now. There can be a large degree of difficulty in vacating a rented room depending of course on the circumstances. Jerzy cannot go until the meth is gone, tethered to the bed, crack & porn, cum-rag laptop, tethered to the cloud of cracksmoke, cloud of unknowing. He knows he will soon believing. Soon be traveling crosstown to Harry round the Middle Earth's———

There can be a large degree of difficulty in placing a call on one's cellphone depending of course on the circumstances. Jerzy overcame them & rang up Harried Middleclass. Hari Krishnleton seemed startled to hear from him. Kept asking Jerzy if he was OK. Not a single mention of the *honeyshot!s* (which was very unusual, to say the least). Jerzy lied, as it did not strike him as the opportune moment to say, "Harry, I have seen the face of G-d, I am bringing to your office the face of G-d." No, that wouldn't do . . . so he lied & said he had the mother of all *honeyshot!s* & would it be all right to bring it by, & soon?

But when?

The when of it was tricky.

His penis stung & bled from marathon motel digital remasturbations, herpetic lesions had no time to heal. He no longer ejaculated, the dick a runny nose that cannot sneeze. All those strung-out strung-together years spent riveted by the front-/hindquarters of porn☆s. All those years thinking but unknowing if he'd seen the face of G-d in the folds of their g-nitals . . . but in the last few days knowing with certitude he had not. It wasn't the cunt, the cunt was the red hairing, all this time he'd been wrong, & now, thankfully, he was more righteous than right.

So he wrapped the 2 faces—for in the end it was true, G-d/Janus had 2 faces because "3 is 2, 2 is 1, & 1 is none"—he wrapped them in blankets & headed out. (Again the difficulty in leaving, but external forces already working on his behalf, taking him by the hand.) He tucked them away in the van then climbed in & dro-blunted. KJ'd too, a booty bump, + Purple Lil Kim'd. Then carefully, mindfully, sacredly, he rolled across town to Harry's.

(1st to Harry's, then to the Gagosian—that was the plan.)

.   .   .

Harry wasn't sure who to call, the police or the paramedics.

Jerzy was grim, grimy, ½dressed. Hair matted. Breath like chlorine. He did not look remotely familiar with the concept or passive activity of sleep. For the moment, Harry believed doing nothing—just listening, paying attention—was the best approach.

"Do you know what these are?"

He held up the blankets he'd carried in under each arm.

"No," said Harry. "Are you going to tell me?"

"Yes—& you might be the *only* one. I was bringing em over to Gagosian but now I think maybe you should just sit with them a while. Only you."

"Okay, happy to. Are they photographs?"

"Yes."

"Celebrities?"

"*Celebrity*, singular. Plural but singular. The ultimate celebrity."

"And who's that?"

"G-d. Janus."

"They're pictures of God?"

Harry remained calm, drawing on his vast experience of watching hostage-negotiators in movies & television shows.

"Of Janus, the 2-headed G-d. Man must invoke Him first, as He is the initiator of human life."

Jerzy propped them against a wall then sat down. Suddenly he looked confounded & grey. Harry thought: *this is the part in the movie where I press the button under the desk to activate the silent alarm.*

Harry stood & said, "Let's see what you brought."

(Be proactive.)

Without glancing at his friend & employer, Jerzy nodded. When he looked like he was going to pass out, Harry transferred him to the floor. Harry's impulse to call 911 was coldly overruled by a quickly growing curiosity.

He began to undo the string around one of the blankets. Jerzy came to long enough to stop him, ordering which direction the pictures should face for maximum viewing impact.

"Be careful."

"Careful of what?"

"Be humble. If you're humble—"

The blankets were off. Because he'd done what Jerzy told him to, only the back of the frames were visible; the images faced the wall.

"OK?" said Harry, seeking permission to continue.

"OK. You can turn them."

The front of each panel was bare, except for a large boutonniere of thick photographic paper stuck to it, & folded in on itself, origami-like. Jerzy nodded out/mouthbreathed whilst Harry went to work unpacking the papery excrescence. Finally 2 enormous images blossomed from each canvas, lying flat—at least 10 × 10 apiece. There was only room to lean them against opposing walls.

Harry stood back.

Too abstract—he couldn't make anything out. Except for in the center of each photo was fused a smaller, unadulterated, *recognizable* photo. Harry took a closer look . . .

How strange! The images grafted onto the very solar plexus of both blowups seemed to be—no, they *were*—those of the telltale panty-sliver of a traditional (blue chip) *honeyshot!* beaver. The clarity & tautness, the drama of silk hose, the moment of automobiliac *egress* suspended in Time, the delicate, classical composition drawing one's eyes toward the single Great Eye of all creation—hallmarks of Jerzy's craft & best work.

But as for the abstractions that *surrounded* the 2 *honeyshots!*———

"I don't quite . . . understand. I can't see . . ."

"Can't you?" said Jerzy.

The unexpected voice, the *presence* of it, startled him. Jerzy held some glossy heaps (*more* folded paper) in his hand. He reached out, offering them to Harry. Jerzy's arm shook: it was scarlet, flecked, bruised by whole brown cities of needlemarks.

Harry took them from him, uncrumpling a printout from Wikipedia, plus two shiny pages torn from a magazine. Some of the wiki passages had been highlighted:

As a god of motion Janus looks after passages, causes the startings of actions, presides on all beginnings and since movement and change are bivalent, he has a double nature, symbolised in his two headed image.[23] He has under his tutelage the stepping in and out of the door of homes,[24] Because of his initial nature he was frequently used to symbolize change and transitions such as the progression of past to future, of one condition to another, of one vision to another, the growing up of young people, and of one universe to another. He was also known as the figure representing time because he could see into the past with one face and into the future with the other. while Janus is Iunonius Juno is Ianualis as she favours delivery, women's physiological cycle and opens doors.[113]

Now Harry *saw*, but still could not *apprehend*.

(Yet there was great skill&beauty in what Jerzy had done.)

But what could it all mean?

"I can't————"

"Those pictures," said Jerzy, helping out his friend, "are of G-d, taken as He stepped from his golden carriage. As you can see, there are *2* of Him: His name is Janus & He has 2 faces. We privileged few bore witness as He arrived for His merciful works."

Jerzy closed his eyes in exhaustion.

Harry dialed 911.

& while the sirens grew louder, the maestro of THE HON-EYSHOT! tried to fathom what kind of madness had led his star pupil to see the face of God in a mantis & a hummingbird.

4th Trimester

Misericordia: the strangling cord

(WITHOUT REPRESENTATION)

The Art of Fiction, Part Three

Bud's

hip surgery didn't go well. An infection required another procedure. A few weeks later, he got pneumonia. He probably picked it up in the hospital. The doctor said, "It happens. We don't like it when it does, but it does."

The narcotics constipated him. He'd never been one to examine his own shit, but fitfully peered into the bowl after each eely expulsion. They were usually curled neatly at the very bottom, guilty dogs avoiding their master's gaze.

Around the time he started to convalesce, Dolly shed her fear of falling. A week after his surgery, she did something she hadn't been able to in a number of years—walked down the two short flights of stairs to Bud's bedroom, unassisted.

Everyone remarked on her high spirits. She began taking outside walks. The caregivers noticed a lilt in her step, a sprightliness. Marta said it was almost as if he took the fall for her, & Dolly's fears along with it.

. . .

As Tolkin had suggested, Bud tried to find comedy in the story of the drowned girl. He played around with the idea of a mermaid but so far nothing gelled. He even netflixed *Splash* to see if it would give him any ideas. He only watched for a little while—it was more fun to chase Daryl Hannah all over the Internet instead. Bud's habit had grown; he was up to three percocets an hour. He was supposed to use the nebulizer a half-dozen times a day, but never did. Twice at most.

. . .

This year's Guggenheim grant winners were listed in a full page of *The New York Times*. He always wondered how they were chosen. The Foundation's website said there was a "Committee of Selection" that consulted with distinguished scholars and artists for guidance in awarding applicants. Among the committee were Toni Morrison, Patti Smith, Steve Martin, Fran Lebowitz, David Simon, Joyce Carol Oates, & James Franco.

. . .

He watched some of *The Real Housewives of Beverly Hills*. One of the wives had just moved, and someone asked her where. She said, "Bel-Air." "Where were you living before?" asked the friend. "Bel-Air," said the wife.

. . .

Michael's New Zealand movie, *Misericord*, had a Facebook page. It already had a release date. One of the producers was known as the old guy who liked to blog as a way of reaching out to fans; he loved live-streaming Twitter "orgies." In the last one he participated in, someone asked about a rumor that the director and star were at each other's throats during the shoot. The producer said the rumor was "Internet horseshit."

Misericord . . .

Odd title. Intriguing word, though. Bud Googled.

1) an apartment in a monastery where certain relaxations of the monastic rule are allowed, especially those involving food and drink, to accommodate infirm monks; 2) a shelf, or "mercy seat," on the underside of a hinged seat in a choir stall against which a standing chorister could lean, during lengthy services (often inscribed with scatological graffiti); 3) a dagger used to administer the mercy stroke to a seriously wounded knight.

Jesus. Infirm monks . . . secret apartments for DaVinci Code-type bacchanalias . . . hidden, porn-carved "mercy" seats . . . a medieval dirk for *coup de grâces* . . . the word was an entire book—say, by Eco or Borges—a novel in itself! In just four syllables and 10 measly letters, it managed to evoke more feeling, more subtlety, more narrative (three acts, ending with a killing!) than Bud would ever be able to conjure in five pages, or 50, or 500.

He lay flat on his back awash in depression, murdered by the word as surely as a knight by a dagger. Only trouble being, it didn't put him out of his *misery.*

.   .   .

Bud was bored and stoned.

Marta picked him up the Forbes Top-Earning Dead Celebrity issue. You had to earn at least $6 million for the year to qualify. Michael Jackson was still riding high.

Tolkin called to cheer him up. He said he went with Brando to the Westside Pavilion to watch a movie by a director whom the kid was interested in. It was in 3D. Michael said that when you walked out, you threw your glasses in a recycling bin that said KEEP 3D GREEN. Michael said it was the best, most insane slogan ever.

.   .   .

He got an email from one of David Simon's assistants, asking for an update on his contact information.

It gave him the idea to update his iPhone addressbook. He was surprised to find his father still in there. Bud kept his old cellphone number, forgetting that he edited the rest, in case he was ever back east and wanted to visit:

. . .

He had a nice conversation with Keira Thompson, head of development at Ooh Baby. She was glad to hear Bud was leaning in the comedy direction on the problematic Biggie project, and happy to be brought into his confidence. He even shared about having some conversations with Tolkin about it. No harm.

He'd read a few articles about the Brainards online, and become curious about the source of their wealth. When they finished with the business side, Bud kind of circled the topic. Keira wasn't skittish about it at all. She said the dad was a genius who found a way to patent "concepts."

"Brando said one of the big things his father came up with was the idea of asking people for the last four digits of their social. Prior to that, people were reluctant to give their whole number over the phone. It made them feel vulnerable. The consequence was that merchants and banks lost billions of dollars a year in sales because people refused to verify. Most of this was before the Internet, Paypal and eBay and what have you, now people give all kinds of personal information to their computers, I know *I* do. Anyway, Brando said his dad told the banks (and *they* told the merchants) to have the person on the phone just ask the consumer for the *last four digits*—psychologically, that made all the difference. People didn't hesitate to ID themselves anymore. He still gets *royalties* off that idea! And there was *another* weird benefit. Brando said the *cumulative time saved* by having people repeat *four numbers instead of twelve* was like HUGE—like, at the end of the year it added up to hundreds of thousands of man hours. So they saved all those *salaries* too! The ones they would have had to pay to have more people working the phones."

.   .   .

Bud unobtrusively recuperated in his very own apartment for infirm monks. Marta did heroic double duty, performing all the functions of an LVN. If the pain was particularly bad, he wasn't shy about using the bedpan. His door had no lock—no way to control the comings and goings of a sleepless, nomadic mother.

One night he awakened from a sedative-induced sleep to Dolly giving him a sponge bath.

"Once you pass 80, it's time to go," she said, *in media res*. He was too groggy to question the surreal scene. "The people who get sick, refuse treatment, then die a few days later—those are the ones who got it right."

"Mom . . . what are you doing?"

"*Sponging* you. What does it *look* like I'm doing? What a *chin* you have! And what *handsome shoulders*. I look at you and see your *father*. You know what kept us together? The *sex*. The *sex* was all we had. You know, you're handsome. You're handsome and you *know* it. *Everybody* knows it—they say, 'Here he comes! Here comes Handsome Bud Wiggins!'"

.   .   .

He put down the novel—alas, the courage to say he was done.

He'd been working on it for years. Finally, he could freely admit he had absolutely nothing to show for it. He used to fantasize about being a literary man, but the literary era was over. When he was a boy, the scene was vibrant. Mailer stabbed his wife and duked it out with Vidal, Capote was a sacred monster, Styron a nasty drunk, Cheever a nasty drunken fag. Now there were only aging wonder-boys like Do-Gooder Eggers, Vegemitey Mouse Foer, & Franzen, the King Rat who preened about spreading Big Brain's ashes in some bandana republic before snitching off his BFF's minuscule frauds of reportage. In one of those phoney *New Yorker* tell-alls masquerading as *elegant meditations*, he diddled himself—with precious, casually *trenchant* reflections on Daniel Defoe, Samuel Richardson & the Novel; on islands & isolation; on the special agonies of bestselling literary men, and the *very* special agony of loving his Hideous Friend—before getting to the cumshot of *how much I loved and invested in him and how much he betrayed me and his wife.* Bud thought it would have been far more interesting if Franzen had fucked the widow, which the essay actually wound up doing. It was a bitchy, addled *Psychology Today*-level treatise that literally posited that D. Footnote Wallace hanged himself as a career move! "In a sense, the story of my friendship with him is simply that I loved a person who was mentally ill." Bud said outloud, *Have you no sense of decency, sir, at long last?* As Fran Lebowitz might jest, "If you think you can write *Saint Genet* but you aren't Sartre—*don't even try.*"

How many copies did *Freedom* sell, anyway?

Like five fucking million————————

I'm done, he said.

The dream is over . . .

His phone rang.

"Bud?"

"Oh, hi Tolkin."

"How's the hip, kiddo?"

"On the mend."

"Listen, I've got some good news."

"Jesus, Michael, you're like the fuckin tooth fairy, it never stops. I love you, man."

"Remember the David Simon meeting you took?"

"Sure. *The Wire* guy."

"Right . . . they're going into production—on the Hollywood project. David told me he lifted a section from one of your stories."

"What stories?"

"What do you mean, *what stories*. From *Force Majeure!*"

"Really? Wouldn't I have heard about that?"

"You're hearing about it *now*. Listen. They're giving you a 'story by' credit—which is a *good* thing. You'll even get paid for it, which is a *very* good thing. Not a lot, but it's WGA minimum. For shared story credit."

"Wow. Cool!"

"You know what this means, don't you?"

"Tell me."

"Remember how he called *The Wire* a novel?"

"Yeah."

"Well, David's calling the new series a novel too."

"Okay."

Bud wasn't following.

"David said that his staff is engaged in writing another *novel* that just so happens to be in the form of a TV series."

"So?"

"So you don't have to finish your book."

"What do you mean?"

"Because it's already *happened*."

"*What* has?"

"Bud, you are now a published novelist! Or *will* be, once your episode airs."

"For real?" he answered.

He couldn't figure out if Michael was joking. He felt dizzy, and his breath was shallow; he'd need to do a round with the nebulizer once he was off the phone.

"Well, by the *Simon* definition you are—which I suppose is as valid as anyone else's. So, pour yourself a glass of champagne and give yourself a toast. To Bud Wiggins, on the occasion of the publication of his first novel. . . ."

"May there be many more to come!"

Hard Time

He

got 36 months, but would do half that if he kept his nose clean. When Tom-squared got busted for distribution, it was her 3rd strike. She gave him up & pled out. He didn't hold it against her.

The scam was simple. They targeted widows in affluent neighborhoods. T² found em on the internet, starting with the hubby obits & working her way back to the wife. She even got their phone numbers & called em up, bogusly wrestling her way into their geriatr. semi-infarcted ♥s. It blew his mind what she could do. The onlys she had trouble with were old ladies who'd already been tapped by the internet-crying Nigger-ians who pretended they were royalty in need.

T would put on a pantsuit & tap on the door and thank them *so much* for being friend & patron of *The Coalition to Stop the Use of Child Soldiers*. Of course they'd say you must be mistaken but Rikki would be standing there in one of those purposefully ill-fitting Salv Army–looking sport jackets. When the grieving geezers protested, a bewildered Tom-Tom whipped out proof in the form of a doctored letter *signed by them* in which they had agreed to house Rikki during his peacemaking trip to America. *He came all the way from Sudan!* Tom-Tom's bewilderment would become exasperation & then anger at the ineptness of her organization's volunteeers. "I hate to do it, but some people are going to be fired over this," she'd say, and by the sad old confused cunt's reaction, she'd know pretty much how well they were going to score.

At this point they'd usually invite them in, it being impolite to keep them afoot on the porch like that. Once settled and properly provided with food & drink, the Double T show-and-tell'd photoshop pics of Rikki with Nelson Mandela; with Jimmy Carter; with Barack & Hillbillary. She even had huge War Child International decals on her attaché, o shit she was *tight*. They took turns raiding the house, at 1st excusing themselves to use the bathroom but over time one of em would simply disappear while the other kept the mourning whore engaged. Before the bust, they fenced about 225K in jewels/gold. Tom-Tom couldn't prove it but was fairly certain it was Cherokee who dropped the dime. She was looking at 7 years; reduced to 3 for ratting out Rikki.

.   .   .

His father was a jailbird who left when he was a baby, and now Rikki had done the same to his own. The irony wasn't lost on him. His parents visited and it pained him to see the look of anguish on Dawn's face. He thought long&hard about it and told Jim he would understand if they wanted to sever parental rights. "No," said Jim. "I appreciate your sensitivity in the matter, but there's not a child on Earth who deserves that to happen to him once, let alone twice."

They brought Nikki to see him. It was just like some of the A&E docs where the family brings babies or toddlers to visit the incarcerated dad. He felt something in him shift. Maybe he'd go to school & become a drug counselor when he got out. (That was what Reeyonna wanted to be, if she couldn't make it as a medical examiner.) He'd talk to Dr Phil about that when he got out. The bottomline was, he wanted to step up to the plate, like the judge said. Handle himself like a man, not a punk. He remembered everything that judge told him. Being arrested like that made an amazing day into one of the worst in his life. Second to ReeRee dying of course.

He was determined. He *would* change.

Fake it til you make it.

· · ·

Rikki had a cellphone in his cell. *A cell in the cell hahahaha.* They were easy to get from trustees or guards if you had the money. His parents always kept his account topped off at $200. For snacks & cigs & shampoo and shit.

The reception was shitty but sometimes you could actually go online. He got a Lana Del Rey youtube & jacked but didn't want to come. He'd jack a while then try to get a pornsite then fail and go back to his Lana jack. After 5 or 6 tries, he got on & pulled down his pants & put his hand on the gluegun. He was in the lower bunk but his cellie was out exercising or whatever.

One of his faves, http://behindthecastingcouch.com . . . it was hard to hear the dialogue but they were pretty much all the same. He never saw one with a pregnant girl before, & he jacked a few minutes before realizing with a shock that it was Reeyonna.

He hit PAUSE.

Reeyonna was so freaked about money, much more than him, probably he thought because of the grudge deal she had going with her mom for cheating her out of her shit. Ree was more practical than him too, & ahead in the nesting dept. Rikki knew how much she wanted to be independent, & the motherfucking casting mother-fucker *played* on that. It was irrational, but he suddenly got angry with himself for never having told her about the shammy site; if he had, she'd never have fallen for it. But why would he? He never even thought about it. She probably went down there around the time Tom-Tom the cuntsnitch was pressuring them to pay rent. He re-membered her coming home one day looking fucked up, & how she stayed in bed a bunch of days & wouldn't tell him what was wrong. He thought he remembered her being worried she was bleeding a little from her pussy too, not a heavy flow, not too worried, but still. But then it stopped. That would have been right around then.

He hit PAUSE again and watched Reeyonna blow the piece of shit motherfucker. Man, this shit was *sad*. Rikki closed his eyes and shook his head. If a year ago someone told him he'd be in jail looking at porn on a contraband cellphone & the porn would be his dead pregnant fiancée giving some sorry-lookin motherfucker head, he'd have fucking laughed. Now he was cryin.

When he opened his eyes, ReeRee was on the desk on her back, being hardfucked. The cam was right in front of her face & she winced as she got pounded. The phone crashed/he lost the signal. Too much of a hassle to get online again. He didn't have it in him to even try. Besides, she wasn't going anywhere. She'd be getting fucked by that lying scumbag forever, until the end of the world, until the end of time.

He lay back on the cot, & couldn't stop his brain from playing the fucked-up images over and over in his head. Prisoners were shouting. Some had conversations, cell to cell. Some were selling wolf tickets, some for real. Others sang, or talkshouted but to themselves. Rikki replayed the ambulance ride in his head. He tried to remember the last words she said to him, but couldn't. He flashed on that scene in the hospital room when he 1st saw her dead. And that dress, she was in that dress, which now that he thought about it was fuckin *weird*. Fuckin ReeRee's mom, what a sick bitch. Criminal motherfucker. Basically, she turned her daughter out. Took her $$$ & made her waddle into that fucking *"casting office"*————— then *oh fuck*

♥ suddenly started beating faster, seeing her in mind's eye splayed across that desk

> *& he takes himself*
>
> in hand

Dead Stardust

In

the months following her daughter's death, Jacquie was hired for a ½dozen portraitures. Two were in private homes. One of them was an 8-year-old girl with cystic fibrosis.

Jacquie thought of moving away. She talked about it with Dawn, who gave her blessing. It was understood that Dawn & Jim were going to raise the girl, & Jacquie felt guilty about that. She had no desire to be a parent again and questioned whether she ever did. Dawn comforted her, tho one can only be comforted so much. Jacquie knew she was depressed but resisted Dawn's suggestion to medicate. She went on the Internet & learned the possible side effects of antidepressants were "new, worse" depressions &/or *suicidal thoughts and attempts*. Jacquie never heard anything so insane in her life—a pill you took for depression that walked you to the gallows!

· · ·

Pieter came to town.

This time, they didn't sleep together. Albie joined them for dinner—the boys got along like a house on fire.

Pieter said he'd be spending more time in LA, working at Gagosian. He didn't bring up Beth Rader nor did he ask Jacquie about her "avocation," for which she was grateful.

He brought her a gift, a beautiful book of full-face black & white portraits. The text was in German. Pieter explained that the artist, a man in his 70s named Walter Schels, had permission from his dying subjects to document moments before and after death. On the left side of the book, the subject stared straight into the camera; on the right, he was dead. Pieter said the pictures were often taken mere hours apart. One was of a young boy who looked so prosaic in life, so beautiful in death. Another reminded her of the photograph she took of Jerilynn & her granddaughter, only in perverse negative: a mother sat on a couch cradling her dead baby in one arm, with her remaining child, a living toddler, riding her hip. The nasal cannula that supplied oxygen to the baby still hadn't been removed. The lovely thing about the portrait was the duality—parity—of the living & the dead. The mom's serene indifference reminded that the opposing states coexisted, were in fact interchangeable. She looked like she was in a trance. The handsome woman gazed off-camera, like she might have been listening to someone, perhaps someone posing the question, *Which one is alive, you or the baby?* Jacquie thought the woman might have got it wrong.

· · ·

She put the house up for sale.

· · ·

She cooked Pieter dinner and got drunk.

He stayed over.

The sex was dirty and bruising. She couldn't remember having so much fun in the sack.

During breakfast, Pieter announced he happened to be "au courant" on her postmortem work. The only person who could have talked to him was Albie; in that same instant, she was certain that Albie had told him about her portrait of Jerilynn as well. Pieter played dumb and she could see the bind he was in. Asking to see the Cedars picture would egregiously violate Albie's confidence—it was one thing for Albie to have spoken in general terms, quite another to have shared about *that*. Such a sensitive revelation might threaten their friendship, and Albie would have known that. While Pieter didn't want to detonate his own relationship with Jacquie, she knew he was willing to carefully navigate any kind of minefield whose end result was being shown the *memento mori* of her baby.

Jacquie already forgave Albie in her head. None of it really mattered anymore. She was getting out of Dodge, bound for Marin. One of her portraiture clients had offered her a guesthouse for as long as she liked. Jacquie thought she might use it as base camp for traveling the world. Hell, the guesthouse was three times bigger than the house she was trying to unload.

"So—do you want to see it?"

He played dumb again.

"It's hanging in the garage."

. . .

A week later, Beth Rader called. Jacquie knew that she would.

Pieter probably told her to wait a respectable few weeks before checking in. Jacquie cut her off at the pass by saying she appreciated her interest but was in the middle of a major move. Beth said Pieter mentioned she was relocating to Mill Valley and that it was one of her *favorite* favorite places, she grew up in Petaluma/Cazadero, bla.

Then she made her play.

"OK, Jacquie, I don't want to take much more of your time. I'm going to be straight up because that's the only way I'm going to feel better, that I was at least upfront & tried my best. And I hope you'll be OK with it because I assume if you're anything like me you prefer just hearing the truth instead of someone just rambling. Pieter told me about the picture of your daughter. And her baby. & let me just say I feel privileged just—that he *shared* it with me. And that you, of course, shared it with *him*. & you need to know he told me about the photograph in the *most respectful way*. The hair on my neck stood up; it's standing up now. It *so moved me*, Jacquie. I just had a nephew pass—of lymphoma—he was just 14, & I wish there'd been some way to *memorialize* that. Not for me but for the mom.

"What I really want to say is *you're a great artist*. You have a body of work that should *not* be ignored. That you're not better known, more *collected*, is criminal. I don't think you've *ever* had representation up to the task—that is my *opinion*—I don't believe you've ever had anyone in your corner who really *understood* the world of Jacquie Crelle-Vomes. The aesthetic, the palette, the precision, the narrative. This new work you've embarked on—& make no mistake, it *is* your new work, whether you choose to *show it or not*, & I don't care *what* you decide, it's *your choice*, I think it would be a *shame* for people not to see it but that of course is *1000%* up to you. Goya had his 'black paintings,' he did them on the walls of his house, never wanted anyone to see them, and they didn't until he was dead and gone. So you can leave them to the wind but *whatever* you do, it's still *art*. Because *art* is something you can't help but make. That's what you do, Jacquie. *You make art.*

"I think you're ready for a show. I really do. Everyone at the gallery does. A retrospective, with the bonus of the new work—again, should you choose to show it. I think it will arouse *tremendous* interest. About where you've been. & where you're going.

"All right, I'll shut up now."

"Beth, it's *very* flattering. And you may be right—about everything. But I've closed that door. What I do, I do for me. I know you'll understand."

"Absolutely. *One hundred percent.* At least I'll sleep tonight—I made my little pitch. *Best of luck,* Jacquie, and you know we're always here. And good luck with the move! Kiss Marin for me!"

. . .

She awakened in the middle of the night thinking about Fergie, the Mill Valley girl with cystic fibrosis. She remembered something her little sister said.

After she died, the mom tried to explain things. Well-intentioned

friends had been coaching her to talk to the sister about Fergie's *journey*, how one day we were all going on the same *journey*. Right after
Fergie passed, a close friend even held the mom in her arms and said,
She's begun her journey. So later that night when the mom tucked her
in, the little sis said, Where did she go? The mom said, *Back where she
came from. Where all of us came from.* The girl said, Where? The mom
nodded toward the ceiling. *Where the stars are. She went to where the
stars are.* The girl asked if Fergie would be cold. The mom said no,
she didn't think so. *Did you know,* said the Mom, *that people are made
from stardust?*

    ☆dust?

            *That's right. People are made from stardust, from
all the light that comes from the ☆s & the sun.*

           Mama, do stars die?

              Everything does.

  But where do they go?

        *Well, stars live a long, long time. And even when they die,
they keep giving out light.*

               But how?

      They just do. It's their nature.

         *When a baby dies in the mama's stom-
ach, is it a dead star?*

          *No, said Mom, on the
verge of losing it. When a baby dies, its ☆dust goes back to be with its friends
again. The other stars.*

        *If Fergie's back with the stars, & all the ☆s
die, even if she dies too, then will she give out light?*

       Yes.

       For a long, long time?

    That's right. Now it's time for sleep.

        · · ·

"Hello, is this Jacquie?"

  "Yes, who's calling?"

"Steve Martin."

"O *hi* Steve! What a nice surprise."

"I usually don't do this—Beth Rader gave me your number. I should add I was holding her at gunpoint."

"Hahaha! No, it's fine—really."

"I was trying to remember the last time we saw each other."

"I think it was—wasn't it at the Central Library?"

"That's *right*. Gee. Beth said you're moving away?"

"Yes! To Marin."

"I love Marin. I just called to say that Beth showed me some images you took that I thought were extraordinary. The young couple with their stillborn."

"Mmmm. Yeah—she's quite taken with them."

"So was I. I know your work, by the way. I've always been a big fan."

"Thank you. Back atcha."

"I've always regretted that I never collected you. I remember how controversial you were—those images of your little girl————————wait. You didn't happen to be at Gus' opening in London at the Gagosian. Gus & James Franco?"

"Gee, I don't think so. But if you find proof that I was, please let me know."

He laughed.

"Your new pictures: I saw Arbus there, but what amazed me is there wasn't that aspect of the grotesque. What you've done is so *tender*—transcendent—& completely unsentimental."

"That's very kind, Steve."

"Beth said you weren't interested in selling any images & I completely respect that. I didn't want you to think that's why I was calling, because it isn't. I'm going to be in LA next week, & was hoping—I'd be honored if you'd show me some prints."

"Next week? I'll probably be up in Marin—————"

"O—————"

"—————but I can come down."

"I can come to you . . ."

"No, it's fine. I'm gonna be commuting for a while, at least until I sell the house."

"That would be lovely," he said, humbled. "& thank you."

"Did Beth mention any of my other work? New work?"

"I don't *think* so. She did say there have been more images taken since the ones I looked at."

"There have . . . Steve, I don't know if you know that my daughter died a few months ago."

"She did tell me that. I'm so sorry."

"I took some pictures of her in the hospital. Pictures of her alone, & of—Jerilynn and the baby—which is healthy and blessed, by the way. She gave me a beautiful little granddaughter, Nikki."

"It's hard to find words."

"I made a series of prints—large-scale, 50 by 60. Is that something you'd be interested in seeing as well?"

"Yes, I'd be honored. And frankly, Jacquie, I'm interested in anything you'd like to show me."

"Let me give you my email."

"Perfect. And would you mind if I bring a friend? I know that James—Franco—would be thrilled."

"Not at all."

"He's become quite a collector. He's gone on an Eggleston bender."

"I saw him not too long ago. He actually may own one or two of my early pieces. The 1st Jerilynn nudes."

"Do you know what I actually think might be great? I'd love to throw you a little dinner party. Just eight or ten people."

"That would be lovely."

"Larry would want to co-host. He's got a beautiful new house in Bel-Air he loves showing off. Beth said he's *very* excited about the new work. What if we did something small? I think the Ruschas are back from Paris . . . Laurene Jobs . . . Joyce Carol Oates and her husband . . . Bob might even come if he's not touring—Dylan. Larry showed him at the gallery in New York. And Tina Fey. We're doing an event at the Nokia—"

"Tina Fey is the funniest woman who ever lived."

"She started collecting. You'd love her. But whether we do a dinner or not, I'd of course love to come see whatever you'll show me."

"I'm thinking—and it's *very* sweet of you to offer a dinner party. But I'm actually thinking—and tell me what *you* think—I'm actually thinking that maybe I could show the work at Larry's house. Maybe mix the two. I could hang the pictures, almost like an intimate gallery show. I'm not sure he has the space . . ."

"O he does! He has the space."

"It might be a better place to show the images than my garage!"

"I think it's a wonderful idea."

"I could even bring the last photos—of my daughter."

"Well, that would be an absolute privilege. For everyone."

During their conversation she'd wandered into the yard, and then the garage, where one of the enormous prints of Jerilynn hung in a temporary frame. Now she was staring straight at it. Her daughter looked so beautiful in the slate grey Alexander Wang—& Nikki lay on her chest in mid-squall.

"Because in a way," said Jacquie. "It's the showpiece."

☆ *Search*

Biggie's

operation was a success. The doctors said he would gradually recover "full powers," though not for a few months.

Telma and Biggie were inseparable. Apart from Brando and the nanny, she was the only one Biggie would interact with. Brando even gave Telma her own bedroom. Gwen was comfortable with it because the children were well-supervised, and Telma did school-work with Biggie's tutor.

Gwen was there a few times a week for lunch and dinner. The story Brando told her about the mother who went away lay heavy on her heart. The father lived in one of the houses on the vast estate but apparently only materialized at night, to pace the grounds. Was he awaiting his wife's return? Or was it for his own death . . . Gwen never saw him, tho when she was over for dinner, did find herself doing a little rubbernecking into the dusky sprinklermist. It was all rather gothic—she couldn't help thinking of the father as Rochester's mad wife, shut up in secret rooms.

. . .

The invitations to cancer galas continued to come in, but Telma evinced no interest. Just before Michael wrapped his movie, he asked

Gwen and her to tea but Telma declined. Telma emailed with Aleisha's mom and phoned the little girl twice a week w/o fail. She accompanied Biggie to the hospital whenever he had an appointment
but otherwise stayed away, quietly abdicating her mayoralty. Gwen
got all kinds of worried communiqués from the RNs, missing Telma
& wanting to know "what was happening."

Gwen didn't say it, but something *was* happening.

Her daughter was growing up.

·   ·   ·

She took the call in her bedroom at the Brainards'.

Her mom said that she and Phoebe were thinking of going to Hawaii for a week, and might Biggie and Telma like to come? Telma
said no, they were in the middle of a big project, but told her mom
she should go enjoy herself, that she'd *better* or Telma would be mad.
While they were talking, a picture of Michael Douglas came on the
television, & Telma told Gwen to hold on while she turned up
the sound. Shia LaBeouf was being interviewed. "Cancer picked the
wrong guy when it picked Michael," he said.

They spoke a while longer, then Telma said she needed to check
up on Biggie. Gwen had already expressed her concerns to Phoebe
about her daughter's codependency; she was afraid Telma swapped
one obsession for another. Phoebe said she thought the bond with
Biggie was a far healthier manifestation of her altruistic spirit than
her relationship to cancer was, which was grandiose & doomed to
end badly. Phoebe said, *Would you try something? I'd like you to try and
stop worrying, for 30 seconds at a time.*

Before hanging up, Telma surprised Gwen by saying, "Mom, I'm
going to marry Biggie one day. I don't know who's going to ask who,
but someone's going to ask *somebody.*"

Telma said an Aloha! & was gone.

·   ·   ·

For the last week, Biggie was having more problems than usual. The doctors said it might go like that; the up and the down of it, until things settled. Telma did flashcards with him every day but sometimes he got tired. He'd say he didn't know certain things, but Telma was convinced he *did*. It could be really frustrating but she knew how to get him to push through.

When she stepped into his room, he was Google Earthing. He was listening to music on his Beats so she was able to kind of creep up & look over Biggie's shoulder, without him knowing. He was in Slovenia, loitering around the parking lot of the Skocjan Caves. (He'd been hanging there with his little "street view man" all weekend.) Biggie told her the caves were created by a sinking river, half on the surface, ½-underground. The wiki said that the subterranean gorge/waterfalls looked like something out of *The Lord of the Rings*.

She was about to let her presence be known when he opened Google & typed

mother

There were 1,341,000,000 hits.

END

David Rosenthal

Nothing to Undo

SARAH HOCHMAN

Acknowledgments

Lily Burk

& Greg Burk & Deborah Drooz

John & Lydia Jane & Lisa Stafford Gladwell, Todd & Emily Horowitz & Elroy & Pebbles Solondz, James Truman & Leanne Shapton & Bunny, David & Carolyn Cronenberg, Ed & Danna Ruscha, Andre Balazs, Wallace Shawn & Deborah Eisenberg, Kate Adair Pohlman, Dr. Gary Bravo & Susan Seitz, Andrew Wylie, Leonard Cohen, Wendy Wall and Claudia Liberman, PG, The Midnight Mission, Salman Rushdie, Bunny & Adolfo, Carlos Castaneda, Father Fabricio Magaldi, James Ellroy, Julius Renard & Darien Donner, Rita & John, Eric Peterson, Bill & Carolyn & Bertie, Marylou Shockley, Hal de Becker Sr. & Hal de Becker Jr., Bob & Lauren Dubac, Peter Feibleman, Seth Flaum & Tamara Blaich, Michael & Wendy Tolkin, Danna & Ben & Rebecca Schaeffer, Jim & Kathleen & Julianna Seligman (and Matty & Herb & the boys), Sherman Alexie, Dr. Bob & Marge & Ted (and the boys), Frenchy Ruscha & Francesca Gabbiani, Dr. Edward Kantor, Jesse Dylan & Susan Traylor, Steve & Kathy Kloves, John Waters, Nadine Johnson, Pico Iyer, Chandra and Billy, Chris and Dori Carter, Susan Kamil, George Meyer & Maria Semple, Nick Marck & Linda Lichter, Mary McMannes, Dr David Bockoff, Mary Ann King, Marta Morales, Francisca, Maria, & Flor, Darren Star, Michael & Lisa & Sean Goedecke, Debbie Reynolds & Todd Fisher & Gloria Crayton & Mary Douglas French, Richard Buckley & Tom Ford, Cyndi Sayre, Chris Silbermann, Mark Gordon, Jim Bartholemew, Brad Spielman, Ron Hugo & Janice Hampton & Jeff Prettyman, Joan Halifax, Bret Easton Ellis, William Gibson, Jenn and Geoff and Ian, Andrea & Joshua, Oliver Stone, Allen & Tracey McKeown & Mabel & Johnny McKeown, Grant Vospher, Bryan & Billie Lourd, Dr. Shawn Nasseri, Dr. Bill Stafford, The Atlantic Group, George Garrett, Gayle & Murgatroyd Boarnard, Dr. Michael Chaikin, Paul Bartel, Cotty Chubb, Cita and Myles Cohen, Harry Shearer & Judith Owen, Dr. Jeremy Fine, Tom Scott, Lynne Scott, Laraine Newman, Glen Goldman, Tony Krantz, Alan Poul, Nelson Lyon, Terry Southern, Terry Gilliam, Ed Begley Jr. & Rachelle Carson, Frank Jones, John Graf, Luma & Lilly & Naqaqa staff, Kevin Nealon &

Suzanne Yeagley, Ed Moses, UCLA Special Collections, Dave Mirkin & Savannah Brentnall, Paul Fortune & Chris Brock, Garry Shandling, Ken Finkleman and Mirjam Cohen, Angela Janklow, Eric & Tanya Idle, Olivia Harrison, Jonathan Carroll, Dana Delany, Christine & Marlene & Guthrie McCarty Vachon, Bob Kaplan & Signe Johnson, Pam Koffler and Russell Fine, John Sloss, John & Kimberly Keefe, "Schultzie," Brian & Cindy Rogers, Anne Thompson, Frank & Berta Gehry, Gerry Harrington, Gil & Janet Friesen, Leonard Michaels, Haley van Oosten, Wilkie McClaren, Leonard Brooks, Collin & Elizabeth Callender, Hughie Dixon, Charley Powell, Gus Van Sant, James Shaheen, Renee Tab, Jennifer Rudolph Walsh, Hudson Marquez & Susan Clary, Iosefo Dramea de Becker, David Rozansky, Father Fernando Mata, Miriam Altshuler, Bill Guthy & Victoria Jackson-Guthy & Ali & Jackson & Evan Minogue, Frank Roddam, Rose & Manfred & Hanna, Jerry Hartman, John Liechty, Ricky Jay & Chrisann Verges, Harvey Purgason, Father Thomas Sells, Darrell & Terri W, Jerry Stahl, Joan Hyler, Gail & Moon Zappa, The Delancey Street Foundation, Tom & Kathy Freston, Wes Craven, Marianne Maddalena, Mary Farley, Hector Babenco, Paul Schrader, Brandon Scott & Rylyn Demaris, Ted Field, Tina Brown, Tina Albert, Anne Thompson, Yoko & Yuko Kanayama, John Kinney, Tamara Masloff, Carol and Tony Monaco, Veronica Godoy, Jirka & Rasmus & Olivia, Alan Bernstein, Mike & Vanessa, Kristy & Damon, Liz & Ted

Bruce Wagner is the author of *Memorial, The Chrysanthemum Palace* (a PEN/Faulkner fiction award finalist), *Still Holding, I'll Let You Go, I'm Losing You,* and *Force Majeure.* He lives in Los Angeles.